BY JEFF SHAARA

The Frozen Hours

A Blaze of Glory

A Chain of Thunder

The Smoke at Dawn

The Fateful Lightning

Gods and Generals

The Last Full Measure

Gone for Soldiers

Rise to Rebellion

The Glorious Cause

To the Last Man

Jeff Shaara's Civil War Battlefields

The Rising Tide

The Steel Wave

No Less Than Victory

The Final Storm

THE
FROZEN
HOURS

THE
FROZEN HOURS

A Novel of the Korean War

JEFF SHAARA

BALLANTINE BOOKS

NEW YORK

The Frozen Hours is a work of historical fiction. Apart from the well-known actual people, events, and locales that figure in the narrative, all names, characters, places, and incidents are the products of the author's imagination or are used fictitiously. Any resemblance to current events or locales, or to living persons, is entirely coincidental.

Published in the United States by Ballantine Books, an imprint of Random House, a division of Penguin Random House LLC, New York.

BALLANTINE and the HOUSE colophon are registered trademarks of Penguin Random House LLC.

Hardback ISBN 978-0-345-54922-8
Ebook ISBN 978-0-345-54923-5

Printed in the United States of America on acid-free paper

randomhousebooks.com

2 4 6 8 9 7 5 3 1

First Edition

Book design by Caroline Cunningham

To my wife, Stephanie, who opened the door to this book after

a meeting with an old family friend, "Peep" Sanders,

who carries the memories found here

The long nights. Too long.

Time stops, frozen in place.

I beg the Frozen Hours for the

Sunrise.

Too many memories

Ice and Death

I'm ready to join my friends.

—A U.S. MARINE ON FOX HILL

CONTENTS

TO THE READER

. . . .

IT'S CALLED "THE FORGOTTEN WAR," but no war is ever forgotten by the people who fought it. In tackling this story (as in my World War II series), I had the enormous luxury of speaking with living veterans. They are of course very elderly men now, who, like all combat veterans, share the experience of facing a deadly and, in this case, an utterly unfamiliar enemy. But this story is not just about combat. There is another enemy here, in some cases far more deadly: the coldest winter in this part of Asia in decades.

You might notice that I do not use the term "police action" to describe the Korean War. That is the label attached to the conflict by an American government deeply fearful that expansion of the confrontation in Korea might very well erupt into World War III. But this story is told not from the government's point of view, but through the eyes of a select group of men who were there, who faced their enemy, or those who carried the awesome responsibility of walking the tightrope between their duty to their men and the wishes of their superiors.

This book is not an attempt to explore the entire Korean War. The focus here is more narrow, which raises a question I grapple with, and agonize over in every book I've written: What do I leave out? By speaking with veterans and veterans' groups, I have been offered wonderful material for an enormous variety of stories, every one as important (and often as painful) to the participants as any other. If I should go further down the road, adding more volumes, possibly creating a trilogy of stories set in Korea, then certainly I can include so much more than you will find here. But this is a single volume, my choice for now, and my responsibility is, first and foremost, to tell you a good story.

This book begins with the invasion of the Korean port of Inchon, in September 1950, and then follows events that extend into mid-December. The focus is primarily on the United States First Marine Division, along with smaller army units and a unit of British Royal Marines. For roughly two weeks, beginning in late November, these men engage overwhelming numbers of Chinese troops around a place we know as the Chosin Reservoir. (I use that name throughout this story, as did most of the Western commanders, since it is the name given to the Changjin Reservoir [the Korean name] by the maps then in use, which were almost always Japanese.) The harrowing tale of that vicious struggle between the Allied forces and the Chinese needs no embellishment. When the temperatures drop well below zero, for men on both sides, staying alive means staying warm, while at the same time engaging in deadly combat with an enemy who is as desperate and as miserable as you are.

If you have read my work, you know that my goal is to take you into the minds of the key characters and tell you the story through their eyes. Here there are three primary characters, two of them Americans: Marine Private First Class Pete Riley and the division's commanding officer, Major General Oliver P. Smith. The third voice is the commanding general of the Chinese field armies that oppose the Marines, General Sung Shi-lun. Also included in this story are characters who are well known to any student of this war: Douglas MacArthur, Lewis "Chesty" Puller, and many others. As well, there are the less familiar, just as important to this story: Marine Sergeant Hamilton "Hamp" Welch, Army Lieutenant Colonel Don Faith, Marine Captain William Barber, and more.

I am often asked about just how these points of view come into being; just how accurate is this story? In every story I do, the events are real, the history as accurate as I can make it. This is a novel by definition because there is dialogue, and you are seeing the events through the eyes of the characters themselves. For me to reach the point where this book emerges, I must feel that I can speak for these men. For that I rely enormously on their own words, their memoirs, collections of letters, diaries, and so on. My goal in the research is not just to get the facts straight, but to get to know these characters as intimately as I can. It is a risky thing to put words into anyone's mouth, especially a respected figure from history—a challenge I accept. You might not agree with my particular interpretation of an event as it happens in this story, and that is a challenge to legions of military historians, as well as the veterans who were there. Controversy surrounds this entire campaign, as it surrounds many of the people involved. There are always *other* points of view, and disagreements abound. In every campaign where disasters occur, there is blame. I have been painstaking in keeping close to the historical record. There will be some who disagree with that record, and I'm prepared to accept grief for that. This is one story. It is not the *only* story and certainly not the *final* story.

Some of you will no doubt feel I have ignored or overlooked the sacrifices and accomplishments of so many other soldiers, airmen, and Marines, other stories, other heroic deeds, other periods of the Korean War that could have been explored. Perhaps I will move into those areas at another time. For now, this is my salute to the men who were forced to wage war through one of the most horrific events in military history, in conditions none of them had any reason to expect. Many, on both sides, did not survive. And certainly, the casualties in any conflict deserve to be honored. But the survivors deserve as much respect. For me, the greatest assets I had were the living veterans or their families who were willing to sit down and talk. At the end of this book is the Acknowledgments section, where so many of those people are listed. I hope you will take a moment to notice that. It is to those wonderfully generous people that this book is also dedicated.

And I hope that, by the end of this book, in some small way this war might be a little less *forgotten*.

JEFF SHAARA, APRIL 2017

LIST OF MAPS

INTRODUCTION

. . . .

FOR CENTURIES, KOREA is a nation of farmers, attracting little attention from the outside world, beyond the immediate interests of its
neighbors. It is the Japanese who consider Korea worth pursuing, and
throughout the latter half of the nineteenth century, the rest of the
world seems willing to concede Korea to Japan. Though the United
States signs a formal treaty of "amity and commerce" with Korea in
1882, there is little enthusiasm for a confrontation with the Japanese,
and when the Japanese occupy Korea in 1905, the American government backs away. Having defeated the Russians in the Russo-Japanese
War, the Japanese have no formidable rivals in the region at all, and so
are now free to treat Korea as they wish. The result is brutal for the Korean people, whose hatred for the Japanese intensifies into a guerrilla
war. But the Japanese are far too powerful, and dissent is crushed.

In 1945, with the dropping of the atomic bombs on two Japanese
cities, World War II concludes and the Koreans ecstatically welcome
their liberation. But the nation suffers from fragmentation, with no official government and no cohesive political infrastructure. Into this void
come the superpowers, the Soviet Union and the United States, who
move in to establish their own spheres of self-interest. In an agreement
solely based on convenience, Korea is divided along what appears on a

map to be the most logical geographical boundary, the 38th parallel, which neatly splits the country in two. The Soviets control the North, the Americans the South. As the conflicts between the two nations blossom into the Cold War, the 38th parallel takes on a different importance, as a border between East and West. Exhausted by World War II, neither side pushes hard for a direct military confrontation, and the Soviets are the first to blink, pulling their troops out of North Korea in 1948. They leave behind a government controlled by their handpicked ruler, Kim Il-sung, who will make few moves without Soviet approval. In the South, the Americans have made a feeble effort to inspire a democratic regime, which is now headed by Syngman Rhee. Rhee professes deep friendship for the United States, but his rule over South Korea is autocratic at best, and a brutal dictatorship at worst. The Americans, eager to support anticommunist governments, embrace Rhee as a valued ally, seemingly oblivious to the abuses he inflicts upon his own people.

As the war of words begins to heat up between North and South Korea, Kim Il-sung quietly builds a vast armada, strengthened by military aid from the Soviets, who come to regard him as a significant thorn in their side. The Soviets are not at all enthusiastic about Kim's saber-rattling, or his poorly disguised ambition to reunite Korea under his own rule. Gradually, Joseph Stalin withdraws direct Soviet support for Kim and Kim begins to seek another ally who would support his goals. He thus forms an alliance with the Communist Chinese, who are now led by Mao Tse-tung.

Comforted by the withdrawal of the Soviets, the American government relaxes considerably, believing that the risk of confrontation in this part of Asia has virtually disappeared. Though American forces occupy bases in Korea, they are a faint shadow of the military that had defeated the Japanese. By 1950, in the five short years since the end of World War II, the extraordinary military might of the United States has been deflated almost completely. Throughout the world, governments are far more concerned that the next great war might begin along the hostile borders that now spread through Europe. What military strength the Americans still possess is mostly positioned where they face off against the Soviets along the border between East and West Germany. Korea, like most of Asia, has become an afterthought.

In Tokyo, the American and Allied occupation forces are commanded by General Douglas MacArthur, who rules over the Japanese as a benevolent dictator. The Japanese not only accept MacArthur's presence, they welcome it, and the American military there is regarded with unexpected affection by the Japanese people. Thus are the Americans convinced that all is well in Asia, and their troop presence in Japan, as well as Korea, is not only weakened but toothless. The troops sent to Korea in support of Rhee are poorly trained and poorly equipped. The South Koreans fare no better, their American occupiers believing that allowing Rhee to control a strong military might in fact create more problems than the Americans are willing to tolerate. While Rhee's army flounders under disinterested American supervision, Kim Il-sung has built the North Korean army into a powerful fist.

In March 1950, the American intelligence community concludes that the North Koreans are preparing an invasion of the South. But those reports are dismissed at all levels of the American government, including Douglas MacArthur. Such intelligence *noise* is regarded with the same lack of seriousness paid to the boisterous threats being made by various communist governments worldwide, none of which are considered legitimate.

On June 25, 1950, the North Koreans open a massive artillery barrage across the 38th parallel, followed by the advance of ten divisions of well-trained and well-equipped ground forces. Backed up by Soviet-made tanks, manned by well-trained Korean crews, the invasion drives southward in four major prongs. As South Korean defense forces dissolve, woefully unable to blunt the invasion, Kim Il-sung tells the world: "The South Korean puppet clique has rejected all methods for peaceful reunification proposed by the Democratic People's Republic of Korea and dared to commit armed aggression north of the Thirty-eighth parallel. The Democratic People's Republic of Korea ordered a counterattack to repel the invading troops."

Though Kim's absurd declaration is mocked in Washington, within hours the American government begins to understand that this invasion is more than meaningless posturing. Petitioning the United Nations Security Council, the Americans push for blanket condemnation of the North Korean attack. The vote is unanimous in favor of supporting South Korea only because the Soviets, who could have simply vetoed the measure, are not in attendance that day. Thus, for the first time in its history the United Nations enter a war, as defenders of South Korean autonomy. The most logical choice to command a hastily formed conglomerate of military forces is General MacArthur.

To those who question this strong show of American resolve to go to war over what many in the United States see as an obscure and insignificant land, President Harry Truman describes this fight as a crusade against the spread of worldwide communism, that the Soviets should be taught that our resolve in this matter is absolute. The assumption in Washington is that the Soviets are pulling all the strings, Kim's army merely a proxy for Soviet intentions to dominate the West, one conflict at a time. No one officially entertains the idea that Kim's only real ally is Red China.

On June 26, one day after the start of the invasion, President Truman receives the following message from Syngman Rhee:

"Things are not going well militarily."

It is a mammoth understatement. Backed by more than sixteen hundred artillery pieces, some ninety thousand North Korean troops have virtually erased any defensive lines the South Koreans can put in their path, and within three days they easily capture the South Korean capital, Seoul. As stunned American and Allied troops begin to mobilize for a defense against the invasion, they are forced into a small portion of southeast Korea, framed by a small mountain range to the north and the Naktong River to the west, around the city of Pusan. Militarily, all that remains of South Korea is a besieged area now called the Pusan Perimeter, an area fifty by one hundred miles, pressed against the Sea of Japan. Though the South Koreans and their allies, primarily the Americans, are pressed into a desperate situation, the North Koreans have overplayed their hand. As they lengthen the distance from their own border, so too do they stretch out their supply lines. Commanded by American army general Walton Walker, the Americans strengthen the defenses along the Pusan Perimeter, while the North Korean juggernaut grows slowly weaker. Though portions of fourteen North Korean divisions press toward the Allied positions, not even Kim Il-sung has anticipated that his army would drive so far so quickly. Despite the jubilation emerging from Kim's propaganda machine, the Allied forces continue to build, forcing a virtual stalemate along the perimeter. By mid-August, Kim's army is outnumbered, though the confidence of the Allied forces remains at a low ebb. Faced with little change to the situation, Douglas MacArthur devises a new and audacious strategy to break the siege. Ignoring his advisors, and the strategists in Washington, MacArthur plans an invasion of his own, an amphibious assault against the western coast of South Korea, at the port of Inchon. MacArthur's plan is to drive American soldiers and Marines inland, far behind the North Korean positions, slicing through any remaining supply lines, thus squeezing the North Korean troops between two major forces. Few officers in MacArthur's camp believe the plan will work, many referring to the odds as "a five-thousand-to-one shot."

On September 15, a force of nearly forty thousand American Marines and soldiers surges ashore at the port city. Facing almost no opposition, they capture Inchon in a matter of hours. The next phase of the invasion begins: crossing the Han River, and liberating the South Korean capital of Seoul. If Seoul can be swept clear of North Korean troops, MacArthur's forces will drive farther inland, cutting off the North Korean troops still waging war along the Pusan Perimeter. There, Walton Walker's Eighth Army is to begin a hard push of their own, a breakout designed to throw the North Korean forces into disarray. If Walker succeeds, the North Koreans will retreat northward, directly into the arms of the forces moving inland from Inchon.

An ecstatic MacArthur reacts to his success by predicting the war's end in a matter of weeks. To many in his command, he has elevated himself to a position of infallibility, a view not shared by official Washington, including President Truman. But victory inspires confidence, and no one is prepared to take anything away from Douglas MacArthur, including his absolute authority over the decisions that will determine the progress of the war.

As the Americans and their allies build up their military presence in South Korea, the Soviets keep a watchful eye on events, seemingly grateful they stayed away. But the Chinese observe as well, anxiously curious what MacArthur's success might mean for Chinese sovereignty.

OLIVER P. SMITH

Born 1893, in Menard, Texas, Smith attends the University of California, Berkeley, graduating in 1916. He is first employed by the Standard Oil Company, but Smith understands the appeal of travel and so, in 1917, he joins the Marine Corps and receives a commission as second lieutenant.

In 1917, Smith marries Esther King, and within three years she gives birth to two daughters.

Throughout the 1920s and '30s, Smith serves in a vast variety of posts, including Guam, France, Haiti, and Iceland, and domestic bases at Fort Benning, Georgia, and Quantico, Virginia.

In 1936, his reputation as an academic is enhanced significantly by his post as instructor at the Marine Corps School at Quantico, Virginia. Nicknamed the Professor, he is considered scholarly and rule-bound, though is highly respected as an expert on amphibious warfare. For the first three years of World War II, Smith remains in Washington, in command of the office of Plans and Policy. But his reputation for efficiency lands him posts in the Pacific Theater, participating in operations at New Britain and Cape Gloucester. In 1944, he is named assistant commander of the First Marine Division and leads his forces onto the beaches at Peleliu, in one of the bloodiest Marine engagements of the war. In spring 1945, he serves as chief of staff to the American Tenth Army during the campaign for the capture of Okinawa.

After the war, he returns to Quantico, is named commandant of the Marine Corps schools, and continues his duties as an instructor. In 1948, he is named chief of staff for the Marine Corps, and assistant commandant.

In June 1950, Smith receives command of the First Marine Division, which includes four regiments and is the sole Marine force sent to Korea in response to the invasion by the North. Unlike many of the army's forces already in Korea, and those hastily assembled to answer the threat, Smith knows his Marines are well trained, many of them veterans of World War II. If the tide is to be turned against the North Koreans, Smith knows his Marines must bear a significant part of the load. As plans for MacArthur's invasion of Inchon take shape, it is Smith's Marines who will lead the assault.

On September 16, 1950, Smith observes the ongoing invasion from the command ship, USS *Mount McKinley,* along with the rest of the Allied high command, including MacArthur. After only a single day, the advance has secured most of Inchon, and has driven more than five miles inland. Smith then does what he has done on so many landing zones in the Pacific. He moves among his men, surveys the faces, the mood, the buoyant morale, all the while holding to the agonizing hope that their astonishing good fortune will continue.

PETER "PETE" RILEY

Born in 1923 in York Springs, Pennsylvania, Riley is an only child. He grows up in the orchard country of south central Pennsylvania, gaining a deep appreciation of the land and its bounty. His family struggles through the Depression and Riley is forced to find work in the orchards. He does not complete high school. In 1940, with little hope for a better job, Riley enlists in the Marine Corps.

When the war breaks out in December 1941, he is in Marine boot camp at Parris Island, South Carolina. His first assignment places him with the Third Defense Battalion at Pearl Harbor, Hawaii, where he is witness to the grotesque aftermath of the Japanese attack. Chafing to participate in the campaigns in the Pacific, he finally receives assignment to the Seventh Marine Regiment in June 1943. He participates in severe combat on New Britain, Peleliu, and Okinawa, where he meets and forms a lasting friendship with Hamilton Welch. Both men continue in service to the Corps after the war's end, when the First Division is assigned to occupation duty in China. In late 1945, as a result of the massive downsizing of the American military, Riley and Welch are both ordered to civilian life.

Riley returns to Pennsylvania and marries high school sweetheart Ruthie Biesecker. They settle in the small orchard community of Arendtsville, where once again Riley returns to the tedious labor of the fruit orchards and processing plants. In November 1946, Ruthie gives birth to a son.

In June 1950, with the sudden breakout of fighting in Korea, Riley responds to calls for veteran Marines and reenlists, reuniting with his friend Welch. He is assigned to Fox Company, the Seventh Marine Regiment, First Marine Division. His commanding officer is Oliver P. Smith. Like many who reenlist, Riley is not completely certain just where Korea is, or just what the Marines are expected to do there.

SUNG SHI-LUN

Born 1907, in Hunan Province, China. As a young man, he attends the Whampoa Military Academy, Guangzhou, China, graduates with high honors, attracting considerable attention from his superiors. As part of his lessons at the academy, he learns rudimentary English.

Sung despises politics, and with the country embroiled in conflicts from the heavy-handed corruption of Chiang Kai-shek's government, Sung is disgusted by the abuses he witnesses on both local and national levels. He considers himself a patriot to China and willingly joins the army of Mao Tse-tung, embarking on the struggle to rid the country of Chiang's despotic rule.

In 1934, he participates in the Long March, Mao's desperate gamble to escape Chiang's military forces. The march, more accurately a military retreat, covers more than five thousand miles and requires a full year. Much of Mao's strength and support comes from the vast numbers of peasants he champions, waging war against Chiang's machine of corruption and betrayal of the Chinese people, bolstered by guns and money from the West. Those who survive the march pledge a loyalty to

Mao that is unshakable, and Mao's command of the Communist Revolution in China becomes unquestioned.

During the vicious struggle against Chiang's forces, Sung is promoted multiple times and builds a well-earned reputation for combat, leading troops in a number of bloody campaigns. In 1949, when Mao's final victory secures control of all mainland China, Chiang flees to the island of Formosa, now Taiwan, where Chiang establishes his republic as a government in exile. Mao's victory is celebrated by communist governments the world over, and adds greatly to the lore that Mao espouses, that the communists are certain to achieve a worldwide revolution.

For his loyalty to Mao, and his excellence in the field, Sung is promoted to full general. When the war breaks out in Korea, Sung shares the belief of many in the Chinese army that the war will never involve China, since most believe that the United States will not hesitate to employ its nuclear weapons, an asset China does not have. Sung also harbors a profound distrust and dislike for the Soviets, an attitude passed down from Mao himself. As the war in Korea evolves in unexpected ways, Sung responds willingly to the responsibilities he is given, and he is assigned to command of the Ninth Army Group of the People's Liberation Army, a force numbering more than one hundred twenty-five thousand men.

As the Chinese government carefully observes events to their south, Sung has one duty. Prepare his army to fight.

PART ONE

"There is nothing romantic about war."

—OLIVER P. SMITH, COMMANDING GENERAL,
FIRST MARINE DIVISION, KOREA

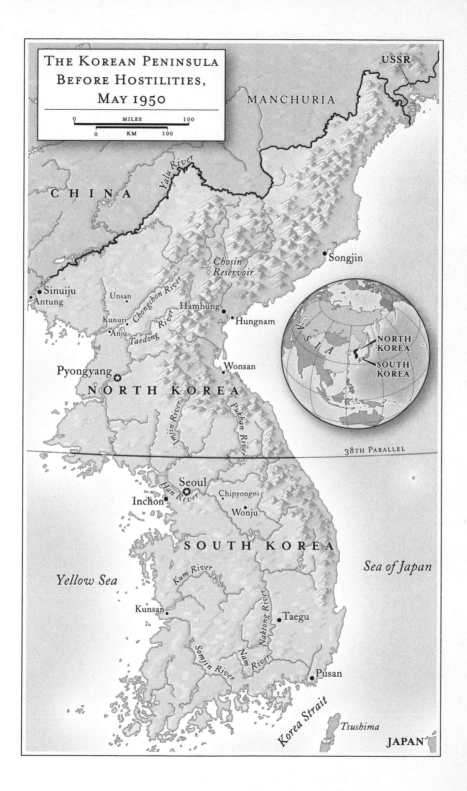

THE KOREAN PENINSULA
BEFORE HOSTILITIES,
MAY 1950

0   MILES   100

0   KM   100

MANCHURIA

USSR

CHINA

Yalu River

Chosin
Reservoir

Songjin

Sinuiju
Antung

Unsan

Chongchon River

Hamhung

Kunuri

Anju

Taedong River

Hungnam

ASIA

NORTH
KOREA

SOUTH
KOREA

Pyongyang

NORTH KOREA

Imjin River

Wonsan

Pukhan River

38TH PARALLEL

Han River

Seoul

Chipyongni

Inchon

Wonju

SOUTH KOREA

Sea of Japan

Yellow Sea

Kum River

Kunsan

Naktong River

Taegu

Somjin River

Nam River

Pusan

Korea Strait

Tsushima

JAPAN

CHAPTER ONE

. . . .

Smith

EAST OF INCHON, SOUTH KOREA—SEPTEMBER 17, 1950

"WHERE'S PULLER? I want to see him, see what's going on. He'll be in the thick of it."

MacArthur seemed to speak to all of them, but Smith had to respond.

"His men went in at Blue Beach, sir. He'll be at his new command post there, certainly." He glanced to one side, saw Ned Almond hanging on MacArthur's words like a sparrow on a telephone wire, a hint of anger toward Smith. Smith tried to avoid Almond's glare, turned to MacArthur again. "The jeeps are waiting. On your command, sir."

"Well, let's go. We delay any longer, this thing might be over before we get to see it."

The aides behind MacArthur laughed, his ever-present audience, Almond laughing the loudest. Smith moved to the door of the crude hut, held out one hand.

"This way, sir."

Smith backed away from the opening, allowed MacArthur the lead, a tradition Smith had learned from their first meeting in Tokyo, a month before. He kept back, allowed the other staff officers to go as well, Almond first, the man ignoring Smith as much as he could. Smith shook his head, then stopped, clamped down any reaction at all, wouldn't show any of them a response. The aides flowed past, the room emptying quickly. He glanced at Craig.

General Edward Craig was, by title, the assistant commander of the Marine division, and so Smith's second in command, a combat veteran whom Smith respected enormously.

Craig said nothing, and Smith glanced at the simple accommodations Craig had established, Smith's folding cot in one corner, the field desk where Craig had spread the all-important maps. Smith reached for his helmet, said, "I suppose I'm off on a field trip, General. Mac wants to see the action. He's asking for the right man."

Craig nodded, a quick smile. "Not sure why General MacArthur seems drawn to Colonel Puller."

Smith shrugged. "He likes fighters. They go back to the last war. Lewie had a few choice comments about Mac, but Mac doesn't seem to mind. Or he doesn't listen to anything a Marine has to say."

"Or he's going to arrest him. Just on general principles."

Smith looked down.

"Then you can have his job." It was a joke, but neither man was laughing. "Got to go, Eddie. Can't keep the man waiting."

He moved outside, saw the others loading up into the jeeps, four vehicles summoned for the journey. There was space remaining in one, directly behind MacArthur, who sat beside a Marine driver who could not avoid a wide-eyed sideways stare. Smith climbed up, wedged his long legs in tightly, looked at the others around them, Almond in one front seat, the others filled now with staff officers and the reporters who had come along with MacArthur. Smith knew the routine, MacArthur handpicking his favorites for the privilege of accompanying the commanding general to the front lines of his great triumph. The Marine drivers all seemed transfixed by MacArthur, but it was Smith who gave the order, a quick wave of his hand.

"Move out!"

The jeeps rolled into single file, Smith shifting his weight, trying to maneuver his legs into some kind of comfortable position. MacArthur turned slightly, said, "Puller, right?"

"Yes, sir. As I said, we're headed to Blue Beach, Colonel Puller's forward command post. He'll be there, certainly."

MacArthur nodded, seemed satisfied, stared forward, the jeep lurching past scattered shell craters, the remnants of the navy's bombardment. Smith couldn't avoid the questions in his mind, sliding between the stabs of discomfort in his legs. Was this all it took? The big guns from the ships unload on them, and the North Koreans just . . . take off? It's never that easy. No, surely they're still out there. Not sure how many. Puller will know more about that. But we're in range of just about any kind of artillery right here, and maybe mortars, too. MacArthur must know that, of course. But if I told him that, offered him caution, he'd just order the driver to go faster, closer. Well, it's his show.

They passed ambulances, other trucks small and large, artillery moving into position. Smith kept his eyes on a long ridgeline in front of them, thick smoke in bursts, spreading out with a light breeze. The thumps from distant artillery came in a steady rumble, the impacts on the ridge mostly from enemy mortars. Smith studied the hill carefully, men in motion, his men, but there was little else to see, the smoke spreading in a wide thin blanket. Up ahead, he saw officers gathering near the road, pointing toward the jeeps. Smith held his hand up, instinct, a message to the driver behind him. He reached a hand out to his own driver, tapped him on the shoulder.

"Pull over here."

The young man eased the jeep to the side of the road, the officers approaching, a pair of cautious MPs among them. They seemed baffled by the strange convoy, but there was recognition, eyes wide, more men emerging from wrecked huts, all of them coming closer. MacArthur seemed to absorb that, gave the men time to assemble. MacArthur glanced toward a reporter's upraised camera, rose slowly, stood high in the jeep, leaned heavily on the windshield, made a slow wave to the gathering Marines. Smith kept his place, knew to wait for MacArthur to leave the jeep. Finally, MacArthur stepped off, and Smith was surprised to see him stumble slightly, a hint of unsteadiness. An aide was beside MacArthur quickly, seemed prepared, but MacArthur held him away with his hand. The man backed off, MacArthur fully in control now, hands on his hips, the ever-present pipe in his mouth. He seemed to pose for a long minute, the camera clicking away. Smith jumped down, no reporter aiming any camera at him. He stumbled himself, a nagging pain in his knees, held himself against the jeep. One of the men moved closer, a captain Smith recognized, Puller's aide. MacArthur said, "Where's Puller?"

The captain looked briefly at Smith, then pointed behind him. "Up on that ridge, sir. There's a good many of the enemy . . ."

MacArthur said, "Then let's get up that ridge." He turned to Smith. "I thought this was his command post."

"It is, sir." Smith looked again at the smoke, a new round of shelling peppering the crest. "I might suggest waiting for Colonel Puller to return."

MacArthur was already stepping out onto the road, moving toward the ridge. The others fell into line quickly, MacArthur leading the parade at a brisk walk, Smith catching up, keeping the pace. He watched MacArthur carefully, could feel the pace slowing, MacArthur not hiding the weariness in his legs. The ridge was steep and dusty, the smoke drifting past, and MacArthur slowed even more, a hint of a struggle. Smith watched as Almond moved past in a rush, taking his place beside his commanding general.

The road narrowed, more shell craters on all sides, rocks strewn about, the wreckage of a jeep partially blocking the way. Smith looked into the jeep as they passed, nothing but charred metal, and he thought of protesting again, but MacArthur stared ahead, slow, plodding pace, saying nothing. Smith glanced back, the line of reporters and aides strung out down the hill, men with pads of paper, more cameras. He knew he couldn't allow this ridiculous parade to just wander out onto the open crest of an exposed hill. The incoming mortar fire came again, down to one side, and Smith said, "Sir, we should stop here. Colonel Puller is certainly close by."

MacArthur took one more slow step, then halted, seemed to fight for air, Almond beside him, pretending not to notice. MacArthur straightened, eyed the crest of the hill just ahead, said, "I want Puller. Find him."

Smith glanced around, saw Marines working mortars of their own, a heavy machine gun dug into a cluster of rocks, one man with field glasses pointing the way, the gunner firing a long burst. More men seemed to emerge from the rugged ground, all of them recognizing MacArthur. Smith felt the need to grab the man and pull him back down the hill, the thought in his brain: This is no place for you.

And then, the booming voice of Chesty Puller. "What in blazes we got here? Oh, for the love of Gertrude. They told me it was you coming up here. You're the only man who'd lead a damn caravan to the front lines." The salute came now, hard and crisp, Puller's chest puffed out even farther than usual. "General MacArthur, it is my honor. Welcome, sir." He looked past Almond at Smith now, a hard scowl giving way to the hint of a smile. "You too, sir."

Smith needed nothing further from Puller, knew there would rarely be formalities between them. He knew that MacArthur had an odd affection for Puller, despite the fact that Puller seemed to bristle at nearly every order MacArthur had ever given him. The thought rolled into Smith's head. Nobody but Lewie would talk to Mac like that and expect to keep his command. Puller knows something we don't. Or, Mac thinks he does.

Smith had known Lewis Puller since their early days at Fort Benning, through several campaigns in the Pacific. The two men were complete opposites in appearance, Puller barely five six, with a thick barrel chest that rode precariously upon two birdlike legs. Smith towered over him, a lean frame standing better than six feet. Their temperament seemed radically opposite as well, Puller a profane and caustic man. But Smith had seen the softer side of Puller, knew him to be a man of enormous heart, and if Puller's first instinct was to jam his Marines into anyplace hot, it wasn't because he was careless with their lives. Puller had absolute confidence that his Marines could do anything he asked of them, and do it well. If men died, well, it's war. That's what men did. But Smith knew that Puller never glossed over his casualties, even if the newspapers portrayed him as the hardhearted and sometimes hard-headed warrior. Smith knew another side of Puller almost no one ever saw, what few newspapermen would find worth writing about. Chesty Puller was extremely well-read, a man who took education seriously. Smith knew they were far more alike than people assumed. No matter Puller's flaws or rough edges, Smith truly liked the man. And clearly, MacArthur did, too.

MacArthur scanned the area, then said, "We thought we'd find you at your command post, Colonel."

Puller stabbed a pipe into his teeth. "This *is* my command post, General. There's a hell of a scrap down that hill."

MacArthur studied the distant ridges, smoke billowing up nearby, more incoming mortar fire. Smith closed his eyes, shook his head, saw Puller watching him. You know what I'm thinking, Lewie. This is insanity.

MacArthur said, "Colonel, your regiment is splendid. First-rate. I am gratified to present you with a Silver Star." MacArthur seemed to rummage through his pockets, then shrugged. "Don't seem to have one handy. Well, my staff will make note of it. So, where's the enemy?"

Puller pointed behind, back to the next ridge. "The sons of bitches are right over there, General. There's no doubt some North Korean officer is up there pointing to all these sons of bitches right here."

Smith flinched, but MacArthur didn't react. His aides came closer, binoculars put into MacArthur's hands. He raised them, scanned for a moment, said, "Seoul is how far?"

Puller said, "Four miles, maybe more."

"How long before you get there?"

"Three or four days."

MacArthur lowered the glasses, glanced back at Smith. "I thought we were pushing them more quickly. We should be inside the city now."

Smith had no answer, knew the timetable had been bested already, wasn't sure why MacArthur or anyone else would complain. Puller said, "Sir, there's a good bunch of those other fellows out there. We pushed 'em back to these ridges, and figured they'd keep going, blow outta here pretty quick. But they've reinforced. Seems like they intend to make a fight out of this. But we'll get there, sir."

MacArthur handed the binoculars to an aide. "I wish they'd come on up here and give us a fight. We'd clean them out pronto. I want that city by the twenty-fifth. You understand that, Colonel?"

Puller took a deep breath, looked at Smith. "We'll do our best, sir."

MacArthur stared out again, his hands planted firmly on his hips. The smoke rose from a new round of incoming fire, the artillery behind them responding, sharp whistles passing overhead.

"Magnificent. You Marines have done the job. I told them back on the ship, the admiral, the reporters. The Marines and navy have never shown more brightly. They'll quote me on that. The world will know. I want a Presidential Unit Citation for these boys." He turned, looked past Smith to the reporters, who had kept their distance. "You hear that? Write it down." MacArthur looked again at Puller, kept his hands on his hips, and Smith could feel MacArthur's pride, the raw satisfaction. To one side, a mortar blast drove the reporters back, a nervous flock of birds, the Marines around them ducking low as well. Another blast came now, farther away, then more, patterned along the crest of the ridge. Smith kept his position, close behind MacArthur, Almond glancing nervously at Smith. He felt the words coming in his head, wouldn't say anything out loud. These are the front lines, General Almond. Get used to it.

Puller stared out through binoculars of his own, called now for a radioman. He turned to MacArthur, said, "Excuse me, General, but I've got some things that require my attention. You want us in Seoul, we need to clean things up out here first." Smith knew Puller's mood, that it was time to go to work. Parades could come later.

After a long moment, MacArthur said, "Excellent job, Colonel. Truly well done." He turned, Almond following in step, both men moving past Smith. But MacArthur stopped, looked again at Puller. "No more delays, Colonel. I want Seoul in hand on the twenty-fifth."

THE HAN RIVER, WEST OF SEOUL—SEPTEMBER 20, 1950

Smith lay flat alongside Puller, both men glassing from the ridgeline down across the lowlands that spread into the city. Below them, Marines poured down the hill in a fresh advance, disappearing into a fog of thick smoke, the rattle of machine guns punctuated by the thump of mortar fire. Smith felt the stirring in his stomach, never enjoyed watching combat, men scrambling straight into the enemy positions.

Puller lowered the glasses, said, "He leave yet?"

Smith kept his eyes on the smoke, caught glimpses of moving men. "Tomorrow morning. He'll fly out. Kimpo's secure, more or less. He'll want his picture taken boarding a plane."

Puller sniffed, said, "You don't much care for Mac, do you?"

Smith brought down the binoculars, thought a moment.

"Never said that. Wouldn't say it. Not even to you."

"That just makes you gutless."

"No. Just careful." Smith looked along the hillside, no one close enough to eavesdrop. "He's not in good shape, Lewie. Seventy years old, and looks every bit of it. There's weakness, fragility. Forgets what he's saying sometimes. It's all about the spectacle, the grand show. He's entitled to that, I suppose. But he's not *right* all the time."

"He was never bothered by whether or not he was right. He sure as hell ain't worried about being *wrong*. Or being old, or fragile, or anything else. And so what? Are *you* gonna tell him to step out of the way? Not even the president's got that much nerve. The Joint Chiefs? They're a bunch of old ladies who'd rather be playing bridge. They don't want to hear anything but good news, talk of victory, the war's over, all of that. Unless Mac decides to lead his own bayonet charge, they're not gonna stand up to him one bit. Well, maybe that's not a good choice of words. They might like to see him leading a bayonet charge. Could solve a problem for them."

Smith lowered his head, stared into scrub grass and gravel. "Stop that, Lewie. There's no one else over here who can lead the men like he can. He's got some . . . difficulties, no doubt. But he inspires. Only man I know who can do that is . . . you. But until there are stars on your shoulder, you're no better off than me. Do what you're told." The word triggered a thought. "By the way, you ever get your Silver Star?"

Puller sniffed. "Some aide brought it up here, expected me to bow down and kiss his feet. I told my staff to send it to my son." Puller stopped. "What's so damn important about the twenty-fifth?"

Smith wasn't sure what Puller meant, then recalled MacArthur. "September twenty-fifth is exactly three months since the North Koreans launched their invasion. I think he promised Syngman Rhee the South Koreans could have their capital back on that date. Makes good press."

Puller said nothing, and Smith knew what he was thinking. Puller raised the glasses again.

"Hell of a way to fight a war. Make sure we win on anniversary dates. What does he think we're doing out here? I'm taking casualties, for God's sake. I can't just waltz into Seoul like it's empty. Those bastards will hold to every block, every house. This is gonna be messy, whether Mac likes it or not."

Smith nodded slowly. "I know. Do what you have to do. Murray knows that, too. The Fifth is moving on past Kimpo. Oh, if you didn't get word, as of today, Litzenberg has the Seventh ashore."

"Good! That puts us at full damn strength. Murray and I will be in position to grab Seoul pretty quick, I think. I'm assuming you'll have the Seventh move up in support. It's still going to be a tough one. The enemy's dug in all over the place."

Smith stared out at the flat ground, flickers of fire, the harsh whine of artillery streaking past. "General Almond insists the entire North Korean army is in full retreat, that they'll be clear of their own border in a few days."

Puller looked at him now and Smith saw the disgust. "You paying any attention at all to what that office boy tells you?"

"Have to, Lewie. He's in command here."

Puller pounded one hand on the hard ground. "Good Christ, O.P.! MacArthur anoints his chief of staff as the next coming of Napoleon, and we're just supposed to bow down and obey him? Almond doesn't know combat from combat boots. You want to know where the North

Koreans are? Ask any of those boys out there. They're up to their asses in North Koreans."

Smith let out a breath. "MacArthur has put General Almond in command of the Tenth Corps, which includes us. It doesn't matter why. So far, this operation has been successful. General Almond deserves credit."

"Oh, he'll take the credit, all right. But if we fall on our faces, it's you who'll take the blame. He's a cookie pusher, and he's really good at kissing MacArthur's ass every night when he goes to bed. That's why he's leading this operation. And that's why there's gonna be trouble. It's not over yet, O.P. Not by a long shot. I'm losing boys out there, and the North Koreans aren't going anywhere we don't shove 'em."

Smith knew everything Puller was saying was true. He had already had enough confrontations with Ned Almond to know that Almond had no grasp of battlefield tactics. But he couldn't say that to Puller, nor to anyone else.

"Look, O.P., I appreciate your predicament. I would only request that you allow your men to do their job the best way we know how. Keep the cookie pushers out of the way."

"I can't keep him away from his own command, Lewie. We'll manage. We have to. No other choice."

Puller went back to his binoculars, the conversation over. There was no argument from Smith. He thought of the command post, that Eddie Craig would have dispatches for him, that Smith would need to follow up with his Seventh Regiment's deployment. They're just boys, so many of them. There wasn't time to season them, and Litzenberg has to know that. I just hope to God the veterans lead the way. He hated Puller's phrase, "cookie pushers," thought of Craig. He didn't know what to expect from me, I suppose. Had to wonder if I was just another office boy. Hope I can prove him wrong on that one. Craig's a good man, seems happy with the job. I need experience with me if we're to do this thing right, somebody who understands combat. At least Puller trusts me. Knows we're all on the same side. The other regimentals, too, Murray and Litzenberg, both good men. And Carl Youngdale, the right man to command the artillery. We'll need them all to be on their toes, no matter how many cookie pushers we have to deal with.

Smith had received a hard dose of the misery that came from Almond's style of command during their first meeting, a month ago in Tokyo. The man had an astounding talent for condescension, Almond repeatedly calling Smith "son," though the two men were nearly the same age. Almond had questioned whether Smith had any actual combat experience, which showed how little Almond knew about the man he was suddenly supposed to lead. Smith had responded with specifics, details of his service throughout so many of the campaigns in the Second World War, which seemed not to impress Almond at all. Only then did Smith realize that Almond had virtually no experience in combat, had, for the most part, been kept on a back burner in World War II. But MacArthur had his reasons for placing Almond in command of the Tenth Corps, and Almond intended to make the most of the opportunity. The Tenth now consisted of two army divisions and Smith's First Marine Division, creating a formidable force against any enemy. Whether General Almond was up to the task was a problem as much for MacArthur as it was for the men who would serve him. If Almond fell apart, or made bad decisions, there could be a far greater price for MacArthur than a missed timetable. But so far, neither Almond nor MacArthur seemed concerned about the gravity of any of the decisions that lay before them. The war was going according to plan, MacArthur's plan. And the word was already seeping out of headquarters in Tokyo that this war would likely be over before Ned Almond or anyone else had a chance to screw it up.

CHAPTER TWO

. . . .

Riley

"GOOD GOD. WHAT IS that smell?"

The boy had his hands clamped over his face, but no one responded to his question. Riley fought the stink himself, looked out over the rice paddy, civilians working the watery field. He pointed, said, "Maybe it's them. Not the rice. It don't stink like that."

Behind him, the sergeant, Welch. "It's the water. They fertilize it with human waste. Don't hardly need a latrine or any kind of outhouse. You just take a dump in your honey pot, then toss it in the fields."

Riley tried to escape the odor, impossible to avoid. Behind him, another man.

"Then they eat the damn rice?"

Welch laughed. "Have to. All they got, I think. You seen any big fat cattle around here? Hell, I heard there's a reason you don't hardly see any dogs. Meat's hard to come by."

Riley shook his head. The dust from the road covered his boots, a gray coating on his green dungarees. He hoisted the rifle a little higher, said, "Hey, Sarge. How come they making us walk?"

"Don't want to bring the trucks up too close to the river. Need 'em back at the seawall, hauling more supplies. The river's just up ahead.

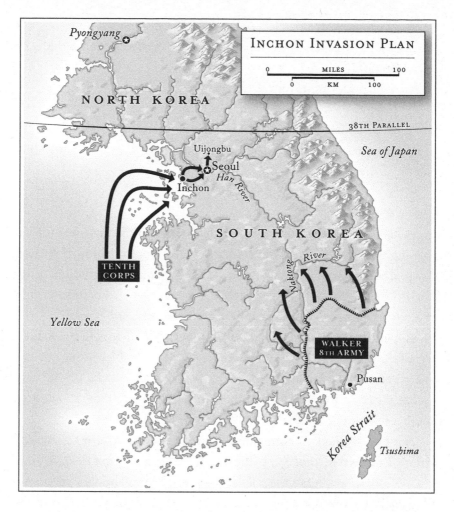

Captain Zorn says we'll be crossing that pretty quick, maybe by morning. I guess they're happy we finally got here."

Across the road from Riley, the boy spoke again. "You think we missed it?"

Riley glanced over at the boy's face, all pimples and short wisps of beard, two fingers clamped firmly on his nose. "Missed what? The fighting? You think we're here for a vacation? You already got a good whiff of this place. You better get used to it. Where you from, anyway? It stink like this back home?"

"New Jersey. Paterson. No, not hardly. Never smelled anything like this. I thought we were the reserve and all. Didn't think we'd actually do any walking."

Riley heard a laugh from Welch.

"Welcome to the Corps, kid. You didn't expect to walk anyplace? Just how dumb are you? They not teach you anything in boot?"

The boy hesitated. "Didn't have boot, Sarge. Not really. A bunch of meetings, more like."

Riley looked hard at the boy now. "Meetings? What the hell are you talking about?"

Welch said, "Heard that a lot, Pete. They brought these kids in for training and didn't have time to teach them a damn thing. Sat them down around campfires like a bunch of Boy Scouts and told 'em ghost stories. That right, kid? What's your name, anyhow? You come with us to Japan? Don't remember seeing you on the transport."

The kid nodded, obvious embarrassment. "Joey Morelli, Sergeant. I stayed outta the way, I guess. Sick most of the time. Never been on the ocean before."

Riley gave a low laugh. "Nothing different about that. I tossed up lunch a few times. What the swabbies called lunch, anyway."

The boy seemed to animate now, glanced behind him to the sergeant. "I wanted it, boot camp, the whole thing. Expected to learn all of it. Couldn't wait to grab me a rifle, show 'em I knew how to shoot and all. They just showed us how to polish boots. Taught us about C-rations. Then we had to board the ship. Maybe fifty of us. They handed me a piece of paper, told me to report to Captain Zorn, that I was with Fox Company. I just done what they said."

Welch said, "Welcome to Fox Company. I guess the captain put you with me so's I keep your head down. You can shoot, huh?"

"Yes, sir, done a good bit of hunting down in the Pine Barrens. Rabbits and such."

Riley shook his head. "Jesus. Good luck with this one, Sarge."

Riley felt disgusted, thought, They're calling these idiots Marines, and they can barely tie their shoes. He heard the sergeant again.

"Not surprised by any of this. It's the new Marine Corps boys. Bring in these slick-faced babies and teach 'em how to shine the general's boots. Hand 'em a rifle and send this one to me. Sergeant Hamp Welch, official babysitter. Tell you what, Private Morelli, you stay the hell out of my way, don't raise your damn head up in front of my riflemen, don't look down a mortar tube, or scratch your ass on a machine gun. Somebody shoots at you, you shoot back."

"You bet, Sarge."

Riley ignored the boy, watched a small cluster of civilians, dirty, sad people, scavenging through a pile of blasted debris. His eyes stayed fixed on the clothing, instinct, looking for telltale bulges, hidden weapons. But the people seemed desperate, tearing through what might have been their home.

Most of Inchon was behind them now, many more buildings still standing than anyone expected to see. They knew there had been shelling, the navy's big guns doing all they could to erase any opposition from North Korean defenses. But the North Korean positions had been vacated quickly, no match for the surge from the Marines that poured off the boats. Riley had been as surprised as the rest of the veterans that there was no beach, that the amphibious landing had used ladders. They expected a storm of fire, the same as it had been in the Pacific, but by the time the Seventh had reached Inchon, the fighting had moved well inland. It was unusual enough to move ashore with no enemy in front of them, but the sight of huge transports perched up high in the mud was an oddity of its own. The tide had gone out quickly, stranding the landing craft like so many enormous toys. The sailors were making their jokes, that someone ought to put wheels on the boats, drive them ashore. Until the tide returned, none of the LSTs were going anywhere else.

Riley had passed through Inchon with the same thoughts as the men around him, that the Seventh Marines had come in too late to accomplish anything, bringing up the rear, acting as a reserve. Out in front, the Han River was already being crossed by the first waves, the men of the First and Fifth Regiments, pushing the North Koreans away from the enormous airfield at Kimpo, what the officers were calling the best airfield in Asia. Riley knew nothing about that, knew only that the road they were on now was supposed to take them to a crossing of the river, the last barrier to the city of Seoul.

All these men knew was the talk from the sailors, that the invasion had been magnificent, perfect execution, the Marines surging up and over the seawall, seeming to frighten the North Koreans away completely. From all anyone seemed to know, the North Koreans around Inchon had been caught completely by surprise, the Marines and now others, men of the army's Seventh Division pushing across the Han River well ahead of schedule. But the sounds from in front of them now told Riley and the other veterans that the North Koreans had not just vanished, that somewhere up ahead there was a fight. Now there were casualties, aid stations along the way that these men could not avoid. Riley had seen all of this before, marches on dusty roads past blasted homes and wrecked villages, civilians like these Koreans swept up in a war few of them understood.

He watched the civilians, most of the people old or very young. The men are gone, he thought. And there's not many young women. Those bastards will have use for them, too. Maybe that's what we're fighting for. Maybe not. They don't tell us much about that.

Riley glanced back toward the sergeant, the rest of the squad leading the platoon, who marched in the vanguard of the rest of Fox Company. He loved Sergeant Welch, that particular kind of affection that veterans knew well, when a man could be counted on to lead, as Welch had proven in a dozen fights across the Pacific. Riley and Welch had served side by side, Welch admitting that his stripes had come from chance, that any man in their company could have earned a promotion for what they accomplished against the Japanese. The most vivid memories now were from Okinawa, civilians caught up in the war that inspired pity as much as outrage. There seemed to be little difference between the Koreans and the Okinawans, all of them victims in one way or another. But Okinawa didn't stink, he thought. Not like this, anyway. Fleas and vermin, maybe. But I bet the North Koreans are just like the Japs. Use their own civilians for cover, for whatever they need. Slave labor, sex. Jesus. They're just savages. He watched a handful of old men in another rice paddy, shook his head, tried to blow the stink from his brain.

Many of the men around him had been through the same experiences as Riley and Welch, places like Saipan and Iwo Jima, Bougainville and Guadalcanal, and nearly all carried those memories in dark places. The biggest talk came from the new recruits, men like Morelli, teenagers who regarded the veterans with envy, a ridiculous thirst for stories of the bloody slaughter of the Japanese. The veterans had learned to tolerate it, though few ever offered more than a casual grunt about anything they had been through. But still, the new men begged for it, and so some of the veterans had learned the art of shoveling manure, giving the new men tasty pieces of stupidity, great tales of war and heroism that most often never happened at all.

The majority of the men of the Seventh Marines were veterans, three battalions drawn together quickly after the North Korean invasion. Many of these men had gone home in 1945, the Marine Corps downsized radically after the war's end, a decision made by President Truman. But with the explosion in Korea, the veterans had been called up once more. In the peacetime years most of them had grown soft, family men who now left behind wives and young children, the old uniforms too snug around thick middles. But the training had come quickly, Pendleton and Camp Lejeune, routines they would never forget. Few of these men hesitated when the orders came, some of them welcoming the chance to leave the boredom of civilian life. Some had it better, good jobs, a pleasant life that erased many of the awful memories of the war. But they all responded.

As the division assembled around the port of San Diego, the new men had joined them as well, but time was critical, MacArthur beating the drum. And so, in short weeks, most of the Marines had steamed across the Pacific to ports in Japan, then mobilized quickly for the last leg, leading the way at Inchon. Whatever training the new men received along the way was haphazard at best, often on board the transports, rifle and machine gun practice off the fantails of the rolling ships, even the mortars launching their rounds into the ocean. The skill of the careful aim would have to come later, a nagging fear within the sergeants and experienced lieutenants, who had to wonder how these new men would react if they actually came under fire.

The highest-ranking Marine in Korea would be the First Division's commanding officer, Major General Oliver P. Smith, a man many of these Marines had served with in the Pacific. Most couldn't really describe Smith, knew him more by name, not like the bombastic reputation of Chesty Puller. Whether or not the Marines would take their orders from MacArthur, at least they had one of their own at the top. And so far, not even the officers, the men like Captain Zorn, had any real idea just what MacArthur wanted them to do. Once Seoul was captured and the North Koreans pushed back across their own border, most of these men assumed they might just board their transports and go back home.

Riley stared out past the fields, could see the river's edge up ahead, a vast fleet of trucks, big guns, engineers and their heavy equipment all in motion. He felt that familiar icy stab, the sudden feeling that he was very close now to something very big, and perhaps very unexpected. Korea was unknown to nearly all of them, some place in some corner of Asia that only the government cared about. It was the aid stations that changed that. For the first time, the sight of wounded men, wounded *Marines* drove home the reality that someone in this god-awful place was trying to kill you, and if you didn't know who or why, it didn't matter. Your job was to kill them first.

They slowed, a two-and-a-half-ton truck moving through, the men breathing more dust. Beside him, the boy again.

"You think we missed it, Pete? Do you?"

The march was halted and Riley tried to hear past the growing sounds of activity along the river. He heard the artillery again, low, sharp rumbles, and he looked at Morelli, pointed, began to speak, to teach, but overhead a sharp, deafening roar, the men ducking instinctively, the dark blue plane ripping past no more than a hundred feet above.

Riley smiled, straightened his back, then his helmet. "I was gonna teach you how to tell a fight from a thunderstorm. There's artillery up ahead, out that way, to the north. Must be the Fifth. But that damn Corsair ain't crop dusting. He's heading up that way looking for somebody to light up. His wings were loaded with rockets."

The boy looked that way, the Corsair long gone. "Geez. Scared heck out of me."

Behind them, Sergeant Welch said, "Fix that nonsense right now. That's the best sound there is in the world. You get caught in a bad place, those flyboys have a way of pulling your nuts out of the muck. They taught you nothing at all, did they?"

The boy didn't answer, and Riley saw more civilians. Rough-looking people, he thought. Like Okinawa. Civilians caught in a war, too dumb or too scared to get out of the way.

Behind him, Welch said, "Riley, take the kid, with Norman and Killian. Check those people out. Make sure they're just locals. They seem pretty interested in something over there." He called out now, toward the front of the column. "Hey, Lieutenant!"

Riley cringed at the word, knew it was a deadly mistake to single out an officer in the field, especially in a place where every pile of wreckage could hide the enemy. He leaned closer to Welch, said, "Jesus, Sarge. What the hell are you doing?"

Welch laughed. "Don't worry about it, Pete. That shavetail needs to learn some things, too."

Riley lowered his voice. "Getting him killed ain't gonna teach him a damn thing."

"I'll let *him* tell me that."

The officer slid back through the widely spaced column, a short, thin man, his eyes wide.

"What is it?"

"Sir, the captain told us to keep an eye out for possible infiltrators. I told these men here to check out those civilians. Most of these huts have been blown to hell, but there's plenty of places to hide. The enemy could be hiding anywhere. I don't trust civilians."

The lieutenant, who wasn't much older than the kid, Morelli, absorbed Welch's advice with a sharp nod.

"Yes. Good. You boys do what the sergeant says. Check those people out, look for weapons. Grenades and such. Lieutenant McCarthy's up ahead, on the radio. He said to pass along the word that we're to wait for orders. The captain's trying to find out where they want us to sit for a while."

Bob McCarthy was the platoon commander, a hard-bitten first lieutenant, the kind of officer the riflemen followed without question. But his adjutant, a second lieutenant, was very new, very green, seemed to follow McCarthy around like a helpless puppy. No one was really sure why McCarthy required another officer hanging around, but the officers usually didn't feel the need to offer explanations. Riley looked at the young lieutenant, said, "We'll handle it, sir."

The others followed Riley toward the blasted ruins, what had once been a large hut, more structures beside it. To one side, Killian, a huge hulk of a man, helmet set back on his enormous head.

"Ain't no enemy around here. We done mowed 'em out of here. Hell, you can see the river out there. Half the Marine Corps's done gone across. The kid's right. We done missed it. Gotta be Old Homer's fault. Damn them officers, anyway."

Riley ignored the comment, had too much respect for the colonel, the man in command of the Seventh. Homer Litzenberg was one of *them*, a Marine since 1922, rising through the ranks to command one of Oliver Smith's four regiments. The nicknames abounded, always: Blitzen Litzen, Riley's favorite. But to most of the men, the commanding officer was always the old man, so, in this case, Old Homer.

Riley glanced toward the big Irishman, said, "It's only been a few days, Sean. The colonel's putting us where we need to be. There's enemy enough to go around."

Killian grunted again. "Hah. So you say. I ain't seen a single Nook since we came off the boats. The fight's way the hell up front, across that river." He moved close to the civilians, two old men, four older women, the Koreans backing away with the kind of exhausted fear Riley had seen on Okinawa. Killian shouted out, "All right! Where's your sons at? Looking to crack the skull of some Yankee-san? They in here maybe?"

Killian lunged forward, used the muzzle of his M-1 to toss aside a piece of wreckage, the heap of debris still leaking smoke. Riley moved away, toward the larger structures, thought, If there's anybody in that junk, they've suffocated. Killian knows that. Likes being the *big man*.

Killian shoved past the civilians, stepped heavily into a heap of straw and lumber, brought the rifle up to his shoulder, aimed. Riley drew up, waited for the shot, thought, No, dammit. No need for this kind of show.

One of the Koreans spoke, an old man, dressed in filthy white.

"Sank you. Sank you. Yankee. You Yankee. Sank you."

Killian seemed to back down, even the rough Irishman affected by the pathetic look of the old man.

Riley said, "That's all the English they know. Count on that. They're scared to death. There's no enemy here."

Killian seemed resigned, said, "Yeah, maybe. Look up there, those other huts. Nooks could be anywhere."

Riley laughed to himself. Nooks. North Koreans. There's always a name.

"Where'd you hear that one?"

Killian's mood seemed to lighten, and he shrugged, all four of the Marines slipping through more of the debris. "Hell, I don't know. I first heard about this mess, I sure thought they wouldn't stand up to fight us. We show up with a few tanks, blow a handful of Corsairs past their huts, they'd skedaddle out of here. I heard that's what MacArthur's saying even now. I just hope we ain't missed out on the show. Damn it all."

Out on the road, Welch said, "Hey! Let's go! We're moving out!"

They followed Riley back to the road, Welch waving them into line, the men keeping several feet between them, good training. Riley saw a strange sick look on the sergeant's face, realized the lieutenant had tears on his cheeks.

"What happened, Sarge?"

Welch pointed to the other side of the road. "Nasty stuff. North Koreans left behind a message for us. For somebody, anyway."

Riley saw two navy corpsmen move into a small hut, the men backing out quickly, curses and shouts, an officer there, a man he didn't know. Riley knew better than to be curious, but it had been so long since he had seen all the varieties of death.

"What they do? Leave their dead behind?"

Welch said to the lieutenant, "Sir, you ought to take your place up front of the platoon. I'll handle things here. Lieutenant McCarthy probably needs you on the radio or something. The men are ready to move out."

The young lieutenant was white-faced, nodded without speaking, stepped away.

Welch turned to Riley, said, "He found 'em himself. Had to be a hero, stick his face into someplace it didn't need to be. I told him there could be trouble. But he's a college boy. Won't listen to some dumb son of a bitch like me."

"Hamp, what's in the hut?"

"Dead civilians. A pile of 'em. Hands wired behind their backs, slit open from crotch to neck. There's a child, maybe six, a couple young girls. One man in a suit. Local bigwig maybe. The colonel will look into it, find out if it's worth reporting."

"Jesus, Sarge."

"Like I said. Nasty. These people are primitives, pure and simple. Taking out this war on their own kind, on civilians. I told the lieutenant, this oughta teach him not to get captured. I think he got that."

Killian was there now, said, "He'll not last long. Hell, what's his name? I forget."

Welch said, "Goolsby. You pay attention to him. He's young, but they sent him out here for a reason. He's got the bar on his shoulder, so you do what he says. If he was a screwup, you can bet McCarthy would have tossed him out, sent him back to the colonel with a note pinned to his ass."

Killian shook his head, stared that way. "Those kind never make it, Sarge. He's already shaking in his boots. Smart-ass college boys. Damn ninety-day-wonders." Across the river, the echoing rumble of big guns was drawing everyone's attention, and Killian said, "There's a pile of artillery letting loose out that way. Sure wish we had Craven out front."

Welch sniffed. "Lieutenant Craven's back home with his million-dollar wound, his feet up in his wife's lap, drinking six beers. You got a wife, right?"

"Yeah."

"Well, you want to grab her soft rump again, you better pay attention right here. Be smart. You know how to keep your head down, and before we're done with this, you'll have reason. Count on it. Now, we're moving up closer to the river. We can jabber about it later." Killian obeyed, and Welch motioned to Riley. "Go on, you, too. Keep an eye on Kane and his BAR. He's got two teenagers carrying his ammo, and I'm not sure any of them know what they're doing. According to our young Lieutenant Goolsby, Captain Zorn got a call from the colonel. When the word comes, we'll cross the river in front of us, help out the First."

Riley said, "You mean, in Seoul?"

Welch tilted his head. "You been taking geography lessons? Trying to take my job?"

"Sarge, a monkey with VD could take your job. I heard the captain talking back at the boats. We're to head out around Seoul, help secure the city."

"I heard the captain, too. Seoul is supposed to be secure already. Big brass has said so."

Riley looked out ahead, focused on the artillery. "That sound *secure* to you?"

Up ahead, the men were moving to the edge of the road, dust rising from a line of trucks. Riley stood to one side, Welch beside him, the red crosses now in view. They moved quickly past, four ambulances, and from inside Riley could hear the soft moans, then a sharp cry as the trucks jolted over the rough road. The last truck was there now, and he saw a corpsman hanging off the rear, blood soaked through the man's sleeves. The corpsman glanced at the Marines along the road, who stared back at him, all of them blinking through dust. The man's eyes met Riley's, a grim nod, the cold stare of a veteran.

Welch said, "I don't give a crap what kind of gift wrapping MacArthur or anyone else is trying to hand us. This fun's just starting."

CHAPTER THREE

. . . .

Smith

SEPTEMBER 21, 1950

"DID THE GENERAL make his departure as scheduled, sir?"

Smith tossed his hat to one side, said, "He left. The schedule belongs to him. So, anytime he leaves, it's on schedule."

He regretted the sarcasm, saw Sexton looking down at the desk. The others turned to their work, a small crowd of officers filling the space in the command post, the silence awkward. Smith couldn't escape a foul mood, thought, I have no time for this. Just don't ask me anything.

From outside, Bowser came in, a bright smile, said, "Did you tell them, sir?"

Smith glared at him but couldn't be angry with Bowser at all.

"Tell them what?"

"If you'll allow me, sir."

Smith wasn't sure what Bowser meant, but he trusted the man with any kind of information, as much as he trusted Eddie Craig or any of the others. Unlike Craig, Bowser had been with Smith for years, serving him now as the division's G-3, the planning and operations officer, and less formally as Smith's assistant chief of staff. It was Bowser who had first briefed Smith on MacArthur's plans for the Inchon invasion, both men surprised that Smith, who would command the actual invasion force, had never been fully included in the planning.

Alpha Bowser had just turned forty, was another of the veterans of the campaigns in the Pacific, and when Smith went to Korea, he was grateful to have Bowser assigned to his staff. Bowser brought a capacity for patience, and as Smith had quickly discovered, when dealing directly with the communications from the Tenth Corps, patience was critical.

"End the mystery, Colonel."

"Delighted to, sir. If you will all take note of this. General MacArthur made his latest farewell to us from Kimpo this morning. As his last official act on Korean soil, for this week anyway, he presented our illustrious commander with a Silver Star. Allow me to congratulate you, sir."

Smith was annoyed, knew that Bowser was spilling out a truckload of his own sarcasm.

"Stuff that, Colonel. A commendation like that is for combat, not for standing around looking official." He looked at the others now, all eyes on him. "Make nothing of this. You understand? General MacArthur seems eager to award anyone at any time the mood strikes him. I will not celebrate such things that are not deserved." No, no. Keep your mouth shut. He pointed toward Sexton, seated at a small table, said to Bowser, "Give the thing to Captain Sexton. Hide it, Captain. No one mentions this again."

Sexton was smiling, the staff clearly not taking his anger seriously.

"As you wish, sir. Should I send it home to your wife?"

Smith tried to remove his gloom, to feel their mood, the entire staff enjoying the scene. He nodded, a hint of his own smile breaking through. "Fine. I'll have a letter for her today as well."

Sexton reached for a piece of paper on the desk, said, "Oh, and this came for you, sir. I suspect Mrs. Smith might already be aware. Hard to keep this stuff quiet."

Smith reached for the paper, said, "What is it now?" He read, Sexton not responding. He read again, wondered if there was some prankster at work. "This cannot be. I never thought that photographer was serious."

Bowser moved up beside him, peering discreetly at the paper, said, "Problem, sir?"

Smith hung his head, the note crumpled in a wad. "I assume all of you know about this?"

There were low mumbles of agreement and Smith looked at Sexton, said, "You may inform Colonel Bowser. I can't do it."

Sexton stood, more ceremony than Smith wanted. "Colonel Bowser, it pleases me to report that our commanding officer, General O. P. Smith, has been anointed as our latest national celebrity. His picture will grace the cover of *Time* magazine for the week of twenty-five September."

Bowser stared for a moment at Sexton, then at Smith. "Good God, sir, you're a star. How'd this happen?"

Sexton said, "It seems that General MacArthur's praise for our commander's performance during the Inchon invasion was heard in all the right places. The reporter was one of the crew that followed the general here and there. Mainly *here*."

Bowser said, "Congratulations indeed, sir. It is certain that your wife will know of this as quickly as the rest of the country. She will be most proud, sir. As are we all."

Smith tossed the note into a trash can. "Just go back to work. The Inchon invasion has only begun. Lest any of you forget, we are taking casualties this very minute. Men are dying so that I can be on the cover of a magazine. I take no pride in that." He knew he had drained away their morale, but would not apologize. This is MacArthur, he thought. This is how we fight his war.

Ed Craig emerged from a smaller room, the space that served as Smith's own office.

"Sir, we have received a communication from Tenth Corps."

"Fine."

He followed Craig back into the smaller room, a young corporal at the desk, pen in hand. Craig said, "You may leave."

The young man stood quickly, made his way past the two officers, and Craig closed the rickety door behind him. Smith said, "What now?"

"Sir, we are receiving reports from the regimental level, particularly from Colonel Murray, that General Almond is issuing orders directly to those commands. *Your* commands, sir. He has apparently made good use of a small spotter plane and is dropping in on the various positions as he sees fit. I am told that the general has gone so far as to order the positioning of individual machine guns and mortar batteries. Colonel Murray is most unhappy with this, of course. Colonel Puller is . . . well, he's Puller. You can imagine his response. Apparently, General Almond feels that by going directly to the front lines, as it were, he can speed things along."

"Bypassing my command."

Craig nodded. "Yes, sir."

Smith felt lava boiling in his brain, clamped it down. "You said you had a communication?"

Craig leaned out over the desk, searched, grabbed a piece of paper, handed it to Smith.

"From General Almond, this morning."

You are instructed to advance with all deliberate speed, capture the city of Seoul as ordered, with a minimum of destruction to the buildings in the city, and hasten the ongoing withdrawal of the enemy. This command anticipates that by your stout show of force, the enemy will make haste to avoid a significant confrontation. There must be no delay.

Smith said, "He said this three days ago."

"And two days ago, and yesterday."

Smith tossed the paper on the desk. "There is apparently some displeasure at Corps HQ that the enemy is putting up a fight."

"I would disagree, sir. There is displeasure that this division is behaving as though there is an enemy in the first place. Intelligence continues to insist that the bulk of the North Korean forces have vacated Seoul and are retreating up through Uijongbu, near the border."

"And yet, General Almond is issuing orders to men in the field engaged in a fight that his own people are telling him doesn't exist?"

"That sounds accurate, sir."

There was a soft knock and Smith turned, pulled the door open: Bowser, no smile now.

"What is it, Colonel?"

"Sir, General Lowe has returned. Wishes to speak with you. Sorry."

Smith looked at Craig, cocked a finger over his shoulder, the silent order to leave. Craig moved past him, tapped him on the back.

"We're with you, sir. Every damn one of us."

Smith stood alone for a long moment, the air thick in the small room, the smell of smoke and paperwork. He reached into his pocket, withdrew a pipe, sniffed the bowl, the tobacco still fresh. He would rarely smoke around any other brass, certainly not MacArthur, and never in any kind of high-level meeting. But there were times . . .

"Ah, General, pleasure to see you again."

"General Lowe. Do come in. Sorry there isn't more, um, luxury."

"Nonsense. Mind if I sit? An hour bouncing in a jeep is a different kind of luxury."

Smith motioned to a small folding chair, Lowe easing down, a slight grimace on his face. Smith moved behind the small desk, sat as well, waited for whatever the man had to say.

Major General Frank Lowe had arrived a few days before, carrying the only authorization required for him to be anyplace he wanted to be. He was there specifically as an observer for President Harry Truman, and carried no authority to lead troops, had no command status, and from what Smith could tell, was perfectly content just watching anything worth watching. Lowe was older than Smith, mid-sixties, but his bearing was similar to Smith's, a tall, thin, straight-backed man. His qualifications came more from his friendship with Truman than from any particular military expertise, even the rank something of a mystery. Lowe had planted himself into Smith's command, had even brought a cot to share Smith's meager quarters. Smith had been anything but happy with Lowe's arrival, but warmed to the man quickly. Lowe had no caginess about him, had freely admitted his reasons for being there, to communicate his personal observations to the president on a nearly daily basis.

"I've been with Colonel Puller today. Quite a scamp, that one. Most accommodating, though. Rather in a mess up there. Making progress despite some rough going. He's inflicting enormous casualties among the enemy, no doubt about that."

"You tell the president all of that?"

"Indeed. As I've said, General, I'm happy to share those dispatches with you."

Smith shook his head. "No. Your position here is clear. I prefer you keep your correspondence private. If I read what you're saying, you might feel you should edit something, some observation about me. That wouldn't be . . . appropriate."

"If you say so, General. But I must say, everything I have observed here will be most satisfactory to the president. He has concerns, of course, and he hopes I can cut through some of the official blather."

The name burst into Smith's head. *MacArthur.* Of course, that's the whole point. Mac will tell Washington what he wants them to hear. At least Truman is trying to go a little deeper than the headlines.

"How long do you expect to be here, General?"

"Please, I do wish you would call me Frank. We may share rank, but mine comes from the discretion of the president. Yours is well earned."

"Thank you. But that's difficult for me. My staff knows I don't usually get terribly familiar, even with them."

"As you wish, General. I'm not certain how long I will be here. Are you willing to offer some prediction just how long this effort will take?"

"As long as it takes."

Lowe smiled. "Of course. Well, then, I might be here for the duration, unless the president changes his mind."

"You'll keep us on our toes, then. Can't hurt."

"I'd rather not have it that way. I'm not here to grade your performance. This is much more about the progress of the campaigns, the effectiveness of our strategy against the communists. What happens in Korea might well presage what happens everywhere else in the world. This is not a vacuum. The Russians are testing our resolve."

"I don't know much about the Russians, General Lowe. I'm concerned with those people out there killing my Marines. My job, unless someone tells me different, is to eliminate the North Korean army. That would be the most effective way to end this war."

Lowe seemed to appraise Smith, said nothing. That will end up in one of his blooming letters, Smith thought. He stood abruptly, felt the need for air.

"Remain here, if you wish. Speak to any of my staff, as you require it."

Lowe laughed. "But stay the hell out of your way, right?"

"Never said that, General Lowe. You are, apparently, my guest. Anything you need, or need to see, just ask. General Craig will see to it."

He moved out the door, eased past his staff, the larger door that led outside. Behind him, Sexton scrambled to catch up, said, "Sir, might I know where you're going?"

"Come with me if you like. Just going outside."

Sexton followed him, and Smith realized the pipe was still in his hand. He lit it now, drew in the luscious smoke, and Sexton said, "How is it, sir? To your liking?"

Smith focused on the scent of the tobacco.

"Yes, quite so." He recalled now, it was Sexton who had secured the pipe tobacco, the one brand Smith preferred, Sir Walter Raleigh. "Thank you, Captain."

Sexton smiled, a short bow. "I put aside a good haul for you, sir. I keep it with my personal equipment. Ought not run out anytime soon."

Smith thought of Lowe's question, *How long?*

"What do you think, Captain? We in for a long haul here? Or you think Tokyo's right, that this thing won't last but a few weeks?"

"No idea, sir. I kinda hoped you could tell me. Maybe General Lowe might have some notion. He's army, right, sir? Does he know what MacArthur's planning?"

Smith enjoyed the pipe for a long moment, said, "He's not about to go any closer to MacArthur than he has to. Right now, he's Mr. Truman's one-man army. The president believes he has to send a spy of sorts out here to find out what's happening."

"A spy? Really?"

"Don't get excited, Captain. Real spies don't go around telling everyone what they're doing. He's just the president's eyes and ears. It's a mystery to me why Mr. Truman needs such a thing. That's what official communications are supposed to do. But apparently, Mr. Truman doesn't believe everything he hears."

"Do you, sir?"

Smith thought of the intelligence reports, G-2 section in Tokyo insisting the North Koreans were just fading away.

"Not a question you should be asking, Captain."

TENTH CORPS HEADQUARTERS—YONGDUNG-PO, SOUTH KOREA—
SEPTEMBER 24, 1950

No one seemed particularly happy to see him, something Smith was getting used to. Almond was leaning low over large maps, spread out across a long table. Various staff moved about, and Smith wondered how many of them actually had something to do. It was never far from Smith's mind that Almond was still wearing the crown of MacArthur's chief of staff. For reasons known only to MacArthur, Almond was continuing to hold two crucial jobs.

At one end of the table stood General David Barr, the commander of the army's Seventh Division. Barr was nearly Smith's age, had enjoyed a lengthy if not terribly distinguished career that went back to World War I. He seemed a pleasant enough man, had shown Smith a willingness to cooperate alongside the Marines as much as Smith required him to. It had not escaped Smith that Barr seemed as unimpressed with Almond as Smith had been.

"General Barr, hello."

Barr offered a weak smile, said, "Is our boundary to your satisfaction, General? On General Almond's order, we have moved our Thirty-second regiment in place even now, covering your right flank. There seems to be some stubbornness on the part of the North Koreans about our liberation of Seoul. I wish your people the best of success."

It was a pleasant surprise, Barr acknowledging that, for now anyway, the job of pushing into the city belonged to the Marines, the army troops acting as protection to the south, along Chesty Puller's vulnerable right flank.

"Thank you, General. We're making progress, but it's a little tougher than predicted."

Both men looked directly at Almond, who seemed oblivious to the conversation. Almond straightened, seemed to notice Smith for the first time.

"Ah, welcome. Good, the party's all here. I had hoped to go over troop dispositions and offer you both some ideas of my own. Tokyo is rather insistent that we pick up the pace a bit. I've instructed both of you to make haste, and there is some concern that things are, um, dragging. There are many eyes on us, gentlemen. The world is watching. We must live up to the reputation that brought us here in the first place. Our gallant troops deserve no less."

Smith nodded along with Barr, thought, Perfect politics. The most important eyes watching *you* are in Tokyo. To one end of the room sat a small cluster of civilians, silent, observant, whom Smith assumed to be reporters. Of course, he thought. Those eyes, too.

Almond spread his arms apart, hands out, as though gathering in the room. "Gentlemen, particularly you, General Smith, I am confident that we will triumph in a timely way, satisfying our assignment as prescribed by General MacArthur. General Barr, you will move the Thirty-second Infantry across the Han River at oh–six hundred tomorrow. Smith, you get your amtracs on the road right now. There is no time for delay. I have taken steps to light a bit more of a fire under the backsides of a few of your officers. Colonel Puller and Colonel Murray are aware of my orders and have agreed to my plans for the envelopment of Seoul."

Smith felt something snap inside him, ignored the others, said in a low hiss, "General Almond, might I have a word with you?"

Almond seemed surprised, said, "You may speak freely here."

"I prefer a private moment."

Almond held on to his blanket of smugness, moved to the far end of the room, the staff making way, the men shifting position to the opposite end. Smith knew it was all he was going to get, and he followed Almond, kept his back to the others. The fury was complete, Smith's hands clenched, his heart beating rapidly, and he hesitated, thought, He wants witnesses.

Smith took in a long breath, tried to calm himself. The words came in a low growl. "General Almond, I am aware you have issued orders directly to my regimental commanders in the field. In the future, I would appreciate it if you give those orders to me, and I will relay them to my subordinates. It is chain of command, General."

He paused, waited for some reaction from Almond. But the maddening smugness remained and Almond said, "I never gave direct orders to any of your command, General Smith. I offered my suggestions as to their deployment, based on my knowledge of events as they are. I assure you, I am not handling your regiments. I am just seeing how they do after *you* handle them."

The wall of arrogance was a mile thick, Smith realizing Almond had the upper hand. He stared hard at the man, tried to find the weak point, the place to dig in, but Almond was too good at this game. He moved past Smith, said to the rest of the men, "If we have no further discussion, my orders are plain, and have been given to your staffs. My goal here is to capture the capital with a minimum of energy expended, by squeezing the enemy until he is forced to retreat wholesale."

Around the room, the others were staring intently at both men, and Smith knew his words to Almond had been heard by all of them.

Almond continued, his voice rising. "If the enemy chooses to continue his futile efforts against us, we must crush him where he sits, and do it with all speed."

Smith moved up beside Almond, said, "And you would have us destroy the city. That is unnecessary. Your orders already issued have called for us to preserve the buildings, not to obliterate the place. I am certain that we can surround Seoul with the troops we now have available, and by cutting the enemy off from escape and resupply, he will have no alternative but to surrender. This enemy will not respect maneuver, a pincer movement, or any other kind of dance. He will only respond in our favor if he has no other choice. The city of Seoul has a million inhabitants. It does not have to be a casualty of this war. Would not General MacArthur prefer we return Syngman Rhee his capital in one piece?"

Almond turned toward him, a different look, grim anger, but he forced a smile, said, "The orders are as written, Smith. An envelopment would take far too much time. I had hoped the enemy would have recognized the hopelessness of his situation by now, and made good his full retreat. If he remains, he will be crushed. This meeting has concluded. You may all return to your commands."

MARINE DIVISION COMMAND POST, NEAR THE HAN RIVER—
SEPTEMBER 25, 1950

The order came after dark, nearly eight o'clock, while most of the Marines were standing down. All of them knew that the dawn would send them out against the enemy once more, another hard slugging match to push the North Koreans through the streets of the capital. But to Smith's surprise, his superior had a new plan.

> Tenth Corps Tactical Air Commander reports enemy fleeing city of Seoul on road north of Uijongbu. Heavy air attacks are ongoing and will continue. You will push attack now to the limit of your objectives in order to ensure maximum destruction of enemy forces. Signed Almond.

"Is this certain? Who did you speak to? Ruffner?"

Bowser nodded. "I spoke with Colonel Chides first, the G-3. He told me that we are to carry out this order as written. I called back and got General Ruffner, and asked him for a reaffirmation."

Smith ran a hand over his forehead, had no reason to doubt Bowser. "Did you explain to those people that attacking at night in an unfamiliar city is not *advisable*? Particularly since there is no indication the enemy is going anywhere across this entire division front?"

"All of that, sir. General Ruffner told me the order had been dictated by General Almond himself, and that it was to be executed without delay."

"Get Murray on the phone. Puller won't take as long to get ready. Call him next."

"Sir, are we to just order the men to march straight into the enemy? In the dark?"

"Those are the orders, Colonel."

As the Fifth and First Marine Regiments scrambled into readiness for the midnight assault, another report came into Smith's HQ. A Marine forward observer north of the city, positioned along the very road the air command had claimed as the enemy's line of retreat, observed North Korean tanks and soldiers on the move. But they were not moving north. They were adding to the strength of those forces already inside of Seoul. Instead of a retreat, it was a counterattack.

CHAPTER FOUR

. . . .

Riley

NEAR THE HAN RIVER—NORTHWEST OF SEOUL—
SEPTEMBER 25, 1950

"WHERE'S THAT KID? Captain wants latrines, and he's the one to do it."

There was little response, the men mostly hunkered down in shallow foxholes, making good use of the darkness to avoid Sergeant Welch altogether. Riley knew Morelli would speak up, the boy just too eager to please.

"You mean me, Sarge?"

It was just the enthusiasm Riley expected, and he knew Welch was smiling, the darkness hiding their faces. Welch said, "Sounds like you. Eight years old, right? My favorite volunteer."

Riley laughed to himself, his knees drawn in tight, his sleeping bag beneath him. Killian sat across from him, both men belching their dinner, an odd mix of C-rations and some kind of local meat, courtesy of some South Korean marines. Killian said, "He'll do it with a smile, too. Don't know why the young are so stupid. Any dirty job, and those kids still think it's a good idea to volunteer."

Riley didn't answer, had dug his share of latrines. He could hear the movement close by, Morelli pulling out his entrenching tool, the telltale clank of clumsy hands working the metal.

"Where, Sarge?"

Riley shook his head silently, heard Welch, "Down that hill there. You don't put the damn things next to where you sleep. Jesus. I want a one-two-three trench. You got that?"

Killian called out, "Hey, Sarge, you better show him how."

Welch was there now, a shadow standing over them. "I got a better idea, Irish. You show him. Right now. Off your ass."

Killian grumbled, stood slowly, knew there was no arguing with Welch. He climbed up from the small depression, disappeared into the dark, the voice of the kid following him.

"One two three?"

Killian responded, "One foot wide, two feet deep, three long. You ask me again, and I'll put you in it headfirst. . . ."

The voices trailed away, and Riley leaned back against the rocky dirt, Welch sitting down beside the foxhole.

"He'll be all right. Just green. Like you on Guam."

The memories came now, a thousand years ago. Riley said, "No greener than you. Around the gills, too. Didn't think one man could throw up that many times."

Welch laughed. "My damn gut's still sore. Didn't think I'd ever eat again."

Riley felt the familiar rumble down low, said, "Hey, maybe you better tell them to hurry it up with that trench. What was that we had for dinner, anyway?"

"Pork. That South Korean officer came through this afternoon, and I guess he hit it off with Old Homer. Sent a flock of pigs our way. I thought we might have an old-fashioned barbecue, but the Koreans showed the cooks what to do. Big mistake, maybe. I always heard Korean pigs weren't fit to eat."

Riley was gingerly caressing his stomach. "I'm not convinced either way. Talk to me in the morning."

"Jarheads! Listen up!" Riley knew the voice of the captain, the low talk all around them falling silent. "Where's Lieutenant McCarthy?"

Welch stood, moved that way, said, "Aid station, sir. Checking on Rickman."

"That's okay. But I want him back quick. Where's the adjutant, the new man . . . oh, hell. What's his name?"

"Lieutenant Goolsby, sir?"

"Yeah. Goolsby."

"He went with Lieutenant McCarthy."

"Of course he did. Ten minutes, and you send someone to get both of them. Right?"

"Yes, sir. What's up, Captain?"

"Orders. There's a bees' nest at division. Whole regiment getting ready to move. All I know. Find your lieutenants."

Zorn moved off quickly, his voice coming again, farther, more instructions for the next platoon. Riley rose up, Welch standing close to him. Riley glanced skyward, a scattering of stars through patches of clouds. He thought of Rickman, the platoon's first casualty. Riley didn't know him well, a quiet man, all business, hit by a sniper on the advance that morning. The bullet found Rickman's gut, the impact dropping the man in a tight curl. They didn't hear the shot, the sniper far away, and the men responded by flattening out anywhere they happened to be. But McCarthy had pulled them back up, a sharp order to keep them moving. Goolsby had scampered all through the platoon, hauling the men back into line, McCarthy watching him with a hard stare. Riley had been impressed by that, the new lieutenant doing the right thing, not allowing the men to slow their own advance by reacting to an enemy that was so far away.

He could feel the men rising up, the fresh foxholes emptying, sleeping bags rolled tight, gear pulled together. Riley did as they all did, responding to the captain's orders.

Killian was back, hard breathing, tossed the small shovel into the hole. Welch was moving through the men, came close now, said, "Well, Irish, I guess you owe me a latrine."

"Yeah, I heard. What's up, Sarge?"

"Orders to move." Welch raised his voice. "Check your weapons. Make sure you got plenty of ammo."

Riley pulled himself up, said, "Captain didn't say anything about fighting. We just advancing?"

"I didn't ask him, Pete. Somebody shoots at your ass, I expect you to shoot back."

Killian grabbed for his gear, cursed, said, "There's mail. Truck just pulled up back by the captain's CP. Damn it all. I'm expecting a pile of stuff from my wife, and my kid's just learning to draw pictures."

Welch said, "It can wait. We figure out where we'll be tomorrow night, that truck will still be there. Why the hell were you at the CP? You planning to dig your hole next to the captain's bedroll?"

Killian didn't respond, and Riley glanced around, said, "Where's the kid?"

Killian kept working, said, "Hell if I know. He followed me back here, I think. I'm not his damn nursemaid."

Riley searched the darkness, shadows and motion, low talk, the muffled sounds of equipment. Beside him, Welch said, "Let it go, Pete. He won't get lost. Scared of the dark, so he'll head for the noise."

Killian made a nervous laugh. "Yeah. Great for a Marine. Run to Mommy when the sun goes down."

Welch moved away, and Riley picked up the M-1, rubbed his hands down the stock, wiping away any dirt, felt the bandolier of magazines around his waist, a quick touch to the four grenades on his chest. He searched the dark again, said to Killian, "You shoulda kept an eye on him. He's too green."

Through the darkness, a stumble, heavy breathing. The voice came now, high-pitched, excited.

"Fox Company? Third Platoon?"

Riley felt a hint of relief, said, "Yeah, kid, you're in the right place."

"We're moving, huh? In the dark? Won't be light for a while."

Killian sniffed. "Hell, kid, it's not even midnight. Just don't fall asleep and run up my ass."

Riley ignored Killian's disdain, said, "Get your gear together. Don't leave anything behind."

"Yeah. Yeah. Okay."

Morelli moved off to his own foxhole and Riley slung the M-1 onto his shoulder, heard Zorn again, with another officer, pulling the men together, hushed orders, the urgency rolling through all of them. There was rifle fire, a heavy machine gun, then more, out to one side. He caught a glimpse of tracers, red, comforting, their own fire, but now the North Koreans were answering, blue tracers, something new. He stared for a long moment, the kid again, close beside him.

"What's all that? We going that way?"

Riley had no time for a lesson, the tension rising inside him.

"We're going where they tell us. You got your rifle?"

"Right here. I'm ready. I'm ready."

The tension in the boy's voice bordered on panic, and Riley grabbed Morelli's bony shoulder.

"Calm down, kid. We start moving, there might be enemy, or maybe not. We might just be moving to fill in empty ground. Stay low, don't shoot at anything unless you're sure. The captain will tell us what's up."

He could feel a shiver in the boy's arm, tried to avoid that himself.

"It's dark, Pete."

"Yeah, kid, it's dark."

The sounds came first, the hard rumble of a tank, the harsh whisper from in front, the men responding by sliding off the road, lying low, blind. Riley felt soft, wet grass beneath him, lay on a slope, his feet in something wet. The roar from the tank was closer, the ground vibrating, voices, strange, foreign. He rose up slightly, strained to see, the great hulk in the road coming closer, and now a heavy foot in the middle of his back. He grunted, rolled, the man tripping, a cry, surprise. Riley pulled the M-1 up, tried to catch details, anything, the man jogging up into the road, more men, the voices growing, and now a bright light, blinding, from the tank.

The firing began, all sides of him, the others in the ditch spraying the tank, the men who kept close to it. Riley felt the desperate agony of fear, searched still for the man who had stepped on him, the spotlight now moving past him, fire on both sides. He fought to see, kept flat, cold screams in his head, the terror of the darkness, held himself low, still, the sounds of a growing fight all around him. The light was out now, the tank peppered by fire from the Marines on both sides of the road, the great beast answering with machine gun fire of its own. The Koreans were shouting, orders, noise, a bugle, the chaos swallowing Riley, swallowing all of them. The road was alive with men, most of them jogging toward the Marines, some stopping to fire, flashes of light, heavy footsteps moving past him in the ditch. He watched them come, searched for the good target, but there were too many, the fire whistling past him from both sides. One man moved up slowly, close, and Riley reached out, grabbed the man's leg, pulling him down in a heap, the man rolling over Riley's body. He pulled the knife, a quick lunge, the Korean crying out, another lunge, soft flesh, the Korean down, beneath Riley, still no sounds, the man's stink engulfing him. Riley's breaths were hard and heavy, thunder in his chest, and he rolled himself upright, to his knees, the knife in one hand, the fury, the hate preparing him to do it again. And now a machine gun opened up, far down the road behind the Marines, the spray of lead ripping above him. He flattened, a silent curse, could hear men hit, falling, hard cries, more Koreans crawling close to him. He let them go, the machine gun fire too close, nothing to do but stay low. There was a massive blast, burst of fire, the tank erupting thirty yards away, the fire illuminating the roadway. Another machine gun chimed in, tearing up the road, slicing through the Koreans who scrambled for cover. He stared at the tank, flames erupting from inside, enemy troops scrambling away, leaving their steel protection. He pulled the M-1 up, no aim, jabbed it into a man's groin as he passed, fired, then rolled over, found another target, easy now, the flames on the tank lighting the scene. He pulled the M-1 to his shoulder, fired again, the Korean a few feet away, falling forward. There were more, coming back along the road, some cut down quickly by the machine gun, most in a full run. He searched for another target, fired again without aim, then again. Now the voices changed, Marines, moving up closer, calling out, rapid fire from carbines and rifles, the machine gun silent. The tank continued to burn, the bodies in the road bathed in orange light, and he stayed on his knees, eyes on the tank, men beneath it, burning bodies.

"Up! Let's go! Spread out into the field! They'll be back!"

He knew Zorn's voice, pulled himself up, stepped down through the muddy ditch, a deep puddle. He struggled to stay upright, keeping his balance, his knees soft rubber. The flames lit the field, taller grass, voices around him, orders, other men moving with him. He felt the water, the splashes high, more orders, men put into position, a line, the men settling down, good cover. He flattened out, water soaking through his clothes, the smells engulfing him, sickening, the sudden clarity, the turn of his stomach. It was a rice paddy.

The North Koreans kept up their advance for several hours, every road or trail alive with troops, more tanks offering them cover and added firepower. The fights were mostly confused and meaningless, but the Marines had the advantage of greater firepower, machine guns moving up quickly, mortars put into place. The surge by the North Koreans began to run dry, exhausted by their casualties, by the tenacity of the men who fought them.

For most of the night, the Marines pushing their way into Seoul itself advanced along dark streets, confronting blockades of rice bags, heavy machine guns seeking targets in a confused melee, casualties mounting on both sides. By early morning the North Korean resistance had seemed to weaken, but the advance was slow, many of the Marines holding tight to the ground they had already earned. Despite the attack orders the Marines had received from Tenth Corps HQ, their own commander understood that a full-blown frontal assault down a hundred narrow streets was suicide. With the Marines digging in, preparing to hold off any new push by their enemy, orders were given for a new tactic. As the sunrise spread slowly over the smoking ruins of Seoul's outskirts, the Eleventh Marine artillery regiment went to work. Pressured to capture the capital by MacArthur's deadline, Oliver Smith used the most effective weapon he had against a stubborn, well-fortified enemy. If the fight between men was mostly equal, the Americans' heavy artillery tipped the scale. Throughout the bombardment, the Fifth and First Marines could only wait, hoping the artillery would do the job. Flanked by the Seventh to the north and the army's Thirty-second to the south, the Americans closer to the city pulled into a tighter arc, pressing the North Koreans on three sides. With daylight, once again, the push would begin through the streets of Seoul. The artillery had weakened the enemy, but the fight would continue, slow yet steady progress by the Marines, whose training had rarely included house-to-house searches.

The Marines facing the enemy did not know of the orders first given to Oliver Smith, that the ancient architecture of the historical city be saved, a gesture of ignorant futility from Ned Almond. Almond's orders had now become a contradiction, his need to satisfy MacArthur forcing him to rush the entire operation. Despite Tenth Corps' fairy-tale hopes that the enemy would simply vanish, Smith and the Marines understood that the city would not be taken without a serious struggle. And so, when Smith called on his artillery, the results were inevitable. The big guns punished not only the enemy, but the historic capital itself. With the Marines renewing their hard push against the battered enemy, they drove down the narrow streets of a city that lay mostly in ruins.

NORTHWEST OF SEOUL—SEPTEMBER 26

With the daylight came a closer examination of the tank, the hole blasted through the turret with perfect aim. Captain Zorn leaned in close, said aloud, "Who did it?"

One of the other lieutenants, the Second Platoon's commander, Peterson, moved up, said, "Speak up. Who did this?"

The men gathered, all eyes on the hole in the tank. Behind Riley, one of the sergeants.

"Sir, my man won't claim it. But I'm pretty sure it was Brubaker. Front and center, Corporal."

Brubaker obeyed, a sheepish grin on his face, said to Zorn, "It was the M-20, sir. Bazooka. Hell of a gun, that one. I musta got lucky."

Zorn stood with his hands on his hips, glanced at Brubaker, then back to the tank.

"We all got lucky, son. You keep that M-20 close at hand. I'm asking battalion for a dozen more. Who was on the machine gun?"

A voice came out to one side, no hesitation. "That was Private Atkinson, sir. One of the heavies."

Zorn looked that way. "Where is he?"

"I positioned the heavies back on that low ridge. He's out to the left."

Zorn stepped away from the tank, stared out to the ridge, called, "Atkinson! You got Spittin' Sally?"

Riley looked out that way, saw a man standing, one arm in the air, the response, "Raht hyar, yassir!"

There was laughter, Riley not sure what any of this meant. Zorn stood out in the road, said, "Some of you have names for your rifles. Not sure I've heard of a name for a heavy machine gun. Gentlemen, our bacon was saved this morning by Spittin' Sally. You get a chance, pay your respects."

Riley didn't know many of the men in the machine gun squad, saw their lieutenant, Hill, a smiling nod toward Zorn.

"Thank you, sir. Atkinson keeps this up, may have to put him in for a citation."

Zorn said, "Don't forget Sally." The laughter came again, the stress of the morning drifting away, relieved by the few moments of humor. Zorn seemed to understand that, called out now, "Move out into that field, take up along the highest ground. Battalion is keeping us along this road, in case the enemy makes another try." He seemed to search, then said, "We got the enemy body count?"

It was Goolsby, unexpected, the youngest officer in the company stepping forward. "Eighty-one, sir."

"Prisoners?"

"Twenty, I think."

Zorn glanced at McCarthy, then stared at Goolsby for a long moment. "Write it down, Lieutenant. I'll give that to battalion. Those kinds of numbers will make Major Sawyer pretty happy. Good ratio. All right, move out up that hill. Eyes open. Dig in. Not sure how long we'll be here. Uijongbu is up that road a few miles. My CP will be set up back behind that ridge. I wanna be close to Sally."

The fight early that morning had been a rapid-fire nightmare, but Riley knew the men had been buoyed by Zorn talking to them, felt that himself. He knew little about the battalion commander, Buzz Sawyer, even less about Litzenberg. But none of them lorded over their commands with that peculiar attitude that seems to tell their men that whatever is happening now is simply an inconvenience, that the senior officers have their eye mainly on a different prize, putting an eagle or even a star on their shoulder. Riley had seen that in the Pacific, officers who ignored everything but the spotlight. Hopefully, he thought, that's not Zorn.

He stepped along a path, men in front of him, and behind him, Killian.

"Well, what the hell happened to you? You smell worse than Korea."

The wetness in Riley's clothes had mostly dried, the odor a part of him now. He looked back, said, "No, you stupid son of a bitch, I smell *exactly* like Korea. Where the hell were you, anyway? I don't see any of that damn rice paddy on you."

Killian was beside him now, gave him a sharp rap on the back. "Brains, skinny boy. Found a good spot on dry ground. Took down a few of those bastards, too. Hell, might give the M-1 a name. How 'bout Deadly Dixie? Maybe the captain'll give me something, too. Those gunneys get all the attention."

"They earn it. The captain's right. That heavy kept us alive. We'd have been trampled by those bastards, no matter how good *your* cover was."

Killian said nothing, both men moving with the others farther up the hill. He saw McCarthy now, Welch and the other sergeants around him. Welch saw Riley, called out, "This way. Take position back of this rise. Dig in. Eat something."

Riley passed Welch now, followed the directions, caught the smell, worse than his own.

"Damn, Sarge, you fall into something nasty?"

"Your mama's bathrobe. Get moving."

Riley smiled to himself, knew he'd have to top that one.

They were spread out in a ragged formation, more than two hundred men, other companies positioned beyond. Down the sloping ground toward Seoul, he could hear the clatter of heavy weapons, that fight not slowing, and he thought of those men, no names, no friends that he knew of. They got none of this, he thought. No time for laughter, for a company commander to test the mood of his men. He stared that way, a low haze of smoke rising over distant houses, saw more Marines moving out on another trail, another battalion adding to the force that was to keep the North Koreans from escaping the city, from slipping away. He was suddenly very tired, realized there had been no sleep at all. He thought of the man he had knifed, fought against ever thinking of that at all. But the moment would find its way down into that hole, join the other memories, the other horrors. One more kill, he thought. Him, not me.

He sat in the hole, shifted himself, pushed rocks out of the way, tossed one out of the hole. Killian was kneeling at the far end of the hole, digging into his bag, and Riley thought of the captain's words: something to eat. He put one hand on his stomach, no appetite at all, his own odor engulfing him. He watched Killian pull something from his bag, a small can with no label.

"Hey, Sean. You ask about the mail?"

"Lieutenant Goolsby said tonight, if the Nooks leave us alone. Ammo carriers be coming up, too."

Riley was surprised. "You talked to Goolsby?"

Killian shrugged. "Well, he's a platoon officer, right? He's sorta in charge. Figure he'd know."

Riley recalled the criticisms of the man from days before, all the talk about ninety-day wonders. "Guess maybe he'll work out okay, huh?"

Killian focused on the can, stabbed it with his knife. "So far. Ain't screwed up yet. But Rickman getting hit bugged him too much. He says it's serious, Rickman's going back to a hospital. McCarthy's okay with it, best as I can tell. But I'm guessing Goolsby's got *green guilt.*"

Riley knew the phrase, shorthand for a new officer's inevitable response when he takes his first casualty. "No time for that. Not after today."

Killian swiped a finger through the open can, which seemed to be fruit cocktail. "Nope. He'll learn. This thing gets hot, won't be time to hand-hold every wounded man. Kinda looking forward to it."

Riley tried to feel an appetite again, couldn't erase the smell. "Why you say that? You enjoy what we went through last night?"

"Sure. Hardest part was finding a damn target. Ain't like deer hunting. You hit one of these yellow bastards, he goes down in a heap. If you miss him, he runs for the hills."

"Sounds like deer hunting to me."

Killian sat down in the trench now, set his rifle upright beside him. "You ain't never killed no deer."

"Once. Well, no, I missed him. He ran like hell. Just like the enemy."

"Where you from, anyhow? Thought you'd be from the city, like me. I went hunting with my family, upstate New York."

Riley said, "Pennsylvania. Apple country. Lots of deer."

"Hmph. Shooting a Nook's no different. Dead's dead."

Riley held his response, thought, You couldn't be more wrong, Irish. The image of the knifing came again, the cries, the hard grunts, the man's smell.

They fell silent now, low talk around them from the others. But with the quiet came the sounds from Seoul, never-ending, skirmishes and raw combat, an excruciating reminder to Riley that the heavy lifting was being done by someone else. He avoided looking that way, nothing to see, could hear Morelli talking to the man in his foxhole, lively chatter about New Jersey. I wonder if he had *fun*, too. I wonder if he put his knife through a man's chest. He closed his eyes, tried to shut down the voice in his head, but the fighting in Seoul rolled on in the distance, a chorus of rattling machine guns, a song from the kind of hell that boys like Morelli didn't know existed.

CHAPTER FIVE

. . . .

Smith

THE JEEP WAS TILTING to one side, making for a nervous ride, made more so by the heavy load on the meager springs. Puller sat in the front seat, Eddie Craig in back, beside Smith. They had come from Puller's new command post in the city, the Duk Soo Palace, but Smith had first come into the city across the Han River on a brand-new bridge. The orders weren't his, the bridge doing nothing for the Marines who were already in the city. The word had come from Tokyo, launching the engineers into a frantic rush. The bridge was to be built specifically for MacArthur, allowing the general to make his entrance into the capital with all the grand spectacle of the conquering hero.

The jeep tottered precariously past a deep crater, the stench of the explosion still rising, Smith holding on tightly to the side. Puller leaned back toward him, said, "Sorry. Busted shock absorber. That'll be fixed. Wasn't time this morning, when we got the word. You'd think there'd be more jeeps, but they were all out doing real jobs. Besides, this one's my favorite."

Smith kept his eyes down the side streets, could see Marines in clusters, aid stations, low-level command posts. The smoke was there, too, some of it from blasted houses, piles of rubble where men huddled, watching civilians searching for anything they could find.

"This is madness."

The words came from Craig, and Puller turned his head slightly.

"Oh, you got that right, Eddie. They made me wear this idiotic helmet, you know. Hate this tin cap, but General Almond insisted, said it'll make me look like I did the fighting. Jackass."

The jeep wound along more potholed streets, a sudden high bounce, the driver grappling with the steering wheel, Puller offering the man a heavy dose of swearing, but Smith ignored that, too, knew the driver was probably used to it. They turned down a wider avenue, rubble to one side, and Puller pointed, said, "Russian tanks rolled through that place there. Half-dozen T-34s. Artillery took care of them, or we did. Surprised me, though. Cost me some good men." Puller paused. "They're veterans, you know. The North Koreans. All that talk about them running away was crap. The prisoners we picked up said they had fought the Japs, some of 'em fought in China. Their weapons weren't new, but they worked just fine. Russian guns, some of ours, too. Didn't think it would be this tough, but I think we'll have this place secure in another couple of days."

"One hour's worth, Lewie. We need *secure* for one hour. By tonight you can do whatever you need to do."

There was a thump of artillery, a hard shriek overhead, then another. To one side, a distant burst of machine gun fire. Craig's word rolled through Smith's brain. *Madness.*

Puller didn't respond to Smith's request, didn't have to. Puller knew as much as any of his officers what still needed to be accomplished. They were only taking this jeep ride now because of orders that could only have come from Douglas MacArthur.

It had been announced on September 27 that two days prior, squarely on the twenty-fifth, just as MacArthur had demanded, the capital city of Seoul had been swept clean of enemy soldiers, liberated as promised, the city now to be handed back in a grand and formal ceremony to South Korean president Syngman Rhee. Around MacArthur's headquarters in Tokyo, the newspapermen had scribbled furiously on their pads as the announcement was made, magnificent news that went out quickly on the wires or by phone, reaching anxious newspapers in the

States, to be swallowed whole by Americans who still weren't sure just what this war was about. But pride ran deep, some of that left over from World War II, the certain expectation that *our boys* would always win, no matter the enemy. MacArthur understood that more than anyone, the power of the positive story, the power of *victory*. To the reporters, the general had offered praise for the Marines, the army, his staff officers, anyone who had contributed to the liberation of Seoul. That the city was still engulfed in fighting seemed not to matter to MacArthur at all.

Madness.

Smith tried to erase the word, saw the government palace looming large in front of them. He rose up in the seat, could see a fleet of staff cars parked in a wide space, great black-and-green limousines transported from Tokyo. Around the parked cars stood guards in white gloves, crisp, clean army uniforms, also from Tokyo. The cars were a surprise, but the soldiers were there because Smith had not agreed with MacArthur's request that the Marines furnish the manpower. It was one more instance of Smith standing up to Ned Almond, each time scraping a raw wound between them, what Smith knew could become a dangerous, career-ending feud. As the jeep drew closer to the wide compound, he could see the uniforms, starched and perfect, thought, Of course he'd dress them up for the occasion. I couldn't have given him that, anyway. Where am I going to get white gloves out here?

There was a guard post at the entrance of the compound, a white-gloved MP stepping out with his hand raised, Puller's driver braking the jeep to a halt. Smith could see that the man was a major, perfect uniform, shined black shoes. Puller rose up in his seat, said, "What the hell is this, Major?"

"Sorry, Colonel. Only official staff cars are allowed to enter the compound."

"Major, my staff car's in Japan. This is a combat zone. We don't ride around on soft seats."

"Sorry, sir. My orders said only staff cars. I can't allow you to pass."

Smith could feel Puller's heat, said nothing, was wondering just what Puller would do. Puller said, "Listen, you oak tree. My boys captured this damn place. I don't give a good goddamn what your orders are. Get the hell out of my way."

"Sorry, Colonel. No entry today. My orders."

Puller shouted to his driver, "Run him over!"

The jeep lurched ahead, Puller flopping down heavily on the seat, Smith pushed backward, nearly tumbling out of the jeep. The MP danced quickly aside, wide eyes, then began to follow, loud shouts. Smith watched the man until he gave up the chase, but Puller was still angry, looked back at Smith.

"We'll stop on our way out, apologize to him, if you tell me to."

Smith shook his head. "Nope. I'd have done the same thing you did."

He knew that wasn't true, saw the look on Puller's face, that Puller knew better as well. Puller stabbed his pipe into his mouth, said to the driver, "Pull over there, Jones, behind that Cadillac. Maybe they'll give you a parking ticket. That'll be fun. You stay here, though. We might be in enough hot water already, and Private, *you're* not dressed properly."

"Thank you, sir."

The man was clearly relieved to be left behind, and Smith thought, I wish I could join you. Puller slid out of the jeep, Smith and Craig behind him, and Craig said, "Colonel, maybe next time? Put your rank on the jeep."

"Why? They make me wear this damn tin cap, they can see my bird quick enough."

They walked past the grand cars, every one polished, some with whitewall tires, the guards seeming protective of their temporary posts. Puller said to Smith, "They have no idea what Marines look like. I'll bet you don't draw a single damn salute."

They were inside quickly, and Smith felt very much out of place, Korean men in suits, a sea of perfect uniforms, nearly all of them army. He scanned the crowd, saw Almond, others, almost none of the army officers familiar. Except MacArthur.

He saw Murray now, with an aide, both men gravitating quickly toward Smith.

"Sir! Glad you made it. We seem to be the only Marines in attendance."

Behind him, Smith heard a grunt from Puller, thought, Keep your head, Lewie.

At thirty-seven, Ray Murray was the youngest of Smith's commanders, and as a lieutenant colonel, was outranked by both Puller and Litzenberg. But no one seemed concerned with the insignia on Murray's shoulder. In World War II, he had earned a pair of Silver Stars and a Navy Cross, had as much combat experience as nearly any officer in Smith's command. There were certainly no complaints how Murray had handled the Fifth Marines since they had come ashore at Inchon.

Smith scanned the crowd again, said, "We have seats for this thing, Ray?"

"Yes, sir. They're starting to file into the assembly hall. I suppose we just follow the flow." He acknowledged both Craig and Puller now, said, "Lewie, it's been a tough couple of days."

Puller grunted again.

"Your boys took Kimpo airfield in a blink. Damn fine work." They followed the crowd into the hall, Smith in the lead. Behind him, he heard Puller again, a low voice to Murray. "I'll be glad when we get this thing over with."

Smith wasn't sure what Puller meant, if he was more concerned with the liberation of Seoul, or what was about to happen right now.

"Gentlemen, if I may have your attention!" It was one of MacArthur's aides, a booming voice from the stage. "Please be seated."

They sat, the room growing quiet, and Craig leaned in close to him, said, "You don't suppose he's gonna start tossing out medals?"

"Shut up, Eddie."

MacArthur rose to the stage now, and across from him, an old Korean, a slight curl to his back, the ravages of age. It was Syngman Rhee.

MacArthur spoke for a half hour, calling for prayer for the success of his men, for the liberation of the Korean capital, for the lives and well-being of every man in his command. During it all, Smith had detected what appeared to be tears streaming down MacArthur's cheeks, a show of emotion that seemed oddly out of place. More than once he thought,

This isn't over yet. The city is still a very dangerous place. But still, the ceremony went on, MacArthur ending his remarks with the Lord's Prayer, only to be followed by the United Nations representative, and a brief speech by the American ambassador, John Muccio. At last, Syngman Rhee took the stage, generous remarks of his own, concluding with the presentation of some kind of document for MacArthur, a gesture of gratitude that inspired another show of emotion.

Throughout the entire ceremony, the thumps of artillery fire punctuated the remarks, some of the impacts on buildings close enough that Smith could hear tumbling concrete. Many of the men in front of Smith reacted with nervous glances, quiet urgency in their hushed voices, Smith knowing that many of these men had never been under fire. By the end of the program, Smith was as eager as Puller and the others to leave, perhaps the only men in the room who understood that the job was still to be completed. It did not escape any of them that through all the talk, the official congratulations, the carefully orchestrated pomp, none of the speakers mentioned the Marines at all.

"I'll be leaving for Tokyo in an hour. I've heard some uncomfortable reports, that things are dragging a bit. Let's clean this up, shall we?"

MacArthur seemed distracted, scanned the departing crowd, a brief nod to a cluster of reporters waiting nearby.

Smith said, "We're doing the best we can under the circumstances, sir. The enemy has a talent for defense, and my men are pushing through the city one house at a time."

MacArthur seemed not to hear him, said, "Just get the job done. What did you think of our presentation? Quite a show."

MacArthur had answered his own question, but Almond broke in, "Wonderful, sir. President Rhee is a wonderful man, most grateful to you for what we have accomplished here. Quite spry for such an old man."

Almond's words flowed like syrup, but Smith kept his eyes on MacArthur, tried not to show any reaction. MacArthur nodded slowly, seemed lost in thought for a moment, then said, "Seventy-five, he says.

They nearly beat him to death in the war. Japanese tortured him. His hands are a mess. He loves us, of course, so we love him back. That's how they think in Washington, you know. He hates Russians as much as we do, so we love him for it. We offer him bouquets and handshakes, those things that make congressmen and newspapermen so very happy." He paused. "They know nothing of what I must do here. Nothing at all. And how they have doubted me!" MacArthur seemed to animate now, brought back to the moment. He looked hard at Smith. "They thought I was a fool. They thought we'd fall on our faces at Inchon." He gestured toward the reporters waiting at the far end of the hall. "Now, look at them. Like schoolchildren, eager for today's lesson. I shall give them one. They will listen, too. Write down every word. Not so those people in Washington. They do not understand what a war is, you know. To them, it's budgeting and arguments over treaties. It's why this country needs men in the field who know how to take command, who can make the decisions, all of the decisions."

Smith didn't know what to say, felt as though he wasn't a part of MacArthur's conversation at all. Almond seemed anxious to respond.

"Yes, sir. Certainly."

MacArthur looked at Almond, as though for the first time, said, "There is much to do still. Orders will be issued. Make ready for the next phase of this operation, General."

Almond seemed to snap upright. "We are quite ready, sir."

"I'll be leaving now. A word to the newspapers first. But I must return to Tokyo." He looked at Smith now, saw Puller behind him with the others.

"Fine work. Truly outstanding. You have earned the gratitude of your nation. I will see to that."

MacArthur moved away, and Smith watched the man's gait, a hint of unsteadiness, a slight shake in MacArthur's hand. Almond moved closer to Smith, spoke in quick, hushed words.

"Clean this place up, Smith. We're going north, and I want no laces left untied. Your orders will come very soon. I expect them to be carried out with all *speed*."

Smith nodded, thought, That word again. "We will continue to do our best, sir."

Almond moved away, chasing MacArthur, who stood tall, the reporters gathering close. Smith had desperate need of a deep breath, backed away, watching the scene, making certain MacArthur didn't suddenly want him by his side. Don't be foolish, he thought. We're not even a sideshow in this place.

As the fighting continued around Seoul, the enemy seemed finally to give way, and another blow to North Korean hopes emerged from farther south. For weeks the North Koreans had waged a vicious war against Walton Walker's Eighth Army, a combination of American and United Nations troops. Walker's forces had taken the first great shock from the North's invasion, had been mostly overwhelmed, shoved backward into a tight squeeze around the southeastern corner of the peninsula, what was now called the Pusan Perimeter. But the amphibious landing at Inchon had accomplished MacArthur's objective, had driven a sharp wedge behind the enemy besieging Walker. As part of MacArthur's overall strategy, Walker's forces were to launch a well-coordinated breakout of their own, coinciding with the amphibious landing of the Marines at Inchon. To the surprise of most of the American military planners, who had been taught by MacArthur to have little confidence in Walker, the Eighth Army breakout of Pusan was successful. Whether or not MacArthur would give credit to Walker, a man he deeply disliked, the breakout seemed to show that the North Koreans, with their supply lines cut, their ammunition running low, their rations disappearing, were mostly used up.

For Oliver Smith, the mopping up soon cleared Seoul of any significant pockets of the enemy, the Marines finally able to stand down, reorganize the smaller units, deal with their casualties. From the time Douglas MacArthur had claimed the liberation of Seoul until the city was actually cleared of fighting, the Marines suffered more than seven hundred additional casualties. Whether anyone in Tokyo wanted to hear that, Smith knew the war in Korea had already become a nasty, bloody affair. In Smith's headquarters, and all through the First Marine Division, optimism followed the victory. At higher levels, many in Korea, Tokyo, and Washington allowed themselves to believe that the retreat of the North Koreans from both Pusan and Seoul meant the end, that diplomats would now take charge, that the two sides would return to some kind of agreement that kept Korea divided along the 38th parallel. But Douglas MacArthur had a very different notion of how this war should end.

CHAPTER SIX

. . . .

Riley

THE PRISONERS CLIMBED UP from the holes, their hands high, Riley keeping the M-1 aimed at the lead man. He saw the face clearly, hard eyes, something about the North Korean that said *nasty*. The prisoner was older than the others, but there was nothing in his clothing that showed rank. To one side, Lieutenant Goolsby made a verbal count, the line lengthening as the prisoners continued to emerge from the blasted hole.

"Twelve . . . thirteen . . . fourteen. God, they smell."

An MP stood close by, another lieutenant, a squad of his men waiting expectantly. Riley saw the youth on their faces, no older than Morelli.

From the deep hole came a woman now, then another, both young, very pretty. The Marines were caught by surprise, the inevitable comments coming.

"Hey! She's a cutie!"

"Whoa, sister. I got your bayonet right here!"

Behind Goolsby, Welch called out, "Knock it off." The sergeant moved forward, closer to the MP officer, said, "Sir, I'd be careful with these. They're more dangerous than the men. They're not soldiers, but I bet they're armed."

The MP seemed annoyed that a noncom could tell him anything he didn't know.

"We'll handle this, Sergeant."

The lieutenant pointed at the first woman, an MP approaching her, his carbine dropped low, a hand out: "Hey there, Missy, you let me check you out, okay?"

The woman spun around, one hand flashing through her filthy dress, the grenade there, the MP lunging forward, tackling the woman, a flurry of dust and shouting. Riley moved forward quickly, but the MPs were there first, the grenade pulled away, a hard punch to the woman's face. The second woman stayed still, watching stoically, and Riley could see the anger, the raw viciousness of her expression.

The MPs spread out now, moving to the male prisoners, no talk at all, no need for words. One was punched hard in the stomach, the Korean curling over with a grunt, collapsing to his knees, twisted pain on his face. An MP pulled the man up by the shirt, ripped it from the man's back, tossed it aside. He glanced at his lieutenant, who said, "Go on. All of them. Strip 'em down."

The MP jerked at the man's pants, sliding them to the ground, another quick jerk, stripping away his underclothes. The Korean stood naked, the MP motioning to the other prisoners with the muzzle of his carbine. They seemed to understand, pulling off their clothes, resigned to their captivity. Around Riley there were low comments, Riley sharing a nagging discomfort. But the MPs were firmly in charge, the clothing tossed aside, the Koreans now completely stripped.

The lieutenant moved to the silent woman, held his pistol in his hand, aimed it at her face, then slowly pointed downward, touching her chest.

"Off."

Riley felt a twinge of sickness, thought, Good God, what's he doing?

The woman glanced at the other prisoners, the men cupping their hands at their groins, and said something in Korean, then pulled at her blouse. In seconds she was as naked as the men, and she turned to the injured woman, a hard shout, short words, the woman undressing as well. No one spoke, the Koreans staring at the men who stared at them, the women seeming more defiant than the men.

The other MPs moved up, poking at the clothing with the carbines, one man bending low.

"Right here, sir. Another grenade. Hell of a knife, too. You were right."

Riley noticed Goolsby, white as a sheet, the MP officer seeing that as well.

"Done this before, Lieutenant. Any dame with a bunch of men, she's either a sex slave or . . . well, one of these. Seen an officer's wife once, traveling with her man, handling a machine gun like a pro. These two . . . they'd kill you quicker'n any man. They can't do much now. There's a truck down the road, we'll load 'em up."

Goolsby nodded dumbly, and Welch said to the MP, "Appreciate it, sir. I'll make sure Lieutenant McCarthy knows about you helping us out. There'll probably be a few more of these folks to handle up ahead."

The MP made a quick nod, moved away, the other MPs motioning the prisoners into line, marching them into captivity.

Riley watched Goolsby again, the young lieutenant trying to gather himself. On the road, more Marines were moving up, the rest of the platoon, another platoon behind them. The prisoners had their full attention, the men offering a chorus of catcalls and hoots. Lieutenant McCarthy was there, and with him Captain Zorn. Zorn moved up closer to Goolsby, said in a low voice, "Let's move out, Lieutenant. This is protocol. No atrocities here."

Goolsby lowered his head, said, "Yes, sir. Absolutely."

Zorn called out, "Fox, Third Platoon will lead the way. Keep it close. Dark in an hour, and we're moving up in support of First Battalion. We'll make camp in a field up ahead. Good work with the prisoners. Move out."

The men were all in motion now, two parallel lines, spread out to either side of the narrow road. The talk started again, laughter, and Riley knew the jokes would come next, the big talkers talking big. He picked up the rhythm of the footsteps in front of him, kept his distance behind Welch, Killian falling in across the road, the routine of the march.

SOUTH OF UIJONGBU—OCTOBER 3, 1950

The foxholes were dug, but this time the men didn't have to rely on C-rations. With Seoul secure, the trucks had come up in support, bringing all manner of supplies, including one of those marvelous luxuries every Marine hoped for: hot food.

Uijongbu had been quiet for a while now, darkness offering what seemed to be a peaceful night, the Marines closer to the town making more efficient progress than had been made in Seoul. The men of Zorn's company were spread out alongside other companies of the Seventh, McCarthy's Third Platoon grateful for the order to enjoy the meal provided by someone higher up the chain of command.

Men were moving about in the darkness, some dropping down into their holes, the click of weapon checks, canteens, low chatty talk. A few yards from Riley, Welch sat against an old tree stump, his knees bent, seemed to be writing, and to one side of him, Killian was doing the same. Riley thought of the mail call late that afternoon, Killian finally getting his wife's package. Riley watched them both for a long, quiet moment, said, "Hey. How can you two see what you're writing? It's dark, for Chrissakes."

Welch ignored him, but the big Irishman took the bait.

"You got something to say, you don't need to see the paper. It just comes out. Poetic, too, some of it. She'll appreciate it, for sure."

"If you say so. Didn't know we had a poet in the outfit. How 'bout you, Sarge?"

"Shut up. I'm thinking."

Riley thought of Killian's package. "Hey, Sean. You inclined to share any of that stuff from home?"

Killian looked up. "Yeah, sure. Cookies. Want one? All I got left is oatmeal. Hammered the sugar cookies soon as I got 'em. Do that every damn time. Brain tells me, Hey, stupid, save some, but my mouth says, Just give me the whole batch."

He shuffled through his backpack, pulled out a small box, leaned out, Riley meeting him halfway.

"Thanks. I owe you one."

"Yep, you do. When these are gone, no telling when she'll send more. Took her a month to send these, and I been begging in every damn letter I write."

"Maybe the poetry will help."

"Can't hurt."

Welch looked up from his own letter, said, "Both of you are gonna end up squatting over that stinking latrine. I seen more jarheads get the trots from home packages than from C-rations. Your gut's not used to soft living."

Killian said, "Cookie, Sarge?"

Welch didn't hesitate. "Sure. Thanks."

Morelli came up through the darkness, always in a hurry. "Hey, Sarge, where's my foxhole? This one?"

To one side, the BAR man, Kane. "Over here, kid. Jeez, somebody get him a map."

Killian looked up at Morelli, said, "Hey, kid, you play poker?"

"Um, no, not really. Played a little on the ship over here. Lost a week's pay."

The Irishman laughed. "That's how it's supposed to work. You pay for the privilege of a good time, getting to know your comrades. Beats doing nothing."

"Maybe. Coulda used that pay. My mama's expecting it, says she's counting on it every month."

Riley wanted to ask, let it go. But Killian wasn't so discreet. "So, you live with your mama? Bet you got a house full of bambinos, and a hot little sister, too, I bet. She like Irishmen?"

Killian laughed, and Riley couldn't help a smile, Welch chuckling as well. The others were offering up comments of their own, and Riley began to feel sorry for Morelli, standing still in the dark, thought, I can see how red his face is from here. He slipped down into the foxhole, said, "It's okay, kid, they need somebody to rag. For now, you're it. We get more replacements, it'll be your turn to dish it out. You'll be the veteran."

Morelli knelt down close to Riley, said in a low voice, "It's okay. I like it, sorta. He's right, though. I live with my folks back in Jersey. No sister, though. Just four brothers, one older. He's in politics."

Riley looked at Morelli through the darkness. "What's that mean?"

"He figured out how to keep from coming over here. Knows people. I told him I signed up on purpose, he went nuts. Said he coulda had me put into any job I wanted. He thinks he's gonna be mayor of Jersey City someday."

"Yeah, great. I'm with you. I'd rather be a jarhead."

Morelli sat close beside him now, keeping his voice low. "You married, Pete?"

"Yep. Christmas makes five years. Little Ruthie." He smiled, let the image flow into him. "Tiny thing. Five feet nothing. Miss her like hell. My boy, too."

"You got a son?"

"Peter Junior. He'll turn four soon. She won't let me call him Pete. Says he's gonna be more respectable than his old man. Get a good education, not like me. She says there's no way he's gonna grow up a Marine. Only one man in the family allowed to spend his days getting shot at. We had a few rounds about that one. I say let the boy make up his own mind." He smiled, shook his head. "Here's some advice for you, kid. Choose carefully what you wanna argue about. Best to let 'em have their way more often than not. When it matters to you, really matters, well, then okay, stand up. Keeps the peace. Peace is good, I promise you. Grew up with war, every damn day. Pop and Mama raising hell about nothing at all. Bad stuff, there."

"What they fight about?"

Riley brought himself back to the moment, the darkness, low sounds around him. "None of your damn business. What you wanna know this stuff for, anyway?"

The boy lowered his head, leaned closer still, a quiet voice. "I gotta tell you, Pete, those MPs today. I never seen that before. None of it."

Riley wasn't sure what he meant, said, "Not likely any of us have seen too much of that. The enemy is bad people."

"No, I mean . . . I never seen *that*. Naked women and all. I couldn't look too long. That musta felt awful embarrassing. All us men watching them. I was raised Catholic. My mama . . ."

Killian was there now, easing into the foxhole. There was no whisper in the man, his voice booming, "How embarrassed would you be if one of those bitches stuck a grenade in your ear? It's the enemy, kid. Get used to it. Any Nooks capture you, they'll stick your rosary beads up your ass. You been paying attention? You see what kind of things they done to their own kind? What's your Bible say about heathens?"

Welch called over, "Enough. You're waking up the whole battalion. Can't concentrate on my letter."

Riley said, "Who's that one to? Doreen or Janice?"

"Not sure yet. Maybe Ellen. I put the name on last, depending on my mood."

Riley leaned back against the side of the hole, said to Morelli, "Let go of it, kid. If that's the worst thing you see over here, you'll be lucky. Besides, I bet God forgives you for looking. Hell, he made those women, right? He made your eyeballs, right?"

Morelli seemed to absorb that, thought a moment. "Yeah, maybe so. I mean, well, yeah."

Killian shifted his weight in the hole, his rifle up beside him. "Unless you're here to play poker, go to bed, kid. You're getting on my nerves."

Morelli leaned low to Riley, said, "Thank you, Pete. 'Night."

He moved off, and Riley said to Killian, "Where'd you get cards? I'll play some. You'll have to tell me what's on my cards, though. Don't know what all those pictures mean, all that other stuff, diamonds and whatnot."

Welch laughed, crawled over closer. "Hey, Irish, you be careful with this one. He cleaned out half the swabbies on the way over here. I think he grew up in a casino or something."

Riley laughed. "Just like to play a friendly game, Sarge."

"It was against orders on the ship, you know. Still is."

Killian said, "Not quite, Sarge. It was *forbidden*. Not quite the same thing as an order. I took twenty off a lieutenant in Baker Company."

Goolsby was there now, the small man coming through the darkness with soft steps. "Let's get some sleep, if we can. Captain Zorn has ordered one quarter watch, and Lieutenant McCarthy assigned Sergeant Welch to pick out the man for first watch. Two-hour shifts."

Welch said, "Irish will take the first watch. I'll relieve him in two hours. Riley can be next. I'll do the fourth. Don't need much sleep. Kane, Baxter. That'll get us to dawn."

Goolsby said, "Very good. See to it, Sergeant."

He moved away, more instructions to the next squad. Killian pulled himself up, said, "Now *those* are *orders*. See you in two hours, Sarge."

Welch ignored the sarcasm, crawled away, and Riley said, "'Night, Sarge."

He shifted his weight, tried to find any kind of comfortable position, knew Killian would be sharp, wide-eyed. He's loud and a jerk sometimes, he thought. But he's a good Marine. Riley closed his eyes, visions of the prisoners, naked bodies and hateful stares, thought of the kid, the shame of it. He'll learn. I hope. Or maybe not. He goes home with no more of a nightmare than that, I don't care what his mama says, he'll be the luckiest son of a bitch in the Corps.

He felt sleep coming, the weariness of the last few days seeping through him. To one side, a voice, jarring, a few yards away, singing.

"Good night, Irene. I'll see you in my dreams. . . ."

Killian stood up. "Oh, for God's sake. Who the hell is doing that? I heard that damn song all the way over here, and I ain't listening to it now!"

There was silence for a moment, then the voice of Lieutenant Goolsby. "Sorry. Just . . . rather like the song."

Killian sat again, and Riley fought to quiet his own laughter, leaned toward the Irishman.

"Nice going, Private. He'd bust you, except you're already as low as you can get. How about you save all that heat for the enemy?"

Killian whispered, "Oh, for Chrissakes. You think he knows it was me?"

Welch called over from his own hole. "Don't worry, Irish. I'll tell him in the morning."

UIJONGBU—OCTOBER 4, 1950

The men of Fox Company were patrolling again, as they had near Inchon, the sounds of the fight replaced by the occasional burst from a
distant machine gun, a thump of artillery somewhere to the north.
Above, squadrons of Corsairs roared past, searching for targets, their
power adding to the morale of the men on the ground. Riley glanced up,
six planes in a loose formation high above, moving north. He always
wondered about the pilots, the *glamour job,* thought, Lucky bastards.
They don't ever have to smell this place. He couldn't get used to the
stink from the rice paddies, but Uijongbu offered new smells, even
worse. The reasons for that were everywhere, decaying bodies buried
beneath blasted homes. Some were North Koreans, left behind, rotting
where they had died. But there were others, civilians, caught in the firefights, trapped by the shelling with nowhere else to go.

Up ahead was a row of crude huts, burnt, whether by design or by
the chance impact of an artillery round. Smoke rose from smoldering
straw, another squad of Marines moving out that way, careful inspection, but there were few places the enemy could hide. McCarthy was
pointing, and Sergeant Welch looked back, motioned in front of him,
this way. The rest of the squad followed him, stepping off the road, and
Riley eyed a flattened fence line, more huts beyond. More of the awful
smell washed over him now, a new kind of putrid, his face twisting, a
hard exhale, futile effort to keep the stink away. Welch reacted as well,
turning his head, and behind him, groans from the others. Welch led
them between two huts, one smashed flat, as though punched by a giant
fist. He pointed toward the other, a heap of mangled straw.

"Check it out."

Riley peered through a gap, what remained of someone's home.

"Nothing, Sarge."

Welch didn't answer, kept his eyes on whatever lay ahead, and behind Riley, a voice, Killian.

"Oh, good Christ."

Riley turned quickly, saw the big Irishman staring out to one side, toward a heap of freshly churned earth. Welch moved that way, and beside Riley, another man, Harper, nearly as green as Morelli.

"It's a cow. Ox, I guess."

The Southern drawl was unmistakable, and Killian stepped closer, stared at the decaying mass, swarms of flies, said, "You sure? How the hell you know that? You a farm boy?"

"Yep. Seen plenty of dead cows. This one's poor, though. Sack of bones."

Riley avoided looking at the carnage, said, "It's no use to anybody now. Hey, Sarge. Over that way. People by those huts."

Welch said, "Let's see what's up."

Riley followed the sergeant, stepped over debris, all of them still cautious. The stink was even worse now, and Riley shook his head, thought, How much of this can these people stand?

The civilians stood in a cluster, a dozen of them, watching the Marines move closer. It was the usual scene, old men in ragged white clothes, old women standing back behind them. There were children, dead stares, hints of fear, tears on dirty faces. Behind him, Killian said, "What the hell's over there?"

Welch turned, motioned them forward, said, "For the love of God."

It spread out before all of them now, the sight every man dreaded, a mass grave. Riley glimpsed the half-decayed bodies, pieces of flesh, black blood and grotesque faces, dark bones covered with swarms of flies. He felt his stomach pull up into a tight curl, one man grunting behind him, dropping to his knees, vomiting.

Riley closed his eyes for a brief moment, another sight he didn't need to absorb. He backed away, the rest of the squad doing the same, looked again to the civilians standing off to one side, mostly silent, the soft whimper of a single child. Welch said, "We've got to report this. Get a good look. Look for uniforms, South or North."

Riley let out a breath, tried to detach himself from the scene. It's just death, he thought. Do your damn job.

The grave was shallow, not much of a grave at all, most of the bodies protruding, blackened limbs, hands with crooked fingers. Rain had drained away much of their cover, grim evidence that most of the bodies were without clothes. Killian said, "No uniforms, Sarge. These folks were executed. Bullet holes in the heads."

Riley saw the same, then more, tiny forms, hard against adult bodies. Welch said, "Oh, Christ. Babies. They've been killed with their mothers. Looks like bayonet wounds. Enough of this." He looked toward the civilians, Riley backing away, doing the same. There was no emotion from the old men, a strange calm. Welch said, "These people were butchered. Bullet holes in the heads. Who did this? You speak English? Who did this?"

One old man raised his arm slowly, pointed up the road, to the north.

Killian said, "Nooks. I knew it."

Welch glanced at him, disgust on his face. "Yeah, genius. You figured it out. I'm getting damn sick of this stuff. This isn't war. It's a horror show. I seen too much of this from the Japs."

Welch started to move again, past the civilians, back toward the road. Riley stepped up, closed the gap between them, said, "You oughta tell the captain, I guess. Somebody's gotta make a report. The lieutenant, at least."

Welch didn't look at him. "Another genius. You think this is one time? Something special? These damn savages can't whip our asses so they take it out on the innocent. Somebody explain to me why. What the hell are these damn Koreans so hot for, that they slaughter civilians?"

Riley had rarely seen Welch this emotional, had no response. He followed the sergeant back toward the road, the others falling into line, keeping their distance, their good training, all of them sharing the same hope, that the North Koreans had truly gone, that the misery of these people could finally end.

UIJONGBU—OCTOBER 7, 1950

The army troops marched past, the usual catcalls, the Marines answering. But these soldiers were veterans, too, most of them from units of the Eighth Army, the men who had advanced from the Pusan Perimeter, now marching northward. For three days since Uijongbu had been cleared of the enemy, the Marines had strengthened their position in the town, more an army of occupation than anything resembling a combat mission. Now the army was moving into position to take their place. The rumors were hot that orders had come for the Marines to pull back, speculation that with the fighting concluded, the enemy had surrendered.

They had gathered at another of the kitchen trucks, enormous buckets of stew, bread, apple pies in stacks, generous slices to each man. Riley did what the others did, heaped his tin plate, seeking out a comfortable place on the rocky ground, another feast he knew not to take for granted.

"Hey, jarheads! Listen up!"

He forced the pie down his throat, the delicious moment interrupted by the cluster of officers standing nearby. He focused first on the familiar face, Captain Zorn, his hands on his hips.

"All right, listen up. Get your gear together. Orders from Division. The whole lot of us are being trucked back down to Inchon, the port."

The cheering erupted, but Riley saw a frown on Zorn's face, knew there was more. Beside Zorn, another officer, familiar, from battalion, one of Major Sawyer's men, who said, "You men have done exemplary work. You should be proud. We've all had a job to do, and that job has been accomplished."

"We going home?"

The call came from behind Riley, more joining in, the cheering again, but Riley kept his eyes on Zorn's face, saw the man slowly shake his head. Zorn waited for quiet again, then said, "No. Get that straight, all of you. This job's not done. We're to wait at Inchon for new orders, telling us where they want us to be. I wish I could tell you we're done here, that our next port of call is San Diego. But the orders only said Inchon. Sounds to me like they're not done with us. That's all I know."

Zorn said something to the officer, who moved away with a sharp nod, and Riley watched him go, thought, He's telling the other companies the same thing. Zorn stood alone now, his arms crossed, watching them, his eye catching Riley. The talk flowed through them all now, rumors springing up from fertile minds, the raw hope that the gloom from Zorn was just part of the job, keeping his company's feet on the ground. Zorn seemed to recognize him, the acknowledgment of a veteran, but Riley did not smile, saw no reason to. He doesn't know what's up, Riley thought. They haven't told him. But I bet he's right. This job isn't done. He glanced around, saw Welch, his hands in his knapsack, organizing.

"What do you think, Hamp?"

Welch kept his stare downward, said, "Nobody surrendered, Pete. We let those bastards get away. We shoulda clamped 'em down in Seoul, wiped 'em off the earth, every damn one of 'em. But we let 'em slip off. Now we gotta go find 'em again."

"But if they went home, back into North Korea . . ."

Welch looked at him, hard, cold eyes. "So what? We took casualties, Pete. Men died, Marines, soldiers. The people back home will want to know what the hell for. Somebody's gotta tell them something good, whether it's newspapers or the government. Just saying, *Hey, everything's fine now. The North Koreans, they all went back home* . . . that ain't gonna do it, Pete. We gotta kill some more people, plain and simple."

Riley looked toward Zorn again, saw the captain standing quietly, arms still crossed, his stare outward, to some other place, whatever might lie ahead.

PART TWO

"I hope we do not have to operate in this country in the winter."

—MAJOR GENERAL OLIVER P. SMITH (TO HIS WIFE),
OCTOBER 1, 1950

CHAPTER SEVEN

· ·

Smith

THE STEAM ROLLED UP around him, wet, glorious heat, the soapy lather sweeping away days of grime. He inhaled deeply, pulling the delicious steam inside of him, breathed it out slowly. His arms hung now by his sides and he leaned his head forward under the shower, blinded by the waterfall that flowed down his face, rinsing away the soap. He opened his eyes, saw a pool of sudsy water at his feet, a slow drift downward through the drain. He allowed himself another few seconds of the watery massage but could not avoid his mind snapping to attention, the harsh reality slapping him that this was only a temporary luxury, a gift from the ship's captain, the privilege of rank. He reluctantly turned the shower off, blinked water from his eyes, paused, took in another long breath, the last of the warm steam, memories of home, more luxuries, all those pieces of life with Esther. He stepped clear of the shower, his brain waging war with itself, one part of him knowing he could slide once more into the torrent of hot water, that no one would question, no one would find fault. But none of this steamy escape could remove the reality of what was happening beyond the bulkheads, the curiosity of his men, the entire division still waiting at Inchon for the order that would put them aboard the ships, following their general to their next port of call. And for them there would be no hot showers.

Smith knew the rumors, the wishful thinking that rippled through the camps at Inchon, that their job was complete. He had ordered his staff to stop that kind of talk, that this war was still theirs to fight. But he could do nothing to stop the euphoria that came from above, the backslapping congratulations flowing out from MacArthur's headquarters, so many untested officers in Tokyo completely convinced that they had won a war. The celebration had spread through the upper levels of the Tenth Corps, a message coming to Smith from Ned Almond that offered effusive praise for a job well done. He had tried to imagine Almond's expression as he wrote the note, whether the man believed his own kindness, or whether Almond wrote with a hard grip on his pen, scowling acceptance that the Marines had earned the praise. Smith tried to avoid meeting with Almond at all, a foolish hope, the Marines still firmly anchored as a part of Almond's command.

Smith dressed quickly, the dread returning. He buttoned up with jerking fingers, tugged the trousers up, the loose waistband revealing his loss of weight. He thought of writing that to Esther but he knew it would inspire concern, worry that he was not eating well, or worse, that he had picked up some Asian malady. No, he thought, she does not deserve worry. But I will write. After all, it is good news, all of it. Success. But I must be honest with her, clear away the junk. She knows full well not to believe what she reads in the newspapers. And *Time* magazine. Good Lord. What is the matter with those people? I'm no hero. Not even close. The Marines were the best-prepared men we could put into the field, and I happen to be at the top. It's no different now than the First World War. Marines called upon to serve as infantry. The Fifth led the way at Belleau Wood. I need to make sure Murray knows that. Make sure he tells his men their own history. It's important. Though, right now, their morale is about as high as it can be. And it's my job to stick a pin in that balloon.

He was fully dressed now, checked himself in the captain's small mirror, satisfactory. I must thank him for this, he thought. For the first time in many days, I don't smell like Korea.

He moved into the passageway, sailors standing aside, crisp salutes,

which he returned. He climbed to the next deck, saw officers, Marines
in a small cluster, cigarettes and coffee cups. They noticed him immediately, faces smiling, Eddie Craig.

"Well, General, you look a good bit more presentable. Fit even by
MacArthur's standards."

He acknowledged the smiles with a brief nod, said, "The staff will
meet in the wardroom in ten minutes, if you please. I'd like to know our
status. I'll request the captain be there as well." He caught a whiff of
something pungent, saw Sexton backing away slightly, self-conscious.
"Make that thirty minutes. I would appreciate it if you gentlemen would
see to your personal hygiene. Even a damp rag will do."

It was his attempt at a joke, but there was no laughter, the men responding with brief sniffs at their clothing. He could rarely tell a joke,
found it difficult to break that pane of glass between them. Craig and
Bowser seemed to be the exceptions, but here, even Bowser kept his
seriousness.

"Aye, sir. If I can find my clean uniform, I'll change. We'll make
ourselves more presentable. Sorry."

Craig said, "There wasn't much time. But you're certainly correct, sir.
We could all use a scrub-down."

Smith regretted the comment now, didn't want them to think he was
scolding them for anything at all. But he had no use for excuses.

"Any effort will be fine. Thirty minutes, then."

He reached another ladder, climbed up to the open deck, a breeze of
fresh salt air. He stepped carefully to the port-side rail, the ship rolling
over heavy swells, and he saw the land spread out along the horizon, the
coastline of South Korea. It can't take us too long, he thought. The captain will tell me when we pass the boundary. I wonder how the men will
react. Word will spread on the transports, some sailor making sure the
Marines find out when they cross the line. No need for secrets here. The
38th parallel might not mean much to them, the land won't look any
different from out here. Likely no one will be shooting at them, either.
If the South Koreans have done their job, the landing will go smoothly,
no enemy anywhere around. There will be one thing very different from

Inchon, though, something even the new men will understand. This time we're not liberators. We're invaders.

He had left the Marines at Inchon making preparations for the voyage, supplies distributed, equipment gathered, the officers seeing to their commands, the men seeing to themselves. They would sail as he was sailing, around the bottom of the Korean Peninsula, eastward, then up to the North Korean port of Wonsan. There the Marines would make yet another landing, securing the port, establishing a base for the next operation.

He felt in his pocket, the unfinished letters, one to each of his two daughters. Get that done tonight, he thought. Esther, too. They're all showing off that magazine cover, sure as the dickens. Rather they didn't do that. He thought of his granddaughter, Gail, yes, she's probably taken that thing to school, waving it around like a flag for all to see. He shook his head. No, let them be proud.

He heard the sound of engines, looked up, a pair of B-29s high above, and he eyed the direction, thought, Japan. Going home. Empty, probably. Aim well, gentlemen. But a new thought jolted him, as it had so many times before, the young man's face, a burst of cold, dragged into his mind by the sight of the big bombers. *You* should be here, he thought. That should be *you,* up in those marvelous birds.

The plane had gone down just before Christmas 1944, his son-in-law Charles Benedict listed officially as missing in action. Benedict had been flying a bombing mission over Mukden, China, the word coming to his family that there was little hope of the crew's survival. The pain of that had been overwhelming, Smith stationed then in Hawaii, so far from home, unable to do anything to comfort his daughter, Virginia. The helplessness of his absence had stayed with him, and so he would never forget to write them, could never escape the nagging fear that if something happened to him, they might not hear of it for many weeks, the horrible coldness of a telegram.

He tapped the folded papers in his pocket. Tonight. Get them done. Tell them only good things. They can read about Ned Almond in the newspaper.

"Well, General, I was told you were enjoying the captain's hospitality. Feel better, I assume?"

The voice was cheerful, the expression on the man's smiling face always seeming sincere.

"General Lowe. Yes, the captain was most kind. You should take advantage of it yourself. Surely he would not object."

"Oh, I have, I assure you, even before we set sail. One thing I have learned quickly is that naval vessels have no shortage of hot water. Their food seems to be superior as well. No offense to *your* staff, of course."

Smith felt Lowe's good cheer, turned again to the horizon, thought, What have we told the president today? Lowe moved up beside him, anchored himself to the rail with unsteady hands, a slight waver. Smith watched him, said, "Are you feeling all right, General?"

"Please, I do wish you could get past your need for such rigidity. It's *Frank.* I'm perfectly happy to greet you always as *General Smith,* but when you call me *general* . . . I'm not altogether comfortable having anyone believing me to be your equal."

"I'll try. Frank. Are you all right?"

"You mean, the waves? The captain advises me to get lots of fresh air and keep my eyes on the horizon. It has seemed to help. Not sure I enjoy sleeping belowdeck, though."

"Stay up here. We'll get you a cot. He's right. The fresh air will help."

Lowe took a deep breath, said, "Damn embarrassing, you know. Never really been a problem for me before. I can't really tell Mr. Truman that his envoy has a weak stomach. You think MacArthur has ever been seasick?"

It was a strange question, and Smith detected more meaning than Lowe might have intended.

"No idea."

"Hmm. I'll bet General Almond has tossed his lunch a few times. Seems the type."

"You expecting a response, General? *Frank?*"

Lowe seemed genuinely surprised. "Not at all. No games here, General. But to be honest, there is concern in Washington that General

MacArthur is relying on his unshakable belief in his own infallibility. There were expectations that Inchon would be his final bow, that he would have no choice but to allow others to take the reins."

"Why?"

Lowe tilted his head. "You are not naïve, General. You know that MacArthur is not as popular in Washington as he is in the newspapers. He is rather convinced that his way of running things is the only way. And he does not pay much heed to anyone who disagrees with him. The man has been a general in this army for more than thirty years. Things can happen to a man who is always in charge, who is never confronted by argument. He has surrounded himself with those who worship him. What does that do to a man? I don't know. Do you?" Lowe paused. "It is an uncomfortable situation. I have received word, and not just from the president, mind you. The Joint Chiefs are afraid of the man. MacArthur tells them what he intends to do, and they decide they'll allow it. Not sure what would happen if they decided not to."

"That's not my concern, General."

Lowe looked at him, another pause. "No, I suppose not. However, I would very much like your view on what is happening right now."

"What do you mean?"

"Your division has been ordered to make a landing in North Korea. Already, South Korean troops are pushing north of the Thirty-eighth parallel, and reports say they are receiving little resistance. There is hope that those troops might end this thing without our own people crossing that border. It concerns me that General MacArthur seems not to care about borders at all. He's giving General Almond another opportunity for headlines. That's how some see it. *Ned the Anointed*, they call him."

Careful, Smith thought. He's testing you.

"Hadn't heard that."

Lowe seemed to read him, said, "Come now, General. I'm not here to pin you down, put your seat in hot water. It's my job to understand what is going on here, beyond the piffle Tokyo hands out. I need you to be honest with me, and I assure you, our discussions are in confidence."

"You, me, and the president."

"Your commander in chief. Doesn't he deserve your honesty as well?

Certainly, your insights. Your position here is crucial to the success of this campaign. And your performance. Almond knows that. He's watching you like a hawk. But he's protected, MacArthur's hand on his shoulder, warding off any criticism. Not so General Walker. Do you know the man?"

"Some."

"Walton Walker can't be happy, wouldn't you agree?"

Smith searched for the right words. "If I was Walton Walker, three stars, and I was told that a two-star, Ned Almond, would not answer to me, that he would operate a separate independent command, I would probably ask why."

"And the answer?"

"You would have to ask General MacArthur."

Lowe leaned again on the rail, seemed more at ease now. "It's no secret, not even to you, that MacArthur dislikes Walton Walker. Doesn't trust him. Walker's done okay, served his men well around Pusan. But his headquarters is a mess, disorganized, men running around with no clear notion of their objectives, or how to obtain them."

Smith was surprised by that, kept it to himself. "I'm not familiar with General Walker's methods."

"No, and you won't be, not anytime soon. You answer to Almond, and only Almond. And Almond answers only to MacArthur. Walton Walker and his Eighth Army might as well be on the moon. It might feel like that, before too long."

"You want me to give you my view about my orders, about the next part of this campaign. You need me to explain to you what MacArthur's doing? You already know."

"Perhaps. I'd prefer hearing it from you. Let's just say the president wants to know who's paying attention."

Smith let out a breath, looked hard at Lowe. "I'm not pleased with your questions, General Lowe."

"Perhaps it is the answers that bother you."

Smith stared out, thought, Perhaps it is. He looked again at Lowe, saw nothing to give him doubts about the man's integrity, no hint of some duplicitous agenda. But still, Smith was careful. It was the sorest point Smith had wrestled with, the contradiction to the training every senior officer had received.

His words came out slowly. "General MacArthur has divided his army. The Tenth Corps is to advance into North Korea east of the mountains. The Eighth Army is to advance to the west. This country is split in two by a backbone, a mountain range that will limit communication and logistics."

"You don't approve?"

"I don't have *approval*. I obey the orders I'm given. If MacArthur is correct, this war will end rapidly, without many more casualties. I must support that optimism."

Lowe shook his head, seemed frustrated. "Marines." He leaned against the rail, faced Smith. "You may enjoy the luxury of your optimism, General. Others are not so fortunate. There is more at stake here than the destruction of the North Korean army. General, do you know what MacArthur told the Joint Chiefs? Allow me to paraphrase. *In exploiting the defeat of the enemy, our troops may cross the Thirty-eighth parallel at any time. . . . I regard all of Korea open for our military operations.* He doesn't mention whether or not it's wise to divide his army in two. He doesn't talk about mountain ranges and backbones. He has rattled the president with his insistence that this cakewalk will end by Christmas. That kind of talk plays well in the newspapers, believe me. Plays well among the troops, too. But the larger concern is just how well that plays in Moscow."

Smith was becoming more uncomfortable now. "I don't know about such things. I've heard no reports of any Russian troops in Korea."

"No. But there is real fear in Washington that the Soviets are waiting, watching, might use this as a provocation for a new war. There is concern that if MacArthur drives his people, *your* people into China, the Soviets will respond in Europe. There are reports of thousands of Soviet tanks poised along the border between East and West Germany. Our allies are praying that this mess concludes as quickly as MacArthur insists it will. But if it doesn't, we're sitting on a big damn bomb, General. What happens here could ignite World War Three."

Smith glanced around, no one within earshot. He looked again at

Lowe, saw no drama in the man, his voice soft and steady. Smith kept his voice low, said, "I've heard none of that. It won't happen. It can't. No one would go that far. President Truman doesn't want that, surely. He can prevent it. His orders must be obeyed."

"The president knows that, of course. The Joint Chiefs know that. But, General, the greater concern in Washington is whether or not Douglas MacArthur knows that."

On October 15, a surprised Douglas MacArthur received an invitation to meet with his commander in chief on Wake Island. The choice of location was seen by those in Washington as a concession to Mac-Arthur, that President Truman's journey would be much longer than that of his general. Whether MacArthur appreciated or even recognized the gesture, he flew to Wake feeling as though the president had trespassed into MacArthur's private fiefdom. The meeting itself did nothing to dissuade MacArthur that Truman was playing politics with the war, that voices of opposition against the president in Washington had forced Truman to demonstrate that he was clearly involved in the hard decisions in Korea. MacArthur realized immediately that the meeting was more for show than for substance, a time-consuming annoyance.

At a formal press conference immediately following, MacArthur repeated to the audience what he had said privately to Truman. His successes were virtually complete. MacArthur was adamant that there was little if any chance of the Chinese or the Soviet Union coming to the support of the North Koreans. MacArthur conveyed the message to the reporters whom Truman had brought across the ocean that the bulk of the American troops would be home by Christmas.

CHAPTER EIGHT

....

Sung

THE ROOM WAS QUIET, all eyes on the older man, who kept his stare downward. Sung could feel the impatience around him, the younger officers chafing at the drudgery of yet another meeting, more clarification of orders they had expected to receive days before. Sung had been through all of this before, long before, the acceptance that the army's resources were so often inferior to the enemy they faced. He had served alongside several of the men in this room, the senior commanders who had learned to endure sacrifice and privation. But others were young, knew little of what it had taken to fight the Japanese, or the great struggle against the Nationalists, the vast armies of Chiang Kai-shek.

Sung glanced to one side, saw the young colonel, Li, drumming his fingers on the arm of his chair. Sung tried to hold in his smile, thought, You were not with us when these things were decided in tents, in shacks, when the enemy was shelling us. Now there is luxury, soft chairs, warm quarters. Of course you are impatient. You have learned none of the lessons that come from struggle. Or pain.

Across the wide desk, the older man's head rose slowly and he scanned the room, his eyes meeting Sung's for a brief moment, no smile from either of them. He spoke now, the words coming out in slow rhythm, precise, well rehearsed.

"Chairman Mao has been very explicit in his orders. We shall be efficient in our obedience of them. It is not the time for hasty judgments, or questions that have already been answered."

Sung glanced again at Li, the younger man responding with silence, a bowed head. Good, Sung thought. It is not the time for unwise protest. He looked at the older man now, said, "General Peng, we will obey. The mission will be one more great accomplishment for our leader. His army shall not disappoint him."

Peng looked at him, still no smile, a short nod. It was the game they had played for many years, a performance meant for the younger men, a script that could have come from Mao's own hand.

Peng Dehuai was the overall commander of the Chinese military forces now, a position granted him by Mao Tse-tung as much a reward for loyalty as anything to do with Peng's expertise as a leader of troops. Sung was grateful for Peng's authority, respected the man as much now as he had two decades ago, the first time Sung Shi-lun had worn a uniform. In the mid-1930s, Sung had served with Peng during the Long March, a year-long military struggle that had become celebrated by every schoolchild in China. Then it was civil war, the beleaguered army under Mao fighting for survival, escaping destruction from the far superior arms and equipment of the Nationalists. The march had taken Mao's troops nearly five thousand miles, allowing them to regroup, resupply, and eventually make war once more against the disorganized ranks of Chiang's army. When the tide turned for good, Mao's success had elevated him to supreme leadership over the entire Chinese mainland. His authority now was unquestioned, fueled by his fierce claims of dedication to the people he ruled, to their history and ancient culture, and more important, their new place in a changing world.

The peasants were told in unwavering terms, great boisterous speeches, that the entire world would become theirs, that the great revolution that had crushed Chiang and the Nationalists would continue beyond China's borders. Most of China's enormous population were peasants, a great sea of humanity that had produced Mao himself, as well as many of the most successful generals from the war, including Peng Dehuai. No one in China was allowed to forget that Mao's glori-

ous triumph had been accomplished by an army that had labored so
long under the boot heels of the wealthy. It was that revolution that
Mao insisted would spread to the peasantry of other lands, the message
so very clear that no amount of Western corruption could stifle their
voices, that everywhere the capitalists ruled, there would be uprisings,
spreading power to the powerless. For the experienced military officers
who had finally defeated Chiang's vastly superior army, Mao's glorious
predictions were embraced publicly, if not always in private. The officers
understood what many of the peasants did not, that despite Mao's insistence that power rested with all the people, Mao was firmly and absolutely in charge. And with the wars now past, the old veterans, warhorses
like Peng Dehuai, understood that survival meant loyalty to Mao.

Sung knew that Peng was as close to Mao as any man in the army,
two old friends who shared the struggles of so many brutal campaigns.
Sung had been through that as well, though he was much younger. He
had earned respect for his command of troops in the field, catching
Mao's eye and Peng's as well. Now he commanded an entire army, the
reward for his loyalty to the revolution, and more important, to Mao
himself. But Sung's affections for Peng came from something deeper
than mere obedience. He valued the older man's experience and wisdom
in the political world as much as the military. He admired Peng's obvious dedication to Chairman Mao, that if Peng had ever disagreed with
Mao's orders, it would never be revealed to any subordinate. The younger
men around Sung had not yet fully grasped the value of that, some of
their brashness seeping through when silence and discretion were far
more useful. If there was a nagging uneasiness clouding Sung's own affections for General Peng, it was that some of the strategies that came
down from Mao seemed to contradict experience, that the great dreams
had clouded military necessity. Peng refused to acknowledge what Sung
could see for himself, that as Mao's power solidified, Mao himself was
changing. With the kind of absolute power that Mao enjoyed, the un-
questioning obedience of all who served him, Mao had seemed to embrace his own infallibility. The most powerful man in China had also
become the most wise. But many of them had memories of those days
when Mao's judgment had been flawed, poor planning, poor strategies

employed in the struggle against Chiang Kai-shek. It was a curious mystery to Sung that Mao's authority was so completely accepted, when the haphazard military decisions continued. Even as Peng's army maneuvered closer to the Yalu River, poised just above their border with North Korea, delays were ordered, betraying the uncertainties in Peking over just how they were to deal with events to the south. There were contradictions, awkward orders, the kind of hesitations that made military men nervous. For the officers it was an exercise in patience, and a wisdom of their own that kept them silent. When Mao's intentions were made clear, the military would respond.

The questions were there, of course, spoken quietly in private places, many of the officers around Sung puzzled by Peng Dehuai's rapid rise to the top command. Peng was respected, certainly, but his predecessor, Lin Biao, had long been Mao's favorite to command the army. In late September, as the first orders had come to maneuver closer to the Yalu River, Lin had suddenly disappeared. The official report claimed that Lin had fallen ill, and more surprisingly, had been sent to a hospital in the Soviet Union. Very soon, Lin had returned, named to command one of Mao's vast field armies. But he was subordinate now to Peng, no one in Peking offering an explanation. There were softly spoken rumors, of course, that Lin had made the deadly error of arguing with Mao, rejecting Mao's strategies for dealing with the problems that had erupted in Korea. The utter collapse of the North Korean army was a surprise, to be sure, but no one had expected that the Chinese would move into Korea to stand alongside Kim Il-sung as an equal partner. Now the public pronouncements barely mentioned the North Koreans at all, as though the Chinese troops were preparing only to defend their own border. With Peng now firmly in command, Sung would follow the orders he had been given, organizing his troops in their new camps along the Yalu, until Peng told him differently.

Peng seemed weary, blinked several times, reached for a cup of tea. He seemed to move slowly on purpose, precise motions, keeping them all still, quiet. The silence was broken by a sudden rap on the door behind Sung, startling him. Peng kept his gaze on the tea, said in a soft voice, "Allow them to enter." The man entered quickly, the door closing

behind him, and Peng said, "General Deng, welcome. I have been waiting for your report."

Sung realized now that Peng had been delaying, keeping them waiting for Deng's arrival. He knew that Deng had been sent off on a discreet mission, but had asked no questions, even though Deng Hua was
a subordinate to Sung, one of his corps commanders.

Deng moved up in front of the room, faced them, acknowledged
Sung now, a short, crisp nod. "Thank you, General Peng. If you will
allow me to present my report."

Peng sat back in the chair, the cup in his hand, seemed to know what
the young general was going to say.

"Go ahead."

Deng took a deep breath, his hands clamped behind him. "Gentlemen, I have just returned from a journey into Korea. My assignment
was to monitor progress of the People's Army there, to observe their . . .
situation. As you know, we have received reports that there have been
reversals, that Kim Il-sung's forces have given away their advantages.
We believe that few if any of Kim's troops remain south of the Thirty-
eighth parallel. These reports were most distressing, as you know. My
orders were to determine just how dangerous those reverses have become." He turned, looked at Peng now, another nod from the older
man. Deng faced them again. "I regret to report that my hosts, the senior command of the North Korean People's Army, had been instructed
not to allow me to fulfill my mission. I was not allowed access to any
field units and was not allowed to travel any farther south than Pyongyang. It was made very plain to me that my presence there was an un-
welcome intrusion." He turned again to Peng. "General, I regret I did
not complete my mission with any success. It is very clear that the
North Korean People's Army is suffering a profound setback at the
hands of the United Nations troops. The government of the People's
Republic does not wish to reveal just how serious those reversals have
become. Any further conclusion would be merely a guess on my part. I
deeply regret my failure."

Sung saw anger in the young man's eyes, thought, Yes, he is not a
man who enjoys wasting his time.

Peng said, "General, you are excused. Do not embrace your mission as one of failure. Your report is most illuminating. It only confirms what Chairman Mao has anticipated from the start."

The guard pulled the door open, Deng marching out with crisp steps. Peng kept his eyes on his cup of tea, said, "Chairman Mao has been most frustrated by Kim Il-sung. Our intelligence predicted that the United Nations troops would invade at the port of Inchon. We informed the North Koreans of that expectation and strongly advised them to make ready to resist such a move. They ignored our recommendations. We know the results. Chairman Mao has no intentions of repeating such a mistake. The North Koreans have chosen to fight their war on their own terms, terms that do not concern us. Until now, the North Koreans have been wholly dependent on the Soviets for arms and supplies. But the Soviets have recognized their mistake as well, and from what we can determine, have withdrawn much of that support." Peng paused, sipped at the tea, looked out at them, scanning the room. Sung waited for more, could see a frown on Peng's face. "You have already been ordered to position your troops along our border. At first, this was to be a defensive posture, so as to prevent the United Nations troops, particularly the Americans, from pursuing an aggressive course that would threaten Chinese sovereignty. We have repeatedly expressed our deepest concerns that should United Nations troops cross over the Thirty-eighth parallel, invading the territory of North Korea, the Chinese people would interpret that as a direct threat to our own interests. As you know, the American puppets who call themselves the army of the Republic of Korea have already crossed the border and are taking advantage of the disgraceful retreat by the North. Despite the unwillingness of Kim Il-sung to provide information as to his own failures, our own intelligence indicates that the Americans have followed in their wake. These reports have confirmed that units of the American First Cavalry of General Walker's Eighth Army have violated North Korean territory. We are certain that this is only the beginning. Chairman Mao continues to be most adamant that such a violation is a direct threat to the sovereignty of our own border and shall be dealt with in absolute terms. We do not fear the puppet army of South Korea, nor do we fear the possible loss of Pyongyang. The greater danger is that those who pull the strings are using this conflict in Korea as a pretense for a far more insidious plan. General MacArthur, who commands the puppet forces of the United Nations, has been indiscreet in his belligerence to Chinese sovereignty. Chairman Mao is convinced that General Mac-Arthur and those who support him from above wish to engage the Chinese people in a war."

Sung absorbed what Peng was saying, the others seemingly surprised. To one side, another of the young corps commanders spoke up.

"General, what actions are we to take regarding the crisis that has directly befallen North Korea? Are they not our allies?"

Sung winced at the question, saw a glimmer of disgust on Peng's face.

"There shall be no actions taken with regard to the government of the People's Republic of Korea."

The man stood now, said, "But are we not committed to assisting Kim Il-sung in the event of such a tragedy? I had thought—"

Peng pointed a bony finger at the man. "You do not *think*, General. Chairman Mao has communicated to the People's Republic that if they wish to be rescued, they can beseech their comrades in Moscow. Chairman Mao has no great regard for Kim Il-sung, and neither do I. The issue is not merely Korea. It is the threat to our border. Is that not apparent to all of you?"

There were nods, the young man beside Sung seated again. Sung glanced at him, saw embarrassment, thought, That was not a good idea. You just revealed that you perhaps have some personal interest in what happens in Korea. I wonder what kind of interest? Someone else shall no doubt ask that same question.

To Sung's other side, Li stood, stiff-backed, said, "General Peng, is it possible, in Chairman Mao's estimation, that the Korean People's Army can continue their struggle by means of guerrilla tactics? Perhaps the army of the North might still be capable of eliminating the Americans' threat to our border by a vigorous defense of their own country."

Peng shook his head. "Chairman Mao does not believe the leadership of the North Korean People's Republic is capable of inspiring their people to such a goal. There is only one issue now. You will receive final orders shortly that will instruct you on exactly when your troops are to advance across the Yalu River and make preparations for the destruction of any forces threatening our borders. It is wholly to our advantage to strike at those troops before they can strike at us. Chairman Mao has told me to expect the final order to be issued at any time. It is therefore essential that you put your troops on alert, prepared to move quickly."

Li seemed surprised, leaned forward. "We're crossing the border? We are to directly engage the United Nations forces? Will the Soviets honor their pledge to assist us with heavy artillery and airpower? Without their assistance, we are at some disadvantage in weaponry. Engaging the Americans—"

"*Sit down.*"

Peng's voice was loud, no room for argument. Li obeyed without speaking. Peng looked at Sung now. "This meeting is concluded. General Sung, you will remain. The rest of you, return to your commands. Orders will follow very soon."

The others stood, the door opening, a hint of cool air drifting into the stuffiness of the room. Sung kept his seat, did not watch the others, kept his eyes on Peng, who sipped again from the teacup. In a short moment the room was empty, the guard leaving as well, the door closing. Peng closed his eyes briefly, Sung keeping silent. After a moment, Peng said, "There is little wisdom in any of them. The young worst of all. But even the experienced ones have forgotten the value of loyalty."

Sung shook his head. "I do not believe that to be true. I have heard nothing of disloyalty to Chairman Mao."

Peng shrugged. "Maybe. But there is uncertainty. They do not trust in our ability to crush our enemies."

"Do you?"

Peng laughed, a glance toward the door. "Of course I do. Chairman Mao wills it, and it will be so."

Sung was careful now. He knew Peng enjoyed his company, seemed to treat him as a son as much as a subordinate. It was the same with many of the veterans, the men who had learned to sacrifice for the greater cause.

Peng said, "You have been hungry, yes? I mean . . . hungry. *Starving.*"

"You know I have shared such conditions. As have you."

"Yes, and you have seen the dead gathering around you, men whose weakness betrayed them, whose spirit would not keep them alive, men who could not embrace sacrifice."

"I suppose so. Yes. We lost nine of ten men on the Long March. It is not necessary for you to remind me of our history, sir."

"Nine of ten. Yes. The tenth man . . . you, me, Chairman Mao. We know what victory means. Not some storybook, slicing the head off the dragon. Not merely vanquishing your rival so you may enjoy the sweetness of his woman. *Victory.* The look in your enemy's eye as you slide the knife into his heart, as you steal his life. The smell of his blood."

Sung saw a hard spark in Peng's eyes, something he had seen before. "Sir, do you doubt my will?"

Peng laughed. "No, my friend. Nor do I doubt your loyalty. To Chairman Mao, and those around him, that is what matters most. I fear that very soon it will be more about your skills as a soldier." Peng paused. "Colonel Li's concerns are accurate. We were hopeful that the Soviets would honor their commitment to provide the military equipment that would balance the scales against the Americans. They have now reneged on that promise."

Sung was stunned. "They have reneged? They assured us—"

"Soviet assurances are like rivers of mud. Soil yourself in it if you wish, but do not expect to drink the water. The North Korean army has become useless, and Chairman Stalin has turned his eyes to other causes. All they offer us now are *advisors,* Stalin's toadies, who have pledged to provide assistance where they observe its need. I suspect, as does Chairman Mao, that these men have been ordered to remain blind to our needs. We shall welcome them into our camps, allow them to see just what our weaknesses might be."

"It sounds as if you are describing spies."

Peng laughed. "And so I am. Chairman Mao certainly believes it so. Here I disagree with him, if only on a minor point. I still believe the Soviets can be helpful to us, and it is in their interest to assist us against our shared enemies. One day they might require some assistance from us in Europe. Chairman Mao is not concerned with a world so far away. But the revolution will one day consume all men in all lands. On that Chairman Mao and I agree completely. We must know who our friends are."

Sung absorbed all that Peng was telling him. "I am not so familiar with such lofty things. I prefer being a soldier."

Peng nodded, a friendly smile. "You are not wrong, my friend. Very soon now, soldiers will be far more valuable than philosophers. The Americans are coming, and we must do what we can to obliterate their threat. I do not require Chairman Mao's wisdom to tell me that. Like Mao, I smell when the enemy believes he is winning, when he convinces himself he is strong, and so he becomes reckless. There is celebration in MacArthur's headquarters. Jubilation that they have crushed the army of Kim Il-sung. Now they will march northward singing their songs, waving their flags."

"Did we not warn them what would happen if they threatened us? Surely they do not wish to risk a war that could engulf all of Asia."

Peng opened a drawer, held up a piece of paper. "This is a letter, offered to me by Chairman Mao's secretaries. I am grateful to be included in these correspondences. Now I share this with you."

He handed the letter to Sung, who took the paper, read slowly. "I'm not sure what this means."

"Look at the bottom. The signature of the Indian ambassador Pannikar. Our people made very clear to the Indian consul that they should communicate our concerns to the Americans. Minister Chou En-lai made very clear on several occasions, through several avenues, that we will not accept any threat to our borders. None at all. Minister Chou stated very plainly that if there was any such threat, we would respond with vigorous force. There was nothing vague about our intentions, none of that ridiculous diplomatic wordplay. Our concerns were clear and precise. If you threaten our border, we will defend our sovereignty. Ambassador Pannikar was most willing to communicate our concerns to anyone in the West who would listen."

Sung scanned the letter. "He says here that they would not listen. He says he was . . . dismissed."

"Ignored, more accurately. The Americans responded by ordering their troops northward."

"I don't understand."

Peng reached for the teacup again. "The Americans believe they can take any action they choose. I have never seen a people with such ... swagger. They defeated the Japanese, the Germans. In the end, Kim Il-sung was little more than a mosquito. And so they believe they are invincible."

Sung put the paper back on the desk. "They have the atomic bomb."

Peng pounded a fist, rattling the teacup. "Yes! That only makes them more arrogant. Incredibly arrogant! A big bomb, capable of destroying a whole city in one moment. We are a nation of farms. How many bombs will it require to destroy all of that? So, the mighty Americans can kill a million of us, perhaps two million. Perhaps *ten* million. And then? We know of sacrifice, Shi-lun. *Nine of ten,* remember? Chairman Mao knows more than anyone on this earth what is required to win a war against a superior foe. All those big bombs and fast planes and mighty cannons. But the Americans lack *belief.* We are fighting for revolution. The Americans are fighting for what? To support a corrupt government in the South? They did that once before, did they not? Chiang Kai-shek sits in his counterfeit palace in Taiwan, alive only because the Americans allow it. Now it is Syngman Rhee, kept alive by fat American artillery. There is no justice to what they do, and that is why we will prevail. They fight for a weak cause. There is purity in us, in our people, in our claim to become a mighty nation again." He paused, seemed to catch his breath. "General Sung, the final order will come as I told the others. But I can tell you this right now. You will continue to command the Ninth Army Group. You will position your forces at the most convenient crossings of the Yalu River, to advance southward on the nineteenth of October. You will use all means to prevent the enemy from knowing your intentions, or your deployment. You will spread your forces to the south and east, protecting the left flank of General Lin's Thirteenth Army Group, as you both advance southward."

Sung absorbed the order, felt a flash of excitement, his heart quickening. "Yes, sir. We shall obey."

"You shall do more than that. You shall relive those days we all miss. You shall once again know how it feels to crush your enemy. And you shall be observed from the highest posts in China. When this is over, your name will adorn great banners."

He felt uncomfortable now, had never been celebrated in public places. "I only wish to do my duty. Do we know just when we might expect contact with the Americans?"

"That is very likely up to you. The Americans will be wandering blind in a strange land. They do not expect to meet us on our own terms. They do not believe we have the resolve to bring this war to them. You shall show them just how mistaken they are."

A new thought rolled into Sung's brain. "Might I expect a Soviet observer in my own camp?"

Peng shrugged. "Possibly. You will of course be the good host."

"Of course. Am I to make known my needs? Am I to allow the Soviets to know my positions, my troop strength?"

"Chairman Mao is not amused by that prospect. But I convinced him that there is no harm. If the Soviets know our situation, they might yet be persuaded to offer us aid. Otherwise, their presence will merely be a distraction. Chairman Mao does not believe Chairman Stalin will ever support us, in any way. I hold to a bit more optimism."

"Then I shall be optimistic as well. I shall do what I can to secure heavy artillery, or air support."

Peng laughed again. "Just lead your troops, Shi-lun. It is not your concern what the Soviets will or will not offer us. Chairman Mao shall see to that. Now go. Return to your troops. Prepare them for what lies ahead. Prepare them for the glory that awaits their victory!"

Sung stood, stiffened, a salute toward Peng. "Thank you, sir. We shall do our duty."

He turned, moved to the door, pulled it open, the guards standing to either side, eyes ahead. The air was cooler now, and Sung placed his hat on his head, saw it was dark outside. He stepped crisply toward the entryway of the great hall, more guards, smart salutes, a group of officers to one side standing still as he passed. The steps led him down, outside, the delicious chill of a cold night, and he glanced skyward, the stars spread out to the horizon. The excitement was inside of him still, the inspiring words of General Peng. Little of that was unusual, many of those words coming from Chairman Mao, unshakable faith in the perfect righteousness of their cause. The troops will know that, he thought. They will trust in their leaders, in why we fight. They will know of our enemy, just what kind of dishonor the Americans carry, their weaknesses, their lack of will.

He moved out across a wide avenue, a flicker of lights from the buildings around the square, another glance skyward.

Still, he thought, a few Soviet planes could be very helpful.

CHAPTER NINE

. . . .

Riley

THE STINK FROM BELOW drove the men to the open deck, desperate for gasps of fresh air. Riley climbed the final gangway with a hard lunge, burst into the open, released the breath he had held as long as his lungs would allow.

"Good God. What the hell, anyway?"

All around him men were dropping, joining more men who had found anyplace to sit in the open air. The curses surrounded him, one man speaking out.

"Good Christ. You smell that? Musta been ten guys with the trots all at the same time. Ten more guys puking. The heads ain't made for this. I can't go near those places. I'll just hold it."

"Or let it fly over the side. You won't catch me down there again, no matter what."

"How long we gotta be on this bucket, anyhow?"

"I'm out of C-rations. Anybody spare some?"

Riley looked at the last voice, familiar, the kid, Morelli. He motioned him closer, made space on the hard deck, said, "Sit down. You better keep any talk of rations to yourself. Any one of these jackasses is liable to toss you overboard."

The boy settled down beside him, seemed strangely cheerful. "Hey,

Pete, I watched the squids today. They were running a whole flock of minesweepers through the harbor. What a job, huh?"

"Picking up mines ain't my idea of a job, kid. They're taking their damn time about it, too."

To one side, Killian crawled to a clear space on the hard deck, said, "I'm with him, kid. I heard one of those tubs got blown to hell. Guess those clumsy-assed swabbies dropped one. I heard the mines are Russian. Figures."

Riley had heard the talk, that the navy's boats were still struggling to clear the harbor.

"Blew up? Didn't hear that. Might explain why the squids are moving so damn slow."

Killian said, "Marines would have had that place cleaned up by now. If I knew my buddies were out here bobbing up and down like turds, I'd sacrifice a few minesweepers to help 'em out."

Riley looked out toward the harbor, still busy with the work of the minesweepers. It had gone on now for more than a week, the harbor at Wonsan too clogged with mines to allow the landing crafts to move in. It was clear to all of them that the North Koreans had been caught seriously unprepared for the Marine landing at Inchon, and so, someone high up the North Korean command had made sure it wouldn't happen again. The enemy's tactic had seemed to catch everyone by surprise. The transports were not expected to be at sea more than a few days, the time it took to transport the Marines from Inchon, down around the Korean Peninsula, then up to the North Korean port of Wonsan. With the delay, the landing craft had been forced to bide their time, much of that in the open water. But they would not merely sit still. Concerns arose about the possibility of enemy planes, Russian MiGs, first and foremost, the LSTs potentially sitting ducks. And so their crews had kept most of the LSTs in motion, motoring back and forth in the Sea of Japan. It didn't take long for the word to spread, that particular talent the Marines seemed always to possess, the art of the nickname. Very soon the entire division was calling their predicament Operation Yo-yo.

But the humor was short-lived. After more than a week of delay, the LSTs had run out of hot food. The supply of soap was exhausted, along with the drinking water in the ship's limited tanks. Bathing had become a distant memory, the men forced to endure the aroma from painfully close quarters. Then a new crisis developed. An epidemic of low-grade dysentery had spread throughout the LSTs, and with that new plague, the heads had quickly become inoperable, unable to handle the volume from so many digestive problems. The one activity that occupied those well enough to move around came from watching the minesweepers. Even now, men gazed out to one side, cursing the slow labor of the navy.

Killian sat down close beside Riley, said, "I seen Kane down below. Green at the gills. The sarge, too. Doc told 'em to get up here, air it out. Not sure Kane's got enough strength to climb anywhere."

Riley shifted away from Killian, said, "Don't need a blow-by-blow. Jesus. You smell worse than I do. Make some space, how 'bout it."

Killian ignored the complaint, and Riley knew it didn't matter anyway. To the other side, Morelli smelled even worse.

A sailor passed through them, a hint of a uniform, crusted with the same greasy smears that coated the Marines. Riley caught the man's odor, so very different, a strong whiff of dead fish. His face curled, a hopeless effort, and Morelli said, "Wowee. Those Japs sure do carry a smell."

Killian cursed, said, "Why in hell we gotta ride these tubs manned by Japs? They got no good ole USA squids handy? I seen one of those bastards at the stern, catching some kind of grubby little fish, acting like he'd hit a home run. I heard they make fish-head stew. I got a hard enough time eating the good parts."

Morelli leaned forward, looked past Riley toward the Irishman. "What kind of fish they catching?"

"How the hell do I know? The kind they eat. The kind that make them stink like that."

Riley closed his eyes, knew he couldn't escape the conversation. He took a long, futile breath, fought the rumble low in his gut, said, "They eat that stuff so we won't steal it from 'em. One of 'em offered to sell me his bowl of soup. There was a fish looking up at me. I passed."

Killian leaned back against the rail. "At least you found one that spoke English. All I been hearing is Jap talk. Nasty critters, too. Keep eyeing me like the war was my fault. They remember what we done to 'em, count on that. I keep wondering if I put a slug between the eyes of some family member, that maybe when I'm not looking, one of 'em might slip a blade between my ribs."

Riley shook his head. "Not hardly. I heard they love MacArthur and all, treat us like kings in Tokyo. They're as happy to be done with that war as we are. Happier still. They ain't gotta fight this one."

"Listen up, jarheads!"

Riley saw Zorn, the others reacting to the captain in slow motion, Zorn's shirt as stained as the men around him.

"We're expecting to land tomorrow. Gather up your gear tonight. Where's Lieutenant McCarthy?"

One of the men pointed down the hatchway.

"He's the one locking himself in the head, sir. Didn't know officers were allowed to smell like that."

There were low laughs, Zorn not smiling.

"Make sure he gets the word. This tub will empty out as quick as we can get it done. It'll be an administrative landing. No enemy around, according to the shore birds. The place is ours for the taking."

Killian said, "Sir, after we take it, can we give it back?"

There were low laughs, but Riley could see that Zorn was in no mood for anyone's attempt at humor.

"Just gather your gear. The quicker we get off this tub, the quicker I can wash my skivvies. Our luck, the first fresh water we'll find will be in those damn rice paddies."

The captain moved away, and Killian leaned back beside Riley again.

Morelli said, "'Administrative landing.' What's that? You mean like paperwork and stuff?"

Riley said, "It means there's nobody there to shoot at us."

"I guess that's good."

Killian sniffed. "Maybe. I was hoping we'd clean out a bunch of those bastards. Built up a fine, healthy hate for those Nook sons of bitches. Don't guess they're any different on this side of their damn country than they were at Inchon. I bet the squids would like to pound a few of 'em, too, after losing a couple of their minesweepers. We're gonna screw around and miss out on the fun again. I just know it."

Riley crawled slowly to his feet, held himself up against the iron railing, looked at Morelli. "No incoming fire is always good, no matter what this moron says." He looked at Killian. "They told us we're supposed to march north. You forget that? They got work for us to do, and you can bet they'll make up for what all we missed at Inchon. We were the tail end on that one. We'll be first in line. Count on it."

Killian leaned his head back, closed his eyes. "Hope so."

Riley glanced toward the hatchway, said, "Guess I'll go below and find the sarge. Hate to see him so damn wrecked. He'll be glad to hear there's not gonna be a fight. The lieutenant, too. They'll feel better when they hear we're finally getting off this crate."

Riley moved to the hatchway, eyed the steps leading below. The smells rose to meet him, and he hesitated, thought, My gear's down there. Gotta do this sooner or later. At least, Korea's gotta smell better after this.

Killian called out to him, "Hey, Pete, I'm taking bets. How long can you hold your breath?"

BLUE BEACH—WONSAN—OCTOBER 26, 1950

The men lined the seawall with jubilant cheers, the Marines curious, no one expecting a welcoming party. Riley could see that many of the men onshore were Marines, the word passing quickly that they were from the First Marine Air Wing, the fliers already establishing a base on an airfield in the port. Others were Korean, soldiers to be sure, seemingly as anxious as the airmen to offer a good cheer for the incoming Marines.

They had ridden off the LST on amtracs, the vehicles hauling them on the short journey ashore. Beside him, Killian said, "Who the hell are those jarheads? And what the hell are they doing here? I thought this was our party."

The men were ordered off the vehicle, and Riley jumped down, his

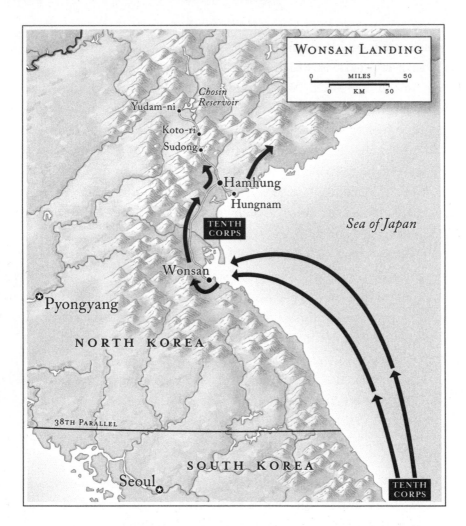

knees giving way, a hard fall into the dirt, his sea bag tumbling to one side. He struggled to his feet, heard the grunts and curses around him, more men doing as he did, their legs betraying them, inelegant landings, men rolling over, all of it now swallowed by the raucous laughter from their audience.

He pulled himself up, lifted the sea bag, but he was too unsteady to swing it over his shoulder. Around him, the men were nearly all down, some climbing to their feet, sea bags scattered about them. Riley tested his knees, stood at attention, felt the weakness again, said aloud, "What the hell?"

Welch was there now, stretching his back, said, "Haven't felt this weak since boot. Jesus. Three weeks on a ship with nothing to do but sit on a head. I guess it hit us pretty hard."

"This is ridiculous, Sarge. We're not even thirty, not like some old fart whose ass is hanging."

The sergeant had one hand on his gut, an uneasy look on his face. "Shut up. I've still got the trots. Need this to clear up right damn now. Feel like my intestines are boiling."

From the onlookers came the calls, all manner of insults, some of it good-natured, some as vulgar as any Marine was used to. Riley looked at the others, the Koreans, let out a small laugh.

"Hey, Sarge. Check out those guys. Somebody's been teaching them our ways."

"What the hell you talking about?"

"Those Koreans. They're giving us the one-finger salute."

Behind Riley, the voice of Captain Zorn. "Cultural exchange program. Bringing them our kind of civilization."

Zorn moved out in front of Riley, more men dropping off the amtracs behind them. Zorn called out, "Tighten it up! Find your damn legs! Get your asses in line! Stand tall! You're Marines, dammit! Show those assholes what Marines look like! What the hell is this? We're out of action for three weeks and we turn into blubber guts? I'll kick all your asses for this. Those flyboys think this is pretty damn funny. Fox Company isn't anybody's entertainment, you got me?"

Riley saw McCarthy move out in front of them.

"Come on, men. They're laughing at you. You heard the captain. We're supposed to be Marines. This is embarrassing, for sure. Fall into line."

Riley tried to stiffen his back, his eyes ahead, saw Goolsby step forward, trying to make a good show, standing with McCarthy. But Goolsby staggered now, turned away, dropped to his knees. Riley closed his eyes, thought, Don't need to see that. Not now. The distinctive sound came, though, Goolsby vomiting, more laughter, more insults coming from the men along the seawall.

McCarthy grabbed Goolsby under the arm and Riley heard him say, "Just sit down. We'll get corpsmen out here on the double."

From the far end of the line, Riley saw a jeep rolling along the formation, heard Killian behind him.

"Hey! It's Old Homer."

The jeep pulled up, stopped with a squeal of brakes, Colonel Litzenberg dismounting. Another officer was there as well, fresh uniform, unfamiliar, and the men fell silent, the airmen as well. One of theirs, Riley thought. Great. Tell everyone what kind of idiots we look like.

Litzenberg stood with his hands on his hips, a stout fireplug of a man. After a long moment, he said, "Men of the Seventh Regiment. This is Major Jacoby, of the air wing. Our reception committee belongs to him. Like many of you, I had wondered why there was no enemy awaiting us here. You may credit the Marine airmen for making our job that much easier. The Koreans as well. These men are part of the Sixth ROK Division. They began the push up this coastline and have done much to secure this port for us." Litzenberg paused, looked down. "I might also add that we had anticipated a reception of a far different nature. We are grateful to the ROK for removing the enemy from the formidable gun emplacements you see around you now. I believe Major Jacoby has something to add. You'll find out anyway, so I thought we'd cut through the scuttlebutt and give you the straight scoop."

Riley saw a beaming smile, Jacoby a head taller than Litzenberg, rocking back and forth on his heels, clearly pleased.

"Marines, it is my regrettable duty to inform you that your arrival here was tardy by only two days. I must say that the men of the First Marine Air Wing thoroughly enjoyed a show that was meant partly for you. It is entirely possible, of course, that there will be a repeat performance, although the entire rig has since left for other bases. Truly a shame, Marines."

Litzenberg stepped forward, and Riley saw a scowl, the colonel as annoyed as Jacoby was pleased. Litzenberg put a hand on Jacoby's arm, said, "You will all hear this in the next few days, so hear it first from me. As it was put to me a short time ago, our delay meant that the port of Wonsan was captured and secured not by the Seventh Marines, as we had hoped, but by units of the ROK, the First Marine Air Wing . . . and I regret to announce . . . Mr. Bob Hope."

Jacoby laughed now, said, "Maybe you won't miss out next time. But it was an outstanding show."

The men reacted as both officers expected, a hard groan and angry calls. The airmen watching them erupted into more cheers. Riley sagged, had heard about too many spectacular visits by Bob Hope, all the way back to his days in the Pacific, none of them Riley's unit could ever attend.

Litzenberg kept his pose, still the scowl, waited for the men to quiet. "We are presently awaiting orders as to our next march. For now, you men will be cleaned up, fed, and made ready. I may not be able to give you a USO show, but I promise you, before we're done here, we'll show these flyboys what we were sent here to do. And where we're going, it's not likely Mr. Hope will be welcome."

CHAPTER TEN

. . . .

Smith

"SO, INSTEAD OF General MacArthur's proposed strategy of crushing the North Korean armies outright, ending this war on our terms, the British are insisting that we should appease everyone concerned by peacefully carving up Korea, creating a demilitarized buffer zone for the Chinese to occupy, all along the Yalu River. Apparently there is some concern among *others* that if we do our jobs and win this war, we will have made things, um, *uncomfortable* for some of the neighboring states. I mean, of course, China and the Soviet Union. It seems that there are those in Washington who wish us to win this war as long as we do not offend anyone doing it."

There was nothing different about Almond this time, no change in the man's amazing arrogance. Smith glanced around, various Tenth Corps staff officers mimicking Almond's disdain for just who these *others* might be. It had been a supreme exercise in patience, but Smith felt it wearing thin, Almond's briefing droning on for more than two hours. There was one spark of optimism that Smith embraced, confident that sooner or later, Almond would finally tell the army commanders and the Marines just what they were supposed to do next. There seemed to be an opening in Almond's self-satisfied pause and Smith said, "Sir, do we have operational maps in hand? I should like to distribute them to my regimental commanders."

Almond seemed annoyed at the question. "Of course. But first I should like to read to you General MacArthur's response to the British proposal."

Smith nodded, said in a low voice, "Of course."

"General MacArthur is very aware that there are those in Washington who wish to handcuff our movements. I, for one, have no idea why anyone should oppose the general's plans at all. I can only attribute this to the dirty game of politics. General MacArthur has assured me that he is far more interested in conducting what we all know to be the dirty game of war. Our mission going forward is to drive rapidly to the Yalu River, eliminating the North Korean army along the way. Despite British concerns that our presence along the Chinese border will cause indigestion among the yellow race, you are to follow General MacArthur's orders, and mine, to the letter." He leaned forward, sorted through a handful of loose papers. "Ah, yes. Right here. To the British idea, General MacArthur has responded to the Joint Chiefs in this way. 'The widely reported British desire to appease the Chinese Communists by giving them a strip of North Korea finds its historic precedent in the actions taken at Munich on September 29, 1938.'" Almond smiled, staring out above them. "Magnificent. Let no one tell you that General MacArthur does not embrace the errors of history. There shall be no such appeasement occurring here. You might think that the British would recall their disastrous efforts to make nice with Herr Hitler." Almond paused. "I might add that I offered some assistance to the general in composing that note."

Smith felt his eyelids growing heavier, forced himself into alertness, glanced over at General Barr, the Seventh Division's commander staring blankly, the same emotionless expressions on the faces of his staff officers. From behind Smith came an abrupt sneeze, which seemed to wake up everyone around him. There was a low groan and Smith turned, saw Bowser struggling with a handkerchief, a whistling blast as Bowser blew his nose.

"Sorry. Bloody awful cold."

Barr seemed to jump on the distraction, said, "General Almond, you did mention maps?"

Almond was still annoyed, waved one hand to the side, motioning for an aide. "All right. Maps. I suppose some of us feel the need to dwell on the mundane. In my role as chief of staff to the general, I have witnessed great things, what I would only describe as a whirlwind of the momentous. So many in Washington fail to see what is being accomplished here. Even Truman . . ." He stopped, seemed to catch himself. "Well, enough about all of that. Captain, please distribute the maps among these men. I suppose marching men need to know where they are marching. If you will examine the lines, indicating your specific units, you will see what we have designed. I intend to have my forces scattered all over the eastern half of North Korea. As you know, the Eighth Army is occupying much of the western half. The goal of course is to sweep up whatever remains of the enemy's forces."

Smith ignored Almond now, took the map, focused, Bowser sliding his chair up alongside him. Bowser sniffled loudly, said into Smith's ear, "I won't breathe on you, sir. Promise."

"You're breathing on me now. Back off."

Bowser obeyed, the chair sliding back. He had a map of his own, Almond's aide completing the task. Bowser grunted, and Smith knew why. Smith said, "General Almond, these maps are in Japanese. Have we none of our own?"

Almond shrugged. "The maps would be the same. Only the names would be different. I give credit to our Japanese allies for providing us with such helpful tools. Their loyalty to General MacArthur is most extraordinary. Are the routes of march, the troops deployments, not clear to you, Smith?"

Smith scanned the map, the red lines showing the Marine units extending northward, concluding at a town called Hagaru-ri. Beyond the town to the north was a three-pronged lake, a reservoir the map named Chosin, created by what seemed to be a dam. Smith felt a familiar twist, a punch of uncertainty. He looked up at Almond.

"This is all too clear. You are intending us to advance some, what?

Sixty miles? Seventy? You have indicated that the First Regiment is to maintain position close to here, while the Fifth and the Seventh move up toward this body of water."

Almond's annoyance seemed to bloom all over again. "More than that, Smith. Your Colonel Puller shall advance southward, protecting the rear of your division down as far as the village of . . . oh, damn . . . what's it called?"

To one side, an aide whispered loudly, "Kojo, sir."

"Yes. Kojo. At least one battalion shall move westward, to the area around Majon-ni. One would think these people could name their towns something more convenient."

Smith scanned the map, his hands with a hard grip on the stiff paper. "Kojo is . . . forty miles to the south. Majon-ni is no closer." He looked at Almond now, who seemed to ignore him, speaking in a low voice to his aide. "General, I am not comfortable extending our lines such a distance."

Almond seemed surprised. "Tell me, Smith, do you not have confidence in your man Puller?"

Smith stifled a low growl, closed his eyes for a brief moment. "I have complete faith in Colonel Puller. But even Puller will object to his regiment being scattered to the four winds. You would have the Fifth and Seventh begin their march to the north, while Lewie is moving in the opposite direction. Support will be difficult at best. Once Litzenberg reaches this reservoir, he will be tied to our supply bases along the coast by one primary road. Do we know the quality of that road? Its vulnerabilities?"

Almond glanced toward his aide. "I told you there would be argument." He looked again at Smith. "Dammit, we have considered this plan in every detail. We have already allowed the enemy to escape our clutches by delaying our advance. That shall not happen again. Your Marines pride themselves on their speed, yes? Their ability to fight off any force with a handful of their own? I've heard all of that bravado. Well, show me why I should believe it. Puller's men will work alongside ROK units to secure your rear, your left flank, and the port of Wonsan. Your other two regiments will drive northward with as much haste as you can muster. Our goal is the Yalu River, and with that, we shall end this war, Smith. Simple as that. I've already passed along the information that, once the enemy has surrendered, or been annihilated, two of your regiments are scheduled to return home. That should put a fire under their backsides, don't you agree?"

Smith looked down. "I will not tell them that. I am much more comfortable having them in fighting spirit, rather than spending their hours each day contemplating home."

Almond looked at Barr. "What about you? Is the Seventh Division not anxious to end this thing? Perhaps show their Marine brothers just how well the army can manage things? I have known very few soldiers who do not carry memories of loved ones with them into combat. Homesickness is a powerful motivator. Don't you agree?"

Barr glanced at Smith. "I prefer to keep such orders within my headquarters, until it is an appropriate time to communicate them."

Almond clamped his hands on his hips. "Is this defeatism I'm hearing? Do you not understand what the job is? The enemy is in chaos, he is retreating willy-nilly. This has become a mopping-up operation, and the sooner we can complete this, the sooner we may all return to our homes and loved ones. Good God, why the doubts? Shall I report to General MacArthur that the Tenth Corps cannot keep pace with the Eighth Army because we fear the enemy is still dangerous? Even Walton Walker understands the prize that awaits him, and I promise you, he will seek any means to embarrass this command. They have already captured and occupied Pyongyang and are certain to reach the Yalu before us if we do not put our people into motion. All right, I have heard enough gloom from you. You have your orders, and I will see them carried out. You will advance with all speed toward the Yalu River, and should you engage the enemy along the way, you shall destroy him. Now go. Dismissed."

Almond left the room, clearly disgusted, his aides in tow. The remaining staff officers gathered behind their commanders, Bowser sneezing again. Barr moved closer to Smith, said to Bowser, "Take care of that cold, Colonel. I imagine we are all to be on our toes for the next few weeks." He looked at Smith now, shook his head. "He does not believe the enemy is dangerous. That could be a mistake."

Smith held up the map. "I am being told to spread my division over dozens of miles, in places we are not familiar with, supplied by a single road. There are a number of towns along the route, and to my knowledge, none of them are secured. I'm not sure just how dangerous the enemy needs to be. There is danger enough in our own arrogance."

FIRST MARINE DIVISION COMMAND POST—WONSAN—
NOVEMBER 2, 1950

Puller was pacing, the smoke from his cigar swirling up around his head. "This is idiocy, O.P. I've got men holding off enemy troops in every direction. What kind of support am I getting?"

Smith kept his eyes on the map, glanced up, saw Sexton on the far side of the room. "Captain, go someplace else."

Sexton obeyed, was out of the room, the door closing.

"I would prefer if you not address me like that in front of staff."

Puller yanked the cigar from his mouth. "My apologies, *General*. But, Christ Almighty. You've got me spread all over creation out there. My battalions are too scattered to support each other. I was told there was no enemy anywhere in the area, and my men are taking fire as we speak. We've run slam into whole flocks of North Korean troops, popping up like so many bands of guerrillas. We wondered what the hell happened to all those enemy who escaped us at Inchon? Well, here they are. We're on *their* ground now, and they don't seem to like it one bit. But Christ, O.P., I was told to expect a nuisance, flocks of Korean jackrabbits that might try to raid our supply posts. It's a whole lot more than that. Right now I'm taking casualties. We didn't expect to have to dig in just to hold a bunch of nameless hills." He paused, a hard glare at Smith. "I know damn well that wasn't your doing. What the hell's happening?"

"I need them to hold on. How much heat are they taking?"

"Enough. But they'll hold. I'm heading down to Kojo right now, kick some colonel in the ass. I heard panic on the radio last night. Won't have that."

Smith studied Puller's expression, tried to see past the man's obvious anger. He wouldn't ask for details, knew that Puller would tell him if the problems were serious.

"Take care of things, Lewie. I need all of you to do the job."

Puller pointed toward him with the cigar. "What job? Just what the hell are we doing here? I'm to protect Wonsan from an enemy that isn't supposed to be there. What am I protecting? The supply dumps here are cleared out, if not by us, then by the damn civilians. The navy's not taking any heat in the harbors. Nobody's shelling their damn boats. They can come and go like they want. My whole damn regiment is doing lunchroom duty, while Litz and Murray go racing off to see who's first to piss in the Yalu River!"

Smith let it go, knew that letting Puller blast away was the best way to handle him. "Take care of business, Lewie. That's all. Tenth Corps has a plan, and it comes straight from Tokyo. We're just a piece of the puzzle."

"What about the *enemy's* plan? Any ideas there? They just gonna let you drive a big damn convoy all the way to the Chinese border, like some flag-waving parade? We should be gathered up, O.P. We have to be able to support each other."

Smith knew he was right. But there was nothing to be discussed now. "Go, Lewie. See to your men. Fix that nervous colonel. Keep in touch with me. I'm going up in a helicopter, meet with Litzenberg. He's leading the way north."

Puller shook his head. "So, Tenth Corps gave you a new toy, huh? I rode in one of those bouncy-assed things. Like sitting on a basketball. Fine, go have fun. Give my regards to the *convoy*."

He recalled Puller's description, "sitting on a basketball," the helicopter tilting wildly to one side, caught by a gust of wind. The pilot jerked the stick, gained control again, dropping the helicopter downward. Below him a small crowd of officers gathered, waiting in the road, one man signaling with his arms toward the makeshift landing zone. The craft settled down now with a soft bump, the pilot cutting the engine, leaning over to him.

"Sorry for the rough ride, sir. The winds are a little tricky."

Smith nodded, said nothing, tried to unravel the knots in his stomach. He slid out of the seat, landed shakily on the soft ground, one hand against the craft, trying to find his legs.

Litzenberg was there now, a short, stocky man, intense eyes, a hard stare at Smith. "Thank you for coming up here, General. Never thought I'd see these things so useful."

Smith glanced at the pilot, who nodded toward him.

"So far. Saves time. You have a CP?"

"This way, sir. We're making good time, but I'm hearing a lot of noise from the locals."

"Let's go inside, Colonel."

Smith's message was clear, no conversation needed for casual listeners. Litzenberg had the annoying habit of arguing when he should be keeping quiet, something Smith had learned to tolerate. Not the time, he thought.

He followed Litzenberg to a ramshackle building, a line of trucks moving past, dust engulfing the waiting helicopter. Inside, Litzenberg pointed to a chair.

"Please have a seat, sir. Coffee?"

"No. Tell me about the locals. What are you hearing?"

Litzenberg sat across from him, two aides spreading a map on a small table between them. "Nervous as the dickens. Farmers, whatnot. They keep telling us there's troops all over the place, waiting for us. We've been picked at a few times, snipers mostly. Nothing to slow us down. If the enemy's waiting to slug us in the gut, they're taking their time about it. Locals keep telling us it's the Chinese. I had interpreters talking to these people, watched all manner of dramatics. These people talk to us like they're terrified, and every time we reassure them that the enemy is gone, they just get louder, preaching doom and gloom. The interpreters seem to think it's all for effect. Every village we've passed through, the people beg us to stick around. We're making friends pretty easy. Kinda strange, since these folks are all North Koreans."

Smith stared at the map, ignored the details, sorted through Litzenberg's descriptions. "You seen any sign of Chinese troops?"

"No. Am I supposed to?"

"Not according to G-2 in Tokyo."

"G-2 should come out here, talk to these civilians. What's his name? Willoughby?"

"General Charles Willoughby. MacArthur trusts him like his own son. I've invited him to come out here, see what's happening for himself. Hard to pry those fellows away from Tokyo. General Willoughby insists we'll have an easy time of this, that the path is open all the way to the Yalu. My job is to take him seriously. Your job is to follow orders."

"Do you?"

"Take him seriously? No choice, Colonel. I've got orders, too. If there are Chinese in this fight, Willoughby insists with absolute certainty that they're flocks of volunteers, sent south to help out their Korean allies. No more, no less."

"Well, it's nerve-racking, sir. We're watching enemy on distant ridges, no one close enough to grab. I'm hoping we can snatch a few prisoners, see what they have to say. My guess is they're North Koreans, but who the hell knows? If there are Chinese troops standing in our way, it's a different fight. I'm no politician, General, but I know something of politics. We start killing Chinese, and the Soviets might not be happy about that. It spreads, like a stain. Next thing, the bombs start falling. Big ones. We could be starting World War Three. That doesn't make me comfortable, sir."

Smith didn't want this, respected Litzenberg too much to watch him get rattled. "I need you to do the job, Colonel. That's all. I've got very specific orders from Tenth Corps. I intend to follow them." He paused. "I intend to follow them with great deliberation. Great care. Precision, if you will."

Litzenberg smiled, glanced at the staff officers around him. "Understood, sir. We shall advance with . . . precision."

Smith stood now, moved to a filthy window, stared out. "I don't know what's out there, Colonel. But until I feel we can readily support each other, I'll not have three regiments strung out across half of Asia. Our first priority is to relieve South Korean elements that have already pushed out in front of us. Maybe those fellows can give us some accurate intelligence. For all we know, Willoughby is spot-on. One part of me hopes that General MacArthur is absolutely right, that this war is pretty much over. I miss my granddaughter, Colonel. I'll be as happy as every private in this division if we get home for Christmas." He turned, looked at Litzenberg. "Keep that under your hat. Your staff, too. I don't need your men thinking they're just biding time out here. Keep them sharp, awake."

"Certainly, sir. I'd be happy to make a wager with you about that Christmas thing."

Smith felt a rising burn of bad humor. "I don't gamble. Don't mention that again."

"Never again, sir."

Smith looked out through the filthy glass. "Road still looks decent enough for trucks."

"For now. Civilians say the road gets hairy a few miles north of Hungnam. If the topo maps are accurate, there are some pretty steep climbs farther north. Might have to put the men on their feet."

Smith saw a hazy form in the window, a man running toward Litzenberg's CP. The door opened with a loud crash, the man halting, coming to attention. He looked at Smith, said, "Sir! They told me you were here. Excuse me."

Litzenberg was on his feet now, said, "What's the problem, Lieutenant?"

The man pulled himself under control, still looked at Smith.

"Sir, begging your pardon, but your staff's been trying to track you down."

"They know where I am."

"Yes, sir. A Colonel Bowser reached us by radio. He was most insistent that you return to Wonsan."

"No message?"

"He wouldn't say, sir. I can raise him for you."

Smith looked out through the window, the helicopter waiting.

"No." He looked at Litzenberg. "Keep 'em moving, Colonel. Eyes sharp. If those civilians keep talking about the Chinese, I'll make sure General Willoughby hears about it. I'll push again for Willoughby to fly up here himself. Maybe our intelligence people can be persuaded to do more than host banquets for Japanese politicians."

Smith moved out through the door, blew through the clouds of dust, more trucks moving past, curious faces watching him. He motioned to the pilot, the man quickly in his seat, firing up the engine, the rotors beginning their slow turn. He slid in beside the young man, pointed with his hand, *Go*, the engine revving louder, then louder still, the helicopter rising slowly, losing touch with the ground. Smith glanced up, his mind focused on the single steel bar, the only connection between the rotor and the rest of the craft, an uneasy lifeline that kept him airborne. He tried not to think of that, stared ahead, the pilot maneuvering out over the first hills, the parade of trucks spread out along the road beneath him. Smith felt a hard chill, pulled at his jacket, couldn't avoid a shiver. He glanced at the pilot, knew the man couldn't hear him, said in a low voice, "Getting colder."

FIRST MARINE DIVISION COMMAND POST—WONSAN—
NOVEMBER 2, 1950

"You certain?"

"Sir, Tenth Corps didn't have much to say, but our people picked up radio traffic from Eighth Army. General Puller has radioed as well, word reaching him through the ROK units in his area."

Smith sat slowly, stared at Bowser, the other aides watching him. Bowser wiped at his nose with a handkerchief, still suffering from the cold, said, "General Almond's HQ says it's only panic at Eighth Army."

"Is it?"

"I don't believe so."

"Me neither. This is pretty specific." He studied the dispatch again, felt a nagging helplessness. "Eighth Army is supposed to secure our left flank. Well, it's pretty clear they're a long way from our flank. And no one seems to be moving this way at all."

Bowser stuffed the handkerchief in his pocket. "It could be blown out of proportion, sir. Some nervous aide putting out an exaggerated call. The kind of thing that drives Colonel Puller up the wall."

Smith slid through the papers, retrieved another dispatch. "This one came from Puller. Seems there's a lot of wall-climbing going on. Everybody's got something bad to say, except Tenth Corps. They're pleased as anything this happened to Eighth Army."

"But do we know what happened, sir?"

Smith tossed the papers to one side, tried to hide a nervous quiver in his hands. He stared past Bowser, the others still silent, watching him.

"All we know, Colonel, is that there's more going on out there than anyone seems to know. And that is a dangerous way to fight a war."

On November 1, as units of Walton Walker's Eighth Army advanced on their mission up the western half of North Korea toward the Yalu River, one unit of the American First Cavalry Division, along with several units of ROK infantry, was suddenly struck by a heavy assault from an enemy no one expected to see. The surprise was complete, although numerous reports had been issued by both air and ROK observers that enemy columns were moving in strength toward the UN positions. Near the town of Unsan, far to the north of Pyongyang, the ROK units were quickly routed, while the American Eighth Cavalry Regiment was surrounded on three sides. In fighting that lasted all that night, the Americans were finally forced to flee into the hills, most of the cavalry units cut off from any support. Despite ongoing reports that no enemy was operating in their area, the Eighth Cavalry's Third Battalion fought a brutal struggle for its very survival, the enemy forces having severed any avenue of escape.

For men too accustomed to pursuing a demoralized and defeated foe, the shock of the assault was absolute. But as quickly as the enemy troops had launched their crushing attack, they withdrew from the fight. The reports flew quickly, the frantic radio calls reaching Walton

Walker that one part of his glorious surge toward the Yalu River had been severely crushed. But the reports offered more than casualty counts. The enemy had left their dead and wounded as well, descriptions reaching Eighth Army HQ, passed on back to Tokyo, that the assaulting troops were not North Korean. They were Chinese.

CHAPTER ELEVEN

. . . .

Sung

NEAR YUDAM-NI, NORTH KOREA—NOVEMBER 2, 1950

THEY HAD ENDED the march while it was still dark, and there would be no fires allowed, no smoke to betray their presence among the hills. It was routine now, the soldiers digging shallow pits, doing what they could to secure a camouflaged hiding place for the day ahead, slipping out into thickets of brush and low trees.

To the east, the first hint of dawn rose in a gray haze over a snow-capped mountain, and he shivered, the sweat of the night's march chilling his skin. He loved the sunrise, watched intently, waited for the first burst of orange that would reveal just how many mountains there were. He glanced upward, the stars fading, and he thought, There are no clouds. It will be a good day for their planes. And so we shall stay here, wait again for dark, and when their planes go home, we shall resume the march.

The tactics were simple and direct: the army would advance only at night. When mistakes were made, the Americans seemed always to be there, swarms of dive bombers, low-flying fighter planes strafing the narrow roads. Often the targets were the innocent, North Korean peasants seeking escape from Sung's troops, a wave of refugees who seemed to fear the Chinese army as much as they feared their own. Soon those people had learned just how dangerous the roads could be, and so they

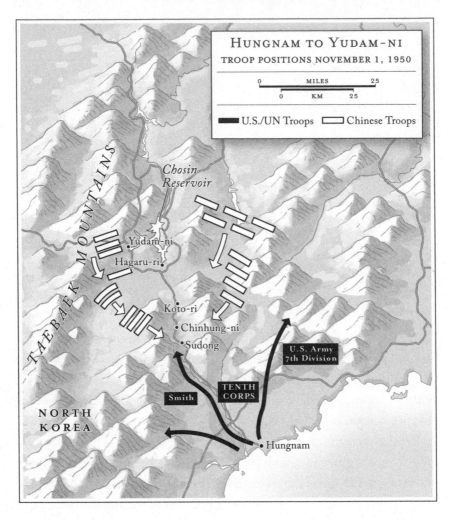

too had spread into the wooded hills, or if they brought wagons, they moved only at night.

A dozen yards down the hillside, officers were gathering together, a cloth bag of rice passing between them. Sung felt the hunger himself, fought it, knew that what he carried in his own satchel would have to last. There was privilege of rank, of course, the coolies with their A-frame packs hauling the rare tins of meat and fish. His orders could direct them to his own camp, providing a feast of sorts for his staff, for those higher-ranking officers who stayed close. But he would not enjoy that kind of luxury, not out here, not while the men around him kept up their strength with a small ration of rice and dried beans. It was pride, theirs and his own, that his army could move on such meager supplies. There were a few trucks, most of them old Soviet vehicles from the last war, unreliable, always requiring repairs that few could manage. When a truck broke down, it would remain by the side of the narrow road, its cargo piled onto the backs of the coolies. He marveled at those men, capable of carrying their own weight on their shoulders, few of them ever speaking, certainly not to him. They went about the bone-crushing labor as though it were their only task in life, and for many that was accurate. Some were North Korean, the officers keeping careful watch on them, concerned with just how trustworthy they might be, whether they would slip away in the darkness, carrying off the precious supplies. So far there had been few reports of that. He rarely saw them on the march, the men hidden by the darkness. In the camp, Sung had been surprised to see a kind of gamesmanship evolving, competitions between them. But no one forgot that those men were the bottom rung of his army's ladder, and there had been brutality, always, low-ranking officers making use of the whip, exercising their own power against men who had no power of their own. Sung put a stop to that when he could, knew just how valuable those men and their A-frames were, the deeper they moved into Korea. For now, the soldiers carried only what they required to fight, their rifles and machine guns, some of them American made. It was the spoils of the victory against the Nationalists, captured weapons from a half-dozen countries. The most common weapon was the burp gun, a stocky machine gun that sacrificed accuracy for sheer firepower. There were American submachine guns as well, the ever reliable Thompson, a close-range weapon for men who understood that when the fight came, it would have to be nearly face-to-face. In every unit came the men who carried the grenades, all shapes, varying degrees of power. Some were merely percussion, a blast that might cripple rather than kill. Others came with a valuable knot of high explosives, and most of those were the potato-masher type, what Sung knew had been a favorite of the Germans in the last war. The elongated handle gave a man leverage, adding distance to his throw, and he had seen to their training, squads of grenade carriers practicing only with the strength of their arms, the accuracy of their toss.

Besides the weapons, most of his men were equipped with the kind of clothing meant to combat the coming of winter, thick padded pants and coats, with a hat to match, heavy earflaps to stave off the harsh, icy winds. They did not wear helmets, another point of pride, the officers knowing that a well-placed bullet could easily penetrate the tin hat worn by the Americans.

There were few boots, the lack of tough leather explained away by the need for stealth, that heavy-heeled boots would likely be too clumsy for men accustomed to lengthy marches. Their shoes were soft canvas, rubber soles, and if they did little to ward off freezing temperatures, Sung had convinced himself and his officers that when the men moved, their feet would warm themselves. The simple answer was to keep them moving.

Sung watched a gathering of coolies farther down the hill, the A-frames standing together, silent men digging into whatever rations they might be carrying. I should order the younger officers to carry those A-frames themselves, maybe just a single night. That should keep those whips silenced. He shook his head. No, you do not do such a thing to officers. You destroy a man's honor by unwise punishment. There is no shame in this army. We shall teach the Americans about shame.

"Hello, General Sung!"

The voice was too loud, drawing stares from the other officers. Sung saw the larger man moving toward him, open coat, a small bottle in his hand.

"Major Orlov. Have you found a suitable place to sleep?"

The Russian glanced toward the sunrise, said, "No. Not yet. In time. It will be a long day. I do not require so much sleep."

Sung wasn't sure just how he felt about the presence of the Russian, assigned to his camp from above, perhaps higher than General Peng. He had tried to read the man, the Russian tall, lanky, too eager to laugh. He spoke fair Mandarin, with a heavy accent that made him difficult to understand. But Sung had spent a great deal of time in Manchuria, had heard enough Russian blended with Chinese dialects to understand most of what Orlov was trying to say.

Sung knew his orders, that the observer was to be regarded as a guest in Sung's camp. So far the Russian had kept mostly out of the way, no questions, the man with little curiosity about just where this army was marching. Sung watched Orlov take a long drink from his bottle, guessed it was alcohol, something Sung and most of his officers never touched. The Russian slipped the bottle into his coat, seemed to follow Sung's gaze at the new dawn.

"A few more days . . . it will get cold, yes?"

Sung nodded, pulled his coat more tightly around him. "We are prepared."

"I see that. Your men wear a double coat. One side brown, the other white. Either way, very useful. If there is snow, they can be well camouflaged."

"There will be snow."

"Yes. I can smell it. Many mornings. At Leningrad, I learned to smell many things, including the Germans. Did you know there is a different smell between German tanks and our own? I should think your enemy here must carry his own odor. If you continue to maneuver in the darkness, your men will learn."

"We will continue to move in the darkness. Likely we shall fight in the darkness. It is the one advantage we have. The Americans are too much in love with their plush sleeping bags, their soft blankets. How is that in your army, Major? Are there luxuries? How badly do you miss your supplies of vodka?"

He stopped, knew he had gone too far. No, you must not insult this man. To his surprise, Orlov laughed.

"I do miss my vodka, yes." He tapped his pocket. "This will not last long, I regret." Orlov paused. "You do not care for my presence, eh, Comrade?"

"I would prefer you address me by my rank. My soldiers are not accustomed to such informality."

"My apologies. My orders were to show you every respect. I am privileged to be in your camp, General."

Sung looked at him, thought, What else were you ordered to do? He looked again toward the rising sun, a harsh glow now bathing the hills with sprays of light.

"I am privileged to have you as my guest." It was the same polite formality that had passed between them since Orlov arrived, just as the army had crossed the Yalu River. Orlov's comment reached him now. "I did not know you were at Leningrad. I assume you were a soldier then?"

Orlov seemed to shrink, more serious now, his voice lowering. "I was a very young lieutenant. I knew nothing of war or Germans or what artillery shells can do to other young men. I learned very quickly."

Sung said nothing, kept those kinds of memories far away. "We all must learn. Perhaps one day there will be no need."

Orlov moved closer to him. "There will always be need. I know your combat record, General Sung. I know of your great struggle against the Nationalists. Your army, even these men here, they march with the pride that comes from victory."

Sung held himself back, felt a pang of caution. "The officers here are veterans, many of them. The soldiers are young. They must still learn."

Orlov nodded. "Yes, I heard one of your commanders saying that the soldiers consider your army to be like a great university. It is all they know, all they are meant to do. You teach them to read, you educate them in the ways of the world. They are better for it."

It was a point of pride for Sung, for many of the senior commanders in the Chinese army, that even the lowest troops learned much about Chinese history, particularly the great struggles of the recent past. Sung said, "They learn of the revolution. They are proud to march under our flag, the flag that reminds them always of their dedication to Chairman Mao."

"Certainly. Well spoken. You have learned as well. I trust such knowledge will give you confidence against the guns of the Americans."

There was sarcasm in Orlov's words, Sung more uncomfortable now. He didn't want this, felt the hard weariness of the long night's march.

He began to ease away, but Orlov followed, and Sung stopped, said, "Major, I must speak with my commanders. They will have reports about this march. I must know the condition of my men before we begin again tonight."

"Of course. I would very much enjoy hearing of this. It is one reason I am here, as you know."

Sung looked at him, studied the man, tried to see past the friendliness of his eyes. "Are there other reasons? Or am I not to ask?"

Orlov held out his hands, open palms. "I am in your service, General Sung. This is your command. My task is to observe for Chairman Stalin, to report what I see, and possibly to offer suggestions to my superiors what the Soviet army might do to assist you."

It was the first time Orlov had used Stalin's name. He studied the man again, Orlov slowly crossing his arms, the grin returning. Sung said, "We are hopeful for such assistance as you can provide. There is a great deal of concern that we engage with an enemy far superior to what our officers have experienced. I make every effort to eliminate such fears. I believe the Americans possess superior weaponry, but I am not afraid of the American heart. They are soft, arrogant." He paused. "I have heard that your officers have concerns as well. There is talk in Peking that you will not help us because you are afraid of what the Americans can do." He hesitated, knew it was a dangerous subject. "My apologies. It is not my place to question the heart of your soldiers."

Orlov seemed unaffected, shrugged. "There is nothing to apologize for. You are likely correct. There is concern in Moscow, as there is surely concern in Peking, that a war with the Americans could destroy us all, the Americans included. It is not about the hearts of men, General. It is about guns. Big guns. Power versus power. Are we willing to assist your government in a fight that might destroy your precious revolution, everything you hold dear? And to what reward? Chairman Stalin has his eyes focused on Europe, on the threat to our sovereignty that still exists on battlefields soaked with Russian blood. The people of the Soviet Union have a great deal of experience with bloody sacrifice. The wounds from the last war are very fresh in our minds. Chairman Stalin is in no hurry to repeat such slaughter, no matter who suffers the most. Your revolution might be centered in this part of the world, but Chairman Stalin is aware that our enemies have great armies of occupation throughout Europe. It is there we must give our greater attention. As much as we would enjoy aiding your efforts, Chairman Stalin must keep mindful of other priorities. He loves his people and does not wish to see them bloodied for no useful cause. Is this war, right here, a useful cause?" Orlov shrugged again. "That decision lies with others, of course. I am but a major. You should understand our concerns, General."

"You know a great deal about Chairman Stalin. It must be an honor to have the privilege of such information."

Orlov said nothing for a long moment, his eyes locked on Sung. "Tell me, General Sung, I have wondered. Your crossing of the Yalu River was most impressive. It was an ambitious operation, and yet the Americans made almost no effort to interfere. Of course, I understood completely why you chose to cross at night. But surely, you expected all of those bridges to have been destroyed by American bombs. It is reasonable to expect the enemy to put obstacles in your path, slow down every move you make."

Sung thought of the crossings, more than a hundred thousand of his men advancing into North Korea without a shot being heard. But he shared Orlov's curiosity about the intact bridges, had expected at least a token of resistance.

"I have no doubt that if we had made our crossing in the daylight hours, the American air forces would have done all they could to impede us. My greater concern was the discipline of the Ninth Field Army Group. I am most proud that my men performed as expected."

Orlov still had the smile. "Perhaps the Americans left the bridges intact because they do not wish to antagonize your Soviet neighbors? I will admit to you that there has been concern in my government that the Americans intend to build bases along the Yalu, to threaten Manchuria and beyond."

Sung measured his words, spoke slowly. "Major, we are miles below the Yalu River even now, and we will continue to march southward until we embrace the American invasion. I do not see how bases can be built on land we have already put behind us."

Orlov shrugged. "I have been told that the Americans might not be aware just what territory you have passed. I have been told that the official dispatches coming from their headquarters in Tokyo reveal no knowledge of your army being here at all."

Sung was surprised, had heard nothing about that. So, of course. The Soviets have eyes in places I will never see.

"You have excellent sources, Major. Are you able to communicate using the stars?"

"My communications have regrettably ceased since we have advanced farther south. I am completely at your mercy, General."

Sung turned slowly away, thought, Somehow, I doubt that.

The radios were nearly worthless, their range cut off by the great hills to the west. But the word had come to his camp, passed along a network of outposts that spread out over the mountains that divided Sung's army from those troops who were moving more toward Pyongyang. He could not know just how accurate the reports were, knew that sometimes reports of combat victory were mighty exaggerations. But he knew Lin Biao, respected the man's abilities to lead any army. If Lin had gone to such lengths to offer him a report, Sung would accept it as accurate. And so would his men.

He gathered the senior commanders, the men seated around an enormous squat tree. Sung had ordered tea, the men grateful for the small treat.

"Comrades, it is a glorious day. I am to inform you that beyond the mountains to our west, the People's Thirteenth Army Group has struck the first blow against the Americans and their puppet armies of South Korea. We have achieved a great victory."

The men called out a salute, their arms in the air, Sung absorbing their good cheer. The questions came now.

"Have the Americans retreated? Have we liberated Pyongyang?"

"Shall we join with them? Will they add to our strength?"

He looked at the voice, one of his youngest generals, a man Sung suspected would one day replace him.

"General Huk, your enthusiasm is welcomed, but there is a great struggle still to be waged. I do not have every detail of the engagements beyond the mountains. While we should draw spirit from General Lin's successes, we must not forget our mission, and what still lies in our path. Our foe is advancing toward us even now. Our observers have reported South Korean troops, along with units of American infantry, advancing along the east coast. But I would also inform you that a large column of American Marines has begun their northward march out of Wonsan. Our orders are very specific. We shall observe them until the time is right, and then we shall destroy them."

As the sun had set, his army rose from the ground all around him, across narrow valleys, stretches of thick timber, tens of thousands of men making ready for the next night of their advance. They had begun to spread out far beyond the few narrow roads, the meager farm lanes that held the attention of the American planes. To their front now lay a sprawling lake, the reservoir that was the water source for farms that stretched all the way to China.

For several days other units had been marching across the rugged hillsides, ordered much farther away from the roads. They were Sung's most forward battalions, probing and scouting, soldiers who were ordered to keep their positions hidden from even the most skilled UN observers. As those units sent their reports back to their commander, Sung ordered more of his army forward, pushing them rapidly southward down both sides of the great reservoir, then spreading them farther out into the hills that rose along both sides of the primary avenue the Americans were using for the march north.

With word of the great success to the west, the bloody blow that Lin's Thirteenth Army Group had struck against the American and ROK troops, Sung's officers were energized even more. But Sung would not yet order any kind of massed assault. As he drove his troops southward, he advanced several of his divisions well past the vanguard of the American march, allowing the Americans to move up between the outstretched arms of a great pincer. To Sung's amazement, as the Marines pushed out along their single roadway, they extended their position, stretching their power into a thin ribbon that extended nearly sixty miles. He was more curious just what kind of strategy the Americans were employing. With each day, the massive advantage of firepower the Americans enjoyed seemed to be diminished, spread farther apart by decisions Sung did not understand. As energized as his commanders were becoming, Sung Shi-lun held them back, ordering only a probing confrontation, a test to learn just what kind of secrets the Americans might be hiding, just what the logic was to their advance. As the Americans continued to spread themselves thin, Sung's primary mission seemed, oddly enough, to be getting easier.

CHAPTER TWELVE

. . . .

Riley

SOUTH OF SUDONG, NORTH KOREA—NOVEMBER 2, 1950

THEIR LOAD HAD GROWN, the new equipment issued as they left Wonsan. Their green dungarees were now a heavier material, said to be windproof, covering cotton long johns many of the Southern men had never seen. The jokes followed immediately, teasing from the Northerners, that back home, civilian long johns had the benefit of a trapdoor, something these long johns didn't have. If there were instructions on just how a man was to relieve himself by maneuvering through multiple layers of clothing, none of the officers had bothered to provide them.

Those men who had grown up in the cold back home already understood layering, and the Southerners were learning quickly the benefit of the variety they wore now. Each man wore an undershirt beneath his usual Marine uniform shirt, covering that with a green denim jacket. The greatest burden they carried now was the heavy parka, a fur-lined hooded coat that hung to their knees. To wear the parka during the march meant more sweating, but carrying it or slinging it over the backpack could be even clumsier.

They carried gloves now, every man wondering just how he was supposed to pull the trigger of his weapon with thickened fingers. And so, many had sliced the fingertip off the wool on their shooting hand. Hanging below their backpack was a thicker sleeping bag, what someone at supply labeled "fit for the mountains." In their packs they carried extra socks, and on their feet the lightweight leather boots had been replaced by what supply had called shoe pacs, a thick wool sole housed inside a watertight rubber boot, designed to keep feet dry. The men soon learned that keeping water out meant keeping sweat inside, that the longer the march, the wetter their socks. Orders had been passed to every man that once they took to the roads, they were to change socks frequently, avoiding the kind of plague some of these men could recall from a very different time fighting in the Pacific. Then it was called jungle rot; after long days in soggy terrain, a man who ignored his feet might find that his socks had become nothing more than a nasty crust that seemed to be glued to his skin. That lesson had been driven into every man who had suffered the agony of having his skin peeled from the bones of his feet. This time the enemy wasn't the steaming heat of the jungle. Wet socks produced a variety of agonies, including blisters, and warnings came that with the coming of winter, wet feet meant cold feet, and if it was cold enough, the result could be frostbite. There were skeptics, of course, many of them the new recruits who had never endured that kind of cold, who imagined the march concluding with feet propped up in front of a campfire. But the officers did what they could to erase those kinds of pleasant expectations, the company commanders passing down the threat that anyone who ignored caring for his feet, or sought to escape to the aid stations with crippled toes, was to be treated with no more regard than the man who purposely shot himself in the foot. Few of the men around Riley seemed interested in testing the resolve of a man like Captain Zorn. But there were others, always the big mouths, who didn't seem to give much heed to threats from officers. To those men, the corpsmen provided incentive of their own, calmly assuring them that a case of frostbite most often ended with amputation.

As they moved north from Wonsan, the nights became chillier, some of that from an increase in elevation. The cursing over the heavier loads began to quiet, the fall giving way to a North Korean winter, the mild days passing quickly to teeth-chattering nights. For now they rode in the larger trucks, the six-by deuce and a half most of these men had become used to. The road itself was crude, hard-packed gravel, patches of hard dirt, and some not so hard, clouds of choking dust that engulfed each vehicle in the column. They rode mostly in silence, the veterans knowing that the trucks were a luxury, that the kidney-bashing bumps were always better than hiking this ground, any ground, on foot. Word had already been passed down that farther on the roads would become steeper, and quite likely more narrow. Rumors flew, sightings of Chinese units, North Korean tanks on the prowl, the men blind in their covered trucks knowing only that they were moving farther into enemy territory.

Riley felt the truck slowing, the sharp squeal of brakes. He sat forward, straightened his back away from the bone-cracking bench seat. Across from him, Welch.

"Looks like the end of the ride. We sure as hell ain't burning much gas. Never seen a convoy move so slow. We could walk faster."

Lieutenant Goolsby was peering through the canvas, voices outside, and Goolsby said, "This is it. Everybody out. What we do this time, two hundred yards?"

It was an unusual piece of sarcasm from the young lieutenant, but Riley knew he was right. For reasons no one would explain to the riflemen, the brass didn't seem to be in any hurry.

The men rose slowly, easing their way back, dropping down. Riley followed, Killian behind him, Riley's turn to jump down to the hard ground. He scanned the countryside, most of it vertical now, and Killian descended heavily, said, "No more orchards. This ain't farm country anymore. Too sloping for rice paddies, for sure."

Riley shouldered his rifle, said, "That just means it'll smell better. Never did figure out what those orchards were growing. Never seen those kinds of trees. Weren't peaches or apples."

The kid was down beside him, said, "Persimmons. Too late in the year for 'em now. I ate 'em growing up. They're great, unless they're green. Pucker you up real good then. We used to do that when we were young. Chomp down on a green one, then wait for our mouths to turn inside out."

Killian sniffed. "Great. Our Guinea is also a farmer."

Morelli kept silent, had learned not to spar with the big Irishman.

Riley ignored them both, stepped farther out off the road, saw a small, flat field to one side, a rough shack to one end. A civilian emerged now, the usual scene, the man old and bent, caped in a simple white garment that matched the color of the man's wispy beard. Riley watched him, the old man staring silently, no expression, the passing of this army just one more meaningless part of what Riley assumed was one more meaningless day. Welch moved out beside him, said, "Most exciting thing happened to that old fart in a while. How the hell does he eat? Nothing growing on this ground. Must have some generous neighbors."

Riley said, "Maybe. There's a hay pile behind his shack. He's got a cow, or ox, whatever the hell they call 'em. He's got it hidden, I bet. Afraid we'll eat the damn thing."

Welch said, "I don't blame him. I'd hide everything I own from this nasty bunch." He looked back behind Riley, said to Killian, "Hey, Irish. You think this one's a threat, too? We oughta search his rathole?"

Killian shouldered his rifle, grumbled. "Don't trust none of 'em. Where's his damn flag, anyway?"

Riley began to move, following the flow of men as they stepped into column, thought of Inchon, the great throngs of Korean civilians, hundreds of them holding up small American flags. It had happened at Wonsan, too, though not as many. But the flags were there, waved by smiling crowds of North Koreans. The show had been inspiring, especially for the newspapermen. But the Marines were more curious than gratified. Riley thought of that now, wondering, Just where the hell did they get the flags? And do they have one for every occasion, depending on which army is marching by? There's Brits here, Greeks, all kinds of troops helping us out. Good old UN. So, did all those civilians get the flags from the UN, some lackey running around passing 'em out? He looked over toward the old man again, called out, "Hey Papa-san, you forgot your flag. You not sure which side we're on?"

Behind him, Killian said, "Yeah, you old Nook. We're the good guys. Come to save the world. You get lucky, somebody'll hand you a loaf of Wonder Bread. You pay enough, I'll sell you a Hershey bar."

"Knock it off. Save your breath for the climb."

Riley glanced at the sergeant, knew that Welch had no patience for

Killian's mouth. Rumbles of artillery fire flowed over them now, the men silent, eyes searching the hills. From behind them Captain Zorn stepped forward, waved one hand, said, "Listen up! There's something Battalion has ordered us to see."

Riley was puzzled, thought, In this place? What the hell is worth staring at?

Zorn directed the men to one side of the road, a harsh order to each of the lieutenants as they passed, keeping each squad, each platoon, to one side of the road. Riley fell into the single line, saw a wide ditch, the men stopping, the words coming now.

"Jesus. What the hell happened?"

"Oh, what the hell? No."

"Keep moving. I want everybody to see this."

Riley looked down in the ditch, saw four bodies, Marines, wrapped in bloody sleeping bags. He moved past quickly, looked away, tried to erase the image, heard the men behind him reacting as well.

"Good God. Those are our boys. Who did this?"

Zorn called out, "They're from First Battalion, the men up ahead of you. The enemy caught them asleep last night. They were bayoneted in their holes, in their sleeping bags. Never knew what hit them. This could be you morons if you don't keep awake and alert. You hear me?"

Riley was angry now, thought, They didn't have to do this. Leaving them there, like some kind of exhibit. We're not rookies, for God's sake. Not all of us. Behind him, he heard Zorn, calling to McCarthy.

"Lieutenant, your men have seen enough. First Battalion is on those big hills to the front, and Colonel Davis has radioed back that the enemy is approaching their position. Last call was that they were beginning to take mortar and machine gun fire. The colonel has his men digging in, trying to find just what the enemy's got in mind. We're in support, and Third Battalion is behind us."

There were more thumps now, a plume of smoke rising up on a hill a mile to the front. Riley kept his eyes that way, followed McCarthy farther forward, the column forming up on both sides of the road. He heard the usual comments around him, nervous chatter, most of that from the new men. Now there were more blasts, far above them on the left, a wide hill, thick with trees, bare on top. He glanced at Zorn, saw the captain staring up that way, a look of surprise on the company commander's face. McCarthy was staring that way as well, more of the officers, all eyes on the closer hill. After a long, noisy moment, Zorn said, "That's Dog Company. They started up that way a half hour ago. What the hell?"

A jeep rolled up, a sliding stop, dust flowing over the men. Riley saw an officer running past him, a sudden stop in front of the captain. Riley knew the man, Lieutenant Wright, Zorn's executive officer.

"Sir! Radio call from Colonel Litzenberg. The trucks have been ordered to withdraw. Fox Company is to climb to the right, take position below the ridgeline, send observation parties higher, see if we can spot any hostile troops to the east of this position. Dog and Easy are out on our left, First Battalion is deployed up ahead."

"I can hear First Battalion, Lieutenant. They're getting hammered. Dog, too. Where's Major Sawyer?"

"Sir, Battalion is establishing a command post just to the rear of this position."

"Fine. I'll do the same at the base of this hill, once we get into position. Stay here, keep any stragglers off this road."

Riley could see movement high on the hill to the left, more Marines climbing from back behind them, spreading up toward the sounds of the fight. Beside him, Welch said, "Easy Company, probably. Go, you dumb bastards. Make yourself useful."

Another jeep rolled up from behind the column, stopping a dozen yards up the road. Farther on, the road curved to the left, sweeping past the snout of the steep hill. The men in the jeep dismounted, and now, from around the bend in the road, a flock of what seemed to be soldiers appeared, moving toward them, some halting at the jeep. There were hands in the air, shouts of jubilation. Riley stared, curious, cautious, the others around him slipping rifles off shoulders. Now they appeared above, to the right, descending rapidly, cheerful men in filthy uniforms.

Welch said, "South Koreans. ROK. Where the hell they come from?"

Riley watched the men swarm down around and through the Marines, realized now most of them had no weapons.

"Marines! Marines. Many Chingese! Chingese!"

The soldiers were pointing back, some up the hill they had just descended, others pointing toward the sounds of a growing fight to the front. Riley looked again to the jeep, saw the ROK troops in a swarm around the officers, saw now it was Sawyer, the battalion commander, others from his staff, one man using their radio. The ROKs were gesturing fitfully, more loud voices, most of that in Korean, and Welch said, "Looks like the major was expecting them. My buddy at regimental said we were supposed to relieve the ROKs wherever we find them. I guess we found them."

One of the Koreans came down the hill close to Riley, thick grime on his face, pointing back up the hill.

"Many many! Go!"

Riley glanced back, saw the two lieutenants, Goolsby moving closer, McCarthy behind him. Goolsby approached the man, said, "What's the story here?"

Welch said, "ROKs, sir. Seems like a happy bunch."

McCarthy was there now, said, "There's a lot more up ahead. The major got the call a while ago from First Battalion. There's ROK popping up in every hole, most of 'em not waiting for us to get into place. We're supposed to be replacing their positions all along these hills. Reports of a good many of the enemy up ahead."

Riley watched the men move past, many more flowing down the hill, dropping into the road, scrambling back toward the south, all smiles.

"They seem happy as hell to be leaving."

One of the men slowed in front of McCarthy, the uniform of an officer, spoke with very little accent. "Many Chinese. Many in the hills. Be prepared."

McCarthy said, "What's your unit? Your rank?"

"Sorry, Marine, I have to follow my men. Many Chinese. Good luck."

The man scampered away, adding to the flow passing by, and Welch said, "Speaks good English. Hell of a hurry. Never saw them run like that from any North Koreans."

McCarthy spat, said nothing, and beside him Goolsby said, "We should tell the captain what he said."

McCarthy began to move up the hill to the right, said, "Count on it. He knows. Battalion knows, too. There's too many of 'em to miss. They've dropped their weapons. I guarantee they were running a hell of a lot faster before we showed up."

Zorn moved through the throng of Koreans, seemed disgusted, climbed up just above the road, closer to McCarthy, one hand pointing up the hill to the right.

"We've got our orders, Lieutenant. Let's go!"

Riley pushed one foot in front of the other, a slow, steady climb. He felt the sweat rolling down his back, sweat in his eyes, felt the soft squish in his boots. He put one foot up against a heavy rock, raised himself one more step, heard the grunts around him, one man stumbling, loud curses. McCarthy was there, a harsh whisper, "Keep it quiet! These hills aren't friendly."

The sounds of the fight still rolled past them, close, the far side of the road, more from the hill ahead. He glanced up, men swarming over the bare ground, using rocks for leverage, the hillside flattening slightly, the ridgeline farther still. McCarthy stopped, looked past him back down the hill, seemed impatient, a hard scowl.

"Halt here. We'll wait for the captain."

The men obeyed gratefully, spreading out, eyes searching the ground all around them. Machine gun fire rattled across the road, a steady chatter, and Riley looked that way, catching his breath, thought, Dog Company. Names came to him now, men he had known before, familiar faces as they passed on various marches. One face settled in his brain, a broad smile, Harper. Damnedest drinker I ever saw. Keep your head down. You still owe me a bottle of Scotch.

Zorn scrambled past, moving toward McCarthy, said, "Keep Third Platoon moving, get to where you can see to the east. I'll have the others spread out along this line, supporting you. Map says this is Hill 727. That might matter to my kids."

McCarthy waved them on, Riley already climbing again, Zorn's words in his head. My kids. You're not the only one, Captain. There's my kid, too.

Welch was up beside him, passing him slowly, said, "Dark soon. We get to where they're sending us, dig a deep one quick as you can."

Riley wiped sweat from his face, kept climbing, the grunts around him louder, no curses now, no one with the energy for griping.

"Right. Just dig one for yourself."

McCarthy was waiting near the crest, waving one arm, spreading them out just behind the highest point. Riley searched for Killian a few yards behind him, saw him jam the butt of his M-1 into the ground like a crutch, pulling himself up, red-faced, sweating. He looked at Riley now, then bent low, said, "My damn boots are full of water."

"Shovel. Let's dig."

Riley slid out of his backpack, pulled his shovel out, looked over the crest of the hill, could see the fight to the north, First Battalion's position bathed in a low fog of gray smoke. But that fight seemed to slow, and he turned to the west, across the road, could see specks of men all across that hill, sparks of flame, drifting smoke.

"Jesus. They're getting hammered."

Welch was there, his shovel in his hand, said, "You don't know who's hammering who. Do your damn job."

Riley dropped the heavy coat, lay the rifle close by, saw Killian drop down to his seat, yanking off his boots. The socks came now, Killian barefoot, peeling away his shirt.

"Gotta dry this crap out. Don't wait for me, dammit. Start digging."

Riley chopped the shovel downward, piercing the rocky dirt, shallow roots of the thin brush. Now Killian joined him, the hole taking shape quickly, others around them doing the same, dirt and rocks tossed in the air. He straightened, arched his back, took a long breath, stared out across the road again. It was harder to see, the glare of the sun in his face.

"Sounds like the fight's slowing."

Killian was breathing hard, said, "Then dig more. We might be next."

From far behind them, Riley heard the rhythmic thumps of a helicopter, and he looked up, the craft now overhead, slipping past, moving out to the east. He stepped down into the foxhole, nearly over his knees, deep enough, watched the helicopter, and Welch was there, breathing heavily, his shovel in his hand.

"Searching for the enemy. If anybody hits us, they'll come up from that way, I guess. Not much light left. Don't know what those idiots are hoping to see."

The helicopter moved out of sight, dipping low past the next hill, and Riley caught the last glow of sunlight still bathing the hillside to the east. That hill was taller, steep and ragged, thick trees painted with the colors of fall, and above them, a bare ridge, the sun reflecting off patches of fresh snow.

Many of the men had stripped down to their undershirts, allowing the sweat to dry, giving time for their outer layers to dry as well. Boots had come off, socks spread out on flat rocks. But with the darkness came the chill, and soon those men had reluctantly redressed, cursing the blanket of cold that settled over them.

Killian was squatting down across from Riley, his usual perch. They munched on C-rations, the first thing Riley had eaten since breakfast. Killian tossed a small can to one side, said, "So, Old Homer thinks we'll have a fight up here? That oughta shut up the damn replacements. Tired of all their bitching about missing out. You take a look at some of these morons? They're ten years old."

Riley didn't respond, but the same thoughts had struck him, new men who didn't seem to know the first thing about being a Marine.

Since the landing in Wonsan, the entire regiment had been beefed up with replacements, some of them with even less training and preparation than Morelli. The officers seemed pleased with the added numbers, but few of the veterans had any confidence that the new men would add anything to the fight. Riley's best hope was that the men around him now at least knew how to aim a rifle.

He tossed aside the remnants of a can of fruit cocktail, said, "Wonder if that helicopter found anybody out there. Pretty quiet, so far."

Killian said, "Sounded like all the fun was other side of the road. Or up north. No idea where the hell we are. Maybe that next hill belongs to China."

"Just keep your eyes open. I'm not ending up like those KIAs back on the road."

Killian shook his head. "That's officers for you. Scare the hell out of the new ones, so they'll fight better. Hell, they might just run like banshees." Killian paused. "The captain's nuts if he thinks that'll happen to me. When I go out, I wanna be staring down the muzzle of some Nook cannon. If you're gonna take me out, by God, blow me to ribbons. Make it worthwhile."

Riley didn't respond, thought of his son. Nope, they'll never find me like that, either. My boy's never gonna hear that his pop died in a sleeping bag. Maybe he won't hear anything at all. Don't go missing, dammit. Ruthie won't never forgive me if I just disappear. But it ain't gonna be because I'm scared. Damn those officers anyway.

Killian drank from his canteen, said, "You'd a thought they'd have more faith in us. They seem to forget just how well we handled those damn Nooks."

"Everything I'm hearing says it's the Chinese now."

"What the hell difference does it make? Nooks or Shambos. They all bleed the same, right?"

Shambos?

Riley knew not to ask. He leaned back against the side of the foxhole, glanced up, stars spreading across the black sky. Peaceful, he thought. Too bad there's gotta be a war.

"You think you'd ever come to this place without this war?"

Even in the dark, Riley could feel Killian staring at him.

"You're nuts. None of us know where the hell we are, exactly. Ain't seen a map in weeks. What's so damn special about Korea? Place stinks worse than my cousin Kevin. And he stinks worse than you."

Riley knew better than to expect anything serious from Killian. He slid his hand up the stock of the M-1, ran a finger over the steel barrel. He knew many of the men had given names to their rifles, treated them like girlfriends. Just do the job, he thought.

Killian said, "I see you. Can't keep your hands off that thing, can you? You been playing footsies with it all day long."

"You're just jealous. I shoot straighter than you."

A few feet away, Welch said, "You don't watch it, I'll make you swap with me. Not sure I'm happy with this damn carbine."

It was an ongoing debate, the value of the M-1 Garand versus the shorter, more compact carbine. The carbine could be set to full automatic, a spray of fifteen bullets that could come in handy in a tight squeeze. But the new men especially were prone to shooting up all their ammunition before they had targets. Riley knew that Welch had better discipline than that, but still, in a tight spot, if the enemy was more than a couple hundred yards out, the carbine was nearly worthless. The M-1 was far more accurate at long distance, reliable, even though it only held an eight-shot clip. Riley had always preferred the M-1, had seen too many carbines clog up, especially in the mud on Okinawa. But he knew better than to talk down a man's weapon. Welch carried the carbine because he chose to, at least for now, and Riley thought, I just hope there's no problem with that thing when you need it.

It had been dark for longer than Riley could tell, no idea what time it was. He glanced upward, many more stars, the cold breeze driving him deeper into his parka. He heard Killian stirring, the change of watches, Riley's turn to rest for a couple of hours. He leaned forward, a soft voice, "Did you sleep at all?"

"Nah."

Killian rustled through his backpack, cursed, and Riley whispered, "Your socks dry out?"

"Not quite. They're miserable. Soaked through three pairs of socks, and I'm gonna make sure they're dry before I put 'em back on. What dumb son of a bitch thought these damn rubber boots would help us fight a war?"

"Same son of a bitch who thought this was a war we oughta be fighting."

Killian's voice always carried farther than Riley preferred, and others around them began to respond, the high-pitched voice of the kid, Morelli.

"Hey, you ought not talk about the president that way. My papa voted for him. Doubt he's a son of a bitch. Not a bit."

Killian said, "Oh, shut up. I'm not so sure it was Truman who thought this up anyway. I hear it's the UN who's really running this show. They tell Old Harry how high to jump and he does it."

To one side, Welch said, "I'm just glad some dumb Irishman's not in charge. You'd have us looking over these hills for leprechauns."

Riley could feel Killian bristle, knew his chin was probably jutting out, a familiar pose. Here we go again, Riley thought. They'll both want the last word.

To the north, a sharp clap, a rattle of gunfire, several sharp thumps, the distant hill erupting again. Welch said, "Mortars. They're hitting First Battalion again. Son of a bitch!"

Riley could see the flashes, streaks of green tracers, something new.

"Hey, Sarge, what's going on? Never seen that before."

"How the hell do I know? Russian guns, I guess. I guess somebody decided we'd gone far enough north."

"All hands! Listen up!" Riley turned, the familiar voice of Lieutenant McCarthy. "Sergeant Halley!"

Riley heard the voice, no one else talking now.

"Sir!"

"Halley, did you spread your squads farther up that way?"

"Yes, sir. I'm heading up there now. We've got a thirty positioned with a good field of fire to our front."

Another shadow, Captain Zorn there now, breathing hard, a hand on McCarthy's shoulder.

"They waited until near midnight, then hit First Battalion again. That's all I know. Make ready to receive ... well, hell, I don't know. Nobody lets their pants down until we hear from the regimental CP. I'll be on the radios back down the hill. Check your walkie-talkies. I'm not jogging up and down this mountain all night long. Where's Goolsby?"

Goolsby emerged from a nearby hole, scrambled closer, a carbine in his hand. "Sir!"

"Keep your eyes all along this ridgeline to your front. We've no idea what's coming this way, if anything at all. But prepare for it! You understand?"

"Certainly, sir."

The captain looked again toward the sounds of the fighting, the roar of machine gun fire blending with the pop of rifles. More mortars came now, a steady series of thumps, the darkness to the north broken by the flashes. Now, new sounds, much closer, to the west, across the road, the chatter of machine guns, more rifle fire. Riley looked that way, nothing but darkness, felt his stomach churn, thought, Dog Company. Getting it again. Jesus.

Zorn moved away now, more orders to the other platoons, the two hundred men of Fox Company spread out along the ridge. Riley rose to his knees, moved the rifle up in front, resting on the uneven ground. More movement now, the hushed voices of the ammo carriers. One man moved up close, a harsh whisper. "Grenades. Captain says take as many as you can throw."

Killian said, "Yeah? How many's that? Five hundred?"

Riley ignored the chatter, grabbed a handful from the satchel, made a small pile beside the rifle, his eyes now hard to the front. The man moved away, and Killian quieted, adjusting himself, the rifle lying close beside Riley's. Far out to the west, the fighting across the road continued, nervous attention focused that way, and Riley said in a soft hush, "Dog's getting clobbered."

"Maybe. It's behind us, even. Easy's there, too. Twice as strong. That's gotta help."

The flashes from the next hill to the north came again, the thunder of mortars, a new round of tracer fire. Riley peered out that way, his helmet just above his eyes.

"Green tracers. Never seen that before. North Koreans' are blue. Ours are red."

"Yeah, Pete, ours are red. Knew that, you moron."

"So, green? New guns? Think the Sarge is right? Russian stuff?"

Killian paused a long moment, said, "It's gotta be the Chinese. Hell, I don't know what kind of stuff they use. But sure as hell, those ROK idiots weren't running home just to see mama-san."

There was hard tension in Killian's voice, unusual, and now movement close beside Riley, Welch crawling close.

"You set? Keep a sharp eye. They seem to like the dark. We're hours from daylight."

Riley glanced toward the sergeant, Welch's voice calm, steel.

"We're set, Sarge. Check on the kid. Check Kane's BAR crew. They're green as hell."

"I know my job, Private."

Welch slid away, and Killian said, "There's a thirty up that way, on that rise to the right. Where'd Kane take his BAR?"

"Right behind you." Riley turned, back behind his right shoulder, saw the shadowy form of Wally Kane, his helpers crouched low behind. "We're not that damn green, Grandpa. You find those bastards, we'll clean 'em up."

Kane was younger, still a veteran, what Riley guessed to be a late starter in the last war. But he handled the weapon well, seemed to appreciate just how valuable the Browning automatic rifles were to the entire outfit. The BAR had been issued with a built-on bipod, said to ensure accuracy by keeping the weapon steady on the ground. But Kane had done what many did, tossed that away, insisting he could fire the piece with more accuracy from his shoulder. It took a man with a strong back to hold the BAR upright for a long stretch, and every man who carried one hauled as much ammunition as possible, increasing his load even more. Thus the assistants, whose single responsibility was to stay close to the BAR, handing off ammunition as quickly as Kane could fire. The BAR was thought by many to be even more valuable to each squad than the light machine guns, which were far less mobile. They all knew that if a hole opened up in the line, Kane, or any of the others, could slip into place with his weapon and do the work of a half-dozen M-1s.

Riley looked down the hill again, more flashes far to the front. Kane talks big, he thought. Not sure I could haul that beast around like he does, but I just hope like hell he doesn't run off. If you do, Wally, at least leave your weapon here. I love emptying a BAR. He kept that taunt to himself, thought, No time for idiocy now. Beside him, Killian whispered, "What the hell's that?"

Riley froze, stared hard, his eyes digging through the darkness. "What?"

"Down there. Movement."

The sounds burst over them now, a screaming chorus of police whistles, a sharp *blat* from a bugle, then another, farther down. Now there were voices, a vast line of men on the hill below them. Riley rose up, searching the darkness, could see them, the shapes growing larger, shadows climbing the hill. The whistles came again, sharp, piercing sounds, Riley gripping the rifle, a cold chill in his spine, his ears ripped by the odd noise. Now rifles popped, muzzle flashes down the line, the light machine gun pouring fire down the hill, streaks of red. Riley jerked the rifle to his shoulder, no targets, just dull shapes, the voices closer, some falling, absorbing the fire from the Marines. But they came on, closer still, a stink washing over him, the familiar odor of rifle fire, and now something new, grotesque, and strange. It was garlic.

He fired the rifle, the muzzle blast blinding him, the tracers from the machine gun giving glimpses of masses of men, all along the hillside, all climbing closer. All across their position, the Marines answered, a storm of fire, the enemy responding with fire of their own, machine guns from distant perches. Riley emptied the rifle, the clip ejected, slammed a new one home without thinking, fired again. Now mortars erupted, coming down behind him, thunderous impacts out to one side, more impacting down the hill. But the Marines were answering with mortars of their own, the blasts spreading out all across the hillside below him. Each blast offered a flash of light, reflections off thick crowds of men, all still

moving forward. The Marines kept up their fire, Riley emptying another clip, the shadows with more form, closer still.

The first grenade landed in front of him, bouncing off his helmet.
He shouted, backed away, his arm in a fast sweep, the grenade pushed
to one side, the blast now, deafening, his head down, face in the dirt.
Riley checked himself in his mind, no pain, no wounds. Thank God.
More grenades impacted all along the line, coming down behind the
crest of their hill, and beside him, Killian began to shout, "Eat this, you
Shambo bastards!"

Riley kept down, turned that way, saw Killian up, throwing grenades
of his own, one after another. Riley felt a wave of panic, sickening, expected Killian to go down, machine gun fire whistling past, close above
him. But Killian's grenades continued downward, the blasts down the
hill, cries of men, more mortar shells falling among the enemy as well.
Riley pulled himself to his knees, lay the rifle down, his hand on the pile
of steel beside him. He jerked the pin from a grenade, held it for a long
second, searching the chaotic darkness, slung it low and hard down the
hill, his face dropping down, the blast finding a target, the flash close.
Killian was firing his rifle again, and Riley tossed another grenade,
heard more shouts along the line, Kane's BAR chattering close to one
side.

There were more shouts up the ridgeline, the enemy rolling up and
over, a burst of firing, men falling. Riley felt a surge of panic, thought of
tossing a grenade that way, but too close, foxholes, his own men. He
threw the grenade down the hill, grabbed the rifle, aimed, thick, hulking
shapes, please God, not one of us. He fired, the hulk falling, more coming up the hill behind. He fired again, heard Killian curse, turned, a man
standing up above him, Killian screaming, his rifle swinging low over
Riley's head, hitting the man low, knocking his legs away. Riley jammed
the rifle into the man's chest, fired, a muffled explosion, searched for
another, saw Killian jamming a new clip into his rifle, firing again, down
the hill. The whistles came again, more of the discordant bugles farther
away. He pulled the M-1 tight against his shoulder, searched frantically,
but the shadows seemed to back away, and now the flashes from the
mortar fire revealed the enemy moving back, pulling away down the

hill. The machine gun fire continued, both directions, spraying the hill out in front of him, and he jerked his head down hard, his face in the dirt. Through the thunderous racket, Riley could still hear the bugle calls, somewhere below, drowned out by the thumps from mortars, their own, the tubes somewhere behind, back down the hill. The tracers continued, mostly red now, and he held the M-1, rose up on his knees, saw the shadows growing faint, farther down the hill, dark shapes, outlined by flashes of bright light. He fired again, no aim, just a broad sweep, emptying the clip, searched for clusters, heard only screams and bugles, the clip popping free. Shouts rolled across the hill around him, the last of the mortar rounds finding targets still, more shouts from behind him, men cursing the enemy, others, the officers, cursing the men who kept firing, wasting their ammo.

He lowered the rifle, put one hand down on the hard dirt, his fingers curling, gripping a rock, a painful fist. He let out a hard cry, tossed the rock down the hill, sat back, collapsing against the side of the foxhole, heard a new sound beside him. It was Killian, the man crying.

The daylight broke to their front, the distant hill an uneven line against a gray morning sky. He had slept, if only a few minutes, heard low voices around him, some of them familiar. He raised his head slightly, a slow drift of thin fog moving over the hillside, felt the chill, looked toward Killian, who said, "You gonna sleep all day? It's supposed to be your watch. Guess we don't need it. It's already light enough to see all hell from here."

Riley eyed his friend for a long moment, wanted to ask if he was all right, but Killian was staring out down the hill, and Riley knew there would be nothing to say. He felt a film of cotton in his mouth, reached for his canteen, a quick swig of cold water, then said, "What time?"

"Four thirty. Maybe. Nothing happening. Damn it all, looks like the Shambos have pulled back. They got a good dose of the United States Marine Corps. It's quiet across the road, too. Dog and Easy are either resting up. Or they're gone."

"They're not gone. We'd know about that."

Killian huffed, said nothing, and Riley pulled himself up, eased the stiffness in his back, his knees, sat in the shallow depression. He blinked, realized the stink was still there, shook his head.

"What the hell is that smell?"

"Shambos."

Riley looked across the ridgeline, scanned the hill down behind them, men crawling from their cover, ammo carriers slipping along, hauling the metal crates, more satchels of grenades. He saw Goolsby, the lieutenant ducking down as he moved across the line. Farther down, closer to the road, was the familiar tent, the battalion CP, and closer, the captain's tent. Men were in motion farther away as well, some down in the roads, a jeep now rolling forward. Killian pointed to one side, said, "Look at that, will you? Those boys let the bastards come inside. Had to be Second Platoon. Jackasses."

Riley saw now, as he had seen during the fight, that the enemy had broken through. The near side of the hill was peppered with bodies, thick yellow uniforms spread halfway down the hill. Down below, Marines were dragging more bodies up the hill, piling them together. He saw Captain Zorn now, moving toward the corpses, Zorn calling out, "Drag 'em up and over the ridge. Put 'em with their pals out front. I want the enemy to see what he left behind."

Riley heard a high-pitched shakiness in Zorn's voice, thought, We all sound like that. He rose up to his knees, climbed to the side of the foxhole, looked out to the far side of the hill, saw a carpet of the odd yellow uniforms. He couldn't avoid the shock of that, said, "Good God, Sean. We killed a pile of 'em."

"Ten piles. Damnedest thing I ever seen. A whole row would go down, another would come up behind it. Didn't slow 'em down. They were tripping over their own dead."

Riley nodded slowly.

"Yeah. Saw that. Grenades did a hell of a job. Guess we oughta thank that ammo carrier."

"Screw him. He was hauling it back down the hill when the fun started. How many you think we wiped out?"

Riley scanned the hillside, saw men down the line doing the same, some standing, weapons by their side, cigarettes and canteens. Riley felt a slap on his back, startled, saw it was Welch.

"Good fight, you two. You didn't forget what it's like to have the enemy give you an old-fashioned banzai, huh?"

Riley kept his eyes on the shapeless bodies, dark, bloody wounds, faces down in the dirt, some staring up, mouths wide. And the smell.

"I guess so," he said. "Didn't feel like that. They weren't like nuts or anything. Just a big damn bunch of 'em. They kept coming, but I heard screaming, too, not that crazy Jap stuff. Just . . . terrified, maybe."

Killian sniffed, pulled out a cigarette. "How the hell do you know that? One Jap same as one Shambo. They charge, we kill 'em."

Welch said, "I'm going down, help check 'em out. Come on."

Killian said, "Take Pete. I'd rather eat breakfast, if it's all the same to you."

Welch ignored him, moved away, down the hill, and Riley followed, almost by instinct. They kept silent, stepped past a half-dozen bodies, black blood, dried pools in the rocky soil. Others were doing the same, a handful of corpsmen checking bodies, some of the enemy still alive, badly wounded. Other men were checking pockets in the thick padding of the coats, and Riley saw McCarthy standing over a corpse, studying a pad of paper. He turned, moved up the hill past them, said, "Orders, looks like. An officer. Maybe big brass. Gotta find the damn interpreter."

McCarthy was gone, up the hill, and Welch stopped, hands on his hips, the two men surrounded by a sea of death.

"They're Chinese all right. All of them. Never seen any North Koreans looked like this. Jesus, look at the weapons. Burp guns. Russian, I bet. And there's grenades all over the place, those damn potato mashers. These boys didn't have time to toss 'em. I guess that's a good thing." Welch moved toward one body, moved a weapon with his foot. "Look here. A Thompson. Where'd he get that damn thing? G-2 will wanna know about that. Grab it."

Riley bent low, his hand on the machine gun, a quick glance at the soldier. The man's hand pulled at the weapon, his face jerking, his eyes opening, then closing again. Riley snatched hard at the machine gun, said, "Jesus!"

He spun the weapon around, pointed it downward, the Thompson responding, a short burst of fire into the man's chest. The soldier seemed to bow up, then settled again, fresh blood in a thick stream flowing over the man's stomach. Welch bent low, his hand on the man's bloody neck, his .45 against the man's skull. Others were moving closer, .45s leveled, questions, and Welch held up his hand.

"No sweat. But check 'em all." He said to Riley now, "Nice going. This son of a bitch might have taken us both."

Riley held the Thompson in his shaking hands. "Been a while, I guess."

"You killed a North Korean with your knife. Wasn't that long ago."

"Didn't have to look at him."

"Get used to it. Don't need you losing your backbone."

Riley stepped away, the Thompson under his arm. "Nope. Just ... didn't think this would ever happen again."

"They don't pay you to think. Let's go. There's C-rations calling my name."

The roar of the planes surprised them both, a pair of Corsairs rolling up over the hill from behind. Riley absorbed the sight, the raw power rolling past, the planes banking to the right, sliding down toward a deep draw in the next hill.

"God, I love those things."

Welch said, "You can bet the Chinese don't. Keep an eye on those two in case they find a target. I bet it's napalm this time. Could be rockets."

Riley watched the planes disappear through the far gap in the hills, heard cheers on the hill behind him, more of the Marines still saluting the pilots. Riley scanned the Chinese again, saw the corpsmen moving through, men with bayonets probing, no one taking chances with any more wounded. He looked again toward the distant hills, said, "That's why they attack at night. Our planes would rip 'em to shreds. Artillery, too. They won't come back in the daylight. That's how they get an edge."

Welch moved away, said, "That, and the fact that there's five hundred billion of 'em. Let's go. But keep your damn mouth shut. You keep figuring things out like that, and they'll make you an officer. I'm never calling you *sir*."

The next night, the Chinese returned, not as many, not as sharp a fight. Once more the Marines took an enormous toll in Chinese casualties. But the fight wasn't completely one-sided. There were dead Marines as well, close to seventy men, with nearly three hundred wounded, a vivid message that this new enemy was far more dangerous and far more dedicated to the fight than a handful of ghostly infiltrators who had bayoneted four men in their sleeping bags.

During the daylight hours, the Marines strengthened their positions, deepening their holes, placing their heavier weapons with the greatest fields of fire. The ammo carriers continued to bring their supplies up the hill, serving as stretcher bearers on the way down for those wounded men who could not walk to the aid station. There weren't many, the Marines knowing they had given the better part of the fight. Still, every man in the regiment knew they had been slapped hard by an enemy none of them had seen before.

The Seventh Regiment had been the first Marines to open the fight with the Chinese, and they had given the enemy a thorough bloodying. Litzenberg had stressed to his officers that a victory over this new foe would send a message that might be heard all the way to Moscow, whether or not it was the opening battle of World War III. Whether that message was heard in Peking, the Marines convinced themselves that the Chinese had surely learned a nasty lesson by tangling with the Corps. And so, as they prepared for a third night of fighting, many of the Marines south of Sudong were not at all surprised when the Chinese did not return. But Litzenberg and his officers did not accept the victory as a cause for celebration. Launching patrols and reconnaissance missions, aided by eyes in the air, the Marines pushed forward, hoping to locate the retreating enemy. The march continued northward toward

Sudong, but the Chinese were nowhere to be found. As effectively as they had surprised the United Nations forces by their stealth in moving south, so too did they use that stealth to withdraw into the rugged ground out of sight of Marine probes. Though MacArthur's head of intelligence, General Willoughby in Tokyo, continued to insist that no more than a handful of Chinese troops were engaged in the fighting, Litzenberg and Oliver Smith were beginning to understand that this enemy was far more than some primitive rabble, and far more numerous than a handful of volunteers sent down to help out their Korean friends. Based on the number of troops that had struck at Sudong, none of the Marine commanders were predicting anything but a lengthy fight.

CHAPTER THIRTEEN

. . . .

Sung

THE STAFF STOOD BACK, his officers knowing his mood. He stared at a cup of cold tea, his hands folded beneath his chin, a deep silence that would keep the others away until he summoned them.

High above the canopy of dense treetops, the sun was glorious in a blue sky, welcome warmth from the deep chill of the last few nights. They were prepared for that, the oncoming winter completely predictable, the men around Sung peeling away the heavy layers of their quilted uniforms. It had been another strenuous night, a rapid march over the steep hills, Sung sweating along with his men. But he kept his uniform intact, an example for the staff that no amount of discomfort would equal what the soldiers would experience. Once more they had made full use of the dark, his staff relocating his camp farther south of the reservoir. It was his response to the continuing advance of the Americans, what his observation posts had reluctantly described as a slogging march, a pace that seemed amazingly sluggish for an army with so much mechanization.

This section of his command area was now occupied by his Forty-second Army, three divisions of three regiments each. The 124th Division had been deployed around the town of Hagaru-ri, placed in a heavy

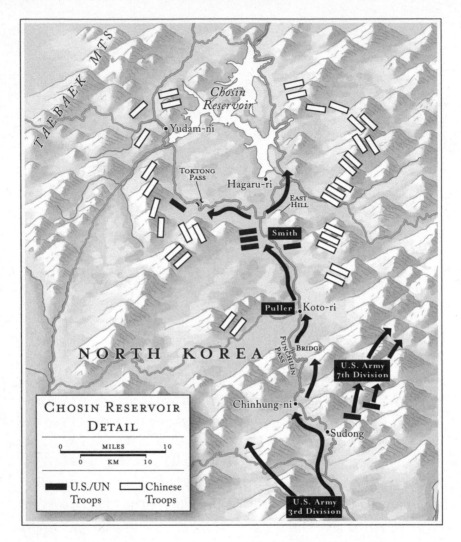

defensive line along the reservoir itself. There was enormous importance
to this part of North Korea, the reservoir and the river that fed it supplying energy for the power plants that even now were transmitting
their electricity northward into China. He had no reason yet to believe
the Americans would alter their northerly course, the Marines keeping
close to their road, the single artery their vehicles could use. That road
ran directly toward the lowest arm of the reservoir, then branched left,
westward, up that side of the waterway. He doubted that the Americans

intended to capture the reservoir itself as some kind of geographical prize. Their advance was most certainly intended to carry them to the Yalu River, and, if Peking's worst fears were realized, they would continue northward, invading Chinese territory. Already he had positioned the 125th Division out to the east of the reservoir, guarding against any advance in that direction, closer to the sea, in the event the American command had decided to pursue the capture of another of the valuable electricity-generating plants near the Fusin Reservoir. In the opposite direction, the 126th Division had been spread out into the rugged hills west of Chosin, protecting the flank of his main position and guarding against the unlikely event the Americans left their main road and foolishly turned their march toward the rugged mountain range that split this part of Korea. But no one in Peking believed the Americans would march very far from the security of their main road, the most obvious artery for transporting their supplies from farther south. Sung agreed. But then, the slowness of their advance had inspired Sung to make a more aggressive move, perhaps catching the Marines completely off guard. He had still not been convinced the Americans would continue their drive north. The pace of their march seemed intended to invite a confrontation, his observation posts high above the main road wary that the Marines were purposefully taking their time by sending smaller units up into those hills, as though feeling out for the enemy's presence. The South Korean troops that had first moved up into the heights had been of no concern to him at all, his field commanders reporting another predictable outcome with any show of force, that once the ROKs realized just who they were confronting, the fight, if there was one, would be brief and one-sided. But Sung knew enough about American Marines to know that they would most likely bull their way into any fight, whether or not it was the wise thing to do. Their sluggishness had offered Sung what seemed like opportunity. If they were so hesitant in their drive toward the reservoir, he would take advantage of the added time the Marines were giving him. Instead of anchoring the 124th at Hagaru-ri, keeping them close to the reservoir, he would push them farther south, all the way to Sudong. The Marines had experienced very little opposition since leaving Wonsan, and Sung suspected that such an easy march would lead to complacency. It was one more symptom of American arrogance, and Sung knew he had to capitalize. As they continued north, the Americans must certainly know that they were being watched at every turn, but he had kept his observers well out of the way. No casualties meant a comfortable march, and *comfort* was something the Americans seemed to value more than anything else.

His new plan had been heartily approved in Peking, General Peng suggesting that Sung's forces offer a display of the raw power behind the Chinese will, a crushing blow that might reverse the American tide completely. To the west, such a blow had resulted in a chaotic withdrawal by several units of the American Eighth Army, a retreat that even now was ongoing. Lin Biao's campaign had already shown more success than Peking had seemed to expect, and Sung knew that General Peng would expect no less from him.

Sung eyed the teacup, focused on a tiny crack, his eyes blinking with a hint of exhaustion. He was rarely sleeping through these long, chilly days, focused instead on the camps, the supplies so very important to men who stayed on their feet. You should nap more often, he thought. It was the same admonition offered by his staff officers, Colonel Wang tending to him like a nursemaid. Sung appreciated the man's intentions, but Sung believed that it was never good to demonstrate such a love of luxury as Wang insisted was appropriate for the army's commander. Meat was provided for at least one meal per day, but nearly always, Sung ordered that away, commanding Wang and the other staff officers to focus their energy more on providing sustenance for the soldiers. But Wang was relentless, and behind Sung's mask of stoicism he felt enormous affection for this young man, who seemed to have no other ambition than serving his commanding general. The game would play itself out after every march, Wang somehow conjuring up a magnificent roast, a hind quarter of a goat or pig, which Sung would order sent down into the hidden camps of the men. Wang would protest, and Sung would insist. Wang knew not to protest too vigorously, and Sung had to keep hidden that the meat was more tempting each time it was offered. His admonition to Wang's protests had been that such a feast would be reserved for the future, once the great victory had been achieved. There was little Wang could say to that.

He was growing impatient, looked around the crude camp, motioned to Wang, said, "Is General Gao aware that I am waiting for him?"

Wang moved closer, a short bow, his voice low. "Quite so, sir. We have expected his arrival at any time."

To one side, Sung saw the Russian, seated at a small fire.

"Major Orlov, you will extinguish that blaze. Have you no regard for our safety?"

Orlov did not hesitate, gathered a handful of dirt, tossed it on the fire, then another, his hand working to wave away the remaining smoke. Orlov stood, uncoiling his long legs, moved closer, said, "My apologies, General Sung. I intended to keep the fire very small, the smoke to a minimum. I have been saving a tin of boiled meat, and it is not a pleasant experience when eaten cold."

Orlov always seemed cheerful, which annoyed Sung even more. He kept his seat, his legs curled on a thin cushion, said, "Care must be taken, always. I should not have to remind you what the American planes can do to us if our location is discovered. Smoke will draw their bombers like rats to a stinking carcass."

"Of course, General. I shall be more careful." Orlov moved closer still, towering over Sung. "I have been curious about one practice I have observed here. Your men ingest a great deal of garlic. In some parts of the Soviet Union, the lands to the east, that is considered a wise precaution against creatures of the night. Specifically, vampires. It is likely you know little of such things. We tend to regard that as superstition, and there is no place for that in our army. I do not wish to insult you, or suggest that you rely on superstition in any form."

"Major, the garlic is for our health. It is widely accepted that garlic holds a great many medicinal properties. The health of this army is important to me, as it is to Chairman Mao. Mao is an enthusiastic advocate for the benefits of garlic. And so am I."

Orlov seemed satisfied, rubbed his nose. "I admit, it has taken me some time to become accustomed to the *aroma* produced by such a practice."

"You should ingest it yourself. Not only will it be of great benefit, but it might relieve your discomfort. You wish to become a part of this army, that will certainly assist."

Sung saw Wang down the draw, scanning off into the woods with his binoculars. Sung frowned, folded his arms. Where is Gao?

Orlov said, "Is there some problem today, General?"

Sung looked up, saw the maddening smile, still wondered how much he could reveal to this man. "I am displeased with my subordinate. Surely that has happened to you."

Orlov chuckled. "Never. There is no displeasure in the Soviet army."

Sung's aide turned, others pointing down a sloping hill.

"Sir, there is a horse team approaching. It could be General Gao."

Sung heard the hoofbeats now, pulled himself to his feet. One of the aides nodded fiercely. "Yes, sir. It is General Gao and his staff."

Sung felt his patience snap, wanted to march that way, held a tight grip on his decorum. He closed his eyes briefly, let out a breath, knew that Orlov was watching him.

Sung saw Gao hand the reins to an aide, adjusting his uniform with the flourish of a man in no hurry at all. One of Sung's aides was close to Gao now, pointed toward Sung, Gao making a show of removing his gauntlets. Sung pulled himself up, rocked slowly on his heels, forced himself to wait. Gao stopped in front of him, offered a crisp salute, with a pronounced glance toward Orlov.

Gao Shu was nearly as old as Sung, another of Mao Tse-tung's loyal veterans. He had commanded the 124th Division since the army had been reorganized, a logical choice based on his experience fighting the Nationalists. But his arrogance seemed to hide greater ambition, the always nagging concern that a subordinate considered himself worthy of far greater command, perhaps Sung's command. Sung knew that, often, that kind of obvious arrogance masked something else: a weakened spirit for the difficult fight. Like many of Mao's troops, Sung had seen something fall away, that perhaps too much had been left behind in those awful struggles against the Nationalists.

"I expected a thorough report from your command much sooner."

Gao stood stiffly, a glance at Orlov, who seemed to know when to withdraw.

Orlov said, "If you will permit me, I shall return to my perch. I should like to enjoy this cold meat."

Sung nodded, looked again at Gao, was surprised to see a hint of tears in the man's eyes. Gao lowered his head, said, "Sir, might we speak away from the camp?"

There was nothing arrogant in Gao's demeanor now, his voice soft. Sung said nothing, motioned toward a cluster of brush, farther up the hill. He turned, Gao following, and Sung felt a punch of sadness. So, he thought, it is true.

The first reports of the clash south of Sudong had carried few details of the struggle. Sung had always relied on his teams of observers, planted high above the fight, officers who would creep forward in the quiet times, absorbing as much information as possible. Some of that information concerned Sung's commanders, carefully weighing just what kind of performance a man could achieve under so much pressure. The responsibility for providing Sung with the more graphic details of the fighting lay with Gao, but now, as they moved farther from the activity of the camp, Sung could feel the kind of emotion from Gao he hoped never to see.

Sung stopped, stared away, said, "I know little of what occurred with your confrontation. You are aware of course that my observation posts can only report now what they see of the American aid stations, their command posts, their ambulances and trucks removing wounded and dead from the field. You are very well aware that I must hear a great deal more from you."

He moved farther up toward the brush, a glance skyward, soft blue and silence, the sunlight reflecting off snow-covered peaks on the hills in every direction. He waited, and finally Gao responded.

"General, at your request, I am here to report on the losses to my regiments. I regret that my division absorbed heavier losses than I had anticipated. For such a cost, I would have hoped to drive the enemy away."

Sung knew that his troops far outnumbered the Marines, though American firepower would always be superior to anything he could offer. Casualties were part of the process, the routine, his officers knowing that, in every fight, sacrifice could mean victory. Sung waited for more, eyed Gao for some signs that this was a show, a performance with some greater meaning. But Gao seemed genuinely moved, stood with his hands behind his back, as though awaiting execution.

Sung said, "You were not ordered to drive the enemy away. You were ordered to strike him with as much energy as your troops could provide. You were ordered to demonstrate to the Americans that we are not to be ignored. You were to provide a message to them that if they continue their outrageous invasion, they shall be destroyed."

Gao absorbed Sung's words, lowered his head again. "I did not expect to pay such a price."

"How much of a price?"

Gao hesitated, and Sung had no patience for another show.

"How much of a price, General?"

Gao kept his head down, retrieved a paper from his coat pocket, handed it to Sung. "I was delayed this morning, as we did not have final accounting. I knew you would want to know in detail."

Sung took the paper, saw columns of numbers, Gao's three regiments listed in order. He scanned the figures, his eyes on one column, his eyes widening.

"You are correct, General Gao. I do wish to know these details. You claim that the Three Hundred Seventy-first Regiment lost eight hundred men? *Eight hundred?*"

"Yes, sir. I wish to suggest that the regiment is no longer fit for active service. It was not so bad in the others. But the enemy was well prepared, and though we did create holes in his defenses and drive a sword into their rear encampments, we could not maintain the breakthroughs. The enemy did not retreat from their positions. He instead was quick to counterattack. His tactics were most effective, and his weaponry is not to be underestimated."

"General Gao, I have never underestimated the weaponry of the

Americans. It is why we march at night. It is why we use stealth in every operation we can. It is why we attack him with overwhelming superiority in numbers."

Gao nodded. "Yes, sir. I understand. I did not expect to lose such a large number of men. They are good men, sir. Perhaps we should employ a different tactic. They made an excellent charge."

Sung stuffed the paper in his pocket, was more annoyed now. "Of course they made an excellent charge! That is what we must do, in every fight! I am not disappointed in the effort of your men, General. Only in the resolve of their commander. There is no *different tactic* available to us." Sung paused, studied the emotion on Gao's face. "Who is the commanding officer of Three Hundred Seventy-first Regiment?"

Gao looked at him now. "Colonel Feng Bo."

Sung weighed the name. "I know him. He was wounded sometime ago, a fight I recall well. He is a hero to Chairman Mao."

"Yes, sir. He was fortunate to survive."

"He is more than fortunate, General Gao. He is chosen by fate. And now fate will choose him again. Colonel Feng is a man who understands what we must do to defeat this enemy. I believe he should be promoted to command the division. You will hand me your sword."

Gao's eyes widened. "Sir?"

"Now." Gao's hands were shaking, the tears returning. He struggled with the belt, and Sung said, "Just the sword. I do not require you to relinquish the scabbard."

Gao said nothing, handed the sword to Sung, a steady flow of tears on the man's face.

"Your weakness is a disease that cannot be allowed to spread. You can be cured of this if you apply yourself to the counsel of Chairman Mao. You have already shown the first step toward redemption. I am pleased that you did not disgrace yourself further by begging me for your command. You will report to Colonel Liu of my staff. He is down below in that deep ravine. He shall find another position for you, as one becomes available. I regret losing your experience. But experience is not enough. You must be willing to do what is required."

Gao seemed to accept his punishment, and Sung was relieved, had no need to humiliate the man. The loss of command would be humiliating enough. Gao saluted him, and Sung acknowledged it.

"If you will permit, sir, I shall find Colonel Liu."

"Go."

Gao stepped away, straightening himself, a show of dignity that Sung was pleased to see. He shall return, he thought. Not a division, perhaps, but some command.

Sung stretched his back, felt the sunlight on his face, absorbed the pleasing warmth.

"Well, that was difficult, certainly."

Sung turned abruptly, saw Orlov standing just above him on the slope, pushing his way through the brush. Sung felt a burst of fury, said, "Major, you will not conduct yourself like some kind of spy. You are a guest of this command, and I expect you to behave with appropriate decorum. What transpires between me and my officers is not for your entertainment."

"I assure you, General, I am not entertained. Forgive me for saying so, but that seemed especially harsh. His troops are, shall I say, massacred? And you would punish him? Just what did he do wrong?"

Sung studied Orlov, who stood close to him now, scanning the sunlit hillside. "Are you so arrogant, Major, that you would ignore my instructions? You are not to listen in on my private meetings with my officers."

"What can happen? I am not in league with the enemy. We are many miles from anyplace you could abandon me. You would have questions to answer about that. I am here only to offer support, General. But I am not a part of your command. As you say, I am a guest. I am independent, and if you allow me to do the job I was assigned to do, we could all benefit."

Sung tried to hold his anger. "What is that *job*?"

Orlov shrugged, the smile again. "Observe. And, if you allow it . . . advise. We are not adversaries, you and I." He pulled a small flask from his pocket, sniffed it, took a small drink. Orlov's face curled, and he shook his head. "Got this from a Korean farmer. Well, no, I will be honest. I got it from one of your soldiers. Not everyone in this army shares your lust for sobriety." He held the flask out toward Sung. "Are you certain you won't have some?"

Sung shook his head, felt defeated, knew that everything Orlov had said was accurate, that the Russians might be far more important to this fight than anyone in Peking desired. And Sung couldn't fight the feeling that in some remote place inside himself, he actually liked the man.

"General Gao did not do anything wrong in the field. Nor did his men. They attacked the enemy and many men died. It is what happens in war. I do not have to explain that to you. General Gao's failure was his sorrow. His regret. He mourns the loss of his casualties. That is a dangerous mistake. It might produce hesitation, uncertainty. His will to make the next attack might be weakened. That is unacceptable."

Orlov slid the flask into his pocket, the smile fading. "It is not wrong for a leader to care for the lives of his men."

"Perhaps not in your army. Perhaps not for the Americans. You are accustomed to grand and powerful weapons. You strike your enemy with massive artillery rounds, with bombs from high above. Since your government has not offered us such assistance, I am forced to use the only weapon I have. My soldiers understand this; my officers *must* understand this. We must rely on stealth and darkness. And most important, we must rely on the power of our numbers. There are eight thousand men in each division, and when we attack, we must engage every man. Every man must carry the fight, from the bugler to the commanding general, and every man must understand the sacrifice and the cost in lives that we must expend in every fight. And we must be willing to give every piece of ourselves to the cause. Such dedication . . . it is the only advantage this army has, perhaps the only advantage China has." He stopped, reached into a pocket. "You are aware of this, of course?"

Orlov nodded, the smile returning. "I have seen a great many field manuals for troops, General. I must say, this one is . . . unique."

"It is written by one of yours, Major. A Russian naval captain, I believe. We have embraced its message, and only made alterations where needed. It is merely a history lesson, a recounting of just why we are fighting this war, what is at stake."

Orlov rubbed his chin. "As I recall, you refer to General MacArthur as a Wall Street house dog, a professional murderer, a war criminal. It says that he has urged his troops to capture whatever spoils they might steal from the kindly people of Korea, including, of course, all the young girls. It is, I would say, delicious reading. I never realized the Americans were such barbarians. I had rather thought my navy's captain had someone else in mind when he authored this, perhaps someone in Berlin."

"You may dismiss this if you wish, Major. But we have adopted this manual for its intended effects on the dedication of our soldiers. I added my own orders, more specific to this fight before us. The American Marine is a rapacious beast, whose lust grows ever stronger as he embraces the pleasure from the punishment and torture he inflicts on the innocent citizen of Korea. I have instructed my soldiers to kill every Marine as he would a snake in his home. Every soldier has read this pamphlet, and if they did not believe it the first time, they will have read it again. And again. If he cannot read, his officers will read it to him."

"I applaud you, General. It is a most effective piece of propaganda. We do what we must, eh?"

Sung thought a moment, said, "Am I accurate in observing that your Chairman Stalin distrusts his military officers?"

Orlov seemed caught off guard, his eyes wide, the smile returning. "In the past, there have been some problems that the Chairman has eliminated by removing certain negative elements."

"Chairman Mao trusts his generals, Major. We are given the task of carrying out the Chairman's vision, serving him with every means he has granted us. In this army, that requires us to use our soldiers as you would use bullets. It is the most effective way, perhaps the only way, we can crush the enemies of China. Right now, the enemy is offering us the enormous gift of his arrogance. He believes he has defeated us in battle. He will celebrate. He will become confident. And so he will become careless. Even now, the American Marines continue their march northward, on a single avenue, extending themselves farther into this difficult land. On either side of their march, my observers are watching, reporting to me exactly what I expect to hear. The strategy we shall employ is one that Chairman Mao perfected during our great struggle. Since you wish to observe us, then you may observe just what we shall do to win this war. I am positioning this army in the shape of a great wedge. It is not as a spear point, but just the opposite. It is a great open mouth, jaws wide, inviting the Americans to continue their march northward as though we are nowhere close. And when the time is right, the jaws shall close. Chairman Mao will celebrate another magnificent military victory, one that will carry China into a new age, where we do not kneel to anyone, not even your Chairman Stalin. My duty is clear, and my superiors are confident that my strategy will succeed. My army shall very soon destroy an entire division of American Marines."

CHAPTER FOURTEEN

. . . .

Smith

THE HELICOPTER CAME IN low over the river, Smith relieved to see the flat landing square appearing beneath him. The chopper settled more calmly now, the pilot easing the craft exactly in the center of the square. Smith waited for the impact, grateful as the chopper settled onto solid ground, allowing himself to relax on the hard seat. The pilot cut the engine, looked toward him with a smile, seemingly oblivious to Smith's tension.

"Here you are, sir. Back home."

Smith tried to return the smile. He slid out from the side of the craft, dropped down, steadied himself as always against the frame, fought to straighten his legs. He knew he was being unreasonable, that this ride had been no different than the others, the pilot skilled at skipping low over the tall hills, maneuvering the chopper through narrow passes. But the craft never felt wholly secure, even the pilots referring to them as buckets of loose bolts. That gave Smith no assurance at all, and more than once he had boarded the chopper only to pinch his fingers around various screws, a foolish effort to tighten whatever it might be that held the craft together.

The pilot had come around to his side, concern showing now on the young man's face, his hand extended slowly, an offering Smith didn't need.

"Can I help you, sir?"

Smith scowled at the young man, shook his head, stood without the aid of the chopper's support. "Not at all, Lieutenant."

"My apologies, sir. I didn't mean to give you such a rough ride. The winds are pretty nasty in those hills."

"No need. It was fine. You're dismissed, Lieutenant."

"Sir, do you mind if I tend to this bird's maintenance? It's protocol. Need to check the fluid levels."

Smith knew that, scolded himself, the annoying uneasiness affecting his decorum. "Fine. Do the job."

Smith eyed the headquarters building, another nondescript place, the former home of what seemed to be a low-level Korean official, that man long gone. He forced himself to steady steps, tried to ignore the painful stiffness in his knee, saw staff officers emerge, the sound of the helicopter drawing them out. He had no need to speak to any of them, the hard scowl on his face backing them away. Bowser was there now, a cup of coffee in the man's hand, Bowser saluting him, a show for the enlisted aides. Captain Sexton emerged as well, said, "Welcome back, sir. Anything you require?"

"I'll have some of that coffee."

"Right away, sir. We have a visitor. Our friend General Lowe has returned."

Smith stopped, couldn't avoid a twinge of alarm, still didn't trust that Truman's man wasn't there for more dirt than he seemed to admit.

"Just bring me the coffee, Captain. Not much in the mood for a visit."

He stepped into the quarters, the usual smell of Korean spices and cigarette smoke, his aides dutifully engrossed in their usual labor. There were two other rooms to the rear, one established as the sleeping quarters for Smith and General Craig. He looked that way, thought, I wonder if Lowe's staying long. The staff glanced up at him as he passed, smiles, short greetings. He nodded them away, moved to the first of the smaller rooms, what served now as his office. Craig was there, behind a small desk, another aide helping him with a radio set.

"Welcome back, General. Happy times at the front?"

It was an odd comment, and Smith said, "Litzenberg has his situation in hand. They're regrouping, drawing up into a more practical position. It's not easy. That blessed road isn't wide enough for a donkey cart. At least the enemy's pulled away, for now."

"I suppose that's good. General Lowe will be pleased to hear that, anyway."

"Where is he?"

"Next door. Your quarters. He has an aide now. They're setting up his sleeping arrangements."

"What arrangements?"

"Spreading out his sleeping bag on the floor, right beside mine. We allowed you the larger space. I know the rules. So, apparently, does Lowe."

There was a grim edge in Craig's words, no smile, Craig returning to work with the radio. Coffee in hand, Smith eased toward the second of the smaller rooms, peered in, saw Lowe on his knees on the floor, digging in a haversack, retrieving a variety of personal items, arranging them in a neat display beside his sleeping bag. His aide stood beside him, the young man noticing Smith, a quick pat on Lowe's shoulder, the aide regarding Smith with boyish terror. Lowe turned, said, "Ah, General! You survived another daredevil mission. Survived one myself."

Lowe rose to his feet, stretched himself tall, said to the aide, "Corporal, this will do for now. Go get yourself some of that coffee, if the general's staff will oblige you."

The young man offered a weak "Thank you, sir," then moved past Smith, flattening himself against the wall as he passed. Smith saw something new on Lowe's face, a hint of despair similar to Craig's. Lowe said, "Do you mind if we close that door?"

Smith stepped into the room, pulled the flimsy door shut with a rattling thump. "You know you can speak freely in front of my staff."

Lowe sat on the floor again, leaning against one wall, his knees pulled up. "Rather keep this between us. It has been a difficult few days."

Lowe had conceded the lone chair to Smith, who sat, allowed himself to sag into the chair. Smith said, "I've just come from Colonel Litzenberg's CP. The Seventh Regiment inflicted heavy casualties on an entire division of Chinese in the hills up toward Sudong. We took casualties of our own, perhaps seventy dead. My division is spread a hundred fifty miles along a road I can't adequately defend. We're ordered to move northward on what the Koreans call a highway, and not too many miles in front of us, that road will be too narrow for nearly every mechanized vehicle we have. My *superior* is extremely unhappy that we have not yet waded into the Yalu River." He paused. "So tell me, Frank, how are things with you?"

It was a rare show of sarcasm, and Lowe let out a breath, said, "I do not mean to suggest that this entire operation . . . this entire war, is not difficult for us all. For *you* all. I am most sorry to hear about your casualties."

"The enemy is more sorry to hear about his."

"Yes, well, of course. I was wondering how well you know Walton Walker?"

"Not very well."

Lowe looked down into his hands, nodded slowly. "Nor I. I know him a bit better now. Spent several days with his command. I suppose you're not so familiar with Hobart Gay."

"Met him. Somewhere."

Lowe peered up at him. "They have problems over there. They took heavy casualties against an enemy that wasn't supposed to be there. General Gay commands the First Cavalry, and I can smell the rats surrounding him. The army always has need of a scapegoat, and Gay's troops took the worst of the assault from the enemy. They lost an entire battalion, for God's sake. Morale is awful, all through Walker's command, and of course, somebody has to walk the plank for that one. I'm afraid it will be Gay. I couldn't say a word. If I bring the president into a situation like that, I'll lose every bit of cooperation from every officer in Tokyo, Tenth Corps, and likely even Walker won't be too happy. I had to keep my mouth shut while I watched Walker's people scramble to create elaborate justifications for every move they're making."

"Why are you telling me this? Nothing I can do. You think Almond cares what anyone here thinks?"

"Sorry. I just had to say it. I'll inform the president all that's happening, of course. But I'll also caution him about jumping into the fray. MacArthur would explode like a rocket on the Fourth of July if Harry Truman told him how to deal with his subordinates. I'm not even sure I should offer the president my own opinion, that the fault isn't with Eighth Army at all. It's Tenth Corps. No effort has been made to move in tandem, to support either flank. There is a gap of nearly seventy miles between Walker's troops and yours." He paused, Smith's expression not changing. "Of course you know that. Forgive me, General."

"You can call me O.P. You've been here long enough."

Lowe smiled, nodded. "No. You're the one man I've come into contact with who deserves to be called *general*. Right now Walker's people are contemplating their possible withdrawal, some of them expecting the order to come from Tokyo that it's time to pull the entire Eighth Army back through the port of Pusan."

"That won't happen. That would be the equivalent of surrender, and MacArthur's having none of that. He'll replace people first."

Lowe stared at the floor in front of him. "You're right, of course. But the morale. No one wanted to talk to me, since they assumed I would relay every swear word to the president. And there were plenty of those. Just before I left, a call came in from Tokyo, the first time anyone there has acknowledged that the Chinese might actually be in this war. I thought Walker would have a stroke, like he wanted to reach through the wire and strangle whoever was on the other end. And even then, G-2 was pulling back from that, claiming that perhaps it was Walker who was mistaken. There is apparently some kind of argument going on in MacArthur's headquarters. No one wants to admit they were wrong about the Chinese being down here."

Smith finished the coffee, set the cup down on the floor beside him. "I can't do much to relieve your anxiety. But I can assure you, the Chinese are out there, and they aren't hesitant about punching us in the nose. We have the prisoners to prove it. According to them, we were hit by a single division, the One Hundred Twenty-fourth. Those prisoners have been talking like the dickens, claims of a dozen more divisions, waiting for us up the road."

Lowe said, "Walker's hearing that, too. You believe your prisoners?"

"Hard to tell. The interpreters believe them. To my mind, it's unlikely that low-level foot soldiers would have access to high-level planning."

"That's exactly what Walker believes. He has prisoners, too, so they tell me. His interrogators don't necessarily trust what the prisoners are saying. Have you spoken to him? Perhaps you two should be coordinating your efforts directly."

"I would *enjoy* speaking with General Walker. I'm sure he and I could fight this war in a way the president would approve. But that's not how it works. Should we want to speak to Eighth Army, we go through Tenth Corps. No one here has the luxury of a direct line to anyone in Walker's command."

"That's insane!"

"If you say so. It's chain of command."

Lowe stared at the floor for a long moment, visible frustration on his face. He looked up at Smith again.

"What happens now? What are your orders?"

Smith glanced at the door, heard the soft knock. "Enter."

Sexton pushed his way in, two cups of coffee balanced in his hands. He handed one to Lowe, then moved to Smith.

"It's really hot, sir. Been boiling for about an hour. Best let it cool a bit."

Lowe sipped carefully, grunted, staring into the cup. Smith took the cup, waved Sexton away.

"Thank you, Captain. That's all."

Sexton backed out of the room and Smith said, "General Almond will visit here tomorrow. When he has new orders, he usually demands that we go to him. When he wants orders carried out with haste, he goes directly to my regimental commanders, company commanders, anyone he can intimidate. I've tried to break him of that habit, with some success. You may of course involve yourself in any such meeting, here, or on the front lines, assuming we can determine where that might be."

Lowe tested the coffee again, his face in a hard curl. "If that requires me to ride in another helicopter, I'd prefer it be here."

FIRST MARINE DIVISION HQ—HAMHUNG, NORTH KOREA—
NOVEMBER 7, 1950

"With the orders I've been given, my division is now spread out over nearly a hundred seventy miles. I am greatly concerned that our fighting efficiency has been severely compromised. It is crucial that we be able to move in support of any vulnerable position. Had Litzenberg's people been attacked by a greater force, he might have suffered substantial casualties. There was no way we could have provided him support from either Puller's or Murray's forces. General Almond, the First Marine Division is a powerful instrument, if it is allowed to be. Scattered as we are, our power is greatly diminished."

Smith paused, expected the usual dismissiveness from Almond. But Almond was glum, seemed to absorb Smith's angry lecture with strange acceptance. Smith glanced at Bowser, the only one of his staff officers in the room. Almond's man, Colonel Gaffney, sat against the wall behind his commander, had offered nothing of his own. Almond kept his eyes downward, said, "Would you suggest drawing your forces more tightly together?"

Smith was surprised, leapt on the opportunity. "Yes! I have insisted on that for days now. Your orders were for the army to replace Puller's people around the ports. My next move would be to order Puller to march north, lessening the gap between him and Litzenberg. The Seventh is already occupying the town of Chinhung-ni, the Fifth is spread out behind them, and Puller is still at Wonsan. As I said, sir, that's a hundred seventy miles' distance."

"The Third Division."

The words came from Almond as though he was reminding himself just who he commanded.

"Yes, fine. The Third Division. Once they move into Puller's area, I would order him to advance northward with all speed. He'll like that, I assure you. He doesn't care for having his people so far removed from the fighting."

Almond shifted his weight in the chair, seemed uncomfortable. Smith stood, stepped closer to him, looking down at the man. He had never felt this way, that Almond was actually listening to him.

Almond said, "How much fighting has there been? I know of the attack at Sudong. Is Colonel Litzenberg prepared for another assault?"

"Yes, of course. But Litzenberg wasn't caught with his pants down. Despite your orders to advance with haste, our own intelligence reports indicated the presence of a great many of the enemy. Litzenberg moved accordingly. The enemy's attack at Sudong was certainly designed to drive us back. Their success against the First Cavalry had no doubt convinced them they could gain a strong upper hand in our front as well." He stopped, thought, Enough of that. No need to be a cheerleader for the Corps. "I do not know exactly what happened with Eighth Army. I do not mean to criticize anyone's command decisions."

Almond seemed oblivious to Smith's show of protocol, said, "The cavalry suffered a great many casualties. The ROK units failed to hold their line. General MacArthur has become aware of the weakness of our allies. It was unexpected."

Smith said nothing. He had a great deal of respect for the South Korean marines, a well-trained and seemingly disciplined force. But the ROK army troops had not distinguished themselves at all, certainly not when facing the Chinese.

Smith glanced at Bowser, who watched Almond with curiosity.

Bowser said, "General Smith, might I point out that the approach of winter will have a direct effect on our operations in the mountains to the north? Supplying our men as they advance farther north could be most difficult."

Smith was grateful for the cue, said to Almond, "I agree. I had hoped that with the Chinese demonstrating a strong presence and a willingness to engage us, General MacArthur would appreciate that the most prudent course would be to stop our advance northward, consolidate our positions below the steeper mountains, and strengthen the defenses around the ports of Wonsan and Hungnam. Colonel Bowser is correct that if we move up into the plateau country north of Chinhung-ni, we could be vulnerable."

Almond kept his eyes away from Smith's, shook his head. "No. General MacArthur would not accept a withdrawal away from those positions we have already occupied. We must continue to demonstrate to the enemy, and to the world, that we are moving forward. You should advance at least as far as Hagaru-ri. Once your division is concentrated, you should be able to prevent the enemy from any major success. General MacArthur has ordered the Eighth Army to secure their position as well. We cannot suffer any more reverses."

There was no enthusiasm in Almond's voice, and Smith knew not to push too hard. He glanced at Bowser again, thought, He's giving me nearly everything I'm asking for. When has that ever happened?

Within two days, orders were received from Tenth Corps detailing how ROK units would move into areas closer to Puller's command, relieving Puller from policing the more southern areas. In addition, the army's Third Division would occupy the port cities, freeing Puller's First Regiment from what had amounted to garrison duty. Puller responded with exactly the enthusiasm Smith expected, the First Regiment quickly put into motion, lessening the wide gap between the extremes of Smith's position. But Almond's orders also included instructions for the Marines to continue their advance not only to Hagaru-ri, at the southern tip of the Chosin Reservoir, but to anticipate movement farther to the northwest, as far as Yudam-ni, midway up the left side of Chosin.

With Smith now able to bring his troops closer together, the first priority was just how the advance Almond still insisted upon could be made more efficient. The road northward was as dismal as reports had indicated, and immediately Smith ordered engineering teams to put their heavy equipment to work, widening the road as it wound through the steeper mountains. Moving the men also meant moving the artillery, tanks, and larger trucks, vast convoys of weaponry and supplies that Smith intended to keep close to his camps. With the supplies now catching up to his troops, Smith ordered vast supply dumps to be constructed along the routes the men had already marched, from Chinhung-ni, through Koto-ri, and finally, as far north as Hagaru-ri. But Smith was not satisfied with the supplies coming from the naval ships at the ports. At Koto-ri he ordered an existing airstrip to be enlarged and improved, suitable for the air force's C-47s, the twin-engine workhorses that could deliver additional supplies as needed, as well as transporting casualties to the hospital ships and medical facilities farther south.

FIRST MARINE DIVISION HQ—HAMHUNG, NORTH KOREA—
NOVEMBER 10, 1950

He felt better than he had in days, the staff feeling that as well, the labor of the headquarters performed without complaint, a smooth flow of paperwork and logistical instructions for the movement of the vast new inflow of supplies. The mood of his staff was buoyant for another reason as well. November 10 was the 175th anniversary of the United States Marine Corps, a date every Marine embraced.

He watched the men move toward him with careful steps, the cake carried between them, placed lovingly on the desk cleared for the occasion. The staff gathered close, and Smith absorbed their mood, the smiles. He slid the pipe into his mouth, tasted the delicious smoke, watched as Sexton hovered close to the cake, now producing a lighter. Sexton looked at him, waiting for approval, and Smith nodded toward the cake, the lighter clicking on, the first two candles lit. Sexton abruptly cut off the flames, lit the lighter again, two more candles, the lighter going off once more. To one side, a young aide laughed, said, "Hey, Captain. You need a stronger thumb to keep that thing lit?"

Sexton straightened, a look of seriousness, said to the gathering, "They don't teach you boys a damn thing, do they? You ever heard the expression, three on a match?"

The officers nodded silently, some of the enlisted men as well. But others, mostly the younger men, seemed perplexed, heads shaking. Sexton looked at Smith, mock disgust.

"What's the world come to, sir?"

Smith held the pipe in his mouth with one hand. "Go on. Tell them."

Sexton assumed an air of authority now, hands behind his back. "In the First World War, the men in the trenches found out very quickly that in the time it takes a man to light three cigarettes with a single match, a sniper across the way could find the range, and make his aim. More than one doughboy died because he was being a nice guy for his buddies, whether it was cigarettes, or, maybe, like right now, three candles. That's a lesson you should learn this way, by me *telling* you, than some commie sniper *showing* you."

The mood suddenly changed, the visual of Sexton's description sinking into the younger men. Smith knew Sexton had gone too far, said, "Just cut the cake, Captain. No snipers here."

Sexton obliged with his Ka-bar, the cake quickly disappearing onto mess plates, paper napkins, most of the men not bothering with a fork. Beside him, Craig took a piece, handed another to Smith, and Craig said, "Should I read the note from Admiral Joy?"

Smith put a forkful of the cake into his mouth, nodded, and Craig smiled, said, "Gentlemen, we have received a most kind letter from Admiral C. Turner Joy, the man most responsible for the navy hauling us into Inchon. We may not have the closest of friends among the ground pounders, but you can be assured that the squids know just who has their back."

Smith finished the square of cake, said, "Just read the note."

Craig held up a paper, read, "On the occasion of your one hundred seventy-fifth anniversary I consider it indeed an honor and a privilege to salute our courageous comrades in arms, the United States Marines, wherever you may be. You can justly be proud of your past record, of your present gallant and heroic exploits in the Korean campaign, and God willing, you will face the future with the knowledge that you have done much toward restoring a happy and peaceful world."

Smith raised the pipe, all eyes on him now. "To a peaceful world."

· · · · · · · · · · ·

It was late, the party concluded, the cake long gone. Smith sat on his sleeping bag, stared at the paper, held the pen poised above. He smiled, tried to picture his granddaughter, couldn't avoid a flicker of sadness. She'll be grown the next time I see her. It happens so fast.

He looked up, saw Bowser in the doorway.

"Sorry, sir, didn't mean to interrupt."

"Come in, Al. Just working on a letter to Esther. Thinking about my granddaughter, Gail."

"How old is she now, sir?"

"Six. But she'll be sixteen before you know it. Seems it's always been like this. I'm off in who-knows-where, and their lives just march on." He stopped, was never comfortable talking about these kinds of feelings. "Sorry. What's up?"

"Nothing, really. The staff is mostly in their quarters. No reports of any major action. Seems the Chinese are respecting our celebration." Bowser paused. "You haven't been outside, have you, sir?"

"Why?"

"Pretty impressive. Temperature dropped about thirty degrees since sundown. I guess winter's finally here. Just didn't expect it to come in all at once."

Smith heard a rattle, looked at the lone window, could hear the wind now. "How cold?"

"Not sure. If it's this cold here, though, pretty sure it's getting a little rough up in the hills. I'm guessing the men will be a little happier with those heavy coats."

The assault against the Marines at Sudong had only deepened what seemed to be a complete shift in strategy, the concern much more now for consolidation and a posture of defense. Smith had used that shift to the advantage of his division, Ned Almond allowing him far more leeway than Smith had enjoyed before.

But the Chinese had seemed to offer MacArthur a new gift. By pulling away from any confrontation with the bruised American units, embarrassed intelligence officers in Tokyo could now point to their original estimates, that the Chinese were in fact a minor force of no real significance. With the disappearance of the Chinese across the entire front, and the reconnaissance teams failing to learn just where they had gone, a buoyant confidence once again blossomed in Tokyo. Urgent discussions about the possible evacuation of American forces from Korean ports were suddenly silenced, replaced by MacArthur's renewed enthusiasm for ending this war as he had always planned.

On November 11, new orders were passed down to both Eighth Army and Smith's Marines. The march would once more be resumed, and there would be no hesitation, no cautious halt for winter. Once more MacArthur was insisting that they drive hard and fast to the Yalu River.

Smith received the order with annoyed frustration. Nowhere in Almond's renewed sense of glee was there any explanation for just how the yawning gap between Eighth Army and Tenth Corps was to be resolved. Despite claims from Tokyo that each force was protecting the flank of the other, Smith knew that as his Marines advanced closer to the Chosin Reservoir, Walton Walker's army units were on the far side of a vast and rugged mountain range, still nearly seventy miles away.

CHAPTER FIFTEEN

. . . .

Riley

THEY AWOKE TO a fresh blanket of snow that painted the mountains around them with the kind of beauty the Marines had forgotten. Once more, the orders were to march north, the road now as steep as the hills they passed, the climb up through what the maps called the Funchilin Pass. The march was slow and methodical, Colonel Litzenberg obeying the spirit of General Smith's order that the advance be deliberate, cautious. With the Seventh still in the lead, Litzenberg had pushed small reconnaissance patrols up into the hills along both sides of the road, discreetly probing the hollows and narrows, seeking out any hidden enemy. There had been confrontations, but they were brief and very limited, mostly scattered posts of Chinese lookouts, sent scurrying away. The men were as nervous as their commander, anticipating another sudden assault from every hidden place. But the Chinese had indeed backed away, allowing the Marines to climb ever higher through the pass. Litzenberg had no interest in the intelligence reports still pouring toward them from Tokyo that whatever enemy they had collided with had most certainly scurried back toward the Yalu River. From Litzenberg down to the privates who trudged their way up muddy ruts in a soggy road, no one paid any attention now to MacArthur's amazing optimism, Tokyo still trumpeting that these men would leave this miserable land in time to celebrate Christmas with their families. Each day's march put them farther from the seaports to the south, and closer to what they all believed would be another fight.

At the top of the pass, the ground flattened, a plateau some three thousand feet higher than the hills they had left behind at Sudong. Bone-chilling blasts of wind now that staggered the men as they marched, slicing through their clothing. The careless quickly learned to fasten their overcoats, the hoods yanked down hard over the wool hats, watery eyes staring down, feet moving in the steady rhythm that matched the man to your front. The march warmed them a little, sweat soaking their undershirts, the columns stopping periodically, orders to the men to change their socks.

A few miles below their goal of Koto-ri, they had marched past a power station, a concrete bridge that carried them over four enormous pipes, man-made waterways that funneled the flow from the Changjin River northward, down through the plateau and valley that eventually led to the great reservoir that the Japanese maps labeled Chosin. But the power plant was merely a break in the scenery, the men paying little heed, even if the engineers among them were quietly impressed. Most of the men strained to hear any sounds of an ambush, hesitating at each sharp bend in the road, the recon patrols still fanning out over the hills above them. By late afternoon they reached the outskirts of Koto-ri, and once more the lieutenants passed the word: Prepare to dig in.

The first two battalions had already spread out through Koto-ri, some of those men patrolling the outlying villages. Like Koto-ri itself, the smaller settlements showed the effect of American air strikes, each village no more than a pothole of ruin along narrow trails.

The town had already taken a new shape, camps set up, tents erected, aid stations and command posts. Trucks were rolling in, a slow procession, one tank moving past, clanking its way farther north. Riley loved the tanks, no one disagreeing with him, the men around him staring as he was, grateful for the power in the steel beast.

They passed men working, shovels chopping into hard ground, a handful of men erecting a larger tent. There were jeeps there, wheels thick with mud, Welch mumbling beside him, "Brass. Maybe Old Homer wants a nap."

McCarthy led them farther into the wreckage, all that remained of the town, more Marines in every open place, familiar officers, the other companies of Litzenberg's Seventh establishing their base. The men mostly ignored one another, but Riley heard the calls from the column, friends seeking friends, and behind him Killian said, "Hey! There's Hooperman!" He was louder now, "Hey, Dog Breath! Your mama let you run loose?"

The man stood knee-deep in a foxhole, shovel now resting on his shoulder. He stared toward Killian for a long moment, then broke into a smile, climbed up, walked toward the road.

"I told you if you ever mention my mama again, I'd polish my bayonet on your nut sack."

"Give it a try, Hoop. I could use the attention."

Up ahead, McCarthy had stopped, was speaking to an officer Riley didn't know, Lieutenant Goolsby leading the rest of the platoon into a small blasted field. Riley hung back with Killian, said, "Didn't know you had any friends."

"Hell, yes! Known this ugly son of a bitch since basic. Corporal Wayne Hooperman, this here is Pete Riley. He'd have made corporal, but he's too stupid."

Hooperman nodded toward Riley. "Pleased to meet you. I don't see any stripes on your arm, Sean. I guess the Corps ain't so hard up they gotta promote big dumb Irishmen."

Riley could feel the man's good cheer, smiled, said, "We passed a goat a ways back. Sean saluted it. Guess he knows his place."

Hooperman laughed, said to Killian, "Hey, I like your friend. Knows you as well as I do."

Killian made a mock scowl. "No friend. Just a rifleman lucky enough to share my hole. I gotta teach him to throw a grenade, not just drop it on his toes." Killian pulled out his canteen. "Glad you're okay, even if you're still the ugliest Marine in Korea."

There was a softness to the Irishman's words, a hint of sentiment that Riley rarely saw. Hooperman nodded, said, "Yeah. We lost a couple men in that last scrap. No fun at all. Hey, you guys are Fox. I knew your captain back in Pendleton. Damn shame he's gone, huh?"

Riley waited for more, glanced at Killian. "What do you mean?"

Hooperman seemed surprised. "The word passed along this afternoon. Zorn's been pulled out, transferred to headquarters or something. He always wanted to be with the big boys. I guess somebody noticed him. You meet your new CO yet?"

Riley was confused, thought, Zorn's gone? He looked toward McCarthy, saw the lieutenant with the other two platoon leaders, and still the unfamiliar officer. Riley saw Welch moving closer, the sergeant hearing the talk. Welch said to Hooperman, "They don't tell us a damn thing till it's over with. There's some fresh-faced captain up ahead, talking to the lieutenants. Guess we'll meet him soon enough."

McCarthy stepped away from the meeting, looked out toward his men, called out, "Third Platoon, fall in here! Take a seat."

The men responded, other lieutenants calling to their platoons, the entire company coming together. Welch kept his voice low, said to Riley, "That's gotta be him. Captain Freshface. They can't leave anything be. I guess officers gotta move around or they get moldy."

Riley kept his eyes on the new captain, a tall, lean man, older, hands on his hips. Riley noticed now, the man's clothing was perfect, dungarees pressed, the jacket seeming to be new. The captain watched as the men sat, appraising them with a hard frown. The chatter grew silent, and the captain moved into the middle of the formation, the company on three sides of him.

"Listen up! I'm Captain William Barber, your new CO. Captain Zorn has transferred. I want you to know, I'm no ninety-day wonder. I started as an enlisted man in World War II. I received my commission in 1943, and like some of you, I ate gravel at Iwo Jima. I took two wounds there, two Purple Hearts. They thought I needed a Silver Star, too. I ended that war as a company commander, and somebody thought I did a good job of it. So my job is to lead you men into whatever scrap the enemy has planned for us. You pay attention, and you'll likely survive. You don't, and you'll end up in a bag. I may not know beans about strategy, but I know a hell of a lot about tactics. Frankly, I'm a hell of a good infantry officer!" He paused. "Who's here from Kentucky?" Several hands went up, and Barber said, "Me, too. Dehart. East of Lexington. Don't worry, you never heard of it. I also need to inform you that effective immediately, we have a new battalion commander. Major Sawyer has been replaced by Colonel Randolph Lockwood. If Colonel Lockwood feels the need to talk to you, he'll let me know." Barber scanned the men closely. "You are a motley group. Pancho Villa's bandits looked more fit than you. That will change. By tonight I want every man cleaned up and shaved. I want weapons cleaned, and you will fall out for a conditioning hike at oh–six hundred tomorrow. This company has too few veterans and too many children. You will shape up, or I'll find you a kindergarten to fit you. You are dismissed."

Riley stared, his mouth hanging open. Beside him, Killian said, "What the hell is this war coming to? You see his dungarees? They're creased, for God's sake."

Riley watched Barber walk away, had nothing to say. Behind him, Welch said, "That's just great. We got us a pantywaist captain who thinks we need basic training."

McCarthy was there now, no smile, said, "Maybe we do, Sergeant. You want to bitch, you go right ahead. But if Captain Barber gives you an order, you will damn well obey it. You got a problem with that, you take it out on the Chinese."

The foxholes were mostly completed, darkness beginning to spread over the field. Riley cleaned his hands in a softening pile of muddy snow, thought of the C-rations in his backpack. I'm so damn hungry, he thought, I might actually enjoy that slop. In the distance came the rhythmic thump of a helicopter, and he stared up, stretching his back. He folded the small shovel, watched the chopper ease down in a wide clearing near the larger tents. One man was signaling, guiding the chopper to rest, and now another chopper appeared, and from a narrow gap in the hills, two more. Riley said, "What the hell?"

Killian was watching as well, others around them turning that way. The choppers set down, a lengthening row in the field, another pair now coming over the closest hill, dropping low near the rest. Killian said, "I bet they're gonna tell us that's how we're moving north. Our new spic-and-span captain thinks we oughta keep our uniforms clean. Hell, no. I ain't riding in those damn things."

Around them, men were laughing at Killian, and Welch called over, "Hey, Irish. I volunteered you for test pilot. Your buddy Hooperman said you were the perfect man for the job."

More laughs, and Riley moved out away from the hole, watched men unloading small crates from each chopper, piling them near the largest tent. Officers were gathering now, the other company commanders, and Captain Barber, the only man with no mud on his uniform. He saw McCarthy speaking to Barber, and McCarthy saluted him, then moved toward Riley at a jog.

"Listen up! I heard this might happen, but I sure as hell didn't believe it. You can thank General Smith and every man on down the line for this." McCarthy paused, took a breath, waited for the platoon to move closer. "In honor of the one hundred seventy-fifth birthday of the United States Marine Corps, headquarters has sent us hot food. Grab your mess kits and form a line."

The order didn't have to be repeated, the men responding with raw enthusiasm. Riley ripped the mess kit free from his pack, slid into the formation, Welch in front of him, and Welch said, "I'll be damned. The brass did something right. I can smell whatever that is already."

In front of them, another platoon had moved into place, and Killian called out, "They better not take seconds."

McCarthy was moving along the line, a rare smile. "Don't worry about it, Private. They're sending plenty." He pointed toward the horizon. "More choppers coming in."

Riley felt the impatience of the men around him, slow steps closer to the food. He heard the thump of the choppers, and now another sound, odd, a loud voice. In front of him, Welch said, "Hey. It's the captain. Good God. That sounds like singing."

The men looked that way, and Barber obliged them, stepping out into the open, his voice booming, reaching them all.

"From the halls of Montezuma, to the shores of Tripoli . . ."

KOTO-RI, NORTH KOREA—NOVEMBER 11, 1950

The temperatures dropped throughout the night, pushed downward by more of the blustery winds. They had been on one-quarter watch, one man in four kept awake for a two-hour stint, the others allowed to sleep. Riley's watch had come early, before midnight, and when he slid into the bag, curling up into the foxhole, the warmth had been perfect. The boots had come off, the socks set aside, dry socks now embraced by the thickness of the sleep bag. Sleep had come quickly, nothing anywhere along the perimeter of the town to cause any disturbance at all.

He had dreamed of Pennsylvania, courting Ruthie, a stroll through the astonishing beauty of a peach orchard. It was his favorite way to soften her up, the peach blossoms holding some kind of seductive powers he could never hope to duplicate. They had kissed for the first time, his eye caught by the flickers of the blossoms in her hair, the soft sweetness of her perfume. He rolled to one side now, heard a loud curse, the words pulling him back to Korea, jarring him awake. It was Killian.

"Holy Christ! My feet are frozen! Damn, everything's frozen!"

Riley felt it now, the burning numbness in his feet, a hard chill that wrapped all around his chest. He yanked at the sleeping bag, but the bag was in place, enveloping him, the cold crushing its way through. He flexed the numbness in his toes, sucked in a hard, cold breath, felt a choking numbness in his throat, put one hand up on his face. He fought to breathe, his nostrils frozen shut, saw the shadow of Killian rising up in the hole, slapping himself with his arms. Riley was shivering heavily now, the iciness of each breath draining away any warmth he had inside. His words came in a quivering croak. "What the hell?"

Killian dropped down again, a vain attempt to curl himself more tightly together. "I know! This is nuts. What happened?"

Around them, men were up and moving, some standing, more arms slapping, cries and curses. Killian said, "Somebody light a damn fire!"

"The hell you don't."

The voice belonged to Welch, and Riley saw him coming, a dark heap coming down in the hole, crushing weight on top of him. Welch was shivering as well, pulling himself up close to the other two, his words in a quick burst. "No fires. Orders. Jesus Christ, it's cold. I can't breathe."

Around them the men were reacting in a growing chorus of shock and anger, Riley still shivering, the sergeant's weight a welcome blanket. Killian was saying something, low, meaningless words, and above Riley, a new voice. "The aid station is back this way! There's heat there!"

Men began to erupt from their foxholes, some of them stumbling on frozen feet. Welch was up now, moving away, and Riley felt the hard cold slapping his face, put his hands tightly against stinging ears. His brain spewed out a chorus of nonsense, shouts inside him, It's just cold! For God's sake, it's just cold! But around him the chaos was growing, a clumsy stampede toward the tents, and Killian was up now, staggering away. Riley looked out from the hole, a hint of dawn rising to the east. He could see the men gathering at the tents, heard the shouts from officers, useless orders to stand down, back away. He thought of running that way, the cold crushing him into the hole, and he curled up tightly again, hard shivering. To one side he saw his socks, laid out to dry the night before. Put them on! He reached out past the edge of the hole, his gloved hands curling around them, no feeling in his fingers, the socks in his hands now, stiff and frozen. This is insanity, he thought. How cold can it be? He reached for his boots, slid them quickly onto numb feet, the soft layers in the bottom of the shoe pacs now hard and icy. He tried to stand, no feeling in his feet, and he stomped one foot on the other, his brain screaming at him the error, his foot bursting into stinging pain. He rubbed at the boots, useless, no feeling still in his fingers, his brain shouting new instructions: Move! He rose up, climbed out of the hole, shivered violently, dropped down to one knee, his teeth in full chatter, nostrils frozen shut.

"Get up! Here!"

He felt a hand under his arm, was pulled up, tried to gather his feet beneath him, find the balance. He wanted to thank the man, had no words, glanced that way, saw only eyes, the face wrapped in cloth, the single lieutenant's bar on the helmet. The hand released him and Riley pushed the words out. "Thank . . . thank you."

"Get over to the aid station. They'll warm you up."

Riley fought the pain, the utter shock of the hard chill in his bones, his lungs. He curled his arms against himself, flexing his fingers, his feet still numb.

"What the hell is this?"

He knew the voice now, McCarthy. "It's ten below, Private. The Koreans call this *winter*."

The abrupt drop in temperatures caused a response that even the men from northern climates couldn't predict. The Marines reacted to the crushing impact of the below-zero weather with what could only be described by the medical officers as shock. More than three-fourths of the two hundred fifty men of Fox Company scrambled to the aid stations, where overwhelmed corpsmen and battalion surgeons could only offer the men the warmth of a heated tent. Men were suffering from dangerously low respiratory rates, a level of hypothermia so severe that the medical men applied various stimulants to pull the Marines from their stunned condition.

The Seventh Regiment had been fortunate to be the first to receive the far warmer winter clothes, but farther south, along the same line of march, Ray Murray's Fifth had yet to receive the heavier gear. Their single advantage was that at the lower altitude, the temperatures hadn't dropped so severely. But Murray's orders were to keep close behind the Seventh, and so, very soon, as his men pushed up through the pass, they would suffer the same misery. As word of the abrupt change in the weather went back to division headquarters, General Smith responded by ordering the supply depots to the south to push forward as much winter gear as could be found.

Once their physical reactions had been tempered, the men of Fox

Company began to adjust to the severity of winter. Though their clothing brought some relief, new problems arose, from frozen canteens to frozen toes. If there was no escaping the cold, the men were comforted in some part by what they saw in Koto-ri. Within days of reaching the town, establishing their perimeter, convoys of supplies began to arrive, driven along the same road these men had climbed by foot. The engineers had done their job, widening and strengthening the pathway, to make way for the large six-by trucks and columns of tanks. Koto-ri rapidly became an enormous supply depot, a protected fortress established by General Smith as a precaution for the continuing advance northward by his division. With the great ports so far behind them, a supply line connected to their advance by a single road, Smith realized what Tenth Corps seemingly did not, that the Marines were more vulnerable with every day's march. If there should be some crisis farther to the south, some danger that could jeopardize that supply line, Smith would provide depots all along the way.

But the men of the Seventh Regiment did not enjoy the relative comforts of Koto-ri for more than a few days. Once more they were ordered to shoulder their gear and resume the march northward toward the Yalu River. Again there was little sign of the Chinese, no significant roadblocks, no attempt by the enemy to stand in their way. And so the men marched farther along the single narrow avenue toward their next goal, the town of Hagaru-ri, at the southern tip of the Chosin Reservoir.

CHAPTER SIXTEEN

. . . .

Smith

FIRST MARINE DIVISION HQ—HAMHUNG, NORTH KOREA—
NOVEMBER 14, 1950

HE CLIMBED OUT of the jeep, stepped down gingerly on frozen feet. The staff was waiting, a helpful radio call alerting them that Smith was close. He moved quickly inside without speaking, a cup of hot coffee pressed into his hands, the heat in the main room embracing him like a powerful blanket. He thought of his escort, the team of jeeps manned by machine gunners, guards against any enemy who might have been observant enough to realize that the small convoy that tracked past them held the commanding general of their enemy.

Sexton was there, concern on the man's face, and Smith said, "Captain, make sure those boys out there get something, too. Feed 'em, give 'em coffee. Send them to the warming tents, or somebody's billet. I'll not have casualties from this weather just because I needed babysitting."

Sexton moved outside quickly, and Smith stood silently, wriggling his toes, the feeling returning. He curled his fingers tightly, pulled his hands close to his stomach, glanced at the staff, hoping no one noticed. It was the old malady, an affliction his doctors attributed to the case of influenza he had endured years before. Smith had not escaped the astounding plague that swept the world in 1918, killing more than six hundred thousand people in the United States alone. He had survived his own battle, but the lingering symptom was a quivering weakness in his hands and feet whenever he had been subjected to extreme cold. And today the cold was extreme.

To Smith's dismay, the helicopters had been crippled, the mechanics working feverishly to solve the problem. The cold had thickened the oil in the crafts' crucial gearbox, rendering the choppers wholly unreliable. For Smith to maintain close contact with his commanders, meetings that were too involved for radios, the only option now was the jeep. Smith had prepared for the dismal trips the same as his officers, heavy coats and scarves, as much protection from the windy ride as could be found. The journey up to Litzenberg's headquarters had taken the better part of three hours, and no matter how much coffee was available at either end, the lingering effects of the trip exposed Smith's dread of extreme weather and brought back the shaking in his limbs. If his staff was aware of that, it wasn't because he would tell them. Weakness of any kind was a plague all its own, especially when his men were struggling to advance through the hostility of the winter by moving on foot.

The progress was still grindingly slow, and Tenth Corps had only partly accepted Smith's explanation that the weather had greatly inhibited the march. Whether anyone around Ned Almond actually believed Smith's reasons for such sluggishness, Smith didn't really care. No one could accuse him of disobedience if his men were moving north. But Almond himself had his own agenda, and Smith was well aware that military considerations, including the physical suffering of his men, were secondary to Almond's sycophantic need to please Douglas Mac-Arthur.

The word had come that morning, even as Smith's jeep carried him southward from his visit to the Seventh in their camps above Koto-ri. Almond was making yet another visit to the Marines' headquarters. The thought was just one more incentive for Smith to advance his headquarters northward, where Almond's visits might become more infrequent.

On the far side of the room, he saw Craig, speaking into a radio phone, Craig eyeing him as he spoke.

"Yes, Colonel, he has just returned. I will share your concerns." Craig paused, and Smith could see he was absorbing a lashing from the other end of the line. "Yes, Colonel. General Almond is due here at any time, and I am certain that General Smith will express what needs to be, um, expressed. Goodbye, Colonel."

Craig put the telephone down, seemed exhausted. Smith said, "Puller?"

Craig nodded. "Tenth Corps still has him chasing guerrillas down there, and he's not happy about it."

"Lewie knows we're putting more distance between his people and the other two regiments every day. I've told him how I'm holding back progress as much as I can, but Lewie feels like he's stuck in the mud. I'll talk to General Almond again. When's he due here?"

Bowser emerged from one of the smaller offices, said, "Just got off the line with Tenth Corps HQ. He's on his way. Colonel Trotter says that the general is greatly pleased to be relocating his HQ to Hungnam."

Smith sagged, tried to hide it. "I expected that. It's protocol. Corps command needs to keep up with the corps."

"Yes, sir. Colonel Trotter says it will be good for us to be neighbors."

Smith said nothing, knew that Bowser and Craig both could read his thoughts. He drank from the coffee cup, the bitterness curling his tongue, the cup now empty except for a smudge of grounds in the bottom. But the cold still ran through his veins, and he ached for more, saw the pot on a small burner in one corner. One of the enlisted aides was up quickly, moving that way, the pot in hand.

"Please. Allow me, sir."

Smith waited for the cup to fill, the shaking in his hand nearly gone. The young man seemed not to notice, and Smith turned away, a soft, "Thank you, Corporal."

He heard the vehicles outside, the heavy rumble and squeal of brakes.

Craig motioned with his hand. "Has to be General Almond. One of the senior mechanics told me he won't let them lube his truck. Likes to make an entrance."

Bowser laughed, said, "Like Patton and his siren."

Smith wasn't in the mood for their playfulness, said to Craig, "The mechanics figure out how to get those helicopters working?"

Craig said, "Thinner oil. They're draining out the usual stuff. Once the new oil supply gets here, they say the choppers will be up to the task."

Smith kept his focus on the commotion outside, thought, Not soon enough.

The door opened with a flourish, an aide pushing inside, back flattened against the wall, holding the door wide open. Smith felt the blast of cold air, waited impatiently, no one appearing. Outside, the voices were boisterous, Almond greeting the men, shaking hands, as though visiting old friends. Smith hunched his shoulders, the heat in the small building sucked away, Almond's staff officer still keeping the door open, oblivious to the reaction of the Marines inside. Almond was there now, stopped in the doorway, appraising, and Smith was annoyed, his usual response to Almond's meaningless smile.

"Please come inside, sir. It takes a while for the heaters to do their job."

Almond stepped in, the door closing behind him, noticeable relief from the staff around Smith. Almond removed his gloves, the coat now pulled off his shoulders by his aide.

"Brisk, eh?" He looked toward Craig, said, "Hello, General. I understand you've been up at the front, prodding Colonel Litzenberg to make better time."

Craig didn't smile, said, "We both have, sir. General Smith and I have made daily runs to each of the regimental commands."

Almond looked down, slapped his hands together, said, "Is that right? With the kind of progress the Marines are making I had thought perhaps General Smith was occupied with other matters."

Smith fought himself not to react, said, "General Almond, my staff has a great deal of work to do here. Would you please join us in my office?"

"Lead the way."

Smith moved toward the smaller office, Craig there before him.

Craig stood aside, Smith sliding into a small folding chair, and he motioned toward another.

"Please sit, sir. No need to be uncomfortable."

Almond stood, his aide standing stiffly behind him. It was a game that Smith was used to, Almond not conceding any need for comfort. Craig knew the rules, said, "Do you mind if I sit, sir?"

Almond folded his arms across his chest. "Certainly. I've been sitting for a while in that infernal truck. Prefer keeping upright, keeping my back straight. There will be time for relaxing when this war is over."

Smith said nothing, wouldn't give Almond any kind of satisfaction. In short seconds, the silence grew heavy and Almond said, "We're relocating Tenth Corps HQ to Hungnam. I would like a company of Marines to serve as guards, security, so forth."

Smith saw the surprise on Craig's face, thought, A show of power.

Smith said, "Why do you require Marines? Is it not better if my men are sent forward? We might need every man we can put into this fight."

"What fight is that, Smith? So far, I have only heard reports of sniping, skirmishes, and an enemy who delights in keeping out of your way."

Smith felt the familiar boil. But, he thought, there has to be more to this visit than a request that could have come by phone. He said to Craig, "Get Bowser."

Craig seemed ready to sputter a protest, but he obeyed, went to the door, a sharp whisper. Bowser was there quickly, said, "Sir?"

Smith kept his eyes on Almond, Almond looking away, and Smith said, "General Almond requires a company of Marines to serve as security for his new HQ here. Find out who's nearby. Murray's people haven't completely taken to the road yet."

Bowser looked at Craig, the same expression of surprise. "An entire company? From the Fifth?"

"Is there some difficulty with that?"

Bowser's eyes stayed wide and he said, "No, sir. I believe Charlie Company is camped just down the road, preparing to march. Captain Jones, I believe. I'll send word for them to stand down, and send word to Colonel Murray."

"Do it."

Smith saw Almond's expression change, surprise, and then a beaming smile.

"You see, Smith? We're in this thing together. There is no need for argument on every point."

Smith looked at Craig, who stared back at him with disbelief.

"Certainly not."

Almond seemed energized now, said, "General MacArthur is most confident that this entire operation shall conclude without major complications. To that end, he has instructed me to make the best use of the assets I have available. There is concern in Tokyo that Eighth Army requires some assistance, that we should spread out closer to their right flank. I will obey, of course, and your men will bear that burden. But no one has told me that we cannot continue on our course toward the Yalu River. I know of no reason that Tenth Corps should not enjoy a share of our ultimate success." He paused, his eyes now on Smith. "I admit to being distressed at the lack of progress your men are making. The Yalu River is there for the taking, Smith. Tokyo has ordered an intense bombing campaign to continue all along the river. Naturally, General MacArthur is aware of the political necessity of avoiding any direct impact on Communist China. But on this side of the border, we are targeting every bridge, every village, every roadway, every avenue of escape the North Koreans can use. Our primary goal is, and has always been, to eliminate the North Korean armed forces in their entirety. And we are continuing to do so. Once your men reach the southern tip of that reservoir, I expect them to advance northward with far greater speed. I want them barreling down that road to Yudam-ni!"

"No."

The word came out in a short burst and Smith saw Craig's eyes grow wider still.

Almond seemed to stumble, leaned toward Smith. "Did you say . . ."

"I said no. I'm not barreling my men anywhere while they're so scattered. Hagaru-ri is a natural rendezvous point, a position we can defend against any sudden assault by the enemy. It is unacceptable to scatter this division in a way that severely hampers our effectiveness. General

Almond, I have expressed the view to you previously that the First Marine Division is a formidable weapon, the most powerful weapon at your disposal. But only if you allow that to be. You continue to insist that General Puller's men engage in a mop-up operation, chasing down fugitive bands of North Koreans. That is the waste of a valuable resource. There are army units assembled to our south who can easily accomplish that mission." He paused, a thought breaking through. "Is it not a good idea to allow the army the opportunity to reap the rewards of such a task? The Third Division has thus far served as a reserve, and they have not been allowed to share the attention that we have received. I would have thought that Tenth Corps would want to spread the glory, so to speak. Allow Third Division to earn their own headlines."

He saw Craig hiding a smile, kept his eyes now on Almond. Almond rubbed his chin, staring away, absorbing what Smith had said.

"I shall consider this. Regardless, you will receive confirmation of your orders to advance to Yudam-ni. Tokyo's concerns about Eighth Army must be addressed." Almond seemed to focus again. "By damn, Smith, you have to push your people harder! If we bomb those bridges, eliminate those villages, make life wholly miserable for the North Koreans, we must take full advantage! General MacArthur is doing his part, and it is possible that Eighth Army is doing theirs. I will not have us falling behind!"

"Sir, do you play chess?"

Smith nursed the pipe, soaking up the wonderful aroma. "Once or twice. Not good at it."

Craig chuckled. "I'll bet. Remind me never to play you. You checkmated Almond pretty effectively."

Smith shrugged, pulled at the pipe again. "Not really. I'm not too sure that what Tokyo has in mind will contradict what Almond's been ordering us to do, what he still expects us to do. It sounds like MacArthur has finally noticed that eighty-mile gap between us and Eighth Army."

"But what's the threat? G-2 keeps telling us that all those Chinese we ran into are a figment of our imagination. Almond still seems to believe that."

Smith held the pipe in his hands, shook his head. "I don't have the first idea what General Almond believes. But he wants to keep this show for himself, wants us to claim as much glory as anyone else in winning the war. If MacArthur tells him to reinforce Eighth Army, he will. But unless they tell him just how to do that, he'll spread us out even further. Count on it."

Craig slumped, his elbows on the small desk. "Where do you suppose the Chinese have gone?"

Smith poked at the dying embers in the pipe. "Nowhere. Litzenberg feels them in his bones, knows he's being watched every step he takes."

"I know. He told me that. We took a ride out near his vanguard, met a recon patrol just coming back in. They saw enemy on every hilltop but couldn't get close enough to get any more details. I tell you, sir, Litz is a nervous wreck. Every night, they get ready for another attack. If he's that nervous, I'm guessing his men feel it, too. The quicker we can move Murray up in support, the better. And Puller . . ."

"We'll get Puller. Even MacArthur knows that if they keep Puller for nothing but mop-up duty, Lewie's gonna blow up in somebody's face. It won't be mine."

Craig laughed again. "And Almond will avoid Puller's wrath, and make sure Third Division gets their share of the headlines. Two birds with one stone, and he wins both ways. You and your chess game."

"If you say so. Have we heard from General Barr?"

"Seventh Division? Not lately. The army doesn't go out of its way to talk to us."

Smith tapped the spent pipe on the edge of the desk. "He will. Barr's a part of this, too, and he's no happier with Almond than I am. They have to include the ROK in any drive to the Yalu, and I don't think Tokyo trusts them to push hard without the army's help. Seventh Division is on our right flank, and they won't just sit still while we get the glory." He paused. "I have to tell you, Eddie. I hate politics. But this war is too complicated to be left to generals."

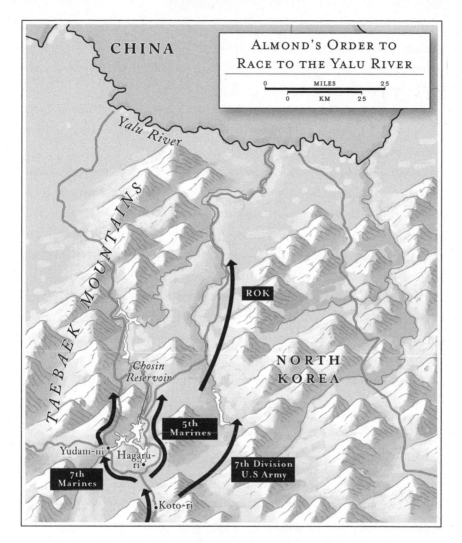

Craig laughed again. "Tell that to MacArthur."

Smith didn't laugh. "He's bombing civilians, you know. Taking out villages all over North Korea, in the name of squashing the North Korean army. Almond said as much right here. Bridges, sure, they're a tactical target. But villages? He calls them hiding places for the enemy. What do those civilians call them? *Home.* I can't believe that any North Korean is happy there are Chinese soldiers in their front yard. The civilians we've seen so far seem happy as the dickens that we're here. We start wiping out villages, bombing targets indiscriminately, those same civilians will turn against us. All those guerrillas we're supposed to be dealing with are leftovers from the North Korean army. But if their civilians join in the fight, or worse, if they decide the Chinese are the better option, things get a whole lot tougher."

Craig looked at him, seemed puzzled. "How? If there are as many Chinese out there as Litzenberg believes, that's trouble enough. How much harm can angry civilians do?"

Smith slipped the pipe into his pocket. "Poisoned water wells. Snipers on every hillside. Scorched earth waiting for us everywhere we try to march. On Okinawa, the Japanese made great use of Okinawan civilians to do their dirty work, freeing up the soldiers for the fight. Same thing could happen here. The Chinese would welcome North Koreans willingly carrying their lunch for them."

Craig had lost the smile now. "Hadn't really thought of it that way."

"Neither has Tokyo. But I bet General Lowe has made a point of this to the president. It's our job to kill the enemy's soldiers. After that, it's the government's job to make the enemy's civilians happy. We don't help that process if we've massacred the helpless."

HUNGNAM, NORTH KOREA—NOVEMBER 15, 1950

As Almond promised, the orders came once again, exactly as Smith expected. To the east, closer to the coastline, ROK units were to advance as rapidly as possible to the Yalu, thus granting them the full propaganda value of liberating their fellow Koreans from the grip of the oppressive communist government. The American army would move in support of the ROKs, primarily units of Barr's Seventh Division. Once the ROKs had wet their toes, it opened the way for the rest of the UN forces, primarily the Americans, to finish their drive to the river as well, sweeping away any enemy troops they encountered along the way. As Smith predicted, Tokyo insisted that the Marines begin to shift their march more to the west, closing the gap between Tenth Corps' left flank and the right of Eighth Army, who would be making their own drive northward. That task would fall to Litzenberg's Seventh. But Almond had held tightly to his own ambitions to have Tenth Corps shove their way north. At the base of the Chosin Reservoir, the town of Hagaru-ri spread out around a fork in the main road, which provided a route up both sides of the reservoir. With Litzenberg moving up the left side, Murray's Fifth Regiment would slide up to the east. While Litzenberg would satisfy MacArthur's apparent nervousness about closing the gap to their west, Murray's Fifth would continue the push as rapidly as possible toward the Yalu, which just might allow Ned Almond to claim bragging rights as to which troops had reached that goal first.

Through all the machinations, Oliver Smith recognized with increasing discomfort that his troops had been spread out like soft butter on an enormous slice of bread. To his relief, Tenth Corps had indeed ordered the army's Third Division to take control of the area patrolled by Chesty Puller's Marines. Immediately Puller was ordered to advance his First Regiment northward, first to secure the ground around the towns of Sudong and Chinhung-ni, and eventually to continue toward Koto-ri, filling in the gap left open by the advance of the rest of Smith's division.

The great supply dump at Koto-ri was only one of several all along the lengthy route from the seaports to the south. Though Ned Almond seemed completely oblivious to the hazards of supplying his troops along such a narrow and vulnerable route, Smith took the precaution of creating more of these supply depots in every place that could be fortified and protected. With the cooperation of the navy's supply teams, enormous convoys were pushed northward, Smith intending that they extend all the way to the base of the reservoir. If more were required farther north, he would create those as well.

The maps showed clearly that Hagaru-ri was a crucial intersection, where the Marines would divide their forces in two directions. It was obvious to Smith that the town be fortified as strongly as any along the way, and once Puller's Marines had reached Koto-ri, some fourteen miles to the south of Hagaru-ri, Smith could then position several of his own units, along with army and other UN forces made available to him, to reinforce and support the advances northward Almond had ordered.

Throughout all the planning, Smith was becoming increasingly concerned that Tokyo and Tenth Corps seemed unwilling to accept that there was an enemy in front of them still, whether or not the reconnaissance efforts had discovered just where they were. The euphoria that spread through the entire theater after the success at Inchon seemed to return, Ned Almond's optimism reinforced by the same spirit coming from Tokyo. The bloodying of the First Cavalry and the Marines' confrontation with the Chinese at Sudong had seemed to fade from the memory of the strategic planners in Tokyo. Even more alarming to Smith, MacArthur's intelligence officers, under General Charles Willoughby, had once again trumpeted their claim that whatever Chinese forces the army and Marines had confronted were minimal in strength and unlikely to pose any additional threats.

The contagious despair that flowed through Smith's headquarters came from his own nagging doubts that no one in Tokyo or at Tenth Corps had any real idea just how dangerous this campaign could still become. Smith embraced protocol as much as any officer in the war, but despite the chain of command that passed down from Tokyo, Smith also answered to what was in his mind a higher authority: General Clifton B. Cates, the commandant of the Marine Corps. On November 15, Smith penned a lengthy letter aimed directly at Cates, bypassing Almond, MacArthur, and his own immediate superior in the Corps, General Lemuel Shepherd, who commanded the Fleet Marine Force, covering the entire Pacific Theater. If there were to be repercussions for his doubts and objections, if Smith's impertinence would possibly end his career, he at least wanted the facts known to the highest-ranking Marine general.

Although the Chinese have withdrawn to the north, I have not pressed Litzenberg to make any rapid advance. Our orders still require us to advance to the Manchurian border. However, we are the left flank division of the Tenth Corps, and our left flank is wide open. There is no unit of the Eighth Army nearer than eighty miles. . . . I have little confidence in the tactical judgment of the Tenth Corps, or in the realism of their planning. . . . I believe a winter campaign in the mountains of North Korea is too much to ask of the American soldier or Marine. . . . We have reached a point now at the south end of the Chosin Reservoir where we will now have to review the situation. . . .

CHAPTER SEVENTEEN

. . . .

Riley

HAGARU-RI, NORTH KOREA—NOVEMBER 16, 1950

"NOT MUCH OF A TOWN. Shacks and stuff."

Riley ignored Killian's appraisal, heard Welch spit the words, "It's Korea, you Irish jackass. You expecting New York City?"

Riley moved farther from the gathering men, could feel too much anger, the kind that brings fistfights. It had been like this for the past couple of days, the increasing tension of the march, each day closer to what every man believed was a certain confrontation with the Chinese. Their edginess was made worse by the brutal misery of the weather, the harsh bite of the bitter winds, brief storms of icy snow. The nights were only slightly better, colder temperatures made bearable by the luxury of the sleeping bags, the men curling up into their foxholes sheltered from the worst of the wind. For those keeping watch, there was no respite at all, two hours of frozen fingers, frozen ears, frozen tears against red cheeks, eyes blinking desperately to see any movement in the darkness. If they had a free hand, the men would breathe into their hands, through their gloves, the only way to keep the worst of the cold out of their lungs.

With their arrival into Hagaru-ri, the weather had tempered, sunshine pushing the daytime temperatures just above freezing. For men who had endured the long nights in cold that was well below zero, forty degrees was positively balmy. Their coats came open now, their boots pulled off, wet socks allowed to dry.

Riley moved away from the rest of the platoon, gazing toward the sunshine, escaping the foul mood of Welch and the others. A gust of wind rolled past him, swirling dust in his face, and he turned away, too late, spit the grit from his mouth. The pain was sudden and searing, his lips split to bloody cracks. He put a gloved hand on his lips, thought, Damn it all! This won't be healing anytime soon. He reached for the canteen, shook it, the slosh of water evidence of a partial thaw. He drank, felt a bath of cold water washing away the grit, thought of spitting it out, No, drink. Can't hurt you. You've eaten plenty of dirt before. He thought of Barber, the new captain backing off from his threats to harden them up by dawn hikes. Says he ate gravel on Iwo Jima. Maybe so. I bet it didn't taste any better than what I ate on Okinawa. Jesus, I hope like hell he isn't some damn martinet, all talk about blood and guts, while he sits in the rear and plays cards.

He walked farther, others milling around, nowhere to go for the moment. The officers seemed content with organizing their command posts, some of the other companies put into position closer to the reservoir, strengthening their new defensive perimeter. He looked that way, could see a glimpse of the wide lake, oddly smooth in the blowing wind. Ice, he thought. Wonder how thick? Back home it would be January before you could walk out on a pond. But it wasn't hardly ever twenty below. He flexed his toes, painfully stiff, thought of the socks. You're wearing all three pairs, you moron. Take 'em off, dry 'em out. Or toss 'em in a fire drum and get some more. There's gotta be supplies around here.

He heard the rumble of a tank, four machines clanking closer. He stepped aside, stared at each one as it passed him, moving out on the road that stretched east of the reservoir. I bet they got heat inside those things. Maybe too much heat. No place to hide, either. He could never watch the tanks without thinking of coffins, the old joke that burying a tanker was cheaper, since they carried their own tombs with them. Not me, he thought. I'll settle for the rifle and two feet. I need to duck, I'll duck. The dust rose up around him, and he covered his face, stepped off the road. Damn. Got me good. He blew at the crud in his nostrils, turned toward his platoon, the men doing mostly what he was, seeing the sights. His eyes settled on the road to the south, more trucks moving up, pulling off to one side, contributing to another supply depot. I guess we're pretty secure, for all that to be brought in here. I'd like to see those boys from the Fifth come rolling in here. The more the merrier.

Litzenberg's Seventh spread out in camps closer to the reservoir, shifting out to the west, making space for Murray's Fifth coming through the valley right behind them. In every open place, tents were going up, some alongside whatever existing structure they could use. The artillery had begun to move in as well, the 105s and 155s rolling past, their officers parking them into formations, preparing them to move once more when the inevitable order came. Other guns were down below the town, ranged on the nearby hills, protection against any sudden appearance by the enemy. But so far the Chinese had kept away, allowing the Marines to move up unmolested to the southern tip of the vast reservoir, building a massive supply depot as formidable as what Smith had moved into Koto-ri.

Throughout the town, aid stations had been established, medical teams inspecting their inventory. The chaplains had established their own kind of aid station, and already men were seeking out the Catholic priest, Father Cornelius Griffin, who was receiving confessions in his makeshift church.

Each company's supply officers had begun to organize the enormous stores of ammunition and every other tool the men would require, from barrels of gasoline and oil to great mountains of C-rations. But not all the rations would be dry. Kitchens were being erected, tubs and pots set over fire pits, the men who watched curious just what kind of luxury the officers might provide them, or if those treats were kept only for the brass.

The engineers had begun work on an entirely new project as well. The Marines watched with curiosity, far out along the edge of the town, green bulldozers and tractors rumbling along a long flat stretch of mostly level ground, great dirt movers scraping the earth, dirt piling high, flattening it out again. The project began to take shape immediately, and the men could see that the effort was lengthwise, a wide and flattened roadway, long enough to serve as a runway. Marine engineers were performing the work that, to Smith's enormous frustration, the army's engineers had refused to do. If the Marines at Hagaru-ri wanted a landing strip, they would build it themselves.

Riley moved closer to the others, heard more of the bickering, another argument between the sergeant and Killian. Goolsby was there now, the smaller man pushing himself into the fray, a scolding as harsh as the young lieutenant dare offer. Killian backed away, Welch still bowed up, Goolsby's hand on his chest. Riley moved more quickly, thought, Careful, Lieutenant. He's got an idiot's temper sometimes. Hate to see him end up in the brig.

Riley watched Welch march off, sitting down on an old wooden box. He moved closer, studied Welch's stare, knew not to push too hard.

"Hey, Sarge. What's up?"

"What the hell do you want? That Irish son of a bitch needs to stuff his skivvies in his mouth. Sometimes I just don't need to hear a load of bitching about nothing at all."

Riley stared out, said, "There's supplies coming in like mad. Maybe some decent food. New winter clothing, maybe other stuff that'll do us some good."

Welch looked up at him, squinted slightly. "Your face looks like you been sleeping on needles."

Riley put a hand on the rawness of his cheeks. "Ice, I guess. Last night, that was rough. Felt like needles. Feels good to get somewhere we can just sit."

"I don't want to sit. I want to shove my bayonet into Charlie Chink's guts. It's been two weeks and all we've done is march. I bet he's out there. Laughing his ass off. Old Homer thinks so. The new battalion chief does, too. Colonel Lockwood. Has his binoculars up to his eyeballs every time I see him. Jumpy as hell."

"Haven't met the man."

Welch pulled out the canteen, sloshed a drink in his mouth, spit it out. "Squat little guy. Short like Old Homer, but round everywhere. If it wasn't for the uniform, you'd think he was mayor of Munchkinland."

Riley laughed.

The wind came in a new burst, swirling around him, dust driven into his face again, grinding at his eyes. He turned away, one hand up on his face, blinking hard.

"Damn it all. How much of this is enough?"

Welch said nothing, and he heard a new voice, the kid.

"Hey, Sarge. Hey, Pete. What's all the equipment doing out there? They been at it all night. A lot of work, for sure."

Riley cleared his eyes, saw Morelli staring out toward the rumbles of the heavy equipment. "Airstrip, maybe. They want supplies brought in, maybe it's better to do it by air."

Welch turned that way, said, "Nah. They're not building an airstrip to bring stuff in. It's to take stuff out. Wounded. We're a long damn way from any hospital. We ain't done with the enemy, and where there's enemy there's wounded."

Riley realized Welch was probably right. Beside him, Morelli said, "I love that big stuff. Used to play with all kinds of tractors and stuff when I was a kid."

The words inspired a memory in Riley, a Christmas present, a very small version of the dozers he saw now. He let that go, had no energy for Morelli's good cheer.

They stood silently for a long moment, the heavy equipment holding their attention, and now, another new voice, Lieutenant McCarthy.

"Listen up! There's mail! That six-by behind those tents. Don't get lost. We're still waiting for orders to dig in."

The men reacted with a sudden explosion of energy, a wave rolling quickly that way. Riley watched for a few seconds, and Welch said, "Well, let's go. It's been two weeks. Ought to be something worth getting."

Morelli didn't hesitate, joined the flow, and Welch looked at Riley.

"You got a bug up your ass? It's mail, for God's sake."

Riley shrugged.

"So, go on. At least one of your fifteen girlfriends might have written you."

"What about you? What the hell's wrong?"

Welch's voice softened, the sergeant knowing Riley's moods. Riley said, "Not sure. Just been thinking about things. You remember Levinson, in Baker Company? We went through boot with him. Okinawa, too."

"Yeah, I think. He the one who went nutso? He never came back, did he?"

Riley pictured the man in his mind, the screaming tantrum that ended only when the MPs wrestled away his bayonet.

"Nope. He got one of those damn awful letters. His wife just ended their marriage, just like that. Hell of a thing to do in a letter. I guess she couldn't take being alone. Or she got bored. It just ripped his guts out."

"Maybe she found some stateside stud. He's better off. Probably in some comfy nuthouse somewhere. What's that got to do with . . . now?"

He looked at Welch, shivered, had kept the thoughts away as long as he could. "I'm scared as hell Ruthie's gonna do that. Always have been. Every time I'm in the field, I think she's starting to hate me just a little bit more. Hell, she's got a four-year-old to handle. He's a load, too. She needs help. Maybe some other *stateside stud*."

Welch stared hard at him, said, "You're an asshole. That woman is as feisty and full of vinegar as anyone I know. When I met her, I thought, Oh, she's cute. Tiny little thing, a stiff breeze'll blow her over. Hell, then I saw her get mad. She's like some kind of she-wolf, protecting her den. I guaran-damn-tee you, she's sitting at home making lists of your chores, your projects, all the things you need to do when you get home. And all the things that little boy needs from nobody else but his dad. And I bet she's writing you a letter every damn day. They'll need another truck just to haul *your* crap. Let me tell you something, Private. You got lucky, and so did she. I seen it plain as day. And she knows it. You better damn well remember it. I'd write her myself, tell her you're down in the dumps, except she might kick my ass for telling her."

"Or I might."

Riley smiled now, and Welch stood, his hand going up to Riley's shoulder.

"Listen. My girlfriends, yeah, they're great. Some real knockouts. I might even see one or two of them when this is over. But, Pete, you've got a *home* waiting for you. I've been in that home. I've seen her look at you. You're *it*. Now get the hell over there and grab a pile of her letters."

He could tell Welch was waiting for him to move.

"Not sure where this came from, Hamp. Just happened all of a sudden. I thought of Levinson, how he came apart. Scares me. We're so damn far away."

"So, you're scared. Me, too. Miserable, cold as hell. You know all that talk about being home for Christmas? They could be right. The Chinks have backed away, and maybe they're backing off all the way to China. Look around you, right here, those big guns, that squad of tanks that rolled through. If Charlie Chink's paying attention, he can see it all. And they got families, too. And, from what I've seen, crappy-assed shoes. This war might be over and we just don't know it yet."

Riley scanned the horizon, one massive hill to the east. He looked at Welch now, saw the concern still on his friend's face. Riley forced a smile.

"It's the *army* brass that's telling us about Christmas. You ever know the army to get anything right?"

Welch slapped him on the back, gave a small push. "Just go read your damn mail. Then you can read mine. I won't remember what half those broads look like. Then you can tell me who's got the better deal."

Riley moved forward, the cold stiffness in his toes slowing him, a slight stagger to his steps. He saw the kid, carrying a long, thin package, beaming smile, more smiles on the faces of the others. Killian came toward them now, another package, his voice loud, boisterous.

"I knew it! You just wait till you see this! I asked, and she came through!"

Killian moved on by, Riley looking at the truck, two men up in the back, handing out the parcels to a pair of men below, names calling out. Riley hesitated, saw only packages, and Welch moved ahead, said, "What you got for Sergeant Welch?"

"Right here, Sarge. Nice little pile."

Welch took the letters, turned to Riley, held them up. "Okay, it's your turn."

Riley stepped closer, saw only boxes, bundles, paper, and string. He felt the nervousness again, tightness in his chest. "I don't see any more letters."

One of the men up in the truck tossed an empty cloth sack aside.

"Nope, that's it. What's your name?"

"PFC Pete Riley."

The man slapped his buddy, said, "So, this is him."

Both men stared down at Riley with leering smiles.

"What's up? There anything for me?"

One of the men in front of him turned, his hand reaching back into the truck.

"We had to make you a pile. Next time you'll get your own bag. Jesus, buddy, what's your trick?"

Riley was curious, saw a thick wad of envelopes.

"Trick for what?"

All four men laughed, and one said, "The whole truck smells like perfume now. There's weapons requisitions that smell like they been to Paris and back. And it's all yours. You musta done *something* right."

Welch said, "They both done something right."

The man tossed the bundle into Riley's hands, the scent of her rolling over him, so familiar, so very wonderful. He gripped the letters, lifted them to his face, saw her in his mind, her smiling playfulness. He stepped back, Welch still waiting, and Welch said, "See? Told you so. Don't ever doubt me again."

"I'll doubt you plenty. It's *her* I won't doubt."

They sat in a small group, silence broken by cheerfulness, each letter bringing some new reaction.

Riley read the letters again, third time around, every one telling him how ridiculous he was for being afraid. He held back a fresh tear, and beside him Welch said, "Good stuff, huh?"

Riley nodded, an unstoppable smile. "My boy's growing up fast. Knocked hell out of some army officer's kid in school."

"My kind of kid."

Riley shook his head. "He misses his old man. So does she. You were right, Hamp. Every bit of it."

Welch said nothing, tossed a handful of his own letters down to his feet, and across from him Kane said, "Hey, Sarge. You mind if I read 'em? I hear all you get is good old nasty ones."

Welch said, "Hell, no." He reached down, scooped them together, shoved them into his coat. "You want good letters, get yourself a bunch of good women. Best if they're . . . enthusiastic."

Riley leaned close, said, "You still telling them you're a general?"

"MacArthur's son-in-law."

Welch laughed, and Riley absorbed that, was relieved to see the humor, spreading now through all of them. Behind him, he heard a shout, turned, saw Morelli running toward them, a long stick of something red in his hands.

"Hey, fellows! Look what my mama sent me. It's a salami!"

Welch grabbed the boy, sat him down beside him. "Careful with that. It might be loaded. It any good?"

"Oh yeah, Sarge. There's a grocer in my neighborhood, Corso and Sons. Makes it himself. The best." Morelli sniffed the salami, all of three feet long, the others staring with wide, lustful eyes. Morelli looked around, said, "Hey, Sarge, you think it would be okay if I passed it around, maybe let the squad have a chunk? Ain't enough for the whole platoon."

Welch pulled out his Ka-Bar, sliced off a four-inch section from the end. "Just what I was thinking."

"Well, good, Sarge. Yeah, pass it around. I can't eat the whole thing."

Welch handed the salami to Riley, who sniffed it, his hand out for Welch's knife. He sliced off a hefty piece for himself, the next man with his knife already drawn. They passed it quickly, a dozen men whittling the stick down to a fat nub, the last few inches returning to Morelli.

Welch said, "You tell your mama she can send everything that grocer makes. She wants, we'll mail her some C-rations in return."

"Sure, Sarge."

Riley nibbled a stiff bite from the salami, a roar of flavor filling him. He looked at Morelli, nodded.

"Good stuff, kid."

The others agreed, comments made through sloppy mouthfuls. Across from Riley, Kane said, "You're okay, kid."

Welch put his arm around Morelli's shoulders.

"My buddy's name is Joey." Welch released him, said, "You learned something, kid. You wanna grease up to a bunch of old jarheads, bribe 'em with food. But keep it coming. We got short memories."

"Hey! Lookee here! I told you! I knew it!"

Riley knew Killian's shouts, saw him walking up toward the group with an arrogant strut. Welch looked down to his feet, said, "Oh, good Christ. What now?"

Killian stood above them, said, "No, Sergeant. It's good *Colleen*. I told you she'd come through. Just look at this."

Riley saw the bundle, brown paper embracing a fat loaf of bread, said, "She baked you some bread?"

Killian leaned the package toward him. "No, Pete. Well, yes. But it's her secret ingredient. Lookee *here*."

Killian reached into the bread, pulled out a small round bottle. Riley was intrigued now, said, "What the hell's that?"

"My favorite Irish whiskey. She knows she can't just ship me a bottle or two by itself. It would end up in some squid's locker. Those bastards all have sticky fingers. So she sticks it inside a loaf of bread. Keeps it from breaking, too. Pretty damn genius, eh?"

Welch said, "She's a hell of a lot smarter than her husband. You see what Morelli did? He got a treasure from home, shared it with his whole squad. Since you told us all about Colleen and her talents for gift-giving, it appears you've got an obligation to your buddies."

Killian took a step back, and Riley saw the pain on his face.

"You serious, Sarge?"

"Listen, Private, you ever want any of these jarheads to cover your ass in a fight, you better learn when to share."

Killian seemed defeated, opened the bottle, took a lengthy sip. He blinked hard, let out a breath. "Hooee. Never better."

He handed the bottle to Riley, who sniffed cautiously, felt the burn rising through his nostrils.

"Holy cow, Sean." He took a slow sip, the fire ripping through his sinuses. He grunted, handed the bottle to Welch, who took his sip, paused, then took another, drawing an audible groan from Killian. Welch fought to gather himself, said, "Good Christ. We hand this stuff out, won't nobody even know it's winter."

Their stay in Hagaru-ri was to be brief, Colonel Litzenberg already aware that orders had been issued for the Seventh to resume their march on the main road that ran northwesterly, alongside the west side of the reservoir, toward the next town of Yudam-ni. From there they would turn on a more westerly course, a road that would carry them across the razorback peaks of the Taebaek Mountains, moving out into the yawning gap between the Tenth Corps and Walker's Eighth Army. Behind them, Murray's Fifth was making preparations to march eastward, far along the opposite side of the reservoir, moving closer to their ultimate goal, the Yalu River.

CHAPTER EIGHTEEN

. . . .

Riley

THE BRUTAL COLD had returned, sweeping down the valleys that framed the reservoir, a thickening layer of ice forming quickly on the surface. The men had attacked whatever labor their officers could find for them, gathering various gear, piling supplies into trucks, the men trying to walk the tightrope of laboring to keep warm, but not so much to build sweat up inside their boots and clothing. It rarely worked.

They began to discover new challenges, especially during the subzero nights. Sleep was still difficult, though the men were adapting to what luxury they had come to appreciate from their sleeping bags. Eating had created problems of its own. The C-rations were mostly frozen solid now, the few exceptions those cans a man could hold stuffed inside his coat, jammed into an armpit, or, when sleeping, pushed down inside of long johns. Frustrated men still attacked their frozen canned goods, chewing on anything they could slice or crack free, swallowing lumps of icy beef stew or fruit cocktail. But that impatience came with a harsh cost, the frozen food causing an unexpected and very uncomfortable intestinal ailment, and a twisted gut created problems of its own. From their first days wearing the heavier winter clothes, the men had learned just how difficult it was to relieve themselves, even the simple act of urination a struggle when digging through so many layers of clothing. The urgency of diarrhea made that task even more of a challenge, some of the men never reaching the latrines, jogging instead into a cluster of brush, seeking relief behind some shack or supply tent. Even then, the task of undoing the dungarees, of digging through layers of long johns, was often too difficult. There was embarrassment to be sure, the taunting ridicule toward soiled pants from the others in every squad, most of them the loud-mouths who had somehow avoided the miserable affliction. But then the ailment would strike them as well, a kind of justice that even the sickest men enjoyed. Very soon, the shared misery became shared compassion, no one teasing a man for relieving himself inside his clothes. It had become one more part of the torment of this astonishing winter.

Through the misery of trial and error, the men discovered that one part of their C-rations seemed immune to the harsh cold: Tootsie Rolls. Riley learned with the others that holding the chewy candy in your mouth would soften it fairly quickly, making it palatable. The added benefits of course were that the Tootsie Rolls gave the men a brief charge of energy, and even better, they tasted good. The supply officers had responded to that discovery with surprising efficiency, a substantial supply available for every man. Along with the ever-present Hershey bars, the men had discovered another treat that was far easier to eat than anything that came in a can: jelly beans.

They formed up into a ragged line, rifles and carbines hung on shoulders, Lieutenant McCarthy moving past, a quick inspection. Riley had welcomed the order to patrol, anything to stretch cold, stiffened muscles, but around him, the griping poured out, the mood of the men as sour as it had been for days. Riley ignored all of that, held his words inside, thought, It's been quiet in these hills. If we gotta go up there, this is a good time to do it.

McCarthy stood at the head of the column now, turned to them, his beet-red face hidden by the fog of his breath.

"Listen up! Recon has struck out in those hills to the north, and they're moving out again to the west. Our orders are to move up in support, protecting their flank, while they hit those ridgelines. There are reports of enemy concentrations out a few miles that way. I don't think we'll be going that far, just making sure nobody's sneaking up closer to where we are now."

McCarthy kept talking, his words trailing away from Riley's hearing, swept off by a new burst of wind. Riley heard more griping close by, a chorus of cursing from Killian, groans from some of the others. He looked down, the hood of the parka clamped around his face, began marching in place, keeping his legs in motion. Whatever order the lieutenant got doesn't matter a hill of beans, he thought. Let's just march. If the Chinks are there, they'll let us know.

He felt the soft wad under his arms, the spare pair of socks. It was second nature now, a second pair always at hand, a third in his backpack. The wind slowed and he looked toward McCarthy, the lieutenant waving them forward, a harsh shout, "Let's move out!"

They marched out along the road to the north, McCarthy moving them in a slow, methodical pace. It was routine now, a slower gait helping keep the socks dry, the sweat off their backs, at least for a while longer. He led them around the first bend, then another hundred yards, Riley keeping his head down, avoiding the amazing wind. He glanced out to the side, toward the reservoir, snow swirling across the ice, thought, Heavy enough for a truck to drive on it, I bet. Somebody else's truck. I'll stick to hard ground.

The column halted, four dozen men drawing up closer, McCarthy pointing up to the left. "Time to climb."

Riley was already warming up, the heft of his clothing giving him more protection now than he needed. There was griping even about that, and he ignored it, had known men who tossed aside various pieces of gear, lightening their loads, only to beg desperately for a handout when their sweat turned cold. He followed the line as it began to move up through the rocky ground, a gentle slope at first. The men in front of him moved in slow, deliberate steps, the pace set by McCarthy, a side hill climb, gaining altitude slowly, keeping the sweat away as long as possible. Riley looked up, small clouds moving past quickly, chased away by the wind. The sky was mostly clear, a piercing blue spreading out above them. There was snow on the hill, but not much, most of that blown into shallow drifts, wrapping around the low brush they stepped past. Farther up, he saw another line of men, easing upward a couple hundred yards farther along the hill. Recon, he thought. I guess so. He wouldn't ask, knew it didn't really matter who they were as long as they were Marines. At least we got some help if we run into the Chinks. He felt his breathing, the stab of cold into his lungs, tried to slow that down, but the climb was growing steeper, the sweat now forming on his back and, of course, inside his boots. He tried to guess how far they had come, knew that didn't matter, either, that McCarthy would lead them wherever it was the captain had ordered them to be. He had started to warm to Captain Barber, the man not hanging as hard to his ridiculous orders to shape up the company. In this cold, exercise at dawn was just torture, and Barber had seemed to understand that he had enough veterans that could shape up most of the new men along the way. Instead of mindless fitness drills, Barber had focused instead on sharpshooting skills, close-range tactics, so many of the lessons most of the veterans had learned in boot camp. Barber understood that these replacements were being shipped overseas with very little of the preparation every commander hoped for. At least by the time Fox Company reached Hagaru-ri, Barber had implanted just a bit more fighting ability into men whose lives might ultimately depend on it.

Riley paused, let out a foggy breath, pushed down hard on a narrow rock, boosting himself up, one hand reaching for a leafless shrub. He saw one man up ahead stumble, saw the frightened look on the man's very young face. Riley watched as he was helped back to his feet, the others pausing just long enough to keep the formation together. God, they're young, he thought. I just hope they had enough boot to do all of us some good. It's bad enough I gotta listen to so much bitching from the veterans. And Welch won't put up with any crybabies. McCarthy neither. This ain't Mount Everest, but sure as hell, some eighteen-year-old out here is calling for his mama because his feet hurt.

"Halt here! Sit down, move up close together."

He saw McCarthy pointing, the ground flattening into a shelf on the hill, a deep gouge in the rocks that offered shelter from the wind. It was a welcome break, the men sliding in close, sitting on the rocky ground, the clusters of dark green huddling together like so many lumps of clay. Riley waited his turn, moved in close to one man, saw it was Welch, a quick nod, Welch ignoring him. He sat, pulled his M-1 in tight to his chest, flexed his fingers. Like so many others, he had sliced the tip off the trigger finger of his glove, and he curled his bare forefinger under, squeezed it with his thumb. Don't freeze, he thought. Might need you. No need to be stingy with the clips, either. They'll give us turds to eat, but they ain't gonna let us run out of ammo.

McCarthy was out in front of them, staring farther up the hill, the radioman kneeling beside him. McCarthy knelt now, spoke into the radio, listened, then spoke again. "What? Repeat. Again! Oh, for Chrissakes."

McCarthy stood, hands on his hips, said, "The radio is crap. This damn cold has wrecked the batteries. Hell, it's probably left over from Guadalcanal."

Goolsby rose up from down the row, moved out toward McCarthy, said, "Think we shoulda brought walkie-talkies?"

McCarthy shook his head. "Tried that already. They won't reach more than fifty yards in these hills. Let's try to make visual contact with recon. Rest time's over. Let's go."

The men began to rise, the platoon following McCarthy once more, out into the open, the climb resuming. Riley felt the wetness in his socks, the sweat on his back already chilling him. Keep moving, he thought. The clouds were completely gone now, the sun straight overhead. But the winds were relentless, the wisps of snow blowing over his boots, the low scrub brush shuddering as they moved past. McCarthy halted them, a brief rest, men sagging, some leaning down with hands on their knees. Riley could see all of Hagaru-ri now, the reservoir to one side, a frosty white, the thickening ice draped with several inches of snow.

McCarthy waved them forward, the men responding, and Riley looked up the mountain, then down to his feet, searched for the next place to step, felt a hard hand pulling his arm. Around him, men were flattening out, and Riley dropped hard, pain in his shoulder, a protest forming in his brain. The hand released him and he saw Welch, down close to him, black eyes staring out past him. Riley turned that way, saw movement on the hill above them, yellow shapes scurrying up, moving quickly out of sight. He felt a jolt in his chest, gripped the rifle, others around him already prone, aiming. McCarthy rose up, motioned up to the left, a harsh whisper, "Goolsby! Take first squad. Go that way. Try to cut them off."

Goolsby was up quickly, a wide-eyed stare at Welch, who rose to his knees, his squad responding. Riley pulled himself up, still the stabbing pain in his shoulder, the impact with an unfriendly rock. They began a steeper climb, Welch moving up beside Goolsby. The hill seemed to roll now, a low dip, then another short rise, and Riley kept pace, felt his breathing in heavy bursts, thought, They could have shot us. You can't see up more than fifty yards.

There was a cluster of low brush, the squad's dozen men moving into cover, Welch holding them up. Welch said something to Goolsby, who responded with a vigorous nod. Welch looked back, searched faces, saw Riley, a quick wave of his hand. He motioned to Kane now, another wave, the BAR man moving forward, a quick glance at Riley. Riley pushed his boots upward, a single step, then another, did as Welch did, the sergeant bent low. They were clear of the brush now, easing over a hump on the hill. Riley's brain was screaming at Welch, Slow down! He glanced back to the others, still lying low in the brush, the face of Goolsby peering up like a startled bird. Riley looked again toward Welch, took another slow step, and now Welch stopped, brought his carbine to his shoulder. Riley moved up slowly, saw what Welch saw, the mouth of a small cave. Welch looked back at Kane, pointed at the BAR, Kane staring back at him, a sharp nod. Welch took another step, then motioned with his hand, *go*. He leapt forward, Riley following, Kane to one side. Welch led them to one side of the cave, dropped, slid in flat beside the opening, the others close beside him, and Riley caught the smell, pungent, unmistakable. *Garlic.*

Welch kept silent, pulled a grenade from his coat, his arm swinging
in a sidearm pitch, the grenade disappearing into the cave. They ducked
low, the blast erupting in a cloud of dirt, and Welch yelled at Kane.

"Do it!"

Kane responded, the BAR at his waist, a spray of fire into the cave.
Riley pointed the M-1 into the opening, waited, searching for movement, any kind of target, the wind sweeping the dust to one side. Welch
started forward, into the cave, barely high enough for a man to stand, no
more than six feet wide. He stopped, pointing the carbine, and Riley
stepped forward, M-1 ready, the smoke still blowing past, choking dust.
Riley searched the space, no one there, Kane now tight behind them,
the BAR reloaded.

Welch lowered the carbine, looked at Riley. "You hungry?"

Riley kept his stare into the dusty hole, saw it wasn't more than a few
yards into the hill. "What? Hell no."

There was commotion behind them, the rest of the squad moving up
close. Goolsby was there, pushing into the opening of the cave.

"What happened? You get them?"

Welch said, "Hey, Lieutenant, could we go back outside? It's a little
tight in here."

"What's that stink? Your grenade?"

They moved out into the cold sunlight again and Riley saw the usual
frown on Welch's face.

"That stink, Lieutenant, is Charlie Chink. Anybody need a snack,
there's rice plastered all over the walls. And a few busted-up bowls.
Looks like we interrupted somebody's lunch."

They had returned to the camp, the recon patrol making the same report they had for days now. The enemy was there, in very small numbers,
and no one seemed to want to fight. But this time there was a difference. This time recon had hauled in a pair of prisoners.

Riley had been as curious as the rest of the squad, the new men in
particular aching to get their first look at just who they were supposed

to fight. They had been taken to a small house, back near Litzenberg's command post, and Riley waited in the cold, Morelli there as well, a half-dozen others around them, most of those from the recon unit. He saw a familiar face, said, "You're Corporal Glenn, right?"

"Yeah. I know you?"

"Riley, Fox Company. You grabbed the prisoners?"

"I was there. We saw them ducking away from you, and we just sat down and waited. You blew up that cave, they got the message, hauled ass and tripped right over us. Six of 'em. These two collapsed, whimpered like babies, so, here they are."

Riley thought, The other four? But Glenn didn't offer, and he knew better than to ask.

"Our lieutenant said we could grab a look at 'em. This is Morelli. He's pretty fresh. Thought it would do him good to smell one."

Glenn looked at Morelli, who offered a sheepish smile. Glenn said, "Take a good whiff, kid. You smell that again out in these hills, you'll know you're close. Hey, there's the interp. I guess you boys can go on in, unless somebody tells you to get lost. I'm going to sleep."

Riley waved toward Glenn as he moved away, and Morelli said, "Interp? You mean the interpreter?"

Riley looked at him, said, "What the hell else could it mean? These Chinks weren't born in New Jersey."

The interpreter was accompanied by a pair of officers, the men moving into the house, more men already inside.

Riley said, "Try to look like you belong here. Come on."

He led Morelli into the house, a guard beside the door, a bored glance at Riley.

Riley said in a low voice, "We were there. We've got orders to observe."

The guard yawned, said nothing, and Riley pulled Morelli by the arm, moved past a small office, a typewriter on a wooden desk. The men had gathered in a larger room, and he kept Morelli back, just outside the doorway. He saw the prisoners, seated on small metal chairs. They still wore their quilted uniforms, but there were no hats, no restraints, nothing binding their hands. Riley thought, They don't look scared. They just look curious. The room was crowded, a pair of officers standing to one side, others that Riley couldn't see. The interpreter was a short, thin man, obviously Asian, and he stood in front of the prisoners, then looked to one side, said with a heavy accent, "I can begin, sir?"

Riley eased forward, peered past the doorway, saw that the man had spoken to Colonel Litzenberg. Riley flinched, thought, Never been this close to Old Homer. He glanced back at Morelli, who stared mesmerized at the prisoners, whispered, "Keep quiet."

Morelli nodded, his eyes still on the Chinese.

Litzenberg said, "Go to it, Captain. See what they know."

The interpreter spoke to the prisoners, what sounded to Riley like a chorus of meaningless noise. He watched the prisoners absorb what he assumed to be questions, was surprised to see a broad smile on one man's face. The prisoner responded now, a chorus of his own, his hands gesturing, pointing, nodding, more chatter. Riley was baffled, thought, These guys aren't anything like Japs. It looks like they're having . . . fun.

The interrogation went on for close to a half hour, the same routine, questions from the interpreter, enthusiastic responses from the Chinese soldiers, the interpreter relaying their answers to one of the officers, who jotted furiously on a legal pad. Through it all, Riley felt drawn into the conversation, the prisoners completely willing to talk about anything the interpreter asked them, offering up as much information as they seemed to have.

The house was growing warmer, Riley starting to sweat beneath his parka, the monotony of the questioning hypnotizing. He blinked hard, shifted his weight, Morelli still close to him. The interpreter ended the routine now, turned to Litzenberg, said, "I've gotten all we're going to get, sir. The conclusion is that these men believe what they're saying, and they insist there are several thousand Chinese troops in the hills to the west, and many more to the north around Yudam-ni. They were part of an observation detail, and they didn't expect us to go up after them. They're both asking for something to eat."

One of the officers looked up, seemed suddenly to notice Riley, and he pointed to the door, said to one of the guards inside the room, "Close that, Sergeant."

The door swung shut in Riley's face, jarring him awake. He backed up, said to Morelli, "Time to go, kid."

They moved quickly outside, the cold a bracing shock, and Morelli said, "Wow! That was amazing! They just talked and talked. I was told, don't never say nothing. Name, rank, and serial number."

Riley searched through the activity around them, said, "Better yet, kid, don't get captured. I think we go this way."

"Hey, Pete. What's that smell?"

Riley caught the aroma, unmistakable. It was cooked meat.

"Let's find out. Try to look official."

He led Morelli toward a row of tents, steam rising from enormous pots, huge platters covered in canvas tarps.

"Looks like you boys are first in line. Step on in."

Riley saw the smiling face of an officer, tried to return the smile, said, "Yes, sir. I guess we're first."

He moved up to the first tent, kitchen workers there with enormous forks, and the officer said, "You forget your mess kit? No problem. There's a few tin plates back here. Here you go."

Riley took the plate, handed another to Morelli, and he stepped closer to the incredible smells. Behind the long table, another officer appeared, another smile.

"What's your unit, boys?"

"Fox Two Seven, sir."

The man wrote something on a pad, said, "Ah, yes, Colonel Lockwood's Second Battalion. He's new. Don't know him yet. Fox Company, eh?"

"Yes, sir."

The tarp closest to Riley was pulled back, and he stared at a massive pile of sliced turkey. Behind him, Morelli said, "Good God. That for us?"

Riley winced, thought, You blow this one, kid, and I'll strangle you. But the officer said, "Of course it's for you! It's Thanksgiving, you know! Division has sent turkey and all the fixings. There's kitchen units set up for every company, even out in the boonies. Ah, here come some more of you boys. I guess the word spread."

Riley saw a herd of men stampeding toward the tents, plates in hand. There were MPs there now, keeping order, lines forming in front of the tents, the aides filling the plates from an assortment of tubs and trays. Riley watched as the man in front of him speared the turkey, flopping it on his plate, another man ladling out sweet potatoes and gravy, others with fruit salad, pieces of mince pie. He watched with pure lust as his own plate grew heavier, a dish of shrimp cocktail the final prize. He felt himself pushed to one side, didn't object, slid away from the throng. All around him, men were shouting, cheering the joy of the moment. Morelli was there now, staring at the feast on his plate, said, "This is amazing, Pete! We gotta find the camp, tell the others."

"They already know. That officer said there were kitchens set up everywhere."

Riley pinched a slice of turkey in his gloved fingers, dropped it into his mouth. He closed his eyes, savored the astonishing flavor, put his face down, licked at the gravy.

Beside him, Morelli said, "Damn. It's cold already."

"Chow down while you can, kid."

Morelli fingered his plate, said, "My fruit's already froze up."

"Eat. Talk later."

Riley shoveled the food with his fingers, the gloves already stiffening with the wetness. He searched for a place to sit, moved away from the crowd, sat down heavily on the ground. Morelli landed beside him, and Riley stuffed another piece of turkey into his mouth, the gravy a thick glue. He fought through it, felt the cold in a lump pushing down his throat, stared at the plate, picked up the slice of pie, tried to pinch it, the pie already a frozen brick.

The entire Marine division had been provided with the luxury of a Thanksgiving dinner, the heavy trucks pushing all the way to Hagaru-ri with instructions to provide a generous feast. As word spread to the various camps, the men responded, gathering dutifully, warmed if only for a few seconds by the great vats of steaming food, pots of scalding coffee. Once loaded down, the men scampered back to their perches, and in nearly every case, the plummeting temperatures won the battle. Before the men could enjoy their Thanksgiving dinner, it had frozen solid.

CHAPTER NINETEEN

. . . .

Smith

TENTH CORPS HQ, HUNGNAM, NORTH KOREA—
NOVEMBER 23, 1950

THE TABLECLOTHS WERE white linen, the aides serving the officers clad in white vests, white gloves, the bowls of steaming vegetables set down between the enormous platters of turkey.

"Sir, right this way." Smith followed the aide to a chair near the end of one of the long tables. "Here you are, sir. Note the placecard."

Smith saw the small folded card on the table, his name written with script no Marine had ever used. He looked for Bowser, saw him at another table, scanning the name cards. Beside Smith, Chesty Puller was grumbling.

"Thank God I'm next to you. Won't have to think up something to say to some ground-pounding desk clerk."

Smith ignored him, watched as the other men began to seat themselves, happy chatter flowing through the room, more than two dozen senior officers from Tenth Corps offering up compliments to their host. The Marine air wing commander, General Field Harris, sat a few seats down from Smith, the only other Marine in the room. Smith caught his eye, saw an uncomfortable frown, Harris silently holding up a silver fork. Smith looked at his own place setting, all of it silver, the plates a fine bone china. The aides were pouring champagne now, and Almond stood at the head of the longest table, a champagne glass in his hand.

"If I may, gentlemen. My mess has prepared a wonderful feast for this occasion, most of it flown in fresh from Tokyo. I've always insisted that my command should have only the best, and on this Thanksgiving Day, I have seen to it!"

Officers raised their glasses, happy murmurs from men in dress uniforms, some of them unfamiliar to Smith. Smith held his glass aloft belatedly, the moment past, and he saw Bowser smiling at him. Smith stared at him, the silent message.

I hate parties. And this party, he thought, is utterly ridiculous.

Beside him, Puller leaned in close, said in a whisper just a bit too loud, "I had a pretty fair Thanksgiving mess planned for my HQ. Somebody found a vulture, dressed it up to look like Tom Turkey."

Smith wasn't sure if Puller was kidding or not. He said nothing, thought of the turkey that had been provided for his own staff by the navy's Admiral Doyle, a generous offering, a symbol of the navy's quiet support for Smith's efforts. And I'm here. China and silverware. And placecards. We're in the middle of a war, for crying out loud.

Puller leaned in again, said, "I forgot to polish my boots for this shindig. I'm not certain, but I think yours are even dirtier. Where'd these fellows get all these class A uniforms?"

"Can it, Lewie."

Smith knew Puller was just as miserable as he was and he glanced at his watch, thought, Just get this over with.

Almond stood again, said, "I understand protocol, of course, and I am eagerly awaiting Chaplain Bryan's blessing for this wonderful bounty. But I cannot help but offer a toast toward the man responsible for all of us being assembled here today."

Smith stirred in his chair, looked at Bryan, the chaplain expressionless, staring down at his plate. This should be your time, Chaplain. Almond should know better, and I'm certain you do. Prayer before toasts.

Almond seemed oblivious to the odd breach of custom, said, "If you will all be seated. There, fine, yes. We are privileged to enjoy the glorious responsibility that comes with this command, and I feel we should give thanks to the man to whom we all owe so much. I offer a salute to our supreme commander, General Douglas MacArthur. . . ."

"I didn't hear you say anything for our supreme commander."

Smith looked at Bowser. "What?"

"Almond's toast."

"I toasted. Just kept it to myself. He breached protocol, you know."

"How?"

"The blessing. The chaplain always goes first. I shouldn't have to tell you that."

"Sorry, sir. You're right, of course. Maybe I was too dazzled by General Almond's eloquence."

Smith ignored Bowser's sarcasm, braced himself as the car jumped, another pothole the driver could not avoid. Smith rode now in a heated station wagon, had succumbed to the need to prevent freezing to death on his many journeys to the regimental command posts. It was a luxury he did not take for granted, passing camps of men engulfed in their coats, performing duties difficult enough for men in summertime.

Bowser sniffed, said, "Why's he do all of that, anyway? He trying to prove he can outdo every supply officer in Korea? Silver and china?"

Smith shook his head. "He did it because he can. That toast was just a reminder that it's MacArthur who *says* he can."

"Food was good. I'll give him that."

"Can't say. Forgot what I ate. Kept thinking about that plain old turkey the navy sent us. I hope the staff had a good meal. They've earned it."

Bowser laughed. "I'm sure they did. With you and me gone, that was two more servings for the rest of them."

Smith tried to wash the experience at Almond's HQ out of his mind, thought, *Thanksgiving should be about family. The only family I have out here are those staff officers.*

"That's where we should have been. I should have told Almond no, that we were too busy, what with the *war* and all." He regretted his own sarcasm, thought of the turkey from the admiral, the far more pleasant feast he had to leave behind. "They know we're headed back. Maybe they saved us some of the admiral's gift."

Bowser looked at him again, laughed, and Smith couldn't help a smile. Bowser shook his head, said, "No chance."

HAGARU-RI, NORTH KOREA—NOVEMBER 24, 1950

The skirmishes were becoming more intense, daily confrontations with Chinese patrols, small-scale fights that seemed to show that the enemy was becoming more aggressive. Smith continued to visit his commanders, grateful that Puller's men had finally caught up with the northern push from the others, most of First Regiment now centered around Koto-ri.

He watched the great machines at work on the airstrip, the engineers keeping them in motion twenty-four hours a day. Beside him, Craig spoke into a radio, the radioman and a squad of guards keeping careful watch on the surroundings. To the east, a massive hill rose up, what Smith had already suspected was a prime overlook for any Chinese observers monitoring progress on the construction. So far there had been little interference, but Smith knew that could change at any time.

Craig handed the radio receiver to the young man beside him, said, "Harris says his pilots are starting to see a great deal more activity to the west. The reports from the Chinese prisoners seem to be accurate. They're out there, for sure."

Smith kept his eyes on a huge bulldozer, scraping the hard ground with a massive steel blade. "They've always been out there. They wanted us here."

Craig pulled at the hood of his coat, covered his head. "What do you mean?"

"That bridge, back down the road. I think of this every time I cross the thing."

"You mean, Funchilin Pass?"

"Yep. The Chinese should have blown it to bits. It would have delayed us for days. But they left it intact. We thought they did us a favor. It was for them, not us. They wanted us up here, doing exactly what we're doing. We're turning cartwheels doing everything we can to prepare for whatever fight we're going to have. We're scrambling to haul supplies up to every depot we've created. We're scrambling to bring the men together."

"At least that's working out."

Smith glanced up, a squad of Corsairs passing high above. "It's better than it was. But don't be surprised if the enemy doesn't figure a way to blow that bridge anyway, now that we're up here. It'll cut us off from supply, from reinforcement. And Tenth Corps has no idea what's going on out here. Almond's too busy waging war with Walton Walker, trying to make points with MacArthur and the newspapers. Who's gonna get to the Yalu first, who's gonna get to brag about victory."

"We got a report from Seventh Division that some of their boys closer to the shore shot up there a few days ago, alongside some ROK. But they didn't have any support, so they pissed in the river and high-tailed it back down."

"I guess they're pretty proud of that *major* accomplishment."

"Probably. It'll look good back home."

Behind them, an aide said, "Sirs, there's a jeep coming up."

Smith turned, was surprised to see Bowser and Sexton, a driver with his face wrapped in a green scarf. Bowser climbed from the jeep, slapping himself with his arms, the customary shiver.

"What are you doing up here, Colonel?"

"Had to see Murray, unscrew some snafu with his supplies. It's taken care of. Captain Sexton caught up with me. Told me we had to find you."

Sexton pulled a paper from his coat, said, "Sir, we got a wire from stateside, passed through Tokyo and God knows where else."

Smith saw concern on both men's faces, felt a sudden tug of alarm. "From my family?"

Sexton seemed surprised at the question. "Oh, no, sir. It's for General Craig."

He handed Craig the note, and Craig read silently, then folded the paper, slid it inside his coat. Smith waited, wouldn't ask, and Craig looked at him, dark worry on the man's face.

"It's my father, sir." He paused, and Smith could feel his emotion. "Forgive me. He has been ill for some time. But this says he suffered a cerebral thrombosis. He's not expected to live more than a few days."

"My Lord, Eddie, I'm sorry. I know you and your father are very close."

Craig seemed to gather himself, faced Smith, seemed more formal now.

"Sir, I would not ask . . ." He stopped, looked down.

Smith said, "We will send a wire to Hawaii. If General Shepherd has no objection, and he won't, I'm granting you emergency leave. Take as long as you need. You need to be with your dad."

Craig kept his eyes down, nodded. "Thank you, sir. This is most important to me."

"No need, Eddie. It's done." He looked at Sexton. "Captain, take General Craig back to HQ, prepare a note for General Shepherd. I'll return as quickly as we can wrap things up here. Colonel Bowser can remain with me for now."

"Certainly, sir."

Craig looked hard at Smith. "Are you sure about this, sir?"

"Get in the jeep."

Craig held out his gloved hand, and Smith took it, a brief stiff shake. Then Craig moved to the jeep, Sexton following, the blanket held up by the driver, Craig climbing into the front seat. The jeep roared away and Bowser said, "That's really good of you, sir. Eddie and his dad . . ."

"I know."

"The staff can handle the load, sir. I can help as your assistant CO if you need me to."

"I know."

"You okay, sir? Don't mean to stick my nose in."

"Alpha, we've got some serious work in front of us. Get on that radio, see if you can raise Litzenberg. I want to know exactly when the Seventh pulls into Yudam-ni. They're supposed to keep going, but I want them to hold up until we can push more supplies their way, same as we've done all the way up here. Tell the staff to make ready to move out of their quarters in Hungnam. I want to know how quickly we can establish my new HQ here in Hagaru-ri. I want the engineers to tell me how much longer it will be before planes can land out there. Tell Puller I want some of his people up here to help secure this perimeter, on the double."

"How many people, sir?"

"That's up to him, for now. He needs to keep a strong perimeter at Koto-ri. He knows how to follow my orders. I tell him what I want done, I don't tell him how to do it. Get on that radio. And tell Litzenberg that once I know he's up there, I'll ride up and have a look."

Bowser moved to the radioman, who handed Bowser the receiver. Smith felt his mind spinning, all the details that swirled around him now. He thought of Craig, wouldn't dig too deeply into the man's emotions. Craig was invaluable, but Smith knew that if Craig's focus was back home, he would be nearly useless here.

Bowser slapped his arms against his sides again, the late afternoon cold settling hard around them. Smith turned again to the heavy equipment, saw trucks with the huge spotlights moving into position, preparing for another night's work. To the side, he heard the radioman, "They're trying to find Colonel Litzenberg, sir. The enemy threw some mortar rounds at the lead of the column. He's coming, sir."

Smith tried to ignore that, thought, Let Bowser do the job. He can handle it. He heard Bowser now, a soft murmur, speaking to himself.

"At least I get to ride in the station wagon."

YUDAM-NI, NORTH KOREA—NOVEMBER 24, 1950

The United Nations' massive compression envelopment in North Korea against the new Red Armies operating there is now approaching its decisive effort. The isolating component of our pincer . . . has for the past three weeks, in a sustained effort of model coordination and effectiveness, successfully interdicted enemy lines of support from the north, so that further reinforcement therefrom has been sharply curtailed and essential

supplies markedly limited. The eastern sector of the pincer, with notewor-
thy and effective naval support, has now reached commanding envelop-
ing position, cutting in two the northern reaches of the enemy's
geographical potential. This morning the western sector of the pincer
moves forward in general assault in an effort to complete the compression
and close the vise. If successful, this should for all practical purposes, end
the war. . . .

"So, we're now part of a pincer?"

Smith read the communiqué again, didn't look at Litzenberg. After a silent moment, Smith said, "We're in a 'commanding and enveloping position.'"

Litzenberg paced the cramped space in the tent, said, "According to General MacArthur. Or is that the word of God?"

Smith wouldn't respond to that, put down the paper. "Murray received this as well. Puller, too. Almond is screaming for a briefing tomorrow morning. I don't think he knew what MacArthur was intending us to do. It's one thing to scamper lickety-split toward an objective. It's quite another thing to work in tandem with another command, to coordinate the assault as one part of a *pincer*."

Litzenberg still paced. "We're spread out across the main road here, positions up in each of the surrounding hills. But it's unnerving. The Chinese are out there in at least two directions and every report tells me they're in force. I'm the left flank of the entire Tenth Corps, and I'm out on a very frozen limb here, sir. Yudam-ni is not a defensible position. I don't have the manpower to cover all the approaches while I'm occupying all that high ground."

He had rarely heard Litzenberg so nervous. More often, Litzenberg was feisty, stubborn, rejecting orders he didn't agree with.

"Colonel, I'm out on a limb of my own. I've been shouted at for weeks now, harangued for moving too slowly. There has been some talk at Tenth Corps that I should be relieved. If I was army, that would have happened already. If Almond convinces MacArthur that we're the reason his marvelous little operation is floundering, it won't much matter anyway."

"Fine! Then have them send the army up here. Let those boys have a crack at the Chinese."

"Can that, Colonel. We're out here because we're the toughest command Tenth Corps has. They won't admit that, but every officer from Hungnam to Tokyo is mighty happy it's us up here and not them. General Ruffner, Almond's exec, he keeps whispering how we need to be cautious of running into a Chinese trap. There's no trap, Colonel. I know, you know, Murray and Puller, every company commander, every platoon commander knows that the Chinese are in these hills, waiting for whatever it is they're waiting for. All I've been able to do about that is what I've already done, draw us up as close together as possible. We dodged a huge freight train two weeks ago when we were scattered out for a hundred miles. I don't know why the Chinese let us get away with that, except maybe they weren't ready for us. But every day that passes, there are more reports, sightings of troop movements, columns of Chinese infantry. The air teams are doing all they can to smother that, but it hasn't stopped the reports. MacArthur says we've cut their supply lines. I'm wondering if that even matters. Maybe they brought everything they need on their backs. Maybe they figure on taking it from us. Maybe, Colonel, this is a one-way street for those people. No one figures on going home. The Japanese were masters of the suicide attack. Maybe, just maybe, the Chinese are planning to give that a try."

Smith had rarely been this animated, fought to control his breathing, the hard pounding in his chest. To one side, Sexton was there, alongside a pair of Litzenberg's aides. They stood silently, frozen in place, no one daring to break the spell Smith had suddenly cast. Litzenberg had stopped moving, said, "Sir, we're doing all we can to prepare for whatever comes next."

"I wish I knew just what that was, Colonel. Maybe when I see Almond tomorrow morning, he'll enlighten us all."

NOVEMBER 25, 1950

As a result of MacArthur's sudden announcement of his pincer strategy, Ned Almond found himself having to mount an aggressive assault in tandem with the attack already under way in the west, the massive push northward begun by Walker's Eighth Army. If Walker required any kind of push, he got it directly from MacArthur, who had visited Eighth Army's forward positions himself, doing what he always did, inspiring the men to the attack. Eighth Army had responded accordingly, three corps advancing northward on a front nearly fifty miles across. At Tenth Corps, Almond's orders were for his left flank, the Marines, to cut across the Taebaek Mountain Range and rendezvous with Walker's thrust as it drove its way to the Yalu River. Even Almond understood that a single Marine regiment was not strong enough to drive through the most difficult terrain in Korea, likely confronting an enemy in unknown strength, in unknown positioning. Though Smith had no confidence in Almond's strategic abilities, the orders now from Tenth Corps at least made sense. Murray's Fifth, pushing slowly up the east side of the Chosin Reservoir, would be recalled, pulled back into Hagaru-ri, and sent out in the tracks of the Seventh. The Seventh would hold up at Yudam-ni, while the Fifth would press forward, right through the town. That decision had been Smith's, who recognized that the Seventh had been engaged in most of the skirmishing and had taken nearly all of the casualties since leaving Wonsan. Once Murray reached Yudam-ni, the Fifth would continue the drive westward, directly across the spine of the mountains.

In the territory Murray would vacate, Almond ordered units of the army's Seventh Division to advance with all speed, occupying the ground east of the reservoir that Murray had taken without a fight.

As Smith continued to shift his forces in accordance with Tenth Corps' instructions, he succeeded in bringing north a single battalion from Puller's First, which was now positioned at Koto-ri. Marching up through the dangerous Funchilin Pass, those men settled into Hagaru-ri as the only combat unit Smith had available for the defense of that crucial junction.

To the east of the reservoir, the army's Thirty-first Regimental Combat Team drove northward, passing through Murray's rapidly marching Marines as they drew back into Hagaru-ri. There was no delay from Murray, whose men immediately pushed up the west side of the reservoir, driving hard for Yudam-ni.

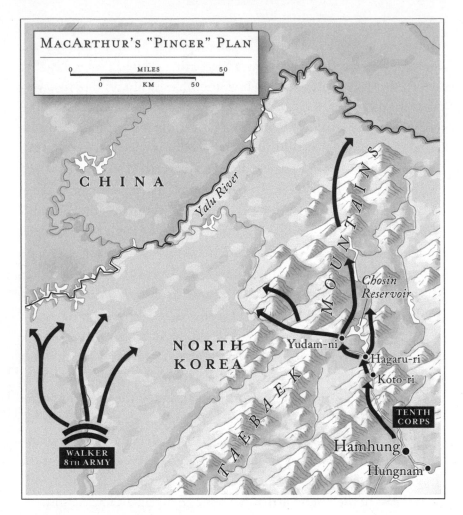

As the troop movements continued, Smith began to breathe easier, if only slightly. Once again the Chinese had offered little in the way of resistance to the shifting positions on either side of the Chosin Reservoir. And more important to Smith, with the Fifth now adding to the strength of the Seventh at Yudam-ni, the Marine division was no longer spread out like a vulnerable snake.

To the west, in Walker's sector, November 24 marked the first full day of MacArthur's grand plan, the left half of the mighty pincer shoving its way across frozen ground, drawing closer to the Yalu. That march had consumed one full day when the Chinese finally showed their hand.

Near the center of Walker's advance, the American Second and Twenty-fifth Divisions found their movement checked by a sudden assault, waves of Chinese infantry, fortified by heavy machine gun fire. As both American divisions struggled to pull together against the onslaught, the situation on Walker's right grew much more serious. There, the ROK Second Corps, three full divisions, were smashed by an even stronger punch from the Chinese forces. Within a few hours, the entire ROK position collapsed, those troops fleeing the field, abandoning most of their weaponry and equipment. Despite Walker's frantic efforts to shore up the position, including the advance of a Turkish unit, the Chinese had quickly achieved complete domination. The collapse of the ROK's forces left Walker's position untenable. With no other alternative, Walker ordered a retreat, pulling his troops southward.

East of the mountains, the Fifth Marines had moved into position at Yudam-ni, preparing to advance through the brutal terrain of the mountain range. Smith's orders had not changed, the Marines intending still to make their rendezvous with Walker's troops as they closed in on the triumphant victory at the Yalu River. With disaster spreading out beyond the mountains, no one at Tenth Corps thought to inform Smith that the army he was supposed to support, to link with for the last triumphant blow against the enemy, was no longer there.

PART THREE

"In campaigns and battles . . . we should not
only employ large forces against small,
but . . . we should concentrate a big force
under, over, beforehand, and alongside the
route which the enemy is sure to take, and
while he is on the move, advance suddenly to
encircle and attack him before he knows what
is happening."

—MAO TSE-TUNG

CHAPTER TWENTY

. . . .

Sung

HE HAD GATHERED several of his senior commanders, allowing them to speak, to reveal their preparations, the positioning of their troops. It was his way of testing their resolve, just who among them was as prepared for what lay ahead as he was. He had few reasons to doubt them, knew that they had all absorbed what had happened to Gao, that any show of weakness could bring the same demotion to them. Already, Gao had been moved to a position far to the rear, supervising a camp of walking wounded, along with ailing troops who had fallen out, too weak to make the treacherous marches through so many of the mountain passes. Sung knew he did not have to mention Gao by name, no need to lecture them on what might happen to them if they showed that kind of weakness or hesitation. The humiliation of losing a top command, of surrendering your sword to your commanding officer, was the kind of shame these men had avoided since they were boys. Now the stakes were so much more important, all of them understanding that bringing shame on your command might mean a firing squad. But Sung had little use for that kind of theatrics. Unlike so many of the leaders he had served in the past, he did not want his camps dominated by fear. That kind of authority had been effective occasionally, when Mao had been in the field. It was Mao's way, prodding his men with both philosophy and punishment. There could be a kind of viciousness to that, a once-loyal officer suddenly eliminated, the victim of his own indiscretion or perhaps a lapse in judgment. Against the Japanese, and then Chiang's Nationalists, Mao had the advantage of his disadvantages, being outnumbered, always regrouping, where poor tactics might be catastrophic, where defeat might mean the collapse of his entire nation. Now, firmly atop China's hierarchy, it was very different, a more benevolent Mao who had granted enormous responsibilities to his generals. The lines of communication remained, radio contact with General Peng, who would certainly relay every important piece of information to Mao himself. But Sung, like Lin Biao to the west, knew that the leash was loose. With the luxury of discretion came pressure to succeed, no one above you to shoulder the blame for failures of your command. Sung had welcomed that kind of pressure, had never doubted his own abilities, even if he suspected weakness in those beneath him. So far, they seemed to have learned the lesson handed to Gao.

As the armies continued their drive southward, Sung had received instruction and counsel, mostly from General Peng, and all of it supportive. From their first day's crossing of the Yalu River, Sung had assumed there would be spying eyes, others in his command who made their own reports to Peking. But so far Sung felt completely comfortable with his decisions, and had no reason to believe that was any different in Peking. The officers who served him seemed to know that as well, a soaring morale that spread down through the ranks of the foot soldiers, even the servants and coolies going about their work with a spirit that smelled of victory. He welcomed that, as much as he encouraged it. Very soon there would be loss of life, the necessary sacrifice coming from men who would accept that as their lasting gift to Chairman Mao.

Many of the men in front of him now had made their journey to his camp on the backs of ponies, a useful tool, and one more piece of living camouflage to confuse the American aircraft. The planes had come every day the weather allowed, teams of two or four or six, swooping low to target anything that could be his army. Occasionally they were right. Many more times they dropped their bombs and threw their rockets into harmless hamlets, abandoned buildings and farmhouses. It made for spectacular display, great fireballs, villages blasted into oblivion, while often the soldiers of Sung's army huddled in brushy fields nearby, close enough to feel the warmth of the explosions. And so both sides waited happily for the darkness, pilots returning to their bases, met with backslapping congratulations, while in the mountains the Chinese rose up from their cover, following his instructions, moving one day closer to the great confrontation.

They were mostly seated, some on cushions, protection from the frozen ground beneath them. Sung tried to ignore the brutality of the cold, a glance skyward, a light snowfall just beginning. He had gone over the maps, each division commander offering details of his position, the fitness of his troops, their eagerness to launch their full-out assault. Sung had held them back from any major assault far longer than even he had expected, their impatience showing through in their discussions. He listened to each man, would give them nothing yet, allowed the commanders more room than usual to express their frustration. Through all the details, so much information, he focused as much on their mood as on their troop positions. In the cold morning, with teacups quickly frozen, he eyed them carefully, searching for hints of anxiety, signs of personal suffering. Surely they know, he thought, that this enemy is something very new, a self-described army of "United Nations," as though by their grandiose label, the entire world was aligned against China. The question rolled into his brain, and he held up a hand, interrupting General Su, one of his division commanders.

"I am wondering if you fear the enemy because you believe his propaganda. Do any of you believe that, because we are said to be isolated from all the world, China will crumble against the might of Western guns?"

The question seemed to surprise them all, the dozen men glancing at one another, searching his words for the trick. Su laughed now, pointed a finger at Sung.

"You are asking if we shall abandon the battlefield, just because the

Americans have larger artillery pieces. My division would not do any such thing. If I believed that they would, I would offer you my head right here."

Another of the senior men spoke, General Bahn, an older man, a veteran of more campaigns than Sung. "Is this a challenge, General? Must you still test the strength of our will? I would suggest that you allow our commands to answer your question for you, to engage the enemy right now. We have maneuvered and delayed, we have strengthened our positions as much as is possible. What more must we wait for? Are you holding our fists in your pocket because you lack confidence? Or is it Peking that lacks confidence?"

Sung debated his response. "I have delayed attacking the enemy because every day that the enemy marches forward, he draws closer to our strongest points. He marches blindly toward his own destruction. I admit to being baffled by their foolishness, and I wonder about the power of their propaganda, that they consider it a wise strategy to convince their fighting men that merely by their presence in Korea, they inspire such terror in their enemies that we shall flee before them."

Another man spoke. "We shall not flee at all. Like General Su, I await the order to attack. My men are eager for the fight."

Sung nodded, put his hands out, as though calming them. This is very good, he thought, exactly what I was hoping for. "I am satisfied with your reports. Word of your efficiency shall be passed back to Peking."

To one side, a man stood, Chao Lin, an older man, who commanded the Sixtieth Division.

"Permit me, sir."

"Yes. You wish to add something?"

"I regret that one of my regiments was careless and suffered the loss of several prisoners to the Americans."

"When?"

"Within the past four days. I have taken appropriate steps to punish the officer in charge. I assure you it will not happen again."

Sung waited for the man to seat himself, said, "Of course it will happen again. We shall capture a good many of their side, as they will capture ours. No one in this army has been ordered to die to the last man. The American soldiers do not understand that, not at all. They have been told that we are a fanatical race, that we are little more than a form of animal life. It is a part of being *Western,* that astonishing arrogance, their belief in their own superiority. I have seen it in their literature, and more important, I see it every day in their strategy. Even now they continue to advance farther into our strongest positions and farther away from their base of supply. I marvel at the willingness of the American Marines to do our work for us. And now they have created vast supply depots within our very position, which we will use to great advantage."

In front of him, General Su rose. "Sir, I mean no disrespect. But you have not told us anything of when we may begin our primary assault. Every day we observe them it increases our eagerness. The weather is becoming difficult. There are reports every day of men who are too stricken with frostbite to be effective. Can you tell us when we are to join the attack?"

Sung stood with his hands inside his coat, pulled them out now, held a piece of paper. "First, General Bahn, commanding the Twenty-seventh Army, confirms that American Marines have vacated their forward positions on the east side of the reservoir and have been replaced by American army troops from the American Seventh Division. General Bahn is as anxious as any of you to begin his assault. Like you, he has been ordered to wait, and observe. That has proven to be of benefit. I do not believe the American army units are capable of resisting us. That, however, is not the most important information."

He made a show of pushing the paper into his coat, then nodded toward his aide. "Colonel Liu, you may have the honor of reading the dispatch received this morning."

Liu stood, had been prepared for this, produced another piece of paper, read slowly, "To General Sung Shi-lun, Commanding, Ninth Field Army Group. On November 25, the Thirteenth Field Army Group launched a significant assault against the greatest concentration of American and Korean troops west of the Taebaek Mountains. This assault was executed with precision and expertise, and was entirely successful. All sections of the American Eighth Army and associated Korean units are in a full retreat. The Thirteenth Army Group is following this victory with an aggressive pursuit, which shall succeed in destroying the enemy invaders. Chairman Mao Tse-tung offers the people's gratitude to our heroic soldiers who have accomplished this victory. Chairman Mao believes that this success should serve as high example to the soldiers of the Ninth Army Group, as you begin your valiant assault. Your goal, as communicated to your commander, is to destroy the American Marine First Division, the American Seventh Army Division, the American Third Army Division, and all associated Korean army units of the puppet government. The people salute your efforts."

Liu kept at attention, looked at Sung with a short nod. In front of Sung, the commanders received the news with wide-eyed surprise, stunned expressions. In front of Sung, General Su said, "Are we certain of this?"

Sung expected that response, said, "This dispatch was received through highest channels and is marked with the sign of Chairman Mao's own hand." He paused. "I am certain."

He allowed them a moment longer, smiles now breaking out, the men turning again to him, the silent question on their faces. He held up his hand, quieting them, said, "Chairman Mao has imparted this lesson to me, and I shall impart it to you. 'Enemy advancing, we retreat; enemy entrenched, we harass; enemy exhausted, we attack; enemy retreating, we pursue.' We have accomplished the first task with perfection. You have all expressed your eagerness to begin the attack. It is now time. By midnight tonight, you will advance your troops into direct confrontation with the enemy forces in your front. You will hold nothing back. If the enemy holds his position, you will attack again until he breaks. When he breaks, you will pursue with the single purpose of destroying him. We shall demonstrate to Chairman Mao just how completely you have learned his teachings. It is time for us to destroy our enemies."

"I must say, very exciting. I had wondered myself just how long you could merely watch the Americans pass by your guns."

Sung scooped a single stick of cold rice into his mouth, warmed it for a long moment, made a difficult swallow. "Major Orlov, if you have questions, you may ask them directly. You may not approve of the answer. But I hide nothing from you."

"I tried a piece of your dried fish this morning. There isn't much else in the camp that resists the cold. I saw one of your aides chewing a piece of rice paper."

Sung slid the stick into the small pile of dense rice, bent low, scooped the rice into his mouth, repeated the same routine, another half-choking swallow. "We shall endure. As we shall prevail."

Orlov pulled his small bottle from his coat, took a drink. "I believe you call that the party line. Your Chairman Mao is quite adept at the poetry of war."

"There is nothing wrong with inspiring the soldiers to do their duty."

Orlov put a gloved hand to his face, brushed at snow on his hat. "So, you inspire a man's mind while his feet suffer a painful death. I was at one of your hospitals this morning. I suppose you would call it that. There was a man there behaving like a doctor. You had at least thirty men laid out like frozen trees, thirty more who still had enough life in them so they could scream."

"You were in Leningrad. You know what cold can do, what kind of challenges it holds."

Orlov pulled at his coat, blew a foggy breath into his hands. "This is not Leningrad. We had snow and ice and the kind of suffering that no man should see. Here? There is death in the air, pushing into a man's lungs. There is death on the ground, beneath your feet. There is no protection, no sanctuary. Look at *you*. You cannot eat your meal without struggling with frozen rice. There is no tea to be had. Boiling water freezes in seconds. If you drank spirits, you would at least warm yourself from the inside."

Sung put the bowl aside, ignored the harsh rumble in his stomach. "What would you suggest, Major? We all go home? Is that what you told your officers years ago? I am cold, I am suffering, I cannot fight. This is too *difficult*."

Orlov breathed again into his glove. "And they would have shot me. As you would shoot your own."

Sung was annoyed. "Do not assume I am Russian, Major. We help our soldiers as we are able. Once the attack begins, they will no longer notice the cold."

"Can't you at least provide them with boots?"

Sung paced slowly, a hard breeze ripping into his furry coat. He tried to hide the effect of that, said, "You are supposed to observe, not criticize. The footwear we use is meant for stealth. It is one of the few advantages we have, the ability to approach our enemies discreetly, to attack at night at close range. The soldiers know that. They are prepared to do what we must do to prevail. We do not have the luxury of fine radios, and so we must communicate with sound, with the bugles and cymbals and whistles. Every regimental commander has his own signals, and his men have been trained to recognize that. I should not have to provide you a lesson in tactics."

He was angry now, watched as Orlov retrieved the bottle again. He tried to keep Orlov's observations at a distance, knew of the horrors of the field hospitals. In the past he had visited them often, comforting wounded men, offering them the gratitude befitting their heroics. But there were no heroics now, not yet, every man crippled by the cold just one more bullet lost, reducing the strength of Sung's army.

"Are you concerned about the prisoners? I heard your General Chao. You seemed to dismiss his concerns about losing a few men to the Americans. I would be concerned about intelligence, that the Americans might gain some valuable information."

"I am not concerned at all. For weeks now we have lost prisoners. This is a proud army, and pride compels men to boast of all they know. How has that changed this fight? I have twelve divisions in these mountains. I outnumber my enemy by a factor of five to one, perhaps more. If the Americans are aware of that, why do they come? They must believe that we are a mirage, an army of ghosts."

"Or, they believe it doesn't matter how many men you have. The Americans in particular, they believe they are invincible."

Sung nodded. "Precisely. And tonight we shall prove to them that ghosts can kill, and that the confidence of their generals is a sad mistake."

CHAPTER TWENTY-ONE

. . . .

Riley

HAGARU-RI—NOVEMBER 27, 1950

FOR THE PAST FEW DAYS, the Chinese seemed to wake up, slipping closer, the skirmishes more intense. An even greater concern was the occupation of a tall hill a short mile up the road toward their next objective, Yudam-ni. It had fallen on Baker Company to push the Chinese away from the vantage point that could have decimated any convoy attempting to travel up the main supply road. After a sharp and brief fight, the Marines gained control of the hill, the Chinese then doing what they had done all along. They disappeared.

Even before Thanksgiving, the orders had come from Litzenberg that once Baker Company had secured the big hill, more of the Seventh would move up that way, advancing northward along the west side of the reservoir. But the orders continued to come, more men from the Fifth moving out that way as well, no one explaining to the men of Fox Company just what those men had been ordered to do. For now the mission of Fox Company had not changed, instructions to serve as a security force. As was typical, the griping came, assumptions that Fox was being punished for some indiscretion, or worse, that Captain Barber himself had asked to have his men passed over for any of the more important tasks. Riley had no idea what to believe, and like the others, he knew only what the officers told him. But even Lieutenant McCarthy was grumbling, low comments suspicious of the captain.

The orders finally came for Fox to follow in the tracks of the others, but still, no one above them offered any satisfactory explanation as to just where they were supposed to go. The scuttlebutt only grew louder when the men observed Captain Barber and the battalion commander, Colonel Lockwood, moving out in a lone jeep, what McCarthy told them was a scouting mission, though the men still grumbled that no one was sure just what the officers were scouting.

Their gear had been stowed, the backpacks assembled, the men gathering, checking their weapons, cursing the cold that made cleaning a rifle impossible. Riley did as he did often, marched in place, a vain effort to keep his feet thawed. Around him others were doing the same, waiting impatiently for the order to move. He saw Lieutenant McCarthy now, and Killian was there, his loud tone piercing even the bustling wind.

"Hey, Lieutenant. How come we gotta walk? There's trucks all over the place."

"If they tell me, I'll tell you. All I know is that Captain Barber went forward with Colonel Lockwood, scouting out the road. The colonel came back, but the captain's still out there. Wherever he is now, that's where we're going. If there were trucks for us, we'd have 'em."

McCarthy moved away and Killian saw Riley, moved closer to him, said, "You'd think as newfangled as we're supposed to be, they'd have a decent way to move us around. My damn feet are already wet. I got spare socks stuck in places I ain't telling you where, and I was writing a letter to Colleen, and had to put it up halfway through. I'm still carrying a turkey leg in my coat that one day might thaw out enough for me to eat it."

Riley saw the chaplain, Craven, moving through the men, welcomed the break from Killian's bellyaching.

"Hello, Chaplain. I guess we're moving north after all."

"Howdy, boys. Yep, count on that. I got it pretty solid that we're headed all the way to the Yalu River."

Killian tugged at his backpack, hoisted it over his shoulders, said, "I tell you what. I'm holding on to my pee, and when we get there, I'm unloading it all into that river, let those Shambos know I been there."

Riley looked at Craven, wasn't sure how the man would react.

The chaplain was smiling at Killian's bluntness, said, "Well, now, Private, you do that if it pleases you. I'd rather like kneeling down beside that water and saying a prayer that the Chinese pull out of this war, so we can all go home."

Craven smiled, nodded toward Riley, moved away. Killian stared after him, said in a low voice, "Figures. Even those Bible fellas pull rank on you."

Riley ignored Killian, pondered Craven's words. "He said we're going to the Yalu. The captain sure as hell ain't gone that far. You think the Chinese are gonna just let us stroll up there without saying something about it?"

"Who cares? We find the Shambos, we'll bust 'em up." Killian looked around. "Not sure how quick we're moving. Maybe I can finish this damn letter."

He hustled off, and Riley shivered, the cold eating through his clothing. He marched in place again, saw Lockwood moving toward his jeep, others with him wrapped in bundles of green. Riley was surprised, thought, Don't see him all that much. Now he's all over the place. They gathered at the jeep, a brief discussion. Riley eased closer, but the talk ended, Lockwood suddenly moving toward him. Lockwood dropped the blanket, yanked his coat closed, an obvious shiver, seemed to make a show of sharing their discomfort. More men were gathering, most of the company, officers calling them forward. Lockwood said, "Here, men! Fox Company!" Lockwood seemed miserable, pulling at his own coat, stomping his feet, and after a long moment he said, "All right, here's the story. Captain Barber is up ahead in the Toktong Pass, waiting for us to join him. The hills there make a bottleneck, the main supply road narrow as hell. It has been confirmed that this company has been ordered to occupy a strong position overlooking the road, to act as security for the rear of the rest of the regiment, and to protect any supply convoys moving north. Captain Barber and I have located that position, some four miles this side of Yudam-ni. The march will cover approximately seven miles."

There were audible groans, and Lockwood seemed annoyed.

"I'll not listen to that! I've gone to great lengths, pulled a few strings, made some promises I likely can't keep. But we've got nine trucks pulling up here in a few minutes."

There were different murmurs now and McCarthy stepped forward, said, "Uh, sir, we were told we had to prepare to move on foot. We were not aware we could ride."

"Of course you'll ride! I take care of my boys. We've got a pair of heavy machine guns joining us, and a squad of eighty-one mortars, too, just for a little more pop. I intend for you to hold that hill, and to protect anyone who moves past it. That's it. Prepare to mount up."

Riley felt energized, watched Lockwood climb back into the jeep. He's okay, he thought. Sounds like it, anyway.

Welch moved up beside him, said, "I guess he set us straight. We're doing guard duty while the rest of the boys hunt down the enemy. What do you think of that?"

"Not sure. They wouldn't send us up there if it wasn't necessary. Chinese could be anywhere, so everybody keeps saying. But Jesus, it's cold. Sure glad we'll be riding."

Welch pulled the hood of his parka tight around his face. "Yeah, maybe. You're right about the cold, and we ain't fighting this war from the back of trucks. I'm wondering about the captain."

"What about him?"

"He's out there by himself on some hill, holding the fort until we get there. I guess he thinks if he has to, he can take on the Chinks all by himself."

TOKTONG PASS—NOVEMBER 27, 1950

The truck ride had been grindingly slow, the convoy delayed by more vehicles in front of them, no one pushing too quickly on the twisting mountain road. Riley tried to settle back into his coat, appreciated the warmth of the cluster of men. Beside him, Killian said, "We're a sad-looking bunch. No wonder Barber hates us. We been volunteered for latrine duty, I bet. Dig out these slit trenches for the rest of the Corps."

On the other side of Killian, Welch said, "Bull. We're going into action. They loaded us up with ammo, and there's more trucks behind us. The colonel's leading us up there, and he wouldn't be riding along if it wasn't important."

Riley looked past Killian, caught a glimpse of Welch beneath the hood. "Since when did you get so much respect for the brass?"

Killian said, "He's bucking for second louie. Talk nice about the officers and they make you one. The reason the colonel's up there is he's the only one here who knows where we're supposed to go. I bet Captain Barber's up on his hillside cussin' up a blue storm wondering where the hell we are. I bet he's got a bonfire going bigger'n this truck."

Riley leaned back against the hard side of the truck, had no interest in getting into some meaningless argument with Killian. Welch said, "They oughta put you in charge. You got it all figured out."

At the rear of the truck, a face appeared, the man climbing up with a heavy grunt, standing tall. Morelli said, "Hey, sir, you better hang on. Truck starts moving, you'll be on your rear end. Happened to me more than once."

"Thank you, son. They tell me we'll be a few minutes yet. There's some artillery up ahead, and they need some time to get them around a sharp turn. I'm Orville Hayes, Associated Press. I don't believe I've spoken to you gents yet. Third Platoon, eh? How're we doing?"

Riley recognized the man now, had seen him around Hagaru-ri, poking his curiosity into anyplace the officers would allow. Riley had no particular disdain for reporters, but there was something highly counterfeit about this man's concerns, Riley as suspicious as many of the others that what he really wanted was some kind of negative poop about the brass or maybe the war itself. The man pulled out a small pad of paper, fumbled with a pencil through thickly gloved fingers. Killian pointed to Riley, said, "Hey! Talk to this one here. He loves reporters. Got some great stories. A real hero, all of that."

Riley pulled himself deeper into his coat, but the man took the bait, leaned low, a gust of sour breath into Riley's face.

"Outstanding! How you doing, Marine? Don't think I've spoken to you as yet. Hate to miss anyone. I assume all of you fellows know I'm trying to gather up as much as I can, to send back home."

Riley glanced down at his boots, thought, One sharp kick, right into Killian's crotch. Remember that. I owe him one. He identified the odor, sour cigar smoke, cutting even through the harsh cold of the frigid air. He saw Welch leaning forward, looking at him with an evil smile, others in the truck speaking out now, confirming what Killian had said.

"Yep, he's your man, sir. Fights bare-handed. Don't even need a rifle."

"Toughest hombre in the platoon."

"I'm scared of him, for sure."

The exaggerated goofiness seemed contagious, the men welcoming something to laugh about. Riley thought, Maybe I should play the part and grab this idiot by the throat.

Hayes put a hand on Riley's shoulder, said, "Quite a character, eh? Excellent. So, where're you from, son?"

Riley tried to avoid the man's breath. "Pennsylvania. Small town near Harrisburg."

"Excellent! Amish country. Your family Amish, then?"

Riley could feel the oiliness of the man's artificial enthusiasm, heard a chuckle from Welch. Riley said, "Not too many Amish Marines, sir."

"Well, yes, that does make sense. It would make a hell of a story, though." Hayes laughed, coughed in the sharp, cold air. "Tell me, son, you have a family back home? How'd you like to give them a rousing cheerio, let them know you're doing fine?"

"I write my wife pretty often. That's good enough."

"Yes, well, that's fine." Hayes paused, a wet cough blowing out in a fog of steam. "You know, your Colonel Lockwood has authorized me to be out here. I was told you boys would cooperate. I don't mean to be a bother, but I do have a job to do."

"Sorry, sir. I don't hear much that comes direct from the colonel. Guess I just don't have much to say."

"Well, let me ask you, son. What's the one thing you wish for out here, the one thing you wish you had?"

Riley thought a moment, the comments growing quiet, the others more serious now, waiting for his response. The question dug through him, stirred something unexpected, emotions he tried to push away. After a long, cold minute, he said, "I want to see tomorrow."

Hayes didn't respond, and Riley tried to ignore him, avoided the thoughts of everything he was missing, of everything that could happen to him. Hayes stared at him for a long moment, then said, "Thank you, Marine."

The silence hung in the air for another long second, all eyes on Riley, who closed his, pulling himself away. The silence was broken by the voice of Killian. "Here's what I want. Write this down. Dry feet. Warm feet. A steak. My dog. My wife. My Packard. My wife again. Another steak. My bed. My fireplace. Maybe my wife again. Pork chops. A baked potato with gravy. Another steak . . ."

The trucks continued their slow progress, climbing, twisting, halting. The reporter was long gone, and Riley wondered if he enjoyed the job, if poking his questions into the faces of fighting men was fun. Has to be interesting, he thought. I guess those fellows gotta keep their heads down, too. He thought of Ernie Pyle, killed near Okinawa, shot down by a Japanese machine gun. Riley never saw Pyle, but knew men who did, who reacted to the reporter's death as a personal tragedy. This guy's not anything like Pyle, pretty sure of that. But he's got a job to do, too. Like the rest of us. And if he's out here freezing his ass off, give him credit for being something besides a coward. I bet he knows plenty of reporters sitting fat and happy in Tokyo. I shoulda talked to him. Not like Killian's stupidity. Maybe he'd mention me, make sure Ruthie would see it. He glanced down to his boots, the ground-in filth on his pants legs. Nope, don't really need her to hear about any of this. Let's just get this over with.

The truck began to move, swung around a sharp turn, and Riley could see a narrow valley, a flat plain between two massive hills. There was a row of small shacks, a narrow field hemmed in by a collapsing fence. He eyed the shacks, instinct, but he thought, Most likely, no one's home. It had been that way along every road outside of the bigger towns since they had begun the climb north of Sudong. He was used to it now, the focus solely on just where the enemy might be, if somewhere on the vast hills, there were Chinese eyes watching them pass by, big fat American trucks, big fat targets. Any civilians were just in the way, an inconvenience, and Riley thought of that now, if the Chinese felt the same way. They can't just shoot them, he thought. The Japs did some of that. Solve their problem by exterminating the pests. Exterminated some of us, too, the POWs. Can't say we didn't return the favor once in a while.

He avoided those memories, every engagement bringing a scattering of prisoners and, nearly always, those men in his unit who took out their revenge. *War crimes.* That's what the reporters kept saying. Nobody asked if we were doing it, too. That guy Hayes didn't ask anything like that. I don't wanna see that stuff in the paper; sure as hell don't want my wife seeing it.

The truck was moving more quickly now, bone-jarring thumps, and Riley stared out past McCarthy, the truck in another tight turn, another truck coming into view behind them.

Morelli caught his eye, the red-cheeked cheerful face, the kid pointing outside.

"The Koreans must go into the towns when winter comes. Not much to do out here."

Riley closed his eyes, waited for it, and finally, Killian obliged.

"Yep, that's it, kid. It's a hotel I've heard about. The Nooks are working heavy construction up in Yalu City. Getting ready for our big liberation Christmas party."

"You think so? Really?"

The laughter drifted through the truck, Killian the loudest.

"No, you moron. They're up there in these hills, aiming their rifles at us. Can't you feel it?"

Morelli was embarrassed into silence now, and Riley knew the redness on his face was more than the cold. He laughed to himself, thought, You'll figure it out, kid. We all did.

The truck jerked to a halt again, a new burst of griping. McCarthy leaned out through the canvas and Riley heard voices outside. The lieutenant dropped to the ground, a quick conversation, then he called back into the truck.

"Let's go. Ride's over. We found the captain. It's time to walk."

CHAPTER TWENTY-TWO

. . . .

Riley

"Good God. I didn't train for this. Where's the damn beach?"

Riley tried to ignore Killian, raised one foot in front of the other, gaining elevation with each step. Most of the men were silent, moving up the steep slope, all of them too aware what sweating could do. Behind him, Killian huffed along, while Welch led the squad alongside the others, all three of Fox Company's platoons making the climb off the main road. At the base of the hill, Captain Barber's aides were raising a tent, alongside a pair of dilapidated shacks. Just above the shacks the hill jutted sharply upward for several yards, where the road itself had been carved out of the hillside. Above that the slope was not as severe, but for men weighed down with their weapons and equipment, the going was slow, methodical, the officers keeping the pace. Through the first part of the climb there were trees, firs and pines wrapping the lower half of the wide hill, the men pushing up through the timber, using the tree trunks for support. But halfway up, the trees gave way to rocky ground, low scrub brush, what Riley had seen on most of the hills in this part of Korea. And without the shelter of the trees, there was nothing to hold back the wind.

Riley glanced up the hill, navigated his way behind Welch, cutting through small rocks, the brush too short to serve as a handle. The trees were well behind them now, and Riley could see the rest of the 240 men, three columns spread out across the face of the hill, mostly faceless men, their hoods pulled tight, protection against the increasing torment from the wind. Behind him, Killian swore again.

"I'm filing a complaint. They pulled me out of the Mediterranean to be here. I ain't no damn mountain climber."

In front of Riley, Welch turned, breathing in heavy bursts. "You bitch one more time and I'll roll you down this damn hill, so's you can climb it again. You read the same damn brochure we all did. Now shut the hell up."

Killian was silenced, Welch climbing again. The slope was easier now, the men reaching the summit, and Riley could see across most of that, a wide span spreading over several acres. The other platoons were gathering, receiving instructions from Captain Barber, the lieutenants passing along just what they were supposed to do. Riley stopped, tried to catch his breath, one hand over his mouth, filtering the frigid air from his lungs. He moved again, keeping up with the others, climbed the last ridgeline, a ragged spine that sliced through the center of the hilltop. Far beyond that he could see another hill, taller, more rugged, connected to their position by a narrow saddle, at least two hundred yards long. Except for that one land bridge, the dome of the hill dropped away into a steep slope in every direction.

"Third Platoon, move out this way." Riley saw McCarthy waving them forward, one arm extended, the men following the order, a single file line along the ridge. They slogged through a patch of dense brush, the hilltop more rugged than the slopes they had climbed. "First squad, right here. Sergeant Welch, arrange your men with a field of fire out that way. The company's forming a wide horseshoe on top of this hill, with both ends terminating down at the road we just left. The captain's command post is there, and he's positioning the mortar teams just up-hill from his tent. First Platoon is the right flank of the horseshoe. Second is to the left. We're the middle. Your squad will be on our left flank. The other two squads will be to your right. There will be a heavy machine gun position on our right, linking us to First Platoon. There's some heavy brush and some pretty rough ground between us, so keep in mind where they are. No blind shooting. You need anything from those boys, talk to Lieutenant Dunne. He owes me a dozen favors, so don't be afraid to ask." McCarthy paused, and Riley saw what seemed to be nervousness, McCarthy laboring to breathe. A new gust of wind swirled up around them, the men huddling closer, Riley moving in with them. He knew there would be more to the instructions, his brain trying to map out just what had led the captain up this particular hill, just why they were here at all. McCarthy scanned the horizon, said, "Dark in a few. I'm betting on snow. The captain's thermometer said twelve below zero, but that's down at the road. This wind is pretty nasty, and it won't get any better, so it's gonna be a long night. Find some kind of cover, anyplace that might break up the wind, but keep all eyes to the front. We're in a circle, everybody protecting each other's asses, even if you can't see 'em. That's it for now. The captain's probably on the radio to somebody in Hagaru-ri, letting them know we're here. He'll be up here soon, checking our position, pretty sure of that."

Welch said, "How about a small fire, sir? Maybe heat up some rations?"

"The wind might make that tough. But the captain's people said they were lighting a big damn bonfire at their CP, so there's no reason we can't heat up our chow. Find a low spot, well back of the crest. Once it's dark, it's lights out. No need to advertise we're up here. You can bet the enemy's out there somewhere, and they've got eyes in the dark, no matter how careful we are. Our job is to keep the enemy off that road and make damn sure that if he tries to cut us off from Hagaru-ri, we make his life miserable. We're the back door to ten thousand Marines. I don't want anybody pushing us out of the way."

There was a rumble from the road below and Riley looked that way, saw a line of vehicles, a half-dozen six-by trucks. He said, "Sir, they sending us more men?"

McCarthy stared down the long hill, said, "Not hardly. That's what we're here to protect. Supply convoys, hauling it up to Yudam-ni. We lose any of those fellows and Colonel Litzenberg will have our asses. You know your job, now do it."

McCarthy moved away, followed by the other two squad leaders.

Welch turned to the rest of the men now, said, "You heard him. This looks like solid rock, so pile up some kind of windbreak if you can. There's a low place right over here, behind that rock. I'll try to get some kind of fire going. We've got a half hour before it's dark, so if you want a tin can heated up, pay attention. Time to change your socks, too."

A harder gust rolled over the hillside, a blast of cold that ripped into Riley's coat. He shook, a hard, uncontrollable shiver, said, "This wind is a pain in the ass. All we need now is snow so we can write home how *pretty* it is."

Killian dropped his backpack, sat heavily, began to work on removing his boots. "Too cold to snow. Learned that back home. It gets down below twenty degrees or so, you got nothing to worry about."

Welch ignored him, went to work with the others in the squad, guiding them into the best position there seemed to be. Riley stood immobile, too chilled to move. He eyed a small flat rock, crouched down onto his knees, pushed one hand on the hard ground, turned stiffly, and sat down. Immediately the cold from the frozen ground began driving up through the seat of his pants, and he kept his head down, the parka tight around his face. He fumbled with the boots, the cold numbing his fingers, his toes too numb to feel anything at all. There was a dusty cloud, coating his gloves, blowing into his eyes, and he brushed it away. But the dust came more heavily now, and he realized it wasn't dust at all. It was snow. He looked at Killian, the man rubbing his toes, a fresh pair of socks in his hands.

"Hey, Weather Man. One more thing you're an expert about."

Killian glanced up, winced, shook his head. "Stupid Shambo snow. Not my fault they got such crazy-assed weather."

Riley pulled his brain into gear, focused on the task at hand, each movement agonizing, the stiffness spreading through him. He tugged at his wet socks, barefooted now, his hands rubbing briskly, drying, a feeble attempt to bring any warmth at all. He tried to wriggle his toes, massaged them roughly, fumbled with a fresh pair of socks, his hands shaking as he pulled them on. He slid the boots on with an urgent tug, kept his toes in motion, fought the stinging pain. He flexed his fingers, jammed his hands inside his coat, fought to breathe, his heart pounding.

Killian grunted out loud, yanking on his boots, and Riley saw the snow forming a light blanket on the man's coat. He looked at Riley, held up his socks.

"Frozen solid already. They'll crack in half, I bet. What kind of idiot came up with this place, anyway?"

Riley tried to control his shivering, said, "I'll agree with you on that one."

The wind blew harder, a sharp groan emerging from Riley's misery, and he turned slightly, saw Welch behind the single rock, struggling with a small fire. Leave it to him, he thought. The only man in this company who can build a fire in a gale. Welch had gathered a pile of small sticks, other men now bringing him larger branches, pieces of a broken supply crate. The flames were barely visible, the smoke whisked away quickly by the relentless wind. Welch knelt low, hovering over the fire, protecting his work, more sticks coming up, adding to the glow. Riley thought of his rations, a can of beef stew he had carried optimistically for more than a week. Maybe now's the time, he thought.

"I'm gonna try to thaw out my chow. The sarge's done a good job."

"Yeah, I got some stew here, somewhere. Kinda tired of eating Tootsie Rolls ten times a day. Hey, who's that?"

Riley followed Killian's stare, saw a hooded figure coming toward them from the low ground. More men were trailing behind, several ammo carriers, each one hauling a pair of steel boxes. The first man reached the high ground, looked their way, moved closer, pulled back the hood of his coat, slapped his hands together. It was Captain Barber.

"Who's lighting that fire?"

Welch stood slowly, a show of reluctance, the wind smothering the low flames. "Sergeant Welch, sir. Until it's dark, the lieutenant and me figured it can't hurt. We can heat our rations."

"It's dark enough, Sergeant. Douse that. You've got more important work to do. I want the men to dig in, prepare foxholes."

To one side, Riley saw McCarthy approaching, his face showing an indiscreet display of wide-eyed fury.

"Prepare with what, sir? We got no TNT up here. This ground's solid rock. Or ice. Either way—"

"No arguments, Lieutenant!"

"We expecting an attack, sir?"

"I don't know what to expect. But we need to be ready for anything that happens. They just ran a phone wire to my CP from down at Hagaru-ri, so, at least for now, we've got communication with Colonel Lockwood. They're nervous as hell about this road. If it gets cut, they're in a world of hurt. Our job is pretty clear, at least for now. Anybody besides Marines moves on that road, or through these hills, blow 'em to hell."

The sound of trucks came again, and Barber looked down that way.

"This could go on all night, or until the enemy tries to stop it. As narrow as the pass is along this hill, it's exactly the place he'll try. Get working. Once the holes are dug, go to fifty percent watch. You hear me, Lieutenant?"

"Loud and clear, sir."

Barber pulled his hood up, marched away toward the Second Platoon. McCarthy stood silently, the griping rising up around him in a windblown chorus.

"Shut the hell up! Shovels out, and get those holes dug." McCarthy looked toward Welch, eyed the remnants of the small fire. Riley moved up closer, thought, Just a minute to warm my damn hands. The lieutenant glanced back toward Barber, seemed to wait for the right moment, then leaned closer to Welch, said, "Sergeant, I've got a can of beans I'd really like to eat. If you're gonna build a fire, do a better job of keeping it hidden. From the enemy, that is. You've got twenty minutes, so make it work. The rest of us . . . Christ, we've got to chop ice."

Welch dropped low, huddling over the still-smoking branches, went to work again. McCarthy looked at Riley, the others, the men staring at him with painful disbelief.

"You heard the captain. Make use of those shovels. Nobody sleeps up here until the job is done. Then, fifty percent watch. And keep your feet dry." He paused. "God help us all."

"FOX HILL"—NOVEMBER 27, 1950

It was nearly nine o'clock, the griping still flowing through the position
in a steady chorus of swearing, made even worse by McCarthy prowling
through the position, testing their alertness. There had been passwords
given, which McCarthy expected to be acknowledged, a common precaution at night. But the men were struggling with their labor, or, if the
holes seemed adequate, they had collapsed into sleep almost immediately. McCarthy's efforts at testing their response to the password most
often resulted in a cascade of swearing from the lieutenant, and several
helmets thumped by the butt of his carbine.

Riley had caught his own share of McCarthy's wrath, his brain
struggling to stay focused on chiseling the rock-hard ground. Gradually
the hole began to take shape, the shovel clanking hard, chiseling splin-
ters of dirt and rock, Killian working just as hard beside him. Riley
stopped, a brief second's rest, said, "This is stupid as hell. We're down a
whole foot. It's gonna take us all night, and then you can bet tomorrow
they'll haul us off somewhere else."

Killian kept working, said, "Hey, it's getting easier. We get down
below the frozen stuff, it's not bad. Come on, keep digging."

Riley wrapped stiff fingers around the short handle of the shovel,
chopped down, solid impact on a hidden rock. The shovel bounced up,
a sharp stinging pain in his hands. Killian paused, said, "Try not to hit
the rocks. It's better in the dirt. Moron."

Riley saw a smile, the Irishman's face red, streaked with filthy sweat.
"If you're gonna give me grief, at least pass along some of that Irish
whiskey."

"Forget it. Ran out the first hour I had it. No help from the rest of
you."

Riley jabbed the shovel down, a scoop of dirt, poured it in front of
the hole. "We get out of this alive, and I bet we'll laugh like hell about
it. One day, over drinks in some posh club in God knows where.
Nobody'll believe us."

Killian tossed up more dirt, the deeper ground softening, said, "Yeah,
we'll be telling war stories to our grandkids. They won't believe a damn

word. Where's that jackass reporter? Ought to have him up here. Maybe take pictures."

Riley jabbed his shovel down, more of the dirt coming up, the hole deepening more quickly. "Pile it up to the front side. Give us cover, if we need it."

Killian dropped down into the hole, dug again, said, "There you go, acting like an officer again. That's what I've been doing all along, genius. Okay, it's about two feet deep. That oughta be enough."

Welch was there now, a quick exam, said, "Good. Captain can't gripe about this one. We found some old holes dug down the face of the hill a ways. This place must have been a Chink position and they left 'em behind for us. That either means they hauled their rice bags out of here or they left those holes on purpose, so they'd know where to find us." Welch looked at Killian. "One of you, go help out Morelli. He's got a bum shovel. Kane's to your right, and I checked the thirty gun to our left. They're fixed mostly out that way, so anything straight to our front is up to you."

Riley felt the sweat on his back growing colder, said, "I'll help the kid, Sarge. Sean can clean up this thing, make it cozy. I could use some damn sleep."

Welch pointed. "Yeah, better you than this idiot Irishman. He's that way, twenty yards. The rest of the squad's in pretty good shape. Not sure what we're expecting to happen, but the lieutenant said the brass is too damn nervous about the road. Not really sure why the Chinks couldn't just go around us. All they have to do is put a few machine guns and a half-dozen mortars on that taller hill over there and there's not much we can do about it."

To one side, the voice of McCarthy. "Sergeant Welch!"

"Here."

McCarthy was there now, held out his carbine. "Check your weapon. Mine's frozen stiff. The gun oil's turned to glue. The M-1s don't seem to be as bad. Where's your BAR?"

Welch pointed, said, "Kane's over there, ten yards."

"Let's check it out. Can't afford to lose the best weapon we've got."

Welch followed the lieutenant, and Riley moved out with them, saw

Morelli's meager foxhole, another man struggling to help. Riley knelt down, said, "You get a little deeper, it gets easier."

Morelli stared at him, trying to see his face, said, "That you, Pete?"

"Of course it's me. Who's your helper?"

The other man stopped digging, sat on the edge of the hole, seemed to welcome the break. "It's Norman, Pete. We've got it. His shovel just fell to pieces. Must be some old army piece of crap."

"You got this, then?"

Norman said, "Can you spare the shovel? The kid needs the exercise."

Riley handed the shovel to Morelli, could tell he was shivering, his words in a chatter.

"Thanks, Pete. You'll get it back."

"I better."

Morelli dropped the shovel, and Riley could see him fumble to retrieve it, his hands shaking. He put a hand on Norman's shoulder. "You get done here, I'd get him into his bag pretty quick."

"The sarge already told me. We're about finished. I'll take care of him; you worry about Irish over there."

Riley turned, saw Killian standing tall in front of the foxhole, realized now the snow had stopped, a hint of moonlight reflecting off the thin carpet of white. Riley moved that way, saw that Killian had no coat.

"What the hell's wrong with you?"

"Drying off. Best way. The wind gets rid of the sweat in a couple minutes."

"It'll get rid of you, too. Get in the damn hole."

Killian kept his pose, arms outstretched, and Welch was there now, said, "Oh, for Chrissakes. He's bucking for the company's dumb-ass award. Put your coat on, Irish. I need your rifle even if I don't need you."

Riley looked at the weapon in Welch's hands. "Your carbine working okay?"

"Not worth a damn. The lieutenant figures we're down to single shot. Kane's BAR is fouled up, too. There'll be no more gun cleaning. The lieutenant's really pissed at himself, says he knew better than to order us to wipe everything down. He's going down the line, checking every piece. Check yours."

Riley raised the M-1, worked the action, replaced the clip. "Seems okay."

Killian was down in the hole now, pulling on his coat. "Already checked mine. Thought about firing off a clip, but I'd probably start a Fox Company war. Some of these kids are nervous as hell."

Welch patted Riley on the shoulder. "You take first watch. Anything to keep him quiet for a couple of hours."

Welch moved off, dropping low at the next hole, more instructions, his words swept away by the wind. Riley looked up, the clouds drifting past the moon, said, "Well, you were right about the snow, I guess. Maybe you're not as stupid as everybody thinks."

Killian curled up tight inside his bag, and Riley knelt, his own bag wrapped around his legs. He leaned the rifle up on the mound of fresh dirt, already frozen hard. He felt a stiff crust on his face, and he blinked painfully, his sweat freezing over every part of him. He wiped at his eyes with the rough sleeve of his coat, a useless effort, dried tears digging into his skin. He cupped his hands over his face, blew a breath, a quick burst of warmth, rough gloves clearing his vision. It wasn't perfect, but he could see down the broad hill, the thin layer of snow barely masking the brush, uneven ground. He pulled the bag up farther, nearly to his waist, touched the rifle, reassuring, one hand pulling the hood of his parka as tight as it could go. But the wind was relentless, numbing cold on his cheeks, more tears clinging in icy flakes around his eyes. He avoided looking upward, but the moonlight told him the clouds were nearly gone, the hillside below him brighter still.

FOX HILL—NOVEMBER 28, 1950, 2:30 A.M.

They had changed shifts, each man welcoming the opportunity to dig down deep into the relative warmth of his sleeping bag. Riley was up again, the cold deadening his senses as it deadened his arms. If his feet weren't warm, at least he could wriggle his toes, the bag still pulled up over his legs. The challenge again was to keep the tears in his eyes from freezing, the hood pulled as tight as possible, as long as it allowed him to see some part of the hillside below. He took the watch very seriously, had known men in the last war who cost lives by falling asleep or focusing more on their own cigarette than on who else out there might see the glowing ash. The officers drove home the punishment for that, of course, a part of every man's training. Falling asleep on watch was punishable by death, though he had never known anyone to carry that out. More likely, a man who fell asleep might be executed by a stealthy enemy.

He had slept for most of his allotted two hours, knew that Killian took his watch just as seriously. If a man could not completely trust his buddy, there wasn't much sleep to be had, especially where the enemy preferred a nighttime assault. For all of Killian's annoying traits, Riley had come to depend on him when it counted most, even if Welch seemed to despise the man.

He looked down at the dark mound in the hole beside him, a hint of snoring, the only other sound but the blustery wind. He tried to measure the time in his mind, thought, Maybe another half hour to go. Hamp will tell me. He crawls around these holes like some kind of rat, popping up when you need him to. He won't let Sean get one minute more sleep than he deserves. He stared to the front again, squinted against the wind, the breeze finding its way down his neck. Damn it all, he thought. Who thought climbing up here, out in the wide damn open, was so damn necessary?

He looked to the side, saw the shadowy forms leaning out above the edges of foxholes all along the hillside, hidden only partially by the low clusters of brush. We'll lose somebody to frostbite tonight, he thought. There's always one, too stupid to follow orders, who knows better than the brass. And they'll peel him away from his socks and chop off his damn feet. The thought made him shiver, and he flexed his toes again, the regular routine, every few seconds testing just how much protection the sleeping bag was giving him. His mind had begun to wander aimlessly, nonsensical, no distraction but the steady blast from the wind. The image of his wife floated past, but that only made him miserable, all that he was missing, all that was waiting for him, and he pushed hard at that, his brain finally settling on a more obvious misery, the cold, how cold, where it might be colder. Hate to be an Eskimo, he thought. They live in this crap all the time. I guess. How the hell do you build an igloo? No Eskimos in this outfit. Maybe one of the new guys. Boy, I bet they're having a peach of a time, right out of Pendleton. Southern California. Welcome to frozen hell, children.

The replacements had continued to come, arriving in trucks even in Hagaru-ri, brought along with some of the men from the First Regiment. They're here right now, he thought. Second Platoon got some of 'em. There's that one big kid, bigger than Killian, another New Jersey kid. Cafferino, Cafferata, something like that. Football player, they say. I guess he'll be good if we mount a charge. Killian'd be good at that, too. Something a little nuts about big guys. Wonder what the Chinese think about that? They're not as puny as the Japs, most of 'em. They must think we're strange, all those big guys. Or maybe we just make easier targets. All right, you idiot, think of something else.

He forced himself to stare down the wide hill, blinked through the crust around his eyes, the tears forming a film of ice against his cheeks. There was a hard shout back behind him, shattering the silence, and he spun around, numb fingers on the rifle. He saw now a shadowy shape, moving fast, a full run toward him, then up and over, hard footsteps on the icy ground. Riley felt his chest thundering, swung around, tried to see down the hill, nothing there, heard laughter, close by, another of Welch's squad.

"Holy Christ! You see that?"

Riley wanted to respond, his hands quivering, a hard grip on the rifle. Another man responded now, closer, the voice of Welch.

"It was a deer. Sure as hell. Caught a good look when it jumped. Hey, Pete. You see that?"

Riley felt a nervous laugh rising up inside of him, the ice in his chest relaxing. "Yeah. Jumped right over me. Scared hell out of me."

"Yeah, I bet. Wonder what scared *him*?"

A different sound came now, an odd chorus far back to the left, down low, muffled by the wind. He wanted to ask, but the others were rising up, weapons coming up, questions swept away by the wind. More sounds came now, low thumps, a chattering from a single machine gun. He kept his eyes that way, kicked out into Killian's bag, said, "Sean! Get up!"

Killian responded, the bag shoved aside, rising up, rifle in hand. "What the hell's going on?"

The sounds increased, a spattering of small blasts, nothing to see, the ground hidden by the curve of the hill. He kept his eyes that way, thought, Sounds like from the road. He strained to hear, a hint of rifle fire, another machine gun. Streaks of green now sprayed over the crest of the ridge, some bouncing high, impacts of machine gun fire on the hard ground.

"Make ready!"

Riley turned abruptly, saw McCarthy moving up to the foxholes. Riley pulled his eyes toward the open hillside in front of him, straining to see, the cold forgotten now. Killian leaned forward, beside him, his weapon pointed forward, said, "Come on, you bastards! Try it right here."

McCarthy was behind them now, his voice cutting through the hard breeze. "There's something going on down below. No word from the captain. No answer on the field phone. Keep your eyes down that hill. If those boys need our help, we'll give it. But the enemy could be any-where. We need some mortar fire up here; light up this hillside. Can't raise anybody on the radio!"

Riley could hear the anxiousness in McCarthy's voice, looked back to the left again, staring at nothing, what seemed like muffled mortar rounds, scattered tracers from distant machine guns. He stared hard down the hillside, moonlight and snow, nothing else there, and now more fire, closer, from the left, Second Platoon. Beside him, Killian said, "They're hitting the captain's CP. They're down on the road. A hell of a lot of good we're doing up here!"

Riley kept his eyes to the front, said, "You don't know that. We've got machine guns there, the mortar teams. Plenty of strength. They need us, we'll know."

"What the hell are we supposed to do? Sit up here and wait for all hell to break out? Sounds like it already has!"

McCarthy seemed to hear him, shouted, "Stay put! Hold this perimeter! We see the enemy in our rear, then we hit them. But right now we have to hold this line and keep watch along this hillside!"

Riley could hear Killian's grumbling, said, "Easy, Sean. Maybe this one isn't for us. You want a damn fight, there's time yet."

He kept his eyes on the new sounds from the left, saw now, far beyond, a flare.

"Hey. What the hell's that?"

Killian stared that way, more flares rising, barely visible in the far distance.

"Oh, hell. I bet that's Yudam-ni. Illumination flares. Somebody's lighting up the world up there. Something's happening, for damn sure. That's not what we're hearing, though."

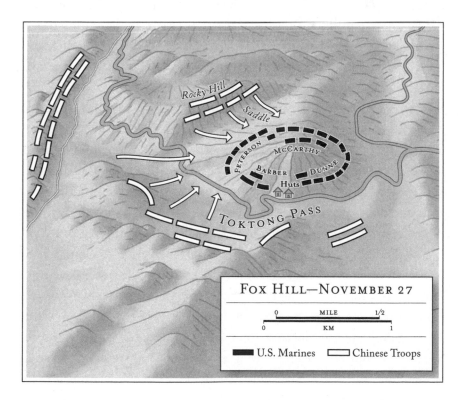

FOX HILL—NOVEMBER 27

| 0 | MILE | 1/2 |

| 0 | KM | 1 |

■■■ U.S. Marines   ☐☐ Chinese Troops

A new shower of green tracers sprayed past, coming from the saddle. A mortar burst impacted behind them, another down to the right, more tracers, the chattering of those guns swept away by the wind. Riley crouched lower in the foxhole, his eyes fixed on the hillside below. The firing seemed to grow on the left, another burst of tracer fire, and now a frantic voice behind them, McCarthy, "They're coming! Give 'em hell!"

Riley gripped the M-1 in his hands, a desperate search for targets, for any kind of movement. But the sounds came first, a chorus of bugles, the crashing of cymbals, and now movement, down the hill. They came in a line, a dozen men, moving slowly, a steady march upward. The machine gun to his left opened, a chattering rattle, red tracers slicing through the men, the line obliterated. Riley stared, dumbfounded, watched another short column farther down, slow progress up the hill, as though no one was watching them. The machine gun opened again, rifle fire down the line, the enemy falling away, some of those men scampering farther down the hill. The bugles came again, somewhere in the darkness, and Riley kept his eyes toward the sounds, scattered rifle fire coming from the men around him. He yelled at the others in his mind, instinctive, Wait! There's nothing to shoot at! He rose up, aimed the rifle, still nothing, then a new sound, close below him, a sharp *click*, a voice down in front of him, and now shadows rising up, a flurry of motion, the ground around him impacted by grenades, rolling, bouncing. The first blast came to one side, then more, mostly behind him, his reflexes pushing his face down below the dirt. He waited, the grenades silent, heard more clicks, and he rose up, saw a man a few yards away jamming the potato masher onto the frozen ground, arming it, the *click*. A new shower of grenades filled the air above him, and Riley crouched low, sheltered by the frozen dirt in front of the foxhole, Killian there as well, loud cursing, his face a shadow. The blasts ripped along the ridgeline, a sharp scream coming from the left, more rifle fire, a brief chatter from the BAR. Killian shouted into his face, "Now!"

They rose up together and Riley looked for targets, but the targets were all around him, men running past, more down the hill, coming toward him. The rifle fire was steady now, every direction, and Riley saw a man scamper straight toward him, a flash of fire from Killian, the man tumbling down, loose grenades rolling into the foxhole. Riley fired the rifle, then again, men running past on both sides of the foxhole, some falling, others pushing past, the bursts from their machine guns silhouetting them. Riley fired again, no aim, the rifle at his chest, his back against the foxhole, his hands shaking, and he focused on one man, running across, behind the foxhole, his burp gun blazing. Riley pointed, fired, the man stumbling down, rising up again, staggering, then dropping flat. Riley searched frantically, another cluster of men moving past, and he fired again, no aim necessary. The clip popped free from his rifle, and he struggled with stiff fingers, pulled another from his belt, rammed it home, jerked the trigger, fired into a half-dozen men standing tall over him. He jammed the rifle upward, fired into a man's gut, then another, Killian answering with shouts, emptying another clip, the cluster of men tumbling down, one man rolling into the hole, crushing weight on Riley's chest. He yelled, pushed the man off, the man still moving, and Riley reached for the knife at his ankle, his fingers too clumsy, the man rising slowly, on his knees, a burst of fire from somewhere close, the man knocked flat. Riley looked that way, saw men crawling, flashes from the other foxholes, a brief gratefulness, silent words, *thank you.* He aimed the rifle again, unsure if it was empty, Killian cursing, then up, firing quickly, another clip, Killian working to reload. From below, more men came in a rush, and Killian aimed downward, eight quick shots, another clip, Riley pointing the rifle, pulling the trigger, nothing, damn! He ripped at a new clip, jammed it in, cursed the gloves, his brain yelling at him to take his time, choose targets, his voice responding, "Too many!"

He emptied the clip again, didn't hear his own rifle, the fire blending with so many others'. But around him, all along the foxholes, men were screaming, hideous sounds, one more sound, Killian, shouting into his ear, "Grenades! Throw all you got!"

Riley crouched low, men still running past, saw Killian rise up, a hard throw, another, down the hill. Riley pulled a grenade from his shirt, ripped at the pin, tossed it low, then again, two more, nothing left.

"Grab the Chink things!"

Riley remembered the man falling, his load rolling into the hole. He bent low, felt in the darkness, his fingers wrapping on the handle of a potato masher. He wanted to ask, How do they work? But there wasn't time, a new line of the enemy jogging up the hill. He jammed the butt of the wooden handle against a rock, heard the telltale click, flung it downward, searched for another, felt only dirt. Killian had his pistol now, quick blasts into men close by, bursts of machine gun fire blowing over Riley's head, some downward, ripping the frozen ground. He thought of the pistol, but the rifle was there, ready, and he emptied another clip, fewer men close by, some running, kneeling. Riley felt his belt, more ammo, several clips, *thank God,* and he waited, searched, saw a man walking up, standing still now, a few feet away, waving to the others, his form outlined by the flashes, the moonlight, the snow, a perfect silhouette. Riley raised the rifle, the blast into the man's head, one more of the enemy tumbling away. He spun around, the fight spreading out behind him, found another shadow, the man standing motionless, as though watching, as though nothing else mattered, the M-1 blowing a flash of fire into the man's back. Men began to flow back past him, down the hill, pulling away, the fight slowing, a burst from the machine gun to the left, red tracers spraying back along the ridge, toward the Marines. Down below, the Chinese seemed to gather up, another line, bugles again, coming again, falling, others driven back, only to return, then driven back again.

The firing was continuous, all variety of noises, the spray of the burp guns, the fire from the heavy machine guns, the BAR, more of the M-1s and carbines all along the hillside. The screams came as well, discordant noise, men staggering close, still firing, more grenades coming in, streaks of fire from machine guns, both ways, splashes of color, Riley's brain struck by the sight, fireworks, like the Fourth of July. . . .

CHAPTER TWENTY-THREE

. . . .

Riley

FOX HILL—NOVEMBER 28, 1950, DAWN

HE WAS AWAKE NOW, stared out over Killian's head, nothing to see, strained to hear past the hard ringing in his ears. The snow had come again, a cold fog settling low on the crest of the hill. Riley sank down into the sleeping bag, gathered up against his legs, tried to flex his toes. His fingers were stiff and stinging, and he looked at the gloves, the bare trigger finger, curled his hand up against his chest. Killian was staring out, the M-1 lying across the hard mound of frozen earth, its bayonet fixed.

"Good. You're awake. It's light enough. You gotta see this. We musta killed them all."

"Doubt that."

His words came in a low grunt, choked away by the painful burn in his throat. He tried to swallow, the pain worse, and Killian looked down at him now.

"Hey! You okay? You wounded?"

Riley had already done his personal inventory, no damage that he could feel. "Don't think so. What's happening? It's awful damn quiet."

"Pretty damn amazing. There's a million dead Shambos." Killian paused. "Looks like a bunch of us, too."

Riley sat up now, a flash through his brain. *Welch.*

"We gotta go down the line, check out the others. We made it through. But there could be wounded, fellows we need to help."

Killian stared out, nodded. "I'll go. You keep an eye out, watch my ass. There's too many bodies out here, and I bet some of 'em ain't dead enough."

Riley straightened up to his knees, still curling his stiff fingers, gripped the M-1. "I got one clip left."

Killian rose up higher, leaned his M-1 against the side of the hole, pulled out his pistol. "That's one more than me, old chum. My forty-five's gotta do. That, and the bayonet. Okay, here I go."

Killian was out of the hole now, crouching low, Riley up, scanning the ground, snow and the bodies of white-clad Chinese. The snowfall was steady, a thick gray sky, hiding the distant rocky hill. Killian moved off slowly, and Riley looked toward Welch's hole, knew only that it had been off to the left. Where the hell are you, Hamp? He wanted to call out, breaking the heavy silence, still fought the burning pain in his throat, breathed into his glove. Along the hillside, the other foxholes were mostly hidden, dark places in the snow. He stared, expected to see others up, like Killian, the usual routine after a tough fight. But no one moved, no voices, none of the idiotic chatter. He turned, watched Killian sliding into the next hole to the right, waited, the hard chill driving into his chest, his heartbeat quicker still. What the hell is this? The words came out from inside, his panic taking charge, a burst of noise.

"Hey, Sarge!"

He stared toward Welch's hole again, then back to Killian, who was head-high in the next hole, staring back at him. Killian shook his head, said, "There's nobody home. Roll up my sleeping bag, would ya? I'm going farther."

Riley stood slowly, unlocked the agony in his legs, gathered up both bags. He tied his up tightly, fastened to his pack, the straps over his shoulders. The M-1 was slid up under one arm, and he crawled up out of the hole. The backpack seemed heavier, dead weight on his stiff back, and he moved the opposite way from Killian, toward Welch's hole, stepped past a white-clad corpse, stopped, a quick look at the Chinese soldier. The man had a clean bloody hole through his forehead, and

Riley didn't stare, thought, Dead enough, turned away, took a few more steps. He stopped, scanned the half-dozen holes he could see, the hillside dropping off into a snowy abyss. Dammit, Hamp, where the hell are you? He took another slow step, the soft crunch of his boots the only sound. There were more bodies now, a pair of Marines, falling together, one man staring up, snow covering his face like a thin sheet. Riley turned away, didn't want to see, cursed himself, forced himself to look, to know, took another step forward, his eyes locked on the man. He knelt, saw through the snow, the recognition now. That's Tilhoff, he thought. Oh, hell. He moved to the next man, pulled at the man's shoulder, rolled him over, the man's chest a frozen pool, pink blood. Troxell. Paul. Oh, Christ.

The bullet whistled past his head, and Riley froze, unsure of the direction. Now more came past, a ripple through the snow in front of him. He dropped low, rolled hard into the closest hole, heard Killian, "You Shambo bastards! Hey, Pete! They're shooting at us!"

He expected Killian to empty his pistol, his usual response, but the silence came again, the soft whisper of the snow. Riley pulled himself up, the foxhole not as deep as his own, listened for any other sound. He saw a helmet in one end of the hole, a dent in one side, picked it up, tried not to see any more details. He raised it slowly above him, moved it back and forth, dropped it down, then raised it again. The air was sliced by machine gun fire, a brief burst, and Riley tried to measure the distance from the sound of the gun. Not close, he thought. Maybe that damn hill. He probably can't see too much. But he knows that if it moves, and it ain't wearing white, shoot it. He thought of Killian. Yeah. Shambo bastard.

But where the hell did everybody go?

"Hey, Sean!"

"Yeah?"

"What you find?"

Killian seemed to hesitate, and finally, "Stein and Stillwell. Didn't make it out of their holes. There's three more back behind. I'm in our hole. Ain't about to leave my backpack. What the hell do we do now?"

Riley peered up, the snowfall heavier now. "I'm trying it this way.

You oughta come with me. Second platoon was over on our flank. Somebody's gotta be out here. Or else we'll keep going, and find our way down to the road."

"If you say so. I ain't staying in this hole, for sure. Too much nasty stuff in here. There's a bloody knife, and a busted-up grenade. Probably had my foot on it all night."

Riley picked up the helmet again, couldn't avoid looking it over. No blood.

"I'm holding up a tin hat. Whenever you're ready, head this way. You'll see it."

He heard the footsteps, Killian's hard grunts, the big man sliding low, coming down into him with a cascade of rock and snow. Riley pulled his legs in tight, not tight enough, Killian crushing him.

"Jesus, Sean!"

Killian crawled to one side, hard breathing, said, "Sorry. This ain't much of a hole."

"They didn't have to park their ox in here, like I did."

Killian reached down, raised an ammo belt. "Son of a bitch. Coulda used these. My M-1's empty. These boys didn't do all that much shooting. Here. Take it."

Riley took the belt, six full clips. "Great. Three for you. Might need 'em." He thought of the two men, ran the names through his head. "I knew Tilhoff from boot."

Killian rubbed his hand over his face, pulled on the hood of his parka. "Yeah, I guess. I try not to make friends. This is why. There's more bodies farther to the right. No sign of the kid, or Kane. They musta pulled out, and somebody didn't give us the word. I guess we were a little busy. God, Pete, I musta shot down half a battalion. Ran out of everything but forty-five slugs. I'm with you. We should head out this way. We find a corpsman, we'll send him up here, check on these guys."

He weighed Killian's words, thought, Maybe we oughta stay. If there's anybody wounded, we can't just run off. But where'd everybody else go? How'd we miss *that* order? How could Hamp just up and leave? Or maybe . . . he didn't.

"We'll have to check 'em all, bring them down the hill, dead or alive. There could be a bunch more we can't see."

"Fine. One thing at a time. Corpsmen and Graves Registration can do their jobs. I'd rather get off this hill on my feet."

Riley kept his anger inside, no time for arguments. He kept his eyes on the snowfall, raised up slightly, said, "Snow's getting lighter now. We can't wait. I think that machine gun's out on the saddle, or beyond. I'll go first, if you want, and if he opens up, we'll dive into anyplace we see. If he doesn't, let's just keep going till we see somebody."

"I always knew you were officer material. I'm ready if you are."

Riley slowly stood, slid the rifle up out of the hole. He climbed out, didn't hesitate, rolled away from the hole, then up to his feet, a hard run, the hood of his coat pushed back, snow in his eyes. He jogged to one side, moved through a pair of tall rocks, then out in the open again, low brush, trampled snow, more Chinese bodies, and he dropped into a hole, gasping through the frigid air. He could hear Killian, the man letting out a hard grunt, another hole a few yards away. Riley tried to catch his breath, fought the cold in his throat, the pain returning. Water, he thought. He reached for his canteen, shook it, frozen solid, what passed now for normal. He sat up, eyed the snow, reached one hand out, gripped the soft powder, held it for a long second, then slid it into his mouth. He worked his tongue, the powder thawing into wet goo, but the taste was awful, as much dirt as snow. He tried to swallow, felt like choking, and he spit, blew out what he could. He let out a breath, looked over toward Killian.

"Hey, Sean. You okay?"

"Yeah. Got a buddy here."

"In the hole? You know him?"

"Not likely. Shambo. Stinking son of a bitch. Garlic and piss."

Riley fought the grime in his mouth, reached for more snow, more careful this time. He poured it from his hand into his mouth, waited for the thaw, the wetness helping, only a little.

"God, Sean. I need water. Canteen's a block of ice."

"Can't help you. Mine's frozen, and there's a bullet hole in it."

Riley took a long breath, shifted himself in the hole. "You ready to go?"

"Lead the way, General."

Riley rose up, saw the snow had nearly stopped. The hillside was bathed in a thin fog, and he eyed the saddle, could see the vague shape of the rocky hill beyond. Hope that bastard's a lousy shot, he thought. He scanned more Chinese bodies, a dozen or more close by, started to climb from the hole, saw movement, one man rolling over, and Riley pointed the rifle, no aim, the man pulling a grenade from his coat, Riley firing, missing, then firing again. The second shot burst into the man's stomach, punching him in a curl, the man groaning, rolling over.

"Shoot him again!"

Riley responded, aimed now, the shot piercing the man's chest. Riley kept his stare on the soldier, said, "He has a grenade. Stay away from him!"

Killian was there now, said, "I ain't got no need to crawl around with no Shambo. Keep your eyes open, I guess. Anybody moves, plug him."

The machine gun fired again, a spray of bullets through the snow beside them. Riley ducked low, heard a husky voice, "This way!"

The voice came from straight ahead, along the edge of the hill. Killian said, "Who the hell is that?"

"Does it matter? Let's go."

He ran hard, heard more firing from the machine gun, searched for the source of the voice. A few yards down the hill he saw a helmet, the man mostly hidden by a slit trench, and he ran that way, the machine gun stitching the ground around him. He slid down now, his backside scraping the rocks, his legs leading him into the trench. He knew Killian was close, said, "Big man coming in behind me!"

Killian crashed in quickly, the men making way. Riley fought his breathing again, saw three men, a handful of wounds, one man in his socks. He was a big man, bigger than Killian, a bandage wrapped around one hand.

"Welcome to our piece of paradise. You ain't much of a rescue team. We were hoping you'd come to get us the hell out of here."

Riley heard the heavy New Jersey accent, no different from Morelli.

"We were hoping you'd do the same for us. I'm Pete Riley. This ugly mother is Sean Killian. What happened to your boots?"

The big man held the wounded hand upright, beamed a broad, friendly smile. "They're down the hill a ways. Didn't have time to get dressed properly when the Chinks showed up. Don't need 'em anyhow. The good-looking one there is Harry Pomers. Ain't worth a damn now that he's shot up. Hell of a linebacker, though. The kid there, he's Smith, though I'm bettin' that's an alias. Too young to be a Marine. Shoots good, I'll give him that. We took out a pile of those bastards last night. They kept coming, we kept piling 'em up. Name's Cafferata. Hector Cafferata."

"I guess that's about it. We'd shoot a pile of 'em, and they'd send a bunch more, and all the while they're tossing grenades at us. I ran out of ammo and ended up using my shovel, whacking hell out of them, sending 'em back down the hill. Old Benson helped best he could, but he got half-blinded by a grenade. Even blind, he helped reload, until we ran out of lead. We skedaddled up here, found this trench, and these two birds. Made a hell of a stand, the lot of us." Cafferata paused. "It was beautiful."

Riley stared, amazed at Cafferata's story. "You batted the grenades back? You some kind of baseball player?"

Cafferata laughed, winced, his good hand massaging the dirty bandage. "Football. World's worst baseball player. I guess we rise to it sometimes. Caught a few, threw them back. One took off my damn finger. Chink grenades ain't too efficient, or I'd be spread out all over this hill. Benson's lucky he only lost his sight, not his damn head. Dumb bastard took off on his own. No, check that. He's the best man I ever fought with. But he's pigheaded. Said he had to get to an aid station, blind or not. Tried to help him, he wouldn't have it, said he'd be okay. Corpsmen running around everywhere, I figured he'd get help."

Cafferata stopped smiling now, a hint of guilt on the man's face. Riley said, "He probably made it."

Pomers said, "Yeah. It was nuts for a while, but the corpsmen were scrambling around here like ants. Grenade smacked me around, blood-ied my head, and this damn corpsman drops in here from outta no-where. Fixes me up, then he's gone again. Never saw him after that. That's just what they do, I guess. Pretty damn useful for a squid."

Riley studied Pomers's wound, blood in a dark stain on the man's face and chest. "Guess we better get you to an aid station, too. We didn't see anybody else. Where'd they go?"

Pomers said, "My squad's mostly down. We got swarmed over, not much we could do to help each other." He paused, and Riley saw a stab of emotion. Pomers seemed to fight it, said, "Order finally came to pull back, but I couldn't move. The kid here stayed with me. Dumb son of a bitch."

Riley looked at Smith, who said nothing.

"Yeah, we got one of those, too."

Cafferata said, "Right at dark, the lieutenant sent Benson and me down low, like a lookout post. Told us if we saw something, we were supposed to haul it back up here, let everybody know. But it was too quick. Never heard the bastards coming. They were tossing grenades as soon as we smelled 'em. Once it started, we got surrounded pretty quick. Hightailed it up the hill, found this trench. And these two morons."

Pomers seemed weak, and Riley watched him, Pomers removing his helmet. There was a bloody bandage around his head, and Pomers saw Riley's look, said, "We were supposed to keep the Chinks off the two thirties. The first one, Ladner's piece, there were too many Chinks. We knocked a bunch of 'em down, but they got the gun. Musta nailed his whole gun crew, too. Ladner wouldn't have given up his thirty for any-thing. Lieutenant's gonna give us hell."

Cafferata looked at Pomers, said, "I'm tired of hearing that crap. The Chinks put everything they had into grabbing those thirties. How many of those bastards do we have to kill before somebody thinks we done all we could?"

Pomers eased the helmet down on the bandage. "We didn't do enough."

Killian spoke now, said, "That's bull. We're still here, and a bunch of those Shambos ain't. Our job now is to find out where the rest of our guys went, and if we can't do that, then we need to kill another pile of those quilted bastards. They can't be far. Maybe pulled back, up on that rocky hill. You can talk all day if you want to, or wait for those sons of bitches to come back. I'd like to see you bat down a few grenades, but this ain't the time."

Riley heard chatter, out toward the saddle. "Hey! Shut up. Listen. What the hell's that?"

Killian was quiet now, the men rising up together, and Riley could see more of the saddle, the fog clearing away. The voices came from that way, movement down one side of the hill, Chinese soldiers gathering, searching the bodies of their dead.

Killian said, "Get ready. We got enough ammo to make a fight of it, anyway."

Riley saw more soldiers farther back, motion up on the saddle itself, another column back on the rocky hill. "Hell, no. There's a whole battalion out there, maybe more. This ain't my day to play Custer. If the company's pulled back, we'll find them. I say, let's move." He looked at Pomers. "Can you walk? Crawl, even?"

Pomers rolled up to his knees. Put one foot down, testing. "I'm ready. Custer's not my hero, either."

Cafferata was nodding his own approval, and Riley looked at Killian.

"Well? You gonna fight this war by yourself? Or you gonna be smart for once?"

Killian stared out toward the Chinese, lowered his head. "Okay. But I swear, Pete."

Cafferata said, "What's your damn problem? The Chinks ain't going anywheres else. You wanna have another party like last night, you just wait for sundown. They don't mind being killed one bit. They just step over their buddies and keep coming. I need some ammo, more grenades, and a better bandage on my finger. It hurts like hell. And I'm damn sure gonna find Benson." He looked at Pomers, the kid, then at Riley. "You ready?"

Riley inhaled, another sharp stab of cold, a hard look at Killian, said, "Let's move out together, then spread apart. Head for the ridgeline. Once you get into some cover, make noise, holler, tell 'em you're a Marine. Make sure anybody out there knows who you are. I don't wanna get gunned down by some nervous kid like Morelli."

They moved as quickly as wounds and stiff legs would allow. The machine guns on the far hill made a brief effort, scattered sprays of fire that didn't find a target. But the Chinese troops seemed more content to hold back, lying low, hidden by the terrain, out of sight of any patrolling aircraft.

The order for the Marines to withdraw had come after the first major Chinese assault, the surprise completely effective. In minutes, openings had been punched all through the Marine positions. The order came first from Captain Barber, Lieutenant McCarthy passing along the only order he could, to salvage what remained of his platoon. Most of the men responded, pulling back over the center ridge of the hill, re-forming down the hill closer to the tree line in their rear. Those who remained were completely engulfed by hordes of Chinese soldiers, or too wounded to respond at all. Even as the Third Platoon was maneuvering to safety, on their left, the Second Platoon had been hit again, another surge by hidden Chinese troops who had swung up the hill from the road below.

With Captain Barber doing all he could to re-form his position and his command, the picture became clearer. The Chinese had come up from the south and east, slipping along the main road, striking hard into Barber's command post. In the chaos that swallowed the position, Barber had managed to pull his command staff up the hill, repositioning the mortars and what remained of the machine guns, his men using the timber for cover, pushing most of the Chinese in that area away. But the Chinese simply moved toward other targets, driving up the hill, maneuvering out along the saddle, completely hidden by the darkness and the rugged terrain. They struck first at the junction between Second and Third Platoons, aiming for the pair of light machine guns anchored there, those crews and the men who protected them, with little chance to hold back the overwhelming numbers against them. In every case, as they advanced into position, the grenadiers led the way, the men whose single job was to slip closely enough to the Marines without being detected so they could effectively throw their grenades. With signals given by their officers, the crashing of cymbals, the notes of a bugle, the riflemen were sent forward, stepping over and past the first line of men to be cut down. Despite the warning from the bizarre noisemakers, several of the Marines never fired a shot, the men who paid little heed to the warnings from their lieutenants to keep alert. As had happened before, those few men who were too exhausted and too cold to do anything but sleep had been bayoneted in their sleeping bags.

For more than four hours the Chinese pushed hard into the front and left side of Barber's horseshoe perimeter. The cost in casualties for the Chinese was horrific, entire columns shot down as they swarmed over and around the Marine positions. Their one success came with Barber's order to withdraw, the Chinese moving up into some of the foxholes the Americans had left behind. But with the dawn, the fighting ceased. The Chinese knew too well that the Americans would once again make good use of air support, and that on this wide hill any movement by a concentration of troops could result in slaughter. Once more the Chinese would pull back into cover, waiting for the darkness.

On the night of November 27, the attack on Fox Company was but one part of Sung Shi-lun's plan to exterminate the entire Marine and army presence in eastern North Korea. The discovery of the Marine outpost at Toktong Pass had been, for the Chinese, a happy accident. The Chinese had already surrounded Marine positions from Yudam-ni to Koto-ri, slicing across the main supply road, completely isolating the American forces into what resembled a loosely spaced string of five pearls. As the Marines at Yudam-ni pushed westward, in obedience to MacArthur's orders, they were increasingly aware that the Chinese were in force in the hills around them. What they could not know was that the Chinese were obeying orders as well.

They had split up, Riley and Killian slipping low, through the snowy brush and scattered rocks, while the others moved out toward their own commands. Riley had given a good-luck salute to the others, concerned that their wounds needed treatment. But they had insisted on moving out toward the aid station on their own, which Riley appreciated. He had no idea where any aid station might be.

Killian let him lead the way, their custom now, the Irishman losing some of his bluster. As they slipped along, Riley kept the best cover behind him, protection from the snipers who picked at them still. He sat down now, the agony of the cold in his lungs, tried to slow his breathing, Killian collapsing beside him.

"What now, Pete?"

He heard the pain in Killian's voice, said, "We gotta be close to somebody. This hill ain't the Rocky Mountains. The only Chinese up here are the ones they left behind."

Killian pulled his boots up close to his chest, a futile grab at his toes. "Damn it all. I gotta get out of these socks. My feet are dead numb."

Riley flexed his own toes, could feel the harsh sting of the wet cold. "Then we gotta move." He heard a voice just past a cluster of small rocks, down a slight draw, whispered, "What the hell's that?"

Killian was up, kneeling, peering that way, the pistol in his hands. Riley moved up with him, the rifle cradled in both hands, and he saw now a pair of men in white uniforms, kneeling low, tugging at a body. Killian said, "Shambos! Take 'em out!"

"What the hell are they doing?"

"Who the hell cares! Take 'em out!"

Riley pressed the rifle to his shoulder, the men no more than thirty yards away. He aimed, the gun sight squarely on one man's back, squeezed the trigger, the man punched down. The other soldier looked around sharply, searching, and Riley saw his face, terrified, Killian with a hard whisper in his ears, "Shoot the bastard!"

The rifle fired again, the man falling over, and Killian was up quickly, hobbling toward them, his pistol held out. Riley stood slowly, moved that way, heard Killian whoop.

"You nailed 'em both, straight through the heart! Bastards were stripping one of our guys."

Riley scanned the distant ridge, said, "Let's go. Snipers gotta be watching us."

The sniper obliged, a sharp crack off a rock beside him, and Riley scooted away, rolled down behind another rock. He was annoyed at Killian now, the man throwing out loud curses toward the sniper. Damn you, he thought. Be smart once in a while. Killian was there now, heavy breathing, sliding clumsily through the powdery snow.

"Hey! Lookee here! They had these old rifles. Seen 'em before. Russian, seven point six two. I bet they work better than any damn carbines. Grabbed both of 'em, and a cartridge belt. I ain't running out of ammo again. You want one?"

"Mine works just fine. You can go souvenir hunting later."

The crack of another shot splattered the frozen ground beside Riley. "Let's go!"

He was on his feet quickly, didn't wait for Killian, made a darting run for a clump of low brush. He slowed, glanced back, the saddle mostly hidden, saw Killian in a limping run. Riley didn't wait, the hill dipping low, another slight ridge to the front, and he jumped up again, a quick dart to the rise.

"Get down, you moron!"

The voice startled him, and he stumbled, fell, Killian coming up behind him, a hearty shout, "Well, we made it! I knew you bastards wouldn't have run off and left us. What the hell you all doing back here?"

Riley unraveled himself from the snow and frozen brush, realized he was flat against a wall of dead Chinese. He backed away, saw men peering up over the corpses, familiar faces, rough beards, weary smiles, black, tired eyes. He crawled up on the bodies, tried not to feel the quilting, the frozen bodies, rolled over the barricade into a slit trench, dropped low, his knees weak, a hand under his arm, another lifting him up.

"Hey, it's Riley. Damn, Pete, we thought they got you. I knew Irish'd make it. Too dumb to get shot."

Riley searched the faces, the voice coming from Kane, the BAR crew there as well. He saw more slit trenches, foxholes in a jagged pattern around them, saw one head rising up, the red-faced eagerness of Morelli.

"Hey, Pete! I was worried about you! Thank God!"

Riley waved a weak hand toward the kid, tried to offer a smile, the cracks in his lips too painful. He saw McCarthy now, crawling low, moving closer, and McCarthy said, "Welcome back, Private. Glad you both made it. You wounded? I'll have the corpsman take a look."

Riley felt a fog settling over his brain, the hands still holding him up, and he focused on McCarthy, said, "Don't think so. Sir, you got any water? Mine's frozen solid."

McCarthy turned, called out, "Goolsby! On the double!"

Riley saw the young man scrambling low, flopping down behind the hole.

"Sir?"

"You call me that out here one more time and I'll feed you to the enemy. You got that, son?"

Goolsby nodded. "Sorry. Won't do it again. What you need, um, Bob?"

"Anything left in your canteen? The good one?"

Goolsby rolled over, slid the canteen out of his belt, held it out toward McCarthy.

"Half-full."

McCarthy took it, handed it to Riley, said, "Here."

Riley shook the canteen, surprised to hear the sloshing inside. He unscrewed the top, raised it to his mouth, caught an odd smell. McCarthy was watching him, and Riley took a quick drink, felt a soft burn. Beside him Kane laughed, rapped him on the back.

"It's okay, Pete. We figured out a remedy."

Riley drank again, and Killian was there now, said, "Hey, save some. I'm as dry as you."

Riley passed the canteen to Killian, and McCarthy said, "You didn't hear this from me, but Sergeant Welch has a knack for thievery. Somehow he found a bottle of medical alcohol. We mixed it in with the ice. Works like a champ."

Kane said, "Makes life just a little more rosy up here, too."

Riley focused on the single word. *Welch.*

"Where's he at? He okay?"

McCarthy said, "Aid station. The platoon took some hits. More than a dozen casualties. He went down to help a couple of the guys get fixed up. Rebbert's down there, with the doc. You two are lucky as hell. The enemy's scattered out all over the far side of the hill, and if their snipers could shoot worth a damn, we'd be wiped out. Mr. Goolsby, make sure they got dry socks. The captain's checking on Second Platoon, and if they're ready to go, we'll be moving out pretty quick."

Killian handed the canteen to Goolsby, said, "We leaving?"

McCarthy shook his head, pulled the hood of his coat up over his head. "Hell, no. We're going back up there, and knocking the Chinks off our damn hill!"

FOX HILL—NOVEMBER 28, 1950, 2:00 P.M.

The charge was quick and efficient, most of the Chinese not willing to stand up to a wave of screaming Marines. More of them had already pulled back to the safety of the deep draws, content to let their snipers

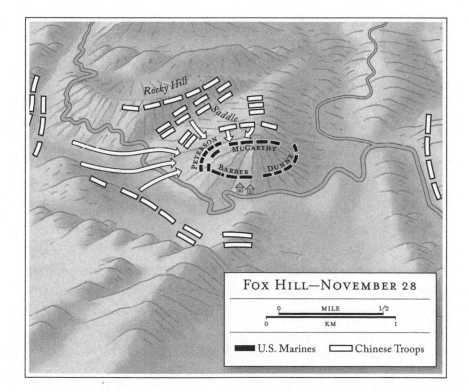

pick at any target they might find, including any man who attempted to return to the holes farthest forward. For now the perimeter across the crest of Fox Hill resembled a football, more than Barber's original horseshoe.

Riley settled into a new foxhole, Killian beside him, Killian pulling off his boots. Riley scanned the hillside below them, the distant ridge-line, no activity for now. But his eyes couldn't avoid the mess that was Killian's toes.

"Jesus, Sean. That looks awful."

"No, it don't. You keep your mouth shut. I'll be okay."

Riley leaned closer, winced. "That's gotta hurt. You gotta get down to the aid station."

"Shut up! I ain't going nowhere. They ain't carting me outta here just cause I got a few blisters."

"Sean, that's frostbite. Your toes are gray, for God's sake. How's it feel?"

Killian seemed to sag, his voice subdued. "It hurts like hell. It was okay as long as I couldn't see it. Or maybe they thawed out. Jesus, Pete. I can't go out like this. You can't say nothing."

Killian carefully slid fresh socks over his feet, and Riley looked down, said, "I won't say anything, not now. But if you can't fight, I'll have to. How you gonna march?"

"We ain't going anywhere no time soon. That's what the lieutenant said. I got these two new rifles, and a pile of ammo. I can kill as many Shambos as I need to from this damn hole!" Killian paused. "You got any Tootsie Rolls?"

Riley poked into his knapsack, mostly empty now, pulled out a piece of candy. "Here. We need to load up on rations. I'm hauling an empty sack. I'm wearing every damn piece of clothing they gave us. Got one more pair of fresh socks, and they're jabbed under my armpits."

Killian slid his legs slowly into his sleeping bag, pulled the bag up to his waist. "Mine are wet, inside my shirt. Whoever said that was the right idea?"

"That's what they told us, Sean. Dries 'em out faster."

"And freezes you to death from inside. I tell you, Pete, we get back home, I'm finding me a beach. I'm gonna stick my toes in hot sand and make my wife bring me drinks all day long. Umbrellas in 'em. Coconut and rum and God knows what else they grow in all those tropical places."

Riley thought of his conversation with the reporter, the only thing that seemed to matter. *Tomorrow.* "I just want to get off this hill in one piece, and walking."

"Been thinking about that. You think anybody knows where we are? I heard the radios don't work worth a crap. We're the back door and all. To what? What if the front door caves in, and all hell rolls this way? What're we supposed to do about it? We got problems of our own."

"You pick up those fancy-assed rifles of yours and you kill Chinese. It ain't hard."

The roar of the planes reached him now, and Riley turned that way, saw a formation of four Corsairs rolling up over the ridgeline to the west. Killian said, "Holy moly! Here they come!" He pointed out from the hole toward the saddle. "Over that way, boys!"

Others were shouting out as well, the infectious excitement of seeing the planes. The formation banked hard, all four dipping low, one lower still, and Riley raised up, strained to see, the plane lower than they were. The single Corsair rose up now, following the contour of the hill, skimmed low over the saddle, banked hard to one side, climbing now, moving past the rocky heights. Killian pounded one fist on the frozen ground, called out, "Don't go away mad! That's where they was hiding!"

Riley watched the other three, circling, now speeding down, fanning out, following the path of the first. Had to spot 'em first, he thought. The three planes seemed to work in perfect unison, a spray of rocket fire, streaks of white ending in blasts among the ragged rocks. Around Riley, men were cheering, and he couldn't help a smile, watched the first plane curl back around, low, along the saddle, pulling up now, a single bomb dropping, but it wasn't a bomb. He watched it tumbling down, bouncing on the saddle, rolling, and now the eruption, a massive ball of fire and black smoke, the saddle plastered with flames. Nearby, Riley heard the word, already forming in his own mind.

"Napalm!"

The cheers continued, the planes curling back, another run, machine gun fire, another rocket attack, the distant ridgeline alive with shattering explosions. Killian shouted out, "Wiped 'em out! Guarantee it! Yee-hah!"

The Corsairs curled around one more time, flying low, roaring past Riley's position, the faces of the pilots clear, goggles and smiles, the planes each dipping their wings, a final salute to the Marines. And as quickly as they had come, they were gone.

Riley kept his eyes on the saddle, the hill beyond, black smoke in a thick haze, drifting off, flames still in patches of brush. He felt his heart racing, realized he was smiling, heard the cheering still around him.

"God, Sean, that was amazing. I'd love to do that, fly one of those things."

The voice came from behind him, moving in close. "You'd smack right into these hills. You're a ground pounder. Leave the flying to the pilots."

Riley turned, saw Welch, no smile from either man. Welch said, "Stritch and Fry are dead. Bryan, too. The aid station's a mess. Half the platoon's been hit. The Second's pretty bad off, too."

Riley saw the painful emotion carved hard on Welch's face, something he had seen before.

Killian said, "That's rough, Sarge."

Riley said nothing, no words coming, a wave of anger, hurt, disappointment. Welch looked at him, said, "Let's go, Private. The lieutenant wants us to check out more of these wounded. Might still be some of our guys alive."

Riley said, "That's the corpsmen's job."

Welch's expression didn't change. "Then we're supposed to check on the enemy bodies, make sure nobody's still crawling around. Let's go."

Riley understood now, there was more to Welch's request than any orders from McCarthy. He climbed up and Welch turned away, walked slowly back through the rocky ground. Riley felt drained of any kind of humor, had nothing inside of him to break the odd tension between them. He followed for a dozen yards, and Welch slipped in behind a larger rock, stopped, waited. Riley was face-to-face with him now, and

Welch stared at him without speaking. Riley felt the anger taking over. He knew what he had to say.

"You left me out here."

Welch looked down, nodded slowly. "Yeah."

"I never thought you'd do that. We been through—"

"We've never been through *this*. Right here. This isn't Okinawa. I got the order to pull out. Goolsby was bawling, screaming that we had to pull back. Damn enemy was all over me, all over the whole squad. Every damn one of the new guys had shot up all his ammo. I had guts blown on me from Stiller. Took a grenade in his chest, I guess. I can still taste his blood. I put my knife through a Chink's neck while Goolsby's hollering the order." Welch paused. "I looked for you. Looked your way. All I saw was Chinks. I figured they got you. Both of you. I pulled Kane out, saved the BAR. McCarthy pulled everybody out he could find. We both did." Welch stopped, one hand up on his face, hiding a different emotion now. "Yeah. I shoulda stayed put. Made sure the whole squad . . . *my* whole squad was pulled out. I thought you were dead. You and Irish both."

Riley felt the anger slipping away, said, "I thought we were, too. I thought you . . . Christ, Hamp, I never had so many enemy so damn close. I don't know how many we killed. Dozens?"

"Captain Barber says he figures five hundred. He's hit, too. Saw him at the aid station. Took one in the leg, I think. Lieutenant Peterson's got it worse, but he's still over there with the Second." Welch looked at him now. "We're still here, Pete. This ain't gonna stop just 'cause we're tired of it."

"Killian wants to go to the beach. Stick his toes in the sand."

There was a gust of wind, Welch pulling his coat tightly around him.

"He isn't going to have any toes. I've seen him limping. That stupid son of a bitch is crippled up."

Riley was surprised, said, "Didn't know you watched us that close. Leave him be, Hamp. For now, anyway. He's good with a rifle. Better than me. I want him next to me."

Welch nodded. "I owe you that."

"You don't owe me a damn thing. Just do your job, Sergeant. And next time, make sure there's nobody left before you *how able* out of here."

Welch nodded, didn't respond, and Riley could see how angry Welch was, all of it directed toward himself. After a quiet moment, Riley held out his hand. Welch seemed surprised, stared down at Riley's gesture. He grabbed the hand, a firm shake, looked at Riley now, said, "I'll do my job. You do yours. Keep your head down, and your feet dry."

"Whatever you say, Sergeant."

Riley looked out toward the saddle, the black smoke nearly gone, small flickers of fire still dotting the brush. There was a familiar sound now, the distant rattle of a machine gun, shouts along the hillside. Welch glanced that way, said, "Back to your hole. I guess the air jockeys missed a few."

CHAPTER TWENTY-FOUR

· ·

Smith

HE WAS GETTING USED to the journeys by chopper, the colder air offering a smoother ride, dampening the harsh thermal currents that flowed around the steeper hills. But with the cold came the need for his heaviest gear, and even that didn't protect him completely from the sharp chill, stabbing hard up his legs, stiffening already stiff limbs.

For days now he had planned to advance his headquarters northward the sixty-plus miles from Hungnam to Hagaru-ri, the most logical location to keep in close touch with his entire command. His Marines were still spread out, from Koto-ri up past Yudam-ni, an infuriating situation he still could not completely repair. Until now his greatest nemesis had been Ned Almond, who continued to base his orders on the amazing delusions that flowed out of MacArthur's headquarters in Tokyo. Regardless of MacArthur's optimistic predictions, from Koto-ri up through Yudam-ni the Chinese had severed each link in his chain, heavy roadblocks of enemy troops slicing across the main supply road in dozens of key locations. It was no surprise to him that the Chinese were planning a major offensive, his own intelligence relying on the talk from the civilians, so many rooted out of their homes by

Chinese troops all along the way. His own patrols had continued to
skirmish with various outposts, those fights becoming stronger in the
days just past. It was essential to Smith that his three regiments continue drawing closer together, to confront what had become a serious
crisis. And yet Tokyo was still insisting that the Marines drive on to the
west, linking up with Eighth Army troops, no matter that those troops
were even now in a headlong retreat southward. But the roadblocks by
the Chinese had been surprisingly effective, and at every link in the
chain along Smith's main supply road, the convoys had been forced to
turn back barely a mile into their journey.

Only a small part of the necessary pieces of his headquarters had
made it as far as Hagaru-ri, the loads of essential equipment, including
communications gear, stalled in the trucks that were penned in with the
main body of Chesty Puller's troops at Koto-ri. If Smith's gear, including his own personal baggage, could not be transported to Hagaru-ri, at
least Smith and his key staff officers could make the journey by the one
means available. Even those men who admitted to a terrifying fear of
the helicopters were soon convinced to take the flight.

He kept his eyes to the horizon, couldn't shake a hard stirring in his gut,
far more than the usual butterflies from the bounce of the ride. The pilot
had obeyed his request, had flown close to the all-important bridge
south of Koto-ri, Smith paying particular attention to its condition,
amazed still that the Chinese had left it intact. Of course, he thought.
They're using it themselves, probably. As long as they make their moves
at night, there isn't much we can do to stop them. And so far, we're not
strong enough in any one place to shove them out of the way.

He shifted his eyes to the side, studied the closer hills, most of them
white. Out front, the ground flattened out, and through a light fog he
could see a blank gray smear on the horizon. Hagaru-ri, he thought. I'm
ready to get out of this thing.

The chopper suddenly dipped, jamming Smith against the Plexiglas
door, his hands reaching out against the windscreen in front. The chop-

per pulled upright, dipping lower now, the pilot making another sharp turn, a shrill voice now in the earphones cupping Smith's head.

"Sorry, sir! We're taking ground fire! Didn't expect that!"

Smith tried to calm the drumbeats in his chest. He looked over to the pilot, saw wide, focused eyes, the young man maneuvering the craft around a tall rocky dome, then a sweeping turn to the right.

"I didn't expect it, either, Lieutenant. Do what you have to do."

"Seemed to be rifle fire. Glad they don't have ack-ack. We'd be in trouble, for sure."

The words came out in a burst of nervousness, but the pilot kept a steady hand on the controls, the chopper climbing, clear of the cluster of hills. Smith tried to relax, studied the ground, nothing but snow, looked ahead to the plain, thought, A mile or less from our lines. Do we know they're out here? Well, yes, of course. Ridge knows his job. Puller wouldn't have sent him up here if he didn't.

Lieutenant Colonel Tom Ridge was one of Puller's battalion commanders, and the man now in charge of the defensive perimeter established around Hagaru-ri. As Smith had ordered at every one of the bases along the main road, Ridge had probed outward, only to find a strong presence of Chinese troops in every direction. Hagaru-ri was already considered the lynchpin of this entire operation, but Ridge had barely three thousand men in position there to defend it. By now Smith had hoped to have Puller's entire force, some five thousand more Marines. But Puller was penned in at Koto-ri, and until Smith could figure out how he would change that, Ridge had to make do with the strength he had at hand. The only help Smith could provide was to order all personnel, including cooks, supply officers, and truck drivers, to shoulder a weapon. It was one advantage the Marines had over the army. Every Marine was trained in handling a rifle, no matter what noncombat job he might assume down the road. Right now, at Hagaru-ri, every Marine was now a rifleman.

The chopper settled low, slowing, and Smith saw the landing pad below, a gathering of men in heavy coats. The chopper set down with a soft bump and Smith gave a brief thumbs-up to the pilot, pushed open the Plexiglas, a heavily gloved hand reaching out to help him. Smith reached back into the chopper, grabbed a small kit bag from beneath his seat. He looked at the aide again, ducked low beneath the chopper blades, put his hands up, sheltering his face, and the man waved him forward, Smith following to a waiting jeep. They climbed aboard, the driver engulfed in his coat like a green mummy. Smith realized the jeep was already running, the vehicle quickly lurching forward. He scanned the area they drove past, a mass of trucks and other equipment, enormous stocks of all variety of supplies. There was smoke swirling upward from a half-dozen large tents, but his eyes were blinded by tears now, and he lowered his hood, thought, Not the time for an inspection.

The door pulled open, a blast of warmth meeting Smith's face as he moved inside. He pulled back the hood, the aide removing his, and Smith realized it was Sexton.

"Welcome, sir. Please allow me to make this official."

Sexton saluted, a brief second of formality, and Smith returned it with a heavy gloved hand.

"Hardly necessary, under the circumstances, Captain."

"I don't agree, sir. Since this is your new CP, I thought you should be welcomed appropriately. This house has been set aside for your quarters. The staff tent is close by, outside. If you like, sir, I can have an aide arrange your gear."

Smith examined the room, one more to the rear, the typical Korean house he was used to. His eyes rested on a squat iron stove, glowing red, the only source of heat.

"That won't be necessary, Captain. The only gear I have is in that single bag. Unless the Chinese have captured it, my van and all my baggage are still in Koto-ri."

Sexton seemed concerned, said, "We'll fix that, sir. I'll have the men pitch in, put together everything you might need."

"I have a toothbrush and a razor. That will do for now. But what I *need* is Colonel Ridge. I need to know what we've heard from Litzenberg and Murray, and I need to know what's happening with the army.

We took ground fire a little south of here, and I need to know our estimation of the enemy's strength. It would be convenient to have some idea just what they're planning next."

Sexton waited for more, but Smith worked now to remove his coat. Sexton assisted him, then said, "Colonel Ridge is out on the perimeter, but he knows to watch for your chopper. The radio tent has been busy all morning, sir. Colonel Lockwood just left, with a convoy, intending to relocate his CP up toward Yudam-ni."

"Lockwood? Why was he still here? Aren't his people already at Yudam-ni?"

Sexton seemed uncomfortable, and Smith had no patience for hesitation, something Sexton knew well.

"I don't exactly know why the colonel was not with his men. But he has been in touch with one company of his battalion at Toktong Pass. That's about seven miles up, halfway or so to Yudam-ni."

"I've seen the maps, Captain."

"They were positioned to protect the main road, to prevent the enemy from seizing a key passage through the hills. It seems the enemy didn't appreciate the gesture. It's Fox Company. They're in some difficulty, sir."

Smith let out a breath. "We're all in some difficulty, Captain. The question now is what to do about it."

"We have walked the entire perimeter, sir. It's not a strong position, but we've done the best we can with the resources we have. We're sitting in something of a bowl, and the enemy is in command of the heights in every direction. The greatest vulnerability we have is to the east, beyond the Changjin River, which flows into the reservoir. The river is frozen and is no obstacle. But that hill is in fact a series of sharp ridgelines and gullies, which offer excellent cover to anyone positioned there. We considered expanding our perimeter in that direction, but we just don't have the bodies. The enemy appears to be in some strength there, and if I was him, I'd use that hill as the base of my assault in this direction. I have one additional company, George, on its way here from Koto-ri, and I had planned to move them out onto that hill. Unfortunately, I don't have an estimate when they will arrive."

Smith raised his eyes from the map, said, "I would not count on their arrival, Colonel. The road north of Koto-ri is in enemy hands."

Ridge looked at Smith for a long moment. "Thank you for that information, sir." He looked again to the map, pointed. "Along the river, the ground is somewhat marshy, though not so right now. I have positioned a battery of six one-oh-five howitzers to cover that area. Closer to the reservoir, we have positioned the remaining men available to us, the service and supply people." He paused. "Sir, I have two rifle companies in key positions, and they're good men. Seasoned men. I can't vouch for the others."

Smith put his hands on his hips, impressed by Ridge's preparations. He glanced around at the faces, familiar officers, most of them from Puller's command.

"I'll vouch for them, Colonel. Our backs are to the wall here, and we have to hold." Smith's eyes returned to the map, and he pointed out to the east of the reservoir. "What of the army? How are they faring? I only heard from the air wing that they were hit as well. Do we know how badly? If they're in a strong position?"

Ridge looked down. "Sir, I can only tell you that General Hodes was here early this morning and insisted that he accompany the Seventh Division's armor and antiaircraft column. The communication lines ceased operation this morning, possibly cut by the enemy. General Hodes informed me that the best way to find out what was happening out there was to see it for himself."

Smith knew Henry Hodes from the various meetings at Tenth Corps, General Barr's second in command of the army's Seventh Division.

"Have you heard from him?"

"No, sir. The only radios he has are those in the tanks. Not sure how effective they are."

"How many tanks?"

"Six, I believe, sir. Shermans."

Smith moved to a small chair, sat down, stared into the dark green of the tent wall. It just gets worse, he thought. The army should never have advanced out so far. We have no idea what's out there. He had a sudden need for coffee, looked around, a small pot on a hot plate in one corner.

"Anything in that pot?"

One of Ridge's aides poured a cup, brought it quickly to Smith. He stared into the dark brew, absorbed the strong smell of something burnt. He raised the tin cup, already too hot for him to hold, then lowered it again. The aide seemed expectant, as though reading Smith's mind, said, "Sir, I can brew up a fresh pot if you'd like. That stuff gets pretty nasty after a while."

Smith shook his head, took a quick tongue-curling sip, said, "No, this is fine. I need better coffee than this, my wife will make it."

Ridge was studying him, said, "If I may say, sir, your presence here will help with morale. The men need to know we're behind them. So far the enemy has kept back, but everyone here knows that could change at any time."

Smith deflected the compliment with a wave of his hand, said, "What have you heard from Yudam-ni?"

"Very little, sir. While we do have radio contact with Koto-ri, we have been virtually unable to raise Yudam-ni at all. It seems likely that their radios are not functioning too well in the cold. We've had battery problems here as well. That, and the difficulty of the terrain between here and there. The air support has been patrolling that area vigorously, and they are able to communicate with our observers on the ground there. I can only report, sir, that last night, and throughout the early morning, the enemy has struck hard from at least two directions. The Fifth and the Seventh have both engaged the enemy on several fronts. From what we can sort out, the fighting has been severe. The pilots also report contact with our position at Toktong Pass. One company as-signed to hold the heights there has been assaulted as well."

"Colonel, I have received those reports at Hungnam. It's one reason I am here."

"Of course, sir."

Smith didn't mean to chastise Ridge, could see that the man had already done an exceptional job laying out the defense of the base.

"Colonel Bowser will be arriving here this afternoon, hopefully with more of my headquarters personnel. He can billet in my house, unless he has other preferences. This command tent will work well, assuming the enemy doesn't currently have us ranged for an artillery assault."

"Sir, I must request that you make available to us the engineers currently engaged in constructing the airstrip. Their rifles could be most helpful. The engineers are working around the clock, their position fully illuminated by spotlights. That seems ... impractical, sir. They could certainly become an immediate target should the enemy make their assault."

Smith shook his head. "No. I want those men doing exactly what they're doing. That airstrip is a priority, Colonel. You can believe we have suffered casualties at Yudam-ni, and before long the same could happen here. We must do everything in our power to evacuate them."

Ridge seemed to accept Smith's priorities, said, "Sir, do you anticipate that we will remain here? That would certainly be a good reason to have an airfield. Supplies could become an issue."

"Colonel, my orders as they stand now are to continue our advance to the west of Yudam-ni. The Chinese have other ideas. All I know right now is that this position is in jeopardy, and quite possibly the same thing can be said for every position we now hold in North Korea."

To one side of the tent, a radio crackled, Ridge's man cupping his hands over the earphones. News, Smith thought. Anything is better than what we have now. He waited, moved that way, Ridge beside him. The man spoke into the mouthpiece.

"Yes, sir. The general is here now. The command tent. Roger, sir. Out." He looked toward Smith, said, "Sir, that was General Hodes. He's coming in. I couldn't make out much more than that. I believe he was in a tank, sir."

Smith turned, moved toward the covered opening in the tent, felt a wisp of icy wind. He turned again, paced in the small area, the others standing aside, watching him. Ridge said, "I can send an aide to bring him in more quickly, sir. There's a jeep right outside, if we can get the engine started."

Smith kept moving, eyes on the hard ground, Ridge's words reaching him now. He stopped, looked at Ridge, said, "The cold?"

"Yes, sir. I've never been in these conditions before. It freezes up anything that moves, including engines. The artillery is having a dickens of a time reloading. The recoil mechanisms on the one-fifty-fives barely work. I watched the artillerymen pulling the guns back into place by hand. Hopefully we won't have to engage in a rapid-fire duel with the enemy. Right now there's no such thing."

"The enemy is enduring this same cold, Colonel. I haven't heard any reports of heavy artillery fire from the Chinese. At least that's one advantage we seem to have."

"And the air. No sign of enemy planes at all. Sir, I spoke to some of the Corsair pilots down south. They were itching to engage Chinese or Russian pilots. I never really understood flyboys, sir. I'll keep my feet on the ground. Even this ground."

The tent flap drew back, the officer rushing inside, clapping bare hands together.

"My God, this is something! The worst I've ever seen!" The man spotted Smith now, offered a hard scowl. "General. Good you're here."

Hodes offered a cold hand, which Smith took, a brief shake. Smith said, "What's the story out there?"

Hodes shook his head. "We couldn't get through. Engaged the enemy a couple miles shy of our goal, far as I could tell. They've blocked the road, blown the bridges, and they're in force all over those hills. The tanks had problems, too. One ran out of gas, others had failing engines. Only option was to fall back."

"You contact your troop positions?"

Hodes sipped the coffee, made a low grunt. "Yes. They've taken at least four hundred casualties. I spoke to Colonel McLean, CO of the Thirty-second. He's in overall command up there. To say he's concerned is putting it mildly." Hodes looked hard at Smith. "General, to be frank, we're in some serious trouble up there. From what we can tell, the enemy has surrounded that entire position. Both the Thirty-first and Thirty-second are out on a pretty dangerous limb. I know that General Barr would approve of me doing this. I am asking that you send assistance, do whatever is possible to pull those boys back here. We have additional forces coming up from the south, but there is no way of knowing when they might arrive."

"The road to the south is blocked. It is unlikely any additional troops can get through with any speed."

"Then I double my request. If we were united here, we'd be a tough nut for the Chinese."

"How many men are up there?"

Hodes seemed uncertain, thought a moment. "Near three thousand, I suppose."

Smith looked at Ridge, saw a glare of concern.

"General, we cannot weaken the perimeter here. There are barely that many Marines here to defend the most important junction in this part of Korea."

Hodes seemed even more surprised now, said, "But we were told that you had two full regiments here, and a third moving up."

"I assume you received your information from Tenth Corps. Were you also told that my orders were to spread out my forces in a flimsy line that is still thirty miles long? The greater part of our strength is, right now, enduring a heavy enemy assault up at Yudam-ni, some fourteen miles north of here. Colonel Puller is still at Koto-ri, and he is taking heavy fire as well." He stopped, tried to control his temper. "General, I appreciate the gravity of the army's situation. But the only way we can mount a force strong enough to eliminate the enemy on the east side of the reservoir is to abandon completely what we have here. That's not possible."

Hodes didn't respond, his gaze dropping. Ridge said, "General Hodes, we could definitely use your men here. Can they fight their way back?"

Hodes didn't look at Ridge, and Smith could feel the man's despair. After a long moment, Hodes said, "I suppose we'll have to."

HAGARU-RI, NORTH KOREA—NOVEMBER 28, 2:30 P.M.

Hodes had returned to his mode of transportation, the tank offering him the only chance to communicate to the army troops east of the reservoir. Smith had eaten a flavorless lunch in his new quarters but would not stay away from the command tent for any longer than he had to. The activity there had continued, Ridge's officers coming and going, maneuvering whatever strength they could assemble into some kind of coherent defensive line. Smith had backed away from those details, would allow Ridge to do his job, a job that had already impressed Smith.

Smith ran the numbers through his head, thought, It's all guesses. The army's taken four hundred casualties, and Yudam-ni has to be as bad, or worse. We've got to have that airstrip, and if there is nothing else in Hagaru-ri worth protecting, we have to protect that. He thought of Puller, his hands full at Koto-ri. I sure could use you up here, Lewie. If there was some way to get your people to jam their way through those hills, you'd figure it out. But then, we might not be able to hold Koto-ri. This isn't a one-way trip here.

He kept Puller in his mind, thought, What would he be doing if he was at Yudam-ni? I can't fault Litzenberg or Murray. They're following orders, my orders. We knew the enemy was out there, and we had to know there was a plan. They weren't just watching us go by. They *let* us go by. They know we're driving for the Yalu. Nothing secret about that. It's all Tokyo talks about. They chose the place, the time. And nobody in Tokyo or at Tenth Corps seems to understand what we're up against. Not sure that I know. I should get up to Yudam-ni, take a good look. It's not time to spare anybody's feelings.

"Captain, is that chopper still on the pad?"

Sexton came out of the back room, said, "No, sir. He's on his way back to Hungnam. Colonel Bowser is scheduled to fly up here."

"Yes, I know. I thought it might be a good idea to fly up to see Litzenberg, check out the situation at Yudam-ni."

Sexton stood in front of him, hands on his hips. "Sir, that's not an acceptable idea."

There was no humor in Sexton's words. Smith knew the look in the man's eyes, Sexton with no tolerance at all for idiocy.

"I was not aware, Captain, that it was such a stupid plan."

"I didn't say anything like that, sir. But you know the book. The commanding general has to maintain contact with all his forces, and right now you are in position to do just that. Taking the risk of flying some bolt bucket up through those frozen hills, with an enemy who's just itching to shoot one of those little birds out of the sky . . . it's unacceptable. And if I wanted to do that, you'd tell me the same thing."

Smith couldn't hide the smile. "I never thought you'd quote 'the book,' Captain."

"*You* would, sir. And I'm betting that Colonel Bowser will agree with me. Forgive me for saying so, sir, but you've got two good commanders up there. There's not a thing you could do for them they can't do themselves."

Smith stood slowly, working the stiffness out of his knee. He knew Sexton had crossed a line, that Sexton would know that, too. He grabbed his coat, slid it on, looked at Sexton, who still stood firmly, his chest poked out just for emphasis. "Don't try this with Puller, Captain. He'll take your bars."

The tent was a hive of activity, the cold blowing in with each man who passed through the heavy flap. The officers were mostly familiar, short greetings from men with better things to do than chat with their commanding officer. Smith stayed mostly out of the way, absorbing every scrap of information, most of it vague and useless, frustrating for everyone there.

He had stopped examining each man's arrival, knew if anyone could offer something substantial, he'd know as quickly as Ridge. But now a new face appeared, a short round man pouring into the tent, wrapped up like yet another mummy. It was Colonel Lockwood. The men stood aside, and Smith ignored their expressions, focused on Lockwood, red-faced, flustered, and certainly surprised to see Smith.

"I didn't know you'd be here, sir. It has been a rather extreme day. Might I have some coffee?"

"Extreme how?"

Lockwood tugged at removing his coat, sat heavily, a coffee cup placed in his hands, the man obviously trying to gather himself. "I had planned to move my battalion CP up to Yudam-ni this morning. I tried to contact Colonel Litzenberg for any additional orders, without success. So we moved out in convoy on the main road, anticipating no difficulty. We had not gone more than a mile when we were confronted by a large number of Chinese, occupying the heights to our front, on both sides of the road. I attempted to remove them, deploying my weapons company to one flank, my headquarters personnel to the other. We had a rather brisk firefight, but it became clear that the enemy far outnumbered us and was attempting to take us on both flanks. I felt I had no choice but to withdraw, and return here."

Smith glanced around the large tent, all faces on Lockwood. "You were fortunate, Colonel. Were your casualties as extreme as your situation?"

"Several wounded. They have been sent to the aid stations. It could have been much worse, I am certain of that."

Smith could see Lockwood's hands shaking as he attempted to drink his coffee.

"Colonel, until we know more of what seems to be happening at Yudam-ni, you will deploy your men here at the discretion of Colonel Ridge."

Lockwood looked at Smith. "Sir, what is happening at Yudam-ni?"

Smith thought, Of course, he has no idea. "The enemy has engaged us in strength. Very likely you ran into a roadblock, meant to keep any of us here from going to their aid. Or, perhaps, to prevent any of them from returning here. Either way we are isolated, as is Colonel Litzenberg."

Lockwood seemed to sink into a deep gloom, and after a brief moment a new thought seemed to burst through him. "What of Fox Company? I placed them at Toktong Pass. I tried to contact them by radio but I assumed the equipment was down."

Smith folded his arms across his chest, shook his head. "I would hazard that the enemy has cut your wire. From all we can tell, your men there are engaged as well. Beyond that, I'm afraid we know very little. Our main concern, the one thing we can attack directly, is the defense of Hagaru-ri. I do not know what the enemy's intentions are, except that they seem to prefer a nighttime assault. We must expect that if they have done so at other points, they will do so here. See to your men. Colonel Ridge will know what to do with them."

"Sirs! A chopper has landed!"

Smith looked toward the voice, the man in a heavy coat backing out of the tent, the flap closing quickly. Smith said, "Bowser, I suppose. A little sooner than I expected."

The flap was pulled back again, a gust of wind inflating the walls of the tent. Smith waited, the flap still open, no one yet there, the nagging memory of another time, the man making his arrival with an entrance reminiscent of his boss. Smith stared silently at the foggy opening, the hard cold wiping away the warmth from the tent's stove. Around him, others were holding down papers, trying to keep their griping out of his earshot. Bowser, he thought, if you're out there shaking hands, I'm going to court-martial you. Two men filled the opening now, the obvious look of aides or, he thought, bodyguards. What's going on now? Another figure appeared, moving slowly, deliberate steps, too familiar.

"Well, this is excellent! I hoped to see my officers at work. I'll just take a look at that map, yes?"

Smith felt his shoulder sag, opened a path to the table. "Welcome, General Almond. This is an unexpected surprise."

Bowser had arrived, but any detailed briefings for Smith would have to wait, all attention focused on Ned Almond. They had moved into the small house, away from the turmoil of the tent, Smith already dreading the thought that Almond would try to take charge of Ridge's defenses.

"Not bad, Smith, I must say. You always seem to find a solid roof over your head."

Sexton had brewed a fresh pot of coffee, three cups on the table,

Almond choosing his after examining all three, a habitual check for cleanliness. Smith glanced at Sexton, knew he had observed the annoying tic, Sexton not hiding his annoyance.

"Thank you, Captain. You are excused."

Sexton faked a smile. "I'll be right outside, sir, standing in the cold, if you need me."

Almond unrolled a map, ignored Sexton, who moved out through the door, a last glance at Smith. He's going to say something stupid one day, Smith thought. Well, me, too.

"General Almond, I said we were surprised by your visit. Do you have specific orders?"

Almond looked at Smith as though for the first time today. "No, not really. I'm on my way to see the army command posts. Colonel Faith's people are up front, I believe, leading the way. The Thirty-first. I'm told he's a good man. I don't want to see any further delays, and I suspect Colonel Faith will get the job done."

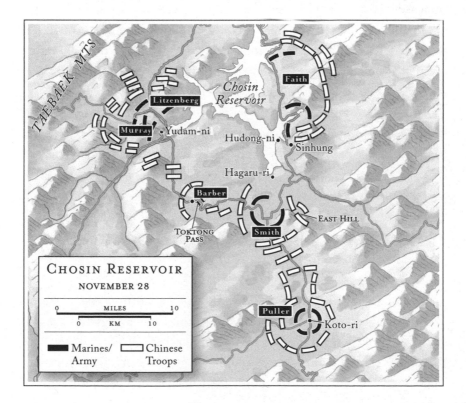

Smith looked at Bowser, saw his own confusion in Bowser's expression.

"Delays for what?"

"The advance, of course. No excuses, just because of the cold weather." Almond looked hard at him. "He's army. Unlike you, he accepts that he has to obey everything I tell him to do."

Smith sat back, stared at Almond, who scanned the map in his hands. After a silent moment, Smith said, "I have sent reports to Corps headquarters all morning. Have you seen them?"

Almond kept his stare on the map.

"I saw reports. You and General Barr. A few others." Almond stopped, seemed to weigh his words, a glance toward Bowser. "Let me tell you something, Smith. I served my country in World War Two without ever receiving the command I deserved. I intend to prove to whoever made that decision that they were flat-out wrong. General MacArthur has granted me an opportunity here, and not you nor anyone else in Korea will destroy General MacArthur's confidence in this command. The entire world is watching us here, Smith. And I will not tolerate defeatism. If the army must carry our banner to the Yalu River, so be it. You had your opportunity for headlines, and instead of obeying my orders, you spout out pessimism. Well, now it's the army's turn."

Smith felt a boiling heat in the back of his neck, fought to keep it hidden. "General Almond, the army position has been under attack. General Hodes has determined they have taken several hundred casualties, and they are in a dangerous situation. The same is true for my Fifth and Seventh Regiments at Yudam-ni. The enemy has struck us hard at every advanced position, and he has mostly surrounded us right here." His voice was rising, and he paused, tried to hold it inside. He looked at Bowser, who shook his head, no help at all. "Sir, we must modify our mission here."

Almond kept his eyes locked on Smith. "So, nothing has changed. Poor morale is still your biggest problem. You have engaged a defeated enemy, and his defeat becomes yours." He reached into his pocket. "See these? Silver Star, times three. You'll not get one of these from me. These are for Colonel Faith's command. One for him, certainly. Morale spreads from the top down, something you've never understood. I will find others in Faith's command who are worthy of the other two. They will appreciate that their commanding officer is aware of their efforts, and will continue to support them. As for the *attacks* you fear, I will tell you, as I will tell Colonel Faith: The enemy who is standing up before you is nothing more than the remnants of a Chinese division fleeing northward. We are going all the way to the Yalu. Do not let a bunch of Chinese laundrymen stop you!"

Almond had continued on his journey up the east side of the reservoir, a Marine helicopter that kept its flight path far out over the snow-covered ice.

Smith was still at the table, the pipe in his mouth, the only piece of joy he had received this entire day. Bowser had examined the rest of the small house, returned now, holding a framed portrait of Joseph Stalin. "This was hanging on the wall. I suppose you saw it."

Smith stared ahead, pulled at the pipe, the pungent smoke wrapping around his gloom. "Put it back up. I told the staff to leave it be. Might inspire us."

"If you say so."

Bowser returned quickly, said, "Mind if I sit?"

Smith pointed with the stem of the pipe. Bowser sat, said nothing, could read Smith's moods better than anyone on the staff. Smith said, "We could use Eddie about now. I can't fault him for caring so about his father. But his timing could have been better. He could go up to Yudam-ni. That's what a second in command does."

"You want me to go up there?"

Smith shook his head. "I need you here. We're short-staffed, and for all I know, we might both need to pick up a rifle."

Bowser seemed to weigh Smith's words. "My marksmanship has always been suspect. But I'll do whatever you tell me to do. Maybe a carbine. Easier to handle."

He appreciated Bowser's humor, always at the right time, the right amount.

"It seems that the best way to communicate with Yudam-ni is by choppered dispatch. I am ordering Murray to pull back from his advanced position and combine his forces with Litzenberg at Yudam-ni itself."

Bowser let out a low whistle. "Almond's orders haven't changed. Murray is to continue moving west, over the mountains. You'll contradict that?"

"The Chinese have contradicted that. The mission has changed, whether or not Tenth Corps understands that or not. From every indication, we are severely outnumbered on every front. There is no more *advance to the Yalu.* We are fighting for survival."

"But what about Almond?"

Smith pulled again at the pipe. "I cannot order Litzenberg and Murray to withdraw out of Yudam-ni and return here, without Tenth Corps approval. But that is exactly what we must do. Our best hope, perhaps our only hope, is that General Almond can be made to understand that."

"How?"

Smith pulled the pipe from his mouth, laid it on the table. "I don't know, Alpha. The man is crazy."

The snow began late in the afternoon, blanketing the men as they sat in their foxholes. The command organized by Colonel Ridge was a jigsaw puzzle of Marine infantry and artillerymen, service and supply troops, army headquarters personnel, and anyone else capable of aiming a rifle. With darkness falling quickly, the word was passed to men who didn't need to be told. Make ready for imminent attack. By nightfall, the Chinese began their assault. As had happened at Yudam-ni, at Koto-ri, at Fox Hill, and around the army position far up the east side of the Chosin Reservoir, the attack began with a chorus of bugles and whistles, cymbals and shouts, the Chinese soldiers pouring out of their hiding places straight into the guns of the American defenses. At Hagaru-ri there were also breakthroughs, holes punched in the defenses that allowed Chinese troops to pour through. But Hagaru-ri offered something the other positions did not. The massive supply dump offered the Chinese soldiers the kind of temptation few of them had ever seen. Instead of pressing forward their assault, routing the Americans completely from the crucial town, the Chinese began to loot the stockpiles, bogging down their attack. In time, the Americans turned the tide, a massacre of men whose mission had been lost in a quest for whatever prizes they could find. By morning the Americans had suffered nearly five hundred additional casualties, but the losses for the Chinese were far worse.

Smith understood that Hagaru-ri would continue to be vulnerable, and that from all indications, the Chinese were intent on continuing their attacks. With the army troops to the northeast cut off in a desperate fight for their own survival, Smith had only one other option for reinforcing his position. The radio link to Koto-ri was still clear, and Smith sent word to Chesty Puller to mobilize any force Puller could spare and send them northward with all speed. Among the troops in Puller's command was a British unit, the Forty-first Independent Commandos, of the British Royal Marines, led by Lieutenant Colonel Douglas Drysdale. Drysdale was an experienced combat veteran of the Burma campaign in World War II who had sought out and was delighted to receive assignment to serve alongside Chesty Puller. By morning Colonel Drysdale's assignment would change. Though Puller had barely two thousand men to defend Koto-ri, Drysdale would assume command of a task force of nearly half of Puller's forces. Accompanied by tanks and a large number of supply trucks, Drysdale would push northward, with no real idea what kind of obstacles the Chinese would put in their way. Smith understood the chances Drysdale would take. Every report reaching Hagaru-ri, from the radio transmitters in Koto-ri and Chinhung-ni, to the haphazard messages passed along from chopper and fighter pilots, told the same story. The Chinese were in strength, surrounding every position the Marines now occupied. With nightfall again settling over the Chosin Reservoir, every outpost, every headquarters, every frontline platoon commander was keeping his men on the alert, waiting for the inevitable attack.

CHAPTER TWENTY-FIVE

....

Riley

THE PLANES HAD come again, but not the blue Corsairs. This time there had been eight P-51 Mustangs, the beloved fighter that had once turned the tide against the German Messerschmitts in World War II. The appearance of the Mustangs was a surprise, and very quickly the air spotter passed the word that they were flown by Australians. Like the Marines who flew the Corsairs, the Australians were fearless, skimming the hilltops, dipping low into the valleys, pouring a devastating mix of machine gun, rocket, and cannon fire on the Chinese positions. As the Mustangs turned away, the Marines cheered them, new respect for an old ally.

The Corsairs had returned as well, but they did not come to help the men on Fox Hill. To the dismay of Captain Barber's Marines, the Corsairs continued northward, word passing again from the air spotter that the planes were destined for Yudam-ni. Barber's weakening radio had made brief contact with Litzenberg's headquarters, and the news both ways was bad. Litzenberg had hoped to bring Fox Company northward, precious strength adding to the forces fending off increasing pressure from the Chinese. But Barber's people had nowhere to go. Throughout the morning, scouting parties had probed the ground in all directions, seeking alternative routes southward that might allow Fox Company to return to Hagaru-ri. But the Chinese were on every hill, in every valley, in every direction. With the road to Hagaru-ri blocked completely, and with no help coming from Litzenberg, Barber knew that Fox Company could very well be wiped out.

It was nearly dark, and already stars were appearing, a clear sign that tonight would be as cold as any they had endured. With the shift in the positions of the perimeter, new foxholes were dug, more slit trenches, the men laboring through the cold, knowing the warmth of their sweat was temporary, that once again the officers would order foot inspections, the men changing their socks as quickly as the work was completed. This time there were no complaints. As they struggled to chop into rock and frozen dirt, Riley and every man around him were aware that Barber's order to dig the holes, so vigorously cursed the night before, had saved many of their lives.

Riley wiped the wetness from his skin with his spare shirt, fumbled with the buttons, his fingers already turning numb. He watched Killian blowing on his fingers, did the same, a brief remedy, allowing him to fasten a single button.

"Christ, Sean, this is nuts."

Killian didn't answer, buried himself in his coat, sat, curling up in a ball, the sleeping bag pulled over his legs. Riley worked the buttons, the shirt finally fastened up completely, and he grabbed his coat, wrapped himself tightly, the hood pulled down hard over his head. He ducked low, shivered, his arms wrapped around him, waiting for the relief, his breathing inside his coat, aimed down over his chest, the only warmth there was. He waited, wouldn't move again just yet, the cold soaking his brain, every part of him, but easing now, his breathing slower, some feeling again in his limbs. He slid his feet outward, the next task, pulled at the boots, his socks soaked with sweat. He grunted, slid them off his stinging feet, tossed the socks aside, the fresh pair going on quickly, his gloved hands massaging his toes. The boots went back on, the cold in the bottom harsh, still wet, and he cursed, said, "What jackass decided these were the right boots?"

Killian didn't look up, the hood low over his face, said, "A jackass who never had to wear the damn things. They say the Corps buys stuff from the lowest bidder. Just once, I'd pay extra to get whatever was made by the most expensive guy. Just once. Boots, C-rations. Doesn't matter."

Riley curled his legs beneath him, sat gingerly, knew better than to put his legs to sleep. "I bet the rifles are the best ones. They make sure of that."

"Like hell they do. I heard the sarge say he had to junk his carbine. He's got a Thompson, the one you grabbed off that Shambo."

Riley knew Welch was a few yards away, another of the fresh holes dug in virtually a straight line across the crest of the hill.

"Maybe. That's fine as long as he's got ammo."

Killian didn't answer, sat quietly, a dark lump at one end of the narrow hole.

The ammo drop had come that afternoon, a single cargo plane swooping in low, pallets of boxes dumped out with barely enough altitude for the parachutes to break their fall. But the ammo had been received with eagerness and cheers, the grenades and mortar shells replenishing supplies that had been nearly exhausted. The rifle ammo had come as well, Captain Barber ordering it to be distributed quickly, every man stuffing his coat with as much as the supply officers allowed. Later in the day a single helicopter had arrived, just long enough to drop a supply of fresh batteries for the captain's radio. For the wounded, the helicopter offered a brief bit of hope of transport off the hill. But the snipers had targeted the chopper immediately, the pilot forced to escape with a crippled engine.

He felt the familiar rumble of hunger, a new thought.

"Hey, Sean, I heard the supply drop didn't have any rations at all. Just ammo."

"You surprised? If we can't fight off the Shambos, we won't be needing much for dinner. That's the kind of thinking officers get paid for."

Riley slid his backpack closer, felt inside. "I got a Tootsie Roll left. A can of something, fruit maybe. I'll split it with you."

"Nah. I still got this turkey leg. Figured I'd suck on it awhile."

Riley laughed to himself, but he knew Killian was serious, thought, He's carried that stupid thing in his pack for nearly a week.

"Good luck. Your spit won't be warm enough to thaw it out. It might stick to your tongue."

Two men were crawling along the hill behind the line, and Riley saw a third man coming up with them, Lieutenant Goolsby. The two men dragged a cloth bag between them, slid closer to a foxhole a few yards away, and Goolsby said, "One per hole. It's Sterno. You only got a half hour, so use it. Thaw out something to eat. Thaw out your fingers, too. But the captain says to kill the fire at eighteen thirty."

The two men tossed a can into each hole, one rolling into Riley's. He grabbed it, as cold as anything around him, was surprised to see Killian produce a lighter, a small flicker of flame. Riley pulled his knife, popped open the lid, held it out, and Killian lit the contents, the pink goo sparking to life. He set the can in the bottom of the hole, one hand close to the meager flame. Killian said, "A half hour. Hell, you couldn't heat a thimbleful of coffee that quick."

Riley gave out a low laugh. "Put your turkey leg over it. Always did enjoy an outdoor barbecue."

Killian sniffed, pulled one boot off, held one stockinged foot over the flame. Riley kept his hands close to the round can, absorbing the warmth. He looked at Killian's foot, said, "How's the toes? You ain't walking too good. The sarge noticed that. He's watching you."

Killian withdrew the foot, yanked the boot on, his face hidden. "Foot's fine. The sarge can worry about *you*."

McCarthy was there now, keeping low, and he knelt close behind the row of foxholes, said, "Listen up. Just got word from the captain. No matter what happens tonight in the next hour or two, *nobody* leaves these holes. The captain's radio worked just long enough to make contact with the artillery battery in Hagaru-ri, a flock of one-oh-fives, supposed to be supporting us. They're gonna range the hills around us in a few minutes. The draws, too." He paused. "They got orders that if we're overrun, they're to turn this hill to mush. Anybody gets up and wanders around, they might turn you to mush, too. If we're going to end up in hell, at least we'll take a pile of Chinks with us. Now keep low. They start dropping shells out here, it's just a show, for now. We've got enough casualties without losing anybody to friendly fire. Okay, I need every one of you to test your weapons. Fire off a round. Now!"

McCarthy was close behind Welch's hole, his voice reaching them all. Riley obeyed, raised the M-1, fired, checked the breech, the next round moving into place. Killian did the same, and to one side Riley heard familiar cursing, Welch.

"Forget the damn carbine. It won't eject worth a damn. I got a single shot and have to screw with the bolt for five minutes to fire the next one. I'll stick with the Thompson."

Down the line, other rifles fired, the telltale burst from a BAR, more curses.

McCarthy crawled along the hard ground behind the line, said, "Find a rag, anything that will work. Get as much lube cleaned out of the action as you can, no matter what weapon you're using. Work the bolt every few minutes. Nelson! How's the thirty?"

The burst of fire came down to the right.

"Not bad, sir."

"Fire off another burst every hour, at least. Those bastards will hit us again, sure as hell, and for whatever reason, their weapons aren't all gummed up like we are. We pulled a bottle of some kind of oil off one of the Chinks. Captain says it's whale oil. I don't know. But their weapons are doing just fine. Grab one if you get the chance. And pay attention to your grenades. Don't just pull the pins. Pull the hammer up before you throw it. They're mostly frozen together, and all you'll be doing is smacking them with a baseball. Fire a round every hour, you got that?"

McCarthy moved away toward the far end of the line, more orders, more single shots ringing out to the left side of the hill. Riley glanced that way, thought, Second Platoon. Pretty close to us. Killian rose up, watching him, his hands over the small flame.

"Ain't very many of us."

Riley had made a count in his head, said, "Half of us got hit, I think. A couple dozen still up here." He looked at the arsenal spread out along the edge of their hole, the Russian rifles Killian had salvaged, another M-1, from one of the Marines no longer using it. "Everybody's got more weapons than they know what to do with. We'll be okay."

"I know exactly what to do with 'em."

Riley didn't answer, looked out past the hole, toward Welch, thought, He's got his own arsenal. And Morelli's with him now. Good. He thought of Welch's words earlier, how the new men had shot up all their ammo. Guess I did, too, back then. They give you a rifle, they expect you to use it. The enemy runs up your ass, he expects it, too. As long as the supply people can drop those crates out here, we'll put up a fight. He wanted to shout over to Welch, thought better of it. He knows I'm here. And he'll take care of the kid.

He turned his gaze to the hillside, darker now, the snow a thin blanket, deeper drifts blown against the scattered rocks. To one side Lieutenant McCarthy had positioned Freddy Nelson's crew, manning a light machine gun, and Riley looked that way, could see the gun surrounded by a low rock pile, and more, the stacked bodies of the enemy. We should have done that, he thought. There's enough dead Chinese to go around. But this hole is deep, plenty of cover. They come, we'll be ready. I guess. He stared again down the wide hill, across the saddle, the distant hill hidden in darkness. They *will* come. Like us, they got no place else to be.

There was an odd smell, and he searched, realized it was close, and he looked down, Killian with his hands out over the soft blue flame, holding the turkey leg.

FOX HILL—NOVEMBER 28, 1950, 10:00 P.M.

The artillery had found their range, Riley watching in amazement as the spotters directed the fire from the big guns so many miles away. All around Fox Hill, the incoming fire had peppered the high ground in nearly every direction, a reminder to the enemy that even in the darkness, they were vulnerable. The mortars had the range as well, the 60- and 81-millimeter tubes spread all around the hill, each squad choosing a likely direction to aim their fire. The mortars launched illuminated shells as well as the usual high explosive, an enormous benefit for the men in the foxholes, offering a glimpse of just where the enemy assault might be forming.

Riley had found an hour's sleep, had the watch now, still embraced by the sleeping bag up to his waist. He could hear Killian's snoring, an odd mix of spits and hisses and grumbles, what might have been the easiest way to make enemies in a barracks. But the sounds kept Riley entertained, helped to focus his mind, keep his thoughts away from the film of icy frost he couldn't avoid around his eyes. The shivering came often, the heavy coat not quite adequate, and as he scanned the darkness, he tried to guess the temperature. He was beginning to feel the difference, just how much pain it caused to breathe, how far down his throat the air would threaten to freeze him. With each stiff breeze that slapped his face, tears would come, turning to ice in a minute or less, gluing his eyes shut. It happened now, and he wiped gently, blew into his cupped hands, directed the warmer air upward over his eyes. Ten below zero meant his tears would freeze in a full minute. Twenty below, half that time. Tonight there were short seconds between the clear glimpses of darkness, and the agony of blindness, his fingers wiping at the raw skin around his eyes yet again.

He shifted his feet in the bag, the cold finding him even down low. God, he thought, it's twenty-five below. Fifty below. Hell, what difference does it make? The damn Chinese don't seem to care. He didn't know that, of course, had wondered with the others just how miserable they could be. Their shoes had been a shock, the thin canvas over rubber soles, offering no protection at all. They gotta keep moving, he thought. I guess that's what they're doing now, marching up and down the hills out there, keeping warm as best they can. He was curious about the quilted uniforms, just how much protection they provided, but few of the Marines had any notion of trying them on. The smell, even in the cold, could be nauseating, the thick stench of rotten garlic. There's bugs, too, he thought. Maybe like Okinawa, the damn fleas, infesting every piece of cloth you found. Well, maybe not. How cold does it have to be to kill fleas? But we ain't taking any baths up here, and we stink just as bad as any of them, even without the garlic.

Beside him, Killian grumbled, a loud snort, and now to one side, Welch said, "Jesus. He's waking up the whole mountain. The damn Chinks can zero in on us just by listening to him."

"Let him sleep, Sarge."

Welch didn't respond, and Riley could hear more of the low talk around him, the men filling the darkness with tall tales, gripes, any kind of distraction from the cold.

There was a strange whine coming from the left of the saddle, lower on the far hill. More whines came now, and Riley stared that way, the talk around him quieting. Now a voice, loud, uneven, broken by the static from a radio transmitter.

"Hello, Marines! You have few numbers, and we are very many. We are surrounding you. You will die very soon. You must all surrender. It is the wise thing. Do not be foolish."

The crackling and hissing stopped and the men began to respond, vulgar shouts across the hillside. Riley heard Killian stirring, the muffled question, "Wha' the hell?"

"Go back to sleep. The enemy's got somebody who knows English. He keeps that up after daylight, somebody'll take him out."

"Marines! Do you wish to die? You must surrender now. Save yourselves. Do not die for the generals in their comfortable homes. They have Korean girls to favor them. You have only death!"

There was a burst from a machine gun down that way, a futile gesture, streaks of red tracers pouring down into the draw. Welch rose up, and Riley heard the familiar cursing, then McCarthy was there, shouted out, "Save your damn ammo! That's what he wants!"

"Marines, think of your wives back home. How they would enjoy you with them. Not out here, where you will only die."

The crackling gave way to the harsh whine again, more feedback, and then the first notes of music. The responses came again, more threats and curses from the men along the hilltop, the music now louder still. Riley stared through the darkness, amazed at the effort by the Chinese, the utter ridiculousness of their propaganda. The music continued, clearer now, his own mind opening up, the music finding its way inside, memories he didn't want. He pushed hard at that, joined in the shouting. There were more rifles firing now, a pair of machine guns. It was a useless exercise against one Chinese officer's seductive plan, just enough awareness of their culture, their homesickness, their emotions. The outrage was complete, anger at the enemy's simpleminded approach, the Marines absorbing the insult that someone *out there* thought a piece of music would tempt them to walk off their hill. But the music continued, and gradually the exhausted Marines realized there was nothing they could do to stop it. And so, with eyes still focused on the darkness, the men began to listen, some of them to enjoy. It was, after all, Bing Crosby. And it was "White Christmas."

Fox Hill—November 29, 2:00 a.m.

The mortars came first, no warning at all, a sudden rain of explosives all along the crest of the hill. Riley dropped low, a spray of dirt and shattered rock coming down. Voices called out, McCarthy, Welch, the unnecessary warning.

"Make ready! They'll be coming!"

Riley waited for a pause in the incoming shells, peered up over the edge of the hole, heard Welch.

"When the hell did they bring mortars up here?"

The words flowed through Riley's brain. If there's more weapons, it means there's more troops. Killian seemed to read his thoughts, said, "I bet they sent reinforcements. We kicked their asses last night."

Riley put one hand up on the hood of his parka, shifted it, clearing his line of sight. He peered down the hill.

"They already forgot about last night. Watch that damn saddle. Both sides of it."

"Thanks, General. I done this before, you know."

Riley felt the hard chill all through him, his nervousness adding to the raw cold. "I know. Sorry."

"And there they come. Look!" Killian called out now. "Hey, Sarge. On the saddle!"

"I see 'em!"

There was a burst of fire from the machine gun to the right, and now scattered firing all along the saddle itself. The mortars began now, pumping their shells over the heads of the Marines, dropping them all along the enemy's position. Riley stared, knew from the sound it was the 60 millimeters, knew that the gunners had already marked their range. The Chinese came in thin lines, advancing at a slow trot, white uniforms not quite disguised by the uneven snow. But the flashes from the mortar fire lit up the entire scene, enemy soldiers falling in clusters, some tossed aside by the close impact of the shells. The machine guns were rattling all along the hill now, the other guns joining in, down to the left. Riley pulled himself down into the hole, checked the M-1, one hand reaching up, feeling for the rows of grenades. He put a hand down on the .45 at his waist, loosened it, took a long breath, then another, ignored the cold that sliced into his lungs. He waited for a long moment, staring into darkness, felt suddenly like crying. It was so familiar, a new surge of terror boiling up inside him, and he fought it, angry at himself, more furious at the enemy. There were grenade blasts now, very close, the first wave of enemy troops doing their job, but the Marines had prepared for that, tossing their own grenades, and now Riley could hear the voices through the sharp sounds, the enemy, wounded men screaming, torn apart. Behind them, more of the mortar rounds came down, streaks of light overhead, bursts of fire all down the hill. He took a long, deep, icy breath, blinked hard, clearing his vision, and the silent voice came now, inside his head, pushing away the fear. He kicked the sleeping bag from his feet, rose up, felt himself shouting, no words, just noise, raw and vicious. The flashes of light were everywhere, and he saw the targets, men tossing grenades, shot down, men on their knees, some with rifles, and behind them more lines of men, moving up the hillside, through fire and smoke, past the screams of their own.

The noise was deafening, the enemy machine guns throwing their green tracers across the ridge, the chatter adding to the chorus of rifle fire and grenade blasts. The fighting swirled around him, some of the enemy finding their way past the line, close-range fire from Chinese burp guns, the answering chatter of the BARs. Riley kept up his own fire, targets close in front of him, still outlined by the flashes of fire from the mortars. With each advance, the Chinese seemed to grow in number, more of them surging past the Marines, collapsing in a storm of fire from men behind the ridge. In front of Riley it was more of the same scene, rows of men shot down, blown aside, the gaps in the enemy's advance filled by more men coming up from behind. All across the line, the orders were shouted out, meaningless words, Riley's terror combining with the raw excitement, adding to the wonder of all that was happening around him. There was no time for thought, for checking the flanks. Throughout the assault, his brain focused on one place, the hillside below him, the relentless charge by an enemy who seemed infinite and unstoppable.

Several times, more than he could count, the Chinese who were able had backed away, re-forming, reloading, Riley using the brief pauses to check his own ammo, the clips in his pocket only a few, the grenades on the ground in front of him down to a pair. As the enemy pulled back, the mortars slowed, darkness returning, and he stared out with furious energy, his hands shaking, spinning cold inside his chest. He steadied his hand by his grip on the rifle, blinked rapidly, keeping his eyes clear. Beside him, Killian seemed to be searching for something, his voice adding to the shouts along the ridge.

"Damn it all! I got nothing left! We gotta fix bayonets!"

Riley forced his eyes off the ridge, looked at him, Killian down low, ripping through his backpack. Riley shouted, louder than he intended, "What is it? You out of ammo?"

Killian ignored him, seemed obsessed with finding something, and Riley could see his rifle leaning up against the side of the hole, the bayonet already attached.

"Get up! Your bayonet's fixed. What the hell's the matter with you?"

"I can't find it! It's gotta be here! They're coming!"

Riley heard too much terror in Killian's voice, and he put a hand out, touched his shoulder. "Sean! Look at your rifle. The bayonet's there."

Killian looked at him now, seemed to calm. "They're coming again. I know it. They're hard to see."

Riley kept his hand on Killian's shoulder. "Yeah, I guess. You need ammo?"

Killian kept low, pulled the rifle in tight to his chest. "I think so. I don't know. They coming again?"

Riley glanced out past the hole, men on the move, wounded being pulled back, a scramble from the ammo carriers. "Here! Ammo here!"

One man stumbled closer, a heavy bag in his hand.

"I got grenades! That's it. Ain't many."

"Give 'em here. Go get more. We need ammo!"

The man dropped the bag, moved away without speaking, and Riley pulled the bag into the hole, not heavy enough, felt through the burlap.

"Half a dozen. That's it. Damn!"

Killian didn't move, sat against the side of the hole, staring at him. Riley laid the grenades out along the lip of the hole, said, "You shoot up all the ammo for those Russian things?"

Killian didn't answer, stood up now, the rifle down beside him.

"Sean, what the hell you doing? Get your ass down."

Welch was there now, crawling low. "What's going on? You need ammo?"

Riley said, "Yeah. I got four clips, six grenades. Not sure about him."

Welch rose up on his knees, pulled at Killian. "What the hell's wrong with you?"

Killian looked at Welch, put one hand up on the side of his head. "You son of a bitch. You hit me with a snowball!"

Riley felt a sickening cold flowing all through him, saw Welch reach out, put a hand inside the hood of Killian's coat.

"Oh, Christ. Corpsman!"

Riley felt paralyzed, and Welch looked at him, his hand extended.

"He's hit. Side of his neck."

Riley absorbed the words, stared hard, nothing to see in the dark. Killian still stood, seemed dazed, and Welch called again, "Corpsman!"

A man ran forward, down on his knees beside Welch, the voice of McCarthy. "Who's hit?"

"Irish. Wet blood."

McCarthy added to the chorus.

"Corpsman!"

Riley felt a new kind of panic, stared at Killian, still standing, staring off, and now another man was there, a mumbling voice.

"Here. Who's hit?"

McCarthy motioned toward Killian. "His neck."

The corpsman slipped into the hole, Riley climbing out, making room. He watched the corpsman pull something from his mouth, the man pulling Killian down gently, Killian settling into the bottom of the hole. The corpsman huddled low, said, "I got him, sir. Doesn't feel too bad. I'll give him morphine, and we'll get somebody out here to haul him down to the aid station."

McCarthy said, "Good. We got plenty of men down. They hit us pretty hard. Sergeant, you know how to handle a thirty?"

Welch answered, "Yes, sir. Been a while."

"You'll figure it out. Nelson's hit, down below. His crew's busted up by grenades. Get over there, man that gun." McCarthy looked at Riley now. "Go with him. You're the crew. Your buddy's gonna be fine."

There was no discussion to be had, the lieutenant's orders clear. Welch was up quickly, the Thompson in his hands, and he said to Riley, "Time to move."

Riley grabbed the rifle, the grenades stuffed into his pocket. He followed Welch, stumbled on the rocky ground, moved past scattered bodies, men in their holes, gathering up ammo, doing what he had done. Welch led him down into a cluster of rocks, one taller, one half of a wall. He saw the machine gun now, bodies scattered around, most of them Chinese. But not all. He moved toward one of the fallen Marines, knelt, stared, helpless, no idea what to do.

"Get your ass over here! There's ammo in those cans."

"They might need help."

"They don't. Worry about them later. We got bigger problems."

Riley saw now, the wide hillside below, movement in the snow, the moonlight catching the rows of men moving out into the open.

"Jesus. They're coming again."

Welch wrestled with the machine gun, said, "Yeah. They're coming. Feed me the belts from this side."

Riley went to work now, felt the heft of the ammo boxes, two full, one partial. "Looks like plenty."

Welch slapped the gun, settled low behind it, aimed, swiveled. "Ain't no such thing, Pete."

The mortars began again, a steady rhythm impacting all down the hill, out on the saddle, the Chinese responding with mortars of their own. The machine guns began their duel as well, the Marines keeping their focus on the enemy troops moving up the hill again, lines of men in white, shot down, more, shot down again.

Welch fired the machine gun, short bursts, seeking targets, the old training. Riley kept close by, feeding him the ammo, and within short minutes, the first box was empty.

The barrel of the gun glowed red, and Welch aimed, stared silently. The Chinese were backing away again, disappearing into the darkness, but to both sides the firing continued. Riley sat on the frozen ground, the rocks to one side offering perfect cover that way. But down the hill, the only cover came from the stacked bodies, pulled into place by Freddy Nelson. Riley hadn't checked the bodies nearby, had no idea if Nelson was one of the dead Marines, or if they were part of Nelson's crew. You don't need to know, he thought.

"How much we got left?"

Riley pulled on the one remaining box, put one hand on the belts inside. "Not much."

"Go get more. While we got time."

Riley stared at him, said, "Where?"

"How the hell do I know? Down the hill, back there. There's gotta be supply idiots down there somewhere."

Riley looked back beyond the ridge, men in motion, corpsmen, litter bearers, others Riley couldn't see clearly.

"Okay. You got ammo for that Thompson?"

"Why? You planning on getting lost?"

"Nope. But ..."

"Yeah, I got five magazines. Leave me your grenades and your M-1."

Riley handed Welch his rifle, then emptied his pockets, Welch gathering up the grenades, laying them out beside the machine gun. Riley started to move, hesitated, said, "Not sure about this, Hamp. Hate leaving you alone."

"I'm not alone, you moron. I got the whole damn Marine Corps up here. Just find me some damn ammo."

Riley moved away toward the ridgeline, visible in the moonlight. He saw litter bearers, and he followed them, called out, "You ammo carriers?"

No one responded, and Riley felt suddenly helpless, moved closer to another pair of litter bearers. He saw the man between them, wrapped in his coat, faceless, and Riley said, "Ammo dump?"

The men kept moving, but one said, "Yeah. Follow me. There's crates down below, by the CP."

Riley stayed close to them, saw men moving in all directions, a spray of green tracers ripping above him. He ducked, instinct, the litter bearers moving away. There was rifle fire to the east, more down along the main road. He felt for his rifle, another instinct, nothing there, realized he had left it with Welch. He kept moving, downhill now, saw the tents, a crush of activity, men laid out in rows, cries and shouts, others kneeling beside them, frantic activity.

"You! Over here!"

Riley realized the man was calling *him,* and he moved that way, the man pointing to one end of a stretcher.

"Kneel down. Grab his feet. He tries to move, hold him tight."

He obeyed, put his hands on the wounded man's boots, a tight grip. The corpsman was doing his work, slipped something from his mouth, Riley watching him intently, the corpsman pulling back the man's shirt at the waist.

"Only way to keep the morphine from freezing, hold it in your mouth. Just hope the damn syringe doesn't crack, or I'll be in Wonderland." Riley realized the corpsman was talking through a mouthful, the man pulling another syringe from his mouth. "Plasma's worthless. Freezes solid, and there's not a damn thing we can do about it. Even if it was thawed out, it's too cold. You'd kill a man pumping that into his veins. They didn't teach this stuff in med school. You a corpsman?"

Riley said, "No. Came down here to find ammo."

"Damn shame. I'm a doctor. I could use a dozen more corpsmen here." He continued to work, then said, "Only good thing about this cold, the wounds freeze up. Man not as likely to bleed to death. Well, two good things. The dead don't smell."

The doctor held a thick bandage on the man's groin, and Riley felt more helpless now, kept his grip on the boots, nothing to do but wait.

"You need me still, sir?"

The doctor stood, stretched his back. "No, go on. The captain'll be okay, I think. Right, sir?"

The wounded man responded with a mumble, and Riley stood straight, recognized the wounded man now, the face lit by a small lantern hanging on the nearby tent. It was Captain Barber.

FOX HILL—NOVEMBER 29, 3:00 A.M.

The ammo cans weighed more the farther he climbed. Around him, the litter bearers and so many others were scrambling past, cries for corpsmen in every direction. He focused on the rocks along the crest, the only landmark he could see, but the fiery blasts added to the blindness from the freezing wetness blanketing his eyes. He stopped, gasping for breath, the cold knifing into his lungs, and he bent low, the hood over his face, tried to find any strength at all. He stood again, the ammo cans in each hand, pushed forward, climbing, tried to ignore the aching in his shoulders. He crested the hill now, flashes of fire in every direction, the impact of the mortars still illuminating the saddle. But it was far out to the left, and he felt that familiar burst of panic, searched for the telltale rocks, strained to hear what might be Welch's machine gun. A flurry of fire whistled past him, and he ducked low, moved down the hill in a clumsy scamper. He stopped, crouched low, looked again for the saddle, nothing there, blind darkness, more flashes of fire cutting above him.

The blast erupted behind him, shoving him over, tumbling him down the hill, his face smacking hard on the frozen ground. He lay for a long moment, a fog in his brain, tried to see, rolled over on his back, the sky above him streaked with fire. He kept still, tested his legs, flexed his feet, pulled one hand into his coat, probing the soft places. No blood, thank God. The ringing in his ears wiped away most of the noise around him, and he waited for another minute, then sat up slowly, still testing his bones. He slid the hood of his coat away, realized his helmet was gone, and pulled the hood forward again, the only protection he had. One hand went to his belt, the .45 there, *yes,* and he squeezed his fingers around the butt, felt for the spare magazines beside it. There was no movement around him at all, his ears letting in a bit more sound, most of the firing farther away. He rose to his knees, another test, pain in his knees from the fall, but not crippling. The fog began to clear, and he could smell the shell that had come so close, the putrid stink of the spent powder. Smells like one of ours, he thought. Okay, don't try to think. You don't know what theirs smells like, either. He searched the ground for the ammo boxes, nothing, rocks and snow. He climbed higher, anxious searching, a sharp blast above him, along the crest, mortar shells, then another heavier blast down the hill, artillery. The lieutenant's word rolled through his brain, *mush.* Okay, time to go. You get hit by a 105, nobody'll ever find you. He scanned the ground once more, no sign of the ammo, and he thought of Welch, furious, waiting with an empty machine gun. Okay, Hamp, take it easy. I'll find you. Eventually. I gotta find *me* first, figure out where the hell I am.

He started to move, saw movement close in front of him, froze, a half-dozen men slipping silently up toward the crest of the hill. The white uniforms stood out in the faint moonlight, the men moving slowly, careful steps. He felt a burst of ice in his chest, kept still, the men stepping past no more than a few yards away, seemingly wandering, no urgency, as though they were lost. There was talk now, Chinese, one man pointing, the others following his lead. They stopped, gathered up, seemed to scan the area, searching for something, one man dropping low, picking up a weapon. He held it at his waist, fired a single shot, a flash in the dark, the sound of an M-1, more talk, another man coming up the hill, joining them. Riley felt a screaming pain in his knees, kept completely still, his eyes crusting over, his breathing slicing into his throat and lungs, the cold returning, invading his clothing. His heart pounded, and he kept his eyes on them, eased one hand in toward the .45, agonizingly slow, a silent shout in his head, Go on, *get out of here*! But the Chinese soldiers seemed content to stay put, another pair coming up the hill, gathering with the others, examining the rifle, more talk. He slid his hand to the bottom of his coat, closer to the .45, and now there was a bright flash, then another, *grenades*. He dropped flat, heard a burst of machine gun above him. He kept still, eased his head upward, strained to see, saw the muzzle blasts from the machine gun. The Chinese were mostly down, cries and grunts, no one returning fire. The rifles came now, ricochets off the rocks. He heard men coming down the hill, faint silhouettes in the dark, *Marines*, saw a burst from a BAR, spraying the Chinese bodies.

"Sons of bitches! We get 'em all?"

"Hope so. Come on. More down that way."

Riley pulled himself up, wanted to shout, anything, held his silence, too dangerous. The men began to move along the hillside, away from him, and now there was a shower of tracers from across the draw, the Marines falling, a sharp cry. The fire went both ways now, a machine gun uphill from him, a duel over Riley's head. He lay flat on the frozen ground, waited an eternity, a minute or more, the guns finally quiet. Riley looked up the hill close by, thought of calling out, his brain holding it in, the thought, You're in the wrong damn place. *Just get the hell out of here*. Find Welch. He slid on his belly, away from the dead Chinese, but there were more bodies in front of him, more smells, garlic and spent powder. He rose up, the moonlight reflecting off a sea of bodies, and he looked up the hill, realized he was far down, no landmarks he could see. There was more firing from the crest, ragged silhouette of rocks, nothing familiar, no sounds but the rattle of the rifle fire. The saddle was far off to the left, and he thought, Move that way, up the hill. That's where we were. I hope to God that's where we still are. I got no use being out here on my own. Dumb son of a bitch.

He clawed his way through the hard rocks, frozen fingers, cold sweat inside his coat. He slid himself uphill now, very slow, quiet movement, staring at the ridgeline. They gotta be there, he thought. We dug in all over that peak. Somebody's gotta be home. He thought of calling out again, no, not yet. Get closer. They need to see you. He crept closer, sliding through the snow, sharp rocks under his belly, staring through the darkness, no movement. He's there, he thought. Somewhere. All right, do this.

"Marine here!"

His voice seemed to explode out of him, and he lay low, waited, heard a nervous voice, very close.

"Who the hell are you? I'll blow your damn brains out."

"Marine! I promise. Third Platoon."

There was silence for a moment, hushed whispers a few yards above him, and now a different voice. "Yeah, asshole? Who won the World Series?"

Riley felt a new panic, his brain screaming for answers. Baseball. Oh, Christ. "Yankees! Beat the Phillies in four!"

There was another silent moment, and the second man said, "Okay, get your ass up here."

He scrambled that way, up on his knees now, reached the foxhole, saw two figures, rifles and grenades. His breathing came in short gasps, frantic words, "Thanks. Name's Riley. Third Platoon."

"Don't care. You're not a Chink. You're in First Platoon area. What the hell you doing out here?"

"Hauling ammo for a thirty. My sarge. Guess I got lost."

"Where's the ammo? We could use some."

Riley lowered his head. "Out there, somewhere."

"Great. Not only are you lost, but you're worthless, too."

"Guess so. At least I knew about the World Series."

"If you say so. We took your word for it. Neither one of us knows hog tits about baseball."

CHAPTER TWENTY-SIX

. . . .

Riley

FOX HILL—NOVEMBER 29, 4:00 A.M.

HE STAYED WITH the two men for more than an hour, but the Chinese had seemed to pull away, the only fire coming from the mortars, occasional blasts of illuminating shells, mostly out toward the saddle. The foxhole was a tight fit, and Riley kept his stare down the hillside, let the others get some sleep. The pains in his knees, the raw scrape on his face added a new discomfort to the misery of the cold, and he dabbed at his cheek, clamped his jaw down tightly, testing if he had lost any teeth. Friendly fire, he thought. Had to be. Haven't heard any enemy artillery anywhere. Not yet anyway. But hell, last night there weren't mortars and now they brought 'em up. I guess. Unless that was friendly fire, too. His eyes strained to see, and he realized there was a light haze of snowfall. There were more details now, the dawn coming on slowly, and he glanced at his new partners, thought, I gotta get out of here. Welch will be going nuts. Or he'll just be pissed. He thought of the ammo cans, back on the hill somewhere. Maybe somebody will find 'em, get some good out of 'em. Hopefully us. He felt stirring close beside him, one of the men waking, and he bent low, whispered, "Hey! If you're awake, I gotta head back to my unit."

The voice grumbled up from below, "Yeah, go on. I guess it's time for breakfast."

The snow was heavier now, and Riley crawled up, one knee on the hard dirt, pushing himself out of the hole. He looked out over the hill, eyed the crest, rocks spread all along, thick brush in patches. He began to move, and the man spoke behind him, low voice, "Hey, Mac. Just so you know. I was gonna plug you. My buddy figured you were okay."

"Yeah, well, thanks to your buddy."

He started to crawl, the ground layered in thin powdery snow. The breeze was coming again, and he could see more detail, realized there was a sharp crevice in the hillside, the brush thicker still. He pushed on, slipped above the thicket, heard a snap of branches, froze. There were dead men all around him, all of them Chinese, and he kept still, one hand moving to the .45. The movement in the brush continued, no other sound, and he drew the pistol, tried to flex his stiff fingers, feeling numbly for the safety, sliding his bare trigger finger into the guard. He rolled over, sat, the pistol pointing into the brush, more sounds, closer, his eyes finding more details in the soft gray light. The man appeared now, crawling, the white uniform, his face down, pulling himself free of the brush. Riley blinked, fought the frost around his eyes, aimed the pistol, waited, the man a few feet in front of him, moving closer. The man stopped, seemed to rest, sinking low, no weapon that Riley could see. One voice rolled through him. A prisoner. Take him prisoner. He waited one more second, then said, "Hey!"

The man popped his head up, wide-eyed surprise, the two men staring at each other for a long second. Riley jerked the pistol upward, a signal, kept the aim on the man's face. The Chinese soldier seemed to understand, moved to his knees, his hands coming up slowly to the top of his head. Riley didn't know what to do, was sitting, his feet extended, awkward position, and the soldier kept his stare on the pistol, Riley struggling to pull his legs closer.

"You just stay put there, pal."

Riley tried to turn around, still aiming the pistol, felt stupidly awkward, the soldier watching him now, a glance backward. The brush behind the man erupted now, another man, a surge of motion toward him, a burp gun firing. Riley shouted, fired the pistol, then again, the burp gun dropping. Now another man was there, down beside the prisoner, a rifle in his hands, firing from the hip, blinding flashes, Riley firing into the man's belly, dropping him. The brush was alive with movement, manic voices, but the men were moving away, down the hill, hidden by the deep cut in the hillside. Riley fired again, aiming at his prisoner, the man crawling away, falling flat. Riley fired again, emptying the pistol, no targets, aiming at noise, and to one side, up on the ridge, a machine gun opened up, chattering fire into the deep draw, splattering the ground, chopping the brush. More men began to crush down the hill, hidden still by the brush, the machine gun finding them, sharp cries. He pushed at the ground with his feet, backed himself frantically up the hill, more fire from the machine gun slicing down in front of him. He wanted to shout, felt the heart-ripping terror, lay flat now, on his back. The machine gun fired again, a shorter burst, then stopped, silence now but for the thunder in his ears. He waited, rolled over slowly, still had the pistol in his hands, peered up beneath the hood of his coat. The machine gun was just off the crest, a formation of rocks, one tall stone.

"Hamp! It's me!"

"Oh, shut up. I figured that out. Only you'd be that damn lost."

Riley rose up slowly, looked back toward his would-be prisoner, the man's chest peppered with holes, his blood oozing out, a thickening pool on the hard ground beside him. Riley pulled himself away, turned, saw several Marines coming down, rifles in hand, faces, one of them the kid, Morelli.

"Jesus, Pete! We thought they got you again! We been watching this bunch, knew they were in this draw. You got 'em to come out."

He looked at the others, Kane, slinging his BAR up on his shoulder, and Kane stared past him, nodded, said, "Good job, Pete. Remind me to take you fishing sometime. You make damn good bait."

Welch called out, "Check 'em out. Make sure they're dead enough. See what they're carrying."

The men moved past Riley, Kane probing one of the bodies with the BAR, firing a short burst. Riley jumped, surprised, and Kane moved to the next man, said, "This one's done. Check him out, kid."

Riley watched with horrified curiosity, Morelli, leaning low, his hand sliding into the man's coat. Kane looked at Riley, saw his expression, laughed.

"Yep, we give him all the good jobs."

Morelli stood now, held something in his hand. "Soap and toothpaste. American stuff, just like the others. And he's wearing that vest."

Riley looked down, didn't know what Morelli meant. "What vest?"

Kane said, "We were wondering why the carbines weren't dropping these Chink bastards. Like the damn slugs was bouncing off. They're wearing some kind of hemp thing. Word went out last night to everybody who's still stuck with a carbine. Aim for the head." He held up the BAR, another smile. "Didn't have that problem myself."

"Get your asses back up here!" Riley saw Welch now, standing at the machine gun, the young lieutenant Goolsby standing beside him. Welch called out, louder now, "There's sniper fire down that way. Get it done, then get back into cover. This ain't a picnic!"

Kane looked again at the handful of bodies, said to Morelli, "Hey, kid. Your turn. Plug each one of 'em. Just to be sure."

Morelli looked at him. "You sure it's okay?"

Kane said, "Captain's orders, kid. Do it."

Riley stood now, eased the stiffness from his legs, said to Kane, "Did the captain really order that?"

Kane was serious now. "I ain't lying, Pete. Too many of our guys were getting nailed by wounded Chinks."

He watched Morelli slip down the hill, probing more of the bodies, and now a single shot rang out, then another, Morelli stepping from body to body, the M-1 pointed down into each man's head. Riley turned away, didn't want to watch that, looked up toward Welch, the sergeant standing with his hands on his hips, observing. The others waited for Morelli to finish the job, the kid climbing up from the draw, looking at Riley with a smile.

Riley moved up the hill, the others spreading out, Welch calling out again.

"Get in your damn holes. The air boys oughta show up pretty soon, and nobody needs to be hunting souvenirs."

The men spread out, moving to their own places on the ridge, and Riley stepped closer to Welch, who said, "Where the hell's my ammo? How'd you end up way the hell out there?" Riley started to speak, felt exhausted relief, adding to the weariness of the long night. He felt the cold engulfing him again, said, "Sorry. Screwed up."

"Yeah, of course you did. I got ammo from one of the carriers. Made him stay with me and do *your* job. The Chinks tried like hell to grab this thirty. Figured out a little trick. Started pulling the tracers out of the belt, so they couldn't find me. They didn't figure that one out yet. Pretty easy to locate a Chink machine gun when he's shooting green at you." He stared at Riley, fixed on his face. "You look like hell. Like that bar fight in Guam."

"Shell came down, knocked me ass over teakettle. Lost the ammo."

Welch put a hand on Goolsby's shoulder, seemed to be checking on him, and Riley was surprised to see blood on the lieutenant's face.

"Same thing happened to him. Percussion grenade. Hey, Lieutenant, you hearing me okay?" Goolsby nodded, sat down now, and Welch bent low beside him. "We better get you to the aid station, sir."

Goolsby seemed to come awake, said, "No. Lieutenant McCarthy is down. I have to stay up here."

Welch stood, said to Riley, "I guess he's in charge, for now. McCarthy's down the hill. Leg's busted up good."

Riley watched Goolsby, saw him shake his head again, trying to blow out the fog.

"Sir, if we get you into a hole, warm you up a little. Might help."

Goolsby looked up at Riley, nodded. Welch helped Goolsby to his feet again, Riley taking him by the other arm. They moved together, the foxholes close in front of them, and Welch said, "Easy. Here you go, sir. Just sit tight. I'll find a corpsman, have him check you out."

Goolsby settled low in the hole. "Thank you, Sergeant. Look after the men. I'll be okay. Just a knock on the head."

There was a scattering of rifle fire down to the far side, and Riley looked that way, said, "Second Platoon?"

Welch reached down, picked up the Thompson, and beside it, Riley's M-1. "Here. Might come in handy. There have been snipers all morning long. The Chinks are lousy shots, mostly. But stay on your toes. No wandering around."

Riley took the rifle, Welch handing him a pair of clips. He slipped them into his pocket, looked back down the hill, the thicket of brush, the bodies of the Chinese soldiers.

"Why'd you make the kid do that?"

Welch pulled his coat tighter, fighting a new gust of wind. "Didn't have to. Turns out . . . he likes it. He's having as much fun out here as that idiot Irishman."

Riley felt a jolt. "How's he doing? Killian, I mean."

"He'll live. Not so some of the others. We took a few more good hits last night. You change your socks lately? Nope. Come on, let's go down the hill. I'll tell the lieutenant we'll try to find him a corpsman. I'm betting they're mostly down at the tents now. A single round took out the captain and Lieutenant McCarthy last night. Last I saw 'em they were both heading down to the tents. Some Chink tossed a percussion grenade right into Goolsby's hole. Lucky to still have his head."

Riley remembered the doctor and Barber now, at the aid station. "I saw the captain. They were working on him."

"They're gonna be working on all of us if we don't get off this hill. Grab whatever gear you need, your knapsack, your spare socks. You probably pissed your long johns, too. You oughta get some rations. There's a big-ass box of Tootsie Rolls down at the aid station. It's pretty quiet for now. Chinks ain't interested in daylight assaults. The air boys keep popping up out of nowhere. Damn beautiful sight. Chinks will wait until dark to make trouble."

Welch was moving off, Riley struggling to keep up, the painful stiffness in his knees, watery cold in his boots. He thought of the tents down below, felt a growling hunger rising in his gut, thoughts of Tootsie Rolls.

The screams caught his attention as they moved past the medical tent, the cries of the wounded blending with the orders called out by the doctor. Beyond was the warming tent, the parking place for the men who had already been treated. Riley stopped, focused on a row of corpses laid out between two fat trees. The faces were covered, the bodies draped with a thin coating of snow. At the tent, Welch said, "How long you gonna stand there? Nothing you can do for 'em."

Maybe, he thought, if I hadn't been stumbling around in the dark.

He knew better than to feel guilty about any of the casualties, that no matter what anyone had done, there was a bullet or a grenade or a mortar shell that could find you. The worst had been the direct hit into a foxhole, a mortar shell obliterating the men who had crouched low, believing they were safe. Haven't seen that yet, he thought. Not out here.

He looked at Welch, who showed him unusual patience.

"Sorry, Hamp. Head's a little foggy."

"Make way!"

Riley turned, saw two teams of stretcher bearers moving quickly downhill, headed for the medical tent. He moved aside, the first team carrying their man inside. The second team halted outside, waited for space, one man saying to Riley, or to no one at all, "Damn sniper. Second Platoon's still catching hell from the west hill. Lieutenant Peterson's up there half-full of lead, still running the show. Hell of a thing."

Riley looked at Welch, said, "Maybe we oughta go back up. Pretty busy place."

"You got a buddy in that warming tent. He's a jackass, but he's still a buddy. I wanna check on the lieutenant, see what's up. And I'm damn cold."

He followed Welch into the tent, not quite warm, but a definite improvement from the cold outside. The sounds were scattered and many, a sharp scream at the far end of the tent, a hard groan rising up from a man to one side. He tried not to see the details, the smells overwhelming him. Welch said, "Here's your buddy. Hey, Irish, you awake, or just goofing off?"

Killian lay on the ground, one of a row of men, each stuffed in a sleeping bag. Riley moved closer, bent low, said, "Hey, Sean. You okay?"

Killian looked up at him, staring through grogginess. "I'm alive, I think."

Riley saw the bandage on his neck, said, "How's the wound?"

Killian was still trying to focus, blinking his eyes, and Welch said, "He's doped up. Morphine. Hey, Irish, how big's the hole in your head?"

Killian shook his head slowly, one hand coming out of the sleeping bag, a clumsy poke at the bandage. "Not bad. Missed the important stuff. But the problem is my feet." Riley could see fear in Killian's glassy eyes, and Killian reached clumsily for Riley's arm. "I'm done for, Pete. My feet are dead. Frostbite. Something like that. They say I can't fight no more."

Welch moved closer, down beside Riley. "You slack-jawed bastard. I want you back up on this hill by tonight."

Riley knew Welch wasn't serious, had heard this kind of test before, pushing Killian to see if he'd push back. But Killian didn't respond, the morphine carrying him off someplace else. Beside Killian, another man spoke.

"Leave him be. It's the shoe pacs. Bunch of us here got nothing left to stand on. I lost most of the hide off the soles of both feet. You thaw out and you know what the hell *pain* feels like. They're supposed to evacuate us, hospitals, all of that."

Killian seemed to doze off, and Riley stood, looked at the other man, said, "You warm enough at least?"

"For now. They keep bringing 'em in, though. And there ain't enough room."

Riley bent down, slipped Killian's arm back inside the bag, pulled the loose top up over Killian's face. The other man said, "Hey, can you do that for me? My arm's busted up, can't move."

"Sure."

Riley pulled at the man's sleeping bag, caught the strong smell of urine now. He looked through the tent, a pair of corpsmen tending to patients, some of them on cots, another row of men in sleeping bags stuffed against one end of the tent.

"I'll get you somebody. Take care of that."

The man didn't respond, seemed to fade into sleep, and Riley was angry now, wanted to call out, order someone to look out for these men. Welch was beside him, seemed to read him.

"They'll get to him when they can. We're just in the way. Come on, we got better things to do. I don't see McCarthy. Maybe in the other tent."

Riley looked at the other men, the few cots jammed together, couldn't ignore the cries, the misery muffled by morphine. He heard Killian's voice, then a soft groan, more words, his name. Riley knelt low again, pulled back the bag, said, "I'm right here. You need something?"

"Oh, God, Pete. It hurts. My feet. They're gonna chop off my feet."

A corpsman was there now, eased Riley out of the way.

"No, they're not. We just gotta get you to the hospital ship. Maybe Tokyo."

Killian calmed, the grogginess settling over him again.

Riley felt a desperate helplessness, said to the corpsman, "You sure?"

The man stood again, said, "You bet. Might lose some toes. There's some a lot worse."

The man moved away, tending to more of the men in the sleeping bags, and Riley caught the hard smell of excrement, felt himself getting sick, tried to stifle it. He backed away, stumbled against a cot, a man responding with a sharp yelp.

"Oh, Jesus. Sorry."

He searched for Welch, saw him moving out of the tent, and the man in the cot shouted now, "Get me out of here! I ain't dying!"

The man reached for him, his hand clawing the air, and Riley backed off, the growling nausea worse, more smells, pushing him past the edge. He turned, hustled out of the tent, collapsed to his knees, vomited in the snow. The tears came now, the despair complete, the horrors overwhelming, the shame of his weakness. He felt a hand on his shoulder, the voice of Welch.

"Get over it. You've smelled worse. Seen worse, too."

Riley closed his eyes, still on his knees, hands down in the snow. "Don't know what happened."

"No sleep, no food, assholes shooting at you all night long. And your buddy's crapped himself. None of us are enjoying this, Pete. Get up."

Riley rose, struggled to his feet, Welch with a hard grip under his arm.

Another pair of stretcher bearers came down the hill, the wounded man bloodied across his face. They moved inside quickly, and Riley said, "Where the hell are they putting all these guys? Outside? What about tonight, Hamp?"

"That ain't your problem. They're doing all they can. The best thing we can do is kill every damn Chink out there, so we can get back to some kinda camp."

"What are you doing here, boys?"

Riley knew the voice now, saw Captain Barber hobbling toward him, a crude wooden splint on his upper leg, a pair of makeshift tree branches for crutches. Two men were with him and one said, "I'll get the doctor, sir. You really should stay put here."

Barber waved one of the crutches at the man, just missing the man's leg. "I'm fine. Too much to do. Get the damn doctor out here, tell him to stick a fresh bandage on it. Go!"

He looked at Riley again. "I said, what are you doing here?"

Welch said, "Came down to see a buddy, Captain. We're heading back up."

"You're Third Platoon, right?"

"Yes, sir."

Barber seemed unsteady on the odd crutches, and Riley could tell that the man was in obvious pain.

Barber said, "I was with Lieutenant McCarthy. We both got hit. His leg's a mess. He's over at the other tent, last I saw."

Welch eyed the heavy bandage on the captain's upper thigh. "Yes, sir, I know. I'm Sergeant Welch. Lieutenant Goolsby's in command of the rifle squads now. We'll be moving back up there right now."

Barber let out a breath, seemed to sag, then forced himself upright. Barber's aide returned now, the doctor in tow, the same man Riley had seen the night before. The doctor knelt close to Barber's leg, said, "Damn it all, Captain, I wish you'd be a little smarter. This is a hell of a wound, and you don't need to lose this leg just because you're stubborn as hell. You damage the artery and you'll lose more than the leg."

Barber scowled at the doctor, said, "Just put a fresh bandage on it. Save the advice."

"All right. Come inside."

"Do it right here. I got no time for your bedside manner."

Riley saw frustration on the doctor's face, saw the man produce the fresh dressing from his coat as though he had already expected to apply it on the spot. Barber raised his foot slightly, the doctor pulling at the splint, the old bandage stripped away, tossed aside. He worked quickly, the fresh dressing applied, wrapped with tape, and the doctor looked up at Barber, said, "If it wasn't cold as hell, you'd have bled to death. You still might."

"It's not warming up anytime soon, Doc. I've got work to do."

Barber looked at Welch again. "Make it quick down here, Sergeant. There's a lot more going on than the problems we've got on this hill. I want all my platoon and fire team leaders at my CP in ten minutes. I guess that means Goolsby. Give him the word."

Barber hobbled away, his two aides flanking him, prepared for a stumble. The doctor watched him go, said, "Not sure what he's trying to prove. He feels guilty getting hit, like he's letting all of us down." The doctor looked at Riley now, no recognition. "You boys looking for someone in particular?"

Welch said, "We found him, sir. Frostbite case."

"There are a lot of those, Sergeant. Not much we can do for 'em out here. I told the captain we need choppers to come in, but the enemy's shooting them up when they try to land. I got work to do, boys."

The doctor moved back into the tent, and Riley tested his gut, the nausea passing.

"Never expected to see this kind of stuff. Feet freezing. Christ."

Welch said, "Never expected to see a Chinese soldier trying to stuff a grenade down my throat, but here we are. Do I have to tell you to change your damn socks?"

"Not anymore."

"Didn't think so. Do it right now. I'll wait. I want to check on Mc-Carthy, and we still gotta hunt down some rations."

Riley sat, went to work on the boots, pulled the dry socks from his belt. He could see down through the trees to the main road, the narrow strip of snow and dirt, what someone thought was so valuable. From across the road he heard a faint chatter from a distant machine gun, scattered rifle fire closer, above him, along the west side of the hill. Welch began to move out through the trees, and Riley followed, heard more of the machine gun fire ripping across the hill behind him, heard the pop of the rifles, saw more stretcher bearers, moving down, another wounded man, one more sleeping bag, less room for all the rest.

The briefing from Barber to his officers and squad leaders was short and to the point. He had finally made radio contact with Colonel Litzenberg at Yudam-ni. Barber relayed the description of just what had happened there, and what still might happen, that both regiments had already endured a crushing assault from the Chinese from nearly every direction. But Litzenberg's message to Barber had been clear. If Fox Company could not move off their hill, and add anything to that fight, it was essential that they stay exactly where they were. If the Fifth and Seventh Marines were to have any chance of escaping annihilation, the narrow road that led back through Toktong Pass had to remain in the hands of Barber's Marines. But there was more to Litzenberg's message. Litzenberg had finally learned of the situation beyond the Taebaek Mountains, where much of the Eighth Army was in a headlong retreat southward. And, for the first time, Barber and his men were told of the situation at Hagaru-ri. There, Chinese prisoners had offered the matter-of-fact detail that some thirty thousand Chinese troops, the better part of three full divisions, were pushing in toward the Hagaru-ri perimeter from three directions. If Hagaru-ri fell to the enemy, the Marines at Yudam-ni, as well as Barber's lone company, would be completely cut off. And there was no one anywhere in Korea who could offer any rescue.

CHAPTER TWENTY-SEVEN

. . . .

Smith

HAGARU-RI—NOVEMBER 29, NOON

HE SAT IN THE JEEP, huddled against the cold, the driver beside him as miserable as he was. Smith kept his gaze on the heavy equipment, the engineers laboring with as much effectiveness now as anytime since the bulldozers arrived at Hagaru-ri. He wiped at his eyes, a hard frost already glued to his face.

"Let's go."

The jeep rolled into motion, a tight turn onto the road back to the command tent. It's not done yet, he thought. But there's enough runway there to support smaller transports, probably the C-47s. Right now I'd settle for the Red Baron in his triplane.

The wounded were overflowing the aid stations, hundreds now, many of them taking turns inside the warming areas, soaking up precious heat from the fat-bellied stoves. There was no room for all of them, not now, the casualty list passing four hundred, more men adding to the count every hour. There was no surprise to that, the Chinese striking hard at the perimeter, especially toward the east, the area around East Hill. But through it all, the engineers had continued their work, carving a magnificent airstrip out of frozen ground.

Smith kept his head down, the only protection from the brutal cold, the jeep turning again, coming to a halt by the large tent. He glanced at the driver, goggles and earmuffs, offered a short nod. "Thank you, son. Find a warm place."

Smith bailed out of the jeep, passed through a pair of guards, men far more miserable than he was, pushed his way into the tent. The coffee came quickly now, the aides knowing exactly what he wanted, Sexton there, offering a can of pipe tobacco.

"Pulled this from the private stock. I saw you empty the last tin. A bit nippy out there, sir?"

Smith took the tobacco, sat, said, "How cold is it?"

To one side, Bowser said, "Thirty below this morning. We think. Thermometer broke. Someone carried it in here just to show me, and the warmth in here just shattered it. I guess. Or Captain Sexton dropped it. I forget which."

Smith sipped at the coffee, pulled the pipe from his pocket. "Well, then, someone needs to find us another one."

Bowser said, "Already on it, sir. They making good progress on the airstrip?"

"They're closer. It's usable. I keep thinking of General Almond handing out medals to anyone he bumps into. It's those boys out there, the engineers, who deserve one. Colonel Partridge told me they're taking turns holding off the enemy. One man drives the tractor, one shoots the carbine. I want the whole world to know what those boys are doing."

Bowser went to the coffeepot, poured a cup for himself, said, "You know, you don't have to go out there yourself. I've volunteered to do it, and I know full well any man here would rather eat this weather than watch you do it. It's no different than going up to Yudam-ni. I really don't understand why you won't send me up there."

Smith lit the pipe, scanned the tent, the staff engulfed in all manner of work, paper, and radios. "Because I want you here. And it's not up for discussion. What do we hear from Litzenberg?"

Bowser said, "It wasn't too bad last night. Not nearly as many casualties. The enemy seems to have calmed down a bit. They could be regrouping, and Litz expects to be hit again, maybe tonight. He and Murray have their heads together, and they seem pretty pleased with your orders."

Smith clamped the pipe in his teeth, thought, I suppose I should be grateful. Litzenberg argues with every order he gets. Now, if they can just do the job. "Any progress on opening the road this way?"

"Not yet. He says the enemy is in strength all along the road, major roadblocks at several points. Air recon confirms that. Murray should have his people back into Yudam-ni by now, if the Chinese let them disengage. They had gotten a mile or more west of the town when they got hit. Weather was pretty stinky up that way earlier this morning, made things tough for the chopper pilots. The fighters are getting through, hitting the enemy positions, when they can find them. You want to give out medals, give 'em to the air spotters. Litz says those boys have saved lives. The enemy wants no part of an air assault, and they button up good when the planes show up."

"What about Fox Company?"

Bowser seemed to hesitate. "Not sure. The air boys say they're still on their hill, overlooking the road. We're dropping ammo, and we've supplied batteries for their radios." Bowser motioned to a man to one side, earphones clamped to the man's head. "Sergeant, anything from Captain Barber?"

The radio man shook his head. "No, sir. I'll try again."

Bowser said, "Try every half hour." He looked at Smith, who saw the worry. "It could just be the weather, or these mountains. Barber's gotta be trying to communicate with Yudam-ni, or us. Let's give him every chance, sir. He knows what those batteries are for."

Smith finished the coffee, stood, tried to ignore the pains in his legs. He appreciated what Bowser was doing, that no matter what else was needed, Smith had to keep his best staff officers close at hand. The priority, still, was Hagaru-ri, and Bowser was as important to him as finding rifles to strengthen the perimeter.

"I'm going to my quarters. Let me know if Barber gets through. Let me know if we hear from Colonel Drysdale. Or anything new from

Litzenberg. Get on the horn to General Tunner, at Air Force Cargo. Tell him we're close to a usable airstrip, and I want every plane in the Far East Command to be gassed up and ready. Well, no, don't tell him that. Just let him know we are very close to asking him for all the help he can send this way."

Outside, he heard the roar of a fighter formation, passing low. Bowser glanced upward, said, "I'll try to reach General Harris. We get out of this place, the air wing will be one reason why. I'll buy him a steak dinner."

"I'll buy him two." Smith paused, a new thought. "I suppose, once we get the strip completed, we'll get a mail run."

He saw the other faces turn, knew that *mail* was a magical word. Bowser said, "Yes, sir, I suppose so. The boys mention it once in a while."

Smith slid into the coat again. "I'll be in my billet. I'll be ready to send a few letters of my own. I want my wife to know I'm not just up here getting a suntan."

He moved outside quickly, the cold blasting him. He hobbled slightly, hoped no one noticed, stepped gingerly through the packed snow toward the small house. He glanced out from the hood of his coat, saw the nearest aid station, slowed his steps, couldn't avoid feeling a familiar gloom, asked himself, How many more were there today? At least I should look in on them. He passed a row of corpses draped in snow-covered cloth, slowed, counted, two dozen. More tonight, he thought. No, let that go. We cannot *fix* this, not yet.

He looked toward the large tent, the tin chimney spitting out a column of gray smoke, swept away by the wind. Stepping carefully, he avoided a smear of ice, stepped to a layer of rice straw spread out, a pathway that led to the entrance of the tent. He stepped inside, a flurry of quiet activity, smells of disinfectant and urine, too familiar. He eyed the doctors, stethoscopes and hypodermic needles, those men ignoring him. A handful of corpsmen were there as well, stepping over the closely packed cots, none of them empty. Smith scanned the wounded men, faces turning toward him, no one speaking. He wanted to give them something, to tell them of the airstrip, the promise that very soon they could be evacuated, a real bed in a real hospital.

Another flight of Corsairs flew over, answered by subdued cheers from the wounded men, one man raising a fist, his own silent salute. I can't add anything to that, he thought. They'll salute *me* when I give them a good reason. Right now, they don't have one.

Behind him, litter bearers moved inside, a doctor coming forward with a bottle of plasma, giving instructions. "We're ready. Lay him over here."

The men obeyed, and Smith kept back, looked at the wounded man, the man's clothing coated with icy filth, black stains, one leg exposed, the man's skin white and frozen. The doctor went to work, one corpsman hanging the plasma beside the worktable, the man's uniform cut away. Smith had seen this before, so often, in the Pacific, wounds festering quickly from the heat. But there was very little blood here, the wounds freezing, the one astonishing benefit of the absurdity of the weather. He saw now, the wounded man was an officer, unfamiliar face, an army uniform. Staff, he thought, one of Almond's clerks. Or a musician maybe. He imagined the scene, the man receiving orders he never expected. Here's a rifle, son. Now you're going to fight. There's an enemy out there who doesn't care what your job is, what you were trained to do. And we don't care, either. Right now, we don't have the luxury of *soft duty*.

"Can I help you, sir?"

He knew the face, the naval doctor, Eugene Hering. Hering had a wide smear of something awful on his apron, looked at Smith with dark, exhausted eyes. Smith focused on the man's face, heard a hint of hostility in his voice.

"This will be over soon, Doctor. The airstrip will be ready for transport planes in a day or two."

"If you say so, sir. Please excuse me."

Hering turned away, moved to the worktable, assisting the other doctor. Smith knew he was out of place here, could offer nothing to help these men do their work. But he could not just leave, said aloud, "We will be out of here very soon. We are doing everything we can."

No one responded, and Smith pulled the coat tightly around him, backed out of the tent.

· · · · · · · · · · ·

He stared down at the letter, reread, erased a word, made a correction, wrote again, "Our clerks were out there with weapons. Our lines held."

He slid the paper aside, thought, I cannot tell her more. I don't have to. She understands. She knows what I do, and how it is done. She knows there is a cost. I should cry to her, sing sad songs? I won't give her that. It isn't a part of me. One day, I will sit with her, and perhaps we will cry. But not now. It's like Dr. Hering. I offer him encouraging words and he stares at me with a man's guts on his hands. How is he encouraged about that? All I can really give any of them is confidence. The men must see that, must always feel that from their commander. It is not enough for me to *hope* that we survive this. We must prevail here. No matter what the fools in Tokyo believe, no matter what they tell us to do, we will *win* this thing. I believe that, and so we will all believe it. We *must* believe it. Yes, our lines held. They *will* hold. And as God is my witness, I will do what must be done to protect these men, to repair the raw, ugly stupidity that sent us out here.

Early that morning, another column of armor moved out on the road east of the reservoir, one more attempt to drive through the enemy's stranglehold on the isolated position of the army's Thirty-first regimental combat team. A few miles northeast of the Marine perimeter at Hagaru-ri, a dozen tanks, commanded by army captain Robert Drake, had held position at the small village of Hudong-ni, close to the shores of the reservoir. Drake's plan was to push the armored column through the Chinese roadblocks, blowing open a path of escape for the troops to withdraw back down to Hagaru-ri. The tanks were accompanied by some three dozen infantry, some of those South Korean troops. But Drake's plan had two major problems. First, the tankers did not have their own forward air controller, and so he could not communicate with the air protection he had hoped for, even as the Corsairs patrolled the skies directly overhead. With no instructions where to place their fire, the Corsairs were partially blind, and ultimately inflicted casualties on both sides. The second problem had more to do with the first effort General Hodes had made to rescue his troops. That column had lost four tanks, one of which completely blocked the only road Drake could use. Drake's alternative plan was to push his armor directly up the hill that guarded the passageway, which was heavily occupied by Chinese troops. But the tanks could not maneuver up the frozen slopes. Faced with a potential disaster to the column, Drake had no choice but to withdraw once more.

A few miles to the north, the Thirty-first's commanding officer, Lieutenant Colonel Don Faith, with no radio contact with the tanks, or with anyone at Hagaru-ri, had no idea that anyone had made the effort to help the twenty-eight hundred men in his command.

The only positive that resulted from Drake's mission was that, now, with no reason to remain at the advance position at Hudong-ni, he ordered the tank column to pull back to the defensive lines at Hagaru-ri, adding to the forces there who had every reason to expect another nighttime attack.

Just before ten that morning, Colonel Douglas Drysdale led his nine-hundred-man task force northward out of Koto-ri. Almost immediately, Drysdale confronted the same obstacles that had faced the Americans along every part of the main road. The eleven-mile journey to Hagaru-ri was sliced through by Chinese roadblocks, troop placements fortified by machine guns and mortars. Facing a far stronger enemy than he had anticipated, Drysdale radioed his situation back to Chesty Puller. Puller responded by ordering a company of nearly thirty tanks out of Koto-ri, to add considerable firepower to Drysdale's column. Drysdale appreciated the advantages the tanks offered, and ordered their commander to distribute the tanks in pairs all along the column. But the tank commander, Captain Bruce Clark, insisted the tanks remain together, a formidable force the Chinese could not hope to stop. Drysdale had no authority over Clark's command, and the tanks remained mostly clustered together, leading the way north.

Clark's men soon engaged Chinese targets all along the route, and though most of those fights were one-sided in favor of the armor, the tanks' slow progress meant that the lengthy column of trucks behind them would move slowly as well. If the tanks were intimidating to the Chinese, not so the column in their wake. With the vulnerable vehicles spread out in a grindingly slow advance, the Chinese attacked the column in several locations, turning a single convoy into at least three separate parts.

Frustrated with the slow progress of the tanks, Drysdale understood what was happening to his task force behind him. The most acceptable alternative seemed to be to withdraw and fight their way back to Koto-ri. But Oliver Smith had a very different view. Reaching Smith by radio, Drysdale explained his situation. Smith, still faced with the desperate need to bolster the defenses around Hagaru-ri, ordered Drysdale to push onward, at all costs. Drysdale responded with typical British aplomb: "Very well, then, we'll give them a show."

Late in the evening on November 29, the vanguard of Task Force Drysdale reached the southern perimeter at Hagaru-ri. With Drysdale were most of the tanks, most of his Royal Marine Commandos, and the company of American Marines. At the rear of the convoy, nearly a third of the column, including many of the trucks and supply vehicles, escaped the worst of the Chinese assaults and pulled back in a desperate escape to Koto-ri. But in the center, fully one-third of the task force could not move in either direction, and throughout one awful night were left to the mercy of the Chinese.

HAGARU-RI—NOVEMBER 29, 10:00 P.M.

The tanks had inspired a raucous cheer, the men along the southern perimeter welcoming the added strength of the armor with a mix of joy and exhausted relief. The Marines were welcomed, too, Tom Ridge's George Company adding to the manpower that Ridge was still shifting into the most vulnerable positions all around the town. But the men at Hagaru-ri had seen these men and their heavy equipment before. What caused the most curiosity, a respectful salute, was the appearance of the Royal Marines. Their dress was different, of course, green berets worn instead of helmets, those men stiffening, a show of perfect decorum as they marched past the men who welcomed them. None carried that decorum with more pride than their commander.

Smith stood, Drysdale saluting him, and he stared at the Englishman for a long moment. Drysdale seemed uncertain now, as though he may have violated some kind of American protocol.

"At your service, sir. It was a bit dicey. I very much regret that we could not advance the entire column. It is a rather dismal outcome, to be sure."

"Colonel, you are wounded."

Drysdale ignored the ripped shirtsleeve, the caked blood soaking through his uniform. "Appears so, yes, sir. Not a problem. You have medical people here, yes? They should be able to fix me up, good as new."

Smith glanced at Bowser, who kept his stare on Drysdale. "Yes, by all means. My aide will escort you to the medical tent. You may report to me when you're up to it."

Drysdale seemed disappointed. "Oh, sir, I'd rather lay out the details now, if you don't mind."

Smith couldn't avoid looking at the man's wounded arm. "Are you quite certain you're up to it?"

Drysdale attempted a small laugh. "Oh, I assure you, sir, I've endured much worse. Never run into an Oriental yet who could pull the starch from a British Marine."

Smith thought, Not the time for this sort of thing. But he seems to mean it. "Very well, Colonel. I am gravely concerned about the condition of your column. Colonel Puller radioed that some of the men and equipment returned to Koto-ri. I suppose we should be grateful for that."

"If you say so, sir. I regret that we could not maintain contact. The enemy was bloody eager to chop us to bits, and with most of the armor gathered in the vanguard, there was little to protect the soft vehicles. I would hope that those who did not accompany me here were successful in escaping the enemy's grasp. I suspect there were losses, sir." He paused, a crack showing in the stern demeanor. "Considerable losses, I'm afraid."

Smith had already received a ragged estimate from Puller, though no one yet could know just what was still happening along the narrow winding road.

"We will do what we can for anyone still out there, Colonel. My greater concern is right here. If Hagaru-ri falls into the enemy's hands, it will jeopardize the entire force we have employed to the north of here. How many men made it through with you?"

"Near three hundred, I am happy to say."

"I would be happier still if your entire force had reached here."

Drysdale seemed subdued now, said, "Yes, of course. As would I, sir. I will bear the responsibility for our losses, General."

"No, you won't. That responsibility falls upon me." He looked again at Drysdale's wounds. "When you are able, you will report to Colonel Ridge. He commands the perimeter here. We will make the best use of your men as we can, I assure you. I am grateful for your efforts."

The compliment rolled out of Smith with no enthusiasm, as though he were greeting the man at a formal dinner party. He was uncomfortable now, still eyed the man's arm. "Really, Colonel, I insist you go to the medical tent. Colonel Bowser, will you ask one of the aides to show him the way?"

"Certainly, sir."

Drysdale saluted Smith again, said, "I shan't be long, sir. I should see to my men, at least for the evening. They have had one devil of a day, as it were."

Smith returned the salute, motioned toward the door, Drysdale moving out with the young aide. Smith waited for Drysdale to leave, felt a chill, the stove not quite adequate to heat both rooms. Bowser stood out in the larger room, said, "He dripped blood all over the place. I'll have it cleaned up, sir."

"Let it go, Alpha." Smith pulled the pipe from his shirt pocket. "What do you make of that fellow?"

"He's British, no doubt about that. He'd rather pass out from loss of blood than admit he might be in pain. We *colonists* should never observe such weakness in one of His Majesty's troops."

Smith had no use for the kind of rivalries that always seemed to rise up. "It was a very bad day, Colonel. Lewie says he counted three hundred men who made it back to Koto-ri. Three hundred made it here. Nothing complicated about the math. Three hundred men are either dead, or grabbed by the Chinese. All of that stiff-upper-lip business. It's their way, for sure. But he knows what I ordered him to do, and he's not likely to forget that. And no matter what kind of foolishness you or anyone else wants to toss around about the Brits, there's nobody on this earth I'd rather have next to me in a foxhole."

HAGARU-RI—NOVEMBER 29, 10:30 P.M.

He sat alone, enjoying the pipe, another letter to Esther forming itself in his mind. You'll read about this one, I'm afraid. I had no choice. No one ever wants to hear that excuse, but it's what I believe. There have been decisions made by others, handed to me this entire campaign, most of them incredible, ridiculous. This one was mine. Did I truly believe we could open that road, that the Chinese weren't as strong there, or that they might just back away? Someone will ask those questions one day. Drysdale is asking them right now, as he wonders if he's going to lose his arm.

The outer door burst open, the guard making way for the wrapped bundle of a man, another behind him. Smith couldn't avoid a nagging dread, rapped the pipe against the chair, stuffed it in his pocket. He waited, saw Bowser's head emerge from the coat, the man red-faced, out of breath, the aide waiting for Bowser to remove the coat.

"Have you two been out doing maneuvers in this cold, Colonel?"

Bowser kept the coat on, was breathing heavily still, tore through a pocket, pulled out a piece of paper. "Sir, this is momentous. Finally, somebody *up there* is thinking straight."

"Up there. Heaven?"

Bowser seemed to miss the joke, said, "Tokyo, sir. MacArthur's HQ. This just came from Tenth Corps. Shall I read it?"

Smith could see Bowser's excitement. "Give it here. You might rip it to pieces."

Smith took the paper, felt the cold on the man and the paper, moved to a lantern.

Effective at once, all elements Seventh Infantry Division . . . are attached to First Marine Division. First Marine Division redeploy one regiment without delay from Yudam-ni area to Hagaru-ri area, gain contact with elements of Seventh Infantry Division east of Chosin Reservoir; coordinate all forces in and north of Hagaru-ri in a defense based on Hagaru-ri; open and secure Hagaru-ri and Koto-ri main supply road. . . .

Bowser waited impatiently, said, "Does that mean what it sounds like it means?"

Smith lowered the paper, absorbed the order. "Someone has determined that they require a single command to dig Tenth Corps out of its hole."

"MacArthur, you think?"

Smith shrugged. "Doesn't matter, does it? I've been handed the results of someone else's idiotic decisions. There's still a finger stirring the pot, though. The middle section . . . Almond is ordering that we rescue the army units. He also insists we return at least one of our regiments from Yudam-ni. I would assume he will allow us to do the latter before the former. We have no one here now we can spare to go driving up the east side of the reservoir. The army's own tanks can't push through. I'm not going to tell Colonel Drysdale that the next duty for his Marines might be the most hopeless task we face."

Bowser seemed frustrated, pointed to the paper. "Sir, they've given you command of the entire situation. Seventh Division included. The whole show."

"Careful, Alpha. Read between the lines. Yes, I am now in command of those troops who, from all we can determine, are presently surrounded by overwhelming numbers of Chinese forces. The most obvious conclusion here is that General Almond has had his mind changed about pushing us on to the Yalu. He can't figure out what to do next, so he's tossing it to me."

Bowser smiled now. "I'm sorry, sir. But that seems to me to be a positive thing."

Smith had the sudden aching need for a cup of coffee, looked out to the waiting aide. "Sergeant, there's a coffeepot in that corner. Will you do what you can to put it to work?"

"Certainly, sir."

Smith sat again, stared at the covered window, could hear the wind rattling the glass. "They haven't come yet, have they?"

"The enemy? No, sir. I can't help but wonder if this cold isn't killing them as efficiently as we are."

Smith shook his head. "No. They're coming. And now I can do what needs to be done. Send in one of the secretaries. I'm preparing orders for Murray and Litzenberg to make immediate preparations to extricate themselves from contact with the enemy at Yudam-ni, to clear the road between Yudam-ni and here. They have worked well together and they can continue to do so."

The sergeant was there now, said, "Sir, I will fetch Corporal Hanley, if you wish. He's good with a pencil."

Bowser motioned toward the door. "Then go fetch him."

The man moved out quickly, and Smith saw more enthusiasm from Bowser, the man's pulsating energy, Bowser starting to pace the room. Smith retrieved the pipe again, could hear the percolating of the coffeepot.

"It could all come down on us, Alpha." Bowser still paced, seemed not to absorb what he was saying. He stopped now, looked at Smith.

"You mean a scapegoat?"

"Of course a scapegoat. Or any other form of goat. Almond thinks he's handing me enough rope to hang with. It's our job to show the men out here, all of the men in this command, that this campaign is a success."

"I don't follow you, sir."

"I could care two hoots how Tokyo or Tenth Corps judges us. But right now, there are near fifteen thousand men out there in this cold who believe somebody's paying attention."

"You've always been paying attention, sir."

Smith picked up the paper, held it up. "Now I can do more than that. Now I can *fix* this thing."

CHAPTER TWENTY-EIGHT

....

Riley

"THIS ISN'T A GOOD SITUATION. But I don't want to leave this ridge. If they can't knock us off here, I'm not handing it to 'em for free."

The others seemed to agree with the captain, Riley hanging close behind Welch, his eyes on Barber's crude crutches. They had gathered back behind the rocky ridge, mostly out of sight of the snipers across the saddle. The Chinese hadn't improved their marksmanship, but any gathering outside of the cover of the foxholes would invite more than just the single rifleman. The air cover had been effective, certainly, and Riley guessed, along with Welch, that in the daylight the Chinese would have one eye focused on the skies above them. But the air strikes had not erased the threat. It was plainly obvious that when the Chinese lost any of their machine guns, it was very soon replaced with another.

Late that afternoon, columns of fresh enemy troops had been spotted out to the west of Second Platoon, on the hill across the road. It was an unusual tactic, not much surprise to their assault, the Chinese coming out of the woods, attempting to cross the main road, driving up the hill nearer the aid stations. But Lieutenant Peterson, Second Platoon's commander, had observed the move along with his men, the columns of troops marching in full view down the draws on the west hill. When they made their strike, it began as it always had, bugles blaring, whistles blowing, but now the Marines were fully prepared. Line after line of Chinese soldiers emerged through the tree line, only to be cut down by the light and heavy machine guns, the BARs and rifles of the men who saw it all coming. The fight lasted no more than a half hour, and to every observer on the hill, it seemed only to have been a one-sided slaughter. Second Platoon lost only a single man killed.

The cold skies had grown cloudy late in the day, the ominous gathering of dense gray that most often resulted in a snowstorm. With darkness falling rapidly, Captain Barber had climbed up along the ridge, finding out for himself what his men already knew. With so many of the Marines hauled down to the aid stations, either wounded or frostbitten, the perimeter was beginning to stretch dangerously thin.

Riley could see the weakness in Barber's face, the man in just as much pain now as he had been at the aid station down the hill. Beside Barber was Lieutenant Wright, his executive officer. Riley didn't know the man at all but, like the others around him, wondered just how long Barber could keep up the effort he was making to maintain control, whether or not Wright would end up taking command of the company. Riley could see Wright's concern, shared it himself, Barber's limp more severe each time he moved along the hillside. But for now, Barber was still in charge.

"I'm not sure what they're up to, but you can bet they'll come back tonight. I don't have the first idea what they thought they were trying to prove in front of Second Platoon. But they stayed off that damn saddle all day. Thank the Corsairs for that." He looked at Goolsby. "Spread 'em out. Put a man in every hole. Full alert. It's the best we can do." Barber paused, seemed to gather himself, finding the energy. He scanned the faces, said, "I had relatives fought with Robert E. Lee at Petersburg. Grant starved him out, and broke his army. That's what we got here, a full-out siege. The enemy believes he's going to accomplish the same thing. But Lee didn't have flying boxcars dropping ammo to his troops. Right now ammo is more important than rations. As long as the air boys can keep delivering, we'll keep killing Chinese. Maybe Chairman Mao will figure out that penning us up in a slaughter pen wasn't such a good idea."

Goolsby glanced at the few sergeants close by, most of them keeping a discreet distance. "Sir, how long do you think we've gotta stay up here?"

Riley saw the frown on Barber's face.

"Son, if I knew that, I'd be a general. Maybe a Chinese general. We'll stay here until we don't have to anymore. Clear?"

"Yes, sir."

Barber glanced at Welch, seemed relieved there was a veteran on the ridge. "Go to work. Gather up what you can from the corpses. Both sides. If you see a weapon that works, the Chinese are just as liable to pick it up as you are. Grenades, anything else. I'm heading over to First Platoon. Lieutenant Dunne is about the only officer on this hill who hasn't been hit. All right, go to work."

Barber hobbled off, Wright and a pair of aides following.

Goolsby looked around, his focus now on Welch. "You heard him, Sergeant. I think you should man that machine gun again."

"I'll take Riley, sir. I need a loader."

Goolsby nodded. "Fine. But make a quick check down the hills, search the bodies again. You heard the captain. Pick up as many grenades as you can find. I'd just as soon avoid what happened to me yesterday. The more you can toss down the hill, the fewer will get tossed back at you. Or me."

Welch motioned to Riley, moved off toward the gun. The others scattered as well, and Riley heard the *ping* off a nearby rock, a sniper taking aim, the men quickening their steps. Welch knelt by the machine gun, worked the action, said, "Not too bad. The cold doesn't seem to bother this thing as much as the carbines. We heat it up a bit, it'll work even better. Check those boxes. Full ones first."

Riley knelt, opened the heavy steel boxes, part of the load dropped by the first cargo plane. "We're good. Three full, plus some. You wanna do a test fire?"

"Hell, no. I'm not sure they've spotted this gun yet, and there's no need to help 'em out while it's daylight. They show up tonight, we'll have plenty of time to test everything we got. How many grenades you got?"

Riley felt through his coat. "Four."

"Not enough. Let's head down the hill, before it's full dark. Plenty of Chinks we ain't really gotten to yet."

"You going with me?"

Welch laughed. "Yeah, sissy boy. I'm not about to turn you loose again. You might end up in Peking. There ain't nothing about a Chink POW camp that sounds like a place I wanna spend my vacation." Welch looked out to the side. "Hang on. I'm gonna make sure Kane and the others know we're out there. It ain't dark, but it's getting there. And that kid loves to shoot up all his ammo. And don't forget, dammit. You see any steam coming out of any of these Chink bastards, it means they're alive. Blow 'em to hell."

Welch motioned him out, and Riley followed, slipped along the gentle slope, past the first of the white-clad bodies. He had learned what to look for, the grenade carriers usually unarmed, carrying a cloth sack. Most of the men closer to the machine gun had been picked over, their odd assortment of rifles now adding to the store of arms along the ridge. Welch pointed toward the thicket, farther down, where Riley had confronted the enemy soldiers. He felt uneasy, didn't really want to see that place again, but Welch was waiting for him, the look that said, *Move it*. Welch bent low, shoved at one of the bodies, picked up a Thompson, a nodding smile toward him. Yeah, fine, Riley thought. It's a treasure hunt. Welch was stuffing something else in his coat pocket, and Riley began to search the ground himself, closer to the deep thicket, stopped at the man he had briefly captured. The man's chest was ripped open, and Riley stared at the pool of frozen blood, an odd pink color, saw now the neat hole in the man's head, where Morelli had finished the job. Didn't need a prisoner anyway, he thought. What the hell would I have done with him?

He heard Welch whispering to him, looked up, Welch holding a cloth bag.

"Magazines for the Thompson. Look here. Still says *U.S. Army* on the bag."

"Lucky you. Now I ain't gotta buy you a Christmas present."

Riley scanned more of the bodies, saw the corner of a cloth bag just visible beneath a man's shoulder. Oh, God, he thought. Here we go. He reached down, a hard grip on the quilted coat, pulled, then harder, the body unmoving, frozen to the hard ground. Guess you can keep it, buddy. He looked toward the next body, heard an odd grunt, saw Welch drop down. He heard the impact now, a string of machine gun slugs skittering on the hard ground. He fell flat, another burst spraying closer by, some impacting the body beside him. He kept his face to the ground, waited for a pause in the fire, and Welch shouted, "Up! Now! He's reloading. Up the hill!"

Welch scampered past him, Riley rising, a hard scramble to keep up. He was above the brush, in the open, the rocks in front of him, and now the machine gun opened again, stitching the ground to one side. He kept moving, a fast run, Welch faster still, a leap into the tall rocks. Riley jumped into cover, a hard landing, sore bones on frozen earth. He heard laughter, somewhere close, lay flat, gasping through the frigid air, the laughter continuing. Welch was flat beside him, still had the Thompson, his breathing in sharp gasps as well. Riley said, "Who's laughing?"

"Who do you think?"

Riley sat up, looked to one side, up on the ridgeline, saw Kane, the crew of the BAR, faces above the rim of their foxholes.

"You know, they got the Olympics in a couple years. You two oughta run a relay."

More laughter came now, all along the hill, Riley leaning his back against the tall rock.

"They can go down there next time."

Welch pulled himself up, one arm lying across the breech of the machine gun. "Bastard thinks he's Milton Berle."

Riley couldn't help a smile, said, "At least you got another Thompson. How many's that?"

Welch moved a white blanket aside, another prize from the fallen Chinese. "This makes four."

"You think I might get to use one?"

Welch seemed to ponder the question. "Well, hell, I found a bag of ammo for 'em. Guess it can't hurt."

Riley took the Thompson from Welch, felt the heft. "Always heard these things were pretty useless. No range."

"How much range you think you need? We're not sharpshooters, you know. You don't want it, give it back."

Riley thought of the night before, then before that, the hordes of Chinese, the fight on all sides.

"Hand me some of those clips."

FOX HILL—NOVEMBER 30, 1:00 A.M.

The supply plane had come again, the big C-119 Boxcar, unloading massive pallets of matériel under white parachutes. It had been nearly dark, the men on one part of the hill following Barber's orders to gather in a circle, each one aiming a flashlight skyward. But the pilot hadn't the aim of the first one, ground fire from the Chinese on the rocky hill keeping the plane much higher than it needed to be. The result was a missed target, many of the pallets falling well down the hill, nearly three hundred yards beyond the perimeter. It was as much a gift to the Chinese as it was to the disgusted men on Fox Hill. The rescue had begun immediately, before the Chinese could fully grasp what a bounty they might have received. The journey down into the wooded draw was dangerous, to be sure, but Barber pushed the men to move quickly, and well after dark most of the supplies were hauled back where they belonged. As if the pilot's inaccuracy weren't cause enough for annoyance, one of the pallets was loaded with what someone to the south must have thought was a precious necessity for the suffering Marines: cans of fresh water. By the time the water was discovered, it had passed beyond usefulness. It was solid ice.

By midnight the Chinese began to open up their machine guns across the saddle, sprays of green tracers peppering the crest of the hill, where the Chinese gunners had ranged their guns throughout the daylight hours. The mortars came as well, not as accurate, impacting in scattered patterns that weren't patterns at all. The Marines kept mostly to their foxholes, accepting that this latest assault was surely the preliminary of yet another massed attack by the Chinese infantry.

• • • • • • • • • •

Riley sat low in the foxhole just behind the machine gun, his sleeping bag again wrapping his legs. It was the first time he had shared cover with Welch in a very long time, another war, another part of the world. There was no talk, the noise from the mortar and machine gun barrage driving each man's thoughts inside. Riley knew there could be no sleep, the captain's orders clear. But the barrage was hypnotic, and Riley felt himself drifting off, soothed by the steady chatter and rumbles of the Chinese fire. He thought of Ruthie and the boy, meeting him at a plane, Philadelphia, maybe. She'll dress like a goddess, he thought. She loves that, standing out in a crowd. And boy, does she. She'll try to be the first thing I see when I come off the plane. Or the train. Hell, I don't know. Maybe they'll let me drive home in a jeep. Just pull up to the front yard and beep the damn horn. Hi, honey, I'm home. Let me tell you about my day at the office. And Peter. So happy to see his old man. He had a jolting thought. What if he doesn't remember who the hell I am? God, no. Can't have that. Need to write her, tell her to show him pictures, every day. Please don't let him forget. And if I don't come home . . . well, do that anyway.

He sat up, wiped at the crusty goo around his eyes. Enough of that, for crying out loud. He looked at Welch, the sergeant's voice rising above the din of the firing.

"You fall asleep?"

"No. Thinking of home. Bad idea."

"Writing a few letters myself. Wonder when we'll get to mail 'em?"

A mortar shell impacted a few feet in front of the hole, and Riley flinched, pulled his head down like a turtle. Too close, he thought. Welch said, "They adjust that one a couple notches and we won't have to worry about it. Shoulda dragged more of those Chinese sandbags up here. We'll do that tomorrow."

There was commotion behind the rocks, and Riley heard voices, eased up slowly, a lull in the mortar fire. There were two men hauling a stretcher, the wounded man suddenly rising up, sitting, the men lowering him to the ground. It was Captain Barber.

"All right, I've had about enough of this! I've ordered the spotter, Lieutenant Campbell, to call back to Hagaru-ri and give us some of that artillery support they say we have. O'Leary's waiting for word from Campbell to fire some star shells so we can range the incoming fire. Sergeant!"

Riley saw another man crawling up closer, a field telephone wrapped around the man's shoulder.

"Yes, sir! I'm set!"

Riley was curious, watched the two stretcher bearers, huddled low now, Barber pushing out, lying flat on the ground.

"Give me the damn phone. Who's this? Campbell? What did they say?" Barber listened for a long moment, said, "Tell Captain Read we're ready." He listened again, then said aloud, "All right, listen up! Four artillery rounds coming in! Wait for it!"

Riley couldn't help peering up, his eyes just above the rim of the hole, staring out toward the saddle. The machine gun fire was relentless from the rocky hill, another spray chewing up rocks down below. The mortar shells erupted over the knoll now, sunlight in the darkness, the star shells drifting lower, the distant rocks bathed in a blinding light. Now the artillery shells came in, sharp slices through the night air, the knoll erupting in four distinct blasts. Riley stared, could see men blown airborne, rocks and equipment blown into pieces. The star shells faded to darkness now, the fiery impacts from the 105 shells passing. Behind him, Barber said, "I'll be a son of a bitch!" He was on the phone again, said, "Wonderful! Perfect! Cease fire! Targets destroyed!" There was a silent moment, and Barber laughed now. "You heard me! *Targets destroyed.* Tell that captain I owe him a cigar."

Riley watched the scene, realized now the barrage had stopped. Welch was up beside him, staring out, said, "What the hell? They hit it the first time?" He turned to Barber now, who sat staring out at the same dark space. "I guess that was some fine shooting, eh, sir?"

Barber said, an announcement to the entire platoon, "That was How Company, Eleventh Marines. Those boys are in Hagaru-ri, seven miles from here. I had hoped they might zero in on those enemy guns after maybe a half-dozen attempts. I was also hoping they didn't blow us to hell in the process. I need to have more faith. Eyes front, boys. The enemy's still coming. But there's a few less machine guns out there to lead the way."

Riley looked again to the front, silent darkness, heard the captain give a subtle order, the stretcher bearers loading him up once more. They moved off, back down the hillside, and Riley said, "He's in rough shape. Woulda walked up here if he could."

Welch adjusted the assortment of weapons in front of him, said, "Yep. Hate to see him go down. Hope the damn doctor pays attention to whatever his wound's doing. I guess he's not such a jerk after all."

"There! To the right of the saddle!"

Riley followed Welch's point, saw the column of white, filing out quickly from the deep draw.

"God, Hamp, there's a million of 'em."

Welch was out of the hole, slid in behind the machine gun, said, "Shut up and handle the ammo."

Welch worked the action on the .30 caliber, the belt in place, and Riley ignored the M-1, gripped the Thompson. Down below, the hillside was covered with a fresh blanket of snow, several inches deep, the Chinese soldiers standing out plainly against the newly clean background. Riley felt the thunder in his chest, watched the enemy spreading out their lines, off to the right, toward the deep thicket. He felt the terror rising up, the uncontrollable panic, his hands shaking, a painful grip on the Thompson. To one side, a voice, Goolsby.

"Make ready to repel boarders!"

Welch laughed, surprising Riley, the laughter contagious. Welch shook his head, shouted, "Aye, aye, sir!"

Riley kept his eyes on the Chinese, Goolsby's ridiculous order bringing thoughts of sailing ships and pirates, a celebrated history, part of the lore of the Corps. *To the shores of Tripoli . . .*

Welch fired the machine gun now, jarring him, and he put one hand on the first box of ammo, watching Welch, both men huddled low. The machine gun spit out in brief bursts, a two-second pause between, then another burst. Now Welch fired in a long, continuous stream, sweeping the ground in front, taking his toll on the advance of the enemy. When the gun was empty, Riley fed the next belt, dragging another up close. All along the hill, the Marines responded to the Chinese advance, their mortars from the backside of the hill dropping a steady rain of explosive horror all along the enemy's lines. For the Chinese, nothing had changed, the grenade carriers moving up first, struggling to draw close enough to toss their one weapon, the Marine rifles, machine guns, and mortar shells wiping them away. Behind the grenadiers, the riflemen pushed forward, walking obediently into the bloody carnage, taking aim at the Marines, who took aim at them. Then the third line moved up, men with heavier weapons, the Russian burp guns and American Thompsons, stepping past so many who had already gone down.

The breakthroughs were minor and short-lived, the Marines now too familiar with the methods of their enemy. For the next couple of hours, the Chinese continued to press, while the Marines, fully stocked with a fresh supply of ammunition and arms, mostly held them away.

With the approach of the dawn, the Chinese effort lost energy, the continuing advances more feeble, until finally they pulled back altogether. Across the hillside, the fresh blanket of powdery snow was again spread with the remains of the men who had been sent up the hill to drive the Americans away. For the Chinese soldiers, the effort had been as costly as any before, and still they came, following orders passed down to them from far up their chain of command. The orders reflected the desperate importance of their mission, to eliminate the Marines who held this hill, opening the way for a stout Chinese roadblock at the most effective chokepoint south of Yudam-ni, the winding narrow passage through Toktong Pass. After three nights of massed assaults, both sides had been bloodied, but the Chinese had absorbed astonishing losses against an enemy they outnumbered by better than twelve to one. On November 30, with daylight breaking on another brutally frigid morning, the Chinese could only regroup yet again and watch from their hidden places as the Marines made ready to receive another attack, firmly entrenched on their solitary hill.

CHAPTER TWENTY-NINE

. . . .

Sung

NORTH OF YUDAM-NI—NOVEMBER 30, 1950, 9:00 A.M.

THE HOSPITAL WAS SET among a thick grove of trees, a small run-down house, the occupant abandoning it to the Chinese. He came to inspire the men, one of those duties a commander should exercise, whether or not he hated the task.

There was no heat, the risk of a smoky fire too great, the American fighters patrolling the area all through the day. He stood just inside, grateful the cold kept the smells away, watched the doctor working on a soldier, a bloodless operation, removing the man's fingers. Sung didn't really want to know why, but there were others, hands wrapped in fat bandages, sitting on the floor of the house, huddled together beneath a number of white blankets.

The doctor completed the task, an aide handling the bandages, the patient seemingly unconscious. Sung was grateful for that, had heard too much screaming from these places. It was one advantage of the cold, that many of the soldiers were brought here nearly frozen, halting the flow of blood from so many wounds. The doctor wiped at his hands, red and raw, stuffing them into his shirt now, a feeble effort to bring warmth to his fingers. Sung waited, had no reason to hurry the doctor, did not require that mindless salute that so many of the officers seemed to enjoy, an exercise of their own power. The doctor turned toward him now, seemed surprised, but his reaction was dampened by his own shivering.

"General, welcome. I would offer you tea, but there is none."

The man was young, Sung guessed twenty-five, too young for what he was experiencing now. Sung had no idea what his medical qualifications were, knew only that he had come attached to the 124th Division, along with a handful of others. The hospitals were scattered, as close to the fighting as the commanders dared. Unlike the Americans, the Chinese ignored the Red Cross insignias, assuming that the Americans in their planes would ignore them as well. Sung agreed with his officers that it was far better to camouflage the makeshift hospitals just as they hid any kind of supply dump.

"I do not require tea, Doctor." He looked past the man, the patient being moved carefully toward the gathering of men, all with the same bandages. "Tell me, Doctor, are those men all carrying the same wounds? They are bandaged alike."

The doctor rubbed his hands against his sides, still inside his coat. "They are not wounds, precisely, sir. These men are like so many others. They were found nearly unconscious, their hands frozen to the steel of their weapons. There is no remedy but to sever their fingers. I suppose the military prefers men to remain loyal to their rifles, no matter the conditions. Their digits are still attached to their weapons, if that pleases you."

Sung looked again at the men seated beneath the blankets, the newest patient set down among them. He would forgive the doctor for his impudence, had no reason to find fault with any man who did this kind of work.

"I am not pleased at all, Doctor. Is this a common problem?"

The doctor shrugged. "It is common enough. The men are suffering more from the cold than they are from wounds. A great many have lost use of their feet. Fortunately, most of those men have died as a result."

Sung looked at the man now, trying to read him. "Why is that fortunate? Bitterness is not a virtue here, Doctor. You will not speak to me in such a tone." The threat was empty, both men aware that Sung would do nothing to remove any doctor from his work.

"I mean no disrespect, General. I do not enjoy my work, no matter that this is a duty I must perform. Perhaps it will please you that these men are ready to begin their journey. I can do no more for them here. They have feet. They can walk."

There was a hint of anger in the man's words, and Sung tried to ignore that as well, his eyes on the men.

"Good. We must wait until dark, and send them north. Do they understand?"

"They have surrendered to the inevitable, sir. Is that not what good soldiers must do? They have not died today, and so they will likely die tomorrow."

Sung pulled the coat more tightly around him, his hands stuffed in the fur-lined pockets. "Doctor, there is no argument. And there is no alternative. They will die here because we cannot feed them, we cannot warm them. If they march north, they have a chance of reaching the Yalu, and assistance. I have ordered that patrols advance south of the river, to rendezvous with these men. There are many others in the same situation, Doctor. It is the only course we have. I need every man here to be fit and capable of fighting. Any man who cannot fight only consumes supplies."

The doctor would not look at him, stared downward. "I understand, sir. It is mathematics."

Sung was impatient now. "Call it what you wish, Doctor. I admire you for doing your duty here, in these conditions. I do not ask that you admire me for doing mine. But I will do what I must. I do not have the luxury of a conscience."

NORTH OF YUDAM-NI—NOVEMBER 30, 11:00 A.M.

In view of our many advantages thus far, I am confident that our mission will be gloriously successful. We enjoy a significant superiority in manpower, which we are using to counter the enemy's air forces and long-range artillery. It would be premature to offer the Central Committee a specific timetable for our victory. However, we are engaging the enemy on several fronts, and we hold the advantage in every position. We offer our most sincere congratulations to General Lin Biao, for the victories he has enjoyed.

He stopped, thought, Yes, offering that kind of praise is a wise move. Lin is continuing to drive the enemy southward, and I must not show envy for his success. His enemy no doubt is a weaker foe than what we are facing here.

The aide waited, paper in hand, and Sung stood now, said, "I believe that will be adequate. Chairman Mao has not expressed disappointment with our efforts here. There is no need to thicken my report with empty promises. Put my words to ink, and bring it to me for my signature. You may leave."

The aide rose, a quick bow, left the small house. Sung continued to stand, staring out through a cracked windowpane. To one side, his two primary aides kept to their chairs, no one speaking. He turned now, said, "I do not anticipate remaining in this place beyond today. We must move closer to our front lines. The troops require inspiration. Colonel Liu, bring me the map of the reservoir, the entire area."

"Right away, sir."

Liu rose, left quickly, and Sung turned to the window again.

"What do you think of my report, Colonel Wang?"

Wang stood, always too formal, said stiffly, "Your message to the Central Committee is excellent, sir. Chairman Mao can only be pleased with our campaign. I see great advancement for you, sir, when our victory is secure."

Sung looked at the young man, said, "Did you rehearse your words again?"

Wang showed surprise, shook his head, and Sung raised a hand.

"No matter. I should appreciate that everyone around here agrees with me. The fact is, Colonel, our progress against the enemy is not adequate. Across the mountains, Lin Biao has driven the Americans and their allies far to the south, and I am quite confident that, if they have not yet done so, they will soon liberate Pyongyang. We have failed to drive the Americans back more than a mile. Our strategy has been sound, and by our maneuvers, we created excellent opportunity. And yet the victory Peking expects of us has been slow in coming."

"Sir, we are in control of the field in every quarter. Your tactics have prevailed. The enemy is entrapped and cannot survive as he stands now."

Sung stared at the young man. "How do you know that? How does he *stand now?*"

Wang seemed uncertain, said, "You have said yourself, sir, we have encircled the Americans in every place they fight us. If they do not die from our guns, they will starve or freeze."

Sung turned to the window again. "You are quoting me again, Colonel. I said those very words two days ago, and probably the day before that."

"I believed you then, sir. I believe you now. As you said to Peking, our advantages will bring us victory, in short order."

Sung kept his gaze outside, the flurries of snow brushing silently against the window. "How many men have we lost to the cold?"

"I am not completely certain, sir. If you wish, I shall order Captain Jin to prepare a report."

"I don't need a report, Colonel. I visited the hospitals myself. My orders are being carried out even now. Any man who cannot fight, but who can walk, will march northward. We cannot continue to feed men who cannot fight."

Wang lowered his voice, as though the small house had an audience. "I had not thought it would become necessary. Is there no transportation for them?"

Sung turned to him, angrier now. "No, Colonel, there is not. How would you handle this? We are unable to bring supply convoys south. The enemy has destroyed the bridges over the Yalu and continues to intercept any vehicles that show themselves on the roads. So, yes, we can move at night. But now there are no adequate supplies of gasoline and spare parts for the few trucks that still operate. Even if we had gasoline, we cannot overcome the cold. Batteries and lubricants do not function in this weather, Colonel. In this part of Korea, there are no supplies of rice or meat for this army to gather, no bounty to be found on farms in these hills. The North Koreans are useless. They despise us as deeply as they despise the Americans." He paused, tried not to be angry at his aide. "Our weapons are no match for what the Americans bring to the fight. Every soldier knows the challenges of fighting an offensive campaign. The Americans fight on the defensive, from holes in the ground, and we have no artillery to drive them out. How many more men must we send into their guns before we exhaust him? I have seen his cargo planes, Colonel. They drop endless supplies of everything he needs to continue the fight. Here, we are running out of every kind of supply."

He stopped, angry at himself, his heart pounding, short, heavy breaths. I do not need to speak this way, he thought. My superiors would not approve.

Wang seemed to wait for an opening, said, "We still have great advantage in numbers, sir. As you said to Peking—"

"What I said to Peking is what Peking requires me to say. They do not entertain reports of our discomfort. They will not hear of our *problems*. There is no counsel for me, Colonel. No one can offer me advice. I have been granted this position, and I will succeed, or I will be . . . removed. I am not yet willing to accept that outcome."

Colonel Liu returned now, a gust of icy wind chasing him through the door. He moved quickly, shivering, spread the map out on the lone table. Sung stepped that way, heard a light rap from outside the door. Liu said, "My apologies, General. Major Orlov requested to know what I was bringing you. I was told not to keep any information from him."

Sung looked toward the door, the anger draining away his energy. "Bring the major inside. I do not need him suffering in this cold any more than the rest of us. Our situation is plain for all to see, even the Soviets."

Liu moved to the door, Orlov moving inside quickly, his fur coat dusted with snow.

"Ah, General. Fine morning. No colder than usual, if you are camped at the South Pole. I understand you are in need of some counsel. Advice, perhaps. I am always at your service."

Sung had long accepted that Orlov seemed capable of reading minds.

"Major, what I require is wisdom. I am confronting an enemy who has proven far more stubborn than I expected. What, may I ask, did *you* expect?"

Orlov shed the fur coat, laid it on one of the small chairs. He rubbed his hands together, moved to the map, scanned the details. Sung was used to the man's theatrics, could feel the drama playing out. After a long moment, Orlov said, "I read over your report to Peking. You are most optimistic. I applaud you."

Sung closed his eyes for a brief moment, thought, No secrets indeed. "I spoke the truth. Chairman Mao expects nothing less."

Orlov looked at him, winked. "He *demands* nothing less. I am quite certain that General Lin's reports are magnificent. Victory upon victory. An enemy who flees before his sword. All very romantic stuff, yes? He is fortunate to have drawn the card he has."

"What card? What do you mean?"

"I mean that the Eighth Army Lin Biao has been successful against is a United Nations force, a combination of commands, a mongrel army, if you will. You, however, are fighting a monolith. Every general in the last war, and the one before that, preferred to fight an enemy of many nations, many cultures. Napoleon said he always preferred fighting *allies*."

"Are you suggesting that because we are engaged with only the Americans, we are at a disadvantage?"

"Aren't you? Look at these Marines who are giving you such trouble. They are trained as a single force. They fight for a single commanding general. They are supported by their own artillery units, and most often, they are supported by their own fighter planes. Is there any place on this map where you have driven the Marines off the ground *they* have chosen to defend?"

Sung felt himself sagging, looked at the two staff officers, said, "Leave us."

Both men hesitated, but Sung gave each a hard stare, the message understood. They moved out, the door clattering behind them. Orlov moved to a chair, sat heavily.

"General Sung, I am telling you what you already know. Your staff knows it as well. Your army knows it. It is your choice of course, to keep Peking from knowing it. A wise precaution, to be sure."

"What is it that I know so well, that is so obvious to everyone here?"

"You will not defeat these Marines with the tactics you are now using. There is a better way. There is always a better way when one is being defeated."

Sung felt the anger returning. "Defeated? You will not insult me, Major, with your speculations. We control every piece of ground, we have the enemy trapped, encircled, and in short order he will either die or surrender. It is only a matter of time. I thought you were here to observe, so that you might convince your superiors to give us more weapons. Instead I hear meaningless lectures. Rather than offer such pessimism, perhaps you can find me a battery of antiaircraft guns, yes? Would your Chairman Stalin be so generous?"

Orlov raised both arms out to the side. "No antiaircraft guns with me today. Sorry. Perhaps next week." He smiled now. "General, I am not your enemy. Yes, I observe. I see difficulties for you. You are losing men at a drastic rate, either to bullets or frostbite. Or is that merely speculation?"

"No one in this army dares speak to me as you do. I tolerate it because I must."

"Are you better off by surrounding yourself with those so eager to please that they would only bow down to you, or speak soft compliments for all you do here? Are you helped by having officers who believe what you tell Peking even as their men die by the score?"

"You offer the obvious, Major. I am doing what I can to inflict greater damage on the enemy. He cannot survive this much longer."

"Can you?"

Sung felt his hands curl into tight fists, closed his eyes. He tried to calm himself, said, "If there is nothing else you wish to say, I must end this conversation. I must communicate with my commanders. We must make ready to continue our assaults against Hagaru-ri. Even now, we are pushing the enemy inward."

"Again."

"Yes. Again. The Marines there are weak, undermanned. It is the most important target."

"Yes, yes. So, why would this assault be different than any before? You left a considerable number of casualties there. Do you anticipate a change from that?" Orlov stood, moved closer to the map. "General, you have not even been able to drive a single company of Marines from Toktong Pass. How many casualties have you left out there? How many more are spread over the ground around Yudam-ni?"

"It is war, Major. Can you advise me where there might be an enemy who is *unarmed*?"

Orlov looked at the map, a finger pointing down. "East of the reservoir. One battalion of the American Seventh Infantry Division. They are surrounded, except for their one flank that rests on the reservoir itself."

"I am aware of that. Am I to be impressed you can read a map? We have already engaged those troops. It would seem your analysis of the enemy here is not correct after all. Those troops are very different from the Marines, an entirely diffcrent command."

Orlov kept the smile. "Yes, they are. At least for now. General MacArthur's people in Tokyo are extremely concerned about those troops. It seems they climbed out a bit far on their limb. No fault of their field officers. It was orders, you know. Just like the American Eighth Army, those people who now flee from General Lin, this lone battalion was terribly excited about participating in a race to reach the Yalu River. The Americans do like their competitions. Now they are in something of a bind, wouldn't you say?"

Sung wanted to ask yet again: How do you know these things? But he knew that Orlov would evade him again, as he had so many times before.

"If you wish me to be impressed, Major, very well. I am. One day we shall have to discuss Soviet intelligence, and your skill at communications."

"One day." Orlov focused again on the map. "General, I understand your frustration. You may treat me with disrespect, if it helps you. But I am not your problem. I am here to observe, as you said."

Sung felt a helplessness, could not deny that Orlov had a firm grasp on the entire campaign. "Major, are you suggesting it is a mistake to attempt another assault on Hagaru-ri?"

"I am suggesting that you not make the *same* assault. You have faced supreme stubbornness at Yudam-ni, at Toktong Pass, at Koto-ri, and at Hagaru-ri. Your primary mission is to destroy the enemy. Why not give your army some red meat?"

"What do you mean?"

"They are hungry for a victory. So give them the best chance they might have. The army battalion is not as well trained as the Marines. Their artillery is not as strong. If you crush the Americans east of the reservoir, you will have an open door to strike at Hagaru-ri from three directions. You have two full divisions facing those army troops, yes?"

"The Seventy-ninth and Eightieth, yes. Another in reserve."

"I doubt you will require your reserves."

"Do I simply ignore the Marines at Yudam-ni, at Toktong Pass?"

Orlov shrugged. "Why not? You have them boxed in, so it is unlikely they are going anywhere. And this weather is your ally. Every day they sit in their foxholes, they die just a bit more."

"As do we, Major. My men are from a part of China that does not feel this kind of cold."

"And yet, you would make them walk home?"

Sung felt a wave of frustration again. "What am I to do? I need every man to be capable. I have limited food, limited supplies of every kind, including ammunition. If they march toward China, there is hope for them. Patrols from the border will be sent south, assisting them. I have ordered it."

Orlov looked down, seemed to absorb the horror of what Sung was explaining to him. "I do not envy you that responsibility, General. I would only advise that you complete your primary mission. That you destroy the enemy with all haste."

Sung turned away, moved again to the window, saw a thicket of small trees buffeted by the wind. His eye was caught by a photograph on the wall, unusual, a Korean family, dressed in city clothes. "Look how they smile. A family outing, an adventure, perhaps to Pyongyang. A happier time. They did not bring this war, and we are here to liberate them. Yet they only fear us."

"Yes, I saw the photograph. Charming. General, you are using that man's home as your quarters. Your soldiers are spread out in whatever tiny kingdom that man's family holds dear. If he had any food or live-stock, you have taken it. If he protests to you, very likely your officers would harm him, or his family. He has fled because he has no choice. It is no different here than it was in Russia. If you care so much, then do what you must to end this. Perhaps then your pleasant reports to Peking will be accurate, a victory that will provide you a triumphant return, bathing you in the glory of the revolution."

Sung looked at him. "You are mocking me, Major."

"I am mocking us all. If you do not succeed here, your career will end in disgrace, a deadly outcome, yes? If you do succeed, they will find one more command for you, another war, another foe, until you fail. Or die. I have always wondered which is better, dying for your revolution or dying as an old man in some hospital."

"The revolution, of course."

"That's what they expect us both to believe, certainly. Either way, you're just as dead."

He saw a crack in the major's arrogance, a surprise.

"We have no alternative, Major. It is the path we have chosen. It is the path assigned to us."

"Then choose your next move wisely, General. I can promise you, your enemies are making their choices as well. And regardless of what you tell Peking, it is their stubbornness that is winning this fight."

CHAPTER THIRTY

. . . .

Smith

HE ABSORBED THEIR DESPERATION, understood their urgency, could feel the sadness infecting both men now, the inevitability of what could become a disaster. Their anxiety was contagious, the kind of helplessness no commanding officer hoped to feel.

"I am truly sorry, gentlemen. But I anticipate another assault tonight, and as you have seen, we are only secured here by a thin line. The fight for the east hill has been ongoing and costly, though I am pleased to say that we have taken a hard toll on the enemy."

He regretted the words, thought, It's not the time for boasting, not even about that.

The two men sat glumly, a glance between them. It was Barr who spoke first, the senior man offering Smith a painful smile.

"General, we appreciate all you are doing here, all you have done throughout this campaign. General Hodes and I both were pleased when General Almond appointed you to overall command here. It certainly made sense. I had thought . . . forgive me. I had *hoped* that events would play out differently. I was not aware that the Chinese had so thoroughly enveloped my battalion, cutting their communication with your people here."

Hodes nodded now, the same grim expression, said to Barr, "As you know, sir, we made every effort to drive a rescue force through to Colonel McLean's command. Even with the power of the armor, it just wasn't possible to make a breakthrough."

Smith watched them both, curious how they felt about the string of orders given them by Ned Almond. He tried to keep his own feelings to himself, but he knew that Barr had suffered through so many of the same meetings, had reacted with discreet exasperation to Almond's utter lack of comprehension, and more, his amazing optimism that all was as he willed it to be.

After a silent moment, Smith said, "I appreciate the gravity of this situation. Had General Almond made the effort to understand just what was happening here ..." No, he thought. Don't do that. They're army men. Somewhere, in some part of both men, they respect Almond as their commander. They have to.

Barr looked at him, a hard stare, said, "I believe you and I have always understood our combined situation, more so than Tenth Corps. There will be time for recrimination later. Right now I have most of two battalions of my command in a serious state. I saw General Almond this morning, before I flew up here." Barr paused, weighed his words carefully. "I was ordered to extricate Colonel McLean's command with all haste."

Hodes stood, angry energy, paced to one side of the room, then stopped, looked at Barr.

"Sir, it seems clear from word we received through the tank radios that Colonel McLean is a casualty. Colonel Don Faith now commands the force. I have not yet spoken to him, and even if I could, I'm not sure what we could tell him. Just how are we supposed to *extricate* anybody? Not even an armored column can get through! Does General Almond offer us some plan, does he have a notion of just how we are to shove aside a Chinese division, so we may open up our route of escape?"

Barr glanced at Smith, said, "Henry, please sit down."

Smith let out a breath, had an ache for his pipe tobacco, thought better of it now. He liked David Barr, knew that the Seventh Division's commander was already suffering under the yoke slung around him by Almond's style of command. Throughout the entire campaign, Barr had seemed a capable commander, and more, a reasonable man. But always there was the weight on his shoulders, obedience to Almond, measured against Barr's own competence, the experience to know just what kind of strategy was called for.

Hodes sat, looked at Smith, said, "My apologies, sir. These are stressful times."

"Neither of you owes me any apologies. Neither of you has made the kinds of mistakes that have put us where we are. I am as obedient to Tenth Corps as you are."

Barr showed a hint of a smile. "Come, now. Had I carried out my orders with the same . . . *precision* that you did, I'd be a mess sergeant now. You wear a different hat, O.P. Almond's not quite sure how to handle you or your Marines. But if you think this latest gambit is wisdom on his part, think again."

"You mean, putting me in charge up here? What would you call it?"

"Expedience. No matter what happens going forward, Almond's off MacArthur's hook. If the headlines back home are bad, it's your name they'll read."

"I know all of that. I'm more concerned with getting my men, and yours, out of this situation. Almond called me this morning, told me you were coming, of course. He also ordered me to extricate my men from Yudam-ni, as though he had just thought of it. I gave that order to Colonel Litzenberg yesterday, and believe me, I am well aware that if those men were here now, we would have the strength to push out toward your battalions."

Barr rubbed a hand on his forehead, as though probing a headache. "I appreciate that, O.P. But I've heard that the road up to Yudam-ni is blocked, as impassable as every other road around here."

"It is. Completely."

"So, did General Almond tell you how to accomplish the withdrawal?"

"Of course not. But he is optimistic that his orders can be carried out. The only avenue open to us is to fight our way through."

Barr nodded slowly. "Best of luck."

Smith shook his head. "It's not luck. It's Litzenberg and Murray, and two regiments of Marines. The Chinese will need the luck."

Barr looked at Hodes, a faint smile. "Never met a Marine yet who thought he was at a disadvantage, no matter who the hell he was up against." He looked at Smith. "I hope your pride is warranted."

"It's not pride, David. It's just how it has to be. There is no alternative. I'm sorry. I don't mean to sound like a recruiting poster."

Barr smiled. "Every Marine does, General. I'm used to it."

Smith focused now on Hodes, could see the gloom in the man's expression. "No matter what Almond's motives were, he's put Colonel Faith's men under my command. That doesn't mean I can do anything about it right now. But I have notified the air wing to give you their full cooperation. I assure you, that will help. It's likely the bombers can open up some gaps, eliminate the enemy roadblocks, and give your men some openings they can use. If your men can fight their way down the reservoir during daylight hours, the air can continuously support them and keep the Chinese mostly at bay."

Smith knew what was coming. Barr said, "And at night?"

Smith hesitated. "For now, they're on their own. I'm sorry, David. There's nothing else we can do."

Hodes stood again, walked to the covered window, faced the wall, hands on his hips. "I was so very close. It's only a few miles. They might as well be trapped on the moon. Don Faith is a good man. If there's any way for him to blast through, he'll find it." He turned, looked at Barr. "But how do we tell Faith that he's on his own, that no reinforcements are coming? He won't know to drive back this way."

Barr rubbed a hand on his chin, said, "I'll tell him. He should also be told he's now attached to the Marine command. He'll have to know to make use of the air support. O.P., might I make use of one of your helicopters?"

Smith was surprised, said, "Of course. What are you going to do?"

"I'm going to go see Colonel Faith. He has to be made aware that we are working on this end to do all we can to get his people back down here. And he's my officer. He's not responsible for the mess he's in. Someone should make sure he knows that."

. . . .

Smith stood outside the command tent, endured the blasting wind, watched Barr's helicopter rise slowly, easing into a slow turn to the northeast. He fought the blinding frost in his eyes, watched the chopper for as long as he could, the craft moving out directly over the frozen reservoir, the pilot keeping as far as possible from the Chinese in the hills.

He still marveled at the helicopters, the odd tool now so terribly useful. What would we have done with those things, he thought, if we'd had them in the Pacific? Just moving the wounded, how many lives might we have saved? Now a division commander is able to fly out to a trapped battalion, to give them instructions face-to-face. He looked toward the construction site, the heavy equipment still working on the runway, no matter the nightly attacks by the Chinese. We need nearly eight thousand feet, he thought. So far, we've got three. Maybe. The Chinese are watching, and surely they know what we're doing, and what a workable airstrip will mean. If I was their commander, I would assume reinforcements would be the first priority. Maybe he thinks about our wounded, *my* priority. Or maybe not.

He looked toward the east hill, the chatter of machine gun fire coming in short bursts, hints of smoke rising from the many hidden places where the Chinese were still battling to shove Ridge's fire teams completely off the hill.

Bowser was there now, bundled in his coat, said, "He get off okay?"

"Yep. Hope he gets back in one piece."

"You'd have to explain that to General Almond, if he didn't."

Smith ignored the comment, said, "We need that hill. Ridge doesn't have the manpower to do what's necessary. That vantage point puts this whole place within the enemy's mortar range. If they had artillery, this position would be useless."

Bowser moved his legs, slowly marching in place. "Anything you need out here, sir?"

Smith turned, saw Bowser's bright red nose, the frost accumulating around his nostrils. "Yep. Springtime. Let's go inside."

HAGARU-RI—NOVEMBER 29, 4:00 P.M.

Barr had returned, the man in a more dismal mood now than before he left. "They're in trouble, O.P. They've already taken a hell of a pounding, and expect more. The enemy has them boxed in pretty tightly. Faith says the last order he got from Tenth Corps was that he was to continue his attack. That was yesterday. He's pretty certain Colonel McLean is dead. McLean disappeared in an advanced position, engaging the enemy."

Smith saw Hodes rise, pacing again.

"Engaging the enemy? Why?"

Barr looked down. "No idea. But Faith has control, as much as anyone can." Barr paused, looked at Smith. "The concern is the quality of the men in that command."

Hodes reacted with a sharp turn. "What concern is that? These are good men, sir."

Barr held up a hand. "At ease, General. The fact is, a good percentage of the men in those battalions are undertrained. Most have never been under fire before. Faith is very well aware that his primary mission, McLean's primary mission, was to hustle along as quick as possible, so they could piss in the Yalu River. No one was told to expect the Chinese to swarm around them like a cloud of hornets."

Smith held his words, thought, Did they not observe the hills? Surely the Chinese were watching every move they made.

Barr shook his head, kept his stare toward the floor. "Colonel Faith has every confidence that he can fight his way south. It's barely five miles, as I understand it. They can certainly make the effort to improve their situation. Faith understands that nothing can come up from this way. He also appreciates your sending him air support." Barr paused. "It's not all roses. Faith didn't temper his opinion of the Katusas. There's fifty or so attached to each rifle company. They've never made a fight yet. They see the Chinese and disappear into the mist. Now, there's no place for them to go, but that doesn't stop them from throwing down their arms and curling up in a damn ball."

It was one disadvantage Smith had been able to avoid. The Korean Augmentation Troops to the U.S. Army were mostly South Korean civilians, many of them grabbed forcefully off the streets of Seoul or any other place where the Korean government could find them. Now they were to fight alongside their American allies, presumably relying on a fiery passion for defending their country. But there had been very little fire in those men at all. The poor fighting quality of the fully trained South Korean divisions had already been experienced by Walton Walker, those divisions the first to flee from the Chinese assault north of Pyong-yang. But the Katusas had no training at all, and their presence did nothing for the morale of the American army troops, whose own confidence was shaky at best. Smith knew what Barr was suggesting, and what Faith was clearly expressing, that if a sizable percentage of your rifle companies simply melted away, it would be difficult at best to keep the rest of your men from catching the same disease.

Smith said nothing, had been fortunate to experience only the added presence of the Korean marines. Those men had been a pleasant surprise, extremely well trained, with the kind of esprit de corps that rivaled the Americans'. Now those marines were farther south, holding fort alongside the American Third Division, spread over the countryside near the North Korean ports.

Smith looked at Hodes, still pacing slowly, knew he was in a delicate place. The rivalry between the branches was always there, regardless of the personalities of the men involved. Barr would never allow that to intrude, not when the situation was as grave as this one. But Smith could see the pride in Hodes's expression, combined with the man's frustration that he had failed to rescue his men not once, but twice.

Smith waited for Barr, who seemed lost in thought for a long minute. He looked up at Smith now, said, "I've never been in this situation before. O.P., I'm not a combat leader. I've served as chief of staff for some good people, and when they named me to command the Seventh, I was chief of personnel for the army ground forces. But I never led those men into a fight. I never had to tell one of my officers, Yes, I know you're surrounded by the enemy, and there's nothing I can do to help you. You're on your own. *Best of luck!* Do you know what it felt like to board that helicopter, and just fly off? I couldn't look at them, all those faces staring up at me."

Barr put his face in his hands, Hodes staring again at the wall. Smith wanted to give them something, any kind of words, but there was nothing there. It's combat, he thought. Men will die. My men, yours. Theirs.

He stood slowly, ignored his own rules, picked up the can of pipe tobacco, pulled the pipe from his pocket, filled it. He thought of apologizing, that treating himself to something he enjoyed was somehow inappropriate. The pipe was full, ready for the lighter, and he waited, the room silent.

And now, a sharp knock on the door.

He jumped at the sound, stuffed the pipe back into the pocket, said, "What is it?"

The door opened slightly, the face of Sexton.

"Sir, General Almond's observation craft has just landed. They radioed he was coming in a few minutes ago."

Smith stared at Sexton, had nothing to say, thought, It just gets worse.

"I want them brought down here with all haste! All haste! The battalion, that fellow up there, Faith? I want them pulled out as well! We have to remove ourselves from this problem, and I want that accomplished yesterday!"

The tent was bulging with men, Smith's staff still at work, no one accomplishing anything beyond their discreet listening to Almond's bluster. Beside Smith, the two army generals sat in front of Smith's own senior officers, all of them summoned to hear what Almond had to say.

Almond seemed to work at catching his breath. "This morning, I was cornered by those damn newspapermen. I told them we had whipped the North Koreans completely, but that the action now ongoing is an entirely new Chinese development. But I will not allow those pen pushers to paint anything we're doing in a negative light. So, the rest is up to you! Smith, bring your people out of Yudam-ni. I want a plan put on paper for the evacuation of the army forces on the east side of the reservoir. I want to know when that blasted airstrip will be complete so that we may begin moving your wounded, and your most vital equipment, out of here. We must evacuate your entire force down to Hamhung. Supply will make large-scale drops, delivering to you everything you would require along the way. This means you may leave behind, and destroy, the greater part of the equipment you have now. Travel light, gentlemen. Make speed!"

Smith had gone back to his quarters, Almond and Bowser following at Smith's request. Almond had seemed to calm slightly after his energetic orders, and Smith rolled the man's speech through his brain, sorting out what might actually be realistic.

"General, perhaps we should move into the back room. Alpha, gather up the chairs."

Bowser moved quickly, the three chairs placed opposite each other, Bowser keeping his own a bit farther from the other two. Smith pointed, and Almond sat, slapping his hands on his knees, a show of nervousness.

"I hope I was clear, Smith."

Smith sat, thought of the pipe, scolded himself, No. "General, you have insisted all throughout this campaign that we move in haste. Had we done so two weeks ago, it is likely my division would have been destroyed. As it stands now, that is still a possibility, but I believe we are moving in the right direction. The speed with which we move will be governed by my ability to evacuate my wounded, including those that will be brought down from Yudam-ni. Once that is completed, we will fight our way out of here, and I will require the equipment we now have on hand, including trucks, jeeps, tanks, and anything else that will aid our operation. I will do my job the best way I know how. It will be dark very soon. You should get to your plane. Do you have any other instructions for me?"

Almond's mouth was slightly open, and he shook his head slowly.

"No, I think you have it under control." He seemed to blink at a new thought. "Oh, yes, the plane. Good idea, yes. I should be off. Godspeed, Smith."

Almond stood, moved out into the larger room, his aide there now, holding open his coat. Within seconds, Almond was out the door.

Smith retrieved the pipe, still full from earlier that afternoon. He flicked the lighter, the aroma engulfing him, warm and wonderful. He looked at Bowser now, was surprised to see a wide smile.

"What?"

"You are my favorite commanding general, you know that? I've had a couple others, but none of them—"

"Oh, shut up."

Bowser chuckled now, and Smith jabbed the pipe into his teeth, said, "He comes up here all full of beans, and orders us to move with lightning speed backward. He gives us a wave of his hand and expects everything to happen as he describes it."

Smith heard an aircraft, glanced up, and Bowser said, "He didn't waste any time. I don't guess his pilot likes flying around North Korea in the dark."

There was a chattering roll of fire, machine guns, and Smith moved out quickly into the larger room, the cook and his aide dropping down to their knees.

"Sir, that's close. Be careful."

More firing came now, another direction, the heavy thumps from incoming mortars. Bowser was there, beside him, said, "They're coming again."

Smith strained to hear, said, "Maybe. Could be probes. It's not late enough for a full-on assault."

The chatter blew past him now, a splinter of wood from the wall, the clank of metal, pots on the cookstove tumbling to the floor. The cook yelped and Smith ducked down, Bowser flattening out to one side of him. Now another round burst through the wall, another ricochet, the cook shouting out some kind of curse.

"Easy, son. Stray rounds. You two, grab your weapons, find Lieutenant Griggs. If they need you on the line, he'll tell you."

The cook sat now, held up a wet pot, a ragged hole through the sides.

"Your dinner, sir. They busted up your cooking pot."

Smith listened, more firing, farther away, the steady rumbles he had heard all day from the east hill. "I'll manage. Go!"

The two men scrambled across the floor, coats snatched down from hooks on the wall. Smith looked at Bowser, said, "You all right?"

Bowser sat up, wiped a hand over his mussed hair. "Too close."

"Only casualty here was my dinner, Colonel. If you wish, grab a carbine. My forty-five is in my bag."

"Not funny, sir."

"I've been under assault before, Colonel. It's never funny."

Bowser crept toward the door, eased it open, the cold air immediate. He closed it again, said, "Looks calm. Most of the firing is to the east."

"I hear it."

"Well, sir, at least you don't have to prove your point to the army. If they've got any doubts whether you can spare anybody to rescue their people, a nice attack from the Chinese ought to convince them we need every hand right here."

Smith stood, eased the ache from his knees, moved toward the stove. "General Barr doesn't need convincing. Hodes is feeling this in someplace deep. Nothing I can do about that." He thought a moment, said, "We've got a Marine air controller out that way, right?"

"Yes, sir. He was left up there, back when Murray pulled out, when the army boys moved up. Captain Stamford, Ed Stamford. Good man."

"I hope so. The air cover might be the best chance those boys have."

Bowser was serious now, said, "You think they're in real trouble? That's near three thousand men."

Smith listened again to the firing, a spray of mortar shrapnel dancing on the roof above him. "Colonel, we might all be in trouble. But I'd rather be here than out there."

HAGARU-RI—DECEMBER 1, NOON

"Six hundred, a few more. It's not good, General. Something has to open up quick, or we'll lose a good many of them."

Smith knew that Hering was never a man to exaggerate, and he had seen the hospitals himself. "I know the situation, Doctor."

"How much longer, then? You can only keep a man on morphine for so long. The plasma we have is just about worthless. Sir ..." Hering paused, seemed suddenly emotional. "If we can't evacuate these men in the next twenty-four hours ..."

"I heard you, Doctor."

Smith couldn't be angry, knew that Hering was as dedicated a healer as any medical man in the service. But the daily frustrations were still building, no different now than yesterday, the day before that.

Hering seemed resigned to his situation, said, "I should return to the hospital. A few of the Royal Marines got hit this morning. Some of them took some white phosphorous wounds. Not sure they'll survive."

Smith nodded, a feeble wave of his hand. "Dismissed. Just keep doing your job. I'll do mine."

Hering turned, left the room, and Smith heard the others in the larger room, a small group of officers, daily reports still to come. He waited for the sound of the door, Hering's departure, tried to find some comfort in the pipe in his mouth, the tobacco growing bitter. He listened to the talk among the officers, a tone of doubt, anxiousness spread all through them, worse now than any day before. His order to Litzenberg had been finalized, the command for the units at Yudam-ni to commence their breakout early that morning. He had heard nothing since, didn't expect to, unless it was bad news. No, he thought, they'll do it. It's one road, and a dozen miles, and they're Marines. This isn't some idiotic order tossed their way by a crowing peacock in Tokyo. They're my men, and I need them here. They need to be here. It's that simple.

He stood, nervous energy, paced slowly, the tobacco not helping at all. Outside, a distinctive voice, his chief of staff, Colonel Gregon Williams. Bowser was there as well, always there, both men doing their own jobs and the duties left behind by Eddie Craig. This will kill Eddie, he thought. He'd want to be right in the middle of the mess, just like Bowser. This might be the toughest assignment most of these men have ever had, ever suffered through. Well, maybe. Hard to ignore what we had to do against the Japanese. How different is it now? A fanatical enemy, hell-bent on wiping us out. Nothing new there. The Chinese probably think the same thing about us.

"Sir, Colonel Drysdale is here. He asked if he could see you."

Smith saw a smile on Sexton's face, felt it himself. "By all means. Send him in here. We have any tea around?"

Sexton still smiled. "He brought his own, sir."

Sexton backed away, and Smith couldn't avoid a lift to his spirits, had come to like Drysdale as much as he already respected him. Drysdale was there now, and Smith was surprised, the man's uniform perfect in every detail, the wounded arm bandaged as neatly as the man's attire. Smith couldn't help a smile of his own.

"Come in, Colonel."

"Thank you kindly, General. I shan't take up your time. I do wish only to report that our efforts to drive the enemy from East Hill have been mostly frustrated. Difficult terrain, to say the least. The enemy's artillery, what there is of it, is tossing some rather nasty stuff our way."

"I heard. White phosphorous."

"Quite so. My men will never complain, sir, but I must speak up for them when I say we have some rather awful injuries. I understand there can be little assistance for our attempts, and your medical people are doing a bang-up job. But I admit to having a weakness for the suffering of my men, when I see little point to it."

"There is a point, Colonel, I promise you. East Hill is a key to our position. I have seen very little of the enemy's artillery in action, but that doesn't mean he doesn't have any. If they suddenly bring up some heavy stuff, East Hill is a perfect location for it. This base becomes indefensible. Even if we can't remove them from the hill itself, we must keep them engaged, let them know we won't let them have the place free and clear. I'm sorry for your men, but, frankly, Colonel, every unit in this command is suffering. If not the wounds, then the cold. I'm not telling you what you don't already know."

"I'm not questioning your command decisions, sir, I assure you. I understand the logic of your tactics and what we are being asked to do. I only wanted to inquire if there might be some relief in the offing, some way to deal with the rather terrible condition of my wounded."

Smith said nothing for a long moment, gave up on the pipe, pulled it from his mouth, rapped the bowl on the arm of the chair. He saw Bowser now, peering into the room, thought, Something else.

"What is it, Colonel?"

Bowser stayed beyond the door, said, "Intel report, sir."

"Anything new?"

Bowser moved closer, a glance at Drysdale, said, "More like confirmation, sir. Colonel Holcomb reports that it is definite that we are facing six full Chinese divisions."

"In total?"

"That's just around Hagaru-ri. There is an estimate of five more at Yudam-ni, possibly as many as three up the east side of the reservoir. Colonel Puller has not yet made an estimate to our south, sir."

"Thank you, Colonel. Dismissed."

Bowser backed away, and Drysdale smiled, a surprise.

"If I may offer, sir, this seems rather a sticky one."

"We're still here, Colonel. The enemy is still on the outside looking in. When the Fifth and Seventh push their way down here, we'll have plenty of strength. Nothing the Chinese have shown us changes that."

Drysdale rubbed his chin, nodded. "I admire your confidence, sir. I share it, actually. I haven't often had the opportunity to stand alongside Yanks, and I admit there are some rough edges that are difficult for my men to accept."

"Such as?"

Drysdale seemed to welcome the opening. "I don't mean to sound critical, General. Certainly not. But throughout the night, your engineers take delight in illuminating the entire landscape while they labor on that airstrip. Invites fire in a reckless sort of way, I'd say. I do understand the urgency, of course." He paused. "I also appreciate the luxury of having adequate supplies of ammunition. But I must point out, sir, that your men seem to delight in filling the air with lead. I have always taught frugality, conserving one's ammunition as long as necessary. Your machine gunners, and those marvelous BARs, they do offer quite a show. I just wonder how useful that truly is, spraying ten thousand rounds toward an enemy platoon when a few dozen would do the trick."

Smith sat now, could feel Drysdale's energy rising. "What else?"

"Well, sir, I don't wish to risk offense. But we pride ourselves on our deportment, the taut ship, so to speak. It is standard practice for our men to shave and tidy themselves up as much as possible every morning. I have observed very little of that among your Marines. Every man wears a stubble of whiskers, and when any of my chaps mentions it, the response is rather boastful on your part, as though the rough edges are a source of pride."

Smith lowered his head, a smile breaking out. "Colonel, I do not question your methods. I would only say that my men are less concerned with appearances. Cleanliness doesn't make them any tougher."

"Certainly not, sir. I intend no insult at all."

"I know you don't. I would only suggest, Colonel, that when this war concludes—and I assure you, it will conclude—that these men will return home to their wives and mothers, and there will be shiny cheeks and enough *sparkle* to go around. As long as your men make the good fight, you may certainly attend to your command any way you see fit. I can also assure you that when it comes to priorities right here, we are pushing hard for morphine and bandages. The soap can come later."

The jeep rolled closer to the first large dozer, stopped, the crew working beside the big machine halting, watching as he climbed out. There were the usual salutes, but Smith wouldn't interrupt their labor, moved past, toward the next machine, saw men standing together, a cluster of heavy coats. They parted slightly at his approach, and Smith searched the faces, the scattering of ragged beards, couldn't help thinking of Drysdale. Beards are warmer, he thought. Should have told him that. He saw the face he sought, the hood of the man's coat pulled back, no salute, the appropriate response so close to enemy eyes.

"Welcome, sir. Good day for working."

Smith looked past the man, the surface of the airstrip spread out far to one side. "Colonel Partridge, they've all been good. I need to bring aircraft in here right now. Tell me something I want to hear."

Partridge let out a foggy breath, said, "We've got twenty-nine hundred feet completely finished. Specs call for five thousand more. It's only been twelve days, General."

"This isn't a gripe, Colonel. A C-47 can land right now, yes?"

"Yes, sir, I suppose so. This wind's tough enough, it should shorten the distance for takeoff."

"That's what I wanted to hear."

HAGARU-RI—DECEMBER 1, 2:30 P.M.

He watched with most of the staff, all eyes on the skies, the light snowfall not enough to hide the patches of blue above them. The winds had slowed, easing the torture from the cold, Smith straining to hear the only sound that mattered.

"There!"

The men around him began to point, and he saw it, clearing the hills to the south. It was a single plane, responding to his orders, the first attempt at a dry run, to test whether the engineer knew his aircraft as well as his ability to build an airport.

He heard the plane's engines now, couldn't help the shaking nervousness, a glimpse toward the east hill, where he knew the Chinese were watching as well. Beside him, Bowser said, "Hurry up, dammit. You're too good a target."

"Shut up, Alpha."

He marched in place slowly, the anxiety of the moment adding to the hard chill in his legs, the aching in his knees forgotten for the moment. He watched the plane lowering, landing gear out now, sinking lower still. He held his breath, the pounding in his chest unbearable, a glance at the east hill one more time, still no violence from the Chinese. There were voices around him now, the men offering their own quiet encouragement toward the pilot, the aircraft, the moment.

The plane drifted lower, held a few feet off the hard ground, the dull roar of the engines growing soft, the plane settling down slowly, a sudden bump, a slight bounce, the wheels now on the ground, the plane moving past the crowd, slowing, stopping, turning in place, the twin props pulling the craft closer. And now the engines were silent, the props spinning slowly, the men around Smith moving forward, chocking the wheels, gathering at the plane's hatch, happy chatter. Smith held back, his eyes a blur, the weakness in his knees spreading all through him, a hard stroke of emotion he knew he couldn't hide. He was alone now, tried to blink through the freezing tears, watched the men swarming the plane, waiting for the pilot to appear. Smith turned to one side, saw Partridge a few yards away, the engineer watching, waiting, a glance toward Smith, a broad smile, the pride in an extraordinary accomplishment.

"I believe, sir, we have an airstrip."

For the rest of that day, five more of the small transport planes made the journey from the bases to the south, each one carrying necessary supplies, each then filled to capacity with two dozen of the most severely wounded men. Only one incident marred the astounding day, one aircraft losing its landing gear, blocking the runway until it could be cleared. By dark, the runs were halted, but Smith returned to his quarters with a brief stop to see Dr. Hering, sharing his quiet joyful confidence that the wounded men would now be served.

Smith knew what Hering knew, that when Murray and Litzenberg brought their units into Hagaru-ri, with the enormous load of their own wounded, the medical facilities would be woefully inadequate. But their work was now made easier by the extraordinary labor of Colonel John Partridge and his engineers. The final piece of the puzzle for the medical teams was the unknown that lay out to the northeast. There the army's beleaguered troops were already confronting a hard crisis of their own, no one at Hagaru-ri knowing yet just how severe that crisis could actually become.

NEAR PUNGNYURI INLET, CHOSIN RESERVOIR—DECEMBER 1, 1950,
    EARLY AFTERNOON

The withdrawal of the army's Thirty-first and Thirty-second Regimental Combat Teams had begun close to noon, Lieutenant Colonel Don

Faith ordering all army units along the east side of the reservoir to assemble for a forceful drive southward, hoping to push through the
enemy that surrounded them. Hagaru-ri was barely ten miles away,
though Faith had wanted to believe that either army or Marine units
had shortened that gap, pushing out to meet him, at least halfway. What
Faith did not know was that General Henry Hodes had given the order
that the forces closest to any rescue, the men who had held to the village
of Sudong-ni, be withdrawn, Hodes and General Barr believing that
their position was too vulnerable and too useless to add any support to
Faith's hemmed-in command.

The order for Faith's men to withdraw had come from him alone,
without any authority received from the base at Hagaru-ri. That would
change, the order finally passed through the haphazard communication
network of aircraft and tank radios, the signal suddenly clearing just
enough so that Faith could understand that General Smith was now in
command, and that Smith had ordered Faith to do all he could to withdraw back to Hagaru-ri. By that time, Faith's men had already been in
motion for more than two hours.

They formed a convoy around a lengthy line of thirty six-bys, plus a
number of smaller trucks. Most of the smaller vehicles were ordered by
Faith to be destroyed, along with most of the remaining supplies, and
the excess clothing and gear carried by the men. The trucks were emptied of their cargo, fitted instead to carry the hundreds of wounded men,
the casualties of four days of assaults by the Chinese.

As the withdrawal began, the Chinese were clearly aware what Faith
was attempting to do, the gathering of men and vehicles plainly visible
from the surrounding heights. Almost immediately, mortar and machine gun fire raked the column, and as the trucks began to file out into
the road, Chinese infantry moved closer, adding their fire to the assault.
Very soon the air support that Smith had promised began to arrive,
twenty Marine Corsairs pouring out their fire along the road, holding
the Chinese away. But the chaos and confusion of the advance under
fire was made worse by one terrible accident, a Corsair dropping a napalm canister that impacted short of its intended target. The fiery blast
spread out through the first ranks of the American and South Korean

troops, engulfing more than a dozen men, some killed outright, the rest suffering the horror of devastating burns. The sight of the blast produced panic in the men who saw it, halting the advance, as Faith's men recoiled from the scene. Some of the Americans scrambled to assist the wounded, helping them onto the trucks, adding to the misery of their human cargo. But Faith and his officers pushed their men and the vehicles to resume the advance, no matter the waves of Chinese fire pressing down from all sides.

For the first mile of their breakthrough from their own perimeter, the Americans were continuously supported by the aircraft, but even with the planes overhead, the column continued to dissolve into a chaotic mob. Many of the men attempted to escape the incoming Chinese fire by climbing aboard the trucks, the untrained South Koreans especially unwilling to stand up in the fight. But the Chinese would not ignore the fat, slow-moving targets, the trucks with their wounded men inside, absorbing as much machine gun fire as the infantry making their way along the road on foot.

Some two hours after they began, the convoy reached the first major roadblock, a wrecked bridge, the vehicles forced to halt. Though some of the drivers attempted to push their way across the shallow frozen marsh, for most of the vehicles the terrain was simply too difficult. Finally, with the Chinese pouring fire onto the men who gathered near the bridge, a single tracked vehicle was put to use, towing the trucks across the marsh one at a time, a process that took the better part of two hours. When the column was finally able to get under way, it was nearly dark.

With most of the column now in complete confusion, the Chinese began to press their advantages, pushing up closer to the flanks and rear of the march. The darkness meant the end of the air support, and with the Corsairs now unable to assist, the increasing pressure from the Chinese pushed Faith's men into further chaos, most of the column now completely disorganized. Though some of the trucks continued to roll, the Chinese had effectively targeted the truck drivers, the sudden breakdowns requiring some of the Americans to demonstrate an astonishing brand of courage, climbing up into the driver's seats knowing they would likely be the next casualty. But the greatest obstacle lay still to their front, Hill 1221, which anchored the strongest Chinese position yet alongside the reservoir. As the convoy rolled up, the infantry who could still advance began to scatter, some men pushing their way up the hill itself, leaving the road and the vehicles behind. Some men re-formed into small groups, some were alone, all of them climbing up through the darkness, some confronted by Chinese machine gun fire, others slipping undetected past Chinese positions. Despite the best efforts of several officers who attempted to organize a strike at the road-block itself, most of the men had absorbed all the horror they could take.

Adding to the pressure from the Chinese closer to the road, Faith's rearguard troops, assigned to keep the Chinese off the tail of the convoy, completely broke down. Many of those men rushed forward, adding to the chaos around the trucks, many more seeking escape by climbing up away from the road. With nothing to hold them back, the Chinese pressed hard into the rear of the column, swarming around the stalled vehicles.

At the roadblock itself, Colonel Faith and several of his officers, including a number of badly wounded men, succeeded in gathering enough troops to drive the Chinese away. With the road now open, many of the trucks continued on slowly. As they reached yet another destroyed bridge, the Chinese pressed even closer and in greater strength, many Chinese troops continuing to reach the trucks themselves. The casualties continued to mount, some of the wounded in the trucks now helplessly exposed to Chinese grenades and close-range rifle fire. As he continued to lead his men through the relentless gauntlet, Colonel Faith became one more casualty, taking a deadly wound to the heart from a Chinese grenade. He died in the cab of one of his lead trucks.

By full dark, it was over. Some of those who survived crossed over or around Hill 1221, linking up with others, all of them walking or staggering toward the perimeter at Hagaru-ri. Others made a different escape, a desperate gamble as they walked out onto the ice of the frozen reservoir, taking aim at the glimmer of light reflected from the engineers, still working their heavy equipment on the airstrip.

Though many of the wounded men in the stalled trucks were pulled out, most of those could not walk on their own. With no one remaining to help, many of those men had no choice but to remain along the base of Hill 1221, only to succumb to their wounds, the cold, or the Chinese who found them. In the trucks themselves, those still alive were virtually indistinguishable from those who had died along the way, the men often stacked three deep. After rifling through the trucks for anything worth salvaging, the Chinese troops burned the trucks, and the bodies of the men still inside.

Throughout the next day, and for three days after, the survivors of Task Force Faith straggled into the Marine lines at Hagaru-ri. The Americans had left behind every vehicle, every piece of equipment, including every heavy weapon, and most of the small arms carried by the troops themselves. Though approximately two-thirds of Faith's men eventually reached Hagaru-ri, the majority of those were wounded, many severely. Roughly one thousand men did not survive, their bodies never recovered.

CHAPTER THIRTY-ONE

. . . .

Riley

FOX HILL—DECEMBER 1, 1950, 1:30 P.M.

DAMN, I'M HUNGRY.

He tried not to do that, his exhaustion scattering his thoughts out in every direction. But the hollow cave in his stomach was worse today, the supply of C-rations nonexistent. His hands were clumsy, stiff, the gloves shredding more each day, the biting cold in his fingers making the work all that more difficult. Riley unrolled the wire, Kane and Morelli holding the other end of the spool, Riley trying to keep his footing in the snow as he backed slowly along the face of the hill. He couldn't keep the thought away, worse with every step, the hollow rumble down low, a twisting ache that now stopped him, the pain in his stomach growing.

Damn, I'm hungry.

Higher up the hill, Lieutenant Goolsby watched them, offering instructions no one really needed.

"That's it. Spread it along that rise there. Stick it in the snow."

The spool emptied, and Riley dropped to one knee, jabbed the steel stake into the ground, no penetration. He tried again, no strength in his arms, the stake ripping a fresh tear in his glove. He looked at his hands, dark red fingers poking through, and he tried to curl them, too numb to feel the pain. He sagged, the weakness overwhelming him now, heard Welch, just behind him.

"Hey! Wake up. No time for taking a nap. That sniper jackass might decide to try again."

Riley tried to stand, his knees stiff, no feeling in his feet, and he stumbled, fell forward on his hands. Welch was there now, his voice hollow, distant, "Hey, L.T., I'm hauling him back to the hole."

Riley felt Welch's hands under his arms, tried to stand, his feet floundering, trying to find the ground. The harder pain came now, a cramp in his gut, and he moaned, the cramp pulling him into a curl. Welch kept his grip, Riley's coat slipping upward, and Welch bent low, shouted into his ear, "Stand up, dammit! Do it!"

Riley tried to see through the fog in his brain, his eyes nearly frozen shut, the numbness spreading, a sharp punch striking him from behind.

"Wake up! Jesus. Let's get him to the hole. There's a can of Sterno, we can make some kind of fire. Maybe melt some snow."

Riley found his feet, a beehive of stinging pain spreading up through his legs. He blinked hard, the ice stuck painfully to his face, tried to speak, his knees curling again, the cramp still pulling him down. He fell from Welch's grip, dropped hard to his knees, the cramp churning harder, and he vomited, grunted a hard cry, gasping for air, nothing at all coming out of his stomach. He cramped up again, another dry heave, felt the sobs overtaking him, and rolled to one side, tried to wipe at his eyes. He was lifted again, more men, his arms stretched over shoulders, his feet dragging the ground, the hillside a blur of white. He heard a voice, Goolsby.

"Take him down the hill, Sergeant. We'll finish here. Sterno's not gonna fix him. If you see a corpsman, drop him there. We need hands up here if we're gonna get all this wire strung."

Welch was close to one side, and Riley started to protest, no, *no*. But the grips were firm, his weakness complete, agonizing helplessness, the worst pain still in his gut. They carried him for what seemed like miles, his mind drifting away, a flash of awareness, the cold, the stinging pains, the churning sickness inside, and gone again, soft sounds, blindness, his eyes frozen shut.

· · · · · · · · · ·

"He's okay. He needs food and water, more than anything else. Body can't function without fuel."

Riley was awake now, blinked, a warm cloth covering his eyes. "What happened? I can't see!"

The cloth was removed, and he fought for his vision, figures above him. He tried to rub his eyes, felt a hand on his wrist, stopping him.

"Nope, don't do that. Skin's raw. It'll only hurt worse."

Riley strained to see the faces, caught the smell, familiar now, the same he had smelled for days. "What the hell is that stink?"

He heard a chuckle, his eyes clearing, realized it was Welch.

"It's you, you moron."

Riley recognized the doctor now, another corpsman standing beside him, and the doctor said, "Actually, it's all of you. This is what happens when you warm up a little. First order I'm giving when we get out of this mess is every man in the company takes a shower. Scrub brushes. Maybe with bleach. Every man who comes in here brings his own smell with him."

Riley tried to see the faces, next to Welch, the kid, Morelli. He had a burst of panic now, said, "Am I hit? Oh, God, my feet!"

He tried to rise, Welch leaning down, a heavy hand pressing him back to the cot.

"Knock it off, bozo. You're not hit. Just loony. And you still got your feet. That's the only part of you that's not screwed up. The kid and I dragged you down here, and you were dead to the world. Thought maybe you took the easy way out."

The doctor said, "It's not all that bad, son. I'm seeing a fair amount of this. You just need something inside of you. Be grateful that's all it is. Plasma's gone, you don't need morphine. I can't explain why we haven't received any rations from all those ammo drops. We've got a few cans left, for emergencies. Here, eat this. Slowly. No gulping."

He saw a spoon coming closer, smelled the sugar sweetness of the fruit cocktail, opened his mouth, the syrup overwhelming him. He choked, sat up, coughed the fruit out, and the doctor said, "All right. Too much. Sergeant, can you or your buddy keep at it? He needs to eat something, and this is the best we've got. I've got people who need me."

The doctor moved away now, and Riley lay back heavily, felt the softness beneath him, glanced to one side.

"Christ, I'm in the aid station."

Welch knelt beside the cot. "It ain't Honolulu. Here. Eat this crap. It's better than the rest of us are getting. We ran out of anything but Tootsie Rolls this morning. And they're being pretty stingy with those."

Welch pushed the spoon to his mouth, and Riley took a long breath, tried to relax, opened his mouth. The fruit was intensely sweet, but he held it in his mouth, warming it, then swallowed carefully.

"Not bad, Sarge. More?"

Welch offered another spoonful, Riley taking the fruit easier now. Above him, Morelli said, "Holy cow, Pete. We thought maybe you'd gone around the corner or something. You was puking and nothing was coming out. You scared hell out of me, that's for sure."

Welch fed Riley another spoonful, said, "It's around the *bend*, you idiot. And he's been out there for a while now." He fed Riley again, said, "You'll be fine. We're all in the same fix, just you had to be the first to get waited on. You ever tell anybody I did this for you, and I'll stick my boots where the sun don't shine. That's it. No more. One can is all they could give you."

Riley savored the last of the fruit cocktail, wiped his tongue all across his teeth. He flexed his toes now, realized he had nothing but socks on his feet.

"Where's my boots? You sure I'm not hit? I remember puking."

Welch held up his boots. "Right here. They got you fresh linings, some dry socks. We were stringing the wire we got in that last airdrop. Captain thinks it'll slow down the Chinks next time they come at us."

"And I just passed out?"

"Hell if I know. I thought you'd curled up and died."

"How long I been here?"

"An hour. Doc cleaned up your face. You're gonna lose maybe a piece of your nose, tops of your ears. He says we might all get that way. Frostbite's not particular, kinda like bullets. But your feet work just fine. As soon as you feel like getting out of this lap of luxury, I need you back on the hill. So, how about right now?"

Beside Riley, a voice, heavy New Jersey accent. "I'd kinda like some of that fruit cocktail. Maybe some beef stew? I'm starved."

Riley tried to recognize the voice, saw Welch looking over toward the next cot. He pushed himself up on his elbows, the man wrapped in his sleeping bag up to his neck.

"You're Cafferoni. . . ."

"Cafferata. Hector. Hey, I remember you. We shared a hole up there, couple nights ago. So, all you did was puke, and they hauled you to a damn bed?"

Riley began to feel creeping embarrassment now, said, "I guess so. Ran out of gas, maybe. This here's my sarge, Hamp Welch. The goofy-looking kid is Morelli. From your part of the world."

Welch said, "Hey, I heard about you. Your buddy Benson came back up on the line. Said you put up a hell of a fight, the first night out, took out maybe half a company. The lieutenant said you played baseball with a dozen Chink grenades."

Cafferata held up a heavily bandaged hand. "Strike one. Son of a bitch blew up too quick. Cost me a finger or two maybe. That ain't the worst of it. Didn't have time to get my boots on, so I fought off those bastards in my bare feet. Not good. They don't know how bad that'll be yet. They found shoes for me, but they're too small. Had to cut off the toes. I'm kind of an extra large."

Riley sat up, tried to ignore the spinning in his head. He saw Cafferata's face now, the large man wrapped like a green mummy. He felt a chill, the tent not quite warm, put a hand on Cafferata's shoulder.

"Hey, you take care, right? I gotta get back out there."

"I'd like to go with you, but they ain't letting me do squat."

Riley stood, unsteady, the doctor moving toward him.

"You all right, son? You can stay here for a while yet, if you're too weak. Not many wounded coming down during the day. Might need the bed by tonight. Most everybody who's staying down here is in the warming tents."

Riley felt Welch slide his hand under his arm, steadying him. He looked at Welch, saw concern, the sergeant's harsh crust betrayed by his affection for his friend. Riley tested his balance, stood upright, said, "I'm okay now. Feel a hell of a lot better. Let me get my boots on." He sat slowly, still testing, the lightheadedness clearing away. "I appreciate the care, Doc. But this bed's for those that need it." He looked at Welch now. "You seen Killian? We oughta check on him."

Welch shook his head. "He's in the other tent. Maybe later. Since you're fit, we gonna get back up on the ridge. Irish ain't much good for anything but taking up space."

Riley pulled the boots on, felt guilty, thought of Killian, wondered just how bad his feet were. He saw Cafferata watching him, said, "I gotta go, pal. We ain't finished the job yet. Next time I see you, maybe we'll be on some beach somewhere."

Cafferata nodded, seemed to grow tired, turned his gaze upward. Riley looked at the doctor, said, "Take good care of that one, Doc. We could use a hell of a lot more just like him."

FOX HILL—DECEMBER 1, 4:00 P.M.

The snow had deepened to nearly six inches, a soft blanket that covered most of the horror that still lay across the face of the hill. Throughout the day, the men had continued to prepare their defensive line, dragging the enemy's dead closer, creating human walls around each of the foxholes. Since daybreak the Chinese had kept mostly quiet, the only real danger coming from the scattered snipers, still positioned on the rocky hill and the other hill farther to the west. For now their heavier machine guns stayed silent, what the Marines believed was the logical reaction to the effectiveness of the air strikes.

Riley had made the climb without help, though the weakness kept his steps slow, inspiring a chorus of playful cursing from Welch. At the foxhole, he had eased himself down, saw the faces of the others watching him, offered them a wave of his hand, no one giving him grief. He could see it in Welch's eyes, the sergeant's toughness not hiding what was going on inside him, inside all of them, the steady collapse of their energy.

He was impressed by the barrier now guarding the hole, saw another row of corpses piled close in front of Welch's machine gun. The bottom of the foxhole was coated with a thick layer of fresh snow, and he squatted, scooped out as much as his fingers could hold. In front of the hole, Welch was tending to the machine gun, jerking on the bolt, firing a single round now, the new routine. Riley watched him, Welch's movements slow and clumsy, betraying the same weakness Riley felt now. From one side, Morelli moved closer, knelt low, precaution against the snipers, held out a pair of gloves.

"Hey, Pete. Here. Use these."

"Thanks, but I got some. The doc gave me a pair."

"I seen those. They got holes worse than what you gave up. Here. These are practically new."

He took the gloves, looked them over, no holes but the missing trigger finger. "Where'd you get them?"

Morelli hesitated, and Welch turned, said, "Don't ask. Just put 'em on. We gotta use what we gotta use."

Riley ripped his away, pulled the new gloves onto his fingers, flexed, looked at Morelli. "Thanks, kid. I owe you one."

"Nah. Here, I found some more Tootsie Rolls, too. Ain't hardly nothing else left to eat. We been checking the Chink bodies, seeing maybe they got some rice or something, but they're about as bad off as we are, looks like. Go on, take 'em."

Riley accepted the gift and Morelli slid away, Welch now looking at him.

"Give me one. Then you eat the rest. Now. Don't need to be carrying your sorry ass back down the hill 'cause you're too weak to fight. The Chinks are coming again tonight. Count on it. You stink as a gun crew, but you're all I got. Kane's handling his BAR by himself, and we only got four more rifles in the squad. Even Goolsby's learning how to shoot straight. I saw him back over the hill, trying out a Thompson. He thinks it makes him look like Al Capone."

"You hear anything about Lieutenant McCarthy?"

"His leg's busted up good. That's all I know. He's still down the hill."

"Heads up!"

Riley turned toward the voice, saw stretcher bearers moving up, their load between them. The man's head rose, a quick motion from one hand, the men lowering him to the snowy ground. It was Barber.

Goolsby was there now, the Thompson hanging off one shoulder, the other sergeants coming closer as well, all of them keeping low behind the taller rocks. Riley watched Barber, felt a stir of nervousness, the captain struggling to sit up, his voice weak.

"Not sure I can make it up here anymore. Told the doc to give me morphine. My hip's busted up pretty bad, and they can't keep it from bleeding. Lieutenant Wright's in charge if I'm out of my head. Keep your eyes sharp. Corsairs are making one more run before dark. We've picked out a nest of those yellow bastards just below the sharp rocks on the far side of the saddle. They might be gathering up for tonight. But we need to get more aggressive, help the air boys do a better job. It's not good enough that they just shoot up the hillside and hope they hit somebody. I want a patrol to get out there and check the damage. If the enemy's still sitting in a hole, take care of 'em. If they're bringing up machine guns, bust 'em up. With dark coming, they won't be expecting us to push out there." He focused on Goolsby, fought for more words. "Lieutenant, take five men with you. Second Platoon will send some men out there as well. Wait for the Corsairs to do the job, then move out there quick. Keep to the right of the saddle. Peterson's men will hang to the left."

Barber seemed weaker still, lay back down on the stretcher, said something to the two men helping him. They responded, lifted the stretcher, moved back along the hill. Goolsby dipped low, crawled forward, pushing through the snow, said to Welch, "I guess it's your squad, Sergeant."

"You don't have to guess, sir. Just order it."

Goolsby nodded. "Right. Not used to it, that's all. Okay, Sergeant Welch, pick four men to go with us. Pick good men. And let's try not to get lost out there."

The sound of the planes came suddenly, the Corsairs rolling up over the hill behind them, and Welch said, "Guess they set their alarm clocks. No time like right now."

There were four in the formation, the tails of each plane marked with distinctive letters, *LD*. Goolsby said, "Love Dog. Lieutenant Peterson told me. Bunch of real characters. I guess we oughta lay low."

The men dropped into their holes, the planes banking sharply, a dry run straight down the saddle. By now the pilots were familiar with the lay of the land, the position of the enemy, very little guesswork. Riley peered up over the edge of the hole, realized his hands were resting on the frozen arm of a dead soldier. He pulled back, avoided looking at any more of the man, kept his eyes on the planes. They climbed now, rolling over, coming back toward the crest of the hill, no more than fifty feet above the rocky ground. Riley watched them pass, saw the face of one pilot, the man looking down onto the Marines, his audience. The planes disappeared behind the hill, long seconds, then came back, one at a time, straight down the saddle. The rockets came first, a spray that blew through the rocky hilltop beyond. The next one followed, more rockets, and then the single tank, hung from the plane's belly, tumbling down, bouncing once on the rocks, and then the explosion, the napalm's massive fireball, the storm of flames curling skyward, swept by the wind. Riley felt himself cheering, the others around him joining in, hands in the air. The planes banked away, circling high above, and Goolsby was there, a hard shout, "Watch the fire! When it dies down, we're going!"

Welch jumped up from the hole, called out along the line, "Kane, Morelli, Norman, Riley. Grenades and ammo. Check it!"

Riley was not surprised by the choices, except for the kid. He knew that Welch would choose the men he had confidence in, and he looked that way, saw Morelli fumbling with a handful of grenades, stuffing them into his pocket. No shortage of ammo, he thought. Just don't forget how to throw 'em.

He climbed up from the foxhole, saw Morelli and the others doing the same, the kid looking toward him with wide-eyed eagerness. They watched the fire, the flames spread out on the far end of the saddle, growing smaller now, black smoke still flowing to the west. Goolsby was out front, rose up, the Thompson in his hands, Welch's words in Riley's head, *Al Capone*. Goolsby waved them forward, then launched himself out away from the foxholes, moving downhill, the others following in line, keeping a gap between them. To the left, Peterson's men did the same, all of them pushing quickly to the saddle.

Goolsby led the way down the hill, and Riley felt the weakness in his legs, jogged with the others, kept up, no one with any more energy than he had. The lieutenant led them down along the right side of the saddle, slipping through rocks, snow-covered scrub brush, stepping past hard-frozen bodies of the enemy. Riley fought to breathe, icy air punching into his lungs, caught the smell of the napalm now, stinking smoke, his breathing harder still. Goolsby raised a hand, held them up, and Riley saw him, red-faced, gasping through the cold. Goolsby pointed up the side of the saddle toward the wide crest, small columns of smoke rising from spots of fire. He stood, waved the Thompson, started forward, and Welch was next, glancing back, sharp motion forward with his hand.

They were climbing again, slow progress, the ground rough, the rocks hidden by the snow, ankle busters, Riley making careful steps, the shoe pacs clumsy, unsteady. He could feel waves of warmth, the fresh stink of the napalm overwhelming, stirring the misery in his gut. He cursed himself, looked down the hill, the deep draw off the edge of the saddle, thick brush, the wooded draw where the enemy had risen so many times before. The woods were quiet, the only sound the breathing of the men, Goolsby leading them through a tall thicket, still below the crest of the saddle. They climbed farther, one man stumbling, Kane, struggling with the BAR, Welch pulling him upright, a slap on Kane's back. Riley kept his eyes on Goolsby, the lieutenant stopping, hands on his knees, then easing forward again, pushing past the ragged hedge of scrub. The others followed in turn, Riley watching everything, eyes on every rock, every tree and cluster of brush. They were close to the smoke now, and Goolsby stopped, stood upright, in the open, staring down, the smoke swirling around him. Riley felt a strange uneasiness, saw Goolsby step back, still staring down. Welch was there now, pulling on Goolsby's arm, the lieutenant staggering away, Welch leading the rest of them up the saddle, into the stinking smoke. Riley followed, saw now what Goolsby had seen. The body was clad in the usual white uniform, the fire moving slowly along the man's legs, the thick quilted cotton burning like the wick of a lantern, the man's bare flesh seared black. The man's face was gone, a black, bloody smear, smoldering fire in what remained of the man's hair. He lay with his burp gun still in his hands, the gun charred, useless. Riley moved past, tried not to see any more, but there were other bodies, a cluster of half a dozen, seated in a circle, down in a depression, each man bent over in a curl, cooked where he sat, hands holding still to their weapons. Up front, Welch fired his Thompson down into a hole, jolting Riley alert. Welch moved on, and Riley was there, saw the wounded man wedged in a narrow gap in the rocks, wounded no more. The breeze rolled up around them now, the stink of the napalm impossible to avoid. One man dropped down, vomited in the snow, and Welch held up, kneeling close to the man, shouting something. Riley kept his eyes on the rocky hill, black smoke, silence, searched for Goolsby. He saw the lieutenant, the Thompson hanging by his side, and Welch was there, more shouts, grabbing Goolsby's coat.

The first shots came from far off, the scattered machine gun fire ripping the air overhead. The response came from Peterson's men, a fight breaking out higher up the saddle. Goolsby seemed to freeze, uncertain, and Welch moved up beside him, jerked at Goolsby's sleeve, said, "Let's go! They need support!"

The men followed Welch, Goolsby taking the point again, finding something inside him. Riley followed, eyed Kane with the BAR, a glance between them, no words, Riley knowing that Kane had the same thoughts. What the hell's wrong with the lieutenant?

The firing across the saddle increased, and Riley could see the Marines, moving up in leapfrog formation, a handful of men passing the others, then hunkering down, the first group moving past. Up in the rocks nearer the tall hill, the Chinese were firing down. Peterson's men were close to them, the Chinese starting to break, scrambling up through the rocks, making their escape.

Welch called out, "Take 'em down!"

He fired the Thompson, too far to be effective, but Morelli knelt, anchored against a rock, aimed the M-1, fired, then again. Riley huddled low, could see the enemy dropping, Morelli doing the job, Peterson's men still putting on the pressure. There was more firing from Peterson's men, aimed down to the left, a fresh fight breaking out, but it ended quickly, shouts from the Marines. Riley saw a man moving toward them, darting quickly along the saddle, keeping low, eyes on Welch. He slid in close, breathless, said, "We've cleaned out a pocket of 'em. They didn't want to stick around. Sergeant Tyler says it'll help if you keep to this side of the saddle. Some of the Chinks dropped off this side earlier. They might try to get behind us."

Riley saw Welch looking at Goolsby, the lieutenant responding. "Yes! Good! We'll keep an eye out over here. You boys be careful over there."

The man looked at Goolsby with curiosity, then to Welch, who said, "He's the lieutenant. We'll take care of our side."

The man nodded, glanced at the others, a brief recognition of Riley.

"Yeah, I'll tell Sergeant Tyler you said so. We already wiped out a squad of those bastards, half frozen to death."

Welch looked at Goolsby, then said, "It'll be dark in a half hour. Don't hang out here too long. We'll secure what we can here, then pull back."

"The sarge is already thinking that. See you in hell."

The man slipped away, the same path back toward the rest of Peterson's men. Riley saw the black concern on Welch's face, another glance at Goolsby.

"Sir, we've got to move up, keep abreast of their position. The captain gave us a job. We're not doing a damn thing just sitting here."

Goolsby seemed angry now, said, "I know what we have to do, Sergeant. Let's move out through these rocks."

They dropped low, Welch pointing to the brush off to one side, the men scrambling that way. Riley pushed himself through the muddy snow, a slushy mess from the heat of the napalm, slid down into the first row of brush. The Chinese machine gun began again, far up on the rocky hill, the fire peppering the rocks around him, pinging ricochets on the rocks along the ridge. He dropped flat, the others doing the same, heard Welch, fiery anger, shouting to Goolsby, "Get down! Keep to the cover! We can't stay here! Get down the slope."

Riley turned his head in the snow, watched the two men, Goolsby staring back at Welch with empty helplessness. Welch moved away now, a quick check of each man, his eyes now on Riley.

"You okay?"

"Yeah. What do we do now?"

"You could ask the man in charge. We've done all we can do right here. The napalm took care of most of the Chinks out here, and Second Platoon did the rest. Barber wanted it cleaned up. It's cleaned up. The longer we sit out here, the more Chinks will figure out where we are. Jesus." Welch lowered his voice. "He should have shoved us out quicker, found the enemy, before they found us. Tyler knew what he was doing. We got no reason to sit here."

Goolsby slid down closer, seemed to gather himself, said to Welch, "Sergeant, we still have a job to do. The captain said to check the drop area. Clean out the enemy."

"Well, sir, if I may suggest, now that every Chink weapon is aimed this way, how about we head back to our lines?"

Goolsby looked at the others, all eyes on him. "I suppose so, yes."

The grenade struck a rock close beside Riley, tumbled down the hill, sliding to a stop in the snow. Riley shouted, "Grenade!"

He flattened out, waited for the blast, but nothing happened. He peered through the crook in his arm, the handle of the grenade sticking up from the snow. Welch said, "A dud. But there'll be more. Don't wait for 'em. Hit 'em now!"

Welch climbed quickly up through the brush, up to his knees now, fired the Thompson, a continuous spray, emptying the magazine. The others moved up with him, more firing, and Riley pushed into the snow, his feet finding rock, climbed the embankment, saw them now, a dozen men, some kneeling, the flash of fire from their rifles, more men moving up from farther up the saddle, grenades now in the air, a shower of sticks tumbling past him. He fired his own machine gun, heard the BAR open up, the enemy tumbling down, the image in his mind, ten pins, from a single ball. The firing continued, one rifle beside him, the clink of the clip, and Welch said, "That's it! Cease fire! Get back into cover."

He slid down through the snow, the others doing the same, Goolsby still hunkered down in the low place.

"Did we get 'em all?"

Riley looked at Goolsby, saw icy tears on the man's face, and Welch moved close to him, grabbed the man's shoulders.

"Tighten up! No time for this! That was one bunch. There's more. Tyler's already got his men pulling back. Let's get back to the hill!"

Riley looked up toward the crest of the saddle, the smell of the napalm still inside of him. He pulled a magazine from his pocket, slammed it into the Thompson, jerked the small bolt, ready again. Welch moved along the hill below him, the others falling into line, and Welch called out to him. "Watch our rear. They know we're here, and they're figuring out what to do about it. You see anybody, shoot everything you got."

Riley kept his eyes on the darkening sky, the ridgeline still quiet. He glanced at the Thompson, his hand tapping the pockets of his coat. Plenty of ammo for now, he thought. What the hell's wrong with the lieutenant? Maybe it's seeing that Chinese candlestick up there. I bet he's never seen napalm up close. Don't need to see it again.

He heard the planes again, the roar growing closer, and he saw them coming up the draw, straight overhead. He had a burst of panic, thought, No, oh Christ, not now! He slid quickly down through the snow, kicked through brush, running now, closer to the others. The rest of the squad had stopped, squatted low, watching the planes, and Riley glanced back, the planes gone now, the far side of the ridge. He was breathing in hard gasps and Welch said, "Easy, Pete. The son of a bitch waved at me. They know we're here. They're keeping the Chinks off our tails. God bless 'em."

The planes returned, the roar of the engines and the hard rattle of their machine guns. One plane peeled off, rolled out to one side, swung around, and Riley watched the nose of the plane pointing straight toward them. He called out, pointed, the others watching the plane, all of them dropping flat. The Corsair was barely twenty feet above the rocky hill, the machine guns opening now, the flickers of fire along the wings. Riley felt frozen, terror enveloping him, but the plane dipped lower still, firing down into the draw beneath them. The plane roared straight over them now, close enough to touch, and Riley felt a hard impact on his head, more falling around him, the men yelling in panic, and Welch shouted, "Shells! Empties, you idiots!"

Riley saw now, pockets of steam in the snow, the spent shells from the Corsair's guns splattering the hillside around them. His legs gave out, and he sat in the snow, reached down, retrieved an empty .50-caliber shell. It was still warm to the touch, and he cupped it in his hands, then slipped it into his pocket. Welch was still standing, said in a low voice, "You got your damn souvenir? Let's get back up the ridge before it's too dark for those numbskulls up there to see who we are. And keep an eye on this draw. That flyboy saw something worth shooting at."

Goolsby was up beside Welch, said, "Let's go. Head back. We'll try again tomorrow."

Riley saw something fragile in the man's face, his voice a weak quiver. He looked at Welch, who returned the glance, said nothing. There was a pop from the draw down below, a single shot, and Goolsby sat suddenly, looked at his hands, one reaching for his shoulder. "Oh! I got stung!"

Welch was down beside him, said, "You hit? Where?"

Goolsby looked at him, then at the others, seemed confused. Riley moved closer, saw Welch push the lieutenant's hands aside, staring into his chest, pulling the coat back off his shoulder. And now, a sharp whistle, the dull *smack*, Goolsby knocked flat on his back. Riley saw the hole, blood in a light stream from Goolsby's forehead, and Welch shouted, "Down!"

They flattened out in the snow and brush, more firing from down below cutting the snow around them. Welch crawled up through the brush, said, "Give 'em hell! Then get your asses up that way. Get to the cover in those rocks!"

Welch rose to one knee, emptied the Thompson into the brush below, Kane firing the BAR, the others joining in. Riley stared, searching for any kind of targets, and he fired the Thompson, aiming low, shredding the brush.

Welch said to Kane, "Give it to 'em again. Then haul your ass up this hill."

Kane reloaded the BAR, fired again, and the others moved quickly up through the snow and brush, slipping into the rocks. Riley watched Welch, who emptied the Thompson one more time, and Riley looked again at Goolsby. He slid down toward the man, one hand on Goolsby's coat, tugged, and Welch was now beside him.

"We can't leave him, Sarge."

"Didn't intend to. Grab his hand."

The fire from below had stopped, Kane above them, firing the BAR one more time. Riley worked with Welch, pulling Goolsby's body up toward the others, toward the safety of the rocks. Two more men now took the job, Kane and Norman grabbing Goolsby's hands, Riley struggling to breathe. Welch had one hand on his shoulder, said between breaths, "Let's go. We chased that bunch off, I think. But they'll be back. Let's get the hell out of here. You okay?"

Riley watched the men dragging Goolsby, making their way up past the rocks, the heavier snow, moving past the frozen bodies of the enemy. Riley saw others, up on the ridge, Marines watching the scene, rifles ready, offering help if the enemy was following. Riley stopped at a fat rock, sat, and Welch looked back at him.

"What's up?"

"Just a minute, Hamp. Gotta get my breath."

"It'll be dark in five minutes. Let's get back home." Welch was catching his own breath, said in a low voice, "He never shoulda been out here. Too green. Irish called it, said he'd never make it."

Riley looked at Welch, said, "We were all green. The lieutenant was no worse than you."

Welch looked at him, said, "He's dead. That makes him worse. Let's go."

Riley looked again at the ridgeline, two more men coming downhill, taking their turn with the lieutenant, the others staring down the hill, searching for any sign of the enemy. Riley struggled to get to his feet, the Thompson heavier still, aching weakness in his knees, his shoulders, his back. He tasted the cold again, the temperature dropping with the setting of the sun, the icy sting returning to his face, the miserable wetness in his shoe pacs. He looked up at Welch, who held out a hand, helping Riley up past the rocks. Riley took a long icy breath, said, "Damn, I'm hungry."

CHAPTER THIRTY-TWO

Riley

THE BREAKOUT FROM YUDAM-NI had begun just after dawn on December 1, Litzenberg and Murray uniting their efforts in a well-organized push that drove them straight into the Chinese troops who had cut off the road to the south. Murray's Fifth led the way, while several units of the Seventh held their position in Yudam-ni, keeping the Chinese troops behind them at bay. The eight thousand Marines moved slowly, methodically, accompanied by a single tank, the only armor they had. To each side of the road, the tall hills hid more of the enemy, and Murray sent his lead troops forward in three prongs, two of them high up, pushing the Chinese back along both sides of the road. The third kept to the road itself, marching with the long train of vehicles that carried the hundreds of wounded. Several miles to their front, both commanders knew they could not just march to Hagaru-ri without passing first through the narrow defiles of Toktong Pass, the most vulnerable part of the march.

Some four miles south of Yudam-ni, short of the pass, one battalion of the Seventh, roughly four hundred men, branched off, leaving the main convoy behind. They were commanded by Lieutenant Colonel Ray Davis, a rugged thirty-five-year-old, a veteran of some of the worst fights the Marines had endured during World War II. With darkness falling late on December 1, Davis led his men up the tall hills to the east of the main road, knowing they would confront heavy concentrations of Chinese, with their only advantage coming from the darkness and all the stealth the Marines could muster. Their mission was not to engage the enemy, but if possible, to slip past him, avoiding a major confrontation that might halt Davis's men altogether. Through the frozen darkness, they were to cross the rugged hills, trudge through the deep passes, and, following maps that were obsolete at best, attempt to locate and rescue the men of Fox Company. Whether there was anyone left to rescue or whether the Chinese had completely obliterated Barber's command was a question no one could answer.

Throughout the night, Davis's men made their way over some of the roughest ground they had experienced. The Chinese they confronted were mostly caught off guard, but there were fights, clumsy and chaotic, the battalion taking casualties Davis had hoped to avoid. Wounded men only added to the challenge, the blinding darkness obliterating any kind of landmark, the men guided by compasses that now failed to work, frozen.

The men struggled to keep to any kind of direction, the hillsides swallowing their bearings, no guidance coming from anyone behind them, no artillery, no aircraft. For a while Davis attempted to guide his men by the stars, but the weariness of the exhausted men made mental exercises required for navigation all but impossible. Trudging onward, stumbling into a surprised, often sleeping enemy, Davis discovered pockets of Chinese soldiers who had frozen to death, unable to protect themselves from the thirty-below-zero temperatures.

As the night wore on, Davis recognized that his men were barely functioning and he ordered a halt, allowing most to rest in the relative comfort of their sleeping bags. But with so many pockets of the enemy around them, sleep was out of the question, and so Davis and his officers moved along the ragged line of march, prodding the men into as much alertness as they could muster. With dawn approaching, the firefights seemed to grow more numerous, and more intense, the confrontations alerting more of the Chinese that their enemy was surprisingly close. Studying his map by flashlight, the bleary-eyed and foggy-brained

Davis continued to guide the men toward what he had to believe was his intended goal. Close to dawn, his radioman was suddenly wide awake, offering Davis exactly what Davis was hoping to hear.

FOX HILL—DECEMBER 2, 1950, 7:00 A.M.

Welch had met with the remaining sergeants who still manned Third Platoon's position, the consensus that at least one of them should check in on the battered Second Platoon, Lieutenant Peterson's command, which had continued to receive the same pressure from the Chinese assaults. As the casualty count mounted, the gaps in the line were increasing, some of the positions occupied by wounded men brought back up the hill from the aid stations, anyone who could still squeeze a trigger. But across from them on the rocky hill, and the wider hill beyond the road to the west, it was clear that the Chinese had continued to regroup, still pushing forward more troops, preparing yet again for their next assault. Fox Hill was defended now by half the force that had first established the line, men whose rations had run dry, whose lack of sleep had dulled the minds, the relentless assaults draining away any strength at all. But still they held to their foxholes, shifting positions, hanging on to the hilltop that Captain Barber had insisted was their only remaining mission. There was no alternative.

Riley had insisted Welch not make the short journey down toward Second Platoon by himself, and surprisingly, Welch did not object. It was one more sign that even the strongest men were losing command of themselves, that the fight they made now was as much by instinct as by following orders. Even if there was no real purpose to the journey, Riley accepted that a walk, even a frozen one, might help wake them both up from the sluggishness of their hunger, might loosen up the stiffness in every limb from the relentless cold.

They stumbled over the snow-covered rocks, and Riley tried to watch the saddle, a useless exercise. The snipers were still active, Riley's brain teasing him into believing he might see them before they took their shot, before the worst could happen. The worst so far had come the day before, the image of Goolsby's death ground into his brain. He had mourned the man's death with paralyzing grief, some of that the product of sleeplessness and hunger. He tried to think of the man's first name, couldn't recall it, felt foolish asking anyone else. He wanted to offer the lieutenant an apology, did so in his thoughts throughout the long night, wondering if Goolsby had known of the rude comments, Killian and the others, "the ninety-day wonder," "shavetail," all those monikers the veterans gave fresh-faced officers. He scolded himself even now, stumbling behind the cover of taller rocks, halting with Welch for a gasp of frozen air. Stop this! He's dead, and you might be, too, if you don't get a handle on this.

Welch moved again, the Thompson dangling from his shoulder, and Riley followed, another glance toward the rocky hill. There had been casualties all throughout the night, some of those from carelessness, or simply bad luck, sprays of machine gun fire that blew into men who might have been away from their foxholes, if only for a moment, trying to stretch, to bring life to dead limbs. He felt guilty for not visiting Killian, but for now there wasn't much point. The wounded were still down there in the tents, more vulnerable now than any day so far, the men on the hill who protected them weakening by the hour. He hadn't even asked Welch about going down, knew instinctively that the energy required for the climb might be too costly, that if the enemy came again that night, he would need everything left inside him to stand tall, to make another tough fight. Killian would understand, he thought. He'd kick me in the ass if I wasn't up here doing the job just so I could hold his hand.

They moved past scrambling supply men, a pair of stretcher bearers, and Riley saw the lines of foxholes facing west, the men barely visible, protected by the mounds of Chinese corpses. He couldn't avoid shivering, his breathing punching his lungs with frigid air. The hood of his parka was clamped tight around his head, the three pairs of socks on his feet less effective with each new gust of brutal wind. He saw a light wisp of smoke, rising from belowground, and Welch halted, searched, a low voice to one side, from one of the holes.

"What's up?"

Welch moved that way, Riley following, the familiar face of Lieutenant Peterson sitting low in a hole.

Welch crawled low, Riley doing the same, both men down in the snow.

Welch said, "Thought I should report to you, sir. No officers on our side of the hill. Not sure if anything's going on we oughta know about."

There was firing out past the rocky hill, distant sounds that echoed faintly. Riley turned that way and Peterson shifted in the hole, said, "Heard that for a while now. It's not aimed this way, so I'm not sure what to do about it. I'm not too mobile right now."

Riley peered down over the edge of the foxhole, the repairs to Peterson's wounds hidden by the heavy coat, the sleeping bag over his legs. Welch said, "You okay, sir? We can still get a corpsman up here if we need one."

"Leave them be, for now. I got half a dozen holes in me, but I'm still here. Unless they blow my hands off, I can fire a rifle. The only officer on the hill not wounded yet is Lieutenant Dunne. First Platoon has had it easy so far. The enemy keeps pushing us from this direction, like he knows we're shot full of holes. If Dunne tries to help us out, shifting any of his people around to this side, the Chinese will see that, and sure as hell, they'll bust up the hill in his sector. They're out there in every direction." He paused, seemed to gather strength. "I heard about Lieutenant Goolsby. Tough."

Welch said, "Yeah. We were there."

"I'll put him in for a citation, if you want to. That's the way it works, sometimes. Dead men aren't too humble to accept medals. Last I heard, Lieutenant McCarthy's doing okay. Nasty wound, but in the right place. Not sure how much longer we're gonna be up here, but at least nobody's bleeding to death. Too damn cold."

Riley said, "How's the captain?"

Welch looked at him, too tired to scold him. Peterson didn't seem to mind the question, said, "His wound's gotten bad. The doc says it's infected, and getting worse. I told him to keep down near his CP. No need for him to risk his stretcher bearers just so he can make an inspection. He's already lost two of his runners."

Welch looked out past the distant rocks. "It's gotten heavier. Who's doing all that shooting? We heard the artillery at Yudam-ni, a couple days ago. But that's not artillery. Too light."

"And too close. No idea, Sergeant. Maybe it's John Wayne and the South Korean cavalry coming to our rescue. Hagaru-ri's the other way, so it ain't help from down there. Right now it's somebody else's problem. We got our hands full holding the enemy off this hill. Get back to your men, tell them to keep doing what they've been doing. Air cover will be here soon, I hope. The captain's radio's maybe got enough juice to last an hour, and he's hoping to hear something from those boys before it conks out again."

Riley heard the sharp zip, the ping of lead off a rock to one side. He put his head down flat in the snow, pressed up closer to one of the corpses, and Peterson said, "Careful. That son of a bitch out there knows I'm here, and he must have some idea I'm in charge. He keeps me honest about every twenty minutes. Keep back to those rocks over that way. That seems to be safe."

"Sir!"

Peterson responded, "Who the hell is calling me *sir*?"

The man fell flat close to Riley, crawled forward, out of breath. "Sorry. Captain wanted me to get up here, tell you what's up."

The man ran out of words, gasping for air, and Peterson said, "So? What's up? MacArthur still saying we'll be home for Christmas?"

"Sir, the radio. We got a call. There's Marines coming this way! You're to order your men to hold their fire if they see personnel out toward the rocky hill."

Peterson didn't respond, a long silence, and Riley could hear the sounds from the distant fight, sporadic now, small pops. Welch said, "I guess that would be them?"

Peterson struggled to stand, another man close by.

"Sir! The sniper!"

Peterson stared out that way, propped against the corpses in front of him.

"I have a feeling that guy has his hands full. He can hear what we're hearing." Peterson looked at Barber's man, said, "Whose Marines? Did they say?"

"First Battalion, Seventh, sir."

"Davis. Figures. He's buddies with Chesty Puller. They're always trying to outdo each other for balls." He paused, stared toward the sounds of the fight, almost nothing now. "He brought a whole damn battalion over that miserable ground just to help us get off this damn hill? I think Chesty will like that."

FOX HILL—DECEMBER 2, 11:00 A.M.

The Corsairs came again, the saddle and much of the rocky knoll bathed in a bright shower of napalm. The men along the ridgeline watched as they had before, grateful for the attention from the air wing, Riley as curious as any of them just what it was like to fly the big blue birds. With the raid past, the enemy's guns had fallen silent, the last firefight erupting close to the rocky knoll on the big hill, the men on Fox Hill surprised to see an eruption of Chinese soldiers boiling up from hidden places, most of them scattering off into the deep draws. Soon after, the men with binoculars passed the word there were troops moving out along the distant ridges, and they were not Chinese. Within minutes, Marines were advancing across the saddle toward them, more men coming up from the low places alongside.

Riley stood in the foxhole, laid the Thompson down, stared with Welch, neither man speaking. All along the line, cheers began to flow out, shouts and greetings, the Marines moving up toward them responding with calls of their own. Welch climbed up without speaking, moved out past the muzzle of the machine gun, Riley struggling to follow. He stepped once more past the walls of bodies, stood alongside Welch, watched the Marines as they made contact with the others along the ridge. Hands went out, more loud talk, and Riley felt a shiver, raw emotion, tried to blink through the frosty tears in his eyes. Two men made their way up the hill straight below them, filthy bearded faces, ragged coats over dirty pants, one man calling out, pulling a can from his pocket.

"Howdy, Marine. They told us you might be hungry. Got some beef stew here, if you want it."

Welch took the can, mumbled something, his voice low, his head down. The man pulled out another can, offered it to Riley, who stared at the man's outstretched hand, the dull green tin. Riley felt the strength go out of his legs, and he dropped down to his knees, sat back on his heels, too weak to raise his arm. The man stepped closer, stuffed the can into Riley's coat pocket.

"Maybe later, then."

The other Marine pulled more rations from his coat, tossed them into the foxhole behind Riley, and after a quiet moment Welch offered the man his hand, said, "What took you so damn long?"

The first man smiled, said, "It's kind of a hike, and there's about five million Chinese tried to stop us. The colonel wasn't sure just what we'd find. It's good to see you boys are still up here. But I gotta say. You look like hell."

Throughout the day on December 2, Captain Barber ordered the preparation for his men to evacuate their position on Fox Hill. The wounded were of course the first priority, their number increasing by two dozen more, the casualties Davis's battalion had taken on their extraordinary journey.

While Fox Company gathered up their own gear, anything worth retrieving, Davis's men continued their mission. The hills around Toktong Pass were still infested with Chinese, men who had kept their distance as they observed this fresh influx of strength. Davis's men were now the aggressors, driving the Chinese away from anyplace around Toktong Pass where they might still pose a threat. Aided by raids from the Corsairs, and blistering fire from the artillery at Hagaru-ri, by nightfall most of the enemy concentrations had been either driven away or destroyed.

With darkness settling over them one more time, the men of Barber's command were poised for the march down off Fox Hill. Of the
240 men who had begun the fight, barely eighty had survived without
wounds.

As Davis's men continued to sweep the surrounding heights, Barber's Marines kept watch on what had been the enemy positions, the
rocky knolls and deep draws where so many assaults had come before.
Instead of the bugles and whistles that had become a terrifying part of
their nightly routine, the Marines were startled by an entirely new
sound, the familiar clanking grind of a lone tank as it wound through
the narrow pass below them. With the tank came the vanguard of Murray's Fifth, followed by Litzenberg's Seventh, and back behind them,
scattered formations of the Chinese still willing to pursue them. But
Barber's men understood that the men coming down the main road
were more than just their own salvation. Word passed quickly that the
evacuation from Yudam-ni was complete, the Marines pushing their
convoy of heavy equipment and wounded men southward, with only a
few miles to go before they reached Hagaru-ri.

CHAPTER THIRTY-THREE

. . . .

Smith

HAGARU-RI—DECEMBER 3, 1950, 10:00 A.M.

THE SURVIVORS OF Task Force Faith had continued to straggle into Hagaru-ri, men alone, others in groups of a dozen or more. The greatest surprise had come out on the ice of the frozen reservoir, hundreds of soldiers fleeing the Chinese by drifting out onto the wide-open, coverless terrain, shuffling through several inches of fresh snow, some carrying the men who could not walk by themselves. As they came into view of the forward observation posts, one Marine officer had reacted by commandeering one of his jeeps, and accompanied by a convoy of vehicles and a team of his own subordinates, he had driven onto the ice, pushing out as far as he dared. Unsure of the thickness of the ice beneath him, and coming under fire from Chinese troops along the shoreline, the Marines had moved in closer on foot, corralling as many of the soldiers as they could, leading them or in some cases carrying them back to the safety of the lines at Hagaru-ri.

Smith had heard about the rescue, was as curious about this new hero as he was the condition of the soldiers who had made it back. The jeep rolled slowly, the driver with a keen eye on the limits of the land, the snow disguising the water's edge. As they passed the last of the low huts, Smith saw smoke, a fat fire roaring near the edge of the ice, men standing close, hands out, bearded faces fixed on the flames that warmed them. Beside Smith, the driver sat hunched over in the jeep, his face wrapped as usual, a swath of green fabric engulfing most of the man's face. Smith glanced behind him, saw the red-faced Captain Sexton, who said, "That's him in the jeep, sir. Colonel Beall."

"I know who it is."

Beside Smith, his driver said, "I heard all kinds of stories, sir. Hard to believe it."

It was an odd comment to hear from the young man, who rarely offered any kind of sound but the occasional groan from the blustery winds that ripped through the jeep.

Smith was curious, looked again toward the fire, the officer paying no attention to his visitors. "Why do you say that, Corporal?"

"Well, begging your pardon, sir, but Colonel Beall is not a man prone to good deeds. I mean, he's rather a tough nut. Every time I have your vehicles serviced, or even cleaned up, I catch all kinds of grief for it. The colonel seems to be unhappy most all the time." The young man paused. "Oh, gee, sir, I didn't mean nothing. Shouldn't have spoke up."

Smith glanced back at Sexton, saw a smile through cracked lips. He was still curious, said to the driver, "I know Colonel Beall, son. Heads up the First Motor Battalion, and there's nobody better for the job. Most of those motor pool fellows aren't happy unless they've got a wrench in their hands and grease on their uniforms."

Sexton said, "I think the corporal here has learned that those motor boys love their steel hardware as much as the artillery or the tank drivers do. I dented up a jeep once, and Beall . . . Colonel Beall threw enough cussing at me to start a forest fire."

Smith heard the humor in Sexton's voice, ignored it. "Both of you need to pay a little more attention to a man's deeds instead of his mouth. Colonel Ridge has made it pretty clear to me that Colonel Beall has saved some lives, and maybe a whole lot of them. I want to hear more about it from him."

Beside him, the driver kept his head down, said, "Well, yes, sir. That's what I'll say from now on, I promise, sir."

Smith looked again at the young man, thought, Not everybody here has to be buddies. And not every officer is a nice guy. I'm not sure what this particular bug is about. Maybe I should keep it that way.

"Stay here, son. Keep the jeep running. Captain, follow me."

Smith stepped out of the jeep, eyed the gathering of men around the fire. There were two dozen or more, ragged and filthy, no weapons, Beall now speaking to the men as though they were there for inspection.

"Pay attention. Warming tents are over that way, and there's rations just past, in the mess tents. Lieutenant Hunt here will show you the way. I'm heading back out, seeing if I can round up any more of you characters."

Smith saw Hunt now, the young officer buried in his coat, responding to Beall's command, herding the troops into a makeshift parade, leading them to a waiting truck. Smith focused more on the soldiers now, some men barely able to walk, assisted by others in no better condition. He let them pass, the lieutenant eyeing him, a sudden salute.

"Sir."

Smith returned it with a gloved hand, said nothing, the soldiers moving past him at a shuffle, most ignoring him. There was no talk, no smiles, and Smith had a sudden thought, the image of prisoners of war, marching off to their camps.

Sexton was beside him now, cold legs marching in place, the futile routine of every one of his staff when he brought them out into the chill. He felt it himself, the usual tremors in his hands, clamped them under his arms, moved closer to the fire, and Beall's jeep. Beall jumped down, seemed to notice the two officers for the first time, and Smith saw annoyance on the man's face, a snarl of impatience.

"What can I do for you two?" Smith said nothing, stood straight, gave Beall the time to study him. He saw it now, the burst of recognition in the colonel's eyes, but Beall was unrepentant, said, "Didn't expect to see you, General. I've got to get back out on the ice. My boys are out there still, hauling in whatever catch we can find."

Olin Beall was nearly as old as Smith, the Hollywood image of the crusty old veteran, with more than thirty years in the Corps. He was one of the very few men Smith had in his command who had actually served in World War I.

"Colonel, I've been told you're doing some fine work out here. How many men have you found?"

He knew Beall would appreciate a minimum of conversation, Beall nodding briefly, the only show of formality he offered.

"Dozens. Lost count, but I'll have a report for you when we're done. They're a mess, General. No fight left in 'em at all. Found a pile of 'em hiding along the shoreline, anyplace they could keep away from the enemy. Some of 'em couldn't walk, frostbite, whatnot. Took some of my trucks out there the last run and hauled a bunch straight to the tents. They're mostly frozen stiff, some bad wounds. Some of 'em are worth a salute, helping the worst of the wounded. Brave damn men. Others. Well, less so. Damn Chinese tried to slow us down, we took out a pile of snipers along the shore. Sir, I need to get back out there. No idea how many more we'll find."

Smith nodded, Beall responding without speaking, jumping into the jeep, driving it himself, spinning around in the snow, a quick surge toward the edge of the reservoir. Smith watched the jeep rolling out onto the snow-covered ice, could see a small truck coming in toward him, had a sudden fear, wondered about the strength of the ice. But the two vehicles passed each other, Beall waving the truck's driver back toward the shore. Smith said to Sexton, "Only advantage to this cold. If that ice wasn't solid, there'd be an even bigger mess."

Sexton shivered, said, "He's not about to lose a single jeep by drowning it. He'd rather drown you."

Smith ignored the comment, said, "He deserves a medal for this." Smith blinked, the ice already crusting around his eyes. He was tempted to move closer to the fire, two of Beall's men stoking it with scrap timbers. But there was a better way to warm himself, where a coffeepot could be found. "Let's get over to the aid tent. I want a better look at some of these soldiers. If there's some officers to be found, I want to know just what happened out there."

"How many more flights are we expecting today, General?"

Smith removed his coat, saw the anxiety in the doctor's face. "As many as they'll send us. There's still plenty of daylight, and the enemy seems to ignore most of the planes."

Hering wiped his hands on his white smock, said, "I'd like to see another couple hundred men out of here as soon as possible. I'm hoping you will allow the lot of the wounded to leave before the rest of the men. That will require a good many of those small transports."

Smith tossed the coat to Sexton behind him, realized the doctor was making an assumption he had already heard from some of the other officers. "Doctor, the men who can fight are not flying out of here at all. Quite the opposite. I've ordered replacements to be flown in on the planes you're using for transport. No point in flying empty boxes up here. We've got new recruits down at the ports, plus there are a good many of the wounded who've recovered well enough to fight. I've ordered as many as possible to be transported up here."

Hering seemed surprised. "Good Lord, why?"

"Doctor, our next mission is to make the move southward, pulling this entire force back to the seaports. We've got far too many vehicles and far too much ordnance here just to leave it all to the enemy. If the Chinese observe us loading up plane after plane with fighting men, all hell will break out. They'll push as hard as they can, disrupt the entire operation, probably with a general assault, and I'm certain they'll do everything they can to knock those planes out of the air. We're fighting our way out of here, Doctor. There's no other way. The replacements will add considerably to our strength."

Hering seemed distressed, said, "Well, in that case, I have a problem to report. I have kept a very accurate count of the wounded men whom we've prepared for evacuation. But we're shipping far more men out of here than I have on my lists. It seems, sir, that there are able-bodied men, including a good many of the newly arrived army personnel, who are doing all they can to hitch a ride out of here, wounded or not."

Now Smith was surprised, said, "That's unacceptable, Doctor. Put a stop to it."

"Well, yes, sir. I'm assuming that some of the men are burying themselves under blankets, and . . . God I hate using the word. They're simply faking it. I came across one man, moans and groans, calling for his mama. I didn't have him on my list, so I had my aide take a look under the cover. No injury, no wound. He admitted as much, begged me to let him go. I didn't have orders not to, so we stuck him on the plane."

"That was a mistake, Doctor. How often has this happened? How many men have you let slip?"

Hering folded his arms across his chest, resigned to Smith's anger. "This morning, I had four hundred fifty men awaiting evacuation. So far we've loaded up better than nine hundred men. I've no idea where they all came from. My tents couldn't hold that many if I wedged 'em in with a crowbar. And I still have two hundred seriously wounded here waiting for a spot."

Smith felt his anger boiling, his jaw clamped tight. "How many of those men have been Marines?"

"You mean, compared to army troops? I can't be sure. It seemed to us this morning that a majority of the men boarding the C-47s were army."

Smith closed his eyes for a brief moment, thought of Almond. You'll love it if I raise Cain about this. One more reason to slam the door on anything the Marines might need down the road. I can hear you bitching now. *All we do is find reasons to fault the army.*

"Put a stop to this nonsense, Doctor." He turned to Sexton. "Captain, have a squad of MPs sent over here on the double. I want an MP on each plane, keeping a tight watch on the boarding. Nobody leaves here who isn't worthy, who doesn't have a pass signed by Dr. Hering. You understand that?"

Sexton stiffened, no sign of his usual good humor. "Completely, sir."

Sexton withdrew, and Smith glared at Hering, the doctor offering none of his usual arguments to Smith's orders. Smith said, "I want the evac area tightened up so much, they won't let *me* on a plane. Check every man."

"It will be done, sir."

Smith tried to calm down, looked across the tent, faces watching him from every cot. He suddenly recalled why he was here, lowered his voice. "Doctor, there's a Marine officer brought in this morning. Captain Stamford. I want to see him, if he's able. That is, if he's still here."

The doctor seemed relieved to change the subject, said, "He's still here, and he's able." Hering checked the clipboard in his hand. "I've got him scheduled to evacuate tomorrow. That last row, second cot from the end."

Smith moved that way, tried to avoid the odors, the soft sounds from those men not quite conscious. He reached Stamford's cot, saw the captain's eyes closed, had a brief argument with himself. Don't disturb him. Well, yes, disturb him. I've got things to do.

"Captain, you awake?"

Stamford's eyes opened, wider now, surprise on the man's face. "General Smith."

Stamford tried to raise his right arm, the instinct for saluting, thick bandages holding him back.

"Leave it be, Captain. How bad are you hit?"

"Doc says I'll live. Guess that's the best news there is. They chewed me up pretty good. The enemy captured me twice, but they're a little sloppy. I got away from 'em both times. Not so some of the others. I lost two of my men, Corporal Myron Smith, Private Billy Johnson. It was pretty bad up there, sir."

"I'm sorry. But I want to hear your take on what happened up there. Is it true that Colonel Faith didn't make it? Or do we list him as missing?"

Stamford shook his head slowly. "He didn't make it, sir. I saw him after he was wounded. It was pretty bad. He caught a grenade. One of his people, a driver, said he died in the cab of a truck."

"Sorry to hear that."

"More sorry than you know, sir. It's not just about being a good soldier. Colonel Faith did everything in a man's power to get his people out of that jam. Somebody let him down, sir. It's not for me to say."

"Say it anyway, Captain."

Stamford seemed to study him for a long moment. "I'll not go on the record with this, sir. There's no future in it."

Smith let out a breath, sat down slowly beside the cot, a glance to the man beside Stamford, heavily bandaged around his face and head. "Captain, there's going to be hell to pay no matter what the facts are. Colonel Faith was part of my command, a choice I didn't make. But the responsibility for what happened up there is on my shoulders. Part of the job." He paused. "And, if nothing else, I would think Colonel Faith's family ought to know if he did something worth mentioning. Now, who let him down?"

Stamford glanced past Smith, no other ears close enough to hear. "They left us out in the cold, sir. Whoever made the decision to pull the tanks away. We made it down to where the armor had been based. I saw a busted-up tank myself at Hudong-ni. If those boys had been there, had they come up to help us out, it might have been different. Who gave that order, sir?"

Smith shook his head. "I can't say, Captain. I won't say, right now. Someone else will ask that question, somebody with more stars on his shoulder than I have."

"Sir, we were cut off completely. I did as much as I could with the air boys, and we took out a hell of a lot of Chinese. But there was no chance for us. The troops just sorta fell apart. They were green, sir, way too green to be sent out there like that. I don't fault the officers. I saw most of 'em go down. Good men, doing all they could to get their men to safety. There were too many Chinese. Everywhere you looked, every bend in the road, the enemy had occupied a ridgeline, a hill. They poured fire on us every yard we moved. I'll not say any more about the army, sir. I've already heard that kind of jabbering, that Marines would have walked out of there with enemy heads stuck on our bayonets. There's too much of that bull already flying around this tent." He paused, glanced around. "There was plenty of bull up there, too. General Almond flew up to see Colonel Faith."

"I know. He flew out of here."

"Well, sir, the general had a pocketful of medals with him, Silver Stars. He gave one to Faith, wanted to pass 'em out like party favors, give one to anybody who stepped up. When he left, Colonel Faith ripped it off his coat, dropped it in the snow. General Almond acted like he was doing us a favor just by showing up. Don Faith knew better. The general might as well have told those men they were being sacrificed, left to the four winds. Is that what the plan was, sir? '*You boys stepped in it, now figure out how to fix things yourself*'? It wasn't right, sir." He paused. "I ought not be saying this to you. When the morphine wears off, I'll wish like hell I'd have kept my mouth shut. Generals look out for each other, isn't that how it works?"

"Captain, nobody's looking out for me. I can't speak for General Almond, and I won't speak against him. But nobody's covering this up, and nobody is going to ignore what happened to Colonel Faith or his men."

Stamford turned his head, looked away. "If you say so, sir."

He could see the pain in Stamford's face, could tell the man was more angry than his wounds could tolerate. There was a pair of corpsmen watching him from across the tent, concern on their faces, and Smith stood slowly, fought the pains in his joints, knew he had taxed Stamford's energy. Stamford looked at him again, blinked wearily, unable to hide the pain, said, "Are you a religious man, sir?"

It was an odd question, but Smith had no reason to keep anything from this man.

"I follow the Christian Scientists, Captain. Yes, I am."

"I just want it known, and I'll put this *on* the record. I swear to you, sir, Colonel Faith did all he could to save his men. They didn't have the equipment, the weaponry, and most of the soldiers didn't have the experience or the training to do the job. And worse . . . it was like God was looking the other way. That's what it felt like. We were marching through the worst part of hell, and no one, not even God, paid any attention."

HAGARU-RI—DECEMBER 3, 1950, 2:00 P.M.

For the better part of the day, the radios had come alive in the command tent, word finally coming down from the main road northward, progress being made by Murray and Litzenberg. The fights were continuous, the Chinese anchored all along the route, but the reports continued to come, the latest that most of the column had pushed through Toktong Pass. Smith had stayed close, heard for himself the struggle of his men who pursued the enemy. By midafternoon the sounds of the fighting could be heard in Hagaru-ri, occasional thunder from artillery, or tank fire, the column halting long enough for the bigger guns to add their power to push away yet another Chinese roadblock. The Corsairs were there as well, formations roaring past, Smith welcoming the power they added to the fight.

He had gathered up most of his staff, no great challenge to that task, his headquarters still undermanned. He studied the faces, Bowser cheerful, as usual, Williams, the others waiting for whatever he would tell them to do.

"Have we heard anything more from the enemy north of here?"

Bowser shook his head, said, "No more than usual. Colonel Ridge hasn't indicated any signs that the Chinese are intending to hit us here. Their focus seems to be on the men coming down the main road."

Smith couldn't hide his anxiousness. "I'm not going to sit here and jabber on the radio while those men slug it out. We're not helpless. I want a force to move out on the main road, shove up as close as possible to the lead of the column, do what we can to eliminate the enemy who we know is standing in their way."

He was surprised to see Colonel Drysdale entering the tent, the usual spit and polish, clean-shaven, his uniform pressed.

"Oh, very sorry, sir. I did not mean to intrude. Just wanted to check on some extra rations for my wounded."

Smith didn't respond, the thought forming in his head. To one side, Colonel Williams said, "No matter. General, if you'll allow, I can see to Colonel Drysdale's request."

Smith shook his head. "I have a better idea. Colonel, are your men in position to embark on an assignment?"

Drysdale did not hesitate. "By all means, sir. My men are ready for any task you wish them to undertake."

"Then undertake this. Put them to the road, northward. I want them to get rid of the enemy troops who are on those closest hills. We've got a heavy column coming this way, and they've taken enough casualties."

Drysdale seemed to light up. "If you mean, sir, that we should open the path for those boys, I'm happy to oblige. Would it be possible to add some of your tanks to our efforts? Casualties are a certainty, as you know. That could help."

Smith looked at Bowser. "Colonel, order the Thirty-first Tank Company to roll out immediately, in support of the Royal Marines. Open that damn road."

HAGARU-RI—DECEMBER 3, 7:30 P.M.

With the darkness came the brutal cold, but Smith wouldn't keep to the command post. He had taken the jeep, others in line with him, moved out toward the limits of the perimeter to the north. The sounds of fighting had mostly stopped, scattered sounds coming from farther up the road, what remained of the struggle for the rear guard to hold the Chinese off the tail of the column. With the darkness, he had ordered Drysdale's men to withdraw, that if the Chinese were to make another assault, it was better if the perimeter was strong, avoiding confusion for the gunners who would target the high places along the road.

He put a hand out, the silent order for the driver to halt the jeep. Smith's eyes had adjusted to the gloomy night, his ears sheltered by the hooded coat, and he slipped the coat back, strained to hear. Around him, the others were doing the same, the men along the perimeter very aware why he was out there in the cold night. Within minutes he heard it, the rumble of trucks, the lone tank, and he stood tall in the jeep, absorbing the sounds. It was one moment of success in a campaign ripe with disasters, one mission fulfilled, by men he knew he could depend on. Their mission was not yet complete, the danger far from eliminated. But now, on this one night, for a long few minutes, he allowed himself to feel their pride, their relief.

They came in column, Ray Davis's men, the First Battalion, Seventh, led by Davis himself. Behind them came the first vehicles, trucks filled with wounded men, jeeps with corpses strapped to the hoods, more bodies lashed to any piece of equipment that could hold them, including the long barrels of the artillery pieces.

They approached the checkpoint, Colonel Ridge's roadblock, one foolish officer insisting that no one pass without offering up the current password. Davis responded as appropriately as he could, that no one in this column had any idea what the password was, and that the best idea for anyone manning the checkpoint was to move out of the way. The officer complied.

Just outside the checkpoint, the Royal Marines had performed one last dangerous task, eliminating an advance by a small body of enemy troops, what might have been a last costly firefight for the men down on the road. Their job complete, Drysdale's men positioned themselves along the line of march, welcoming the Americans with calls of good cheer, as well as cigarettes and chocolate bars.

With barely a quarter mile to go before entering the perimeter, Colonel Davis ordered a halt, passing the word that any man who could march would now do so. Obeying the call, the trucks held back, the Marines, including dozens of walking wounded, forming up in column. At Davis's command, they began to march once more, moving past the respectful salutes of the Royal Marines.

In his jeep, watching them come, Oliver Smith gave himself up to the moment, his own emotions wrapped around those of his men, as Davis's Marines, ragged and filthy and unshaven, made their way into Hagaru-ri, singing the words every Marine knew so well.

"From the halls of Montezuma, to the shores of Tripoli . . ."

CHAPTER THIRTY-FOUR

. . . .

Riley

HAGARU-RI, NORTH KOREA—DECEMBER 4, 1950, 3:00 A.M.

ALL ALONG THE MARCH, Riley had stayed close to the truck that carried so many of the wounded men, including Killian, who rode in the same truck as Lieutenant McCarthy. Around the truck were more wounded, men who could walk, no one trying to hitch a ride if it meant crowding those men who were so worse off.

They had come into Hagaru-ri several hours behind Davis's First Battalion, but the greeting they received was no less emotional, and no less enthusiastic. The British were there still, passing out hot coffee, which very quickly lost its burn. For men who had not tasted coffee in days, the cooling off was welcome. Tender faces also meant tender mouths, bleeding gums, and cracked lips. For some, including Riley, the lack of real food had drained their appetites, digestive systems impacted or shut down completely, most of the men unable to make use of a latrine since the assaults had begun. The medical staffs seemed to understand just how poor these men had become, that beneath the layers of frozen crust on their uniforms and faces, malnutrition and dehydration could create one more kind of bedridden casualty. But if a man was fit enough to avoid a visit to the aid station, the staffs guided them in another direction, where the hot food waited.

Riley followed the scent, not even his chapped and burnt nostrils able to disguise what was emerging from the mess tents. He followed Welch through the flaps of the big tent, the smells overwhelming now. Besides the amazing odors was the heat, and Riley felt swallowed by warmth, stopped, stared with tired eyes at the men who had already swarmed around the mess tables. They sat in long rows, some of the men barely holding themselves upright. Around them, the mess orderlies slid mounds of food in a steady procession in front of anyone who had the strength to empty his plate. Riley stepped closer, one hand on Welch's shoulder, trying to keep upright, staggering unsteadiness in his knees.

"Hey, you boys. There's seats over here."

Riley followed the voice, a smiling orderly with his hands on the backs of a pair of metal chairs. Welch stepped that way, Riley following numbly. They reached the chairs, and Welch sat heavily, Riley sliding in beside him. Across from him, a familiar face, one of Barber's aides, the man shoveling something thick and gooey into his mouth, a drool flowing down through the thick stubble on the man's chin. There was a plate put down in front of Riley now, and he absorbed the sight, had a sudden sense that this wasn't real, one more illusion after days of nightmares. No one was speaking, and Welch stuffed a fork into the pile on his plate, Riley fumbling for the fork with the fingers of his rotten gloves. He looked at his hands, tugged at the gloves, pulled them free from his swollen red fingers, tried to pick up the fork, dropped it, and across from him the man said, "Just use your hands, if you have to. Worth it. Best damn pancakes I ever ate."

Riley put his fingers on the soft mass on his plate, probed, the man smiling, then stuffing a blob of food into his mouth. Beside him, Welch mumbled something, slid a large can toward him, and Riley saw now it was syrup. His mind seemed to wake just a bit more, the smells drilling into his hunger, the juices in his mouth beginning to flow, uncontrollable, his tongue pushing through the dry crust on his lips. He reached out, took the can, poured the syrup clumsily across his plate, the thick liquid pouring out onto the table, an instant mess. He set the can down, wiped at the spill with his fingers, glanced around, embarrassed, heard the orderly behind him.

"Don't worry, sport. There's plenty more. Just eat up. More coffee here?"

The orderly put two coffeepots on the table, some of the men reaching out, pouring a steaming brew into tin cups. Beside him, Welch said, "You gonna eat those things, or do I have to show you how?"

Riley grabbed the fork again, stabbed a thick wad of pancakes, now a soft, gooey blob, stuffed it into his mouth. Across from him, more smiles.

"See? Told you so. Cures what's wrong. I'm stuffed to the gills. There's more of us coming in. I'll make room. Enjoy that, while you can."

The man slid back, moved away, happy talk toward some of the others. More men were coming into the tent, like Riley, moving toward the table with wide, puzzled eyes.

He was more energized than he had been in days, the rich sugar from the syrup rolling through his veins like gasoline. The darkness was complete, no stars, just the usual wind, and he felt like returning to the mess tent, his mind embracing the astonishing luxury of the pancakes. But the corpsmen had cautioned them all, especially any man whose bowels had shut down, don't overdo it. What goes in had to come out eventually, and already some of the men were suffering the agony of diarrhea.

He watched more men coming out of the mess tent, a stark contrast to those still going in, men groaning in the darkness with hands on their bellies. He couldn't help smiling, thought, Whoever thought of making up those pancakes gets a Medal of Honor. If they'd have told us that's what was waiting for us, we mighta beat hell out of the Chinese a whole lot sooner.

He stood alone in the cold dark, wasn't sure just where to go, Welch off searching for officers, someone to tell them where they were supposed to be. All around the compound, men were standing in groups, huddling together against the windy cold. There were walking wounded as well, corpsmen guiding those men to the aid tents or the larger hospital, what seemed to resemble a ramshackle schoolhouse. Riley felt the cold again, leaking into his coat, his toes numb, his hands stuffed into his coat pocket. He looked toward the aid tents, trucks parked nearby, one more being unloaded, the stretcher bearers moving quickly, a doctor pointing the way. He had no idea what Killian's truck had looked like, just one more out of dozens, but the guilt came now, a full belly, the stickiness still on his fingers. They must feed the wounded, he thought. Got to. His mind was racing now, thoughts of Captain Barber, the lieutenant, and all those men who had been carried off the hill in closed-up sleeping bags. Already, the Graves Registration people had gone to work, logging the names, checking them against the rosters from Fox Company, other companies, so many men hauled down from Yudamni. There were the missing, too, two men from Third Platoon simply gone, no sign of them, whether they had been captured, or simply buried in some snowy hole under a mass of Chinese bodies. Riley had been a part of the search, the team discovering one other corpse, a Marine from First Platoon who had moved out too far, cut down by the enemy, freezing stiff before anyone knew he was gone. All along the march down from the pass, he had thought of what they had left up on the hill, the amazing scene, so many Chinese bodies spread out across every stretch of open ground. Someone had made a count, Barber's aides maybe, estimating a thousand enemy soldiers scattered in front of the guns on Fox Hill. Davis's First Battalion had been the first to see that, their approach bringing them over the mass of enemy dead. Those Marines had offered salutes for that, raucous congratulations to the men of Fox Company for a job well done. They're still up there, he thought. Nobody buried them, nobody hauled 'em off. And one day it's gonna be spring. Then what? Somebody goes out there and finds 'em? Not a job I'd want.

"Hey, Pete. You get some pancakes?"

He knew the voice of Morelli, saw the kid bounding toward him, more energy than usual.

"Yeah. I won't eat for a week."

"I know. Me, too. Haven't had coffee that good since I left home. You might wanna go back inside. Just as I was getting up, they starting putting out beef stew, noodles, and God knows what else. It's like Christmas dinner and Easter Sunday rolled into one."

"Not me, kid. Had all I could handle. What the hell time is it?"

Morelli shrugged. "Maybe three. I'm gonna wait for dawn, then have breakfast."

Riley wasn't in the mood for cheeriness, but he couldn't escape Morelli, the kid beside him now, an overeager puppy. Riley said, "The sarge is off finding out what's up. You oughta go look for him."

Morelli didn't get the hint, said, "They say we're leaving this place pretty quick. I also heard we're supposed to stay here until spring, holding the fort and all. The enemy's getting ready to hit us hard. Someone said that, too. Someone else said the war's over, the enemy's done quit. There's an army unit got busted up out east of the reservoir. I heard they might want us to go up thataway. Someone else—"

"And someone else said there's a truck full of gorgeous Hollywood stars on their way here, just to lay a wet kiss on you. Jesus, kid, you oughta know better than to listen to all this crap. When they want us to move, or fight, or eat more pancakes, they'll let us know."

"I know. I just . . . I wasn't sure I'd ever see any of this again. Look how many we are. Two whole regiments made it back here. Or what's left of 'em. You see all those British guys, all spiffed up, like right out of a picture book? One of 'em slapped me on the back, handed me a pack of cigarettes. Guess I'll start smoking. Don't wanna hurt anybody's feelings."

Through the dull glow from the lantern light, he spotted Welch, moving toward him, a hard scowl on his face. Riley was grateful for the distraction, said, "What's up, Sarge?"

"They've got a pile of warming tents set up for us over that way. The captain's in that big tent right there. He's not in command anymore."

Riley felt a jolt. "Why?"

"He's shot up too bad. I talked to Lieutenant Abell, the new CO. He's from First Battalion. The captain and Lieutenant McCarthy are both being shipped out. Peterson, too. They're finding somebody to take over Third Platoon from the replacements that are coming up here. Transports are hauling new guys in from the ships. Looks like we might get another ninety-day wonder."

"Jesus, Hamp."

Welch stared away, and Riley knew him well enough to know he was holding back emotion. Riley said, "It might not be all that bad. There's probably some good officers still back in Pendleton."

Welch still stared away. "Yeah. Like Goolsby."

Riley didn't want to think about him, had tried not to recall the image of the man's wound, the small river of blood freezing to his forehead.

"I think we oughta go see the captain, if it's okay. And I wanna find Killian."

Welch looked at him again, nodded. "Yeah. I miss that Irish idiot. Maybe his wife's sent some more of that good hooch."

Welch started toward the larger tents, Morelli hanging back. Riley looked at him, motioned with his hand.

"Come on, kid."

Welch led the way to the tent, men emerging with empty stretchers, another truck rumbling up close. Riley looked that way, the faint light from a handful of lanterns reflecting off a mound of bodies lashed to the truck's hood. The driver jumped down now, his arm bandaged, the man staggering to his knees. Riley moved that way, caught the man before he collapsed in the snow. He called out to the corpsmen, "Hey! Right here! He's hurt."

The stretcher bearers moved out from behind the truck, a man hauled between them, one of them calling out, "Corpsman!"

Another man appeared out of the big tent now, and Riley stood back, the corpsman kneeling down, talking to the driver, reaching into the man's coat, one hand on the man's neck. The corpsman backed away, still on his knees, the driver tilting slowly, falling to one side. Riley moved closer, said, "Hey, what the hell? Help him inside."

The corpsman looked at him, then away, stood slowly, held out one hand, covered in wet blood.

"He didn't make it. Hole in his chest. Musta had just enough left in him to get his buddies here. I been seeing this all night. Just about every truck driver is shot up. This one's a hero."

Riley felt a hand on his shoulder, the voice of Welch.

"You can't fix it, Pete. Let's go inside."

Riley kept his eyes on the driver, felt the agonizing helplessness, so familiar now. Like Goolsby, he thought.

"Yeah. I gotta see Killian. Make sure he's okay."

They moved into the tent, more stretcher bearers coming out past them, another truck rolling up, a squeal of brakes, another load of wounded, more corpses tied to the hood.

He didn't expect to see tears, Killian's words coming out in a spray of cursing.

"They're shipping me out! Damn it all! I might never walk again, that's what one jackass said. Crippled up forever! On account of these damn shoe pac boot things."

Riley stood silently, Morelli beside him, Welch coming up now.

"Hey, Irish. Guess you'll get your Purple Heart. I talked to that guy in the white coat. He says you're going home tomorrow."

It was Welch's effort at cheerfulness, and Killian said, "Keep the damn medal. Give me back my feet. What's my wife gonna say? They gotta give me a fake foot, maybe half a leg."

Killian's voice was carrying, faces looking that way, and Riley felt uncomfortable now, said, "You're going home, Sean. Ain't that enough? You're alive, for Chrissakes."

Killian turned away, the tears still flowing. Riley glanced at Welch, expected anger, saw it. But Welch spoke in low words, his voice calm. "I just saw Captain Barber. He took a bad wound on his thigh, just below his groin. *Walking* may not be the worst thing he misses. There's a guy over there who's lost half his face. A half dozen down this next row missing a whole limb, some more than one. Tell *them* how bad your wife is gonna feel."

Killian looked at Welch, then lay back, closed his eyes. After a long moment, he said, "I don't wanna go home, Sarge. I know I'm not all that busted up. But you guys are the whole thing, you know? I got nothing back home. I couldn't hardly get a job before, and now I'm a gimp. Everybody in this place says how great it is that I'm not dead." He paused. "Up on that hill . . . I kinda felt like it was the right place to cash it all in. Like it was my time. I ain't never done anything in my life that felt as good as that. When those Shambos were close enough to smell, God, Sarge, it was *fun*. Now, I have to go home and be . . . normal."

HAGARU-RI—DECEMBER 4, 9:00 A.M.

As they waited for the planes to land, the medical aides had laid the wounded under thick piles of rice straw, each man inside a sleeping bag, no one complaining, even if they were cold. Some of the men were unconscious, heavy doses of morphine, others more excited to be awake, their wounds not erasing the joy at the sight of the C-47s that would haul them south.

There were others, too, the quiet ones, and Riley saw faces looking at him, could feel the guilt, the odd need to stay out here, that even if they couldn't fight, they didn't want to leave their units, or abandon the men who had shared the foxholes. Riley stayed close to Killian, neither man speaking, Riley fighting the cold, while the Irishman fought his tears.

The plane touched down, the ground crews moving quickly, and Riley watched as the plane disgorged its passengers, a dozen men who stepped onto the icy tarmac like green sausages. Replacements, he thought. He was curious about them, saw men with bandaged hands, their coats worn, dirty, others cloaked in everything fresh. Maybe they're ours, he thought. God, I hope not.

Welch had learned that Fox Company had barely sixty effective men, but Lieutenant Abell was anticipating a hundred new faces. And none of them will be Killian, he thought. They'll be like the kid, too eager and too stupid, and it will take blood and bullets to teach them anything.

"Okay, load 'em up!"

Riley stood back, the crews moving to the wounded men, sweeping away the straw, each man carried quickly toward the open maw of the plane's belly. He looked again at Killian, saw red eyes staring back, struggled to say something, anything that would matter.

"Hey, Sean! They got nurses on those hospital ships, you know." There was no response from Killian, and Riley felt idiotic. The crews worked their way down the row, the man beside Killian carried off now. Riley moved closer again, put a hand on Killian's arm. "Time to go. It'll be okay. Your wife will be happy as hell to see you. I promise."

Killian nodded, more tears, said, "I know. I hate leaving this. That's all. Maybe they'll fix me up and I'll be back."

"Go home, Sean. Go plant some flowers and mow your grass, and maybe hatch a couple more kids."

"You sound like Colleen. That's what she wants."

"It's what we all want. Some of us just don't know it yet."

The stretcher bearers were there now, a quick glance at Riley, and one man said, "Heads up. You're the last one on this run. Another plane coming in a few minutes."

Killian held out a hand, and Riley took it, a hard squeeze. The bearers paused, but Riley could feel their impatience, no one enjoying the cold. He backed away, Killian up and moving, the rumble from the plane's engines sweeping away his words. Riley watched as he was loaded on the plane, felt a man moving up beside him. He glanced to the side, saw Welch, who said, "He gone?"

"Yep."

He saw now, Welch holding a package, and Welch said, "Mail run. Came in this morning. Looks like his wife sent another loaf of bread."

Riley looked out toward the plane, moving away now, rolling out toward the strip. "Guess he wouldn't need it anyway."

Welch shook his head. "Nah. They'd have taken it away from him. Regulations, and all."

Riley looked at the fat package, Welch staring at the plane. Riley said, "So, what say we go drink a toast. To Irishmen everywhere."

"In a minute."

Riley heard a crack in Welch's voice, both men watching the plane taxi to the far end of the strip, a hard roar of the engines, the plane moving slowly, gaining speed, lifting off as it passed by. They were both silent, stood for a long moment, and he looked at Welch, the thick grime through the man's ragged beard, red eyes, and icy tears.

CHAPTER THIRTY-FIVE

. . . .

Smith

"OH, LORD. HE'S BACK."

Smith looked up from the papers on the small table, saw Bowser at the window. There was a loud clatter from the next room, a voice calling out, "General Smith! General Almond wishes to see you outside on the double."

Smith sat back in the small chair, said, "I was just about warm. How many of our dead have we shipped out today?"

Bowser kept his gaze out the window. "Forty-six. Eight more are wrapped and ready. He's talking to the men. Anyone who will stop long enough to listen to him."

"Make sure those eight get on the planes today. I know Doc Hering has more wounded he wants out of here, but I want the corpses moved out just as quick. I don't intend to leave trucks or artillery here, and I'm sure as hell not leaving the dead."

Bowser looked at him now, knew Smith was serious. "I'll see to it. The last plane in, one of the R4Ds, had another handful of replacements, some of the lightly wounded from Hungnam. And the reporters keep flocking in as well."

Smith pulled himself up from the chair. "I don't give a hoot about reporters."

Sexton was at the door now, said, "Sir, there's a lieutenant here who says General Almond doesn't care to be kept waiting. They're looking for you to meet with him outside."

Smith felt tired resignation, said, "You may tell the impatient lieutenant I'm coming."

"You just told him yourself, sir."

Smith saw the man peering in over Sexton's shoulder, ignored him, saw his coat in Sexton's hands. He turned, Sexton holding the coat, Smith sliding his arms into the sleeves. He looked at Bowser, saw the hint of a smile.

"Don't be so smug. You're coming, too. He might have questions I don't feel like answering."

Bowser retrieved his own coat, said, "I had no doubts, sir. I aim only to please."

"Don't we all."

He moved out past Almond's young aide, still ignored him, Sexton holding the door open, a blast of cold wind greeting Smith as he stepped outside. He saw Almond, a half-dozen men gathered around him, an audience that Almond was addressing with obvious enthusiasm. Smith moved that way, his men responding by backing away. Almond saw him now, said, "Ah, Smith! You receive my congratulatory letter this morning?"

The letter had come that morning by wire, a gush of praise for Smith and his regimental commanders, as though Almond had never been angry at anyone in Smith's command.

"We did. Thank you."

"Nothing to it. And there's more. I should like the lot of you to receive the Distinguished Service Cross. Perfectly appropriate, under the circumstances. Can you pull them together? The colonels, Murray and Litzenberg? Perhaps your artillery man, too."

"Colonel Youngdale."

"Sure, him, too. But be quick about it. I have a rather busy schedule today. I do intend to visit Colonel Puller on my way south, so no need to bother him with this now. I'll save him the trip up here."

Smith absorbed Almond's good cheer, thought, Does he know just how many Chinese are sitting between here and Koto-ri? Well, no, he flew above it all. He looked at Bowser, said, "I suppose we should get the word to all three commanders. Tell them to meet here on the double."

"Well, damn it all!" Almond was searching his pockets, obviously frustrated. "It seems I only have the one medal. Well, Smith, here it is. You might as well take it. I can have others sent up here for the rest of you."

Smith held his words inside, fought the temptation to tell Almond just where to put the medal. Beside him, Bowser leaned in closer, said, "Sir, how about Colonel Beall?"

Smith smiled to himself, said, "General Almond, as much as my senior officers and I appreciate your gesture, we can wait for another day. However, I would very much prefer to see Lieutenant Colonel Olin Beall receive that medal. He was in command of our efforts to rescue a good many survivors of Task Force Faith. Pulled in a sizable amount of the battalion right off the ice, under the nose of Chinese snipers. Exemplary job."

"Beall, huh? Sounds good. Newspapers will like that. Take some of the sting out of the reports about Faith's, um, problems. Find him for me, will you?"

Smith looked at Bowser, who moved away quickly.

Almond looked again toward the small gathering of Marines, as though hoping once more for an audience. Smith felt the cold slicing through every seam in the coat, said, "Sir, might we move this inside?"

Almond weighed the request for a long second. "No. This won't take long, and my aircraft is waiting. I told the boy to keep the engine running. Helps with the heat." Almond seemed to have a sudden thought. "My chief of staff, General Ruffner, tells me you're removing your dead from here. Taking up a good bit of space on the cargo planes. That a wise move?"

"It's the only move. I'll not leave anyone behind, if I can help it. These men deserve a proper burial."

Almond shrugged, seemed unwilling to argue the point. Smith had already received a protest from Ruffner, paid no attention to the man's reasoning, that such *cargo* was taking up space from goods far more use-ful. If either Ruffner or Almond decided to blow this into something larger, Smith knew that the reporters would leap on the story. And Al-mond would lose. Smith was becoming miserable now, had forgotten his thick wool hat.

"General, I'm going back inside. If you require my presence for your ceremony, I'll return."

He didn't wait for a response, moved toward his quarters, Sexton opening the door. Smith said, "I suppose it makes him more of a warrior if he stands out there and gets frostbite. Colonel Beall can have his medal. He earned it."

Sexton hung the coat up beside the door, said, "Sir, when Colonel Beall finds out he's getting his medal by listening to some speech out in that wind, he might teach General Almond a few words the army's not heard before."

HAGARU-RI—DECEMBER 5, 1950, 10:00 A.M.

The staff saw her first, Smith detecting a low whistle from the house's main room. He looked out that way, heard another whistle, and now, Sexton, eyes wide, standing in his doorway.

"Sir, you're not going to believe this. That dame is here."

Smith had no patience for mysteries, said, "What *dame?*"

He heard the door now, the creak of the hinges, a hard slam, a cho-rus of voices. And one particular voice, responding to the obvious atten-tion. It belonged to a woman.

Sexton glanced behind him, held the stare for a long second, then looked back at Smith. "*This* dame, sir."

She was there now, no formal request, just pushing past Sexton as though he was merely in the way. "Maggie Higgins, General. *New York Herald Tribune.* Mind if I sit in on a few of your discussions? I like to go right to the heart of it."

Smith felt pressed back in his chair, her presence as full of energy as anything he had felt from Chesty Puller. She was tall, younger than he expected, and even in fatigues, Smith could see why the men reacted to her. For men who had not seen anything *female* in weeks, she fit the definition perfectly.

"Miss Higgins, I had heard you were in the theater. I didn't think you'd land here. This isn't exactly the kind of place I'd expect a woman. . . ."

"I knew you'd throw that at me. Let me tell you something, General. I'm just as capable and just as willing to take risks as any man in the press pool. I've interviewed boys while they were bleeding, or being shot at. They didn't give me a Pulitzer Prize because I've got great legs. I hope you don't intend to keep me from doing my job."

He felt overwhelmed, sat up straight. Behind her, he could see a variety of faces, his aides, overwhelmed in ways of their own. He stood, tugged at his jacket, his brain screaming caution.

"Miss Higgins, I have far more to worry about than a flock of reporters. But that doesn't mean you are not my responsibility."

"I intend to march out of here with your men. It's the best way I can get an accurate story of what their experiences have been like. The American people are begging for the story, just what it has been like for these men. It's no secret that this could have been a very different kind of story, a postmortem. The men who fought their way out of certain disaster deserve to have their stories told."

"You may write whatever you please. But you will not march alongside my men."

She seemed to grow angrier now, hands on her hips. "You would discriminate against me because I am a woman. I expected as much."

He let out a breath, glanced up behind her, hoping to see Bowser. "Miss Higgins, it is precisely because you are a woman that I cannot have you marching in column with my men."

She made a sound, was red-faced now, and he felt a surge of desperation, called out, "Where is Colonel Bowser? Find him!"

"Is my being a woman a threat to you, General? Do you feel I am too fragile to march?"

He felt anger himself now, took a deep breath, the word rolling over again in his brain. *Careful.* "Miss Higgins, I am not threatened by you or any other woman, except perhaps my wife when she's royally angry. I am well aware that you being here is a distraction, as are *you*. My men have a difficult job in front of them that will very likely involve heavy combat. There will also be casualties due to the cold, frostbite cases, and whatnot. Should you become injured in any way, I know how my men will respond. Their attention will be diverted. They will do all they can to ensure your safety, or they will compete to see who will take care of you. I am sure that these men would go to any length to take care of you, and we haven't time for that kind of business. Such a distraction could be dangerous, if not to you, then to my men. I won't have it. You will board the next plane out of here."

Bowser was laughing, and Smith held his scowl, was in no mood for it.

"Where were you?"

"I came as soon as they found me. But you appear to have weathered the storm."

Smith jabbed the pipe into his mouth. "She'll write this up, you know. Paint a picture of me like some sort of barbarian. We don't need this kind of nonsense, Alpha. Not one bit!"

Bowser laughed again. "We're Marines, sir. To most people that makes us barbarians. No harm will come, surely."

"She wanted to go out with the troops. Can you see that? These men haven't seen an American woman in ages."

"She's a comely lass, too. Oh, there would be fistfights, I'm sure."

Smith looked at him, still the scowl. "Nothing's funny about this, Colonel."

Bowser looked down, stifled the smile. "I apologize, sir. But you have to admit, she added a little spice to your day."

"I don't admit any such thing. Make sure she gets on that plane. She's taking up a wounded man's space. Somebody down there should have stopped her before now."

"I don't think anyone had the guts."

Smith felt his anger calming, Bowser's good humor contagious. He tasted the pipe, allowed himself to enjoy the smoke, and Bowser said, "She's spitting mad, that's for sure. But she'll get over it. I heard the other reporters talking about her. None of 'em are as fired up to march out of here as she is. I'm guessing she'll be waiting for us down the road a ways."

Smith pulled the pipe from his mouth. "Where?"

"Well, the rest of 'em are mostly going to Koto-ri. I imagine she'll do the same." Bowser laughed again, and Smith knew why, the scene forming in his mind. "I'd love to be there to see it, sir. I wonder if she'll march into Colonel Puller's HQ with that much vinegar."

Smith couldn't help a smile. "I hope so. At least I was polite."

HAGARU-RI—DECEMBER 5, 2:30 P.M.

He had promised the reporters a news conference. There were few secrets to protect, the operation in front of them straightforward. Litzenberg would lead the way south while Murray's men did what they could to sweep the enemy away from the east hill, protecting the march from the rear.

Around him now, Colonel Ridge's perimeter had been enormously strengthened, the Marines in Hagaru-ri numbering nearly ten thousand effectives. The Chinese had seemed completely aware that any assault now would be even more costly than their attacks thus far, and so the enemy was keeping mostly quiet. The one primary sticking point for the position at Hagaru-ri was the east hill, where enemy troops continued to make themselves a dangerous nuisance. It would be Murray's job to sweep them away, removing eyes as well as guns from the best vantage point the Chinese now had. As long as the Chinese seemed content to hang back, the movement out of Hagaru-ri might not be as dangerous as what the commanders had already dealt with at Yudam-ni. And if the Chinese made an effort to attack the town, Smith had planned on heavy air support, the Corsairs and air force planes poised to blanket the enemy's positions. Any aggressive assault by the Chinese would have to absorb the kind of firepower the Chinese had seemed increasingly unwilling to chance.

He moved across the frozen ground, his boots cracking the thin sheet of ice that seemed to drape over every surface. The entire convoy from Yudam-ni was now safely in Hagaru-ri, and Smith had ordered them to rest and refit as much as possible, allowing both Murray and Litzenberg forty-eight hours to put their men back into shape. With the refit, including weapons and warm-weather gear, was the matter of distributing the replacements who had been flown up from Hungnam, close to six hundred men now, rebuilding the platoons and companies that had lost so many of their number. The newly healed wounded would of course return to their units, while the new men would be assigned where they were needed most.

The able survivors from Don Faith's command had been formed into a temporary battalion numbering close to four hundred men. Smith had no idea how effective those men might be in a fight, and already there were rumblings among some of the Marine officers that the army troops should simply be kept out of the way. Smith would entertain none of that, knew that these men had seen the worst a war can be, most all of them losing friends as well as commanders. There had always been the friction between the services, and now Smith began to hear that many of the Marines were unhappy marching alongside the soldiers, many of Faith's men offering no enthusiasm at all for another stiff fight. But Smith had no patience for squabbles. The soldiers were still capable, had been regrouped and rearmed, and in the campaign Smith had planned, their numbers were certainly needed. If they were unwilling to fight on, that was a mindset Smith couldn't fathom.

He thought of Almond's last boasting pledge, as the man moved out toward his small plane. *I'll give you all the B-17s and B-29s you need. We'll open up a clean path all the way to the ocean.* Smith felt a growl inside of him, thought, Almond looked like he was about to break down and cry, as though there was some kind of gooey sentiment attached to such an offer. I suppose that's how he thinks. It's all so simple. Bombs and big guns, and the enemy will melt away. Victory, just like that. Have none of them learned what kind of enemy this is? I wonder how many of these newspaper people think the same way.

He was astounded to learn just how much press coverage the plight of the Marines was receiving in the States, that every news report began with the certain doom that was swallowing the First Marine Division. So, he thought, if it's not MacArthur telling them we've won this thing before it even began, it's MacArthur or someone else telling them that all is lost. Why don't those people wait until the story ends, one way or the other, before they tell the whole country how bad off we are? I suppose I'll get my chance to preach about that right now. He stopped, looked at the large tent, saw a team of MPs, eyes watching him, men doing their job. Smith hesitated another moment, thought, God, I hate interviews.

"If you have any further questions, I'll do my best to give you a straight answer. I expect all of you to board the planes by tonight and return to, well, wherever it is you came from. I do not need civilians marching alongside men under fire. And I assure you, we will be under fire. We will begin our advance very early tomorrow morning."

"Sir, you used the word *advance*. Shouldn't we describe your next operation as a retreat, or perhaps simply a withdrawal?"

He detected a British accent, one of a half-dozen reporters that had gathered in the larger tent.

"We're not doing either one. Where the enemy is blocking our path, we will confront him. As you know, we are surrounded, and so we will have to fight our way out. I have issued attack orders to all my commanders. It just happens that this time, we're advancing in another direction."

Within twenty-four hours, the reporters had made the best use of the wire services, telephone, and any other communication line that would carry their stories. Very soon after, the word filtered back to Smith's headquarters, various responses coming to him from the quote now attributed to him, a ringing cry that began to appear in headlines in every newspaper that carried the story. For Smith, the twist to his words was

amusing, and unlike so many misquotes attributed to military commanders, he saw this one as positive. The language now was a bit raw for
his taste, but the sentiment conveyed his message perfectly, a message
that he intended more for his own men.

"Retreat, hell. We're just attacking in another direction."

CHAPTER THIRTY-SIX

. . . .

Riley

HAGARU-RI, NORTH KOREA—DECEMBER 6, 1950, 4:30 A.M.

THE BONFIRES HAD BEGUN the day before, anything not carried off by the Marines and army troops to be destroyed. The orders were specific and detailed, the order of march, the assignment for Murray's Fifth to remain behind, long enough to prevent the enemy from striking at Hagaru-ri, until the entire force had cleared the area. To the surprise of Riley and everyone around him, Fox Company was chosen to move out first, leading the way south, the point of the entire convoy. The trucks would follow, spread out all through the column of marching men, while up the hills to the right, Marines from the Seventh's Charlie and Baker Companies would clear away any Chinese troops who attempted to interfere. Above the road to the left, the army's newly formed Seventh Regiment, what remained of Task Force Faith, would tackle the job. If there were doubts about the army's abilities in a fight, the orders had mentioned nothing about it. Immediately behind Fox Company, four Sherman tanks were fueled up and put into line, though in the deep freeze of the predawn, the crews were struggling to fire up the engines. But the schedule was precise, and so, as the tanks finally coughed to life, the men of Fox Company were already moving out.

The goal was to reach Chesty Puller's perimeter at Koto-ri, and in between lay elements of five Chinese divisions, with at least nine road-blocks identified by reconnaissance planes.

Riley was shivering, nervous energy, the cold filling his lungs as energizing as it was painful. He had never thought about going into combat again, the *next time,* but like most of Fox Company, he accepted that their job was not yet complete. No matter how many they had killed, no one believed the Chinese would simply turn around and go home. Within an hour of leaving the southern perimeter of Hagaru-ri, the Chinese made it very clear that they were still on the heights, and still intended to make a fight of it.

Riley's arms were clamped tight against him, his breathing in hard bursts, no one talking. He kept behind Welch, his usual place in line, Morelli across from him. He had missed Killian immediately, the idiotic chatter that livened up any march. But the men close to him now were silent, some of those the replacements, nervous and excited men, who had welcomed the order to lead the way. He had met most of them, brief exchanges, and like the other veterans, Riley made very little effort to buddy up to anyone. Some of the new men were older, leftovers from World War II, many of those volunteering in response to the awful news that flowed across the pages of stateside newspapers. Their arrival at Hagaru-ri was mostly without fanfare, the grim acceptance of veterans that they were needed, warm bodies to fill the gaps left by so many casualties. The new recruits were wholly different, and Riley had seen too much of that already, boisterous backslapping introductions from boys who thought they were men. But the weather offered a rude slap that the *adventure* for these new Marines was not what they expected. Very quickly, the new men appreciated the value of the heavy coats, and many did what Riley had done long before he reached Fox Hill, tossing away the helmet, relying instead on the wool hat and the hood of the parka to prevent frozen ears.

It was mostly dark, the hint of dawn showing a gloomy blanket of fog over the hills around him. He kept his gaze downward, shielding his face from a steady spray of windblown snow. Another glorious day, he thought. Maybe it'll keep the Chinese in their caves. He had a new thought, sweeping away his optimism. Or maybe it will keep the Corsairs from seeing anything on the ground. Christ, nothing glorious about that.

There was scattered firing up the hill to the right, a brief exchange, silence now. He felt the jump in his chest, one hand gripping the rifle close beside him. Already? Maybe we woke 'em up. Surprise, Chinamen, now get the hell out of our way. We got someplace better to be. He felt the weight of the excess ammo on his belt, in his pockets, thought, Hope I ain't gotta use it all up. The Thompson was gone, Riley relying again on the M-1, much more useful at long range. He felt the tug of the fully loaded backpack, thought, It's only a few miles away, so why'd they tell us to load up with so much stuff? He thought of the fires again, understood why the supply officers had opened up the PX, offering the men as much as they could carry, free of charge. From bitter experience, the veterans grabbed up things they could eat, and not the canned goods that turned quickly to blocks of ice. They had learned by now that candy was far more useful, thawing out in your mouth, and so they grabbed up enormous amounts of caramel and chocolate bars, and of course, Tootsie Rolls. He had scooped up as much of that as the others around him, encouraged by the supply officers. Like a Christmas sale at Sears, he thought. *Half off, one hour only.* Ruthie goes nuts for that. Not sure I'll ever want to look at another candy bar, even free ones.

He could see glimpses of the hill to the right, like so many others, tall and wide, little cover but scrub brush and snowdrifts. He heard more firing up to the right, thought, That's supposed to be Charlie Company. He looked ahead, past Welch, Lieutenant Dunne's First Platoon already up past a curve in the road. He glanced up the hill again, still nothing to see, thought of the Chinese. They had to know we were doing this, he thought. They saw the bonfires, surely. We either burn that stuff or let them have it all, and that's probably not a good idea. I wonder if they know what a Tootsie Roll is?

He heard the rumble of the tanks coming up from behind, saw a man moving back toward him, breathing a thick fog. It was the new

CO, Lieutenant Abell, halting in the road, waving toward the lead tank. The tank slowed, and Abell climbed up onto the rear of the machine, dug out the intercom telephone, shouted something, still shouting as the tank rolled past Riley. Abell climbed up on the tank's turret, pounding angrily on the hatch, and Riley heard the words now, "Open the damn hatch, you jackass!" The tank stopped now, the hatch opening slightly, Abell's face down low, hot talk Riley couldn't hear. The lieutenant backed away, jumped down, and the turret began to turn, the big gun pointing out to one side of the road. Riley was curious, followed the aim, saw a small cabin barely visible against the hillside, a hint of movement there, and the tank's gun erupted, a loud *thump*, the cabin shattered in a fiery blast. Abell shouted out toward Welch, "Take your squad up there. Check it out. Eyes open!"

Welch called out, "First squad, up the hill! Let's go!"

Riley followed, questions in his mind, a half-dozen men moving with him. They ran as quickly as the shoe pacs would allow, Riley already gasping for air, the usual burn in his throat and lungs. They were there quickly, and he kept his eyes on Welch, saw him pointing the Thompson toward the wreckage of the cabin. Riley saw the small fires, the remnants of the blast, and scattered through the wreckage, bodies of the enemy.

"You heard the LT. Keep your damn eyes open!"

Riley studied the Chinese soldiers, some of them in mangled pieces, was surprised to see two of them cloaked in American coats. "Hey, Sarge! You sure they're Chinese?"

Welch pushed into the shattered timbers, reached down, rolled one man over, said, "They're Chinks. I guess they been souvenir hunting, too." He called out, "Now listen up! You didn't even know these bastards were up here! Lieutenant Abell spotted them. They're just letting us pass by for now. Seen this before. They just watch us, then when we think we're safe, they smack us from behind. Or the men behind us, the trucks, think we've cleared the way, and they get slammed from the flanks. Keep your eyes alert. It's full daylight soon."

Riley knew most of that was aimed at the new men, and he moved closer to Welch, a low voice, "Did you spot them?"

Welch slung the Thompson on his shoulder. "Hell no. I was kinda enjoying the peace and quiet. I guess we gotta figure they're out here on every damn hill."

"I suppose we owe the lieutenant for this one. They coulda hit us hard."

Welch moved to another body, kicked it lightly. "That's why he wears the silver bar. Let's get back to the road. We're holding up the whole works."

The Chinese were firing from behind a burnt-out jeep, other wreckage blocking the road. Riley had rolled down low in the snowy grass, close beside the road, more firing coming down from the hill to the left. He pulled himself small, no cover at all, the chatter of machine gun fire raking the road beside him. The men around him were returning fire, and Riley slid the M-1 up to his shoulder, peered up carefully, then down flat again. The roadblock was just past a curve in the road, two hundred yards away. In front of him, a loud shout, "Where's that damn tank?"

More men were calling out, and Riley heard a loud grunt, too familiar. He turned that way, saw blood on the hood of the man's coat, a large rip across the back of the man's head. He felt a jolt, shouted out, "Corpsman!"

"Not now! He's had it!" He knew the voice, Welch, sliding up close. "I saw him hit. He raised up his head, and I was just about to give him hell. The bullet went through him, hit me in the arm."

"Who . . . ?"

"New guy. That Georgia cracker. Christ, this hurts."

Riley felt a burst of alarm, scanned Welch's coat. "Where? You hit bad? You need a corpsman?"

"Don't think so. His brains slowed it down. My coat did the rest. Mighta busted a bone."

"Let me see it."

"Go to hell. We got an enemy up there. Find somebody to shoot at."

A machine gun opened up on the heights above them, the icy road peppered again. Riley pulled himself in tight, felt Welch beside him, rolling over. The Thompson fired now, then stopped, Welch shouting, "He's right above us! That clump of brush. Take him out!"

The men on both sides of the road responded, a chorus of firing, and Riley saw the muzzle of the machine gun protruding from a brushy thicket. He slid the M-1 up, aimed, fired, then again. The machine gun went silent, but he saw the grenade now, a high arc, tumbling down, bouncing on the hard road. Others saw it as well, shouts, *"Grenade!"*

The blast sprayed him with hard dirt, and there was more rifle fire, another machine gun opening up from the roadblock ahead. Riley gasped for air, the cold forgotten, saw Welch's face, crusted with dirt and ice. Welch said, "You okay?"

Riley took a long breath, said, "Think so. A few feet shorter and we'd have shared that grenade between us."

"Yeah. Where the hell is that tank?"

The answer came now, behind them, the hard thump of the gun, a blast impacting the roadblock. Another came now, and in front of them, a shout, "Up! Hit 'em!"

The men began to rise, Welch up quickly, Riley beside him. In front of them, two dozen men surged forward, and Riley saw Kane moving to one side, the men in front of them falling flat, firing steadily. Kane stayed up in the road, flattened out behind the BAR. There was more fire from another BAR, Kane joining in, and behind them, another hard thump from the tank. Riley kept on his stomach, just off the road, saw Welch rise, firing the Thompson. He aimed the M-1, fired, no targets, just the blackened wreck on the road, movement beyond.

The voice came again, from up in front. "Go! They're running!"

The men rose up again, a hard scamper toward the roadblock, no enemy fire. Riley ran as quickly as he could, gasping cold air, Marines reaching the roadblock, firing farther down the road. He stumbled, cursed the clumsiness of the shoe pacs, saw a body to one side, men low around it, kept moving. He was at the wrecked jeep now, collapsed to his knees, searched the slopes to both sides, saw men up on the high ridges, Marines, pushing forward. Around him, the harsh order, "Cease fire! Save your ammo!"

The rifles went silent, and he saw Abell, peering up past the jeep.

More men were coming forward, and Abell waved them out to both sides of the road. Behind Riley, the tank was rolling closer, and Abell squatted down behind the jeep, called out, "Good job! You've taken out your first roadblock. Gather up, prepare to move out!"

Riley thought of the dead man, saw Welch, said, "We should check on that guy, make sure he's not wounded."

Welch pointed back, and Riley saw a pair of corpsmen, slipping quickly between several downed men.

"They'll figure it out. We got better things to do."

"What was his name? I don't remember."

Welch seemed to think for a long second, shook his head. "From Georgia. Talked with a mouth full of molasses. Just came in yesterday. They'll grab his dog tags."

Riley looked back that way, a half dozen wounded, said, "Jesus. His first day?"

"It happens. You know that."

"Yeah. I guess. How's your arm?"

"Nothing. Hell of a bruise, probably. I guess I owe that fellow something."

A man jogged forward now, moved toward Abell, said, "Lieutenant, sir?"

"What?"

"Sir, Lieutenant Dunne's dead, sir. Back there a ways."

Riley saw shock on Abell's face, unexpected.

"Good God. You sure, son?"

"He's dead, sir. There's no doubt."

Riley looked at Welch, who dropped his head, and Riley said, "He made it out of Toktong Pass without a scratch. They said he was the only officer who did."

Welch said, "So did we. No one's wearing a lucky charm out here."

Behind Welch, Abell said, "The trucks are moving up. Let's load up the casualties."

· · · · · · · · · ·

They had marched more than three miles, more roadblocks, more casualties. Up on the ridges on both sides of the road, Riley could hear the firefights, some brief, some more intense. But the greatest distraction was the air cover, the Corsairs and other bombers unloading on pockets of the enemy wherever they were found. From the men down on the road, the blasts of rocket fire and fiery bursts of napalm brought cheers, and outbursts of amazement from the new men. The aircraft hit the roadblocks as well, adding enormous firepower that swept away most of the enemy resistance. For most of the day, the fighting was brief and sporadic, the enemy content to strike quickly, then fall back, unwilling or unable to make a strong stand.

As dark began to settle over the heights around them, Abell passed the word. The order had come from Litzenberg that the company was to keep going, advancing as much as possible, even in the darkness.

Riley kept his eyes on Welch, the steady rhythm of his footsteps. There was little else to see, the roadside dotted with occasional huts and run-down farmhouses, most of them wrecked by artillery or torched by fire from the planes. For much of the day, the tanks had moved forward, leading the way, and Riley tried to feel comfort from that, but there were doubts as well. Some of the men kept close to the big machines, warmed by the stinking exhaust, for most, a welcome trade. Riley was too far back in line, and with the darkness settling in, he thought of the tankers, a job he never wanted. But now those boys are warm, he thought, and they're buttoned up tight. Not a bad place to be when you can't see a damn thing. Ain't seen much the Chinese have that can hurt those fellows, as long as they keep their hatches closed. Wonder what they can see from inside the damn things. Or maybe they don't bother looking. They leave that to us.

The fighting on the darkening ridges above had grown quiet, a surprise, especially with the planes returning to their bases. He saw Welch wave a hand, move off to one side of the road, the column slowing. Riley moved up beside him, felt the misery of cold, wet socks, said, "We gotta change socks, Sarge. We stopping for long?"

"Hell if I know. Something's up. Hey, what's that?"

Riley listened, nothing, but Welch held up his hand, the men around him silent. Riley heard it now, a faint voice, "Help! American!"

Welch pointed. "There. Easy. Spread out."

Riley saw Abell now, the lieutenant moving closer to Welch.

"What is it?"

"Somebody in one of those huts. Maybe. Not sure. Could be Chinks."

The voice came again, slightly above the road, and Riley could make out the group of small huts, the voice more distinct.

"American!"

Abell said to Welch, "Check it out. Careful. Those bastards speak English when they want to."

Welch began to climb off the road, the rest of his squad following. The call continued, high and faint, coming clearly from one of the huts. Welch moved that way, waved the others out in a wide formation, a quick glance at Kane. Welch whispered, "Get up here. You see Chinks, you unload that thing."

Kane moved forward, out to the left of Welch, the BAR held ready. Welch leveled the Thompson, Riley up to the other side, the M-1 pointing, four more men out past Riley. He ignored them, kept his eyes on the darkened hut, dim light, an odd stink. Welch dropped down to one knee, still pointing the Thompson, said, "Hey! You wounded?"

"Oh, God. American. Yes, help."

"So who's Ted Williams play for?"

"Red Sox. Red Sox!"

"Who the hell are you?"

"Jim Kalin, Corporal. George Three One."

Welch absorbed that, said, "Come out."

"Can't. Can't walk."

Welch pointed at Riley, motioned him forward. Riley let out a cold breath, his heart pumping, crept forward, the rifle ready, pushed the muzzle into the opening of the hut. In the faint light, he saw the man, lying up against one side of the small hut, bodies beside him.

"Thank God. Thank God."

Riley glanced around the hut, nothing else, called out, "I got him."

Welch was there quickly, a glance at the man, then a hard shout, "Corpsman!"

Riley moved to the man, the pungent stink overwhelming, Kalin stammering now, a pool of emotion.

"Oh, God. Thank you. Check these fellows. I think they're dead. But check."

The corpsman was there now, and Riley recognized him, Rebbert, a longtime veteran. Rebbert moved quickly, kneeling close to Kalin, said, "Can you feel your legs? Are you wounded?"

"No. They busted me up good. Can't walk."

Riley bent low, one hand probing the other men, each one cold and stiff.

"Sorry, pal. They're gone."

Kalin said something, too low to hear, and Rebbert said, "Let's get him to the trucks. We'll have to carry him."

Welch moved in, Riley beside him, Welch calling out, "Morelli. Make yourself useful."

The kid was there now, breathing heavily, and Welch said to Kalin, "It's okay, sport. We got ya. How long you been here?"

They hoisted Kalin up from beneath his arms, a sharp cry.

"My legs. Oh, damn."

Rebbert said something unintelligible, and Riley could see him pull something from his mouth, a syringe.

"Here. This will help."

The needle went in, Kalin calming immediately, and he said, "Four days, five. Not sure. They gave me a couple potatoes to eat. I tried to help the others, thought we'd all just freeze. They left us. Didn't come back."

They had him upright, Welch leading the way out of the hut, a fresh burst of cold enveloping Riley. They moved slowly down the hill, Kalin's legs dangling, dead weight. On the road, the column had continued to move, trucks in line, moving slowly. Rebbert called out, one truck stopping, a squeal of brakes, the group carrying Kalin to the rear of the truck. Riley saw inside, men with fresh wounds, two men laid out with sleeping bags over them. Abell climbed up, said, "Lift him up here."

They hoisted Kalin into the truck, the man out completely now, a wounded man making space. Abell said, "How many more are there?"

Welch said, "Just him, sir. Three more didn't make it."

Behind Abell, one of the wounded men said, "Jesus. What happened to him?"

Welch said, "He's been out here for days. Chinks left him behind. Try to keep him warm, okay?"

The man examined Kalin, said, "Hey, pal, you're gonna be all right now. Holy cow, he's a Marine. What the hell's he doing out here?"

Abell said, "He's part of Task Force Drysdale. Road up ahead is a mess. Burnt trucks, bodies all over the place. Let's move out."

Abell jumped down, moved toward the front of the truck, tapped the passenger-side door, the truck lurching forward slowly. Riley kept pace, the smell easing, replaced by the sharp chill from his breathing. They moved as quickly as Abell could walk, and Riley saw the rest of the platoon, familiar faces, men scattered out along both sides of the road. It was almost full dark now, and he heard low talk, caught a new smell, burnt vehicles, saw one group of men in a tight knot, Abell moving that way.

"What's up?"

The men made way, and Riley saw now bodies in a pile off the side of the road. They were white, crusted with snow, and naked. Abell knelt low, a small flashlight in his hand, said, "They've still got dog tags. All right, let me grab one of the trucks, somebody who's got room. Then we'll put 'em aboard."

There were groans from some of the men, and Riley ignored that, knew it had to be the new men. He studied the corpses for details, wounds long frozen, smears of dried blood. He thought of the Chinese, wearing American parkas, thought, They're wearing everything else, too. He was grateful for the darkness, no faces, and he looked toward the column of trucks, saw Abell in the road, halting one. The lieutenant moved quickly to the truck's rear, then waved the men closer, *this one*. Riley bent low, flexed his fingers, slid his hands beneath one of the bodies. Other men joined him, Welch beside him, the men working together, lifting, the frozen bodies separating. They carried the first man to the truck, the corpse twisted, one arm extended, the body pushed up into the bed of the truck. Abell was in the truck, pulled the man as far back as there was room, more men bringing the next body, then the rest. Riley went back to the pile, but more men from the platoon had joined in, the dead all retrieved. He felt exhausted, the squishing cold in his shoe pacs miserable, and he felt for the spare socks, tucked into his belt. Up ahead there was a burst of machine gun fire, flashes of light. The shouts came now, men scattering, a sharp blast erupting from the bed of a truck. The rifles began, the chatter of a BAR, the hillside across the road alive with flickers of light. Riley dropped down, rolled the M-1 off his shoulder, crawled off the road, a narrow strip of grass. He backed into the slope, turned the rifle outward, another blast beneath another truck, the word in his mind, *grenade*. The machine gun fire came down from the heights, streaks of green tracers, most of it pouring into the column of trucks. There were shouts, orders, the trucks moving again, then stopping, doors jerked open, men climbing up, new drivers, answering the commands, *keep moving*. A six-by rolled in front of him, and he saw men swarming around it, white coats, his brain screaming, *Chinese!* To one side, a Thompson fired, spraying the side of the truck. The men in white tumbled down, another grenade erupting, the flash illuminating the scene. More Chinese troops moved out into the road, some of them trying to board the truck. The truck stopped again, one man firing a burp gun into the cab, and Riley fired, the man falling back. More rifle fire came from the edge of the road, the Chinese caught in a crossfire, some running away, still on the road, cut down. More were moving up the hill, a retreat, the BAR chopping men as they ran, Riley finding targets, emptying the clip. He rammed another into the rifle, sighted a man scrambling up the hill, the man stopping, his arm up, tossing a grenade. Riley fired, the man collapsing, a long second, the grenade erupting close by.

The firing began to slow, but there were new flashes high on the ridge, the army troops engaging the enemy, intercepting the retreat of the Chinese from the road. Riley sat still for a long moment, thunder in his chest, his back against a slope of frozen ground. There was a chorus of screaming around him, shouted orders, panic, wounded men. One truck was burning, the fire lighting the entire scene, men working to pull wounded from the burning truck, and he felt a jolt of energy, stood, moved that way. There were a dozen men, some pulling the wounded away from the truck, others trying to get close, the fire now too hot, swallowing the truck. He felt helpless, weak, stared into the flames, stepped closer, past the bodies, the corpsmen working in a frantic rush, more wounded tended to, one man dragged to the side of the road, another laid beside him. Riley couldn't see that, wouldn't look at the faces, the wounds, his eyes on the flames, and he moved closer, slow steps, drawn by the heat, the delicious warmth on his face.

Throughout the night, the enormous convoy inched its way slowly south. As they had done so many times before, the Chinese positioned themselves for ambush, or rolled down to the main road in a breakneck assault. The firefights continued, the Marines and the men of the army's newly formed battalion shoving their way through pockets of the enemy. Not all the Chinese were spoiling for a fight. In many encampments, the Americans crept forward to find huddled groups of frozen enemy soldiers, men who had died because their orders kept them on the hills, waiting to confront an enemy they did not live to see. Many of those Chinese units were the same troops who had ambushed Task Force Drysdale, and were still occupying the heights above what the Marines now called Hellfire Valley. The signs of Drysdale's fight were still in evidence, scattered corpses from both sides, the hulks of wrecked vehicles, shoved aside now by the heavy equipment that cleared the way.

By dawn on December 7, the men of Fox Company could still see hordes of Chinese troops high up above them, but most of those troops were engaged with the Americans sent up the hills to find them. The fights continued, scenes of bloody awful horror, the Chinese again driven back. The convoy was repeatedly struck, machine gun fire, mortar rounds, more destruction and more casualties, some Chinese troops positioned close to the road itself, close enough to lob grenades into masses of wounded, or riflemen who only targeted the truck drivers. Throughout the morning, the convoy kept in motion, fits and starts, tanks and rolling artillery working to keep the enemy away.

Behind them, in Hagaru-ri, the men of Murray's Fifth engaged the enemy, a brutal and bloody fight that finally pushed the Chinese back, allowing the final battalion of Murray's regiment to join the convoy. The rear of the column continued to receive heavy assaults from the unending numbers of Chinese on the heights, hard fights for the Marines that were aided again by the tanks and artillery, as well as brutally effective air strikes. They left behind the smoking remnants of the base at Hagaru-ri, worthless now to the Chinese troops who swarmed into the supply depot, finding only heaps of ash from a hundred bonfires.

By late morning, the men of Fox Company reached their goal, leading the way for the entire convoy, passing through Chesty Puller's outposts that guarded the way into the next link in Oliver Smith's shortening chain, the town of Koto-ri.

CHAPTER THIRTY-SEVEN

. . . .

Smith

KOTO-RI, NORTH KOREA—DECEMBER 7, 1950

HE STAYED AT HAGARU-RI until the operation was well under way, would not just leave the men behind until he was confident the Chinese around the base could do little more than throw themselves uselessly into Murray's guns. Once Litzenberg offered assurances that the leading elements of the convoy were certain to drive through the last of the enemy roadblocks, Smith and his staff officers boarded their own aircraft for the short journey to Koto-ri.

Murray was confident that when it was safe for his last few units to join the march, they would have no difficulty holding off any enemy incursions from behind. As one of his final responsibilities, Murray would leave Hagaru-ri only after destroying as much of the airstrip as possible, and any other asset the now-empty base might offer. The Chinese would certainly swarm into the town, and if they chose to waste time searching through piles of rubble, that was fine with Smith. The convoy, numbering nearly a thousand trucks, jeeps, and ambulances, was hauling everything of military value, including of course the vehicles themselves. To suggestions, especially from Tokyo, that the airstrip be used to evacuate the men by flying them out piecemeal, as had been done with the wounded, Smith offered a flat refusal. Abandoning the

massive amount of equipment, including the artillery, tanks, and vehicles, would be a bonanza for the Chinese and a devastating morale
crusher for Smith's troops. Smith knew there were desk jockeys in
Tokyo sharing the doomsday sentiments of many of the stateside newspapers, who regarded this campaign as a disastrous failure. But Smith
would hear none of that. His newly celebrated battle cry, which still
brought a smile, was, in his mind, completely accurate. This was not a
retreat. It was an attack in another direction. To fly the men out, abandoning their equipment, would change that completely. As the men
prepared for the march south, Smith heard the talk, the enthusiasm
for accomplishing this new mission, no different than their enthusiasm
for anything he had asked them to do before. He had no interest at all
in suddenly taking that away. They had walked in. They would walk out.

To more moderate suggestions that the men should take advantage
of their transportation, riding the trucks instead of marching the eleven
miles to Koto-ri, Smith understood what many staff officers in Tokyo
did not, that packing trucks full of men, allowing them to sit still in
frigid conditions, would drain away their ability to react to a crisis. If the
journey was uncontested, the far more pleasant ride would make sense.
But Smith had to anticipate that the Chinese along that eleven-mile
stretch would do all they could to crush the convoy, as they had already
done to Task Force Drysdale. Any assumption that the Chinese would
simply lie back was erased the first mile out of Hagaru-ri. To arguments
that the convoy could make far better speed than the pace of marching
men, Smith knew very well that the condition of the road, added to the
misery of the weather, meant that speed was a luxury they wouldn't
have. Smith knew that even in decent weather, the trucks would be easy
pickings for Chinese mortars and machine gunners, his men crowded
together nothing more than ripe targets. Marching among the trucks
meant better security for everyone in the convoy.

He had thought of walking with the men, one of those morale
boosters that sounded more effective than they truly were. In fact, the
business of reorganizing the division, of planning the next phase of the
operation, had to be well under way even before the men reached Koto-

ri. Chesty Puller had already prepared a large command post for Smith and his staff, and now the engineers were tackling a problem farther down that Smith had anticipated for weeks.

Some three miles south of Koto-ri, the Chinese had finally destroyed the bridge that spanned a deep gorge in Funchilin Pass, creating a major obstacle for the Americans once they began their next drive southward toward Hungnam. Smith was certain the Chinese would fortify the hills around the deep chasm, hoping to crush the Marines and army troops as they bunched up, helpless to move. Smith had to wonder if the Chinese command truly believed the Americans would allow themselves to march full speed toward a nearly impassable roadblock, only to halt in a ten-thousand-man traffic jam while their officers scratched their heads figuring out what to do next. But so far, the Chinese had shown very little imagination in their tactics. By finally blowing the bridge, it was clear to Smith that the Chinese would continue to do what they had done now for weeks, full-on frontal assaults. By creating a difficult roadblock, the location of that assault seemed pretty clear.

The solution to the challenge lay once more with the engineering team led by Colonel John Partridge, the man responsible for the extraordinary success in building the airstrip at Hagaru-ri. This time Partridge was faced with the task of rebuilding the bridge, assisted by the fortunate presence in Koto-ri of a team of army engineers, led by Lieutenant George Ward. Ward had significant experience with the construction of Treadway bridges, prefabricated steel spans, with plywood platforms strong enough to support a tank. The gorge, nearly thirty feet wide, could be bridged easily once the right equipment was brought into Koto-ri. On December 7, while Litzenberg's men were still fighting their way south, the engineers received a total of eight bridge sections, enough for two full bridges. The spans weighed nearly two tons each and were dropped at Koto-ri by parachute, each span hauled by a C-119 Flying Boxcar. The next task was to clear the pass around the gorge of a formidable force of Chinese whose purpose was to prevent any kind of crossing at all.

KOTO-RI, NORTH KOREA—DECEMBER 7, 1950

"Not sure where we're going to put them all. I guess I should have paid more attention to just how many people you already had down here."

Puller drank from a coffee cup, shrugged. "We'll manage. We've got tents ready, mess areas, medical teams. I assume we're not going to remain here for long. We can certainly supply the men by air as long as we need to, but I'm assuming you'd rather have the men go to the mountain than have the mountain brought up here."

Smith stared at the map, Puller's wisecrack slipping past him. "Do we know how strong the enemy is around that bridge?"

Puller sat back, toyed with a half-spent cigar. "Plenty. My suggestion is to send the fresh troops I've got here down that way. Chinhung-ni is about seven miles below those hills. I can order my First Battalion there to move north. The enemy will be squeezed from both sides. Won't matter much how many they are. They can fight for those hills, or die trying. We can grab those hills pretty easily, and once the enemy is out of the way, it's a clear shot to Chinhung-ni. The convoys can push across the bridge pretty quick, if there's nobody shooting at them."

Smith leaned back, one hand on the pipe in his mouth. "Just like that."

"You don't agree?"

Smith appreciated Puller's total confidence, even if there could be a significant cost in casualties.

"How secure is Chinhung-ni?"

Puller stabbed the cigar into his mouth, crossed his arms over his chest. "Right now, my First Battalion is being relieved by some part of the army's Third Division. That was always the plan. We didn't really think we'd be bringing everybody back down the same road we went up. You were so fired up about your people being spread out all over hell and gone. Now you're bitching because we're all rammed together?"

Smith knew there was nothing angry in Puller's words, saw the rough hint of a smile. "Lewie, I'm just doing my job. Tenth Corps is going to pick apart every detail of this entire operation. Count on it. If there's one mistake, my backside is gonna boil for it."

Now he saw anger, Puller's expression changing abruptly.

"I won't put up with that crap, not one bit. There hasn't been a campaign in any war in history where somebody didn't hunt up a scapegoat for anything that went wrong. But there's fifteen thousand, hell, twenty thousand fighting men gathering up in this place who would be happy as hell to tell those mush-brained bastards just what we've done here. You didn't give the orders that got us into this pickle jar. The newspapers, by Christ, they're telling the American people that this whole outfit is gone, wiped out, and you can believe that Tenth Corps or those morons in Tokyo might still believe that. Or, since we're doing just fine, thank you, they're trying to figure out the best way to put perfume on a hog's ass and lead him in a parade down Fifth Avenue."

Smith smiled, couldn't help marveling at Puller's confused choice of words. "What on earth are you talking about?"

Puller was fuming now, tossed the cigar into a large tin can. "One day I'm gonna run this show. Find a way to keep the damn politicians out of our nose hairs. Your problem, O.P.? You're a nice guy."

Smith glanced at the various staff officers, the command post part of an enormous hospital tent. The men had gathered, the junior officers keeping back behind the senior staff. But all eyes were on their commanders. Smith said, "You have work to do, gentlemen?"

Bowser was sitting close by, grinning, his usual expression. "Not really, sir. The boys are still coming in here, and Murray's people are on the march. Until they complete the trip and we can tally up our casualties, there's not much else that Colonel Puller hasn't already done for us."

Puller kept his arms crossed, grinned past a fresh cigar. "See? Somebody needs to tell MacArthur that Marines aren't just sons of bitches. We know how to *run* a war, not just fight one."

From the far side of the tent, a pair of aides came forward, and Smith looked that way, said, "What is it?"

They halted, a young sergeant speaking out.

"Sirs, the newspapermen are pushing pretty hard. They want to know details. The MPs are keeping them back, but they're mighty pushy, sirs." The other man elbowed the sergeant, a sharp whisper. "Oh, yes, that broad. She's pushy, too."

Smith looked at Puller. "Maggie Higgins?"

Puller blew out a cloud of smoke. "She said you'd authorized her being here. Pain in the ass."

Smith thought a moment. "I've no patience for this crap, Lewie. Here's what I'm *authorizing*. Put her on a plane, quick as you can. And send along anyone else you think is a pain in the ass. I tossed her out of Hagaru-ri already. This is too important, and we're too close to success here. I don't care about how good a reporter she is, and the fact that she's a woman. She's a distraction, whether she likes that or not. Am I clear?"

He knew he didn't have to be that stern with Puller, the browbeating more for the rest of the staffs. Puller kept the cigar in his mouth, nodded.

"She's been pretty pissy about being treated differently because she's in a combat zone."

Smith was fully annoyed now. "Bull. I'm treating her differently because there are twenty thousand young men around here who haven't seen a good-looking woman in weeks. Months maybe. She'll be the prime attraction, men stepping all over each other to get an interview, or maybe just stare at her."

Puller shook his head. "One reason I didn't give her too much grief is that she's so damn disagreeable all on her own, and I figured the boys would find that out themselves. She's already gone around interviewing wounded men, ignoring what kind of shape they might be in, like their damn misery isn't as important as giving her their full attention. More than one of the boys has fallen asleep while she's holding court. She might be pretty, but she's not making any friends here. Maybe this will teach her something about humility."

Smith was in no mood for this. "Lewie, she's already distracting *you*. How many reporters are here? A dozen? Name them. I can't. We're not here to humble civilians. If you're right, she cares more about her reputation than the boys she's talking to. Get her the hell out of here."

Puller nodded. "Yes, sir."

Across the tent, more men were moving in, and Smith looked that way, had a nagging dread of some new disaster. The group moved his way and Puller said, "Those are Murray's boys. I know that major, Simmons."

Smith knew the men as well, stood, felt a surge of energy. They stopped, four men, ragged dirty uniforms. The major said, "Sir, Colonel Murray is pleased to report that his lead elements have entered Koto-ri. I can verify that, sir. I led them."

Bowser stood, moved out to the far end of the tent, and Smith watched him for a long second, not certain where he was going. He looked at Major Simmons now, said, "Welcome. How much difficulty did you have? We received several radio calls, a good bit of resistance all along the way."

"Yes, sir, there was. The air cover helped, and the artillery boys used those one-oh-fives in short-range combat, point-blank fire. Damnedest thing I've ever seen, sir. The enemy pushed hard all along the road, and we chewed 'em up pretty effectively."

Smith couldn't avoid feeling nervous relief. "Major, there's warm food in a number of mess tents. Grab some, if you like."

The man smiled, and Smith saw the weariness, the grime on the man's bearded face.

"Will do, sir."

Bowser returned now, said, "Excuse me, sir, but I heard something odd. It sounded like singing. I checked on it." He looked at Simmons. "Major, I assume those are your boys out there."

"Yes, sir. I can shut 'em up if you wish."

Bowser seemed apologetic now. "Oh, no. I was just curious. They're singing some pretty, um, raw stuff."

Simmons smiled now, his pride showing through. "Colonel, the men are quite accomplished in adding their own lyrics to some pretty dull songs. Colonel Murray encourages it."

Smith was curious, looked at Bowser. "I'd like to know what they're singing."

"You sure, sir? It's rather amazing just how profane ... well, you know, sir."

Smith laughed, knew Bowser was too efficient at protecting him.

"Colonel, I assume they have chaplains who've heard this stuff? If it's all right by them, it's all right by me."

Simmons spoke up now. "Actually, sir, it's a couple of the chaplains who wrote the stuff."

The fighting around Funchilin Pass began early on December 8, made more difficult for both sides by a vicious snowstorm that limited visibility and movement. Worse for the Marines, the storm kept their air cover away. But Puller's suggestion and Smith's plan for squeezing the Chinese between two halves of a vise proved enormously effective. By dawn on December 9, with the weather clearing, the Chinese had either been wiped out or had withdrawn on their own from the site of the destroyed bridge. With the word coming back to Koto-ri of the successful push, the engineers took over. By four that afternoon, the lead vehicles of the enormous convoy began crossing the bridge. After a temporary delay, caused by a near disaster for one of the heavier bulldozers, the bridge was made fully passable. Throughout that night, nearly fourteen hundred vehicles and most of the Marine and army troops made their way across the span.

Puller's final responsibility at Koto-ri was to perform the same task Murray had accomplished at Hagaru-ri, keeping the Chinese away from the perimeter of the base until the convoy had cleared the area. In the process, the airstrip successfully evacuated some six hundred new casualties, most of those from the fighting they had endured on the journey down from Hagaru-ri.

With the perimeter of Koto-ri secure and the crucial bridge fully operational, Smith knew it was time once again to move his command post south, this time returning to the port of Hungnam, the exact location where his headquarters had been established when this campaign had begun.

He boarded the helicopter, watched as Bowser led a half-dozen men toward an idling C-47. His pilot was unfamiliar, Smith absorbing a slight jolt of discomfort from that. But the young man smiled at him, said, "On your command, sir."

Smith pulled the coat tightly around him, pointed upward, the pilot revving the engine, the chopper rising quickly. They topped the tallest structures, the pilot turning, aiming south, and Smith felt a tug, a hard pull inside of him. He put a hand on the young man's arm, said, "Over that way. Past the tents. Just a few seconds."

The pilot obeyed, the chopper swinging around, easing slowly over the encampment. Smith looked down, saw crews of Puller's men gathering up everything worth carrying, loading it on the vast rows of trucks. The pilot looked at him, uncertain, and Smith kept his eyes on the ground, pointed ahead, the chopper sliding farther along, no more than a hundred feet above the ground.

"Sir, the enemy's been raising Cain with every aircraft flying out of here. We go much closer to those hills, we're pretty sure to take fire."

Smith ignored the caution, searched, held up a hand now. "Hover right here."

The chopper slowed, and Smith saw the freshly churned ground, already frozen, an enormous grave.

"We had to leave some men here, son. One hundred thirteen of them. Buried them right there. The airstrip wasn't adequate to fly 'em out. I hate that. Hate it with every bone in my body. We'll get 'em out one day. I promised them. We'll get 'em out."

The pilot looked at him with wide eyes, nodded slowly. "Yes, sir. I'm certain of it, sir."

Smith kept his eyes on the mass grave, felt a sickening twist in his stomach.

"We'll get 'em out."

CHAPTER THIRTY-EIGHT

. . . .

Sung

NORTHEAST OF HAGARU-RI—DECEMBER 10, 1950

THERE WERE SIX PRISONERS, bandaged and crippled, huddled to-gether in a small hut. Two of Sung's men guarded them, showing more menace than the prisoners required, Sung aware it was more for his benefit than for any threat that these men would attempt escape. He studied them as they studied him, caked filth on bearded faces, bloody clothing, rags wrapped on their feet.

Sung looked at the aide beside him, said, "What happened to their boots?"

The man shook his head. "I do not know, sir."

Sung thought, Well, I know. Whoever captured them took their boots and anything else of use.

"Have we been able to speak with them?"

"None of them speak Mandarin, sir. Our interpreter, Mr. Hong, has not been seen in several days. We believe he deserted."

Sung looked at the man. "Where would he go, Colonel? He would join *these* men, fight against us?"

"I do not know, sir."

"I hear those words far too often, Colonel. What do we know of these men? They do not appear to be Marines."

"They admit to being American army. We understood that much from what they said."

"Two of them carry wounds."

"Yes, sir. We treated them as best we could. We have very little to offer our own wounded."

"That is not a reason to ignore the treatment of prisoners. Have their wounds cleaned, bandaged again. We are not war criminals, Colonel Liu."

"Yes, sir. Right away."

Liu backed away, moved quickly toward the medical area, and Sung dropped to one knee, looked hard at the faces, eyes staring sharply at him. He saw fear as much as anger, was gratified by that. He fought for the words, the scattered English he had absorbed so many years before.

"Your war is past. You will be freed soon. I do not need to keep you."

He waited for a response, the men perking up a bit to his words. One man nodded toward him, a hesitant *thank you.*

"You may speak. We want no secrets from you. We offer you only sanctuary. You are no different than us." He stopped, struggled to find the words he sought. "You do not have to fight for your warlords. Men who get rich on your blood. You do not have to fight for the generals, for your government. You can return to your army, spread this joy. There will be a new war. The people fighting the government. Tell your soldiers, your friends. They can end this war if they turn their guns to their own officers."

Their expressions did not change, but one man took a long, grimacing breath, said, "Go to hell."

Sung waited for more, saw nothing coming from the others. He stood again, saw defiance from them all, a surprise. Liu returned, one of the medical men in tow. Sung watched the doctor go to the first prisoner, a clean bandage in his hand, but the soldier pulled away, angry words, too fast for Sung to understand. The doctor tried again, the prisoner protesting loudly, slapping the man's hand away. The doctor looked at Sung now, said, "What do I do, sir? They will not allow me to treat them."

"Doctor, treat them when you can. They become weaker, or their pains become greater, they will allow it. We shall release them when it is appropriate to do so." Sung spoke to the men again in his rough English. "We will not harm you. We are not your enemy."

The first prisoner looked up at him, said, "I told you to go to hell."

Behind Sung, Colonel Liu said, "They must believe we're poisoning them, or torture perhaps. Your orders were clear, sir. We have already returned a number of prisoners who were well cared for. Surely their soldiers will understand that we mean them no harm, that this struggle is for all soldiers. How do we teach them of the revolution, sir? How do we make them understand?"

"Colonel, you must have faith in the revolution. These men will remember how we treated them, and they will return to the abuse of their masters. We have planted a seed in them. It is all we can do." He paused, studied the men again. "But I admit, I thought it would be easier convincing them."

SOUTH OF HAGARU-RI, NORTH KOREA—DECEMBER 11, 1950

"Sir! This way!"

He nudged the horse over the snowy trail, followed the man's wave, saw the cave now. All along the climb he had passed bodies, nearly all of them his own. He tried not to see that, but the horse saw it for him, stepping gingerly through the frozen rocky ground, avoiding the snow-covered corpses. The cold was relentless, and he pulled himself into his coat, a futile effort to keep the wind away. Behind him, staff officers rode as he did, while out to both sides a company of guards climbed on foot, keeping themselves in formation, a veil of protection. The guide motioned again, pointed, and Sung climbed down from the horse, handed the reins to his aide. The guide waited for him, stood aside, the opening of the cave partially blocked by a pile of rocks and rubble, someone's attempt to add cover. He hesitated, staring into the ragged maw of the cave, then dipped his head slightly, moved inside.

The cave opened up to a wide hollow, some of that man-made, the preparation his men had labored over to keep hidden from the American aircraft. He blinked in the darkness, just enough light to see why they had brought him here. The cave was filled with soldiers, nearly thirty or more, an entire platoon, their weapons stacked neatly to one side. Some appeared to be sleeping, pale white faces, others staring ahead. All had their legs pulled up tightly, were huddled close together, their quilted coats embracing each man, the customary flapped hats on their heads. He studied them, expected any one of them to suddenly acknowledge him, the usual deference, a respectful salute. But they stayed silent, none of them moving at all, nothing in their eyes but frozen death.

He backed out of the cave, stood for a long moment, thought, We must mark this place. It would be easy to forget this hill, this cave. Now it is a tomb, and we shall be respectful of that. He looked up past the opening, the hill wide and steep, rocks and frozen scrub. He looked back toward his horse, his aides waiting for him, and he moved that way, said to anyone who could answer him, "Are there more caves on this hill?"

No one responded, and he knew it was a foolish question, that very likely the only men who knew of the caves were the men who had sought out their protection, and if there were more like this one, they too had become tombs.

He climbed up on the horse, the aide handing him the reins, no one speaking. Among the staff was a young captain, a man who had been punished by his colonel because he had lost his soldiers, unable to explain what had happened to his command. Sung had been nearby, making the slow, plodding ride down the valley to Koto-ri, had interrupted the colonel's tirade, a threat of execution screamed into the terrified captain's face. It was an overreaction from an officer who surely carried some blame himself, one small failure in a vast campaign of failure. Sung had stopped, inquired, the young captain begging him for leniency, offering an explanation that the colonel had tossed aside with a self-conscious smugness. But Sung saw something of substance in the captain, a story that offered more of tragedy than incompetence. And so he had made the climb up the great hill, led by one of the captain's men, a witness ignored by the colonel. And now the story was confirmed.

He looked toward his aide, said, "Colonel Liu, release the captain. He may return to his command." He looked at the young captain now. "Do you still have a command?"

The young man did not look at him, kept his eyes downward. "Sir, I have only six men from my company. There are others who died in the night, and the night before. The storm caught us on the march. We were already down to sixty men. They performed admirably, sir. I regret I could not prevent their loss."

"So do I. You may go. I shall inform your colonel that you are without blame. If he wishes to find fault for our losses, he may express that to me. The *blame* is mine."

KOTO-RI, NORTH KOREA—DECEMBER 11, 1950

The fires were still burning all throughout the town, and he moved into a wide square, the wreckage of what had been a hospital. The stink was putrid, burning bandages and bedding, a smoldering mass of gauze and linens and too many things he did not need to identify. He dismounted the small horse, walked slowly toward a scattered heap of empty steel barrels. Gasoline, he thought. What they didn't require for their trucks they could use to ignite their fires, to destroy anything of use. I suppose I would have done the same.

Down one of the narrow avenues of the town, men were gathering, a cluster of quilted uniforms, poking through more of the rubble. They seemed cheerful, boisterous talk, and he watched them for a long moment as they found small treasures. One man made a loud noise, held up what seemed to be a large hammer, the others saluting him, then returning to their own search. He was curious just why they were so joyful, but stayed away, would allow them to continue searching. They have very little, he thought. Perhaps they will find food, somewhere in this wreckage. Weapons we have in abundance, even if our ammunition runs low. Does that matter? There is no longer an enemy.

The staff kept back, knew him well, that when he was like this, pensive, silent, he was not to be interrupted. But the Russian had no such tactfulness, dismounted a horse of his own. Sung avoided looking at him, a spectacle of opulence in his thick fur coat. But he will offer his opinion, Sung thought. After this day there will be opinions in every quarter. I cannot avoid it.

Another group of soldiers emerged from a side street, carrying all manner of junk. They saw him, seemed too giddy for discretion, one man calling out, "General! It is a wonderful day! We salute your victory!"

He waved to them, knew his aides would try to silence the men, scold them for such a lack of respect. It hardly matters, he thought. But still, they should continue to do their job.

Orlov was there now, kicking through more of the rubble the Americans had left behind.

"So, you have won a great victory."

There was sarcasm in Orlov's voice, and Sung expected it.

"You would mock me, even now?"

Orlov feigned surprise. "General, it is not my place to pass judgment on your accomplishments."

"Yes, yes, you are merely an observer. That tune has grown quite stale, Major. You did not ride into Koto-ri with my staff just to observe. In this miserable country, one burnt-out town is so like another. There is no charm in this place. Even the people have gone, following after the Americans like hungry dogs. We liberate them, and they flee."

"So, you have liberated them? I suppose that will be the message to your people. Chairman Mao will no doubt send joyous tidings to Moscow, trumpeting the glorious successes of his armies over the imperial stooges."

Sung turned to him, angry at the man's interminable smugness. "What would you have me do, Major? My army has eliminated the American threat. We have driven the enemy from the soil we vowed to protect. Even now, they rush to their ships, desperate to escape the destruction we have levied upon them."

Orlov smiled. "Very well said, General. Those would be the very same words you would put on paper, then, in your report to Peking?"

Sung looked again toward the soldiers, more men flowing into the town, some gathering at the fires, seeking the warmth. The air of celebration continued, officers moving among their men, high spirits and salutes.

"Yes. I will tell Peking what Peking requires me to say. They will tell your Chairman Stalin, and everyone else in this world, the very same thing. The Americans have been humiliated. We are victorious."

Orlov rubbed a hand through his rough beard. "Forgive me, General, but I don't hear *victory* in your voice."

Sung kept silent for a long moment, still did not trust this man. But there was no one on his staff, no one among his senior officers he could confide in. He glanced upward, the sky clear and blue. No aircraft today, he thought. Not here, anyway. This place is now in the past.

"Tell me, Major, in your army, is there great ambition, jealousy, men who seek opportunity for their own advancement?"

Orlov glanced at the soldiers, said, "Of course. Men who have power always want more. Do you fear your officers? Or is it the politicians in Peking whom you fear?"

"There is no fear in Peking. All is secure there, all are obedient to Chairman Mao. Men of ambition have no place in the revolution, and are soon removed. Chairman Mao has secured his place."

"Yes, I suppose so. Moscow is a very similar place."

"But the army is very different. There is a way to rise, to advance above others, to gain more power, more authority. I have been very fortunate. But there are some in my command who see what we have sacrificed, who will use that to make reports of their own, and they will not be so positive."

"I have always wondered, General, how many knife blades you had to slip into the ribs of *your* rivals."

Sung looked at Orlov, saw only seriousness now. "I have done no such thing. I have advanced by my deeds, by my performance. It is the best way. I have no guilt for my position."

"And yet you fear your officers."

He moved away, his eyes on soldiers, some falling into formation, officers gathering up their men. Orlov followed, and Sung felt a different kind of fear now, wondered if Orlov carried knives of his own. He stopped, no one close.

"What I fear, Major . . ." He paused, looked again toward the soldiers. "What is the *truth* here? My soldiers will be told they have won a great campaign. They will believe that, because they have no choice. We are trained all our lives to believe what our superiors tell us. In that we are no different than the Americans. I spoke to prisoners, offered hope that they need not fight for the imperialists any longer. They most certainly did not believe me. Their indoctrination is as powerful as ours, no doubt." He stopped, felt uncomfortable now, watched Orlov for a reaction. But the Russian offered no comment, and Sung understood now, *He knows more about that than we do.* "Major, no amount of lessons from above can alter the fact that there is failure here, *my* failure." He raised his hands, pressed his fingertips together in a sphere. "The enemy was trapped. They were surrounded. My strategies were sound. And yet they were allowed to escape. Already there is talk from my generals, for all that we have lost."

"But Peking will ignore that. You said it yourself. The Americans are fleeing to their ships. Every newspaper, every government in the world will acknowledge *that* truth."

"There is another truth, Major. I lost a third of my army. The casualties who did not die by the guns of the Americans have frozen to death, or they have been so crippled from the cold they can never fight again. I have lost the fighting effectiveness of three full divisions, and possibly, when we gather together, reorganize, that number will grow. Entire regiments no longer exist. There are officers with no one left to command, soldiers with no one to command them. There are men in these hills that we will never find. A great many men."

"Will you be punished for that? How will Peking explain that to your country?"

Sung looked down, shook his head. "Peking does not concern itself with casualties. I have believed that it was the only way to command an army, not to concern oneself with the death of soldiers. But there were so many deaths. And we let them escape."

Orlov stared at him, black, piercing eyes. "They might end this, right now. This was a distasteful campaign to the capitalists, no profit to be made here. Korea is not worth such a cost. You feel that way, surely the Americans do as well. They might very well board their ships and sail home, and they might even find some way to save face doing it."

Sung shook his head. "No. I have seen them fight. They will come back. And we shall do all of this again. Perhaps not here, perhaps to the south, perhaps in the summer, when men suffer not from the cold, but from the heat. And more men will die, and more divisions will be lost, and again Peking will celebrate my accomplishments. And perhaps next year, the war will end. Or the year after." Sung felt a thick wave of sadness, looked toward the smiles of his men, the celebration, great crowds gathering at the bonfires, officers leading the men in songs, raucous cheers, the morale of an army eager to fight again. "Or perhaps, Major, it will never end."

CHAPTER THIRTY-NINE

. . . .

Riley

HE HAD WALKED ACROSS the Treadway bridge in blind darkness, guided by the helping hands of Marine engineers, low voices that kept the men focused on the plywood beneath their feet. Riley had no idea just what lay below the bridge, how deep the gorge, was grateful for that. The fighting had continued most of the way south, but there was none of the intensity of the journey they had taken toward Koto-ri. Now what seemed to be scattered units of Chinese were more content to lob their mortar rounds toward the convoy from the heights, far fewer of them descending on the road itself. The effort of the walk was as severe as any before, the night of December 10 the coldest yet. Riley had only heard talk about that, Lieutenant Abell jawing with some higher-ranking staff officer along the route. With the Chinese keeping mostly away, checkpoints and command posts were more visible, but none of them mattered to Riley or the men around him. As they pushed slowly into the village of Chinhung-ni, there had been an odd inspection, a large command tent manned by men in clean uniforms. There was warm food as well, though it was nothing like the feasts of pancakes and stews they had left behind. Even in Koto-ri, the rations were plentiful, the men encouraged to chow down, supply officers explaining that what they didn't eat would be burned. Along the route, with brief firefights still erupting along the high ground, Riley walked with the same rhythm as before, following Welch in front of him, the occasional glance to the man across the road. The misery was still there, the lengthy hikes made even worse by the never-ending pains in his feet. None of that was helped by the weight of what felt like a brick that he hauled inside him, low in his gut.

At Chinhung-ni, they passed by army units, the men assigned to replace Chesty Puller's First Regiment. The Marines were mostly too exhausted to pay any attention to the soldiers, catcalls and lewd remarks flowing over them, the custom when the two branches crossed paths. But several of the soldiers made a deadly mistake, a boastful cry that the army had come up to rescue the cowardly Marines, who were too panicked to stand up to their enemy. If few had the energy for a knock-down brawl, the officers recognized a new threat, several of the men around Riley reacting to that particular insult by sliding rifles off shoulders, muzzles aimed at the offending soldiers, that particular horror clamped down by a scramble of words from the sergeants. Though the insults continued, the worst offenders began to temper their words, aware that quite likely, the sudden reaction by the Marine officers had saved lives.

South of Chinhung-ni, the road sloped downward, Riley not remembering that he had hiked this road the other way, nothing of the landmarks around them now familiar at all. What had been ugly scrub and ragged homesteads were just as ugly and just as ragged now, changed only by a light coating of snow, or scattered bodies of Chinese troops. Some of those lay in the road itself, corpses crushed by the wheels of trucks, the tread of the tanks, flattened almost beyond recognition.

They rounded yet another sharp curve in the road, and he eyed the smoldering wreckage of another truck, men retrieving the human cargo from the rear. He passed the cab of the truck, glanced that way, saw what used to be the driver, the cab charred and stinking, no one yet retrieving the blackened corpse. He looked down, blinked that away, too tired to be sickened by a sight he had seen too often now.

"Hold up!"

He stumbled, stopped, the ache in his feet worse by standing still.

Up ahead, men had gathered, and he tried to be curious about who or why, his curiosity as numb as the rest of his brain. He looked to the side of the road, a place to sit, no one yet giving the order to move off the road. Welch turned to his squad, men as half-conscious as Riley, and Welch said, "Lieutenant's got something going on. Make ready. Could be Chinks."

Riley looked to the side of the road, the remnants of a hut, thoughts of the Marine they had rescued. "Hey, Sarge. Maybe we should take a look."

Welch looked that way, nodded wearily. "Yeah. Let's check it out. Kane, you and Riley."

Riley stepped over a low mound of icy snow, slipped, adding to the misery in his feet. Kane was beside him now, silent, holding the BAR at his waist, and Riley said, "Just don't shoot me in the ass."

He moved to the hut, heard a soft cry, jolting him alert. "What the hell? Hey, Sarge, somebody's in here."

Welch was awake now as well, moving that way, the Thompson in his hands. He stopped beside Kane, said to Riley, "Okay, easy."

Riley felt the churning jitteriness in his stomach, pushed into the timbers with the muzzle of the rifle. The cry came again, very soft, very high, and he was suddenly dreading what he was going to find. He hesitated, Welch behind him.

"Go!"

Riley lifted the remains of a wooden door, saw now a very small figure, buried beneath a scrap of a blanket.

"Holy cow. Sarge, it's a kid. A little kid."

Welch was there now, the others moving close, the small, filthy face looking at Riley with raw terror. Welch knelt low, pulled at the blanket, the child crying out.

"Jesus, kid. I'm just trying to help."

Riley bent low, said, "Easy, Sarge. You'd scare hell out of me, too. Here, kid, just need to take a look. It's okay."

The child responded to Riley's softer tone, still the fear, tears now, a faint whimper. The blanket pulled free and Riley felt suddenly sick, dropped to one knee, closed his eyes. Welch said, "Oh, Christ. His feet. They're just ice. He's got a hell of a wound, up his leg."

Riley couldn't speak, the child's whimpering slicing into him, a man behind him calling out, "Corpsman!"

The corpsman was there now, familiar face, Rebbert. "Whoa. What we got here? Oh, God."

Rebbert moved in close, the child too weak to protest, and Welch stood, said, "Back off. Let him do what he can."

Riley forced himself to stand, eyes still closed, a step backward. Rebbert spoke to the child now, soft comforting voice, the whimper continuing, and Riley turned, moved back to the road. He saw Abell now, the lieutenant's arm in a sling, a wound from the fighting the night before. Abell seemed annoyed, said, "What's the holdup?"

Welch pointed silently, and Abell looked that way, shook his head.

"Can you do anything?"

Rebbert looked back toward the road, and Riley was surprised to see red, tearful eyes.

"He's done for, sir. Frozen extremities. He gets warm, his wound will just bleed out. If we can fix that, the pain will kill him. I can't give a little kid morphine."

Abell put his hands on his hips, said, "We'll try. Who wants to carry him?"

Morelli raised his hand, said, "I'll do it, sir."

Rebbert covered the child again, stood, said, "I'm telling you, sir, he's done for. The legs are infected, his hand's frozen stiff. Sir, there's nothing we can do. Nothing will fix him."

Abell seemed angry now, frustration boiling over. "Damn it all! Carry him anyway." Abell turned away, moved toward the front of the column, stopped, said, "Listen up! Radio says there's a pile of locals, refugees, coming out from every hole. There's already a pile of 'em following the march. Don't shoot anybody just because they got slant-eyes, you hear me?"

Welch stepped up toward the road, looked at Abell, said, "What the hell do they want, LT?"

Abell shrugged. "They don't want to be Chinese, I guess. Battalion says keep an eye on 'em, watch for infiltrators. There have been Chinese soldiers slipping along with 'em. If they're surrendering, grab 'em. If they try anything, then you can shoot 'em."

Abell moved away now, and Welch gave a last glance to the men at the hut, moved into the road.

"Let's go."

Riley looked toward the hut, saw Morelli bending low, Rebbert lifting the child, the child letting out a hard cry. Morelli was talking to the child in low whispers, Rebbert wrapping the blanket around the small body. The whimpering came again, then quieted, and Riley felt relief, thought, He's okay, I guess. Rebbert worked on the child for a long moment, then said, "Hey, Sarge. It's no good."

Welch was angrier now, impatient. "What's no good? Get him out here. The kid wants to carry him, he can carry him."

Morelli lowered the bundle to the frozen ground, kept to his knees, soft words. Rebbert put a hand on Morelli's shoulder, said, "Sarge, I told you. It was no good. The child's dead."

Welch said, "What do you mean he's dead? Just like that?"

Rebbert pulled Morelli up by the shoulder of his coat and Riley saw dull shock on Morelli's face. Morelli said, "He just quit. Stopped breathing. He was stiff as a board, damn near."

Riley closed his eyes again, didn't want to hear any more. He shouldered the rifle, looked up along the ridgeline above them, saw Marines moving out that way, the constant push to protect the column. He flexed his stiff toes, icy wetness, the twisting misery in his stomach. Behind him, Morelli moved back to his place in the march and Riley heard sobs, Morelli, his eyes down. They began to move again, the sounds returning, a truck to their front, more behind, and along the roadside, another string of shattered huts.

The refugees had been as Abell described, a gathering parade of misery, old men and women, suffering children, and the younger men who tried to blend in. Many of those were soldiers who had given up the fight,

Chinese and even North Korean troops, some not bothering to hide their uniforms or coats. Many of those were injured, light wounds or, more likely, severe frostbite. But there were others who still knew their duty, who worked their way close to the column of Marines, close to a truck of wounded men, only to toss a grenade, pull a burp gun from inside their clothing. There were casualties, but not many, the infiltrators not surviving long, the Marines offering no mercy to the enemy who had shown none.

As they continued the downhill march, Riley ignored the harsh shrieks of the heavy artillery shells passing overhead, big guns in Hungnam still engaged, the artillery impacting pockets of Chinese troops all along the main road. Behind them, Murray's Fifth again brought up the rear, those men cleaning up the last remnants of whatever stand the Chinese were still willing to make. As the Marines reached the outposts north of Hungnam, the Chinese finally backed away. The officers already in the port city had no idea if the enemy had been ordered to stand down by their commanders, or whether the smaller units had withdrawn on their own, conceding that the great struggle was past.

HUNGNAM, NORTH KOREA—DECEMBER 12, 1950

The beards were still there, the men only slightly more clean, no one with any real incentive to change out their uniforms. At the medical tents and the larger hospitals, men gathered to ask about friends, seeking any information they might find.

Riley had stood in line for more than an hour, an unsatisfying and fruitless effort to learn something about Killian. He moved across an open field now, tents lined up to one side, a formation of parked trucks behind him. He wasn't sure just what to do, had eaten all his uncertain belly would absorb. He thought of returning to the bivouac, had heard there would be another mail run later in the day. The letters from Ruthie had been waiting for him, four in all, perfume and sweetness, a photo of mother and son beside their Christmas tree. He carried that now, slid into his shirt, argued with himself if he should do that, if keeping her so close would only make him more homesick. I'm here, he thought. And that sure as hell ain't changing anytime soon. But by damn, I do love looking at both of 'em. One day soon, I hope to God, it's all three of us.

"Hey, Pete!"

He knew the voice, saw Welch limping toward him. Riley waited, watched him, knew better than to scold him.

"Howdy do, Hamp. How you feeling?"

"Hurts like hell. Not bad enough for morphine, and I don't want that crap inside me anyway. I guess if McCarthy hadn't gone down, he'd have chewed on my ass to check my feet more. You find out about Irish?"

Riley shook his head. "They got nothing on him here. Said he probably flew straight to Japan, with the worst foot cases. I'll track him down sooner or later."

Welch was serious now. "Not likely. I heard all that garbage about us being shipped home. It ain't happening. They're loading us up on those tubs out there, moving us down to Pusan. It'll be a while before the rest of us go home."

Riley felt a punch in his chest. "So much for being home for Christmas."

"I never believed that anyway. I heard from the LT, Eighth Army got way more busted up than we did. They couldn't even hold on to Pyong-yang. The whole UN force has pulled back below the boundary with the North. Brass is saying the Chinese won't stop there, that maybe in the spring, we get hit even more."

Riley absorbed that, said, "So, we're back where we started from."

"Yep. Everybody's waiting to hear what MacArthur is gonna do next. Meantime, we gotta get shipshape. They just put up a flock of shower tents back behind the truck park. I've gotta get rid of this fur on my face. And you could use a good dose of soaping, too."

Riley pulled the photo from his pocket. "Yeah, I guess. Look here. Ruthie sent this. She had her pop get us a Christmas tree. She and Peter decorated it all up. He's grown, Hamp. He's up to her waist now."

Welch scanned the photo, smiled, held it for a long minute. "God, he looks like you. Poor kid." Welch kept his eyes on the photo, no smile now. "I want me one of those, Pete. I want the whole package."

Riley was surprised, saw more seriousness than he expected. "Hell, you got fifteen names in your book. Just pick one. You're a war hero now. They'll go all gooey just hearing about it."

It was a joke, but Welch didn't smile.

"Maybe. Maybe not. One of these days, they'll send us home. If I get out of this thing in one piece . . ." He paused. "I need your help, Pete. Maybe Ruthie can ask her friends, find someone worth talking to. I mean, real talking. They don't need to kick their shoes off after five minutes. Kinda don't wanna do that stuff anymore."

Riley saw Welch still staring at the photo. "Sure thing, Hamp. Ruthie's got a pile of friends. It'll work. One I know of, really nice girl. She's a knockout, too. Pretty sure she's not like any of those in your book. From what Ruthie's said, I'm pretty sure she's kept her shoes on."

"Thanks, Pete. I'll remind you about that when we get home."

"You won't have to. Ruthie will start working on you first thing."

Welch handed the photo back to Riley, and Riley caught the look in Welch's eyes, a smile now. Welch reached a hand out, slapped Riley's arm. "You need a shower."

CHAPTER FORTY

. . . .

Smith

SMITH STOOD OUT in the breeze, a soft chill wrapping him, the light jacket not quite adequate. Around him, the camps were in full bloom, great rows of tents, larger tents where food was being served, and the medical and evacuation facilities, the final stop for men not yet assigned to the hospital ships offshore or the larger facilities in Japan.

He watched the men, some in groups, some alone, wandering as though they were lost. He kept back from all of that, would allow them the brief respite, disorganized and scattered, with no particular place they needed to be. In the larger tents, he knew the papers were flowing, Bowser and the other senior staff tracking down the various units, the weaknesses, the holes, sorting through the massive details of rebuilding the First Marine Division.

He didn't know yet what the next assignment would be, if Ned Almond would still be in command, if the division would even remain a part of Tenth Corps. It was a respite for him as well, a brief pause from the orders, the duties, the job. He had already pondered what might happen now, if he would protest serving under Almond again, just how much noise he could make and still keep his career. He has to know what we did out here, he thought. He's not stupid, after all. He's just not . . . *leadership*. He should go back to Tokyo and do what he did before, shining Mac's shoes, cleaning up paperwork jams. MacArthur has to know where Almond's better off, where all of us would be better off.

The wharves were frantic with activity, ships of all sizes, guarded by the warships offshore, patrols of aircraft overhead. He moved that way, energized by the chill, and he did not ignore the irony of that, the temperatures here so much warmer than what his men had suffered around the Chosin Reservoir. He had learned that the altitude there was more than three thousand feet above where he stood now, and in the winter that part of Korea could be one of the coldest in all of Asia. I knew that, he thought, before we ever began the march. But I didn't really know, none of us could.

He had seen the reports of the numbers of frostbite cases, crippling and in many cases permanent damage, worse for many than the wounds from enemy bullets. They'll write about it, he thought, the men, the reporters. They should. No one should ignore what those men went through.

The letters had reached him from home, most from Esther, a chronicle of her days of fear and uncertainty, fueled by the newspapers and all those voices who had no real knowledge of just what was happening. He thought of her, couldn't help a smile, moved closer to the water's edge. He kept far away from the activity, focused on the calm sea, caught the salt smell, even now, in winter, memories of Hawaii. We will do that again, he thought. Without a war, without generals and newspapermen and casualty reports. My girls, too. It would be amazing to watch my granddaughter grow up. Maybe I can keep the boys away, at least for a while. He smiled. That didn't work so well with my daughters.

Don't do that, he thought. Every one of these boys wants to go home a whole lot more than they want to be here. And they've earned it more than you. They've gone through more kinds of hell than any of us expected, and unless the commandant tosses me overboard, there's still too much to do out here. There's still a war, and it's a whole lot nastier than any of us thought. For now, I've still got my command. And every man in this place still salutes me. They know what we did, even if Washington's trying to figure it out. He thought of Truman's man, Frank Lowe. He's been holed up with Walton Walker for a while, while Eighth

Army tries to pull itself back together. Maybe they had it worse than us. There was nothing about what happened over there that smelled like anything but a flat-out retreat. But don't you say that, never. Not once. Not to Lowe, not to your own officers. It's too easy to make enemies, and nothing good comes from that. No matter what Ned Almond might believe, the only *contest* going on here is between us and the Chinese. And we're not done yet. Sorry, Esther, but Hawaii will have to wait. He fingered one of her letters in his pocket, recalled her words, could see her face as he read them.

"Your march is being called many things. 'An attack in reverse,' 'a fighting march to the sea.' But the description I like best is that it is a 'splendid moral victory.' I think it was just that, and I am very grateful."

No, he thought. It is so much more than that. So much talk about disaster, about our mistakes and flaws and poor decisions. So much about the quality of our enemy, and how badly we underestimated him. So much about suffering and loss and blame. They must be told, they must know what I know. There was no defeat, no tragedy here. It was war, and the men in this command didn't just survive and escape. We were outnumbered and outmaneuvered, and yet we persevered. He looked toward the camps again, a swarm of activity around the tents. None of those men believe we were *defeated*. They came down from that reservoir, those hills, with purpose, and that purpose remains. This war will go on, and they will need us, somewhere, and very soon. And no matter anything that has happened, we will be ready. And we will do the job. And *that* is our victory.

AFTERWORD

· ·

THROUGHOUT THE EARLY MONTHS of 1951, the Chinese make every effort to exploit their gains, filling the void left by the withdrawal of American and United Nations forces across all of North Korea. Though the Chinese recapture the South's capital of Seoul, they are not content to maintain a position that pushes the boundary southward well below the 38th parallel. Mounting a number of major offensives, they continue to wage war aggressively, against an enemy who has finally learned just what kind of foe the Chinese have become. As a result, the Americans and their allies continue to build up their resources, and thus their defensive lines.

The war settles into a brutal stalemate, though there are voices in the American high command, notably General James Van Fleet, who insist that the Chinese are vulnerable to another all-out effort to drive them back to the Yalu River. But Washington is leery of a tactic that has already failed in a spectacular way. The goal, stated discreetly, is to return Korea to the status quo that existed before the war, reestablishing the boundary between North and South at the 38th parallel. It is a solution that inspires no one.

Though combat erupts along the various fronts, there is a realization on both sides that with the Americans insisting on maintaining a "limited war," without the potential for nuclear weaponry, peace can only be achieved by negotiation. According to historian David Halberstam, "No one knew how to end it. The war had settled into unbearable, unwinnable battles. It had reached a point where there were no more victories, only death."

In July 1951, peace talks begin at Kaesong, northern South Korea, and eventually are moved to Panmunjom, close to the border itself. But while the United Nations negotiators push for a resolution, the Chinese are distrustful at best of any offer or suggestion that does not originate in Peking. Worse for the negotiations, Joseph Stalin is firmly behind the Chinese, and believes that a protracted war will weaken his primary communist rival, as well as his adversaries in the West. The negotiations drag out for close to two years, while on the battlefront, blood continues to spill.

With the election of Dwight Eisenhower in 1952, the new president makes clear that he wants nothing to do with the deadly drudgery of the unwinnable war he has inherited. Events take a dynamic turn when, in March 1953, Stalin dies, throwing the Soviet Union into political chaos. Without the Soviets to back up their threats, the Chinese begin showing flexibility. It is South Korean president Syngman Rhee who now slows efforts at peace. Rhee has greater ambitions than presiding over half of Korea, though the Americans are adamant that the boundary must remain intact. The alternative is more bloodshed and a far longer war, which no one in the West will accept. Rhee threatens to continue the war against North Korea on his own, a threat that is laughably toothless.

The last great fight takes place in spring 1953. Known as Pork Chop Hill, the fight symbolizes much of what has taken place for the prior three years: a meaningless battle over meaningless ground that takes the lives of far more soldiers on both sides than any victory could justify. It is the American general, Maxwell Taylor, now commanding the Eighth Army, who orders the Americans to withdraw, thus conceding the hill to the Chinese. The propaganda value of such a grab has become utterly irrelevant to the Americans, who only wish the fighting to stop. On July 27, 1953, the truce begins.

One bright moment during the protracted agony of the truce is the delivery, by the North Koreans, of the 113 corpses buried by Smith's Marines on their evacuation from Koto-ri.

Predictably, the Chinese trumpet their supposed victory, while in the West, the war is as quickly forgotten as the media, and the fighting men themselves, will allow. To this day, the 38th parallel is a military hot zone, two mighty armies facing off over a no-man's-land, where a single spark might ignite the war once again.

Despite Chinese claims of overwhelming and lasting victory, a casual observation of the state of affairs for both North and South Korea might tell a different tale. South Korea is one of the most vibrant economies in Asia, with strong financial and cultural ties to the West. The South Korean people enjoy one of the highest standards of living in all of Asia. In contrast, North Korea is possibly the most repressive and isolated society in the world, where the starvation of the citizenry is an acceptable condition of militarism.

If there is an honest victory to be claimed in Korea, it is by Mao Tsetung, who demonstrates his willingness and his ability to confront the West militarily, and survive in the process. If there is defeat, it comes to the American methods of fighting a war that secured victory in World War II. By 1945, the Americans create the largest and most destructive fighting machine the world has ever seen, capable of not only defeating but annihilating any enemy. By the 1950s, that machine has been rendered weak by the nation's conscience, the shocking realization that the nuclear capabilities now in possession of a number of nations are capable of destroying all of humanity. The restrictive philosophy of "limited war" now governs American leadership's hesitation about ever using its nuclear weapons again. That policy is tested severely once more, in Vietnam, a decade later. While fierce debate rages (then and now) about the wisdom of tempting a nuclear holocaust, the unwillingness thus far of the two superpowers, the Americans and their Russian counterparts, to risk a war that could erase humanity, goes beyond philosophical debates. As has happened in the American Civil War and World War I, the technology for mass destruction has far outpaced man's ability to maintain the peace. To this day, Korea remains an open sore, a war that had no end, where men with guns watch each other across walls of barbed wire.

GENERAL OLIVER P. SMITH

"This campaign is perhaps the most brilliant divisional feat of arms in the national history. Smith made it so, through his dauntless calm, his tender regard for his regiments, and his unshakable belief that rest when needed, rather than precipitate haste, was the only thing which would bring his men through the greatest of combat trials. In battle, this great Marine had more the manner of a college professor than a plunging fighter. But our services have known few leaders who could look so deeply into the human heart. . . . His greatest campaign is a classic which will inspire more nearly perfect leadership by all who read and understand that out of great faith can come a miracle."

—BRIGADIER GENERAL S. L. A. "SLAM" MARSHALL—
MILITARY HISTORIAN

"The performance of the First Marine Division . . . constitutes one of the most glorious chapters in Marine Corps history."

—ADMIRAL JAMES H. DOYLE

"They have gone. We could not stop them."

—GENERAL SUNG SHI-LUN

With the Chosin Reservoir campaign concluded, a great many civilian and military observers invite Smith to voice his displeasure with his former commander, Ned Almond, but Smith chooses what many describe as the high road, and rarely speaks out negatively about the trials he endured serving under the thumb of Tenth Corps. Smith says, in part, "I did not desire to enter into any controversy, and declined to discuss the matter." However, one of Smith's most trusted staff officers, his G-3, Alpha Bowser, writes, "I feel to this day, and will feel until I go to my grave, that if the enemy had possessed good intelligence and good communications [Tenth Corps' orders] would have resulted in the First Marine Division, and most of the Seventh Division, never returning from that place."

Though many have labeled the sharp disagreements between Smith and Almond as the typically tiresome interservice feuding, most impartial observers concede that the clashes between Smith and Almond had much to do with Almond's fanatical loyalty to Douglas MacArthur, and his belief in MacArthur's infallibility. Orders from Tokyo rarely took into account actual conditions in the field, and the complete failure of MacArthur's intelligence arm to present an accurate picture of conditions caused orders to be passed through Ned Almond that took no measure of the quality and disposition of the enemy they faced. Smith's recognition of this very likely saves the lives of most of his division and a sizable percentage of the army troops under his command.

Smith continues in command of the First Division through its next major engagement, Operation Dauntless, which begins April 21, 1951. Once again, the Marines and one division of ROK troops are ordered to push northward, attempting to reclaim territory in central Korea now occupied by the Chinese, territory seized as part of their overall success throughout the Korean winter. As before, the Marines and Korean troops easily advance, only to be surprised by a sudden massive onslaught from hidden Chinese positions. Though the Marines hold well and inflict significant casualties on the Chinese, the ROK unit collapses completely. The resulting breach in the position creates a crisis for Smith's regiments. But their position, though bloodied, holds. Once more, the Marines cause enormous casualties to an enemy who outnumbers them, blunting the Chinese offensive.

Just prior to March 1, 1951, Smith receives word that he will be replaced in command, though he is allowed to continue throughout the April offensives. On May 1, with the Marines' position secure, Smith is relieved, replaced by Major General Jerry Thomas.

Upon leaving his command, Smith is awarded South Korea's highest military honor, the Korean Order of Military Merit, presented by President Syngman Rhee. Smith leaves Korea for Hawaii, where he is awarded the Navy Distinguished Service Medal. He also receives confirmation of his Navy Distinguished Service Cross, the medal Ned Almond had attempted to give him at Hagaru-ri.

Expecting to be called to Washington, a custom for commanders returning from a war zone, he is instead ordered to Camp Pendleton, California. Smith begins to understand that disagreeable currents are flowing through the capital, and he writes to his wife, "The atmosphere of Washington has not changed. All hands are still spending a lot of their time fending against the other fellows. There is still the search for the hidden meaning behind the words."

As Smith is never a self-promoter, he is confronted by the egos and sensitivities of his peers, including his superiors, notably Lemuel Shepherd. Shepherd is enormously popular, as well as ambitious, and anticipates being promoted as commandant of the Marine Corps, replacing the soon-to-retire Clifford Cates, the highest-ranking Marine. But as Smith's accolades pile up, including prominent mention in stateside newspapers, it is clear to Shepherd and every other high-ranking officer in the Corps that Oliver Smith is the newest and most recognized Marine hero. Shepherd begins to feel that Smith is jockeying for the job of commandant, something Smith denies. But the fragility of the egos around Smith prove ugly, and he is rarely invited to speak, and thus be celebrated, at official military or governmental functions. Rather, Smith is excluded from official Marine Corps operations and policy discussions, and the reputation he earns in Korea fades into history. Historian David Halberstam describes Smith as "one of the great, quiet heroes of the Korean War."

Smith's wife, Esther, joins him at Camp Pendleton, where Smith is instrumental in creating the Marine facility at Twenty-nine Palms, now the nation's largest Marine Corps installation. While at Pendleton, Hollywood approaches him, enlisting Smith's input into what becomes the film *Retreat—Hell!*, which is released in 1952. The film is well received, and *Variety* describes the film as "a top-notch war drama." Smith quietly acknowledges that the title, attributed to his now-famous quote, is a bit more graphic than what he had actually uttered. Hollywood ignores the comment.

After two years at Pendleton, he is named to command of the Atlantic Fleet Marine Force, in Norfolk, Virginia. Still considered a threat to the ambitions of other higher-ranking Marine officers, Smith does not seek any further advancement, content to spend his remaining time in the Corps with men his junior. Those relationships become some of the most important of his life, and he is surprised at the impact he has made on so many subordinates. He retires in 1955, and while attending the obligatory farewell dinners, Smith is astounded by the outpouring of affection he receives from junior officers, who are quite clear just what his influence has been, and how he should be remembered. He tells a friend, "From a purely personal standpoint, what has given me the greatest satisfaction has been the discovery, sometimes inadvertently, that I have enjoyed the respect and confidence of those who have served under my command."

He and Esther settle in Los Altos, California, an idyllic retirement for a man who has endured unimaginable pressures as a combat commander. "Retirement has some compensations: no deadlines to meet, no speeches to write, no wondering when some untoward incident will upset the apple cart, and time to do some of the things you have not had time to do while on active duty." But the pleasant retirement with his wife and closest friend is not to last, as Esther dies in 1964.

Contenting himself with gardening and the occasional visit from a military historian, Smith dies in his sleep on Christmas night, 1977. He is eighty-four. In his home office, on the wall behind his desk, is a map of the Chosin Reservoir.

"I know of no officer in the U. S. Marine Corps who has contributed more to the splendid reputation of that service than General Smith. He is without a doubt, one of the ablest generals of his time."

—ADMIRAL JERAULD WRIGHT

"There was a magnificent leader, that O. P. Smith."

—GENERAL MATTHEW RIDGWAY

PRIVATE FIRST CLASS PETE RILEY

He continues to serve Fox Company, and in January 1951 is promoted to corporal. Promoted again to sergeant in 1952, he serves until February 1953, when a vehicle accident causes severe injury to his back. Riley is discharged and returns home to southern Pennsylvania.

Unknown to Riley, his friend Hamilton Welch recommends him for a Bronze Star, which Riley receives in 1955.

In 1956, Ruthie gives birth to their second child, a daughter, Annabelle. Their son, Peter, graduates from Cornell University in 1969, completes a doctorate at Stanford, and is today a prominent physicist.

Riley finds employment with a major fruit processing plant, remains on that job for twenty-six years, retiring in 1979. Always active in veterans' reunions, he and Ruthie settle in Gettysburg, Pennsylvania, where he becomes a licensed battlefield guide for the National Park Service. He retires from that activity in 2005, and he and Ruthie enjoy a peaceful life to this day.

In 2007, Riley fulfills a lifelong dream when he satisfies the necessary requirements and finally receives his high school diploma.

SERGEANT HAMILTON "HAMP" WELCH

Welch returns home to Corning, New York, but finds little to keep him there. He follows Pete Riley's advice and allows Ruthie Riley to open doors into a social life. Settling in Chambersburg, Pennsylvania, Welch finds employment at a lumberyard and eventually lands a position as a park ranger at Harper's Ferry National Military Park. At Ruthie's urging, Welch begins a relationship with Doris Brown, and the two are married in March 1957. They have three children.

Welch retires in 1985, devotes time to fly-fishing in the streams across Pennsylvania and beyond. He dies of heart disease in 2004, at age eighty-one.

PRIVATE FIRST CLASS JOE MORELLI

The young man serves Fox Company throughout the remainder of the war and is discharged from the Marine Corps as a corporal in 1954. He returns to his family's home in New Jersey and settles in New Brunswick, where he applies to and attends Rutgers University. He graduates in 1959 with a degree in political science and remains at Rutgers as an instructor and then a full professor until his retirement in 1997.

In 1957, Morelli marries Gina Costello, and they have six children. He dies in 2011, of cancer.

PRIVATE FIRST CLASS SEAN KILLIAN

Killian recovers from his damaging case of frostbite, which leaves him with a severe limp for the rest of his life. He returns home to New York, eventually settles in Vero Beach, Florida. He and his brother open a hardware store, which offers him a moderate income for most of his adult life.

In 1955, his wife, Colleen, gives birth to a daughter. Colleen dies of cancer in 1981.

Killian retires, sells the business in 2000, and lives today in Stuart, Florida.

PRIVATE FIRST CLASS HECTOR CAFFERATA

Cafferata is sent to a hospital in Japan where he recovers from the severe damage to his feet from his barefoot combat experience on Fox

Hill. The wounds to his hand from an exploding grenade are not reparable, and Cafferata endures crippled fingers for the rest of his life. His actions on Fox Hill are considered extraordinary. During the night of November 27, 1950, Cafferata fends off nearly a full battalion of Chinese soldiers, killing a good many of them. By recovering and throwing the grenade that damages his hand, he likely saves the lives of several of his comrades, all without the benefit of his shoes or coat.

He is medically discharged from the Marine Corps in September 1951. For his extraordinary actions on Fox Hill, Hector Cafferata is awarded the Medal of Honor by President Harry Truman in November 1952.

He dies in 2016, in Venice, Florida, at age eighty-six.

GENERAL SUNG SHI-LUN

Despite the lessons he absorbs from his failures against the Americans and Allies during the Chosin campaign, Sung reluctantly follows instructions from Peking, that the strategy of all-out confrontation should continue. The Chinese launch several offensives against Allied positions in the South, absorbing an astonishing number of casualties. Sung continues to lead his troops in what soon become hopeless assaults against an increasingly better-equipped enemy. The resulting stalemates and the slow churn of victories for the Allies provide momentum that leads eventually to the protracted peace talks.

In 1954, Sung maintains his rank, is widely regarded as one of China's finest military tacticians, which he does not publicly dispute, though he is quietly grateful he is never again called upon to lead an army in the field.

He retires from the army in 1969, returns to his home in Shanghai, avoids the purge of Mao's Cultural Revolution, which removes so many prominent military officials from their positions, including Sung's friend and mentor, Peng Dehuai.

In 1989, during the violent protests that take place in Tiananmen Square, he bravely speaks out against his government's oppressive tactics. "Since the People's Army belongs to the people, it cannot stand against the people, nor kill the people. It must not fire on the people and cause bloodshed." His protest is ignored.

He dies in 1991, at age eighty-four, and is buried in Shanghai.

MAJOR DMITRI ORLOV

Though Sung Shi-lun harbors nagging suspicions about Orlov throughout his presence with the Ninth Army Group, Sung is never made aware that his suspicions are accurate. Orlov the "observer" is a far more influential member of Stalin's military, and is in fact not a major, but a major general in the Soviet army. Orlov returns to Peking in late December 1950, where he quietly supports Sung's fading reputation, which adds considerably to Sung's longevity in the Chinese military. Orlov returns to Moscow in February 1951 and reports to Stalin on conditions and tactics of the Chinese army, which does nothing to bolster Stalin's enthusiasm for joining in the war as allies of the Chinese.

But Orlov's observations about the inherent weakness of Chinese efforts points to the utter lack of air support, something Stalin begins to take seriously. Though Soviet MiG fighters have been deployed to bases in Manchuria as early as November 1950, their pilots are primarily North Korean and Chinese. Orlov's observations convince Stalin to discreetly assign a larger number of Soviet pilots to the air war, though the Soviets do not officially reveal their involvement.

Orlov continues in service to the Soviet army until Stalin's death in March 1953. Though Orlov attempts to keep clear of the political turmoil that follows, he is considered Stalin's man, and is thus forced into retirement. He lives out his life in Ukraine, with his wife, Anya, and dies in 1985, at age eighty-one.

GENERAL DOUGLAS MACARTHUR

Arguably one of the most colorful and popular military commanders in American history, he is never far from severe controversy. Though he will always have his admirers, some fanatically so, his critics are equally passionate in their disregard for the man's skills as a strategist. Never to be regarded as open-minded, MacArthur's utter disregard for the view-points of his superiors becomes his undoing. His distaste for following counsel or eventually orders from the Joint Chiefs of Staff causes enormous friction between his command in Tokyo and Washington, but MacArthur possesses an almost magical ability to intimidate, so much so that his superiors feel powerless to interfere in his control of the United Nations forces in Korea. His brilliant gamble that results in enormous success at Inchon only cements his authority, and inspires him to believe utterly in his own genius.

He is betrayed by many of those who serve him, including most prominently his intelligence officers, which fail completely to understand who or what kind of enemy they are facing in Korea. Fed blatantly erroneous reports by officers who seek only to gain his praise, MacArthur is not completely at fault for the astounding lack of awareness of Chinese intervention in the war, at a time when men on the front lines, including Oliver P. Smith, see a very different war than is being described to them from above.

It is MacArthur's blithe dismissal of his president, Harry Truman, that causes his ultimate downfall. The two men generally despise each other, but Truman begins to understand that MacArthur's dislike extends much further, into a general disregard for Truman's authority as commander in chief. Though Truman tolerates MacArthur's arrogance, he cannot ignore the potential danger that MacArthur's belief in his own authority might portend for the country. MacArthur speaks openly of the use of nuclear weapons against either China or the Soviet Union, and though Truman reluctantly concedes that possibility, it is not a stance the president is willing to speak of publicly. MacArthur, on the contrary, is far more indiscreet in recommending an all-out war against China, which would include massive invasions of the Chinese mainland. That policy is not viewed favorably by either Truman or America's allies, most notably the British, who begin to see MacArthur as a dangerously uncontrollable force.

The final straw comes for Truman when it is learned in Washington that MacArthur has privately expressed to officials from both Spain and Portugal that he was willing to order the invasion of China without full authorization from Washington. Though MacArthur disputes that account, it is a possibility that Truman cannot chance. Though he understands MacArthur's enormous public popularity, Truman makes the decision that relieving him is a political gamble Truman must take. Despite the sudden reluctance by the Joint Chiefs, who seem anxious to defuse the controversy by minimizing MacArthur's perceived crimes as nothing more than errors in judgment, Truman feels he has no alternative. On April 11, 1951, Truman relieves MacArthur of his command and replaces him with General Matthew Ridgway. A political firestorm erupts across the United States, newspapers and congressmen who support MacArthur calling for Truman's ouster. Truman's popularity rating drops to barely more than 20 percent, the lowest for any sitting president in United States history. For a long week, there is considerable anxiety in the Truman White House that MacArthur might ignore the order, and there is talk in Washington that MacArthur might in fact rally his enormous support and march on Washington, inserting himself in command of the government. But such talk seems overblown when MacArthur leaves Tokyo and returns home on April 18. He is then invited to address a joint session of Congress, during which he offers the now-famous quote, "Old soldiers never die, they just fade away." It is a moment of drama rarely equaled in American history. Support rallies around the general for a run for the presidency, and MacArthur joins the campaign in 1952. But his lack of campaigning skills and his political support cannot match that shown for another heroic general, Dwight D. Eisenhower, who wins a landslide victory.

In 1952, MacArthur and his wife, Jean, move into the Waldorf-Astoria hotel in New York City, and later that year he is elected chairman of the board of the Remington Rand Corporation. Still respected for his vast military experience, he is sought out for counsel by Presidents Eisenhower, Kennedy, and Johnson. He vigorously advises the latter two men against involvement in Vietnam.

He dies in April 1964, of biliary cirrhosis, a liver disease, and at his own request is buried in Norfolk, Virginia. He is eighty-four. Jean dies in 2000.

The accolades and historical celebration of MacArthur's life and career are lengthy, including more than one hundred military decorations from the United States and other countries around the world. Much of his reputation is earned, and there is ongoing debate that much of it is achieved on the backs of others. Like others before him, from William T. Sherman to George Patton, the controversy at least inspires discussion and examination. It is this author's suggestion that characters like Douglas MacArthur are a crucial component of American history. In what can often become a dreary study of names, dates, places, facts, and figures, it is essential that there be personalities worth remembering, for good or otherwise. Douglas MacArthur is certainly that.

"I didn't fire him because he was a dumb son of a bitch, although he was, but that's not against the law for generals."

—HARRY S. TRUMAN

"That little bastard [Truman] honestly believes he's a patriot."

—DOUGLAS MACARTHUR

"He got his first star in 1918 and that means he's had almost thirty years as a general. Thirty years of people playing to him and kissing his ass, and doing what he wants. That's not good for anyone."

—GENERAL JOSEPH STILLWELL, 1950

"If MacArthur had had his way, the cost to the moral credibility of the United States around the world would almost certainly have been historically disastrous."

—HISTORIAN MAX HASTINGS

GENERAL EDWARD "NED" ALMOND

Almond never accepts blame or even responsibility for the failures of his command in the fall and winter of 1950. It is a view not shared fully by his supreme commander, Douglas MacArthur. After the Chosin campaign concludes, Almond's authority is severely curtailed, and true to Oliver Smith's wishes, the Marines never again serve under Almond's authority.

Almond serves adequately as Tenth Corps commander throughout the campaigns of 1951, and is generally praised by General Matthew Ridgway as an aggressive field general. But he never receives public praise and attention, nor the affection of his troops that always embraces Oliver Smith.

Throughout his life, he maintains steadfastly that his orders to advance blindly toward the Yalu River came from MacArthur, that he only obeyed what he was instructed to do. But he alters his own history in his description of the campaign as little more than a reconnaissance in force, and in 1976 he writes, "we had been caught in a mess by an unknown enemy strength which battle action could only determine." Once that strength was determined, it fell upon MacArthur, and not Almond, to order the withdrawal southward, which Almond acknowledges, though he continues to ignore and deflect criticism for his command decisions.

He leaves Korea in late 1951, is promoted to lieutenant general, and becomes commander of the Army War College in Carlisle, Pennsylvania. Almond retires from the army in 1953 and goes into the insurance business. He dies in 1979, at age eighty-six, and is buried at Arlington National Cemetery.

CAPTAIN WILLIAM BARBER

Fox Company's commander recovers from his wounds in Japan, returns to the States in spring 1951. He requests and is assigned to the Marine Corps recruitment center in San Diego, serves in that post until his promotion to major in July 1952. His service carries him to Fort Benning, Georgia; Camp Lejeune, North Carolina; and Quantico, Virginia; as well as service as a naval attaché to the United States embassy in Bangkok, Thailand. He is promoted to lieutenant colonel in 1960 and is assigned to Okinawa as commanding officer of the Marine's Third Reconnaissance Battalion. He returns again to the States, is promoted to full colonel, and serves in a variety of prestigious positions at the Marine Corps Headquarters. He eventually is named commanding officer of the Second Marine Regiment. His active-duty career concludes in 1970, after a tour in Vietnam as psychological officer for the Third Marine Amphibious Force.

After retiring, Barber becomes an analyst for the Northrop Corporation and settles in California. He dies in 2002, and is buried in Arlington National Cemetery.

William Barber's career is punctuated by his astounding command of the action of Fox Hill. Outnumbered five to one, his company fends off repeated attacks by Chinese troops, with best estimates concluding that more than one thousand of the enemy are killed in the process. Of his 240 men, only a few dozen leave Fox Hill without wounds. Despite his severe wounds, Barber continues to command the action, until the pain and worsening infection render him completely immobile. For his heroics, William Barber is awarded the Medal of Honor by President Truman in August 1952.

COLONEL HOMER LITZENBERG

He is awarded the Navy Cross for his command during the Chosin campaign. In mid-1951, Litzenberg is assigned to Marine Corps Headquarters in Washington, D.C. He serves in a number of administrative posts, including command of the Marine Corps Development Center at Quantico. He briefly commands the Third Marine Division, and in 1954 is named inspector general of the Marine Corps. He commands at both Camp Lejeune and Parris Island until his retirement in 1959.

He dies in 1963 at age sixty, and is buried in Arlington National Cemetery.

COLONEL LEWIS "CHESTY" PULLER

"All right. They're on our left. They're on our right. They're in front of us, they're behind us. They can't get away this time."

—COLONEL LEWIS "CHESTY" PULLER

Arguably the most celebrated and admired Marine in the Corps' history, Puller is awarded five Navy Crosses and one army Distinguished Service Cross, the only man to receive so many awards at that level. He is promoted to brigadier general in January 1951, major general in 1953. He returns to the United States in mid-1951, commands the Third Marine Division, then is named to command of Troop Training Unit, Pacific, in California. In July 1954 he is named commander of the Marine Second Division, at Camp Lejeune, North Carolina.

He suffers a stroke, and retires from the Corps in 1955. He survives until 1971, and dies at age seventy-three. He is buried in Christ Church Cemetery, Saluda, Virginia.

"I'd like to do it all over again. The whole thing. And more than that, more than anything, I'd like to see once again the face of every Marine I've ever served with."

—COLONEL LEWIS "CHESTY" PULLER

COLONEL ALPHA BOWSER

One of O. P. Smith's most trusted staff officers, Bowser earns considerable respect as a primary staff officer for commanders throughout much of his career. He returns home to the United States in May 1951, serves in his position as G-3 (Assistant Chief of Staff, Operations and Plans) at the Marine base at Camp Pendleton, California. After serving briefly as chief of staff of the Marine Third Division, Bowser is named to the staff of Supreme Headquarters, Allied Powers, Europe, in Paris. In July 1955 he is assigned to San Diego, serves on the command staff of the

Pacific Fleet Amphibious Force. In 1956 he is promoted to brigadier general and named to command the Marine Recruit Training Command in San Diego. Promoted to major general in 1960, he serves as commanding officer of the Marine Base at Twenty-nine Palms, California, and later serves as commanding officer of the Marine base at Camp Lejeune. Promoted to lieutenant general in 1965, Bowser is named to command of Fleet Marine Force in Norfolk, Virginia, until his retirement in June 1967.

He settles in Kailua, Hawaii, and dies in 2003, at age ninety-two.

GENERAL WALTON WALKER

The beleaguered commander of the United States Eighth Army is cruelly regarded by history, especially as that history is written by Douglas MacArthur, who never respects Walker's abilities leading troops. After his army's breakout from the Pusan Perimeter, Walker is blamed for allowing a great many North Korean troops to escape northward, despite MacArthur's planned envelopment formed by the Inchon invasion. Overwhelmed by the surprise assault by Lin Biao's Chinese forces, Walker withdraws the Eighth Army back below the 38th parallel, conceding to the Chinese the North Korean capital of Pyongyang. It is a militarily sound move, allowing the Eighth Army to both survive and regroup. MacArthur does not agree. Though many of his troops speak highly of Walker's command, he is never allowed to redeem his failures in the summer and fall of 1950. On December 23, near Uijongbu, South Korea, he is killed in a jeep accident. He is sixty-one. Walker is buried in Arlington National Cemetery.

He is succeeded in command of the Eighth Army by General Matthew Ridgway.

GENERAL FRANK LOWE

President Truman's "eyes" in Korea continues his various informal inspection tours, though he develops a clear friendship and respect for Smith's Marines beyond any other group. In late December 1950, Lowe writes Truman that the Marines should never again be placed under army command, which, logically, endears him to Oliver Smith. Lowe also issues a blistering report on the poor quality of the South Korean troops, laying blame at the feet of Syngman Rhee, whom he faults for rampant corruption. He returns to Washington in April 1951, having performed exactly as Truman had hoped, especially with added insight into the mind and performance of Douglas MacArthur, which contributes enormously to the eventual climactic confrontation between the president and his commanding general.

In his final report from Korea, Lowe says, "The First Marine Division under the command of O. P. Smith is the most efficient and courageous combat unit I have ever seen or heard of."

When Lowe departs, he leaves behind a gift to Colonel Alpha Bowser: a heavily armored jeep, armed with a .50-caliber machine gun, and most important to Bowser, soft seats. The two men remain friends for years after.

Later in 1951, Truman demonstrates his appreciation for Lowe's service by awarding him the Distinguished Service Cross.

COLONEL DOUGLAS DRYSDALE

He recovers from his wounds, continues to lead his Royal Marines throughout the United Nations campaigns against the Chinese throughout 1951. He continues in various commands until his retirement in 1962. Drysdale and his men are awarded the Presidential Unit Citation by Harry Truman, and in 1954, Drysdale is named an "Honorary U.S. Marine" by Marine Commandant Lemuel Shepherd. His own government recognizes his heroism, awarding him the title of "Member of the British Empire" as well as the "Distinguished Service Order."

He dies in 1990, in Norfolk, England, at age seventy-four.

LIEUTENANT COLONEL DONALD FAITH

For his extraordinary leadership throughout the desperate escape attempt from overwhelming Chinese forces east of the Chosin Reservoir,

Colonel Faith is awarded a posthumous Medal of Honor. Though re-criminations are many after the campaign, no amount of blame is di-rected at Faith for the devastating losses under his command.

"In terms of the collective memory of the American people, the Korean War is not just forgotten. It was not remembered in the first place. . . ."

—HISTORIAN ALLAN MILLETT

ACKNOWLEDGMENTS

. . . .

I AM OFTEN asked about research sources. The following is a partial, and invaluable, list of published firsthand memoirs:

The Coldest War, by James Brady
The Three Day Promise, by Donald K. Chung, MD
We Were Innocents: An Infantryman in Korea, by William D.
 Dannenmaier
Once Upon a Lifetime, by C. I. Greenwood
Brave Men, by David H. Hackworth
One Bugle, No Drums, by William B. Hopkins
Reminiscences, by Douglas MacArthur
Colder Than Hell, by Joseph R. Owen
The Korean War, by Matthew B. Ridgway
Years of Trial and Hope, by Harry S. Truman

I am deeply grateful to the following historians, whose published accounts of the Korean War all contributed to the necessary research:

Henry Berry
Clay Blair

Burke Davis
Bob Drury and Tom Clavin
T. R. Fehrenbach
David Halberstam
Eric Hamel
John W. Harper
Max Hastings
Robert Leckie
William Manchester
S. L. A. Marshall
Allan R. Millett
Martin Russ
Jim Wilson

Most especially, I am deeply indebted to the following, who offered unpublished firsthand accounts, or other significant avenues of research that proved essential in the writing of this book:

John A. Blazer, Savannah, GA
Walter E. Cohan, Vero Beach, FL
James R. Conway, Atlanta, GA
Fred Denson, Athens, GA
William T. Dunn, Reedsville, VA
O. W. Ervin, Littleton, CO
Robert Ezell, Los Alamitos, CA
Lyn Gillet, Poulsbo, WA
William Gerichten, Kernersville, NC
John Edward Gray, Mount Ulla, NC
Jim Griffith, Flemington, NJ
Bob Harbula, West Mifflin, PA
Larry Hochfeld, Tamarac, FL
Jack Ingram, Columbia, MD
Seamus Kilty, San Anselmo, CA
Tom Lewis, Albuquerque, NM
Leroy Martin, Rivervale, NJ

Emma McSherry, Gettysburg, PA

Dick Olson, Green Valley, AZ

David Palluconi, Fairfield, OH

George "Chip" Peifer, Roseville, CA

Charles Penick, Vinton, VA

Erick K. Poeschl, West Milford, NJ

Marvin L. Pollard, Roanoke, VA

Eugene "Peep" Sanders, Gettysburg, PA

James R. Saul, Danville, VA

Win K. Scott, Waynesville, NC

Stephanie Shaara, Gettysburg, PA

James A. Van Sant, Santa Fe, NM

Dr. Stanley I. Wolf, Bethesda, MD

I offer a very special thank-you to Gail B. Shisler, Fairfax, Virginia, the granddaughter of General Oliver P. Smith. Shisler is the author of an outstanding biography of the general (*For Country and Corps*) and made herself available to me for advice and consultation. She graciously provided me with CDs of General Smith's verbal, unpublished memoirs, which were an essential tool in the telling of this story.

And I am forever indebted to the members of the Chosin Few and the survivors of Task Force Faith, many of whom have passed away during the writing of this book.

ABOUT THE AUTHOR

Jeff Shaara is the *New York Times* bestselling author of *The Smoke at Dawn, A Chain of Thunder, A Blaze of Glory, The Fateful Lightning, The Final Storm, No Less Than Victory, The Steel Wave, The Rising Tide, To the Last Man, The Glorious Cause, Rise to Rebellion,* and *Gone for Soldiers,* as well as *Gods and Generals* and *The Last Full Measure*—two novels that complete the Civil War trilogy that began with his father's Pulitzer Prize–winning classic, *The Killer Angels.* Shaara was born into a family of Italian immigrants in New Brunswick, New Jersey. He grew up in Tallahassee, Florida, and graduated from Florida State University. He lives in Gettysburg.

jeffshaara.com

ABOUT THE TYPE

This book was set in Caslon, a typeface first designed in 1722 by William Caslon (1692–1766). Its widespread use by most English printers in the early eighteenth century soon supplanted the Dutch typefaces that had formerly prevailed. The roman is considered a "workhorse" typeface due to its pleasant, open appearance, while the italic is exceedingly decorative.